Protector of the Grove

BOOK ONE

PROTECTOR OF THE GROVE

NICHOLAS SEARCY

Cover design by Jason Nathaniel Artuz

ISBN: 978-1-0394-7222-8

Published in 2025 by Podium Publishing
www.podiumentertainment.com

Protector of the Grove

1

WAITING FOR THE END TO COME

Elijah Hart ran a hand over his hairless head as he tried to ignore the curious or disgusted glances originating with the plane's other passengers. His lack of hair wasn't really the issue—not by itself, at least. Instead, the real problem was the lack of eyebrows; he'd never really considered how much the presence of those two short tufts of hair affected the way someone looked. Not until he'd lost his, that is. In addition to the alien absence of hair on his brow, he was also afflicted with sunken cheeks, red-rimmed eyes, and a pallid complexion. One look, and anyone who knew anything would recognize precisely what he was.

He sighed, drinking in the stale, antiseptic atmosphere. He hated flying, but not because he was terrified of crashing. No—it was more the act itself. The sudden jumps and jerks, the steady drone of the engines, the cramped confines of the cabin—it all added up to a particularly uncomfortable experience that, if he had any choice in the matter, he would have avoided.

But some things were more important than the avoidance of discomfort.

"Elijah!" came his sister's voice, jerking his attention back to the tablet in his lap.

"Shit. Sorry," he mumbled, locking his eyes on the screen. "Chemo brain, I guess."

Alyssa shook her head, pushing a lock of blonde hair back behind her ear before saying, "I wish you would have waited for me to come pick you up."

Before Elijah had been diagnosed with cancer and forced to undergo the horrors of radiation and chemotherapy, he and his sister had looked strikingly similar. Now, though, when Elijah looked at his sister's sandy-blonde hair and clear skin, he couldn't help but be reminded of all he'd lost.

Of everything he'd yet to lose.

"It would've just been a waste of money," Elijah said with a tired sigh. "There's no point in you paying for a flight all the way out to the island when I'm perfectly capable of sitting in a plane by myself for a few hours."

Of course, Elijah didn't mention the half dozen times he'd had to race—or hobble, given his distinct lack of energy—to the plane's lavatory to vomit. The treatments had torn him apart, leaving him a shell of his former self. And though he'd recently finished his last round of chemotherapy, he still hadn't had time to completely recover.

And he never would, either. What the treatment hadn't destroyed, the disease itself had. Soon, it would all be over. Or that's what the doctors had said, at least. It was the reason he'd left his home in Hawaii to fly back to Seattle where he'd grown up. He didn't want to spend what little time he had left drugged out of his mind in hospice care. Instead, he wanted to spend it with the only family he had left—his sister, her wife, and their son.

Still, just because he preferred going home to lying in a hospital bed didn't mean he was happy with his circumstances. As much as he wanted to see Alyssa and her family, the last thing he wanted was for them to see him wither away and succumb to cancer. He'd have preferred to be remembered as he'd been—vibrant and alive. Not the husk he had become.

"Elijah, I—"

The tablet stuttered, then went dark. At the same time, the lights in the plane's cabin went the same way, leaving the passengers mired in complete darkness. Someone screamed. Others gasped. Most of the reaction was confined to a low murmur, though. There was no point in panicking.

Elijah felt something dig into his forearm, and it only took him a moment to realize that the clawlike fingernails belonged to the woman next to him. He was just about to say something comforting, but his words were cut off when his stomach jumped into his throat as the plane dropped.

There were more screams.

Elijah's heart pounded, and his stomach clenched.

And then he realized what was wrong. The hum of the plane's engines had ceased when his tablet stopped working. Had they been struck by lightning? Or was there some other mechanical issue? He didn't know enough about planes to figure it out. Instead, as was the case with everyone else on the plane, the panic had truly begun to grip him. His fingers wrapped around the armrest, squeezing the hard plastic with every ounce of his meager strength.

Elijah had long since come to terms with his own mortality. Death was inevitable. He would just have to confront it a little earlier than most. And though he'd spent a few weeks after his diagnosis railing against his own fate, questioning why he'd been chosen to die an early death, he'd slowly made peace with leaving the world behind. After all, what choice did he have? It was coming for him, regardless of how he felt. Whether it was in a few more weeks or a scant few minutes shouldn't have mattered all that much to him.

But it did.

With everyone else panicking all around him, Elijah couldn't stop himself from reacting similarly. It was simple human nature at work, and as the plane continued to plummet, his heart raced out of control. He murmured, "It's going to be fine. These planes can glide for miles without power. It's going to be okay."

"Y-you think so?" asked the woman beside him, her voice small, quiet, and terrified. Elijah couldn't see her—it was night, and with the plane's lights having stopped working, he was almost entirely blind. Still, he remembered her being an attractive redhead, and she spoke with an Irish accent. She'd introduced herself out of politeness, but after a four-hour flight, most of which Elijah spent mired in self-pity, he couldn't remember her name. He wanted to say it was Gwen or something like that, though that might've been completely wrong.

"I think—"

Elijah never got the chance to finish his statement because, only a moment later, something wholly unexpected flashed before his eyes. A disembodied block of text appeared:

Your planet (Earth) has been touched by the World Tree. Scanning . . .

Elijah blinked, thinking that he'd suddenly gone crazy. Perhaps he'd hit his head and hadn't realized it. "What the . . ."

He never finished that question, either, because a moment later, a different message replaced the first:

Scan complete. Grade: Unranked.

"What is going on?" demanded the redheaded woman. "What does this mean? Who's doing this?"

Elijah had no idea how to answer that, so he remained silent. Regardless, the fact that she'd seen the messages as well meant that he wasn't going crazy. Unless her response was part of his delusion. Either way, he didn't have much time to offer any words of comfort because a third notification came closely on the heels of the second:

Due to lack of energy and mass, planet (Earth) will be adjusted to multiversal standard. Selective randomization of terrain will occur as mass increases. Stand by for insertion of planetary core . . .

None of it made any sense to Elijah, but the information never had the opportunity to marinate because, only a second later, the world shifted. The already pitch-black cabin somehow grew darker, and suddenly, Elijah felt more alone than he ever had in his entire life. He couldn't feel anything. Not the plane's sharp descent. Not the fingernails digging into his forearm. Not the ever-present weakness and nagging nausea he'd felt since the night after he'd first started his treatments. Nothing. Nor were his other senses working properly. The sounds of panicking passengers and the buffeting winds were gone.

No antiseptic ozone smell assaulted his nose. There was nothing. Instead, he felt as if he was floating in an absolute void.

Fortunately, that disconcerting lack of sensory input only lasted for a couple of instants before he was distracted by yet another disembodied block of text:

Planet (Earth) has been accepted for integration into the Cua'ti Sector. Indigenous population given access to the System.

Elijah tried to shake his head, but without any senses, he wasn't sure if it did any good. In fact, he wasn't even sure if he had a body in that strange void. He did his best to ignore the existential terror that came with that thought, distracting himself with the information conveyed by the blocks of text. It didn't make any sense to him, but he also couldn't deny that it was happening. After all, the woman sitting next to him on the plane had seen the odd notifications, as well. Unless it was all a hallucination brought upon by the combination of his disease and the treatments he'd undergone, it was all really happening.

And the implications were terrifying. Specifically, the parts about randomization of terrain. His mind jumped to scenes from various disaster movies he'd seen, and he wondered if the entire world was experiencing a great earthquake or some other massive upheaval. If that was the case, how many were already dead? How many would die?

Before he could wind himself up even further, Elijah was confronted with yet another notification:

Scanning human (Elijah Hart) for aspects. [Nature] aspect found. [Martial] aspect found. [Scholar] aspect found. Generating class choices . . .

It didn't take much internal investigation for those so-called aspects to make sense to Elijah. The [Nature] aspect was probably the most fitting, given that, until he'd been diagnosed with cancer, he had spent his adult life working as a marine biologist. Moreover, he had always felt a certain connection with nature that he'd never been capable of putting into words. Ever since he was a kid, he'd always felt more at home in the wilderness than surrounded by so-called civilization.

The same could be said for the [Scholar] aspect, which probably came from his years in college and his career as a scientist. The incredible amount of study required to attain a doctorate had clearly left its mark on him. Since then, his work as a marine biologist had only thrust him deeper into the life of an academic, albeit one who spent more time in the field than in a laboratory.

Finally, he considered the [Martial] aspect. That probably made even more sense than the one awarded for his time stuck in the trappings of academia. After all, Elijah had spent much of his youth playing one sport or another. He wasn't always the best at any of them, but he was naturally agile, and what he lacked in sheer physical size, he made up for in Dexterity. However, his first love had always been boxing. He'd never been an elite fighter, but that didn't matter; he loved the sport, and as a teenager, most days saw him down at the gym.

In college, he hadn't had time to continue boxing, but he'd picked it back up in the years since getting his doctorate. He didn't train as hard as he once had, but he still put in plenty of time. To see that acknowledged by the so-called System—whatever it really was—was more than a little gratifying.

Of course, Elijah couldn't be entirely certain any of it was even real. It could have just been a hallucination. Or perhaps he was already dead, and the whole thing was the result of his last few neurons flashing out of control. In either case, he wasn't given enough time to get into those sorts of existential questions. Instead, he focused on the latest notification to appear before him:

You have been awarded four choices of class archetypes. Choose well because this decision will forever affect your path.

"Well, that's not ominous at all . . ."

He felt certain that he'd spoken, but he couldn't actually hear the words. They might've just been thoughts, for all he could tell. As soon as he'd finished reading the last notification, another appeared:

Archetype: Warrior
A versatile melee archetype, proficient with most weaponry. Features bonuses to durability, Strength, and learning martial techniques.

Required Aspect:
[Martial]

Sample Class Choices:
{Berserker}, {Guardian}, {Knight}, {Brawler}, {Gladiator}

First Skill:
Heavy Blows

Compatibility: 51%

The next was:

Archetype: Researcher
Research is the root of all academic pursuits. Features bonuses to memory, calculation speeds, and observation.

Required Aspect:
[Scholar]

Sample Class Choices:
{Librarian}, {Tradesman (Various)}, {Philosopher}, {Doctor}

First Ability:
Knowledge Repository

Compatibility: 63%

Elijah's eyes found the third option:

Archetype: Druid
The druid is a defender, ally, and cultivator of nature. Features bonuses to natural Regeneration, Ethera density, and One With Nature.

Required Aspects:
[Scholar], [Nature]

Sample Class Choices:
{Bard}, {Preserver}, {Fury}

First Spell:
Touch of Nature

Compatibility: 94%

"It feels like a video game," he mumbled to himself. He didn't even think about the fact that the words were lost to the void.

Archetype: Ranger
The ranger is a hybrid between the druid and warrior archetypes, with strong ties to both the martial and natural paths. Gives up true mastery of either path in favor of versatility. Features bonuses to durability, Regeneration, and One With Nature.

Required Aspects:
[Nature], [Martial]

Sample Class Choices:
{Predator}, {Tamer}, {Trapper}

First Skill:
Natural Instincts

Compatibility: 89%

So, his choices were between becoming a Warrior, Researcher, Druid, or Ranger. The first seemed pretty self-explanatory, and if Elijah was reading the description correctly, it would eventually branch off into something more specialized. Given his background as a boxer, he was particularly intrigued by the {Brawler} options. However, he was a little thrown off by the seemingly low compatibility of the archetype.

The second choice, Researcher, was at first easy to dismiss, but the archetype's descriptions had hinted that magic was now going to be a real thing. As crazy as that sounded, it was much easier to accept when he was floating in a void, deprived of all senses, and seeing a bunch of notification boxes about classes, archetypes, and the randomization of Earth's terrain. And that wasn't even considering the messages concerning Earth's core and increasing the planet's mass.

So, with the assumption that magic was real, what sort of secrets could a magical Researcher unlock? The archetype had also mentioned {Tradesman (Various)} as class choices that branched off from the Researcher archetype. And Elijah had a suspicion that the System wasn't talking about electricians or plumbers. If his experiences in a materialistic society were anything to go by, that might be a route to wealth or importance.

Not that either of those things really interested Elijah. So long as he was comfortable and doing something about which he could be passionate, he was happy enough. Even so, the Researcher was worthy of consideration, and he couldn't dismiss that archetype out of hand.

Next, he considered the third option—the Druid archetype. He really didn't know what such a path might entail, but by the required aspects, he could surmise that it might be some sort of natural wizard. Or a scholar focused on the study of the natural world. A plant mage, perhaps. Whatever the case, he didn't know enough about it to choose it. After all, if the notifications were to be believed, these decisions were permanent. And while he didn't necessarily expect to survive much longer—even in the calm void, the plane's descent loomed large in his mind, and he still had terminal cancer to worry about—he would need to make a rational choice. And without further information, there was no way he could choose the Druid archetype.

For the first time in his life, Elijah wished he'd spent his youth playing video games like his friends and classmates. However, he'd been too busy with sports—or with his family's weekend camping trips. That hadn't left much time for more than the occasional game, but even that was enough to highlight the similarities between this System and some of the rules that governed role-playing games. Perhaps if he'd spent more time with them, he'd be better prepared to make appropriate choices.

Finally, he moved to the last option—the Ranger. It was a blend of the Warrior and Druid archetypes, which made the choice seem very appealing. However, Elijah couldn't help but think that there should be some sort of drawbacks to the class. He found himself focusing on the description, which said it gave up true mastery in favor of versatility. That planted a seed of doubt.

For a long time, Elijah stared at the descriptions, torn between his choices. Indecisiveness strangled his mind, and he found himself incapable of making a decision. It would have been different if he'd had all the information, but those paltry archetype descriptions highlighted just how ignorant he was.

Suddenly, another flash of text interrupted his internal debate:

Insertion of planet core successful. Due to proximity to high-energy sectors, planet's (Earth) mass and energy adjusted. Randomization of terrain complete. New grade: C.

Next, the void suddenly disappeared, replaced by the chaos of the plummeting plane.

A feminine voice mumbled, "Oh, God . . . What is going on?"

"I don't know," Elijah answered, his own voice quivering with fear. He still hadn't made a choice, so he turned his attention inward. When he did, he saw the same options laid out before him. Warrior. Researcher. Druid. Or Ranger.

They all had their benefits, and he was certain that they would all have deficiencies, too.

Meanwhile, the plane found some stability, and it leveled off. The shaking stopped, and Elijah heard more than a few sighs of relief.

It was all temporary, Elijah knew. They'd been an hour and a half away from Seattle when everything went dark, which meant that they were still hundreds of miles out to sea. He had no idea how far a plane could glide, but he suspected it wouldn't be that far.

Someone shouted over the din of tense murmuring: "Okay, everyone—please remain calm. I've spoken to the pilot, and he says everything is going to be okay. We've lost power, but he thinks—"

Just then, something slammed into the plane, ripping a giant gash in the fuselage. Everyone screamed, and Elijah caught sight of a huge shadow with a hint of feathers before the plane resumed its sharp descent. Elijah's heart once again jumped into his throat as the plane dropped like a rock.

A few unlucky passengers had been torn from their seats and sucked out into the dark night. The wind whipped by, adding to the panic, and Elijah clutched his armrests with all the Strength he could muster. It wasn't much.

Another furious impact tore yet another gaping hole in the plane, and Elijah was close enough to see one of the wings cartwheeling off into the air. Nearby passengers were ripped free, and they disappeared into the darkness a moment later.

That was when it hit him.

He was about to die. They all were. And there was nothing anyone could do about it.

If the crash didn't get them, then whatever had ripped the plane apart would pick up the slack. The introduction of the System had given a brief glimmer of hope, but reality had come crashing back in a hurry. He was already dead. Between the cancer, the impending crash, and the creature outside, he knew his remaining time was numbered in seconds.

That expectation was proved true when, a moment after that thought flitted across his brain, the sound of screeching metal filled his ears as the creature tore into the plane once again. This time, Elijah was one of the unlucky ones who'd been close enough to be thrown free of the plane, and an instant of chaos later, he found himself falling through the air.

The starry night twinkled above him as he watched a monstrous, birdlike shape rip into the plane and tear it to pieces. An explosion erupted as something ignited, and Elijah got a brief glimpse of the monster. It was a bird, though its size beggared comprehension. Its wingspan was comparable to the plane's, and it was equipped with talons the size of an economy car.

Elijah didn't have the chance to see much more before his fall abruptly ended with a splash and unconsciousness brutally smothered his awareness. His final thought before he completely surrendered was that he still hadn't chosen an archetype.

Perhaps he never would.

2

DEATH OF FAMILIARITY

What the hell is going on?" gasped Alyssa, staring at the disembodied blocks of text. It was too dark to see, but after that brief period of nothingness, she could feel Carmen's comfortable presence next to her in bed. "You saw it, too, didn't you?"

"I . . . I did," Carmen answered, her hand finding Alyssa's. She squeezed it tightly. "Could this be real?"

Alyssa had already gone through the tunnel of disbelief and come out the other side. No matter how she looked at it, she couldn't see how the situation could be anything but real. It was one thing if it was just her experiencing it, but the combination of the loss of power, the strange period of nothingness, and the fact that Carmen had been through the same thing confirmed the reality of it all. So, she chose to treat it as such. If it turned out that she was crazy, then she would just deal with spending the rest of her life on antipsychotic drugs in a mental institution.

"What choices did you get?" Carmen asked.

"We'll go over it once we figure this thing out," she said, reaching over to her phone. Fortunately, it still worked, though there was no signal. Still, it gave her a light source. "I'll go check on Miggy. He's probably terrified."

With that, she slipped off the bed and, using the light on her phone, headed out of her bedroom, down the hall, and into her eight-year-old son's room. Thankfully, he was more than fine. In fact, he was grinning from ear to ear. When she asked if he was okay, he said, "What's going on? Why's the power out? It's not even raining. Can we play Scrabble?"

Of course that was where his mind would go. For one reason or another, he saw any power outage as an opportunity to play board games, which he loved. Probably because he usually won.

"Everything is fine," she said. "Did you see any . . . uh . . . boxes?"

"Huh?"

Clearly, he hadn't. Alyssa had no idea why that would be, but that lack of comprehension seemed par for the course. So, she played it off, then led him into the house's living room. For some reason, she had a very bad feeling, like there was something dangerous right around the corner. Part of that was due to the oddness of the situation, but she also knew just how irrationally people tended to act in any emergency.

"Okay, so what did you get?" Alyssa asked as she walked into the room.

"You first," Carmen said, her feet curled under her on the couch. It was an incongruous position for someone with her particularly muscular physique.

Alyssa rolled her eyes. "Fine," she said, glancing at the boxes she'd so far ignored. After the ones talking about Earth being connected to the World Tree—whatever that meant—was the one mentioning aspects.

She read it, then said, "I got three aspects. Martial, Faith, and Scholar. You?"

"Scholar and Magic," Carmen said, obviously disappointed. Even if the situation seemed a little ridiculous, she clearly took it just as seriously as Alyssa.

"What are aspects?" asked Miguel.

"We're not sure," Carmen said. "But for your mom, Martial makes sense."

"Because she's a policewoman?"

"And because I've spent years practicing judo and jujitsu," Alyssa said. "I used to go to the boxing gym with your uncle, too."

The mention of Elijah brought with it more pain than she'd expected. If his plane had lost power . . . No, she didn't want to think about that. Where he was concerned, it was easy to sink into a pit of depression, what with his illness. She was prepared to say goodbye, but that didn't mean it was easy.

Faith made sense, too. Especially since her brother had been diagnosed, Alyssa had spent quite a bit of time praying. She rarely went to church—most of them didn't especially approve of how she lived her life—but her religion was still important to her.

Scholar was easy, too. She'd just finished her master's degree in criminal justice, and she intended to pursue her doctorate, as well. It was mostly so she would look better when it came to promotions at work, but that didn't change the fact that she'd spent quite a bit of her life studying.

For Carmen, the Scholar aspect made even more sense—assuming that it was, as Alyssa suspected, a comment on the lives they'd led. Carmen held her own doctorate in history with a specialization in primitive skills. So, most of her life had revolved around her education. As for Magic? Well, that was a mystery, but hopefully one they could solve by going through the rest of the notifications.

"And your archetypes?"

"What's an archetype?" asked Miguel, snuggling close to Carmen.

"In this instance, I think it refers to an overall classification. But we're not sure, Miggy," said Carmen. "Hopefully, we can figure it out together."

He nodded along, and Alyssa said, "I got Warrior, Priestess, and Researcher. You?"

"Priestess? Ugh."

"Don't knock it. It says one of the sample classes is a Valkyrie."

"Sexy."

"Ugh," groaned Miguel.

"What did you get?" repeated Alyssa.

"Two choices. Tradesman and Sorcerer. Both of which are bullshit. I mean, it wouldn't make me so angry if your classes didn't have feminine suffixes. But you got priestess. Why couldn't I get Tradeswoman or Sorceress? I mean . . . Come on."

"I guess they didn't get the memo on gender equality."

"Obviously. So, which one are you picking?" asked Carmen. "Priestess, right?"

Alyssa shook her head. "I'm tempted," she said. "Valkyrie does sound cool. But I don't know . . ."

Indeed, looking at her choices, she was torn. Given the vague feeling of unease blanketing her mind, she had no intention of choosing Researcher. With the power outage and the messages she'd read, it seemed a foregone conclusion that things would get more dangerous. And as a police officer, she was duty bound to meet that danger head-on and protect the populace.

So, her choices were between Priestess and Warrior. She looked at the first description again:

Archetype: Warrior
A versatile melee archetype, proficient with most weaponry. Features bonuses to durability, Strength, and learning martial techniques.

Required Aspect:
[Martial]

Sample Class Choices:
{Berserker}, {Guardian}, {Knight}, {Brawler}, {Guard}

First Skill:
Heavy Blows

Compatibility: 77%

Then, she looked at the one for Priestess:

Archetype: Priestess
Faith is versatile, lending power in a wide variety of ways. Features bonuses to Regeneration and Ethera.

Required Aspect:
[Martial], [Faith]

Sample Class Choices:
{Valkyrie}, {Apostle}, {Chaplain}, {Paladin}, {Inquisitor}

First Skill:
Word of Power

Compatibility: 63%

"Do you want my advice?" asked Carmen.

"You know I do."

"Take Warrior," she said. "The other one sounds fancy enough, but I know you. You're a fighter. I can't imagine any other archetype describing you any better than that."

"But what if the other one's better?"

Carmen rolled her eyes, then raked a hand through her black hair. "You always do this," she said. "Remember when we used to have time to play games together? You would always second-guess your choices. But believe me, Alyssa—you won't find a better fit than Warrior."

"What about you?" Alyssa asked, pushing the choice aside for the time being.

"Tradesman all the way," she said.

"Really? You don't want to sling fireballs?"

"I mean, yeah. But you know me. I'd rather make things, you know? Besides, I get the feeling that the world's going to need people who can build things," she said. "You read those notifications, right? Randomization of terrain? I mean, if I were a betting woman, I'd put money on the reason the power's out is because the grid's fucked."

Miguel gasped. "You said a bad word."

"And I'll probably say a lot more before this is finished," Carmen said.

"Carmen."

She rolled her eyes. "Fine. I'll put a dollar in the swear jar in a minute," she said. "Of course, money's probably useless right now."

"What? Why?" asked Alyssa.

"That always goes first, doesn't it? With the power being out, credit cards and stuff are useless. The same for paper money. Haven't you ever watched a zombie movie? Society's about to collapse, Alyssa," she said.

"This is not a zombie apocalypse."

"You know that for sure?" Carmen asked. "I mean, maybe not the zombies. But I just got told by a magic box only I can see that I could be a Sorcerer. So, who knows what's going to happen? My point is that apocalypse rules are definitely in play. Food. Water. Shelter and security. Those are the priorities."

"You think it's going to get that bad?" Alyssa asked. As a police officer, she had training for that kind of scenario, but she'd never really taken it seriously. Sure, she was prepared to respond to active shooters and terrorist scenarios, but the full collapse of society definitely seemed a bit far-fetched.

Carmen shrugged. "I have no idea, but I think it's possible," she said.

"Okay, so first thing's first," Alyssa said, deciding that it was better to treat it as an apocalyptic emergency and be wrong than the opposite scenario. "We need to catalog our supplies. You and Miggy go to the kitchen—"

"Did you seriously just tell me to go to the kitchen?" asked Carmen with a grin.

"This isn't time to joke, Carmen."

Once again, Carmen rolled her eyes. "Fine. But I want it on record that you're no fun. I mean, assuming we're not crazy, we just got offered magic powers. Or at least I did," she said. "That's kind of a dream scenario for me."

"Except the apocalypse part you just predicted."

"Well, the world has too many people, anyway," she remarked. "Maybe Roy will get eaten by a zombie. Or turned. Then, I can legally blow his head—"

"Carmen!"

"Who's Roy?" asked Miguel.

"Someone your mom knows from work," Alyssa said, referring to the head of Carmen's department. He was a blatant misogynist who constantly questioned her work, belittled her at every opportunity, and had even come on to her on more than one occasion. "He's not important."

"Unless I need to rid the world of a Roy-shaped zombie."

"There aren't any zombies."

"You don't know that."

Alyssa let out a long-suffering sigh. "You're a child."

"I'm young at heart, which is why you love me," Carmen pointed out.

"Anyway—you two take stock of the food," Alyssa said, moving on. "I'm going down to the basement to get . . . other stuff."

That was where she kept the gun safe, which, given what Carmen had predicted, seemed extremely important. Even if it wasn't a zombie apocalypse—which sounded silly even in the context of what had happened so far—there was every chance of looters and other violent lawbreakers. And even if she had no intention of exercising lethal force, she was prepared to do whatever it took to protect her family.

"Aren't you forgetting something?"

"Huh? What?"

"Your archetype. You really should choose something. You get bonuses to your stats and stuff," Carmen said.

"Stats? Like a video game?"

"Yup. Just like a game."

Alyssa shook her head, then confirmed her choice to become a Warrior. When she did, she got a notification congratulating her on it, then another window opened soon after:

Name	Alyssa Hart		
Level	1		
Archetype	Warrior		
Class	N/A		
Specialization	N/A		
Alignment	N/A		
Strength	6		
Dexterity	7		
Constitution	5		
Ethera	4		
Regeneration	4		
Attunement	None		
Cultivation			
Body	Core	Mind	Soul
Unformed	Unformed	Unformed	Unformed

"What does all of this mean?" she asked. Before Carmen could answer, another notification popped up, telling her that she had ten free attribute points to spend.

"It means that all that weight lifting I did was completely useless," pouted Carmen. Indeed, that was her primary hobby and means of stress relief, and her physique showed it. She'd never been one for heavy cardio, but she had long since cultivated a body studded with bulging muscles. Of course, some of that was mitigated by the fact that she was, at best, an inch over five feet tall.

By comparison, at nearly six feet tall, Alyssa was extremely tall for a woman, and though she worked out as well, her routines were more for endurance, resulting in a much slenderer physique.

"Kind of depressing, really," Carmen remarked. Then, she perked up, adding, "But on the bright side, I put all my points into Strength. So, I can probably lift a car now."

"Ugh. Didn't think it would be smarter to . . . you know, spread the points around?"

"Nope!"

Alyssa shook her head, and after spending a few moments reading what each attribute did, decided to follow her own advice, allocating two points into each category. As soon as she did, she let out a gasp as a wave of what could only be called rejuvenation swept through her.

"That's the good stuff, right?" said Carmen, still grinning.

Alyssa didn't answer. Instead, she focused on the fact that, if she could feel something like that, then the chance—slim though it was—that it wasn't real became even more unlikely.

In the middle of her thought, something banged against the door.

She flinched. Carmen grabbed Miguel, clutching him with her thick arms.

Then, a familiar voice called out, "Alyssa! It's me! Open up!"

Alyssa let out a sigh of relief, then crossed the living room to the door. When she flung it open, she saw a tall, broad-shouldered, and athletic man in his mid-forties.

"What's up, Chief?" asked Alyssa, looking past him and the petite blonde woman clutching his arm. The street was dark.

"Shit is going to go wrong real quick out there," Roman Cain said. He was both the police chief and her neighbor. "Thought we all might be safer together."

Of course, Alyssa knew that he hadn't come for his own good. Rather, he'd done so for his wife, who was good friends with Carmen.

"Yeah. Probably for the best," Alyssa said, stepping aside. "Come on in."

3

CASTAWAY

Elijah dreamed of his puppy, Fremont, nipping at his legs as he read a book. The dog was a rambunctious thing, still untrained, and full of energy and cuddly love. Slowly, his rational mind intruded on the pleasant dream, telling him that his dog hadn't been a puppy for years, that he'd been forced to rehome him when it became clear that the cancer was incurable. Doing so had been almost as emotional as when his oncologist had informed him that the treatments weren't working. That he only had a few more months to live.

Gradually, Elijah's memories distorted, and the puppy's nipping bites became something altogether more painful. Punishment for the abandonment Fremont had doubtless felt at being left with a neighbor.

Suddenly, Elijah's eyes fluttered open as pain lanced through his leg. He kicked out, but the pain only increased. Moreover, there was something digging into his arm, too. He spasmed, waving his arms and legs as he tried to dislodge whatever had assaulted him, eventually jerking himself free and clamoring away.

His hands found scant purchase on the slippery rocks and gravel as he crawled away, and he vaguely noticed the steady lapping of waves. The unmistakable smell of the sea. The biting ocean wind.

That's when his memories began to assert themselves. The plane. The cancer. The System.

Gasping, he pushed himself to his knees and looked around. As he'd suspected, he was on a rocky beach, but only a few dozen feet away, there was an incredibly dense forest. The sky was gray with clouds, and the steady sound of the waves, accompanied by a strange clicking sound, filled his ears. He turned his attention in the sound's direction, and his eyes widened at the sight.

At first glance, it was just a crab, little different from thousands of others Elijah had seen throughout his life. However, it differed in a couple of notable ways. First, it was a perfect example of a purple shore crab. Dark maroon in color, it had stout claws, which bore slightly darker spots. However, unlike its more typical brethren, which were usually only a few inches across, this one was the size of a cat.

Elijah scrambled backward when he saw a dozen more of the creatures bearing down on him, each of similar size. But they followed; judging by the frayed edges of his pants—and the wounds beneath—the little scavengers had thought him dead, and they'd been feeding off of him.

More importantly, they didn't seem all that enthused about losing their meal. The first few scuttled forward in a sideways shuffle, and when Elijah didn't react, the rest followed. He reacted on instinct, kicking out with bare feet. Apparently, he'd lost his shoes at some point, though he didn't have time to lament the loss. Instead, the whole of his attention was occupied by defending himself from the horrifically huge crabs.

He connected with the first, his foot hitting its incredibly hard shell. It did little damage, but the thing couldn't escape the reality of its small size, and the momentum of the kick sent it sailing through the air.

But it also opened Elijah up to the rest of the crabs, which assaulted his legs with their oversized claws. Snapping, ripping, and tearing—it wasn't long before his lower legs were a bloody mess, with ribbons of flesh hanging off in strips. A few of the claws had cut right through his muscle, stopping only when they reached the bone.

Elijah panicked, kicking out with renewed fury, but his Strength waned with every blow. Whether it was blood loss, his preexisting conditions, or simple fatigue, he didn't know; what he did know was that he couldn't continue in that manner. So, after he kicked another one away, he levered himself to his feet, then leaped, pushing off with all his Strength.

He barely cleared a few inches.

But it was just enough that when he descended atop the closest crab, he felt the thing's shell crack and crunch beneath his bare feet. The shards of shell pierced the soles of his feet, but he didn't allow himself to stop, stomping down as hard as he could. Over and over, until the creature had been reduced to a slurry of shell, crabmeat, and its juices.

Seeing the other crabs surrounding him, Elijah stumbled away, scrambling over the rocks as best he could. He left a trail of blood and bits of ruined flesh behind, but adrenaline drove him forward and into the trees. He glanced back to see that the crabs had descended upon their fallen fellow, and he sighed in relief.

Still, he kept going into the thick forest, only collapsing a few dozen feet in. Crabs wouldn't go too far inland, so he felt like he was safe. Even so, the presence of the abnormally large crabs was a troubling thing.

But it was nothing compared to his ruined legs that increasingly refused to follow his commands. A few more feet, and he tumbled to the ground. Elijah dragged himself forward until, at last, he could turn over and rest his back against a pine tree.

Finally, he let himself relax, and in that moment, another block of text appeared before his eyes:

Congratulations for defeating your first foe. Status unlocked (accessed via mental command). There are many ways to advance in this universe, and killing is only one of them. Explore the System to discover your own path to power.

Elijah was both alarmed and relieved to see that his memories on the plane hadn't been a hallucination. Relieved because one of his most potent fears was losing his mind. He'd watched his grandmother descend into dementia, and those memories had stuck with him ever since. He'd experienced some mental decay during his treatment—a side effect colloquially known as chemo brain—and he'd have rather died than go through any more decline in his mental faculties.

After a second, during which he grew increasingly lightheaded, Elijah decided to distract himself from the pain by taking a look at his so-called status. When he thought of it, another box appeared. However, this one was divided into various categories. He studied it:

Name	**Elijah Hart**		
Level	**1**		
Archetype	**Druid**		
Class	**N/A**		
Specialization	**N/A**		
Alignment	**N/A**		
Strength	**3**		
Dexterity	**4**		
Constitution	**1**		
Ethera	**4**		
Regeneration	**7**		
Attunement	**None**		
Cultivation			
Body	**Core**	**Mind**	**Soul**
Unformed	**Unformed**	**Unformed**	**Unformed**

Below the status was another box, which said:

You have ten (10) attribute points to spend. Each level you gain will grant you two more points to spend as you wish. Upon reaching level ten and gaining a class, each level will come with an automatic allocation based on your class. Some classes will grant additional free attribute points. Choose well. All decisions have consequences.

That was comforting, at least. Elijah had no context for what the numbers on his status page really meant, but he suspected that threes and fours weren't high. Most of that could be attributed to his disease, which had sapped his muscle mass like nothing else could. But the one point in Constitution was more than a little troubling.

Obviously, he knew what Strength and Dexterity were. One represented physical power, while the other was probably representative of his coordination. And Constitution was likely tied to his body's durability. Regeneration was self-explanatory, as well, and he felt certain that it governed his ability to heal. That it was his highest attribute was both comforting and a little disappointing.

Comforting because it meant that, if he managed to survive for any length of time, healing quickly would almost assuredly prove invaluable. Disappointing, though, because his other attributes were so low.

Even though he had a good idea what each category meant, Elijah focused on Strength, which brought up a new box:

Strength:
Determines physical might.

That was in line with Elijah's expectations, so he quickly moved on to the next attribute:

Dexterity:
Determines coordination and reaction speed.

Again, that made perfect sense, given the word's definition. However, what was left unsaid was that, between the two of them, they represented a much larger concept. Strength wasn't just about lifting heavier things; instead, it described explosive movement, as well, which in turn would determine how quickly he could cover ground. However, without coordination, that ability would be useless. With both high Strength and Dexterity, he would be able to move incredibly quickly. But if either of them lagged behind, his speed would suffer.

Next, he looked at Constitution:

Constitution:
Determines the body's stamina as well as resistance to physical and magical damage.

This was the third piece of the puzzle and confirmed that all three of the physical attributes worked together. Strength gave him power. Dexterity gave him coordination. And Constitution would give him the capability of harnessing those attributes to their fullest effect. Without it, he could easily envision a scenario where he quickly ran out of stamina. Or one where his body simply couldn't endure the strain.

He would have to keep that in mind going forward, lest he grow lopsided and incapable of using his attributes properly.

Ethera:
Determines the size of the pool of energy used to empower magical spells, skills, and techniques.

Ethera was the first of the attributes to truly surprise him, but the description was as straightforward as he could've asked it to be. As was the case with the numbers representing his attributes, he had little context for what it really meant, though. If he ever got a spell, skill, or technique, he would be able to experiment and find out more. So, he moved on to the final attribute, Regeneration:

Regeneration:
Determines physical healing as well as Ethera recovery.

This was another surprising attribute. In addition to the effect he'd suspected upon reading the name, it also determined how quickly his pool of Ethera regenerated. It didn't take a genius to figure out that it would be incredibly important, and it wasn't difficult to imagine a scenario where he had a huge pool of available Ethera, but once he used it all, it might take him an eternity to regenerate it.

With a sigh, Elijah leaned back, staring at his status screen. As he did so, something nagged at him, niggling at the edge of his awareness, like he'd forgotten something very important. Then it hit him.

He hadn't chosen an archetype, but there it was on his status screen. Druid. The System had chosen for him.

With focused thought, he found that he could cycle back through his notifications, and as he did, he found the moment he'd dreaded:

Due to failure to choose an archetype within twelve (12) hours, one has been chosen for you. Choice made due to compatibility.

Then, there was another notification informing him that he was now a Druid, whatever that entailed. The decision had been taken out of his hands, but for some reason, Elijah wasn't upset about it. In fact, it felt entirely appropriate. Perhaps the System knew what was best for him, after all.

On his status sheet, Elijah focused on his archetype, and yet another table opened before his eyes.

Archetype: Druid **The druid is a defender, ally, and cultivator of nature. Features bonuses to natural Regeneration, Ethera density, and One With Nature.** **Required Aspects:** **[Scholar], [Nature]**	
Spells	
Touch of Nature	**Harness the power of nature to heal yourself or an ally.**

This notification was the most welcome one he'd yet seen, and he couldn't help but let out a sigh of relief. However, just because he had the spell didn't mean he knew how to use it. And given that he had precisely zero experience with magic—or Ethera, as it had been called—he didn't like his chances of figuring it out. Still, given the state of his legs—and his body in general—he felt certain that Touch of Nature was the key to his survival.

First, though, he decided to use his free attribute points. With his body ravaged by cancer, he felt that there was only one choice. He wouldn't get such an influx of attribute points anytime soon, so if he was going to fix himself, he needed to do it now. Even then, he wasn't entirely certain that it would work. Was the damage already done? He had no idea. But until he felt like the cancer was gone, he would continue to invest his attribute points appropriately.

At first, he considered investing them in Regeneration, though that just didn't feel right to him. That attribute was already pretty high, and he was still dying. No—if he wanted to make it through the cancer, investing in Constitution seemed like the better option.

To that end, he flicked his mind at his status screen, mentally willing it to add his free points into the Constitution attribute. Once he was finished, a new box of text appeared before him:

You have spent your free attribute points. Would you like to make this allocation permanent?

Elijah hesitated. If he was wrong, he was probably sentencing himself to death. So, even though he felt confident in his reasoning, he mentally retracted the attributes until only one had been allocated. Then, he confirmed it, bringing his Constitution up to two. He didn't feel that it made any difference, so he added another. Then another. He kept going until he reached five points, only stopping because he finally felt something changing.

Suddenly, his body clenched, his every muscle going taut. It only lasted a few seconds, and when his muscles finally loosened, he felt better than he had in weeks. Probably better than at any time since he'd begun his treatments. That was all the confirmation he needed before slamming every free point into Constitution.

That was a mistake.

A strangled groan escaped from between Elijah's lips as he went completely stiff. His body trembled with exertion as he felt vitality flood his body. Blessed, agonizing life. Minutes later, when he went limp, he let out a long, quivering sigh of relief. His body was still weak, but it was a natural weakness, not unlike he'd felt after spending a couple of hours in the gym. It was a far cry from that feverish lack of Strength he'd felt for the last few months.

Was he certain that the cancer was gone?

No. But he had reason for hope. And sometimes, that was enough to change a person's entire outlook on life.

4

NECESSITIES

I think we have enough for a couple of weeks, so long as we ration," said Alyssa, looking over the stacks of canned food on the table. There were other dry goods, as well, but not nearly as many as she'd hoped. "Makes me wish I'd made a Costco run before, you know, the end of the world."

Roman shook his head, saying, "I'm not that worried about food. We have the garden out back, too. What really concerns me is water."

Alyssa looked away, then ran a hand through her hair. It was so difficult to wrap her head around the fact that the world had changed overnight. However, when the sun had risen, she'd gone outside to survey the damage, and she'd been shocked to discover that, instead of the familiar skyline of Seattle, all she saw on the horizon was mountainous wilderness. The rest of her neighborhood was still there, and though she saw hints that the nearby town of Easton had survived, she anticipated that she'd only seen the smallest fraction of the changes that had taken place.

Further supporting that assumption was the fact that utilities hadn't been restored, meaning that in addition to the lack of power, cellular service had been suspended. Probably due to issues with the cell towers. But that wasn't an immediate concern. The biggest issue was that, because of the transformation of the terrain, water service had been cut, as well.

"Lake Eden is only a few miles away," Alyssa suggested. "And we can set up some buckets for rain collection for the short term."

"And if it doesn't rain?" asked Roman. He glanced toward the basement's ceiling, almost as if he could see the others in the house above. He took a deep breath, then said, "I think we need to go to the store."

Alyssa leaned forward, hands on the table, and sighed. As a police officer, she'd often had to deal with shoplifters, and during some periods of civil unrest, she'd had to respond to looting, as well. So, what Roman had suggested didn't really sit well with her. However, it wasn't as if she was contemplating stealing televisions and cell phones. This was a matter of survival.

Still. It just didn't feel right.

But considering that the world as they knew it had just ended, her moral quandary felt more than a little silly.

"We only take what we need," she said.

Roman shook his head, then put his hand on her shoulder. "I don't like it, either," he said. "It's been less than a day, and already, we're talking about breaking the law."

"I'm aware."

"But the thing is—this isn't anything like what we've been trained for," he said. "This is survival."

"I just told myself the same thing," she stated.

"And if we don't do this now, there's not going to be anything left," Roman pointed out. "We need to take care of our immediate survival. You have Miggy. I have Trish. And I'm going to do whatever it takes to make sure they get through this. Next to that, legality doesn't matter. Hell, I'm not sure morals even come into it."

Alyssa shook her head. One day. That was all it had taken. And if they were thinking that way, then everyone else was, too. The moment that thought crossed her mind, she knew that the situation was going to quickly deteriorate.

Easton had never had much of a criminal element. That was why she'd moved to the suburbs in the first place. But when people got desperate, social order had a way of being tossed by the wayside. Roman's suggestion proved that.

The real problem was that Alyssa couldn't really counter it. Food and water were going to be issues. That was a fact. And given the choice between watching her son die of dehydration or hunger and following the law of what may well have been a fallen civilization, she knew precisely which option she was going to choose. So, in that context, Alyssa said, "We need to get going soon. Manning's isn't huge, and if we take too long, it'll be picked clean."

With that decided, Alyssa and Roman went upstairs to inform the others of the plan. Everyone agreed that it was the right course of action, but predictably, conflict reared its ugly head when they realized that they were going to be left behind.

Trish said, "It's just a mile or so. What could go wrong? I don't want to be cooped up in this house, and I'm sure Carmen doesn't, either."

"It might be dangerous," Roman said. "Think about it. None of us have really tried out these abilities, but—"

"I tried mine," Carmen pointed out. "I mean, Bind isn't meant for fighting or anything, but—"

"Nobody said anything about fighting," Alyssa interrupted.

"That's because you don't want to admit the obvious," Carmen countered. "But I think what Roman was going to say is that people are probably panicking right now. And they have magic abilities. More than that, some of them have definitely come to the same conclusion you two did. Given that, there's a good chance that they'll try to keep others from taking resources that might ensure their own survival."

"It's been less than a day!" Trish insisted. "You act like all of society is going to collapse just because the power is out."

"Trish . . ."

"You haven't been outside yet, have you?" said Carmen.

Alyssa added, "Trish, this is way more than just the utilities being cut. The whole world has changed. Did you even read the notifications?"

"I skimmed them," she admitted. "Something about World Trees and whatnot. Seemed like nonsense."

Alyssa massaged her forehead in frustration. "You did pick an archetype, though, right?"

"Yes. Roman made me choose Healer."

Alyssa let out a sigh of relief. Then, she said, "Okay—I think it's best if we figure out what everyone chose and test out our abilities before we start running around. Like Carmen said, it might get dangerous out there." She looked around, then went on, "Guess I'll go first. I picked Warrior. And the ability I got was Heavy Blows."

She navigated to the ability's description:

Heavy Blows	Increase the damage of your melee attacks by 5%. Toggled personal augmentation.

"It just says it increases the damage of my attacks by five percent," she explained. "Apparently, it's a toggled personal augmentation, whatever that means."

"Self-buff," said Carmen. All but Miguel narrowed their eyes in confusion. "Oh, come on. None of you play video games? It's obvious."

"I only play sports games," said Roman.

"I like *Candy Crush*," Trish stated.

Alyssa asked, "You really think this System is like video games? I mean, what are the odds of that?"

Carmen shrugged. "I mean, there are probably all sorts of explanations that would make sense," she said. "Maybe the System seeded the ideas a long time ago, guiding us so that it would make sense when we were touched by the World Tree. Or—"

"That sounds like the World Tree is some kind of sexual deviant," said Trish.

"It's a tree . . ."

She shrugged. "Still not the best phrasing," Trish persisted.

Carmen rolled her eyes, then said, "Anyway. My point is that the explanations don't really matter. It is what it is, and I get the feeling that if we keep questioning it, we're going to end up dead. Accept it, adjust, and move on. Or that's what I intend to do, at least. So, in that spirit, I took Tradesman, and my first ability is Bind. It lets me bind two materials together."

"What use is that?" asked Roman.

"For combat? Nothing that I can think of," Carmen answered. "But for making things? I mean, it should be incredibly useful going forward."

"You took a noncombat option? That's the stupidest thing—"

She crossed her arms and interrupted, "I also put all my extra points into Strength. So, watch what you say, big guy."

"Calm down," said Alyssa. "I'm sure Carmen can pull her own weight and then some. Besides, people who can make things are going to be valuable. You've got to see that, chief."

Roman shook his head. "Whatever," he said. "Guess I'll go next. I took Marksman. Ability I got was Aim, which I can use to increase the damage of any ranged attack by thirty percent."

"Wow. That's . . . That's nice."

"I don't think it works on guns, though," he admitted.

"Why do you say that?"

He shrugged. "Instinct? I don't know. It's weird. I just . . . know. Does that make any sense?" he asked.

Alyssa said, "Kind of. My ability kind of came with something similar. I sort of know how to use it, at least. Yours is probably the same way."

"Stop trying to make sense of it," Carmen advised. "Just accept it."

"Probably for the best," Roman said, shaking his head. Then, to Trish, he continued, "Alright, babe. Tell them what you got."

"It's called Mend. I can . . . I don't know . . . I guess I can heal people with it. Just wave my hand and they'll get better? It feels kind of like it would be strong, but . . . it also comes with . . . I don't know. Sort of, like, if I cast it, I won't be able to do it again for a little while."

"Cooldown," provided Carmen. Everyone looked at her, and she said, "Game term. Sorry."

"What about the kid?" asked Roman, gesturing down the hall where Miguel was asleep. He'd tried to stay awake, failing spectacularly. "He get an archetype, too? And what are we going to do with him when we go for supplies?"

"He didn't see anything but the initial notification about the world changing," Alyssa answered. "And if we're all going, we need to take him with us."

Roman shook his head. "That'll complicate things."

"Nonnegotiable," said Carmen.

"Fine. But if it's dangerous out there . . ."

"I'll take care of him," Carmen stated.

Alyssa was quick to voice her own agreement. While Miguel wasn't her biological child, she'd helped raise him since he was a toddler. So, in every way that mattered, he was as much her son as if he'd come from her own genes.

Roman shook his head, saying, "But if you're taking care of him, you're going to be distracted when we might need you to—"

"Drop it," said Trish. "Just drop it, okay? If we had kids, I'd want to keep them close, too. Especially if things are as bad as you say they are."

Roman had clearly been outvoted, so as his wife had suggested, he dropped the topic. Instead, they all went out to the backyard, where they spent a little time practicing their abilities. From Alyssa's perspective, there really wasn't much to practice. She just had to use her ability, and it would remain active indefinitely. Perhaps there was some other limiter, but if there was, she couldn't find it.

Trish's limitations were far more prominent, and after spending almost an hour testing things out, they determined that the cooldown after using Mend was nearly fifteen minutes.

"Feels crazy to complain about magical healing, but that seems like a pretty harsh cooldown," said Carmen, pressing two old fence boards together. They stuck, which seemed to be the limits of what her own ability could accomplish. "Still, I guess we just save that for emergencies."

Roman, who'd retrieved his hunting bow from his house next door, shot an arrow at a target he'd set up at the other end of the yard. It was only a few dozen feet away, and when he loosed the arrow, it whipped across the lawn with the speed of a bullet, tearing through the target—a fake deer meant for hunting practice—and hitting the shed behind it.

"Damn," he said.

"Impressive," agreed Alyssa.

"Haven't shot this thing in years. No time for hunting, lately."

Indeed, Roman had been promoted to police chief only a year before, and since then, he'd been putting in seventy-hour workweeks. That he was home when the world went crazy was just a stroke of good luck.

After everyone had gotten comfortable with their abilities, Carmen went inside to wake Miguel up while everyone armed themselves. Roman and Alyssa both strapped their service pistols to their hips, while Trish was given a shotgun. She handled it with some familiarity, reminding Alyssa that the other woman had spent her fair share of time at the range.

Carmen carried an old softball bat and an ancient revolver that had belonged to her father. Despite its age, it was in good condition, and like Trish, Carmen knew her way around some firearms.

The only one who was unarmed was Miguel. No one wanted an eight-year-old running around with deadly weapons, after all. Still, he put himself to use by carrying spare ammunition and bottled water in his backpack.

Thus prepared, the group set out for their local market.

5

BEYOND REPAIR

Alyssa kept her hand on her pistol as she walked down the center of the street. Behind her followed Carmen, their son, Miguel, and Trish. Bringing up the rear was Roman, who was holding his bow.

With her shotgun in hand, Trish complained, "Is all this really necessary?"

"Maybe. Maybe not," Carmen said. "But I've watched enough zombie movies that I'm more than willing to be overly cautious."

"There are zombies? Cool," said Miguel.

"I still can't believe you let him watch *The Walking Dead*," Alyssa muttered just loud enough that her wife could hear it.

"In my defense, I didn't expect him to like it so much," Carmen remarked. "Especially after the first season when the quality went downhill."

"I liked it!" Miguel countered.

"Because you're eight, and you don't have taste. It's not your fault. You just haven't experienced enough variety to know when you're watching trash," Carmen stated. She reached out to ruffle his black hair. "But I still love you even if your taste leaves a lot to be desired."

He dodged to the side, avoiding her hand as he whined, "Mom . . . C'mon . . ."

Alyssa ignored their back-and-forth as Carmen teased their son. Instead, she focused on her surroundings. It had been a troubling discovery to find that none of their vehicles worked. Even Carmen, who knew a bit about working on cars, had been stumped as to why they were inoperable. She'd tried to change the batteries and even inspected the spark plugs, but everything appeared to be in working order. They just wouldn't start.

So, the group had been forced to head out on foot as they sought supplies at the local grocery store, Manning's Market. It was only a couple of miles away, so they reasoned that the trip shouldn't prove too arduous.

By the time Alyssa and the others reached the end of their street, she was beginning to rethink that assessment—chiefly because of the hole that had been ripped in the side of one of the houses.

"How did we not hear that?" she asked, ready to draw her pistol. She also had an old machete sheathed on her other hip, but she hoped she wouldn't need to get close to whatever was capable of tearing a hole in a building. "What even could do that?"

"I don't know," said Roman, having already nocked an arrow. "And I don't want to find out, either."

The house was barely standing, with a good portion of the roof having collapsed when something had torn through a load-bearing wall.

"We need to check it," Alyssa said. "In case someone inside needs help."

Roman started to respond, and judging by his expression, he intended to argue for ignoring it. It was strange, how quickly he'd abandoned his role as a public servant dedicated to the safety of the townspeople. But then again, judging by what she'd seen so far, the town didn't really exist anymore. Not in any way that mattered, at least.

"If someone's hurt, I can help them," said Trish, already moving to cross the lawn.

"Honey, don't—"

She turned, backpedaling for a moment as she said, "It's fine. It was probably just a—"

She never got the chance to finish her thought before something came tearing out of the house, moving so fast that Alyssa had difficulty tracking it. In the space of a second, it was already bearing down on Trish.

She screamed and tried to run, but as panicked as she was, she only got a step before stumbling. And then, the creature was upon her, latching on to a hastily raised forearm. Blood misted, and the sound of a breaking bone filled the air, accompanied by Trish's agonized shout.

And then gunshots sounded.

Alyssa fired once. Twice. Then three times. Each shot took the furry creature in the ribs, but it didn't release Trish's arm. Suddenly, an arrow sprouted from just behind its foreleg. Then Alyssa heard the thwap of a bowstring before another joined the first.

It yelped, releasing Trish, who fell to the lawn where she clutched her arm as a mewling sound escaped from between her lips. But Alyssa only had eyes for the creature before her.

It resembled a wolf, though it was at least the size of a pony. And its coloring was different from any canine she'd ever seen. Predominantly black, the thing's fur had green-and-blue streaks, as well, which gave it a distinctly alien appearance. Alyssa advanced, firing her weapon over and over again as she emptied the magazine into the monster.

It didn't die, though.

Instead, it leaped to its feet and stumbled back toward the house. It never got to its destination. As Alyssa fired her gun, Roman continued to loose one arrow after another until, after seven, it finally slumped to the ground. Still, it wasn't dead, though that wouldn't last much longer. Alyssa had been hunting with her father enough that she could recognize when an animal was on its last leg. Soon, it would bleed out.

She wasn't willing to trust that assumption, though. So, Alyssa strode forward, dragging the machete from the sheath at her waist, until she stood over it. Then, without further hesitation, she reached back and chopped into the monster's neck. The blade cut deep, splattering blood on her pants, but the monster still clung to life. So, she swung again, and at last, it perished.

Breathing hard, more from panic than exertion, she turned and demanded, "What the ever-living fuck was that?"

No one paid any attention to her, though. Instead, they'd all descended upon the injured Trish. When Alyssa joined them, she saw that the other woman's arm was misshapen, covered in blood, and had bones sticking out in multiple places. More, it looked the wolf creature's claws had clipped Trish's upper thigh, which was gushing blood. Clearly, it had hit an artery.

"You have to use your ability," Carmen was saying.

"Spell . . ."

"What?"

"It's a spell. Not an ability . . ."

"Whatever it's called, use it now or you're going to bleed out!" Carmen spat.

It made perfect sense, but still, Trish looked at Roman and waited for his approval before she closed her eyes and cast her spell. Alyssa felt something stir, almost like an ephemeral wind, before Trish's body erupted into golden light. When it faded, her arm was entirely healed, and the bleeding had stopped.

"Whoa," gasped Miguel, his eyes wide as saucers. "Magic."

"Trish," said Alyssa, holstering her pistol. As she shoved her machete back in its sheath, she spat, "What the hell were you thinking? You saw a house that looked like a monster had torn through it, and you thought you should just traipse across the lawn without any sort of precautions?! What the fuck was going through your head?"

"I . . . I don't know . . . I just thought I could help," she sobbed. "I didn't think there was a monster. Why would I think there was a monster? I just thought . . . I don't know . . . I don't know what I thought . . ."

"You didn't think at all!" Alyssa growled. "This isn't—"

"Enough," interrupted Roman, reaching out to grab her by the arm. "She knows that what she did was stupid, Alyssa. Just leave it. Nobody's hurt, so we can just—"

Alyssa pulled away. "She just wasted her spell. That means she can't use it again for a while."

"It wasn't a waste," said Roman. "But it's done now. We can't undo it, so we just have to keep going."

Alyssa clenched her fists in frustration. If they didn't take things seriously, they were all going to die. However, harping on Trish's mistake wasn't going to change anything. Hopefully, the woman had learned her lesson.

"Fine. But we need to do better."

"Agreed," Roman said, a steely glint in his eyes. He glanced at the pile of fur that had once been a monster, then asked, "So . . . What was that?"

"Looked like a wolf," she said. "Sort of. Lots of things were wrong, though. Its snout's too short, the fur is all the wrong colors, and its legs are a little longer than normal."

"And it's the size of a pony," added Carmen, her hand on Miguel's shoulder. She wasn't going to let him get too far away, especially after what had just happened.

"That, too."

Carmen reached down to help Trish up, saying, "It's a monster. Doesn't matter where it came from. Maybe it's a wolf that got mutated. That wouldn't be that surprising, given the fact that Trish here just cast an honest-to-God healing spell. Or it could've been brought here from somewhere else. It might've just manifested for all we know. The point is that it doesn't matter for now. All we need to know is that the world just got a lot more dangerous, right?"

"The people who lived there are probably dead, too," Alyssa said, gesturing to the ruined house. "If they're not, they ran away. No way they fought it off."

"You don't know that," Trish said, wiping her tears. She must've forgotten that she was coated in blood because she left red smears across her cheeks.

"If they had fought it off, it would've been injured. And I'm pretty damn sure doors couldn't stop that thing. Hell, walls would barely slow it down," Alyssa stated. "If they were still in that house, it would've killed them. Same with any other houses we see. Let's just go to the store, get what we need, then head back home. We can hole up there until . . ."

She let the statement trail off because the idea of rescue seemed absolutely ridiculous. The city was gone. If those notifications were to be believed, the whole world had been randomized. That meant the army wasn't coming. No—they were all alone, and if they wanted to survive, they needed to do so on their own.

Perhaps someone would eventually come. The government still existed, after all. But Alyssa expected that it would be a long time before they got around to rescuing anyone.

"What are you thinking?" asked Roman.

"I don't think we should go back to the house," she said. "Not permanently, at least. We need somewhere more defensible."

Roman didn't immediately respond. Carmen and Trish did, though. Neither were terribly supportive of the idea, but that wasn't surprising, given their personalities. Carmen was concerned with uprooting Miguel, while Trish still wasn't convinced they needed to move at all.

Miguel, for his part, seemed excited about it.

"Where?" asked Roman.

"I don't know. Maybe the elementary school?" she suggested.

"Too open."

"The bank?"

"Too small."

"The station?" was her next suggestion.

Roman tapped his finger against his chin, then said, "You know what? That would probably work. It's got size. It's closer to the lake, so we would have an easier time getting water. And it's sturdier than any house."

Indeed, the police station was made of brick, and it was a FEMA-approved shelter. That, plus the fact that it was equipped with a sturdy fence and a relatively huge arsenal of weapons made it the perfect choice.

"Plus, we kind of need to go there, anyway," Roman said. "Once we're sure Trish and your family are safe, we need to start working on the rest of the town. The station's the best place to do that."

"Sounds like a plan," Alyssa said. She wasn't nearly as concerned with her duty as she was with making certain that Carmen and Miguel were safe, but she hadn't abandoned it altogether. "Store first. Then back to the house to gather our other supplies. We probably need to spend the night there before heading out first thing in the morning."

Roman nodded.

For their part, the others only made minor objections. However, they were quickly convinced when Alyssa pointed at the house, reminding them that a monster had ripped its wall to pieces. After that, they fell into line.

So, with that, the group continued down the street as they made their way to the grocery store. When they reached the market over an hour later, they found that more than a few people had already picked it clean. There were still some supplies to be had, but it was far less than any of them hoped.

In the end, they had to be satisfied with one cart full of canned goods, another shopping cart filled with bottled water, and another with a variety of dry goods. Thus supplied, the group started back to the house, studiously ignoring the evidence of fighting they passed along the way. A few storefronts had been bashed in, and a couple of houses had taken even more damage than the one where they'd encountered the wolf monster.

Still, they didn't see any other people, which they all found more than a little curious. Alyssa hoped that they were all just hiding, mostly because she didn't want to think about the alternative.

Finally, they returned to the house, where they set about arranging everything they might need to take with them when they left for the station in the morning.

6

MAGIC AND DANGER

Elijah looked down at his ruined legs. The crabs had really done a number on them, and unless he figured out how to use his new spell, he'd be in real trouble. Even if he'd managed to overcome his cancer—which he was still unsure about—he still had to concern himself with immediate survival.

His legs were caked with dried blood and dirt, which didn't bode well for staving off infection. In addition, huge chunks of muscle were missing, snipped away and eaten by the oversize crustaceans. His legs had been so ravaged that he questioned whether he could even walk without the advantage of adrenaline pumping through his veins.

He extended his hand and whispered, "Touch of Nature."

But nothing happened, which made him feel extremely foolish. After trying a few different techniques, most of which involved contorting his fingers in various ways, Elijah sagged back against the tree and closed his eyes. Now that he'd calmed down a little, he was beset by wave after wave of agony originating from his legs. There were smaller injuries across his body—the crabs hadn't confined themselves to a single place, after all—but they were insignificant next to the fiery pain in his lower legs.

There was something beyond the pain, though. Something almost soothing. Something comforting. He focused on that sensation, delving deeper and deeper until he finally recognized what he sensed.

It was nature.

He remembered the description that had come along with the Druid archetype, which had claimed that it included a bonus to One With Nature. At the time, Elijah hadn't known what to expect from it, but now, leaning against that tree in the middle of a forest, he felt more at home than he'd ever felt before in his life.

In the past, Elijah had been no stranger to the outdoors. As a child, he'd grown up camping and hiking with his parents, and he'd continued that positive relationship with nature when he'd chosen his career as a marine biologist. Often, during a hike or when he was sitting on a boat in the middle of the ocean, he'd found himself looking around in abject wonder and appreciation for the natural world. Sometimes, it was the result of gazing at a particularly vivid sunset. Or seeing a mighty storm on the horizon. Maybe overlooking a raging river that cut through a deep canyon. It had happened so many times that the scenes themselves tended to blend together. But the feeling remained.

Now, it had been dialed up to a hundred, and as a result, he didn't just feel an appreciation for nature. Instead, it was a connection. He was no longer standing outside, a spectator looking in; rather, he was a part of it. Another piece of the ecological puzzle. Simply put, he belonged.

He let out a sigh, and for a long moment, Elijah simply basked in that feeling. It overwhelmed his pain, ushering it into the back of his mind. The agony was still there, but in the face of that overwhelming sense of belonging, it was a pitiful thing that barely even qualified as discomfort.

Then, suddenly, that oneness with nature faded away, little by little, until it was only a vague awareness. A metaphysical anchor that kept him moored to the natural world.

But more than that, it gave him some insight into his own being, which was divided into four distinct pieces. There was his physical body, weak but vibrant with potential. Then, his mind, a snarl of errant thoughts and determination. His soul, an ephemeral web that suffused his entire body, almost like a second circulatory System but far more complex and infinitely more meaningful.

The last piece drew his attention more than any other, though. At the center of who he was, there was a gleaming ball of energy. Physically, it was located in the center of his chest. Spiritually, it was at the intersection of his soul; each pathway inevitably stemmed from that sphere of power, the thickest and most powerful of which ran to his mind.

It was all connected, but that core was the driving force behind everything. So, he focused on it. A second later, he let out a ragged gasp. The energy contained in that core wasn't just overwhelming. It was domineering. But even the brief glimpse Elijah had managed told him that it was the key to everything. So, marshaling his willpower, he shoved his attention back into the core, keeping one thing on his mind.

Touch of Nature, he thought. When he did, a surge of power rushed through his soul. It built for a long second until, at last, it flowed into his hand. Elijah opened his eyes to see that his fingers glowed with a soft, verdant light.

Trembling, Elijah reached out to touch the most egregious wound on his leg, where the crab had torn a three-inch chunk of flesh from his calf. If he'd been capable of washing out the dirt, debris, and blood, he felt certain he would have seen bone. But when he touched the wound, the green light surged, blanketing it in a warm glow. Then, the flesh began to writhe, bits of muscle and skin growing out in tendrils until they connected with the other side. One after another, looking like fleshy string, they mended together, and as they did, they pushed the foreign substances out.

But it wasn't easy. In fact, holding that concentration was one of the most difficult things Elijah had ever done. If it wasn't a matter of survival, he might not have managed it. However, it was, so he did, keeping the energy—no—the System called it Ethera—flowing through his soul and into his mind, which somehow converted it into the spell.

After a few moments, he couldn't hold it anymore, and with a gasp, his core sputtered, and the Ethera ran dry. Still, when he looked down at his leg, he saw mostly unbroken skin where the wound had once been. There were plenty more up and down his calves and on his feet, but in mere moments, he'd managed to completely heal a wound that should've taken weeks to mend.

Elijah sighed in relief and sagged against the tree. Its presence was comforting, like an old friend who'd wrapped him in its warm embrace. For a moment, Elijah considered simply giving in to his exhaustion and closing his eyes. However, it only took the memory of waking up to being eaten by giant crabs to disabuse him of that notion. So, he sat there, regulating his breathing as he concentrated on his core.

Slowly, it refilled, but it didn't generate the Ethera itself. Instead, Elijah's mind seemed to have become a funnel, absorbing the energy from the environment and channeling it through his soul down to his core. The key seemed to be keeping his mind clear; otherwise, he could sense the rate of recovery slow to a crawl. Overall, it took almost ten minutes for him to refill his Ethera reserves. Once his core was full, he repeated the process on his other wounds, stopping only when he ran dry of Ethera.

It took most of the rest of the day, but by the time the sun began to dip toward the horizon, Elijah was healthier than he'd been in months. He was still weak—remarkably so—but he didn't feel sick or injured. He couldn't be certain if the cancer was actually gone, but he felt well enough that it gave him some hope for the future. Perhaps he wasn't going to die, after all.

Not immediately, at least.

But the fact of the matter was that, even if he was healthy, he was still stranded in the wilderness, alone and with no supplies. And if the size of those crabs was any indication of what to expect, the wildlife had been affected by whatever had turned the world upside down, as well. It wasn't outside the realm of possibility that things were much more dangerous now than they had been when he'd left Hawaii.

Even so, there was cause for optimism. He was still weak, but he'd just used an actual magic spell to heal wounds that should have been crippling in his current environment. Without Touch of Nature, those wounds would have soon gotten infected, and given the state of his immune System, he would have succumbed not long after that. Now, though, he had a new lease on life, and he wasn't going to waste it.

So, he gathered all the knowledge he'd managed to compile over decades of camping and hiking, and he began to make a list of what he needed to do if he was going to survive for longer than a couple of days.

The first thing he did was check his pockets for his phone, which proved completely unfruitful. It must have fallen out when he'd hit the water. Or while floating in the ocean, perhaps. It wasn't unexpected, but still, the inability to simply call for rescue was disappointing. In any case, he moved on to the other necessities for survival.

First, he needed water. Then shelter. Fire. And finally, food. Luckily, the biome seemed to suggest that he was still in the Pacific Northwest, which meant that water should be plentiful. Shelter might be a little more difficult to find, but given the time of year, food should be abundant. Sure, mushrooms and berries weren't always appetizing, but they would sustain him until he could find something else.

Fire would be the most difficult, especially without specialized tools like a ferro rod or a lighter. Even so, he'd made fires from scratch before, and though the environment was incredibly wet—there were places in the Pacific Northwest that were classified as actual rainforests—he hoped he could put those long-dormant skills to good use.

For now, though, Elijah needed to explore his surroundings to see if he could find a ready source of fresh water. So, after inspecting himself for wounds one more time, he pushed himself to his feet. The surge of energy he felt upon standing was enough to make him stumble, and he pressed one hand to the pine tree, steadying himself.

He just wasn't used to feeling . . . good.

If anything, that highlighted how adaptable people could really be, that he'd managed to keep going for as long as he had. But now, he didn't have to worry about that.

He hoped.

With a sigh, Elijah shook his head, reminding himself that he didn't have much choice in the matter. Before, he'd been completely incapable of changing his fate. The cancer was terminal, and he'd accepted his death as inevitable. However, now that it seemed to be gone—or at least weakened enough that he'd been given a fighting chance—he felt free. But it was all an illusion. If it still decided to kill him, there was still nothing he could do about it. So, he chose to focus on the things he could affect—mainly, the items on his list.

After taking a deep, steadying breath, he pushed away from the tree and trekked inland. It was slow going, mostly due to the density of the forest, but Elijah was an old hand at picking his way through the wilds. So, he made gradual progress until the sound of a stream filled his ears.

By that point, the forest had descended into dusk, which made finding shelter almost as much of a priority as finding water to quench his thirst. Still, he trudged forward until he stumbled onto a small stream. It was only a few feet across, but it flowed extremely quickly across the rocks that made up the streambed.

Elijah collapsed next to the water, cupping his hands and taking a big gulp. He knew he should have taken the time to boil it, but he was hoping that the combination of his high Constitution and the healing power of Touch of Nature would be a match for any sickness that came from the microbes in the water. Regardless, he didn't have much choice in the matter. Every piece of wood he'd seen during his trek through the forest had been soaked through by the incessant humidity and the frequent drizzling rain, meaning that he'd have to get lucky if he wanted to start a proper fire.

After drinking his fill, Elijah sat back and focused on the sense of One With Nature, and he was surprised to find that it was subtly different than it had been closer to the shore. Stronger, in some ways. But gentler, too. It was as if there was some sort of calming presence watching over the area.

And he got the impression that it would be stronger the farther inland he traveled.

As curious as Elijah was, though, he was in no shape to investigate. Night was on its way, and he needed to find some sort of shelter before that happened. Being alone in the wilderness in the dark was one thing, but trying to sleep in the rain was even worse. So, he reluctantly pushed himself back to his feet and followed the stream uphill.

As he did so, Elijah continued to look for a hollow or an overhang that might prove to be decent shelter for the night. But to his eternal surprise and good fortune, only twenty minutes later he found himself staring at something wholly unexpected in such rugged country.

It was a cabin.

It was old and decrepit, and the roof looked on the verge of collapse. But soaked through, tired, and with night nipping at Elijah's heels, the cabin looked like a godsend. He ambled forward, tripping over a root along the way, but he maintained his balance until he reached the wall.

The cabin itself had been constructed of a series of horizontal logs, with the gaps filled in with mud. The roof was of similar construction, but a layer of moss and leaves would provide insulation. A metal tube, rusted and barely holding together, extended from one of the walls, and Elijah reasoned that it must be the cabin's chimney.

"Hello?" he called, sure that he was wasting his time. The cabin was in too poor of shape to have housed anyone in a long while.

That impression was further cemented in Elijah's mind when he began to circle around the structure, and he saw that half of it had, indeed, collapsed long ago. He shook his head, wondering what had happened. How old was the cabin? Why hadn't the owner fixed it? Where were they now? A hundred similar questions raced through Elijah's thoughts, but there were no answers forthcoming.

So, he carefully climbed over the debris, making certain not to impale his bare feet on anything particularly sharp, and looked around inside. There wasn't much there. An old pot that might be good for boiling water or, eventually, cooking. A rusted knife that didn't look sharp enough to do anything with. And the remains of some rotted furniture. Altogether, it wasn't much better than if he'd found a cave.

But for now, it would have to do. Tomorrow, he'd have to find food and a better place to sleep so he could regain his Strength and prepare for whatever came next. He still hadn't decided if he wanted to continue his trek inland to look for civilization or if he wanted to stay put and wait for rescue.

There were merits in favor of either course of action. On the one hand, most survival guides would have told him to stay where he was and wait for rescue. There were plenty of exceptions to that rule, though, and in any case, everything he'd seen on that plane suggested that the world had experienced significant upheaval. It would be a bit naive to expect someone to rescue him.

But as Elijah settled down in the most intact corner of the cabin, curling up, he decided that that was a decision better made after a good night's rest.

7

MANY PATHS TO POWER

After a night filled with fitful sleep, Elijah woke to a world of pain twisting through his stomach. He clutched at his midsection and, as cramps assailed him, heaved the meager contents of his stomach onto the ground beside him. There was precious little there—mostly liquid, in fact, which gave him some clues as to what had happened. The water he'd drunk the evening before had obviously been contaminated.

"Stupid," he muttered, thinking back to his decision to drink the water without even trying to boil it. But in his defense, he didn't really have the means to start a fire. And until he'd found the cabin, he hadn't had anything in which to boil any water he managed to collect. For a healthy person, the tainted water might not have been that impactful, but his immune System had been devastated by the deadly combination of cancer, chemotherapy, and radiation, and despite the effects of his increased attributes, he clearly wasn't fully recovered.

Once his stomach stopped twisting and turning, Elijah sat up and closed his eyes. The pain was still there, but he needed to move past it. He had plenty of experience in that arena, what with everything he'd been through while fighting his disease, so it wasn't that difficult to concentrate on the ball of energy in his chest. With an effort of will, he mentally embraced the Ethera in his core, grasping at it with his consciousness.

The shock was like dunking his entire mind in frigid water. Or molten lava. It was difficult to tell the difference, the feeling was so intense. However, he pushed past that shock, wrapped his core in his willpower, and pulled. As he did so, he muttered, "Touch of Nature."

His hand lit up with verdant energy, and when he laid it on his rebellious stomach, the spell flowed forth and back into his body. For only an instant, Elijah could follow its path, but soon, it left his perception behind. However, a few seconds later, he felt the spell take hold as it healed the damage inflicted by whatever parasite had twisted his stomach into knots.

The spell only lasted for a few moments, but by the time the green energy dissipated, Elijah felt better than he had since before being diagnosed. He wasn't so naive as to think that his little spell could cure cancer; based on how long it had taken to heal his legs, he suspected that it didn't have nearly enough power to do that. Instead, it felt like confirmation that the attribute points that he'd allocated into Constitution had been well spent.

Was he cured?

He had no idea, but he intended to investigate it further. Even if he hadn't been completely healed, he'd made progress. And for now, that was enough to give him a jolt of optimism and energy.

So, with streams of morning sunlight cutting through the forest's dense canopy, Elijah pushed himself to his feet and stretched aching muscles. Whatever benefits he'd gotten from Touch of Nature, it had done nothing to counteract the effects of sleeping in such an uncomfortable position. Not that he would complain too much. Not only was he alive, but he had access to magic.

Plus, there was still that slight tingle in the air giving him a trickle of energy and a sense of belonging. He didn't quite feel at home, but he wasn't nearly as distressed as being stranded in the wilderness should have made him.

After a few minutes of stretching, Elijah thought back to the simple list of things he wanted to accomplish. The first part was to catalog everything he'd found in the ruined cabin. It was all trash, but in the wilderness, even garbage could be useful.

A rusted knife. A pot. And a few piles of wood. There was also a coil of rope, but it was so rotted that he wouldn't trust it to hold even the meager weight of his cancer-ravaged body. Overall, it wasn't much, but it was better than he could have expected. The pot, in particular, would be incredibly useful when he managed to start a fire.

Clutching the rusted knife in his hand, he arduously hacked off the shredded hems of his pants, carefully putting the cloth in his pockets where he hoped they would dry into decent tinder. It wasn't a great idea, but everything else in the forest was perpetually damp. He had some other thoughts on how to get around that, but for now, he would take the steps he could and hope for better luck in the future.

With that done, he scoured the area around the cabin for a walking stick. Fortunately, a storm had come through sometime in the past few days, breaking plenty of limbs. So, Elijah had no difficulty finding a stout, mostly straight branch that could serve as both a walking stick and a means of protection from any nearby predators. Of course, he didn't think he was going to fight them off. The best he could hope for was to use the stick to establish some distance before he ran away.

As he'd searched through the forest, though, Elijah got the distinct sensation that he was being watched. However, no matter how often or how quickly he turned, he saw nothing. Perhaps it was only his imagination playing tricks on him.

Or maybe some apex predator who'd been transformed alongside the rest of the planet was stalking him.

He shuddered at the thought. There were plenty of predators native to the Pacific Northwest. From bears to wolves and everything in between, they were dangerous enough before the influx of Ethera had transformed the planet. But if they'd been affected like the crabs? The last thing Elijah wanted to run into was a van-sized brown bear.

Regardless, he didn't have much of a choice in the matter. If he was going to live—or maybe even thrive—he couldn't just stay huddled in that ruined cabin. He needed kindling. He needed firewood and food. Otherwise, he might as well lay down and die.

So, marshaling his courage, Elijah set off into the woods. All the while, sticks and rocks stabbed him in the feet, but he ignored the discomfort. None of it drew blood, and he could always use Touch of Nature to heal any damage at the end of the day.

As he walked, he kept an eye out for reasonably dry sticks, picking them up when he stumbled upon them. He also kept a lookout for birch trees, hoping to use their bark for tinder. On that account, he was unlucky.

Still, he was fortunate enough to find some red bunchberries and a huge chanterelle mushroom. Elijah used the front of his shirt to carry them as he continued his exploration. That same feeling of being watched followed him through the forest until he finally broke free from the brush and into a wide meadow.

The clearing was about two hundred yards long and about half again as wide, but it was completely clear, save for a single huge oak tree that towered hundreds of feet into the sky. However, as impressive as that sight was, Elijah was more concerned with the wispy white dandelions dotting the small prairie.

He couldn't help but smile as he realized that he'd found his tinder. It wasn't perfect, and he'd have to gather hundreds of the cottony white seeds, but there were plenty available. Gleefully, he crossed the meadow and began collecting his bounty, shoving the seeds into one of his pockets.

His happiness at finding such a ready supply of tinder was so intoxicating that he almost didn't notice that the feeling of belonging that had suffused the entire forest had only grown stronger. But once he did, he immediately knew the source. He looked up at the tree towering over the meadow.

It called to him.

And before Elijah realized what was happening, he found himself stumbling across the meadow. When he reached the tree, he extended a trembling hand and laid it on the rough bark of its trunk. A soothing sensation filled Elijah's entire body. Suddenly, his muscles relaxed. His mind cleared. And the fatigue that had been building from the moment he'd woken up fell away.

Then, he felt a presence.

"Hello," came a high-pitched voice.

Elijah jerked his head up, and he saw . . . something growing out of the lowest branch. At first, he thought it was just another limb, gnarled as it was.

However, as he looked closer, he saw that it had taken the shape of a tiny six-inch-tall person. That person, though, was made entirely of branches that had grown together. It had no defining features, and one of its wooden hands clutched at the trunk.

"Did I startle you?" asked the tree creature.

"Uh . . . N-no," Elijah said, his voice hoarse from lack of use. "What . . . I mean . . . Who are you?"

The creature cocked its head to the side as if thinking about Elijah's question. Then, after a few seconds, it said, "I am the tree, and the tree is me. I only took this form so I could communicate with you."

"Why? Not that I'm . . . ungrateful," Elijah said. "It's just that I've never spoken to a tree before."

"A druid who does not speak to trees? How?" it said. Then, it leaned forward, never taking its arm from the trunk. "Ah—I see. You are very weak. New to power. Understandable. But this will not do. My protector cannot be so weak."

"Protector?"

"Indeed," said the tree. "You are a druid, and this is your Grove. Therefore, you must protect me."

Elijah had no idea what to say to that. In fact, the whole encounter was so strange and unbelievable that he was unsure what to even think.

"I have decided to help you."

"What? How?" he asked.

"Information," the tree said. "Now, sit. I will guide you to your first breakthrough. It is not much, but it will give you a better chance of survival."

"Breakthrough? What kind of breakthrough?" he asked, cursing his own ignorance. He didn't know anything about the new form the world had taken, and that lack was going to get him killed. So, he decided to wring as much information from the tree as was possible.

"Cultivation, of course," said the tree creature. Somehow, even without any facial features, the thing was able to convey that it considered Elijah something of an idiot.

"I have no idea what that means," he said. "I saw it on my status sheet, but—"

"Heavenly Status," said the tree.

"Uh . . . Okay. My Heavenly Status, then," Elijah corrected himself. "Anyway, I don't know if you realize it, but this world just got . . . I don't know . . . transformed, and there's no manual or anything to tell me what's going on."

"A newly integrated world?" the tree said. "Of course. Now I remember. That is why the Ethera is so thin. It makes perfect sense."

The tree creature sat down on the branch, then cupped its chin in one hand. "Hmm. So, you know nothing of the System? That is both a boon and a curse," it said. "You have an opportunity to grow very powerful, but with that power will come responsibilities." It looked up. "If you survive, of course."

Elijah swallowed hard. He'd already surmised that the new world would be dangerous. If he had magic, then surely others would, as well. And judging by what had happened with the crabs, the wildlife would be affected, too.

"I'll do whatever it takes," Elijah stated. He'd made peace with his impending death, but that didn't mean he intended to lie down and give up. He felt like he had a new lease on life, and he wasn't going to let it go without doing whatever he could.

"Very well," said the tree creature, sounding pleased. "But I am limited in how much information I can convey. The System does not prohibit charity, but there is an established System whereby newly integrated worlds can gain knowledge."

"I'll take whatever I can get."

"Yes, yes. You have some spirit in you," the tree said. "With how weak your body is, you will need that. In fact, I think that is where we will start."

"You want to heal me? I've been sick for a while, and—"

"No. And yes," the tree stated. "It is more complicated than that. Think of it more as I will be guiding you toward the tools that will allow you to heal yourself."

"Like Touch of Nature," Elijah reasoned.

"No. With cultivation."

"You keep saying that word like I should know what it means," Elijah countered. "But if you want me to plant something and help it grow, I'm not sure I have the tools or the—"

The tree sighed, a sound like wind whistling through its branches. Or perhaps the wind really was rustling its leaves. Elijah wasn't sure, and he didn't have much opportunity to figure it out because the tree said, "Cultivation is a System whereby a sentient being improves themselves. There are four categories—Body, Mind, Core, and Soul. They are intertwined but separate. Dependent on one another, but capable of progressing independently."

"O-okay . . ."

The tree went on: "Your body is the easiest, but in your situation, it will be the most impactful. Without it, you will likely die within a month or two."

"The cancer?"

"A disease, yes. I cannot sense any other specifics."

Elijah shook his head. So, his efforts at raising his Constitution attribute had been wasted, and the resultant spike of energy was unrelated. He hadn't been healed at all.

It wasn't really unprecedented. There had been times after his diagnosis when Elijah had almost felt normal. Usually, those moments were brief, and they usually coincided with distractions. Now, he realized that the plane crash and all the changes he had experienced had probably caused such a moment.

"What do the others do?" he asked.

"Your Mind dictates how quickly you can funnel Ethera into your soul," it said. "Together with your Regeneration attribute, it determines how quickly you can refill your stores of Ethera.

"Then there is your Soul, which determines how quickly you can bring that Ethera to bear via spells, abilities, and skills."

It went on: "But the Core is the most important aspect of your cultivation. At its most basic level, it is where you store your Ethera, and when you cultivate it, you increase the potency of your Ethera. However, it will also influence your entire path, which is arguably more important."

"Why don't we improve that one, then?" Elijah asked.

"Because you are not ready," the tree said. "In addition, without advancing your Body cultivation, you will surely die, regardless of the stage of your core. And finally, it requires more than this world is currently capable of providing."

"But what—"

"To tell you more than that would be to risk the ire of the System," the tree stated. "For now, all I can do is put you on the path. Learn this lesson well because your life will depend on it."

"I . . . I understand."

"Good," the tree said. "Now, let us begin."

8

CLEARING THE STATION

Alyssa knelt in the park across the street from the police station. Next to her was Roman, with the other three a few feet behind. She asked, "What do you think?"

"It's not good," he said, clutching his bow. Alyssa noticed that his knuckles were white, and if she was honest, she didn't blame him even a little. On their way through town, they'd seen plenty of evidence that the world as they knew it was gone. They'd even had to fight a couple of battles, though with Alyssa's Heavy Blows–empowered machete and Roman's bow skills, none of the mutated creatures had lasted long.

Thankfully, they hadn't seen anything like that first wolf monster they'd encountered.

"Do you think it's another wolf?" she asked, still studying the shattered glass of the front door. "Or something worse? Maybe one of those huge raccoons?"

"I don't know," he admitted, running his hand through his hair. He looked as bad as Alyssa felt. Just like her, he took the little town's safety as his personal responsibility, and they'd seen plenty of evidence of just how thoroughly they'd failed in that endeavor. Not that they could have predicted that the world would be transformed overnight, but still, it hit them both extremely hard.

Especially when they'd seen the bodies.

So far, there had only been a few, and they were so chewed up that they were unrecognizable. Even so, no one in their little group had been unaffected.

Alyssa rested her hand on the grip of her pistol. Not because she thought it would do much good. If nothing else, the trip across town had proved just how ineffective firearms were against the transformed creatures. Even the raccoons, which seemed to be the weakest monsters they'd encountered, took an entire magazine to put down. The machete at her hip had proved a much more reliable weapon.

The same was true of Roman's bow.

Even Carmen's shotgun, which she'd gotten from the gun safe in their basement, hadn't done much, and she'd been forced to fight with the old softball bat. It hadn't lasted long, and she'd replaced it with a solid-steel crowbar, which, with her Strength, was devastating.

The one who'd taken it worst was Trish. She was a nice enough woman, but she just wasn't built for the apocalypse. Prone to panic and incapable of acting in a crisis, she was more of a liability than an asset. Even her ability to heal couldn't change that.

By comparison, Miguel was taking the end of the world remarkably well. Certainly, he was frightened. What eight-year-old wouldn't be? But he'd proved his mothers' son, and he'd responded to the dire situation by searching for ways to make himself useful. At present, he was the group's pack mule, carrying extra ammunition and a few bottles of water.

Their other supplies were in shopping carts they'd taken from the market.

"We're going to have to go in soon," Alyssa said, glancing at the sky. The sun was almost to the horizon, which meant night would soon be upon them. None of them wanted to be outside after sunset, which meant they needed to clear the station out, then secure it so they could hole up for the night.

In the morning, they would establish more permanent defenses.

"I know," Roman stated, shaking his head. "I don't like it. There's something in there. I know it."

"Does that change anything?" Alyssa asked. "We can't go back."

Indeed, the house was miles away, and it would take at least twenty minutes to reach any other building that might offer any security.

"I'm aware. I'm just not looking forward to what we have to do."

"That's fair."

"Where do you think everyone else is?" he asked. They'd only seen a few townspeople along the way, and none of them seemed keen on doing anything but barricading themselves in their houses. Even when Alyssa had offered to protect them, they'd remained silent. Not for the first time, she recognized that being a police officer didn't exactly engender trust. The relationship between law enforcement and the general populace had been shattered, and it seemed that the end of the world hadn't changed that.

Alyssa shrugged. "It's probably not healthy to think about that right now," she said. "Okay, so here's what I'm thinking. I'll run in there and—"

"By yourself? No chance."

"Just listen, alright? I'll run in there. I got that new ability," she said. Indeed, she'd gained a level along the way, and it had granted her a new ability:

Charge	**Dash forward at 200% your normal speed for three (3) seconds. Your next attack will do 30% more damage.**

"I can go in, see what's in there, and if I get in trouble, I'll use Charge," she said. "That way, I can lead them out here, where you'll be waiting to fill them full of arrows."

"It sounds dangerous."

"More than taking Trish and Miggy in there?" she asked. "Because I don't know about you, but I have no intention of letting my son in that building until I know for sure there aren't any monsters. Too much can go wrong in an enclosed space. If keeping him safe means I have to take on a little more, then so be it."

Alyssa had worked with Roman for almost five years, so she knew him well enough to recognize the sour expression for what it was. He didn't like the plan, but he also had no alternative proposal. The reality was that the trip across town had taken a lot longer than any of them could have anticipated, and now, they were overextended. With night coming, they didn't have a lot of choices.

"We could go back to the bank," he said. "It's less than a mile away."

"There are probably monsters there, too. You saw that hole in the front window," Alyssa reminded him. Indeed, they'd only passed a couple of buildings that hadn't been breached, and none that were close enough to reach before dark. "You know I'm right, Chief. This is the best option. Besides, you can set that new ability of yours up, too."

"I don't trust it," he muttered.

"Embrace the magic, chief," she said, forcing a grin she didn't really feel. "That's all we can do at this point."

Alyssa understood his reservations. It was one thing to use something like Heavy Blows, which just made her better at something she was already doing. But to manifest a trap out of nothing? That was enough to hammer home just how much things had changed. Sure, the monsters did the same, but it required a different sort of response than being able to use magic.

Or Ethera, as every notification seemed to remind them.

In Roman's case, his second ability—or spell, as it was categorized—let him set a magical trap that hobbled any hostile creature that passed through. The effect didn't last more than a few seconds, but the one time they'd tested it, the spell had worked extremely well. How it differentiated between enemies and allies was still a mystery, but it managed it all the same.

"Let's do it, then. Daylight's burning," he said, replacing his cap.

"Probably should let them know the plan," Alyssa said, nodding to the other three. They were far enough away that they had been incapable of hearing the exchange.

"I'll take care of it," Roman stated. "You need to get moving. We'll be ready when you come out."

"Alright."

With that, Alyssa stood, then looked back at Carmen. She nodded at her wife before taking a deep breath and turning toward the station. She and Roman strode forward together, but he didn't pass through the door. Instead, he knelt before it, holding his hands out and casting his spell. Meanwhile, Alyssa stepped into the lobby, holding her machete in one hand and the pistol in the other.

If everything went according to plan, she wouldn't need either. Not inside the building, at least. Outside was a different story, and she didn't want to think about the immediate future. It was attention she couldn't spare.

So, she crept through the familiar lobby, passing the receptionist's desk and into the office space. There, she saw ten desks, each sporting a computer monitor. Beyond was an interrogation room, a break room, and a couple of storage closets. On the other side stood the chief's office.

Alyssa stepped softly, keeping her breathing as even as she could. It had been a long time since she'd hunted, but she hadn't forgotten the lessons her father had taught her. Sure, Elijah had always been the more skilled outdoorsman, but Alyssa hadn't lagged too far behind. So, she channeled those skills as she cleared the area, finding nothing.

Next, she checked the outer rooms, finding more of the same. Which was to say, nothing. In fact, Alyssa was starting to think that, perhaps, whatever had broken into the station had already abandoned it.

But she knew better.

Besides, there was still one level left to clear. The basement contained the holding cells as well as the armory, which meant that there was plenty of space downstairs to host any number of horrors.

So, after taking another deep breath, Alyssa approached the stairs. Opening the door, she poked her head inside.

And nearly gagged.

There, sprawled across the floor, was a half-eaten corpse that had once been one of her colleagues. By his skin tone, it was Jerome, one of the other deputies. Alyssa didn't need to check for a pulse to know he was dead. Not only was he completely stationary, but he was missing a third of his torso. Nobody could live through that.

Still, after making certain that nothing was going to jump out and try to eat her, she knelt beside him and collected the magazines at his belt. Ammunition would soon grow scarce, and there was every chance that she would need it. After all, whatever had killed Jerome was probably still around.

Taking a deep, steadying breath, Alyssa continued down the stairs. Notably, Jerome had clearly tried to climb to safety, as evidenced by trail of blood-soaked stairs. Alyssa ignored them, instead focusing on her surroundings.

Which was a good thing because, as she hit the staircase's switchback, something launched itself at her. But it didn't come from below. Instead, it descended from the low ceiling, spreading bat-like wings as it snapped at her with slavering jaws. With so much adrenaline coursing through her veins, she responded with incredible alacrity, slashing out with her machete.

The monster—and it could be nothing else—screeched as the blade bit deep into its furry body. But it still got its claws into her forearm. Alyssa screamed as she tried to dislodge it, banging the monster against the wall. Yet, despite her frantic efforts, it held fast. So, she jammed the pistol against its bulbous body, then squeezed the trigger.

The weapon discharged with an earsplitting and unmistakable crack, which was soon followed by another. And another after that. The monster went wild as she emptied the entire magazine into the creature. Blood and fur misted into the air, but it held on until the very end.

Finally, after she'd discharged every single round into the monster, Alyssa banged it against the wall. Over and over until, at last, its screeches became burbling wheezes. Then, at last, it fell free.

Alyssa stared at it for a long moment, unsure of what she saw. The monster was bat-like but with humanoid characteristics. Especially its face, which looked almost simian.

But she didn't have time to study it because the sound of a dozen flapping wings filled the air as more monsters ascended from below. Alyssa didn't hesitate to turn and run. She'd gotten the creatures' attention. Now, she just needed to lead them outside where, hopefully, her allies could finish them off.

That was easier said than done, though, largely because she had a flock of monkey bats trying to kill her. Dashing up the stairs, she had to duck under one such monster, then lash out with her machete to knock another out of her way before she could get through the door. Once she'd made it through, she used Charge.

Instantly, her body responded.

Alyssa had run track in college, so she'd always been relatively fast. But the speed she achieved after using Charge was something else altogether. If she ran any less than thirty-five miles an hour, she would have been incredibly surprised. However, that speed came with a cost—chiefly, that she had difficulty changing direction. For a few steps, she was fine, but then she clipped one of the desks, which sent her spinning. With so much momentum, that spin took her into one of the walls, where she caromed into another desk. But she still kept moving forward, eventually stumbling into the lobby and through the door.

The bat monkeys weren't far behind.

Charge dissipated, and she tumbled to the ground. She tried to turn it into a roll, but her movements were graceless, and she ended up sprawled across the pavement of the parking lot. Behind her, the bat monkeys screeched, the sound accompanied by the steady thwap of Roman's bow.

Meanwhile, Alyssa heard Carmen let out an inarticulate yell, and when she finally righted herself, she saw the stout woman swinging her crowbar at the disoriented and slowed bat monkeys. In the waning light, they looked like true monsters, largely because there was no way anything like them had ever existed on Earth.

But with Carmen's incredible Strength and Roman's steady aim, the flock of creatures soon fell.

Vaguely, Alyssa was aware of someone kneeling beside her. Trish reached out and used her Mend spell. Vitality flooded through Alyssa's body as her wounds closed. Instantly, her mind snapped into focus, but it was unnecessary. The monsters were all dead.

Roman and Carmen rushed over, and from somewhere, Miguel appeared with a bottle of water.

Alyssa looked up and said, "That definitely didn't go like I planned."

"You think? God, you're an idiot," groused Carmen.

"*Idiot* is a bad word," Miguel offered.

"I know, sweetie," said Carmen, tousling his hair. "But sometimes, bad words are appropriate."

"Is it clear?" Roman asked.

"I think so," Alyssa answered, pushing herself to her feet. Despite the healing, she was still a little unsteady. "I saw Jerome. He didn't make it."

"Shit. He was a good man," Roman stated. He sighed. "He won't be the last, though. Let's get inside and find something to block the door."

And with that, the group grabbed their carts full of supplies and headed into the station. Hopefully, it would prove more secure for them than it had been for poor Jerome.

9

AN INTRODUCTION TO CULTIVATION

What do I call you?" asked Elijah, still looking up at the tree creature.

"I have no name, for I am only a sapling," it said. "Regardless, this is the last time we will speak for a long span. I am nearly at the end of my available energy."

"Oh."

Elijah had no idea how to respond to that, so he'd decided to keep his mouth shut. As his father always said, it was better to remain silent and be thought a fool than to speak and remove all doubt. It had originally been an Abraham Lincoln quote, but Elijah's father had adopted it as a mantra.

Elijah missed the days he'd spent with his father. Most of the time, they didn't even talk; instead, they'd just sit in nature and enjoy one another's silent company. By contrast, his mother had been the talkative type whose base demeanor bordered on mania. She could be exhausting, but her good-natured attitude and kind heart had made it endearing rather than annoying.

Everything would have been so much easier to bear if they were still around. But fate had other ideas, and almost a decade past, they'd died in a brutal car crash. Back then, Elijah had just graduated high school, but he remembered it like it was yesterday.

He shook his head. It was neither the time nor the place to think about such things. If the tree creature was running low on energy, then its time was limited. Elijah needed to get as much information out of it as he could manage. He looked up and asked, "So, what do I do?"

"Sit," said the tree.

Elijah did, crossing his legs under him. The tree was surrounded by a carpet of green-and-yellow moss that had felt particularly luxurious on his sore feet. Sitting atop it was even better, and he found himself relaxing. Or perhaps that was just the tree's presence, which had put him at ease the moment he'd laid eyes on it.

"Put your hands on your knees," it said. "Then close your eyes."

Elijah followed the tree's instructions, feeling a bit silly. He'd tried meditation a few times, but he'd never achieved anything close to a quieted mind. Still, he'd tried it enough that he could recognize the trappings.

With his eyes closed, Elijah could feel everything even more clearly. That pull he'd felt back in the cabin was even more potent now, telling him that it had originated with the tree. However, he also felt a sense of connection that he couldn't quite wrap his head around. Like he was part of something far bigger and more complex than he could understand. But rather than feel overwhelmed by that reality, he instead felt immense comfort. It was as if all he had to do was just let go, and he could throw away his individuality in favor of—

"Listen to me, young one! Hear my voice!" thundered the tree with far more volume and authority than it had before. "Do not surrender."

It took a few more moments for Elijah to latch on to the tree's continuous instructions, but when he did, he felt overwhelmed with what he'd been about to do. In seconds, he'd nearly given up on everything that made him an individual.

"The Call is strong here," said the tree, its voice far gentler. "That you can resist it at all is a testament to your individualistic nature."

"The Call?" asked Elijah.

"Of nature," the tree stated. "Of the collective. We call her the Mother of All. But that is your first lesson, young druid. To become one with the Mother is tempting. It will feel natural. But that is not our path. You must resist, or you will lose yourself. Do you understand? Do not surrender."

"I . . . I understand" was Elijah's response. And he did. He was horrified that it had only taken him a few seconds before he'd almost willingly sacrificed his individuality in favor of joining with the Mother.

"You must feel her presence," it said. "But you must not let it overwhelm you. Try."

Elijah focused on that feeling, keeping a firm grip on his own identity. It was difficult, and it took quite a while, but with every breath, he let himself more fully perceive the energy surrounding him. In his mind's eye, it was green, but that was just a construct of his imagination. Still, it helped. For a while, it continued to try to convince him to surrender, but now that he was aware, he could resist The Call. Barely. However, with every passing moment, it was a little easier.

"Now, look closer," the tree intoned. "Separate the Call from the Ethera."

Elijah followed the tree's instructions. For a long time, he didn't even know what he was looking for, but as the minutes passed into hours, he began to recognize a subtle difference between the energy and the presence of The Mother. It still felt like her, but it was separate. Completely different from the Ethera in his core.

"I see it," Elijah said, completely unaware of the sweat pouring down his hairless face. In fact, he was so deeply enmeshed in his trance that he could barely perceive the passage of time.

"Good. Reach out with your awareness and drag the Ethera toward you," said the tree. "But do not absorb it through your Mind. Surround yourself with it."

That was much more difficult. Elijah could barely even follow what the energy was doing when his Mind harvested it from the air and funneled it down into his Core. When he'd done it before, most of the process was automated; he'd just had to give it a nudge. But interrupting that process and forcing the energy to do something else? That was extraordinarily difficult.

Still, Elijah bent his will to doing just that, concentrating the entirety of his being on keeping the ambient Ethera from entering through the vortex in his mind. In the end, his will acted as a one-way door, letting the suction of the funnel act on the Ethera but not letting anything through. Hour after hour passed, but he didn't let up.

Eventually, the gathered Ethera began to pool around him, growing ever denser as it clung to his body. One layer after another, it condensed further and further until Elijah could hardly breathe.

He pushed harder, packing the energy around him until it had become a cocoon of Ethera.

"Hold it there," said the tree, a note of strain in its voice.

Elijah complied, focusing every ounce of his will on keeping the energy as densely packed as he could. And then an avalanche of Ethera crashed into him. He almost lost control as the pressure built far past what he could handle. But the new onslaught of energy was more controlled.

"Now, condense it!" roared the tree, its voice so powerful that it sent reverberations throughout Elijah's body. "Focus your will on harnessing the Ethera and compacting it into your body!"

Elijah pulled with his will, focusing on the tree's instructions. He didn't stop to wonder how he was doing any of it. Indeed, if he had, he would have felt like he'd gone insane. Or perhaps that he was concussed. But he didn't have any room for such thoughts in his mind. He could only do as the tree ordered.

Even so, he almost lost his grip when his entire body erupted into agony.

It was as if he'd descended thousands of feet underwater without any protective gear. The human body just wasn't meant to withstand that kind of pressure, and it felt like he was on the verge of implosion. His bones creaked, and his organs felt like they were about to rupture.

If he could have stopped it, he would have. But the Ethera had taken on a mind of its own, increasing the pressure exponentially with every passing second. Elijah tried to scream, but he couldn't open his mouth. And even if he could, there was no air in his lungs.

He was dying.

He knew it. The tree had tricked him into willingly walking to his own doom. But Elijah didn't have the willpower left to curse his own naivete.

Eventually, the pressure leveled out, but that was little relief for Elijah. He couldn't move. He could scarcely think, much less try to break free as the Ethera began to solidify around him. In the beginning, it felt like a dense fog, but then it was like being submerged in water that, in turn, became gelatinous. At some point, it turned completely solid, then crystalline, where it settled.

Elijah wanted to scream. To rail against his captor. But he couldn't marshal the willpower, and even if he could, he was frozen in place. He could only await his fate.

Like that, time passed. It could have been hours, days, months, or even years. Perhaps he would sit there, trapped in that crystalline prison for all eternity.

And then, suddenly, there was a cracking sound, followed by the sensation of immense power washing through him. Another crack. And then another.

Over and over, tiny fissures appeared in the crystal. Elijah still couldn't open his eyes, but he could feel tiny surges of relief with each crack. Then, finally, the crystal shattered, and he fell over, gasping for breath.

That's when the smell hit him.

It was like rotten garbage and sewage rolled into one horrible odor. Lying on his side, he retched, but only a little water came out. Coughing, he pushed himself to his hands and knees. Hanging his head, he muttered, "W-what did you do to me?"

"Nothing," said the tree. "I merely provided a little push. You did this to yourself. That is how cultivating the body works."

Elijah slowly sat up, shifting away from the tiny puddle of vomit. However, when he looked down at the blanket of moss that had surrounded the huge tree, he was distressed to see that the once-green-and-yellow carpet had become black and shriveled, almost as if the life had been sucked out of it.

Then, he looked at his hands, which were covered in a black tar-like substance. As distressing as that was, he was more concerned with the state of his fingers. Over the course of his chemotherapy, his body had been ravaged by the toxic chemicals, but the most troubling side effect was when he'd started to lose his fingernails. His toenails had soon followed, but by that point, he had been distracted by other, more pressing issues.

Now, though, his nails had returned, and what's more, the skin he saw beneath the tar-like substance had lost the pallid, sickly complexion that had been with him for months. In its place was healthy skin.

"What happened?" he asked, confused. He'd thought the tree had been trying to kill him. Or, perhaps, to feed off of him in some way. But now? He wasn't so sure.

"You have broken through to the first stage of Body cultivation," the tree said. "You will be stronger, faster, more durable, and healthier than you've ever been before. That substance covering you is impurity made manifest and purged from your body. Whatever disease from which you suffered has now been cured."

Impurities. Elijah guessed that much of what had been purged from his body had been related to the chemotherapy he'd undergone. To confirm what the tree had said, Elijah opened his status:

Name	Elijah Hart		
Level	1		
Archetype	Druid		
Class	N/A		
Specialization	N/A		
Alignment	N/A		
Strength	3		
Dexterity	4		
Constitution	11		
Ethera	4		
Regeneration	7		
Attunement	Nature		
Cultivation			
Body	Core	Mind	Soul
Wood	Unformed	Unformed	Unformed

Elijah shook his head. Not only had he picked up an Attunement—whatever that meant—he'd also progressed his Body cultivation from Unformed to Wood. The next question seemed obvious, so he asked, "What comes after Wood?"

"Stone," said the tree. "But you will have to find an area with much denser Ethera if you want to progress. As it stands, even if you were fortunate enough to find such a place, attempting to take the next step would kill you."

"What? How am I supposed to progress, then?" asked Elijah.

"So impatient" was the tree's response. "Barely taken one unsteady step on the path, and already, you want to run. The first—and easiest way—to ensure that you are ready to progress is to gain levels. You can do this in a variety of ways. Killing other creatures is the most common, but any use of your skills or spells will count toward your progression."

"Like a video game . . ."

The tree either didn't hear Elijah's muttered interruption, or it simply chose not to acknowledge it. It continued, "The other method is to acclimate yourself to increasingly denser Ethera. To do so, you must repeat what you did here today. Over and over, improving bit by bit until you can take the next step."

Elijah's eyes flicked to the other categories of Core, Mind, and Soul. So, he asked, "What about the others? How do I progress my Core?"

"I cannot answer that," said the tree. Its voice had already grown dimmer, and Elijah thought it looked even smaller than before. "What I did here was the limit of the assistance I could give, and even that was toeing the line between what is and is not allowed. Any further, and . . . it would not be good."

"What else can you tell me?" Elijah asked. He was grateful for the help the tree had given him—even if it was only limited to ridding his body of cancer and the impurities associated with the radiation and chemotherapy—but he wasn't averse to pushing for more. After all, the more information he could get, the better prepared he would be to survive. Perhaps he could even get to Seattle and find his sister and her family. Though he sensed that with how much the world had changed, that might be a far-off goal.

"Nothing," said the tree. "I can only wish you luck on your journey. When next we speak, I hope to see that you have progressed."

"But—"

The tree creature shrank before Elijah's very eyes, growing smaller until it was only a small protrusion atop the branch. At the beginning of their conversation, the tree creature had claimed to be an extension of the tree, and now, it had retracted.

He leaned back, trying to wrap his head around what had happened. He'd been healed, and if what the tree had said was true, his cultivation had given him a stronger body. What that meant—beyond the basic understanding that it was better—was still a mystery, though. He'd have to do some testing.

But first, he needed to head back to the stream and clean himself as well as he could.

Then, another question hit him: How long had he been in that crystalline chrysalis of condensed Ethera? It had felt like an eternity, but other than looking up at the sky, which was just as overcast as always, he had no context by which to tell time. He wasn't that hungry or thirsty, so maybe it had all been in his head.

The bushberries and the mushroom he'd gathered, as well as the dandelion fluff, had gone the same way as the carpet of moss. None of it was rotten, but rather, it was more like they had become blackened shells of what they'd once been.

Perhaps the tree had sustained him somehow. Either way, it didn't affect what he needed to do. So, he pushed himself to his feet and started back the way he'd come.

10

THE FIRST STEPS

Elijah ran his hand over his head, feeling a light stubble that should not have been there. After all, hair just wasn't supposed to grow that fast, was it? When the plane had crashed and the System had descended upon Earth, he had been completely bald, his hair having been sacrificed at the altar of chemotherapy. By his count, only a couple of days had passed since then.

Except for the chrysalis.

He had no idea how long he'd been in there. It could have been days. Years. Months. Or it might've been mere hours. His only hints were his budding hair growth, which wasn't really as informative as it could have been. After all, his entire body had changed—he could feel the Strength coursing through him—was it really so unthinkable that cultivating a body of Wood might prompt some rapid hair growth?

Letting out a sigh, Elijah left the majestic tree behind and went about restoring his stock of dandelion fluff. He might have been cured of his cancer, but his needs were still the same. He needed water, food, and a fire, and that was just the beginning.

After gathering two pocketfuls of fluff, Elijah headed back into the woods. On the way back to the fallen cabin, he realized that he'd left his walking stick in the meadow. However, because he expected to find that it had become an empty husk, just like the moss, berries, and mushrooms, he chose not to go back for it. He would just find a new one.

So, as he walked, he kept an eye out for three things. First, he wanted more mushrooms and berries. They wouldn't be enough to sustain him indefinitely—he knew he needed protein and fat—but they would go a long way to staving off hunger while he sorted out his other needs. Second, he wanted a new walking stick. It wasn't absolutely necessary, but he'd always carried a stick while hiking, so it felt right to have one now. Besides, a stout stick could function as an impromptu weapon if he encountered something dangerous. And third, he wanted to gather fallen branches for firewood.

Only a few minutes into the woods, Elijah found more bushberries. It wasn't surprising; the little red berries were all over the place in the Pacific Northwest. He'd hoped to find some blackberries, too, but he hadn't been that lucky yet. A couple of minutes later, he found a clump of lion's mane mushrooms, which were white and looked a little like bunches of cauliflower. Not for the first time, he silently thanked his father for teaching him about foraging in the wilderness. Otherwise, he'd have run the risk of gathering something poisonous.

But that begged the question—was his new body of Wood susceptible to poison? He had no idea, but it would be foolish to assume that it wasn't. So, he kept gathering until he finally reached the cabin. Once there, he carefully placed his meager stash of food—a few handfuls of bunchberries and the lion's mane mushrooms—on the ground and grabbed the old pot he'd found when he'd first moved into the cabin. It was a little rusted, but he estimated that it would hold a couple of quarts of water. Being that it was his only viable container, he knew he couldn't be terribly picky.

With that in hand, Elijah trekked back to the stream, and after spending quite some time washing the black gunk from his body and clothes, he gathered a potful of water. It was going to be such a pain, going back and forth. It was late in the summer—assuming that he hadn't been in that chrysalis for months—so the only real danger was the unforgiving terrain. But it was navigable. In the winter, though? That would be a different story altogether.

Elijah found himself hesitating.

He'd gotten sick after drinking the water last time, but that might have been the remnants of his fight against cancer. It didn't necessarily mean that the water was contaminated. Sure, the smart thing to do was to take it back and boil it. However, with the size of the pot, only drinking water that had been boiled would see him spending the majority of his time going back and forth to the stream.

The way he saw it, he had three options. Just suck it up and resign himself to wasting so much time when it might not even be necessary. He'd learned enough about wilderness survival to know that any time he spent doing that would be time he couldn't spend finding food. He'd gotten lucky with the bunchberries and the mushrooms, but as the weather turned, those would slowly disappear. He needed to stock up, or he'd end up starving to death. And that meant spending as much time as possible gathering food.

The second option was to move his camp. But on the first day, he'd looked around, and he hadn't seen any likely shelter. Sleeping out in the open was out of the question. It might work out well enough for now, but the moment the weather turned, it would become a death trap. The old cabin wasn't perfect, but at least it had most of a roof that would protect him from the weather.

The third choice was to simply drink the water without boiling it. It was clearly the most convenient option, but that didn't mean it was the right one. After all, he had gotten ill the last time he'd tried it. But that might've been the cancer or the remnants of failed chemotherapy. The water could have been perfectly potable.

In the end, his decision came down to his ability to heal himself with Touch of Nature. Certainly, being forced to do that wasn't particularly pleasant, but it was a nice safety net if the water was contaminated. If it was, he would just have to use his lone spell to heal himself.

But he was also banking on his new body of Wood. His attributes hadn't changed, but he'd already felt a qualitative difference in his Strength and stamina. So, it wasn't out of the question that he would be more resistant to waterborne diseases and parasites.

He hoped that was the case, at least.

So, Elijah bent down next to the stream, cupped his hands, and drank. The water was clear, and it tasted cool and fresh. But he knew better than most that that didn't mean anything. The water still might make him sick, but he had a way to easily fix that. Sure, he'd lose a bit of hydration if he woke up vomiting, but that was a small price to pay for the convenience of simply drinking from the stream without the necessity of boiling the water.

Once Elijah had drunk his fill, he cleaned the pot as best he could, then used it to carry some water back to the cabin. When he got there, he dug out a shallow pit, surrounded it with gathered stones, and leaned the sticks he'd collected together into a pyramid shape.

It wasn't ideal, but surviving in the wilderness without supplies never was. You had to take what you could get. To that end, he searched the cabin for a likely piece of wood. There were a few options around the collapsed wall, and he chose the least rotted board he could find. With that done, he settled down and used the old, rusted knife to carve a notch into one side of the board. It took a while, but beneath the rust, the four-inch blade was sturdier than Elijah could have expected.

When the notch was finished, he let out a sigh of relief. Before, even that much work would have left him exhausted. And while he was frustrated and tired after a long day of trekking through the woods, he still had energy to spare. That, as much as anything else, told him that he'd left the effects of the cancer far behind.

Back in the meadow, he'd gathered a few pieces of thick horseweed, which he intended to use as a spindle. So, he stripped them down and selected one roughly as big around as his pinkie. Then, he carved a small dimple in one end; it was intended to increase airflow—a tip he'd learned from his father.

So, with all of that set up, Elijah carved a divot on the inner edge of the notch he'd cut into the board. With that done, he was ready to attempt to create his first coal. He'd done it before, but that had been under ideal circumstances while camping with his father. Now, though? He had suboptimal tools, barely acceptable materials, and a damp environment. Even if he did manage to get a fire going, it would take a lot of work.

But Elijah knew that his life would eventually depend on that fire. Not only would it provide warmth during the chilly nights, but it would also allow him to cook any food he managed to find as well as keep most predators away. He didn't know if the transformed animals in the area—none of which he'd actually seen, aside from the enlarged crabs—would be afraid of fire, but he was banking on their natures remaining static. At least for now. Who knew what else would come?

Elijah shook his head and focused on the task at hand. He couldn't plan for everything; he just didn't have enough information. So he could only take it one step at a time, combatting any changes as they presented themselves.

He set a bit of dandelion fluff on the divot, then followed up with the dimpled end of the spindle. Sitting cross-legged by his poorly constructed firepit, Elijah set about creating a coal from which he could start the fire.

Friction fires were fickle in the best of times, but using a homemade hand drill was an acquired skill. Still, Elijah had done it before, and even if it had been quite some time, he hadn't forgotten the technique. Twisting the spindle between his palms, he rapidly rotated the stick of horseweed. For a few minutes, nothing happened, but eventually, small tendrils of smoke started to drift up from the wood. Nothing caught, though, so he kept at it.

He'd optimized the process as much as he could, but that wasn't saying a lot. So, it still took quite some time before, finally, he created an ember. Leaning forward, he added more dandelion fluff to the coal. It caught easily and burned quickly, so he kept adding to it until he had a nascent flame.

Carefully, he pushed forward and placed that flame in the pile of twigs at the bottom of the pyramid of sticks in his firepit. Then, he added some more dandelion fluff.

It caught, and he pumped his fist in celebration before adding more and more sticks to the growing flame. The fire wouldn't be much with the fuel he had available, but it was proof that he had remembered his father's teachings.

Elijah sat back and admired the growing fire for a long moment before he looked at his hands. He'd always had plenty of calluses, but his battle with cancer had kept him abed for weeks at a time. So, his tender hands had developed a couple of blisters.

But he had an answer for that, didn't he?

Focusing on his core, Elijah dragged some Ethera into his soul before embracing his spell, Touch of Nature. His hand glowed with verdant light, and before his very eyes, the blisters healed. After that, Elijah inspected the rest of his body, looking for any other injuries, but he found none. The transformation that had come with his body of Wood had left him completely healed. Only the blisters he'd gained while making his fire and a few light scratches on his feet needed healing.

As he finished his inspection, the fire roared to life, finally eating into the pyramid of sticks he'd created. He added a few bigger pieces that he'd foraged, then turned his attention to the food he had gathered.

The bunchberries were mildly sweet but didn't really taste like much else. And the mushrooms had a thick, earthy flavor. But Elijah wasn't in any position to be picky. He needed a lot of calories to survive, so he'd take whatever he could get. Still, he had to admit that he wasn't a particular fan of mushrooms.

As Elijah sat there, he began to make plans for the future. Some of his needs had been met. He had water. A little food. Basic shelter and fire. But there was a time limit on most of it. Foraging for wild edibles was a good start, but it wouldn't sustain him for long. Besides, those sources would be gone soon after the weather turned. He needed something else. Preferably meat.

That's when he thought of the crabs.

He'd already killed one of them, and they hadn't seemed that difficult to find. Perhaps they would offer a ready source of protein. He also had some ideas about how he could go about fishing in the nearby ocean. There were some hurdles he'd have to clear—like making some line and creating a hook, not to mention finding the right spot—but he felt confident he could make it work. It just might take a lot of trial and error.

Meanwhile, he'd need to build up his shelter, both for protection against the wildlife as well as the weather. He also needed to explore some more; rare was the environment that had been completely untouched by man, and he hoped that he could stumble across something he could use. Perhaps some plastic bottles had been washed ashore. Or an old barrel, maybe. The possibilities were endless, and Elijah knew he couldn't afford to ignore any potential means of survival.

Just like that, he realized that he'd already made his decision about whether or not he intended to stay. Certainly, there were merits to setting off into the wilderness in search of civilization, but ultimately, he'd decided that it was better to stay put at least until after he made it through the winter. Maybe then, he'd be able to make such a journey with some degree of confidence.

As Elijah sat there eating bunchberries, he continued to make plans for how he was going to survive. Idly, he wondered how the rest of the world was getting by, but ultimately, he couldn't afford to split his focus. He needed to concentrate on keeping himself alive, and then, once his survival was assured, he'd be able to spare thoughts for others.

11

CRAB

Throughout the night, Elijah kept adding fuel to the fire, so by the time morning came, he was still tired, and his meager store of firewood had been vastly depleted. But he'd managed to keep it going, so there was a chance that he wouldn't have to go through the grueling process of creating a friction fire again. Of course, he'd have to make sure it had plenty of fuel while he went about the tasks he had planned for the day, but that was unavoidable.

There was a reason most survivalists never left home without a ferro rod, after all. Starting and maintaining a fire was hard but ultimately necessary work. Elijah was only thankful that he had plenty of experience with it. Otherwise, he'd have a lot of cold nights ahead of him, and his chances of survival would have plummeted.

Either way, the moment the night turned to dawn, Elijah was up and stretching. He was sore from the previous day's exertions, but not nearly as much as he might have expected. He almost felt like he had before his body had been ravaged by cancer, radiation, and chemotherapy. He still wasn't quite there, but that bone-deep weakness that, for months, had been his constant companion had disappeared.

As he stretched, he went over his tasks for the day. His first goal was to refresh his store of firewood. It wouldn't be easy because he could only really gather fallen limbs and sticks, and most of those had been rotted by the constant humidity and frequent rainfall. However, it was all he could do until he could create some tools. He had some plans for how to do that, but he knew it would all be trial and error; he had no experience with that kind of thing, so he expected that it would probably lean more toward the latter. He could figure it out, though. If cavemen could do it, then he could, too.

But that wasn't a short-term task. For now, he needed to focus on immediate survival. So, after getting loose, Elijah set out from the cabin and started gathering fallen branches and sticks. Like that, he spent most of his morning until, finally, he had accumulated a sizable pile inside his cabin. Most of the wood was wet, but he hoped that the protection of the cabin's roof would give everything a chance to dry out.

After feeding a bit more wood into the fire, Elijah went searching for another walking stick. Or staff, given that he intended to use it in his upcoming crab-hunting expedition. It took another couple of hours, but he eventually stumbled upon a birch tree whose limbs would make for a fine staff.

He only had to get to them first. The few that had fallen to the ground were long since rotted, so he had no choice but to climb a few feet up the trunk and somehow cut a limb loose. He even saw a likely target that wasn't that far out of reach.

Fortunately, the tree itself wasn't that big around, and with his newly recovered Strength and endurance, Elijah found it fairly easy to climb. Then, once he reached the limb, he wrapped his legs around the trunk and got to work. With his hands free, Elijah placed the rusted knife's edge on the branch, then used a rock he'd recently gathered to hammer out a cut.

With his legs burning from the exertion, he continued at it until he'd made a sizable notch that dug a quarter of the way through the branch. If he wanted to make it all the way through, he'd be up there for hours, and he knew his energy reserves wouldn't last that long. So, without much other choice, he took a deep breath, then reached out to the branch with both hands.

Finally, he let go with his legs and swung free. The branch held for a split second before a loud crack filled the air. Then, Elijah fell half a dozen feet to land on the leaf-strewn ground. The impact knocked the breath from his lungs, and he felt something in his ankle twist, but he'd accomplished his goal.

In normal circumstances, it would have been stupid to do such a thing. The chances of injury—which were obviously well-founded, judging by the throbbing in his ankle and what he suspected were a couple of broken ribs—were too high. However, Elijah had a healing spell in his pocket, and because of that, he'd already decided that he could be a bit reckless with his body. So long as he didn't incapacitate himself by hitting his head or something, he felt confident that he could heal himself from whatever injuries he might sustain.

Still, there was the pain to worry about, but it was a small price to pay, given that something like the staff would improve his chances of survival.

But it was easy to make that kind of judgment before he actually had to endure it. Now that he felt the consequences of his actions, he'd begun to question whether or not he was an idiot. Even so, what was done was done, and he had more than enough experience dealing with pain and discomfort. Not only had he spent quite a lot of time in the boxing gym—and all that entailed—but he'd also been through the horror that was cancer and chemotherapy. He could handle the pain of a twisted ankle long enough to heal it.

Still lying there, Elijah looked inward and grabbed the Ethera in his core, dragging it into the pathways of his soul. Once he was flooded with the magical energy, he embraced his lone spell. He placed his hand, which glowed with verdant Ethera, on his side and used his spell to heal the broken bones.

The first application didn't do the trick, but the second pushed the pain into the background. A third, which exhausted the Ethera in his core, finished the job, letting him breathe freely.

Sighing, Elijah sat up and inspected his ankle.

"That's definitely not a sprain," he muttered through gritted teeth. In the time it had taken him to heal his ribs—which was no more than a couple of minutes—the ankle had already started to turn purple. It was also swollen to twice its normal size. Perhaps it was broken, as well.

That really brought home the stupidity of his actions. Just because he could heal himself didn't mean that he was invincible. While it would doubtless help, he had a limited amount of Ethera at his disposal, and regenerating it took time. Time he could have spent trying to accomplish the hundreds of other tasks he needed to button up before he felt his survival would be assured.

Lying back, he let out another deep breath. Magic was helpful, but it wasn't the cure-all he'd hoped it would be.

Elijah let out a little chuckle. He'd only been using magic for a day or so, and already, it felt mundane. It was just another tool in his tool belt, not a miracle that would solve all his problems. Perhaps in the future it would be more impactful, but for now, it was too limited to do much more than heal small injuries.

As he lay there waiting for his Ethera to regenerate, Elijah's mind wandered. And then, suddenly, the feeling that something was watching him returned. It was buried within that pervasive sensation of belonging that had come courtesy of his druid archetype, but it was there all the same. Slowly, he turned his head in the direction he thought it was coming from, and he saw a brief flash of movement in a nearby clump of trees.

Then, it was gone. The feeling. Whatever was stalking him. Everything. Only his One With Nature remained.

Clearly, he wasn't alone in the forest. That wasn't really a surprise, but he'd hoped that he could avoid any major predators. There was a chance that whatever had been following him was just a curious herbivore, but he felt almost certain that that wasn't the case. After all, a simple deer wouldn't have sent a chill up Elijah's spine.

Probably.

It was just further evidence that he needed to curtail his risky behavior. If something attacked him while he was injured, he wouldn't last long.

For the next few minutes, Elijah kept his inner eye on his core while his physical eyes scanned the area. But nothing came, and eventually, he was able to heal his ankle. It took four uses of Touch of Nature, which told him that the injury was much worse than he'd first suspected.

"Stupid," he muttered to himself as he climbed to his feet. He inspected the branch he'd risked everything for. It was long—probably ten feet—straight, and about two inches thick. A little bigger than Elijah preferred, but he hoped to whittle that down. Eventually. For now, though, it was a good stick.

Using the same method he'd used to notch the branch before taking it down, Elijah arduously undertook the task of bringing it down to size. It took a while—most of which was spent banging the rock into the knife blade—but he managed to cut a roughly five-foot section. He also carved one end into a rough point; for what he planned, it needed to act as both a spear and a staff, but it couldn't be too delicate.

He dragged the rest back to his cabin, where he intended to cut it into firewood.

Waste not, want not, he thought, tossing the unused portion into the corner. He'd get to that later. For now, hunger gnawed at his belly, and he wanted to use his staff for its intended purpose. So, after popping a few bunchberries into his mouth and taking a quick trip to the stream, where he washed his face and drank his fill of water, Elijah slowly made his way back to the beach.

There, the crabs waited, looking entirely disoriented.

It wasn't a surprise. Purple shore crabs usually lived under rocks, and their diets consisted mostly of algae and the rare small animal. So, suddenly being the size of a midsize dog was understandably disorienting to the creatures. As a result, they milled around, their instincts telling them to find rocks to hide under while their size prohibited any such action. In a way, it was sad.

Or it would have been if Elijah hadn't recently woken up to a herd of them desperately trying to eat his legs. No—not trying. Succeeding. He'd had the wounds to show for it, too.

Clutching his stick, Elijah knelt down as he studied his intended prey. The monstrous crustaceans were big enough that they were a threat, but their disorientation meant that they had yet to adjust to their new size. If they had, the things could end up being a real terror—especially if they were capable of traveling inland.

Elijah could easily imagine a scenario where a horde of giant crabs swept through the area, devouring everything they found. Including him and his cabin. But he couldn't worry about that right now. He wasn't there to cull the population. Instead, he just wanted some meat.

So, he watched and waited until one of the crabs separated itself from the others. It skittered down the shore, which was comprised mostly of slippery, wet rocks. The crab was completely ignorant of how it had made itself into attractive prey.

Elijah felt something ignite in his mind. When he was younger, he'd spent quite a lot of time hunting and fishing with his father. Those were some of his fondest memories. But back then, he'd never felt as focused as he did at that moment. It was like the spirit of a great predator flowed through him.

He stalked forward on bare, silent feet. Holding the staff in both hands like a spear, he followed the crab until it was almost forty yards away from the rest of the group. But still, it wandered, stopping ever so often to nip at some bit of kelp. Any other time, Elijah might have remembered how many nutrients he could get from seaweed, but in this instance, his mind was laser focused.

One step after another, he moved forward, steadily gaining on the brownish-purple crab. His progress was slow, but that was intentional. He didn't need to go quickly. He just needed to do it right.

Finally, when he was only feet away, he pounced, swinging his staff at the comparatively delicate backmost leg. His first strike connected with a solid crunch, but the crab whipped around without any hesitation, nearly latching on to Elijah with its enormous front claw. He dashed to the side, narrowly avoiding the skittering creature, but it scuttled after him.

He ran, quickly outpacing the oversized crustacean. When he was twenty feet away, Elijah looked back to see that the crab had lost interest. Apparently, even if it had grown quite a bit, it hadn't gotten any smarter.

So, Elijah circled back around until he was once again behind the crab, then stalked forward and repeated the process. This time, he put a little less force into the blow so he could maintain control and avoid the creature's response. Once again, his sturdy stick hit with a solid crack, and he darted away. The crab's pursuit came much more slowly this time.

Elijah's hit-and-run tactics continued until, at last, all of the beast's legs were broken, rendering it almost completely immobile. Still, it wasn't dead. In fact, judging by its barely audible hisses and whistling screeches, it was in quite a lot of pain. It was a cruel way to kill something, but without proper tools, there was nothing more Elijah could do.

But he didn't have to prolong the kill.

So, he carefully approached its rear once again and, using his stick as a lever, flipped the crab over onto its back. It tried to snap at him, but Elijah had expected that, so he was already backing away and circling back around to the rear.

Once there, he approached the helpless creature, located the proper position, and used his staff like a spear. It took a handful of strikes to get through even its softer underbelly, but eventually, he pierced through the shell and severed the nerve center closest to its head. Then, he repeated the process on the one near its rear, killing it. Throughout the whole process, the crab snapped its claws ineffectually, but so long as he was careful, Elijah didn't have to worry about that.

Still, what he had done was an incredibly inhumane way to kill something. But given his lack of equipment, there was no other way to do it.

Sighing, he looked down at the crab's corpse. He wasn't looking forward to processing it, but he knew that it would only be a matter of time before the other crabs sensed the presence of food. So, taking out his rusty knife, Elijah bent down and got to work.

12

AN UNSEEN THREAT

Elijah studied the results of his efforts, which had been arranged into separate piles according to their intended purpose. The first was simple enough; it was comprised of a couple of crab claws, each the size of a small animal. Beneath that chitinous exterior was at least a few pounds of white meat, which Elijah hoped would see him through until he could supplement his diet with fish. He'd considered harvesting the rest of the crab, but he'd run into two problems.

First, crab had a tendency to turn rancid very quickly, and he had no way to preserve the meat. Even the amount he could get from the claws was pushing it, and he wouldn't dare eat it after twenty-four hours. Even with his ability to heal himself, he wasn't interested in getting food poisoning from bad crabmeat.

Second, the other crabs had eventually noticed the smell of nearby carrion and, like the opportunistic scavengers they were, had quickly come scuttling in Elijah's direction. So, even though he'd only managed to break off the creature's claws and legs, he wasn't able to do much else without drawing the ire of the oversized crustaceans.

But he wasn't too upset. The crabs didn't seem like they were going anywhere, and he already had proof that he could efficiently hunt them. If his other plans for food failed, he felt confident that he could always get more crab. In the future, as the weather turned colder, perhaps he could even use it to bolster his stores of food for the winter. That wasn't one of his immediate concerns, though.

The next pile held various bits and pieces of the crab's shell that Elijah intended to fashion into needles and hooks. It would take some doing, but he was nothing if not adaptable. Plenty of ancient people had used bones for hooks, and while crab shell was a lot more brittle, it made up for its unsuitability by being readily available. With as much chitin as he had harvested, Elijah was sure that he could make it work.

After harvesting the crab, Elijah had been forced to flee the shore and head back to the cabin, where he'd piled his treasure trove of food and potential building material. Then, he got to work.

The first thing he did was pop open one of the shells by cracking it with a few blows from his walking stick. Normal crab claws weren't that difficult to crack, but Elijah soon found that these purple shore crabs hadn't just gained size. They'd gained durability, as well, and even in death, their shells made for an extremely tough material. He couldn't help but wonder if he should be saving them for some sort of armor; after all, he'd already discovered that the wilderness was dangerous. Having some protection wouldn't go amiss.

But he tabled that thought in favor of focusing on his task, and eventually, his efforts bore fruit in the form of a cracked claw. Once its structure had been compromised, it was much easier to get to the meat within. Elijah picked the shards of the shell away, then carefully gathered the white meat. It seemed tougher than most crabmeat he'd encountered, but as far as he could tell, it seemed edible. So, he tossed the meat into his pot.

The second claw he left alone for the time being. For now, it would keep better inside the shell—at least until morning, when he intended to eat it for breakfast.

Once Elijah had a potful of crabmeat, he set it over his small fire and waited on it to cook, stirring it every so often with his small knife. To be sure it was completely done, Elijah overcooked it by quite a bit, but that was because he knew the dangers of eating undercooked crab. Just because he had the ability to heal himself didn't mean he wanted to tempt fate.

Besides, he had a couple of plans for his Ethera, and healing himself because he ate the wrong things didn't factor into them.

Eating the crab was not a pleasurable experience. Certainly, it would provide him with the necessary proteins and fat that mushrooms and berries couldn't give him, but he lacked the tools to prepare it properly. As a result, it alternated between mushy, salty, and burned. Elijah had to keep reminding himself that it was necessary in order to keep himself going.

Once he'd choked down his meal, he headed back to the stream to wash his pot and rinse the taste out of his mouth. Along the way, he stumbled upon some more berries, which he quickly gathered and ate.

Just before he reached the stream, Elijah felt the hairs on the back of his neck stand on end. Something was watching him. He knew it the same way he'd felt the tree. Whether it was his connection to nature or something more concrete, Elijah had no idea. But he didn't dare ignore it.

Slowly, he turned a circle as he searched for whatever had followed him. As he did so, his mind ran amok, conjuring images of mutated versions of all the predators native to the region. Bears, cougars, wolves, and coyotes were at the top of the list, but there were plenty of other, smaller creatures that could pose a danger—especially if they'd grown the same way the crabs had.

Suddenly, he thought of a man-size mosquito, and he nearly started running right then and there. But he stopped himself, even if he couldn't keep his heart from beating out of his chest. He could only hope that the System hadn't chosen that route.

For a long few minutes, Elijah continued to study his surroundings, but he was no more successful in finding his stalker. Then, the feeling of foreboding disappeared, leaving him sweating profusely as his heart hammered in his chest. For another five minutes, Elijah didn't dare move.

Then, finally, he managed to steady his breathing and refocus his mind. Whatever had been there—and he was sure it was something—had chosen not to attack. And if he wanted to survive, he couldn't afford to let fear dictate his actions.

Of course, it was one thing to think that and another to overcome the sense of palpable terror he'd felt. Even the remnants were potent enough to keep him rooted in place. But slowly, Elijah managed to shake it off and continue along toward the stream. By the time he'd reached it and started cleaning his pot, he had convinced himself that it was all just an overreaction to an overactive imagination.

Mostly. But in the back of his mind, he knew it was real. The fact that he'd felt it multiple times since washing ashore was as much an indicator as the visceral feeling of being watched. However, the more time that passed, the easier it was to push that certainty aside in favor of the necessities of survival.

Once Elijah finished washing up, he trekked back to the cabin. The moment he entered the area, though, he realized that something was wrong. He crouched, holding his walking stick in one hand and the pot in the other. Neither were great weapons, but he wasn't exactly spoiled for choice.

The forest was deathly silent as he crept toward the derelict cabin. No birds sang. No squirrels chirped. Even the insects seemed to have gone dormant.

Flattening himself against the cabin's most intact wall, he slid forward, inch by inch, until he could see the interior. It was completely unoccupied. His fire still burned, low but merry in the waning light of approaching evening. But it all felt wrong. Like the space had been violated. It took Elijah's conscious mind a moment to catch up, but when he did, he let out an audible curse.

The remaining crab claw was gone, and in its place were a couple of faint tracks. Elijah slowly moved into the cabin and investigated the site of the theft, and he was unsurprised to see feline paw prints in the soft earth. And they were huge—far bigger than he would have expected from a mountain lion or a bobcat, which were the only big cats native to the area.

But that didn't really mean anything, did it? The crabs had grown. Why couldn't a bobcat? Or worse, a cougar?

In the back of his mind, though, Elijah considered another option. The tree that had guided him through his cultivation had clearly come from somewhere else. It wasn't a native to Earth. So, it stood to reason that the System had brought new dangers to the area.

Obviously, Elijah couldn't be certain. He didn't have enough information. But he also couldn't discount the possibility that the region was now home to a superpredator like a tiger or a lion.

Fear gripped him, cold and palpable. He knew he wouldn't stand a chance against something like that. Especially not with only a stick and a pot to defend himself. Sure, if he was wounded, he could use Touch of Nature to heal himself, but that seemed a poor substitute for combat ability.

That's when Elijah decided to implement his budding plan for self-improvement.

He had woeful attributes, especially in Strength. His Body of Wood had helped with that, but it was clear that if he wanted to survive, he needed to address his weaknesses. The most straightforward way to do so was to go out and kill things; he'd felt a bit of foreign Ethera enter his body when he'd killed the crab, and he'd intuited that it was something akin to experience from a video game. But it wasn't much, and he sensed that he'd have to kill quite a few more if he wanted to progress in that manner.

The tree had also explained that he could gain levels via other actions associated with his archetype, but he hadn't felt any influx of Ethera when he'd healed himself. So, that ruled out a plan for intentionally injuring himself and reaping the Ethera from healing the wounds. If he was honest, Elijah was glad for that. That kind of path, even if it had proven effective, would have been too disturbing.

So, that left him with one other possibility. He could do things the old-fashioned way. Elijah was no stranger to working out, so he knew that, so long as he had fuel for his body, he could slowly strengthen himself. In addition, he could cut down his recovery times significantly by using Touch of Nature to heal himself. He had no idea how soon he could expect gains, but he suspected that it would be fairly quick.

In the meantime, he would continue to survive. Thankfully, the native predator hadn't disturbed Elijah's pile of chitin, so he could still enact his plan to create hooks and needles. Once he had those, he could make some rudimentary fishing line from some dogbane he'd seen in the tree's meadow. It wouldn't be nearly as strong as synthetic fishing line, but it would still be better than trying to unravel the threads of his remaining clothing.

Elijah settled down close to the fire and went to work. Normally, he'd have carved the hooks from wood, but the crab's chitinous exoskeleton was too appropriate to pass up. From a mundane crab, the shell would've likely been too brittle, but for this evolved version, it almost had the texture and Strength of plastic. Besides, there had been some spines on the underside of the legs that were nearly perfect for hooks. All it took was for Elijah to separate them, then whittle them down to size—a tedious process that took time and concentration but little actual skill.

Eventually, he managed to create his first hook. He held it close to the campfire's light and grinned. It wasn't ideal—not like a metal hook would have been—but it wasn't bad, either.

By that point, night had truly fallen, but Elijah wanted to get a few more hooks made before he went to sleep. In the end, he only got three finished, but he was happy with them all. So, having accomplished his goal, he curled up in his corner of the cabin and went to sleep.

The next morning, Elijah awoke feeling somewhat refreshed. He wasn't certain if it was the effect of having a filling meal, or if his body was just getting stronger, but he felt better than he had since before his diagnosis. Which was good because he had a lot of plans for the day.

The first few hours he spent doing various calisthenics and lifting some heavy rocks he'd found near the shore. And if he hadn't believed his status before, he was soon convinced by his weakness. Still, he sensed that his body was stronger and more durable than it should be, likely due to his cultivation. He intended to exploit that, pushing himself far past the point of exhaustion with each exercise.

After a few hours, he spent a while resting and healing himself with Touch of Nature, and he was surprised to see that his status reflected his work. His Strength had risen by a single point. If he could continue along that track, he could truly make some gains.

Once he felt up to it, he set out toward the meadow where he'd seen the dogbane. When he got there, he noticed that the tree was still dormant. However, it still radiated a sense of calm power, letting him know that it was no normal tree—not that he would have made that mistake, anyway. One look was all it took to put the lie to any notion of normality.

But he wasn't there to gape at the tree. Instead, he gathered an armful of dogbane, which were red-stalked weeds that, when picked apart, could make for decent cordage. Having accomplished that, he headed back to his cabin, where he intended to start the process of making fishing line.

The trip was uneventful, save for Elijah stopping from time to time to pick various berries or edible fungi. He even found some rose hips, which was a nice discovery. More importantly, he wasn't beset by that same fear he'd felt near the stream, which was enough to put his mind at ease.

Finally, he reached the cabin and relaxed. It remained completely undisturbed, which was reassuring after the previous intrusion. Elijah could only hope that his good luck would continue long enough for him to ensure his survival.

13

SAFE HAVEN

Alyssa stood on the roof of the police station and gazed out across the parking lot. There, she saw a haggard group of people waiting in front of the crude brick wall Carmen had built. It was rough, but at almost six feet high and half as thick, it had proved to be very effective in the weeks since it had been built.

"What do you think?" asked Roman, who'd taken a position beside her.

She glanced his way. The past couple of months had been difficult for everyone, but Roman had been hit particularly hard by all the death they'd seen. After that first night in the police station, they'd set about creating a safe haven, and along the way, they'd picked up quite a few survivors. At present, their little community, which had extended well past the station by virtue of a series of hastily built structures behind the main building, numbered in the hundreds.

And more seemed to come every day.

"I don't know," she said. "Same as always, right? Take them in, interview them, and then watch them closely."

"That method doesn't work," he said, clearly referring to a recent incident where a few recent additions had plundered the stores of supplies. The group had escaped before anyone even knew they'd stolen anything. Where they'd gone, no one knew, but Roman wanted to hunt them down. Everyone else had talked him out of it.

"What's the alternative?" Alyssa asked.

"Martial law," he said. "Curfews. Strict rationing. Rewards for good behavior."

"You make it sound like a prison," she said. He'd spent the first part of his career working at the local jail, so the fact that he'd gone down that road wasn't terribly surprising.

"Same concepts."

"And you think that's fair?" she asked.

"Fair has nothing to do with it," he answered. "Look around, Alyssa. This isn't a world where we get to worry about personal freedom. We all have to work toward the greater good, or we won't survive. You know that as well as anyone else."

Indeed, she'd seen more death in the past two months than she'd ever thought possible. The first few days had been particularly hard on the local townspeople, and it was only through luck that their little group had managed to survive. She'd heard stories about monsters breaking into houses within a few hours of the world's integration, and what's more, she'd seen the results for herself. The reality was that they had suddenly found themselves in an incredibly dangerous world where support was a distant concept. They had no choice but to take care of themselves.

But that need had brought to light an additional problem—they all had different ideas about how to go about it. Roman leaned toward a strict policy where everyone was expected to pull their weight, and if they didn't, they'd be left behind. Understandable, considering what was at stake. By contrast, Alyssa wanted to leave people to their own devices—at least for the most part. Sure, she expected people to work for the greater good, but she had no interest in forcing them to do things against their will.

And she would never kick anyone out of the compound they'd established. Roman would, and without even a hint of guilt. If someone wasn't pulling their weight, they were worthless to him.

Again, Alyssa didn't exactly disagree with that assertion. She knew how close they were to tipping over the edge. But she didn't think someone deserved to die just because they were incapable—for whatever reason—of working toward the greater good. Some lacked the skills. Others were barely functional after losing friends and family. Only a few refused for selfish reasons.

"I think we need to go down and let them in," Alyssa said.

"We're going to have to figure this out eventually," Roman stated. "We need a System. We're getting too big to be on the honor System."

Alyssa nodded. "Then we get everyone together and hash it out," she said.

"Or we tell people how it's going to be, and if they don't like it, they can leave," he responded.

"We can't do that."

He sighed. They'd had the discussion more than a few times, and he clearly didn't want to revisit the debate. So, he said, "We'll figure it out later, then. For now, we need to get those people inside."

With that, the pair descended from the roof via a ladder that led to the ground. Then, they headed toward the gate. Like the wall Carmen had constructed, it was a crude thing made of plywood and rebar they'd found at a construction site just outside of town, but it did the job well enough.

They pulled it open.

"Oh, thank God!" said a shabby-looking fellow armed with a shovel. He sported a few wounds, as did the rest of his party. There were seven in all—two of which were women—each looking like they'd been through hell. "We heard there were people here, but I wasn't sure what we would find."

"Where did you hear that?" demanded Roman.

"Uh . . . Around? There was . . . I don't know . . . We ran into a group a few days back," the man said, running his hand through greasy hair. "They told us about this compound. Said it was safe."

"Nowhere is safe," Alyssa stated.

"R-right," he said, glancing at Roman. The former police chief held his bow at the ready, and he already had an arrow nocked. He hadn't gone so far as to draw it back, but the threat was clear in his expression. The refugee asked, "Can . . . Can we come in? We've been walking for two days, and—"

"What are your archetypes?" Roman asked.

"What?"

"Archetypes. What are we dealing with here?" Roman repeated.

"Uh . . . I'm a Ranger. Martha is a Mage. Two Warriors. Two Scholars. And a Tradesman."

"No Healers?" asked Alyssa in obvious disappointment.

"And two Scholars? Useless," Roman added.

One of the women spoke up: "We're not useless! I'm a historian, and I think—"

"Nobody cares what you used to be. Or didn't you get the memo? The world ended two months ago. Now all that matters is if you're useful," Roman said. "That means fighting. Gathering. Healing. Building things. Can you do any of that?"

"N-no . . ."

"Then you're useless. But that's fine. We need manual laborers, too."

One of the men said, "But I have a doctorate! I can—"

"In what?"

"Uh . . . French literature . . ."

"Right. Useless."

Alyssa wanted to speak up, but they'd agreed to present a unified front. She didn't like how dismissive Roman was, but division was even worse. So, she held her tongue. Meanwhile, Roman told the group of refugees the rules. They weren't onerous. No fighting. No stealing. Everyone worked toward collective survival, and if they were attacked—which wasn't common, but it wasn't unheard of, either—everyone was required to contribute to the defense in one way or another.

"Food is earned," he went on. "You work, you eat. You don't work, you starve. You refuse to contribute, you can take your ass elsewhere. We've got no use for freeloaders."

"We'll work," the leader said.

"Damn right you will," Roman stated. Then, his expression softened, and he extended his hand. "Roman Cain. This is Alyssa Hart."

"Cain? That sounds familiar," said the man.

"Used to be the police chief," Roman said. "Before everything went to shit, I mean. Not much use for those kinds of titles these days, though."

It was at that moment that Alyssa saw a flicker of movement as something streaked toward the open gate. She couldn't see what it was, but she had been in enough fights in the past couple of months that she didn't hesitate to act. Yanking the machete from the sheath at her waist, she used Charge and dashed forward to meet it.

As she did, she used her newest ability, which she had acquired upon reaching level three. Stomping on the ground, she let loose with Shock Wave, sending an invisible pulse of force to hit the monster. It didn't do much, just stunning it for a split second, but it was enough to give Alyssa an opening. She used it, slashing down with all the force she could muster.

And considering that she'd put all her free points into her physical attributes, the power she could bring to bear was considerable.

The creature—which looked like some kind of monstrous weasel—took the blade on the shoulder. The momentum of the overhand attack knocked it into the ground. And a moment later, an arrow took it in the eye, killing it instantly.

Alyssa's Charge dissipated, and she slowed to a stop. Her eyes darted back and forth. Sometimes, the monsters moved in packs, and she wanted to ensure that the weasel had been alone. She saw nothing, suggesting that it was a lone hunter.

Then, once she'd ensured that there were no other threats, she reached down and grabbed the monster by the tail. In one swift motion, she hefted it and slung it over one shoulder before turning to the stunned refugees.

"Good fur. Winter's coming, and we're going to need all the materials we can get," she said.

Indeed, the monster was almost four feet long, which meant that its pelt would make for a decent blanket. They had access to quite a bit of cloth—by virtue of looting the abandoned homes and the handful of businesses in the town proper—but no one could afford to turn down any resources.

"Come on in," said Roman. "We'll get you settled."

With that, the stunned group came through. Alyssa sheathed her machete, then dragged the gate closed, locking it in place. Then, she told Roman, "I'll go drop this for Carmen. She can probably make something with it."

He nodded, and as he led the group into the main building, Alyssa circled around to the left. Soon, she caught sight of Carmen, who was wearing nothing but a sports bra, a pair of shorts, and a heavy leather apron. The other woman was busy stoking a forge. Alyssa took a moment to admire her wife's muscular form before she remembered that she had a dead animal over her shoulder. Once she did, she strode forward and, when she reached the smithy, deposited the animal carcass.

"Really?" Carmen said, cutting her eyes at the corpse. "Right in the middle of my smithy?"

Alyssa shrugged. "Don't know where else to stick it," she said. "You want me to process it?"

"Go nuts."

Alyssa did just that, pulling a knife from where it was strapped to her thigh. Then, she commenced with gutting, skinning, and quartering the animal. It took a while, and when she'd finished, her arms were covered in blood up to her elbows. But it was worthwhile, and not just because of the pelt. The meat looked perfectly edible, which would come in handy considering the shortage of food.

"I have no idea how you can do that," Carmen said, handing Alyssa a bucket of water. "Just watching you makes me want to vomit."

"Grew up hunting with my dad," she said with a shrug as she washed the blood off.

"New arrivals have any decent skills?"

"Not sure. There was a Ranger, so maybe he can help with defense and hunting," she said. "A Mage. A couple of Warriors. And a Tradesman. Two Scholars, unfortunately."

Alyssa didn't precisely agree with Roman about what to do with the less useful people in their budding community, but she couldn't deny that she was more than a little disappointed with the Scholars.

"Oh, maybe I can get an apprentice," said Carmen.

Alyssa shrugged. "Maybe," she agreed. "What are you working on, anyway?"

"Boar spear," Carmen stated. "I think I've got the blade shaped. I just need to get it sharpened and attached to the haft."

"Nice," Alyssa said. She could see the use of such a weapon. Many of the monsters they fought were just mutated animals who charged blindly when they were disturbed. For that kind of situation, you couldn't get much better than a boar spear.

"Glad you approve because I made it for you," she said.

"Someone else might—"

"Didn't make it for anyone else. I don't give two shits about all those other people. All I care about is that you and Miggy stay alive. That's why I made it," Carmen said.

Alyssa sighed, then rolled her eyes. "So noble."

"I'll leave the nobility to you," Carmen said.

"Whatever. You going to be here much longer?" she asked.

"A few more hours," Carmen said, glancing at the sky. Night was still quite a ways off. "But save some of that weasel, yeah? Miggy hasn't been getting enough meat."

"Will do," Alyssa responded. That was one thing they definitely agreed on. No matter what else happened, the boy was their first priority. She leaned in and kissed Carmen, then said, "Don't work yourself to death."

And then she headed back toward the main building. There was still a lot to do, after all.

14

THRIVING

Elijah hacked at the block of wood, careful to hit it just right. Over the last couple of months, he'd had plenty of practice, but even so, losing concentration would be disastrous for the results. He spared a glance for the pile of firewood propped against one corner of his shelter and reconsidered that word. Disastrous.

For weeks after washing ashore, every action had been one of life and death. When he'd killed his first crab, when he'd made his first tools, and finally, when he'd caught his first fish—the stakes had been incredibly high. But now? He had a stock of smoked fish, a horde of berries, and a store of mushrooms. Food wouldn't be an issue anytime soon; in fact, he felt confident that his cache would last him through most of the winter, and if he continued to gather food, he wouldn't even need to ration.

He looked down at his crude axe. The blade was made of chipped flint, sharpened and refined over the course of a week. It wasn't his first such tool—they had a habit of cracking if he used them too roughly—and he was certain it wouldn't be his last. The same went for his stone knife and spear, the latter of which had yet to even see use. Regardless, he could always make more. He'd found a nice vein of the stuff in a nearby cliff, so he wouldn't soon lack for material.

Elijah sighed, flexing his shoulders. Over the past six weeks, he'd made incredible progress regarding his overall physical condition. Some of that was due to his usage of Touch of Nature that reduced his recovery times to mere minutes rather than days. But he also felt confident that his Body of Wood had played a part, as well. When he turned his mind inward, Elijah got the feeling that his body wanted—or needed, perhaps—to be stronger. Whatever the case, the result was explosive muscle growth that had left him nearly as strong as he'd been before his cancer diagnosis.

It was a good thing, too, because there was no way his weakened body could have survived for more than a couple of weeks. Getting stronger and healthier hadn't been a mere desire; it had been a necessity for survival. And Elijah had thrown himself into it accordingly. The results spoke for themselves.

Elijah didn't have access to a mirror, but from what he could see of his arms, legs, and torso, his entire body was lean and corded with compact muscle. He'd never look like a bodybuilder; wilderness survival didn't lend itself to packing on mass. But he did look—and more importantly, feel—healthier than he had in recent memory.

More importantly, Elijah's constant fishing and crab hunting had had another side effect. Each kill had netted him an accumulation of foreign Ethera. With the fish, it was barely noticeable. A thimbleful compared to the crabs' cup. But he'd killed a lot of fish, and the pool of Ethera had slowly grown until Elijah felt as if he was going to burst. Soon—maybe the next time he went fishing—he was certain that he would gain a level. And with that, he'd get another two points to improve his stats.

He couldn't wait because he already knew where those points were going to go. First, though, he needed to finish his daily chores—chopping firewood and gathering water—before he could go fishing.

An unrelated shiver ran up his spine. In the past, he would have panicked. But over the weeks, he'd grown used to his stalker. If it really wanted to kill him, it would have done so already. With each passing day, Elijah had grown stronger and gotten better equipped. His axe and spear weren't ideal weapons, and he was certain that they wouldn't give him the edge he needed to survive an encounter with the still unseen feline predator. However, he was confident that he could at least wound it. Perhaps the creature knew that, as well.

Or maybe he was just anthropomorphizing it by attributing human intelligence and reasoning ability to an animal.

Either way, if the cat—and he was fairly certain that's what it was—wanted to kill him, it had already had plenty of opportunities to do so, and with less risk than he now presented. Besides, he had an agreement with the creature. Sort of.

Slipping his axe's haft through his belt of twined dogbane fibers, Elijah grabbed the fruit of his day's labor and piled it into a neat stack inside his shelter. The cabin had undergone almost as drastic a transformation as his body, and he'd used a series of logs from trees he'd cut down, branches, and moss to enclose the space. At the time, it hadn't been wholly unnecessary, but with every passing week, he drew closer to winter. That, in turn, meant that he needed a much sturdier home to stave off the incoming weather. It also served as rudimentary protection from any wildlife that might come sniffing around. It had been the work of a rough couple of weeks, but he'd finally gotten it to a passable, if not completely comfortable, state.

With his firewood put away, Elijah sat on the stump he'd dragged inside the shelter and let out a sigh. For a moment, he just sat there, gathering his thoughts. That was one of the issues with living a solitary life. Often, he'd lose himself in his inner thoughts, and he wouldn't even realize that he'd been staring off into space for some indeterminate amount of time. Usually, his thoughts weren't elaborate. Instead, they were mostly comprised of half-forgotten memories from the distant past.

Ultimately, that was a good thing. He'd had a good childhood with loving parents who would have done anything they could to support him. Certainly, they'd passed away before their time, which was anything but pleasant, but he'd long chosen to focus on the good times they'd shared rather than the devastating loss of their passing.

So, as he sat there, he found his mind drifting back to when his father had taught him the rudiments of boxing, to when his mother would take him out into the woods where she helped him to identify various wild edibles. Or when the entire family would visit the farmers market. Little things all, but they were enough to keep his spirits up.

Idly, he found himself wondering how his sister was coping. What was life like in the cities? She didn't live within Seattle's city limits, but it was close enough that she wouldn't have escaped the problems that came with a metropolitan area. The world had irrevocably changed. There was magic now. If what had happened to the plane was any indication, modern technology had probably failed. He'd lost his phone in the crash, but he suspected that even if it had survived, it would've been rendered into nothing but a useless brick. Likely, everything else was the same.

Elijah wasn't so naive as to think that humanity would react well to the changes. He'd seen people turn into savages after more mundane natural disasters, so it stood to reason that, with survival on the line, people would head down an even less civilized route. Of course, there were plenty of people who would support their neighbors and friends. Good people always outweighed the bad, in his experience. However, he also knew it only took a few people willing to enforce their will on others to enslave a much larger population. Human history was evidence of that.

He shook his head. Down that line of thinking was nothing but despair, which was a very real threat in his situation. Elijah needed to keep his spirits up, lest the isolation and brutal environment be allowed to replace it with despondency. If that happened, he'd soon surrender to depression and wither away. And he refused to let that happen.

The best cure for that kind of thing was to keep busy. To create manageable goals. To take the wins he could get. So, he ran his hand through his lengthening hair, closed his eyes, and took a deep, centering breath before climbing to his feet. He pushed his makeshift door—which was made of sticks that had been bound together with his homemade cordage—aside and ducked outside the shelter. His main fire burned merrily in its pit, reminding Elijah of his half-finished project. He glanced toward the back of the cabin, where he'd been building a fireplace with stones and clay he'd harvested from the stream. It was arduous work, which meant he'd limited his efforts to only working on it a bit each day, but it was coming along. Hopefully, he would finish it by the onset of winter.

Flexing his shoulders, Elijah dragged Ethera from his core and sent a pulse of Touch of Nature through his body. When he'd initially used the spell, he'd done so with very focused intent, which was perfect for healing wounds. However, over the past month and a half, he'd discovered that he could use it without intentional direction. When he did, the Ethera of the spell spread throughout his entire body, healing the minute tears in his muscle fibers that came from exertion, curing his fatigue and hastening his recovery by a large degree.

Usually, it took a couple of pulses, but that wasn't a big deal. He had Ethera to spare, considering he only had the one spell. Hopefully, that would soon change, but he really couldn't be sure when he'd get another spell.

Grabbing his spear, a coil of line, and a wooden container he'd carved from a piece of stump, Elijah set off toward his fishing spot. He took a circuitous route, heading toward the snare lines he'd laid; they had yet to be successful, but he hoped they'd soon bear fruit in the form of small woodland creatures he could eat. Thankfully, the hares and squirrels hadn't been transformed like the crabs. Otherwise, he'd be in real trouble.

He checked his snare lines, but he'd once again failed to catch any prey. However, he did find a stand of mushrooms that he could add to his stash back at the cabin. He slipped each morsel into a satchel he'd crafted from woven grass and lined with his shirt. Soon, he'd have to find some sort of replacement clothing, or he'd die from exposure. At least the weather hadn't really turned yet, even if Elijah knew it was coming.

Slowly, he made his way to what he referred to as his fishing hole. Nestled on the shore almost a mile from where he'd battled the crabs, it was characterized by a deep pool almost thirty yards across that connected to the sea by a narrow channel. The best spot from which to cast his line lay atop a large boulder that he wouldn't have been able to climb without his recent physical gains. Now, though, so long as he was careful, it wasn't difficult, and he soon found himself threading his homemade hook with his similarly handmade line. Once that was done, he baited the hook with a piece of rancid crab, then tossed it into the water.

Once it had settled, he wove the line around his arm, from elbow to palm, then started to gradually pull it in. The first cast was unsuccessful. So was the second. But on the third, he got a bite. However, when he pulled it in, he saw that the fish had only taken the bait. That was the problem with his hooks—well, one of them, at least. They only managed to do their job about half the time.

But Elijah was persistent, and on the tenth cast, he finally pulled in a fish. Like most of the other fish he'd caught over the past six weeks, it appeared to be a steelhead trout. However, it had clearly been mutated just like the crabs had been. Its fins were larger, its body sleeker, and its teeth much more prominent. But fortunately, this mutated variant still tasted the same as every other trout

Elijah had ever eaten. More importantly, despite looking like it would be a fearsome predator in the water, it had the same weakness that afflicted almost every other marine animal—it couldn't breathe outside of the water.

Elijah pulled it on top of the boulder, but he gave it a wide berth as it flopped around. He'd have preferred to end its suffering with a swift strike from his axe, but when he'd tried that with the first fish he'd caught, it had ended with the thing flopping around at the wrong time and latching on to his forearm. Without Touch of Nature, he'd have quickly bled out from that wound, so he'd decided to simply let the fish suffocate from now on.

Still, it wasn't a pleasant thing to watch, even if he knew it was necessary. He'd never been particularly averse to hunting or fishing, but watching an animal suffer was something wholly different. Even so, he forced himself to watch. Part of that was practical—he wanted to be alert in case the fish got close to the edge; he couldn't afford to lose it, and he would throw caution to the wind to avoid that eventuality. But the other reason he made himself watch was because he wanted to be aware of the cost of his own survival.

Elijah had long since come to terms with hunting and consuming other animals. Back in the civilized world before the System descended and changed everything, it was possible to avoid eating meat. And for the past few years, he had—mostly. But there was a marked difference between eating meat because you liked it and doing so because you needed the protein and fat if you wanted to survive.

That shift in his mindset had given Elijah some insight into the natural order. Animals didn't care about the morality of killing another animal for food. They just did what they had to do. In that way, nature was brutal. However, most animals shied away from wanton killing, as well. For them, there were no trophies. Just a meal and another day of survival. Elijah had gradually adopted that mindset as his own.

When the fish died, he felt an influx of foreign Ethera flow from the trout and into his mind, where it spread through the branching conduits of his soul and, finally, into his core, where he felt something shift. He gasped at the resulting flash of power, and when it settled, he didn't need to see the notification to know that he'd reached level two.

Elijah let out a sigh of relief. Now, it was time to see what benefits a level brought with it.

15

SNARING ROOTS

Elijah sat on the boulder, the trout forgotten as he looked at the notification that had come with the jolt of power to which he'd been subjected after reaching the second level. It said:

Congratulations! You have reached level two, earning two (2) free attribute points. Would you like to allocate free attribute points?

Elijah already knew what he had planned, so he slotted the two points into his Regeneration attribute. His reasoning wasn't complicated; Regeneration was the only attribute that did two things. First, it would help him heal from wounds more quickly. He already had Touch of Nature for that, but there had been plenty of times when he hadn't wanted to waste his limited Ethera on minor injuries. Now, those nagging issues would heal that much more quickly. But more importantly, the second function of the Regeneration attribute was what he was really after: Ethera Regeneration. The faster he could regain the energy he spent, the more he could use Touch of Nature.

Besides, he was already gaining physical attributes like Strength and Dexterity via his frequent workouts. He had a suspicion that that wouldn't last forever, though, so he wanted to get as much as he could out of his routine before investing any points in the physical attributes.

After assigning his attributes and confirming his choices, Elijah opened his status to inspect his gains. And he wasn't disappointed. His Regeneration had increased by two points.

Name	**Elijah Hart**
Level	**2**
Archetype	**Druid**
Class	**N/A**
Specialization	**N/A**

Alignment	N/A		
Strength	6		
Dexterity	5		
Constitution	11		
Ethera	4		
Regeneration	9		
Attunement	Nature		
Cultivation			
Body	Core	Mind	Soul
Wood	Unformed	Unformed	Unformed

After he reached level three, Elijah intended to invest an additional point in Regeneration before focusing on Ethera. Once that was up to ten points, he would start working on his other attributes. Hopefully, by then, he would know the limits of his physical training, which would give him enough information to make the right choices. The same line of thinking told him to get everything to ten, then specialize from there based on his experiences.

Indeed, there was a part of him that just wanted to throw everything into his physical attributes. Being stronger, more coordinated, or more durable never hurt anyone. However, because of his archetype, he expected that he would become increasingly more reliant on his spells. Those required Ethera, and he was almost certain that he'd eventually outgrow the meager size of his core. No—for better or worse, he was on the path of a spellcaster, and aside from being fit enough to survive, he needed to assign his attributes along those lines.

Fortunately, there was no ambiguity about what each attribute did, so he could make his plans with at least some degree of certainty.

Sighing, he closed his status before opening a new window. This one described his archetype and, more importantly, the spell that came with his new level. How he knew he'd get one, he wasn't sure, but that knowledge was firmly entrenched in his mind.

Archetype: Druid
The druid is the defender, ally, and cultivator of nature. Features bonuses to natural Regeneration, Ethera density, and One With Nature.

Required Aspects:
[Scholar], [Nature]

Spells	
Touch of Nature	**Harness the power of nature to heal yourself or an ally.**
Snaring Roots	**Call upon nature to summon a snarl of roots to bind your enemies' movements.**

That had potential, depending on how strong those roots turned out to be. Certainly, it could help him kill the crabs—or, more importantly, help him escape if he made a mistake. Even with his experience and a proven technique, killing the crustaceans was no sure thing. More than once, he'd picked a fight he couldn't win and been forced to retreat, frustrated and wounded. But with this new spell, perhaps his hunting would become safer. And given that Elijah's survival was balanced on the edge of a knife, safer was always better.

He ached to try it out, but there were no enemies about. So, he reluctantly went back to fishing. And over the next few hours, Elijah had decent success, catching four more fish, which he gutted and cleaned before tossing the offal into the water. Then, with his catch in hand, he set off back toward the cabin, where he intended to use some of the wild herbs and mushrooms to make a fish stew. It wasn't the tastiest thing around, due to a lack of proper spices, but it was better than his initial attempts at cooking the crab.

Along the way, though, a familiar foreboding sent a shiver up his spine, and he let out a sigh. He knew his stalker had returned—no surprise there; even when he didn't have a basket full of fresh fish, it rarely let him walk through the forest unobserved.

"Come for your tribute, huh?" he said as calmly as he could. Still, there was a slight tremble of fear in his voice. He liked to think that he and the cat—whatever it was—had an understanding, but the fact was that he could very well have been fooling himself. It was a wild animal and, judging by his senses, almost assuredly far deadlier than he could hope to be. He had no idea what was going through its mind.

Even so, now that he'd started down this path, he knew that trying to stop wouldn't be smart. So, he grabbed three of the fish and tossed them onto the ground before saying, "Eat well, your majesty."

Then, he backed away. There was a rustle in the nearby brush before a huge shape appeared. Elijah's jaw dropped as he beheld the creature. In a lot of ways, it looked like a panther. But he'd seen panthers before, and none of them were even half this monster's size. In fact, this creature was closer to the size of a tiger than the panthers Elijah had seen.

But that wasn't the only thing that made him wary. It also had a few characteristics that distinguished it from any other panther—or other animal—Elijah had ever seen. For one, everything about it seemed exaggerated. From its musculature to the size of its teeth or claws, it was all too much. On top of that, it bore a white stripe down its spine that branched down to its ribs, slowly fading into black.

And then there were its eyes. Emerald green and glistening with intelligence, they told Elijah that he wasn't dealing with some mundane animal. Like the tree, this creature was magical in nature.

More than anything, Elijah wanted to turn and run. While pursuing his doctorate, he'd worked as an intern at a local zoo. And once, he'd seen a lion turn on one of its keepers; it had been a massacre that the woman had barely survived, and that only because the animal hadn't really been interested in killing her. If it had been, there was no chance she would have made it.

And this creature was almost twice the size of a typical lion. It also moved with unnatural grace, telling Elijah that its bulk wouldn't slow it down. If he ran, it would pounce, and there would be nothing he could do about it. Even with the local wildlife having been transformed, this creature was an apex predator.

The panther stepped forward, its green eyes locked on Elijah. It moved slowly. Carefully. And with deadly silence. Elijah's heart thundered in his chest even as a cold sweat broke out across his brow. If the panther attacked, he could use his new spell. He had his spear. And he was almost as fit as he'd been before his cancer diagnosis. But instinctively, he knew none of that would matter. He was inferior in every single way, and he only lived because it chose to let him live.

It ducked its head and snapped up one of the fish. It swallowed it in a second before eating the second. Then the third. Before Elijah knew it, the panther had finished eating the overlarge trout.

Then, it shifted its gaze to Elijah's basket.

It wanted more.

He swallowed hard before slowly retrieving one of his two fish from the basket, then tossing it toward the panther. The fish landed only a few feet away from the panther, but it didn't even look at it. Instead, its eyes remained locked on the basket.

"Oh, come on . . ."

A low growl cut him off.

With no more complaining, Elijah threw his remaining fish toward the huge panther, who snapped both up just as quickly as it had the first few. Then, without any hesitation, it turned around and melted back into the undergrowth. In the space of a second, it was gone.

Elijah stood there for a couple of minutes, unable to move. He could barely even breathe. But then, resentment set in. He'd just wasted half the day so he could feed a giant cat.

Now, he had no choice but to go back to his fishing hole and hope he could catch something else. Sighing, he did just that, and by the time he reached it, the sun had already passed its zenith and was heading toward the horizon. In a few hours, it would be dusk, so he knew he'd only have time to get a single fish. Maybe two, if he was lucky.

"Unless that stupid cat decides to shake me down again," he muttered, tossing his line into the water. Almost immediately, he felt a nibble, and he grinned. Perhaps his luck was changing.

He tugged on the homemade string, wrapping it around his elbow. But the fish on the end of the line wasn't going to come in without a fight. Still, Elijah was an old hand at fishing, and he continued to work the line until he felt it go slack. At first, he thought that the line had broken—it wouldn't have been the first time, and he knew it wouldn't be the last.

But then, he saw a dark shadow in the water before, suddenly, something burst forth from the waves. Elijah only got a brief view of scales and sharp teeth before he threw himself backward. He tumbled off the boulder and to the ground below and, by some miracle, managed to keep from breaking his neck.

When he looked up, he saw an abomination looking down at him.

It was dark blue-green in color, with four arms, glistening scales, and a face that looked like it belonged to some bottom-dwelling monstrosity. The monster—and it definitely was a monster, there was no doubt—screeched at him before launching itself into the air.

For a split second, Elijah froze.

But then, instincts born of uncountable hours in the boxing ring took over, and Elijah dove aside. His brief hesitation cost him, though, and a line of fire erupted across his back. He screamed as he was sent rolling across the rocky shore. With adrenaline coursing through his veins, he ignored the worst of the pain as he pushed himself to his feet.

The monster looked at him, then against all odds, its hideous face split into a wide grin. A chill ran up Elijah's spine as he realized that the thing wasn't just a monster. It was that, but it was so much more. It raised one of its claws, then licked Elijah's blood away. Its smile widened.

Elijah had a brief moment to take stock of the situation. His spear was atop the boulder, so it was out of reach. He had the flint-bladed axe at his waist, but it was barely even sharp enough to split wood, much less cut through that thing's viridian scales. So it was useless.

No—if he wanted to survive, he had only one option: He had to run.

So, as the creature advanced—in no apparent hurry—Elijah embraced the Ethera in his core and pushed it into the webwork of channels that constituted his soul. Then, he cast Snaring Roots.

The Ethera left his core in a rush, taking all but a third of his reserves, but it went to good use because, a moment later, thick brown roots erupted from the ground, snaking around the monster's legs. They twisted and turned, ensnaring its entire lower body.

Elijah didn't stay to see how far the spell would go because he knew he only had a narrow avenue of escape. So, once the creature was trapped, Elijah turned and ran, crashing through the underbrush and stumbling over exposed roots. Already, the blood loss was getting to him, but he couldn't afford the time needed to stop and heal. So, he continued to run, hoping that the monster would be reluctant to follow him inland.

But only fifteen or twenty seconds later, Elijah heard the sounds of the creature's pursuit. He pushed himself, but he just wasn't fast enough. He tripped over a rock he should have been able to avoid, and he went tumbling down a slight incline and into a shallow depression. When he looked up, he saw that the monster had already closed with him. His spell had briefly slowed it down, but it was completely insufficient against such a powerful creature.

Elijah scrambled back, searching for a weapon. A stick. A rock. Anything.

He came up empty-handed, and once again, the monster grinned its sickening grin before stepping forward.

At the end of his rope, Elijah embraced Touch of Nature, hoping to heal the wound in his back so he could try to fight the monster off. In the back of his mind, he knew it was useless. With the size of that monster—it was at least seven feet tall and dense with muscle—and the way it moved, he didn't stand a chance. Even if he'd been armed, those scales looked tough. Perhaps if he'd had something more potent than Snaring Roots, he would have been able to hold his own.

But he had none of those things, so he was almost assuredly going to die.

That was okay, though. Elijah had made peace with his own mortality long ago. On that plane, he'd been ready to die; the fact that he'd gotten even a few more weeks was a miracle.

Still, none of that meant he was going to go down without a fight.

The Ethera in Elijah's core drained away, fueling Touch of Nature as the wound in his back healed. It wasn't perfect; it would probably break open the moment he moved. For now, though, it would have to be enough. He'd reevaluate if he somehow managed to survive against the monster.

As the viridian beast slowly advanced—it seemed to be savoring Elijah's fear—he pushed himself to his feet and squared his shoulders, ready for whatever came next.

16

AN ANT AMONG TITANS

Elijah had managed to close the wound on his back, but with the viridian monster slowly gaining on him, he had other things on his mind. His core was empty, and it would take at least an hour before it recovered to full capacity. And even if he survived that long, he had no way of defeating the creature. It was too fast. Too strong. And those scales were far too durable. His only other spell, aside from Touch of Nature, had already proved insufficient.

No—he knew that, unless he managed some miraculous feat, he was going to die. After everything that he'd managed to survive—from cancer and the plane crash to carving his own place out of the wilderness—it was frustrating to think that it had all been for nothing.

But that wasn't true, was it? The moment he'd recovered from what the doctors had called incurable cancer, he'd accomplished the impossible. Further, there likely weren't that many people who could have survived his experiences after being stranded in the wilderness. Not only was the forest an inhospitable place, full of dangers both hidden and obvious, but he'd even managed to kill a few of those monstrous crabs. He wasn't quite thriving, but he wasn't that far off, either.

If only he'd chosen an archetype with more combat potential, he might have been capable of standing against the scaled monster.

But that wasn't necessarily true, either. Without the ability to heal himself, Elijah would have died a dozen times over. And even if he had managed to survive as another archetype, he didn't think he could have done much against the creature slowly walking toward him.

Its aura reminded him of the panther with whom he'd made a tentative truce. But it was also wildly different. Elijah had no idea if he was imagining the auras of the two creatures, but given that magic had been thrust upon the world, he was prepared to believe that what he felt was real.

Either way, with the panther—or whatever it really was—Elijah felt a sense of connection. It was subtle, but something told him that, while it wasn't a native to the area, or even Earth, it still belonged. It was still a part of the wider tapestry that constituted the natural world. But the newcomer was something else entirely. It felt like an outsider, and for some reason, Elijah thought of a virus. A corrupting influence that was both part of the natural world and apart from it.

Of course, that wasn't quite right, either, and he didn't have the time to contemplate what any of it meant. Not if he wanted to maintain any hope of survival. Slim though it was, Elijah knew that that hope was contingent on his persistence, on his refusal to give in. The moment he surrendered and accepted his fate, he would die. But so long as he kept fighting, that hope would survive.

So, he steadied himself and drew the flint-bladed axe from his makeshift belt. It was a poor weapon, but even that was better than facing the thing with only his bare hands.

Squaring his shoulders, he gripped the rough haft tightly and muttered, "You want some of this? You're going to have to earn it."

To his horror, the monster let out a wheezing sound, which to Elijah's ears was unmistakably a laugh. Whatever confidence Elijah had managed to muster faded.

Then, before Elijah could hype himself back up, the creature pounced. Its claws flashed as they cut through the air, and it was all Elijah could do to dive out of the way. A ripping, tearing sound preceded a great crash as the enemy shredded a nearby tree—a reminder that if those claws made contact with his comparatively soft flesh, there was little he could do.

Elijah rolled to his feet just in time to see the tree tip over with a massive crack and the sound of snapping branches. Fortunately, the monster hadn't counted on that, and a moment later, the huge trunk of the tall pine tree thudded down right on top of the monster. Even that seemed insufficient against such a mighty creature, but for a few seconds at least, it was stationary.

That was Elijah's moment. He dashed forward, a battle cry on his lips as he raised his homemade axe. He brought it down with all the Strength he could gather. His aim was true, and the flint blade found a home in the monster's unprotected side. However, Elijah's heart jumped into his throat when he saw two things.

First, his axe shattered into a million pieces, the shards exploding out from the point of impact. A few of them buried themselves in Elijah's unprotected skin, but most went sailing into the surrounding forest.

But more troubling was the second thing Elijah noticed—the blow, mighty though it was, didn't even leave a mark.

No, that wasn't true. He'd managed to leave the tiniest of scratches—so small that it might have been Elijah's imagination—on one of the monster's scales.

It hissed and gurgled, leveraging its four muscular arms beneath the heavy tree trunk. Its claws bit deep into the bark, and it pushed. Meanwhile, Elijah took those few seconds for the opportunity they represented, and the moment he recovered from his ill-advised attack, he rolled to his feet and took off at a sprint.

One second passed. Then two. Three. He scrambled over a fallen tree and slid down a slight hill, his passage eased by the ubiquitous moisture that seemed to cling to everything. When he reached the bottom, he regained his feet and continued his flight, hoping to put as much distance as he could between himself and the unassailable monster that had pegged him as prey.

A handful of endless seconds passed before Elijah heard the sound of pursuit. Still, he ran—because what else was he supposed to do? He couldn't fight that creature. He couldn't hurt it. He couldn't endure its attacks. He was lucky that he'd managed to survive as long as he had. He dodged between the trees, panting as much from fatigue as from the panic filling his heart.

The monster chose a different track. Judging by the sounds of snapping branches and falling trees that dogged Elijah's path, the creature had chosen to simply run through the various obstacles native to the densely forested wilderness. That was probably the only reason it didn't immediately catch him. With its size and single-minded pursuit, it was far less suited for forest traversal.

But that didn't mean it wasn't gaining on him.

In the end, his doom came in the form of a particularly well-camouflaged root that Elijah never even saw. One second, he was sprinting through the forest, and the next, he was tumbling through the air only to land on his chest. His momentum took him into an awkward roll, and he ended up colliding with a solid berm composed of roots and tightly packed earth. The impact dislocated one of his shoulders and took a few square inches of the skin of his arm.

More troubling was the fact that he'd stopped moving.

Terror gripped him as he tried to scramble to his feet, but the pain in his shoulder made it difficult to focus. On top of that, that arm was useless, which threw off his balance. Still, he grasped at exposed roots as he tried to continue his flight. But by then, the monster was upon him.

Insanely sharp claws bit into his legs as the sound of the creature's hissing laughter mingled with his screams of agony. Elijah lashed out, but he might as well have been kicking a boulder for all the good it did. Even so, he squirmed and kicked as the monster reached down with curious delicacy and turned him over.

Oh, God—it wanted to see the look on his face as it killed him. That was the only explanation. Elijah's screams turned into a defiant, yet trembling, roar as he continued to resist. But it was useless. The monster was unstoppable. Unassailable. Unbeatable.

It leaned close, its fetid breath filling Elijah's nostrils. Then, a forked tongue slithered out from its lipless mouth to trace a line along Elijah's cheek. It shivered in pleasure. Elijah pressed himself against the ground as he desperately tried to put as much distance as he could between the creature and himself, but it was useless. The ground was as immovable as the creature was inescapable.

The monster was also done delaying the inevitable.

Dim light glinted off the reptilian creature's viridian scales, shining with a dark green-blue tint as it unhinged its jaw and opened its mouth. Row after row of teeth glistened in that yawning abyss as it opened wider and wider. Elijah punched out with his good arm, but the monster didn't even flinch at the blow. Why would it?

It leaned forward. Inch by inch, Elijah's death crept closer until he could see the blackened flesh inside the creature's mouth.

He closed his eyes, resolving to go to his death with stoic defiance.

But then, a whisper of a sound greeted Elijah's ears, and suddenly, the weight of the monster's grip disappeared. A mere second later, the sound of splintering trees filled the air, and Elijah flung his eyes open to see two titans locked in furious battle.

The panther had pounced on the monster's back, its claws biting deep into its scaly hide. Black blood misted the air as the panther subjected the creature to a furious onslaught of raking claws. Those impenetrable scales split. Its blood flowed. And the monster wailed in hissing agony.

A moment later, the panther lost the advantage of surprise, and the monster regained its balance, reaching back and gripping the panther's glossy black fur. But the lithe animal wasn't so easy easily caught. It dodged with feline grace, its claws continuing to rake at the monster's scaly hide.

But it didn't do so without picking up a few injuries of its own. The panther was agile and deadly, but the enemy wasn't without advantages of its own. And it used them as it clamored to turn the tide of battle, its own natural weapons ripping into the panther's fur and tearing through its dense muscles.

The panther spat and hissed under the assault, but it didn't let up. Most predators would give up on a hunt if it proved too dangerous, but the scene Elijah witnessed wasn't one of two animals engaged in a natural battle for survival. No—it was a pair of bitter enemies who were compelled—whether it was by choice or instinct, Elijah had no idea—to fight to the bitter end.

Using one arm, he dragged himself farther away, but he didn't take his eyes from the fight. It seemed to go on for ages, but Elijah knew that less than a minute had passed.

The panther leaped away from the monster's sweeping claws, narrowly dodging the attack before it bounded off a nearby tree, changing directions. The tree swayed under the cat's massive weight, and the panther rocketed toward the scaly creature. It tried to react, but the cat was moving too quickly. The panther's claws flashed. Once. Twice. Three times in less than a second. And when it jumped away, the viridian monster's throat had been destroyed.

Pitch-black blood flowed from the gaping wound, smothering its shimmering scales in stygian blackness. It stumbled to its knees, falling forward only to barely catch itself with an outstretched arm that extended to the black-blood-soaked ground. Its claws dug furrows into the soft earth, but with a gurgling, hissing roar, it climbed to its feet and faced off against the cat, who was patiently waiting in the shadows. Elijah could only see hints of its tail's movement and shining green eyes, but he could easily imagine it crouching for its next pounce.

The monster staggered forward, leaving a trail of black blood.

The cat knew it only had to wait it out, though. Its enemy was already weakened, and the viridian monster's Strength fled by the second.

But then, the monster seemed to remember its original prey, and it turned toward Elijah. Even with its blood gushing from the wound on its stubby neck, the creature managed its horrifying imitation of a smile before it turned its body in Elijah's direction.

Elijah shuddered. The monster was on its last legs. Its life was going to end. There was no stopping that. But just as surely, it didn't intend to die alone. Elijah's hand crept to a small hilt at his waist.

The flint-bladed knife was not a weapon. Comprised of a single stone that he'd arduously filed into a point before wrapping the narrowest end with his homemade cordage, it was barely even a tool.

But it was better than his bare hands. So, with his good arm, he reached down and yanked it from his makeshift belt. Brandishing it in the monster's direction, Elijah pressed his back against the berm and pushed himself to his feet. The monster continued to advance, its pace slowed not by a desire to prolong Elijah's horror, but by its diminishing Strength.

Elijah was content to wait. Every second that passed brought it closer to death. Perhaps, if he was lucky, it would fall before it even reached him.

He was not lucky.

With a burst of speed that constituted the last of the monster's Strength, it dashed across the short distance. It reared back, its claws glistening with the panther's red blood. But Elijah didn't wait for its attack. Instead, he marshaled the last bit of his own remaining energy and leaped forward, leading the way with his homemade dagger.

He knew it wouldn't cut through the monster's viridian scales, but he wasn't aiming for those. Instead, he thrust his knife deep into the wound wrought by the panther's sharp claws. It sank into the creature's black flesh, biting deep until it collided with bone. The monster flinched back, losing its balance as Elijah crashed into it.

Elijah screamed as he was thrown free, rolling on his already injured shoulder. He could feel the ripping tendons of the abused joint, but he couldn't stop himself.

After a second, he skidded to a stop, and it took him a few more moments to gather his wits and look back at the scene of the battle.

And what he saw brought a grim smile to his face. He was so elated that, at first, he didn't even notice the gaping wound drawing a line across his belly. But within a few seconds, fire erupted in his stomach, and he looked down to see his innards falling out.

Even more disturbing, when Elijah looked up, he saw his protector slinking forward. The panther had sustained a host of wounds that Elijah hadn't noticed during the battle, and beneath its glossy black fur, he saw hints of white bone. Half its face had been massacred, and it moved with a pronounced limp.

Gathering his intestines, Elijah realized that he was about to die. Stomach wounds weren't immediately fatal, but when a person started spilling his guts, it was only a matter of time. Soon, he'd grow weak and pass out—if not from the wound itself, then from shock or blood loss. So, even if he managed to recover enough Ethera to power Touch of Nature, he wouldn't be conscious to use it.

But that was okay. He'd done well for himself, and while he knew he was about to die, he'd stood his ground. And that unstoppable monster was now dead. He only hoped that the panther would survive, which, judging by its wounds, didn't seem likely. It approached, looked at him out of the corner of one baleful green eye, then flopped onto the ground with a pained sigh.

Elijah's eyes drooped as he felt the pool of sticky blood gathering beneath him, and finally, he began to dip into unconsciousness.

17

RESURGENCE

Before Elijah dropped into unconsciousness, he saw a familiar notification that jarred him back to awareness.

Congratulations! You have reached level three, earning two (2) free attribute points. Would you like to allocate free attribute points?

It was followed closely by another:

Congratulations! You have reached level four, earning two (4) free attribute points [four (4) total]. Would you like to allocate free attribute points?

Two levels? That didn't make any sense. He hadn't done anything. Sure, he'd jabbed his now-ruined homemade knife into the monster's neck, but Elijah felt certain that he had only hastened its demise. The panther had been the real killer. But the evidence was right in front of him; the System had given him credit, and the resulting Ethera had pushed him to level four.

As he continued to bleed out, Elijah's mind turned sluggish, and his ability to focus slipped further and further away. It was like wading through thick mud just to force his status open and allocate his attribute points. When he finally managed to wrangle his mind into doing what he wanted, he shoved the free attribute points into Ethera, bringing his total up to eight.

Immediately, Elijah felt an influx of magical energy as his core doubled in size. Thankfully, the upgrade didn't just provide capacity, but rather, it gave him an amount of energy equal to what he'd get from four Ethera, leaving him with a half-full core. The influx was a heady sensation that nearly drove him to distraction, but he once again harnessed his concentration and forced himself to cast Touch of Nature. The healing spell soothed the injury in his stomach, dragging his intestines back into place and sealing the wound. But before it could do much more than patch things up, Elijah's core ran dry.

He was still gravely injured, and any movement would threaten to tear the wound open, but he'd bought himself some time. His survival was now all but assured, provided he didn't run afoul of any other monsters.

Elijah glanced at the corpse of the scaled creature that had attacked him and shivered. That, of course, brought with it a significant amount of pain. That monster had come out of nowhere, and even with his newly strengthened body and magical powers, it had been completely out of his league. Without the panther . . .

The panther!

The enormous cat was lying only a few feet away, its breathing shallow and its eyes filled with agony. And it wasn't surprising. The panther had killed the monster, but it had also paid the price. Shallow wounds decorated its entire body, but Elijah's eyes were drawn to the three much more serious injuries it had sustained.

The most troubling was a long gash down its side. At least two feet in length, and gaping open to expose the panther's ribs, it was a ghastly wound that, even in the best of times, would likely spell a wild animal's doom. If infection didn't set in, then perhaps it would have a chance. But given the foul odor coming from the now-dead monster, Elijah considered that unlikely.

Next, one of the panther's legs was turned the wrong way, and Elijah saw its broken bones bulging beneath its sleek skin. Finally, the semiaquatic monster had ripped a chunk of the panther's face off. In short, the huge cat had almost assuredly given its life to save Elijah.

Or perhaps it made more sense that the monster was its mortal enemy. After all, though Elijah had been paying tribute to the panther in the form of a daily fish or two, he'd never gotten the sense that it liked or accepted him. In fact, it had always seemed on the edge of killing him outright. The idea that it would protect him, except as a side effect of its true intention, was almost laughable.

But still, Elijah owed the animal his life.

It was at that moment that he made a choice. If he recovered enough Ethera before the panther succumbed to its wounds, he would try to heal it. If not, then it just wasn't meant to be. With that in mind, Elijah settled back against the tree and waited on his Regeneration to refill his core. Slowly, his mind began to churn, drawing the ambient energy in before sending it through his soul and down into his core. The process was both soothing and distracting enough that he wasn't overwhelmed with the pain of his still-serious wound.

To further distract himself, Elijah opened what he'd begun to affectionately refer to as his spell book:

Archetype: Druid **The druid is a defender, ally, and cultivator of nature. Features bonuses to natural Regeneration, Ethera density, and One With Nature.** **Required Aspects:** **[Scholar], [Nature]**	
Spells	
Touch of Nature	**Harness the power of nature to heal yourself or an ally.**
Snaring Roots	**Call upon nature to summon a snarl of roots to bind your enemies' movements.**
One With Nature	**Draw power from nature.**
Eyes of the Eagle	**Briefly enhance your eyesight with the power of a fearsome raptor.**

As had been the case with both level one and two, he'd gotten spells for each of his new levels. One With Nature seemed a bit ambiguous, but the second spell, Eyes of the Eagle, seemed fairly straightforward. And, for now, completely useless. Perhaps there would be a situation in the future where having telescopic vision would help, but at present, it would do nothing to help him.

What's more, he couldn't spare the Ethera to test either spell out. However, One With Nature was definitely intriguing. Drawing power from nature could mean just about anything. Would it let him rapidly regenerate his Ethera? Or perhaps give him an influx of Strength? The possibilities were endless, and his speculation occupied his mind until he'd recovered a little more than half his Ethera.

Once he'd done that, Elijah pushed himself away from the tree and slowly shifted closer to the panther. By that point, it had been almost an hour since they'd killed the monster, but the cat had yet to succumb to its wounds. Still, its breathing was labored, and Elijah saw pink-tinted foam around its mouth. Clearly, it had internal injuries in addition to the visible wounds.

In short, it was dying.

Elijah aimed to change that.

When Elijah laid his hand on the animal's paw, its only reaction was a shift of its eyes and a slight tensing of its muscles. Perhaps that was the extent of its capability. Closing his eyes, Elijah pulled Ethera from his core, channeling it through the webwork of his soul, and into his spell Touch of Nature.

He gasped.

Healing someone else was clearly very different than healing himself. For one, he couldn't just place his hand on the appropriate spot and hope for the best. Instead, he needed to know what he wanted to fix before he could heal it. Thankfully, as a trained biologist, Elijah was very familiar with animal physiology, and it didn't take him long to find the issues. Even without the magical awareness that allowed him to sense problems, Elijah would have had a good idea of where to start. With it, he could pinpoint the issues in mere seconds.

That's when the other difference between healing himself and healing others surfaced. When targeting himself, Touch of Nature had always felt like being wrapped in a wave of soothing energy that both healed and revitalized him. But with the panther, it felt like he'd just poured a glass of water into a vast ocean. Even with his senses and experience as a scientist guiding him, Elijah knew it was going to take more than a few casts to heal even the least of the panther's wounds.

But Elijah was nothing if not persistent. So, he focused on the cat's internal injuries first, using his gathered Ethera to mend the wounds. He managed three casts before his core ran dry once again, but he'd managed to stanch most of the internal bleeding. It was less effective than he'd hoped, but it was a start.

Over the next day and a half, Elijah fell into a rhythm. Once his core refilled, he would cast Touch of Nature on himself a single time, then use the remainder of his pool of Ethera to repeatedly heal the panther. As he did, he learned a couple of things. First, so long as he kept his mind clear, he could regenerate his entire core in two hours. Sometimes, it varied by a couple of minutes, but he chalked the variance up to his inability to keep proper time. After all, he didn't have a clock to consult. If he let his mind wander, his Regeneration took a significant hit, so he did everything he could to keep his thoughts from wandering too far afield.

The second thing he learned was that the panther was vastly more powerful than him. Elijah had no notion of its level, but it was so far above him that it might as well have been a god. But it was mortal, just like him, and he knew that without his help, the cat would have quickly succumbed to its wounds. It seemed to know that, as well, and even after Elijah had healed it enough to keep it from dying, it remained in place.

Gradually, Elijah mended both his and the panther's wounds until, after almost two days, the job was done, and he slumped in exhaustion. Hunger gnawed at his belly—after all, he hadn't had time or concentration to spare for gathering any food—and fatigue weighed down on him like he carried a mountain on his shoulders. Fortunately, water hadn't been as much of an issue, given that it had rained intermittently throughout the process.

The panther pushed itself to its feet, testing its mended leg. Elijah had left it for last, as much to keep the panther in place as because it was the least life-threatening of the cat's many injuries.

"Yeah, it's healed," he said tiredly. His own wounds had healed much more quickly, allowing him to focus entirely on the panther.

The cat locked its glistening green eyes on him for a long moment. Then, without even a nod of thanks, it padded away, disappearing into the shadows.

Elijah sighed. "You're welcome, I guess," he muttered.

Then, he turned his attention inward to address a notification pushing against his mind. When he did, his jaw dropped.

Congratulations! You have reached level five, earning two (2) free attribute points. Would you like to allocate free attribute points?

Another notification soon followed. And then another. Three levels, putting him at seven. That gave him six extra attribute points to allocate, but even more exciting than that, he'd gained three new spells. It was a nearly overwhelming degree of advancement, and he quickly opened his spell book to investigate his gains.

Archetype: Druid **The druid is a defender, ally, and cultivator of nature. Features bonuses to natural Regeneration, Ethera density, and One With Nature.** **Required aspects:** **[Scholar], [Nature]**	
Spells	
Touch of Nature	**Harness the power of nature to heal yourself or an ally.**
Snaring Roots	**Call upon nature to summon a snarl of roots to bind your enemies' movements.**
One with Nature	**Draw power from nature.**
Eyes of the Eagle	**Briefly enhance your eyesight with the power of a fearsome raptor.**
Ancestral Circle	**Create a place of power.**
Nature's Bounty	**Encourage the growth of plants.**
Storm's Fury	**Call forth the power of a storm and harness its might.**

The first spell felt powerful, but the description didn't give any hints as to what it was supposed to do. Creating a place of power sounded great, but how did it benefit him? He would have to try it out if he wanted to discover the answer to that question.

The second spell, Nature's Bounty, at least seemed more straightforward, and he could already see how beneficial it could be. A good portion of his diet depended on foraging, but what if he could create a garden and accelerate its growth? It would change everything about his life in the wilderness.

The last spell was clearly Elijah's first attack spell, but beyond that, he wasn't sure what to expect. Storms were deadly, sure, but he wasn't certain how he was supposed to use such power to fight his enemies.

Elijah shook his head as he pushed himself to his feet. While healing himself and the panther, he'd rarely moved from that position, and he'd grown stiff. In the past, he'd have had quite a bit of difficulty sitting still for that long, but in the throes of his quest to mend his savior's wounds, moving around had been the last thing on his mind.

Then, Elijah remembered that he still needed to allocate his six free points. He did so, splitting them between Ethera and Regeneration, bringing them to eleven and twelve, respectively. His original plan had been to focus on his physical attributes once he got Ethera and Regeneration to ten, but he'd never expected to gain so many levels so quickly. He still wanted to get the most out of his physical training, so he'd chosen to focus on his magical attributes for now. Once Strength and Dexterity plateaued—if they did at all—he would reevaluate his plans.

For now, though, Elijah had some spells to test. First up was One With Nature, but when he embraced the spell, channeling Ethera from his core and through the pathways of his soul, he got a big shock. His jaw dropped as a cascade of information spread across his mind, telling him how the spell worked.

Grinning, he said, "Oh, that's good. Really good. This could change everything."

18

THE POWER OF A DRUID

Elijah felt Strength flow through him as he felt the effects of One With Nature take hold. More, for the first time, the spell came with understanding. It felt as if he'd suddenly remembered a long-lost memory, and the result was that he knew how the new spell worked. And he was impressed.

The effects of One With Nature were threefold. So long as he remained in contact with natural earth, the spell would enhance his physical attributes. His new understanding wasn't specific about the exact degree of enhancement, but he could feel that it was significant. Further testing would need to be done if he wanted exact information, though.

The second facet of the spell's enhancement came in the form of natural healing. It wasn't even close to rivaling his other spell, Touch of Nature, but it would go a long way toward staving off minor injuries and the effects of fatigue. More importantly, the effect it would have on his physical training would almost assuredly be profound.

Finally—and he suspected, most importantly—the spell came with a sense of connectivity with the natural world. He'd felt a version of that the moment he'd awoken with his new archetype. However, One With Nature enhanced that feeling a hundredfold. More than that, though, he could sense the forest's aura of life far more keenly, and within a few feet, he almost felt as if he could identify individual organisms.

But he suspected that he'd have to grow much stronger for the spell to reach that level, if it ever did. For now, though, he took comfort in the feeling that he was that much closer to belonging in the forest. Elijah also got the feeling that it would protect him from natural predators, at least to some extent. If he antagonized them, they would still react with vicious certainty; however, he felt that they wouldn't instigate anything.

Of course, Elijah suspected that something like the panther would be unaffected. He had no gauge or context for its power, but he knew it was too far above him to succumb to any attack or spell he could muster. Not that he wanted to try—no, he'd been disabused of that notion when he'd witnessed the battle between the panther and the monster. That was a battle he had no interest in fighting.

After testing One With Nature, Elijah glanced at the monster's corpse. It had begun to decompose within an hour of its death, and now, it was little more than a mass of discolored refuse. In the beginning, he'd harbored notions of harvesting its impenetrable scales and using it for armor, but even if it hadn't rotted into a state of uselessness, Elijah was more than a little put off by both the smell and the sense of wrongness that radiated from its body. Even in death, it didn't seem like it belonged in the world, and he wanted nothing more than to let it rot so that it would cease its corrupting influence.

Mostly, that aura of corruption had faded, but Elijah still wanted to get away as quickly as he could. So, after a few more seconds, he headed in the direction of the stream. As he did so, he marveled at how much stronger and more vital he felt.

"Could definitely get used to this," he muttered. The spell's effects had nearly doubled his physical ability, making traversal through the forest trivial. Soon, he reached the stream, where he stripped off his soiled clothing and washed it as best he could. The endeavor was only a moderate success; the monster's black blood seemed to have suffused everything, right down to the tiniest of fibers, but he did what he could.

Next came his body, and though the water had grown much colder since his first encounter with the stream, One With Nature made him much more durable, so he barely felt the stream's frigid embrace. Without soap or something abrasive, it took quite a while before Elijah was satisfied with his relative cleanliness, but when he stepped out of the stream, he felt refreshed in a way he hadn't since awakening on the shore after the plane crash.

After dressing, Elijah made his way back to the cabin, which was much the same as he'd left it. The fire had been extinguished, and it looked like some small animal had rooted around in his food stores. Not unexpected after two days but still disappointing. Before Elijah got down to trying his other new spells, he set about the task of restarting the fire. He might not have needed as much protection from the cold as he had before using One With Nature, but he still didn't want to go through any more nights without a fire.

Summer had already faded, and he knew from experience that fall could turn into winter in a matter of days. So, he needed to be prepared for it.

As he worked, Elijah continued to feel his way through One With Nature, and along the way, he discovered that, once cast, it would remain in place indefinitely. However, he also sensed that his body only had room for a single augmentation of its nature. Part of that feeling came from the information he'd been granted alongside the spell, but he could also feel the subtle way the spell stretched his soul. Any more and it would collapse.

But that was fine by Elijah. He didn't have any other augmentations to cast, so he didn't have to worry about it. For now. Perhaps he'd have to revisit the problem in the future, though.

In any case, once Elijah restarted the fire, he took a few minutes to test the other new additions to his spell book. After One With Nature, the next one on the list was Eyes of the Eagle, which gave him a brief duration of telescopic vision. After casting it for the first time, he looked down at the ground and could see everything as if it was under a weak microscope. It wasn't powerful enough that he could see microbes or individual cells, but he suspected that wasn't the purpose. Instead, it was meant to give him the means to see long distances, and he expected that it would accomplish that goal very well.

The next new spell was Ancestral Circle, which, for now, proved useless. However, like his other spells, it did come with a thorough understanding of the spell's purpose. And that was enough to make Elijah's jaw drop.

Unlike Elijah's other spells, Ancestral Circle required significant preparation. Once he chose an appropriate spot—and the moment he understood the requirements, he knew precisely where he wanted to put it—he would have to plant a series of trees in a perfect circle. Then, he would have to empower that circle with his spell. Once that was done, the true purpose of Ancestral Circle would be available to him.

And it could be summed up in one word: teleportation.

It was limited, but the idea was that he could use the second portion of the spell to instantly transport himself from anywhere in the world to his circle, which the burst of information he'd received with the spell referred to as a Grove. He could only do so once a week, but it was an incredible ability.

Still, it would take a vast amount of work to create his Grove. He was so eager to get started that he very nearly set off to his chosen spot right then and there. But good sense won out, and he moved on to the second-to-last spell he'd received after healing the panther.

Nature's Bounty was far more straightforward than any of his other spells. He only had to channel his Ethera from his core and through his soul before casting the spell, and it would cause rapid plant growth within a ten-yard radius. Of course, to plants, rapid meant that it would only take weeks for a plant to reach maturity, but that was still a huge boon. Already, Elijah's task of growing his Grove had gone from being a project of years to one that might only take months. Doubtless, the two spells were intended to be used in tandem.

Finally, Elijah's exploration of his spell book reached Storm's Fury. Ever since learning that his transformed world was one of magic, Elijah had imagined being a grand wizard and slinging fireballs at his enemies. Of course, he knew that wasn't what being a Druid was all about, but even so, he'd become enamored with the fantasy, and he'd found himself hoping that his path would include something of the like.

And now, it did.

Standing a couple dozen yards away from his cabin, Elijah sighted in on a rock he'd placed twenty feet away. Then, as he had with every other spell, Elijah dragged Ethera from his core and pushed it through the pathways of his soul and into the spell he wanted to cast. And for a split second after he released it, nothing happened.

Then, suddenly, a bolt of lightning tore through the forest's canopy and hit the ground five feet away from the rock. Electricity spiderwebbed across the ground for another few feet before dissipating, leaving only a few tendrils of wispy smoke snaking up from the point of impact.

Elijah grinned.

On the one hand, the spell seemed incredibly powerful. He knew the power of that much electricity, and he could surmise that it could be a potent weapon. But on the other hand, he'd missed his target, and badly. Clearly, he needed to practice.

That was okay, though. He was nothing if not persistent, and it wouldn't take a significant shift to add target practice to his exercise regimen. The only big problem was that the spell was incredibly Ethera hungry, and it had taken almost a third of his capacity to cast it a single time. Not ideal, but Elijah was used to that.

Once he'd finished exploring his new spells, Elijah set about replenishing his food stores, gathering mushrooms and berries as he walked around the forest. Eventually, his path took him to the meadow that was home to the powerful tree that had eased the cultivation of his Body of Wood. When he arrived, he noticed something peculiar—the meadow was perfectly circular; it was as if it had been made to accommodate his Grove.

Perhaps it had. Or maybe the tree had influenced the area for that purpose. Whatever the case, it was precisely what Elijah needed. He'd already decided to use the tree's thick aura to his advantage when placing his Grove, and the discovery was just further evidence that he was on the right track.

But with the sun dipping toward the horizon, he didn't have time to get started just yet. Instead, he gathered more berries, some dogbane for more cordage, and a few dozen acorns that had fallen from the tree. The arboreal spirit that dwelled within still seemed dormant, but Elijah hoped that it would awaken soon. After all, if it had guided him through the process of cultivating his body, then it was probably full of other useful information.

Once he was finished, Elijah trekked back to his cabin, where he enjoyed a meal of berries and mushrooms before, at last, releasing One With Nature and letting himself fall asleep.

When Elijah awoke the next day, he held off on reapplying the augmentation as he went through the daily regimen of exercise he'd established before the fight against the viridian scaled monster. However, instead of being confined to physical exercise, he interspersed target practice into the routine. He still had to stop and concentrate before he could focus enough to cast Storm's Fury, but by the end of his workout, he'd progressed noticeably. His aim was still lacking, especially if he rushed through it, but he'd found that the process of casting the spell came quicker every time he did it. It was still alien, but like any process, it was on its way to becoming instinctive. Now, he only had to spend the time necessary to push it over the edge to where he could use the spell without thought.

Of course, that wasn't something he could accomplish in mere hours. Instead, it was a task of weeks. Or perhaps months. Maybe it would even be years. But stranded in the wilderness, he had time to spare.

More than that, he had plenty of motivation to get it right. After all, that monster had come at him out of nowhere, and if the panther hadn't saved him, Elijah would have been slain. Even with the cat's help, it had been a close thing. The new world wasn't benign. It was deadly. And if Elijah wanted to avoid ending up as some monster's lunch, he needed to grow more powerful.

To that end, he redoubled his efforts and leveraged every ounce of his focus as he continued to practice his aim, one lightning bolt at a time.

19

NOT ALONE

Elijah crouched at the tree line, watching the crabs scuttle across the rocky shore. Then, he tossed a bit of fish entrails only a few feet away from the most isolated crustacean. It took the creature a moment to notice it, but when it did, it wasted no time before skittering across the rocks and gobbling it up. That's when Elijah tossed another bit of fish guts a little farther away. After the crab found that one, too, he repeated the process. That's how, a few feet at a time, Elijah led the crustacean away from its fellows. Once it was sufficiently isolated, he struck.

Not with the homemade spear in his hand but with magic.

A thin bolt of lightning, barely visible in the harsh light of the winter sun, descended from the sky to hit the crustacean in the center of its muddy-brown shell. It let out a shriek as it convulsed, its limbs spasming out of control as it flopped to the gravelly ground.

But Elijah knew from experience that it wasn't dead. It would take two more strikes—and all the Ethera in Elijah's core—for the monster to succumb. He quickly recast the spell, to similar results. Finally, he finished it off with a third cast. Elijah sighed.

For all the excitement he'd felt when he'd gotten his first attack spell, it had proved to be a bit of a mixed bag. While the spell did allow him to hunt in relative safety, it wasn't nearly as powerful as he'd hoped it would be. Clearly, the Druid archetype was no mighty wizard, even if it gave Elijah a single attack spell.

Rising from his cover, Elijah trotted to where the crab had died, then set to harvesting it. He'd done so dozens of times over the past eight weeks, so he found the task boring but ultimately necessary. After all, with the onset of winter, the fish had retreated into deeper waters, leaving his once-fertile fishing hole desolated. The crabs—along with his stores of mushrooms and berries—were his only consistent source of food. Sure, Elijah managed to kill a few hares and squirrels here and there, but those instances were so infrequent that he knew he couldn't rely on them when it came to his survival.

Of course, if things got really bad, there were always the bugs he felt crawling through the earth. They wouldn't be pleasant, but Elijah expected that they would provide some sustenance. Still, he wasn't quite at the point where he needed to resort to eating insects. He was tired of crab, but it was still better than eating crickets and grubs.

"Yeah. My standards are sky-high," he muttered to himself. Other animals had no problems eating bugs. It was the same with many human cultures, as well. But Elijah found the idea disgusting. Even so, he knew that if he got hungry enough, he'd start digging through the dirt like any other hungry animal. Only, he had an advantage; with One With Nature, he could feel everything within a few feet, and the ground was no barrier to the ability. No—he was perfectly suited for bug hunting. He just didn't want to do it.

So, he hunted crab. Fortunately, there seemed to be an endless number of the creatures—which didn't seem all that surprising. Purple shore crabs had always been very populous, and the onset of the System hadn't changed that. At first, Elijah had wondered if the creatures would simply starve—after all, with greater mass came the need for a more plentiful food source—but that problem had been solved by the corpses of sea creatures that regularly washed ashore. Most were half rotted and bore severe wounds, but the crabs didn't seem to mind. They had always been scavengers, after all.

Soon enough, Elijah finished harvesting the crab, putting the meat in a huge basket he'd woven from sticks, dried reeds, and leaves. Once he'd finished, he set the basket aside and repeated the process, killing and harvesting another crab. He didn't need the meat for himself, but still, he felt compelled to feed—or perhaps pay tribute to—the panther, which he'd only seen a handful of times over the past eight weeks.

Gathering his huge basket—it was at least three feet across—Elijah began the trek back to the cabin. About halfway there, he felt the presence of the panther bearing down on him. It wasn't as suffocating or terror-inducing as it once had been, but it was still enough to make him sweat. He set the basket down, then piled half of the meat on the forest floor.

"Your tribute, your majesty," he said, his voice loud and slightly mocking. "Feels sort of like it should be the other way around, though. You're the mighty hunter, right? You should be feeding me."

The forest stilled, and a wave of oppressive power washed over Elijah. Unperturbed, he said, "Fine, fine. You're the king around here. I know my place."

The feeling disappeared. Elijah wasn't certain if the cat could understand him—he suspected that it could, after a fashion—but he didn't really care. The panther hadn't killed him yet, so he didn't think it was suddenly going to change its mind over a snarky comment. Besides—Elijah had studiously held up his end of the bargain by providing food. The cat had no reason to kill him.

But it was still a wild animal, wasn't it? As such, it was unpredictable. There was no telling what might set the panther off. Then again, it was far more intelligent than any wild animal Elijah had ever seen—even dolphins or chimps. So, applying his previous experiences might not be the best idea.

Whatever the case, they seemed to have a mutually beneficial arrangement, and Elijah wasn't going to do anything to mess that up. So, he added a few handfuls of crabmeat to the pile before saying, "There you go. Next time one of those monsters attacks, remember who feeds you, yeah?"

Predictably, the panther didn't give voice to its agreement. Nor did it show itself at all, and without the cat's oppressive aura, Elijah would have thought that he was talking to empty air. But he knew the cat was there. It had heard him. And he suspected that it understood. That would have to be enough.

With that, Elijah continued back to the cabin. Along the way, he kept an eye out for mushrooms and berries, but with the onset of winter and his constant foraging, he found nothing. It would have been troubling if he hadn't amassed a significant store of food.

And it had finally gotten cold enough that he didn't have to worry nearly so much about spoilage, even with the crabmeat. That was a boon, even if it came with the decidedly less pleasurable side effect of him being cold all the time. He'd tried his best to guard against it, making rudimentary clothing out of woven grass and the few rabbit pelts he'd managed to acquire, but it was mostly ineffective.

Still, with his increased Constitution, as well as the constant enhancement that came with One With Nature, it wasn't so bad. Even though the days had continued to grow colder, he felt that, unless things got much, much worse than was normal for the Pacific Northwest, he would survive. It wouldn't be comfortable, but that was true of most of his life now.

After storing everything away in raised boxes he'd carved, Elijah added some more wood to his fire, then set off toward his budding Grove. The trip was mostly uneventful, save for when he ran into a rapidly decomposing monster corpse. It looked different than the one he and the cat had fought. Smaller. And somehow less oppressive. However, it was still an alien creature that could—and would, if it got the chance—rip him to shreds. Thankfully, the panther seemed to take hunting them as its personal mission, and over the past eight weeks, Elijah had run into a handful of other monster corpses.

Leaving it behind—there was nothing useful about it—Elijah continued on his way until he reached the Grove. In some ways, the meadow containing the huge tree was the same. The dimensions hadn't changed, nor had the tree itself. However, about thirty feet from the natural tree line, there was now a ring of saplings. They were barely taller than Elijah himself, but even that much growth was so abnormal as to be considered miraculous. Part of their rapid growth was due to his daily usage of Nature's Bounty, but Elijah suspected that it was also a characteristic of the trees themselves. After all, they'd come from acorns he'd gathered from around the majestic tree at the center of the meadow, and he knew good and well that it wasn't normal.

The ambient Ethera of the area had also increased significantly, and Elijah could keenly feel its nature aspect. It was soothing and energizing, and it increased the Regeneration of his core significantly. Normally, it would take him two hours to regenerate the Ethera in his core, but in the Grove, it was cut down to a quarter of that.

And that increased Regeneration had allowed him to make abundant use of Nature's Bounty, which in turn had continued to increase his Regeneration. It was a perpetuating cycle, and one for which Elijah was extremely grateful. Without it, his Grove would have taken much, much longer.

After completing two circuits through the circle of saplings, Elijah went deeper into the Grove until he reached ten neat rows of turned soil. From that soil sprouted dozens of small plants that would, Elijah hoped, eventually become berry bushes that would, in turn, make gathering food much easier. But the bushes were in their infancy, and it would be weeks before they bore fruit. Still, the fact that they'd sprouted at all was a good sign for Elijah's long-term survivability.

Elijah planted himself in the center of his nascent garden, crossing his legs and activating Nature's Bounty. His spell's range was just wide enough to encompass the entire garden—by design—so, once activated, he only had to sit and keep it going. That's what he did; however, as he did so, he focused on the network of pathways and channels that constituted his soul. It was metaphysical in nature, so his only concept of how it worked came from feeling the Ethera as it traced its way through the network. However, a few weeks before, he'd discovered that he could guide and accelerate the process, dumping extra Ethera into the spell and making it more potent.

Or that's what he thought. There were no manuals to read, and Elijah could only go by what he felt. But he expected that it was one of the reasons behind the garden's rapid growth. In any case, it didn't seem to be hurting anything, so he kept at it, pushing at the boundaries of his soul's pathways.

That was how Elijah spent the next few hours until his soul started to ache. The first time he'd discovered the process, Elijah had pushed through the pain. A mistake, as it happened, because he'd eventually pushed himself too far, resulting in an inability to use any Ethera at all for the next two days. So, the moment he felt that ache in his soul, Elijah cut the spell off.

Looking up, he saw that there was still plenty of daylight left, so he decided to explore a little. He still had little concept of the area beyond his immediate surroundings, so he'd resolved to spend a bit of time each day in exploration. Before he started, though, Elijah knew he needed to refill his core. So, he waited about twenty more minutes before he set off toward the east.

Clutching his new homemade flint-bladed spear, Elijah trekked inland through the dense forest. One hour passed, then two. Along the way, he gathered the few mushrooms and berries that had managed to stubbornly resist the effects of winter. He also saw signs of game, but he didn't run into any animals.

Eventually, though, Elijah crested a small hill only to find himself atop a sheer cliff that dropped off at least two hundred feet. Below him, the canopy of the forest ran on for at least a couple more miles until it abruptly ended at the sea.

"It's an island . . ."

Indeed, Elijah could see the curve of the shore a few miles in the distance. Of course, it still could have been a peninsula, but he didn't think that was the case for some indefinable reason. In any case, Elijah could see more land stretching across the horizon in the distance. Miles of turbulent sea separated Elijah from the mainland, but at least he wasn't stranded in the middle of the ocean.

Finally finding a use for Eyes of the Eagle, Elijah embraced the spell, then channeled Ethera from his core and through his soul. Immediately, his vision sharpened, and he could see the distant shore as if it was only a few hundred yards away.

And what he saw was both troubling and exciting.

It seemed that he was not as alone as he thought he was.

20

NEOPHYTE SOUL

From the top of the cliff, Elijah studied the encampment across the strait separating his island from what he expected was the mainland, and what he found was inexplicably infuriating. With Eyes of the Eagle, he could clearly see the beginnings of a primitive town nestled at the foot of a mountain. The low-slung buildings had been constructed of seamless concrete—or some magical variant, he expected—from which grew thick smokestacks that were steadily belching black clouds into the otherwise pristine air.

The town was surrounded by thick forests not unlike what Elijah had found on his island, but the inhabitants had waged a war against the flora, clearing large swaths of trees in the process. No doubt, they had been used as fuel for their fires. Or perhaps they'd been used to construct the sturdy-looking barges moored at the town's simplistic dock. Either way, the sight filled Elijah with a degree of sorrow he couldn't adequately describe.

He'd never really been an environmentalist—not like many of his colleagues. Certainly, he'd always tried to conserve where he could, and he had never been an unrepentant polluter, but he also knew that environmental issues were far more complicated than the hardcore activists wanted to admit. In a vacuum, it was easy to tell people to drive electric cars or eschew eating meat, but those were solutions only available to a select few. Others had to do what they had to do, regardless of environmental consequences.

That wasn't to say that Elijah didn't want to hold industry accountable for their profit-driven choices. He did. He just understood that things were far less simple than they might appear to be at first glance.

However, when he looked upon that decimated forest and the billowing black smoke, he felt a degree of anger he'd never felt before. Clearly, that was his Nature aspect—and the connection that came with his archetype—screaming at him. He did his best to push it to the back of his mind, but it was difficult.

The fact that the inhabitants of that town didn't appear to be human helped, though. Elijah didn't know what any of them were called, but he saw creatures that reminded him of stereotypical fantasy dwarves, gnomes, and goblins, all of which were working together.

Soon, Elijah noticed a flood of the small-statured creatures pour out of what he thought was a mountain cave. Upon further inspection, though, he saw that each of those people—if indeed, that was the right word—was carrying a mining pick. After that, it didn't take much longer for Elijah to notice the carts full of unrefined ore, though he was too far away to utilize his limited geological knowledge to identify what it was.

Elijah stood there, watching the town from miles away, until he could confidently say that the entire settlement was a mining operation. Likely, the chimneys belching clouds of billowing black smoke were connected to smelters, which would extract metal from the raw ore.

More than that, though, Elijah saw that the refined metals were taken to the biggest building, which looked more elaborate than all the rest. For some reason, he didn't think he was looking at a warehouse. The building was too elaborate and far too small to serve that purpose. And given that his own spell, Ancestral Circle, had a teleportation component, it didn't take him long to guess that the alliance of dwarves, gnomes, and goblins had access to something similar.

Or perhaps he was wrong. He was still far too new to the transformed world to understand what was and wasn't possible. However, he felt unreasonably confident in his assertions.

For a while, Elijah wondered what he should do. The distance from the island to the town wasn't short; at least ten miles, but probably more than that, separated him from the coast. So, it would not be an easy trip, even if he managed to construct a raft of some sort. He never even considered swimming; seeing the transformation of the trout, with all their extra teeth, was enough to dissuade him from that notion. And that wasn't even considering that the monster that had almost killed him had come from the sea. Who knew what else was down there?

After a while, Elijah realized that, while the discovery was interesting, it didn't really affect his situation. With the inability to cross the strait, the best he could do was create a bonfire and hope they saw it. Then, he'd have to hope that they were friendly, which wasn't entirely likely, given that the town's inhabitants weren't even human. No—nothing had changed, save for the fact that he needed to be on his guard.

Which was the same as always.

As the sun began to dip toward the horizon, Elijah reluctantly turned away and started back toward his cabin. Fortunately, he'd long since mastered traversal through the thick foliage, so he made good time back to the Grove. There, he did a circuit around the clearing, keeping Nature's Bounty active, before he retreated to his cabin where he prepared some stew, which was comprised of seaweed, crabmeat, and mushrooms.

So, the same thing he ate most days.

As he sat there spooning the stew into his mouth, Elijah was struck by a deep sense of longing. It wasn't the first time he'd missed his old life and, more importantly, people, but after seeing civilization so close, the feeling came back with a vengeance. With their setup, the dwarves, gnomes, and goblins were probably eating like kings. Even if they didn't have access to teleportation—which, for some reason he couldn't explain, he doubted—their area was probably home to plenty of game. Deer, wild hogs, and a multitude of other edible animals were native to the region, and the thought of enjoying a nice venison steak filled Elijah with a deep sense of longing.

Of course, he also missed his friends. He wished he could talk to his sister. Or her family. Idly, Elijah wondered how everyone else in the world was doing. Were they struggling to survive, just like him? Or were things easier in the cities? Were there even cities left? The world had supposedly been rearranged, so there was no guarantee that there hadn't been more changes.

He sighed.

For now, mere survival was difficult enough. But what about the future? Would he be content to remain an island hermit for months? Perhaps years? No. He needed more than that. He needed a purpose. The problem was that Elijah had never been burdened with anything of the sort. After his parents had died, he'd thrown himself into his schoolwork, eventually getting his doctorate despite not really being passionate about marine biology. Sure, it was interesting enough, and he did enjoy it, but only as a job. It was never a purpose.

But now, magic was real. The impossible was now possible. Not that long ago, he'd spoken to a tree. With a mere thought, he could call lightning from the sky. Not to mention his healing abilities. He had power. The question was how he wanted to use it.

The problem was that he didn't know the answer to that fundamental question, and he wasn't sure if he would figure it out anytime soon.

Not that it was urgent. Staying alive in such an unforgiving world was hard enough to occupy most of his focus. So, for the time being, he just had to keep going, and that wouldn't change until at least the spring. With that thought, Elijah let sleep overtake him.

When he awoke the next morning, he embarked on his daily routine of exercise and target practice. At first, his physical attributes had improved, but they'd stalled out at nine points, which just seemed to confirm his suspicions that if he wanted to go past ten, he would need to allocate his points appropriately. Still, with his ability to heal, he felt better than he had since college. He was only thirty years old, but they'd been a hard thirty years filled with sports injuries. But with constant usage of Touch of Nature, the remnants of those injuries, which had presented themselves via nagging aches and pains, had faded to nothing, leaving him whole and hale.

If he'd had proper nutrition, Elijah would have been in the best shape of his life.

After his target practice, Elijah headed to his nascent Grove, where he completed his daily circuit powered by Nature's Bounty. The saplings seemed to have grown a few inches, and his garden of berry bushes had continued to sprout. Soon enough, he hoped to have a proper Grove. Once it crossed whatever arbitrary threshold that was imposed by his spell—or maybe the System itself—he would be able to test out the teleportation feature.

Once he'd finished his circuit, Elijah settled down next to the majestic tree at the center of the clearing, where he recast Nature's Bounty, pushing extra Ethera into it. The pathways of his soul flexed, expanding minutely with every pulse of energy only to return back to normal a moment later. However, they did seem a bit thicker than they had the day before. It might have been his imagination—or wishful thinking, perhaps—but his soul seemed a little sturdier. The pathways a little wider. It was as if the previous day's exertions had stretched them enough that some of the benefits remained.

In some ways, it wasn't unlike his daily exercise. Repeated exertion seemed to be the key to channeling more Ethera through his soul, which he hoped would allow him to cast more powerful spells.

Or maybe he was doing things completely wrong and he was on the verge of ruining his pathways. He had no way of knowing. But what he was doing felt right, which was enough to keep him going.

Over the next six weeks, Elijah continued the rhythm of his existence. Even as the weather grew colder and more inhospitable, his days maintained the familiar cadence of improvement and the necessities of survival. From time to time, he'd go back to the cliff, where he continued to observe his neighbors. The town grew, with many of the buildings gaining an extra story or two. And whether it was imagination or not, the population seemed to increase, as well. So, too, did their impact on the environment.

Elijah seethed as he watched the forest's retreat, but he had no idea what to do about it. Nor was he sure if he truly cared if they cleared a little bit of the woodland. There were plenty of trees out there, after all. But he felt what he felt, artificial or not, and he couldn't escape it.

Toward the end of the sixth week, though, Elijah had a breakthrough that cut right through the monotony.

It happened as he sat next to the tree at the center of his Grove; the saplings had continued to grow, and they were on the verge of becoming proper trees. He could feel his spell teetering on the edge of activation. But that wasn't the source of his breakthrough. Instead, that distinction belonged to what he'd begun to refer to as his soul cultivation.

The pathways of Elijah's soul had continued to thicken; the effect was only minute, but even a small change was cause for celebration because it allowed him to channel more Ethera into Nature's Bounty, which in turn caused the spell's radius to increase. In the beginning, it had only been about ten feet wide, but now, the circle's diameter was at least fifteen feet.

Following the same pattern he always did, Elijah flexed the Ethera, pushing against the boundaries of his pathways. They stretched, but he felt that they could take more, so he continued to shove more Ethera through them. Then, suddenly, something snapped.

Elijah gasped as the Ethera ran wild, tearing down the limits imposed by his pathways. In the space of a second, his entire soul began to degrade under the influence of the tidal wave of Ethera. Panicking, he tried to stem the flow, but his cultivation System had no interest in following his commands. Instead, Ethera flooded through his mind, dragged into his soul from his surroundings. Meanwhile, the energy in his core came in from the other side, and when the two energies met, they did so with explosive force.

The world felt like it was ripping him in two. Elijah screamed, but it was useless. He could hardly think amid the pain, much less find a solution to the problem. Over and over, those two opposing forces crashed against one another, sending agony arcing through Elijah's body, soul, and mind.

It went on for a subjective eternity as the Ethera tormented him. Before, Elijah had considered the energy benign, but free from the confines of his cultivation System, it was an incredibly destructive force. Especially when the two different flavors—the wild Ethera and the energy from his core—clashed.

But Elijah endured. He couldn't have said how. He didn't know why. He just clung to his life with as much fervor as could muster as he maintained the grip on his sanity. And slowly, the clashing energies transformed his pathways.

But they didn't grow wider. In fact, they were destroyed completely, and the loose Ethera was freed to rampage through his body. But as the seconds turned to minutes, and minutes turned to hours, the transformation took hold, and suddenly, he crested the peak, and his body—or his soul—started to absorb the Ethera. At first, it only took a trickle, but soon, that trickle became a torrent.

Then, finally, Elijah's soul drank the last of the Ethera that had been raging through his body, and he collapsed. When he did, a new notification appeared in his mind's eye:

Congratulations! You have cultivated a Neophyte Soul!

He only had a moment to study that notification and smile before unconsciousness overtook him.

21

NERTHUS

Elijah awoke shivering in the middle of the night. Winters in the Pacific Northwest could be brutal, and it seemed that his island was no exception. Fortunately, his initial investment into the Constitution attribute had combined with his Body of Wood as well as One With Nature to give him significant protection from the elements. He was still cold—after all, the temperatures had dropped well below freezing—but his experiences told him that he was at no risk of frostbite or other issues related to overexposure. Of course, even if that wasn't the case, he had Touch of Nature to bail him out, though that seemed like a waste of Ethera.

With a groan, he opened his eyes to see an incredibly clear, starlit sky. That was one thing about being stranded in the middle of nowhere—there was no light pollution, so there was nothing to obscure the tapestry of stars. In a way, it reminded Elijah of being out to sea, though even those experiences had been marred by the occasional drone of an airplane or a satellite streaking through the atmosphere. Now, after the onset of Ethera and the transformation of the planet, there was nothing of the sort. And in all the ways that counted, it was both terrifying and objectively beautiful.

After all, while there was incredible beauty that had come with the transformation of the Earth, it also came with the knowledge that everything people had worked toward for thousands of years had been cast aside in the space of an instant. Elijah had no way of knowing for sure, but judging by the way the plane had crashed, technology no longer worked the same way it had before. No more electronics. No more cars. No telephones or computers. They'd been shoved back into the Stone Age.

But along with the dissolution of technology came Ethera and magic. So, hopefully, people had begun to adjust. There was no telling how many different archetypes were out there, and if Elijah's own abilities were any indication, there was plenty of reason for optimism.

There was also a call for cynicism, as well. Elijah wanted to think the best of people, but he was realistic enough to know that they wouldn't always cooperate with that optimistic expectation. Instead, they would act according to their own self-interests. Sure, most people would try to help others. And only a few would turn on their neighbors.

But it really only took one person with power to ruin everything. One man or woman who chose to take advantage of those weaker than them could do untold damage, especially with the escalation of power that came with the influx of Ethera. That's what Elijah feared more than anything. A magical tyrant so strong that no one would oppose them—it was a horrifying prospect.

Not that it really mattered for now. Aside from his distant neighbors across the strait, Elijah was alone. There was no one to oppress him, save for the environment itself.

For a long while, Elijah just lay there, his body still feeling as if it was in a state of flux. Certainly, he could already feel the changes that had come with his Neophyte soul. However, he was more than a little afraid of looking at the changes—which seemed extensive—wrought by his heedless pursuit of improvement. In hindsight, his actions had been stupid. He had no idea what he was doing, and because of that, it wouldn't have been surprising if he'd crippled himself. In fact, if he'd had the wherewithal to form rational thoughts while in the middle of his soul's transformation, that was exactly what he would have expected. But against all odds, he'd succeeded in yet another cultivation upgrade.

He opened his status:

Name	**Elijah Hart**		
Level	**7**		
Archetype	**Druid**		
Class	**N/A**		
Specialization	**N/A**		
Alignment	**N/A**		
Strength	**9**		
Dexterity	**8**		
Constitution	**11**		
Ethera	**11**		
Regeneration	**12**		
Attunement	**Nature**		
Cultivation			
Body	**Core**	**Mind**	**Soul**
Wood	**Unformed**	**Unformed**	**Neophyte**

Idly, he wondered what he should do with his future attributes. He'd very much reaped the benefits of having a bigger pool of Ethera and increased Regeneration. But he also knew that, without physical attributes, he wouldn't stand a chance against more powerful creatures like the viridian monster or the panther. He hadn't forgotten how much stronger and faster they were, after all. To stand up to that level of might, he needed as much of a boost to his Strength, Dexterity, and Constitution as he could get.

It was a conundrum, and it was one he didn't expect to solve in the near future. Nor did he need to. After all, he hadn't gained a level in a while, and if he had his way, he wouldn't be fighting any more major battles anytime soon. Sure, he got a trickle of Ethera from his crab hunting, but it wasn't nearly enough to progress at any appreciable rate. It would take a concerted effort to change that, and in the middle of winter, he couldn't afford to devote himself to such a thing. Survival was hard enough without adding the danger that came with hunting for levels.

So, Elijah turned his attention to the pathways of his soul, and he was more than a little surprised to find that they were completely gone. For a moment, he wondered if the System had gotten things wrong. It had claimed that he'd progressed, and because of that, he'd expected to find a minute increase in the size of the channels that carried his Ethera throughout his body. However, that just wasn't the case.

The only thing that kept Elijah from panicking was the fact that nothing really felt wrong about it. So, he tested it the only way he knew how, dragging Ethera from his core and casting Nature's Bounty.

A flood of Ethera poured out of his core, infusing his entire body. A moment later, the spell activated, and when it did, Elijah could feel that the diameter of the area of effect had more than doubled. But it didn't feel any more powerful.

So, Elijah let it drop and cast Touch of Nature instead. Before, the cast had taken almost two seconds, but now, it only took half that. He tried out his other spells, finding similar results. It seemed that, for his constantly channeled spells, it simply increased the area of effect. For Nature's Bounty, that was an incredible boon because it meant that he could affect more plants at once. For something like One With Nature, though, the effect was somewhat muted and only really influenced the sensory bubble around him.

With spells like Eyes of the Eagle, Storm's Fury, or Snaring Roots, the transformation of his soul merely made them activate much more quickly. Definitely useful, if not life-changing.

"You have only begun to walk the path of a cultivator," came a voice from nearby. Elijah didn't need to look up to know that it belonged to the tree spirit. "For now, you are merely setting your foundations."

Elijah glanced at the familiar form sitting on the branch. It seemed a little bigger, but it was hard to tell in the middle of the night. Even with the moon and stars casting the glade in silvery light, it was difficult to see more than shadows.

"What?" Elijah asked.

"The first steps are unique," the tree spirit stated. "You are not truly a cultivator until you have reached the first stages in body, mind, soul, and most importantly, your core. However, you are progressing well, as is proper for the protector of my glade."

"Huh?" was Elijah's response. "What are you talking about? Protector? I'm just trying to survive here."

"You have drawn an Ancestral Circle around my glade," the spirit said. "Using my seeds, no less. When the saplings reach maturity, our bond will be complete."

"What bond?" asked Elijah.

"It is a symbiotic connection," said the tree spirit. "Your Grove will become more powerful, and with it, the speed of your cultivation will increase. However, that power does not come without obligations. You must become my guardian, protecting me from those who would harvest my wood and drink my sap in hopes of growing stronger."

"Is . . . Is that possible?" Elijah asked.

"It is," the tree spirit responded. "Deplorable and shortsighted though it is, there are those who act as parasites, consuming all they see. Doing so will grant power, but it is fleeting. Harmony is the better path, though it is often slower."

Elijah could intuit a little from the spirit's explanation, chiefly that harvesting and consuming natural resources like the tree would grant power, though it would be a one-time gain. And perhaps it would only be temporary, though Elijah expected that that wasn't the case. However, he'd already experienced the effects of cultivating under the tree's branches, so he knew that that was a path to Strength, as well. Though, according to the tree spirit, it was slower, yet sustainable. The optimal path seemed obvious to Elijah, but he could also see how quick gains might be appealing, as well—especially if growing stronger more quickly would mean survival.

But Elijah had no interest in quick gains. Nor did he have any inclination to somehow harvest the tree. Doing so seemed abhorrent, and not just because of the effects of his archetype, though it surely influenced him. Instead, his reticence was born of the knowledge that the tree spirit was a sapient creature. Killing it and consuming its power—however that might be accomplished—was grotesque.

Still, Elijah understood people well enough to know that he might just be in the minority in that opinion.

"What do I need to do?" he asked. "And what should I call you? I don't want to keep thinking of you as the tree spirit, you know?"

"Hmm. I have never had a name," the tree responded. "Perhaps . . . Nerthus. Yes, that name feels right. Nerthus."

"Okay, Nerthus—is there anything I need to do? Or should I just keep helping the other trees grow? Also, are they going to be like you? Sentient, I mean? And how do I progress my other cultivation? Like, my Mind and Core," Elijah rambled. After his ordeal with laying the foundations for his Soul, he felt a little giddy—almost like he'd drunk too much coffee.

"No—you are doing enough," Nerthus said. "The saplings may one day develop spirits but not for a very long time. Regarding your cultivation . . . I cannot say. I am limited in what information I can give a newly integrated native."

Elijah was a little disappointed, but he wasn't really surprised. Nerthus had been helpful, but it had always been limited in terms of what information it could convey. But that was fine. Elijah would have loved to hear more, but he'd been doing okay so far.

Mostly. Aside from a few speed bumps like almost getting killed by a huge, scaled monster from the ocean. Which reminded him . . .

"While I've got you here," Elijah said. "A few weeks back, I ran into this monster. Or I guess it ran into me. It was huge, scaly, and just felt . . . wrong. Like, just looking at it made me nauseous. Anyway, it almost killed me, but there's this panther who lives in the area—we've got kind of an understanding—and between us, we managed to take it down. But it started to decompose almost immediately. None of the other animals I've killed have been like that."

"That is because that was not an animal," responded Nerthus. "It is one of the Voxx. Creatures from a different realm. They come through portals and corrupt the very land they walk upon. As weak as you are, if you managed to survive an attack . . . perhaps you will be a better guardian than I hoped."

"Where do they come from?" asked Elijah.

"Some come from temporary portals," Nerthus stated. "Those are rare. I suspect that is the origin of the one you encountered. However, there are more permanent . . ."

Nerthus trailed off, and the entire tree trembled. "I am not permitted to say any more than I have," it stated. "I am sorry, guardian."

Elijah shook his head. He'd have preferred more information, but he understood that the tree spirit was limited. So, he resolved to be happy with what he could get. However, just when he was going to ask another question, the spirit said, "I must rest now. Perhaps when you complete your Grove, I will be able to remain longer."

"I . . . I understand," Elijah said. "Thank you."

"No, guardian. Thank you," stated Nerthus, its voice trailing off as it retreated into the branch upon which it had been sitting. Soon, it looked like nothing so much as another knot in the wood.

Elijah sighed. He had learned quite a bit from that short conversation. First, it was incredibly important that he continue to try to explore the other facets of his cultivation. He'd already laid the groundwork with his Body and Soul. Now, he needed to work on his Mind and Core—though that would take some doing, because he didn't even know where to start.

Second, he'd learned of the existence of two sets of enemies. There were the people who would want to harvest creatures like Nerthus; for some reason, he expected that the coalition of dwarves, gnomes, and goblins he'd seen across the strait would fall into that category, but he had no real basis for that intuitive leap. Still, with how unconcerned they seemed to be about their environment, it seemed to fit. The other—the so-called Voxx—were a far graver threat, probably to everyone, regardless of how they chose to interact with the world.

And third, he'd discovered that Nerthus's existence—as well as Elijah's choice of where to grow his Ancestral Circle—gave him a significant advantage. He didn't know what form that advantage might take, other than to aid him in his cultivation, but he expected that it would be important.

But more than the information, Elijah was most grateful for the opportunity to engage another being in conversation. Sure, talking to a tree was a poor substitute for human companionship, but doing so had soothed his mind and soul to the point where he actually felt optimistic about the future.

Of course, the moment that thought skittered through his mind, he remembered just how tenuous his situation was. Certainly, he'd managed to find a way to survive, but that was contingent on everything remaining the same. Which was incredibly unlikely.

22

WOODWORKING

For the next few weeks, Elijah fell into a rhythm. With winter tightening its grip on the area, the days shortened, and the nights grew longer. However, to his surprise, the cold didn't seem to bother him much at all—which was a good thing because, aside from a makeshift blanket he'd stitched together from rabbit hides, he had little protection against the elements. Certainly, he'd closed the cabin off by piling moss and leaves across a few upright limbs, but he'd never been much for bushcraft. He knew some of the basics, and he could survive passably well, but Elijah knew he'd never be much of a builder.

So, his continually decreasing susceptibility to the cold was more than welcome, though he had no idea if it was due to his Body of Wood or his increased Constitution attribute. Perhaps it was both. Either way, it significantly increased his chances of surviving through the winter.

Fortunately, the crabs didn't seem to care what time of year it was, so his hunting continued apace. However, he did worry about the lack of vitamins and carbohydrates in his diet. He did what he could to supplement his meals with seaweed that he gathered from the shore, but it was a poor substitute for a balanced diet. When his cache of berries and mushrooms ran out, he'd be in real trouble.

Which was why he'd taken to spending much of his day trying to force his garden to grow. It was going well, and the bushes had nearly reached maturity, but it would still be some time before they sprouted anything edible. The same could be said for some wild onions he'd planted nearby.

To pass the time while he sat in the middle of his garden blasting the plants with Nature's Bounty, Elijah busied himself with whittling. It was something he'd picked up from his father, but he hadn't practiced carving in quite some time. Years, in fact, so he was more than a little rusty—an issue that was further exacerbated by the lack of a proper knife. He had his stone-bladed knife, but it was nowhere near as good as working with a steel blade. Still, so long as he went at it deliberately, he could carve something approaching recognizability.

His first attempt had been Fremont, the dog he'd been forced to give away, but that had come out looking more like a child's interpretation of a horse. Which meant that the only recognizable traits it bore laid in the fact that it had four legs and the proper basic shape. Still, with basic survivability taken care of, Elijah had quite a bit of free time—and he'd have more as winter truly embraced the island. So, he'd kept at it.

And day by day, he improved. Even as his technique grew more practiced, his focus shifted, as well, and he stopped trying to carve figures. Instead, he wanted to replace his walking stick with something a bit more elaborate.

Which was how he found himself combing the forest for the perfect material. The hunt hadn't gone that well. The branches he'd found were almost all rotten, and even the ones that weren't were bent too far out of shape to be useful for his purposes. Still, he persisted until he found a wrist-thick branch that had only just fallen from a hickory tree. Elijah had no idea why it had fallen, but he suspected it had something to do with the fact that the base looked as if it had been chewed through by some small animal. Couple that with the winter winds that periodically swept through the island forest, and it wasn't that difficult to figure out.

Branch in hand, Elijah trekked back to his cabin and set about straightening it. In the beginning, he only had some vague ideas about how to go about the task, but he did know that it had something to do with saturating the wood with steam. Through trial and error, he'd come across a decent, if labor-intensive, method of steaming the wood, then bending it into the proper shape.

Before he'd advanced his Strength, Constitution, or Regeneration, Elijah never could have kept it up for long enough to make the shapes stick. And even with his improvements, he was forced to periodically use Touch of Nature to stave off fatigue. He was also aided by One With Nature, which accentuated his physical capability to the point where he suspected that he'd reached the peak of human potential. Perhaps he'd even exceeded it. Whatever the case, it worked, even if it was a grueling process that took days. It would have been much easier if he'd had clamps and proper woodworking tools, but out in the wilderness, that simply wasn't the case.

Either way, it was good practice for his spells and an even better workout. After two days of working on straightening the stick, Elijah's Strength finally ticked over to ten. His Dexterity still lagged behind by a couple of points, but he had some ideas about how to remedy that—once he finished his staff.

Once the staff had been straightened, Elijah set about carving some decorations into it. When he started, he just focused on the process, uncaring about the result. Afterward, he would liken it to absently doodling; however, it wasn't long before his little stone-bladed knife seemed to take on a mind of its own as it carved fanciful designs in the sturdy staff. Soon enough, it started to take shape, and only when it was half finished did Elijah realize what he'd taken for inspiration.

The staff looked remarkably like the tree spirit's limbs—as if someone had intertwined dozens of small vines into a single structure. At first, Elijah was surprised that his mind had taken him in that direction, but the more he thought about it, the more appropriate it seemed. So, he continued along, only now he was conscious of the direction he wanted to go.

As he carved—a process spanning weeks and consisting of him steadily scraping the barely sharpened stone blade against the wood—Elijah found himself continuing to flare Touch of Nature. As always, he kept One With Nature active, as well, and often, it was accompanied by Nature's Bounty as he coaxed his garden into maturity.

Once he'd finished the process, the staff looked almost natural, as if it had been grown rather than carved. In addition, even when Elijah let his spells fall away, it practically pulsed with what he'd begun to consider his own flavor of power—a result of its constant exposure to his Ethera, no doubt.

But it needed something else.

And Elijah knew precisely what that something was. During his exploration of the wilderness, he'd stumbled upon quite a few beehives. More than once, he'd considered pilfering the honey—not only would it provide a bit of variety to his diet, but the hive would give him access to beeswax, which had all sorts of uses. However, he'd so far decided against it because he had no apiculture skills.

And Elijah had no interest in getting swarmed, even if, from a rational perspective, he knew he could heal whatever damage a few stings might cause. With his advancement in Constitution and his body cultivation, the bees might even be incapable of penetrating his skin.

Of course, that was assuming they hadn't evolved like the crabs had. Some animals had appeared mostly unaffected by the planet's conversion, but others had been completely transformed. For instance, most of the hares he'd encountered were just normal rabbits, but he'd caught a few glimpses of some rabbit-like creatures that actually had horns. Who knew if the bees he'd stumbled across were similarly transformed? He'd observed them a few times, and they didn't look any different, but there was no way of telling if they had other new defenses. Perhaps they were even more venomous than normal, which was a terrifying thought. It was one thing to get a painful sting, but it was something else entirely if they were suddenly deadly.

Even so, Elijah had come to trust his ability to heal, and he'd decided to attempt to harvest one of the hives. To that end, he'd chosen one close to the stream; if they swarmed him, he intended to cut and run, submerging himself in the frigid water until they lost interest. But he hoped it wouldn't be necessary.

Using an ember he'd carried from the cabin, Elijah started a small fire at the base of the tree where the hive was located. Then, he added green pine needles to make the fire smoke more than normal. Finally, he waved the smoke in the direction of the hive. He only had a vague idea of how it was supposed to work, but he knew that smoking the hive was the most effective method. So, that's what he did, waiting for a few minutes until he scrambled up the tree and, using his stone-bladed knife, cut a huge chunk of the honeycomb away.

Thankfully, the bees in the hive were incredibly lethargic, and though he picked up a few stings, it was nothing like the swarm he'd expected. Before long, he'd filled a shallow wooden bowl he'd carved with the stuff, and he retreated, using Touch of Nature to heal the stings he'd received.

"Easier than expected," he muttered to himself as he made his way back to the cabin. Along the way, he felt the presence of the panther, but he said, "No fish right now, your majesty, and I don't think you want to eat beeswax."

Still, he left a big chunk of it out, just in case he was wrong about cats and their tastes. After all, he wanted to do whatever it took to stay on the panther's good side because he'd seen exactly what happened to things that drew its ire.

When Elijah made it back to his cabin, he stoked the fire and placed the honeycomb into a pot of water. Then, he set it to boiling. Once the honeycomb had melted, he strained the soupy mess, then repeated the process until, at last, he had a disc of golden wax. Grinning, he set it aside and retrieved his staff.

Fortunately, Elijah's father had taught him how to make his own finish, which combined beeswax, turpentine, and linseed oil. While it would have been much easier to simply go to the store and buy the materials, Elijah had learned how to gather and prepare the proper materials from their sources. The linseed oil had been the easiest because flax—especially in the quantities that he needed—wasn't difficult to find. After that, it had been a simple process of drying the seeds, then crushing them. It would have been better to boil the result, but that came with a host of problems, chiefly that it was difficult to do so without the oil combusting. There were ways to avoid that—primarily additives—but Elijah didn't really know how to source them. So, he'd decided to simply use the raw paste, even if it wasn't ideal.

The turpentine had a similar issue in that, ideally, it needed to be distilled, but Elijah had chosen to simply boil it and hope for the best. The results were mixed, but he expected that it would work well enough.

With the various ingredients in hand, Elijah added them together like his father had taught him, resulting in a paste that he hoped would seal the wood of his new staff. Sealing wasn't absolutely necessary, but he had time to kill and a desire to do things properly. After creating the sealant, Elijah dipped a corner of his shirt into the mixture and started massaging it into the wood.

He went slowly, and it took him most of a day to finish the process. Meanwhile, he continued to use his various spells, almost on instinct as much as because he needed them. Finally, with his hands cramping despite his constant usage of Touch of Nature, he finished.

And when he did, he got a couple of surprises.

First, the weeks' worth of carving the staff had resulted in his Dexterity increasing to the point where it matched his Strength. That was somewhat expected, even if he'd been too distracted to pay much attention to it. However, the second surprise was that the System recognized the completion of the staff with a notification:

Congratulations! You have created a unique item, [Staff of Natural Harmony]! This item will serve to enhance any spells, skills, or techniques with a nature aspect.

Grade: Simple.

"W-what the . . ."

Sitting in the center of his budding Grove, where he'd been flaring his Nature's Bounty, Elijah was dumbfounded. He'd simply meant to carve a cool-looking walking stick, but it seemed that he'd overshot that mark by quite a bit.

Excited, he monitored his spell, but its area of effect hadn't grown by a single inch. In fact, it seemed exactly the same as it had before he'd finished the staff. And he knew good and well that Nature's Bounty had a nature aspect. It was right there in the name! So that meant he was doing something wrong.

After a few minutes of frustrating experimentation, Elijah figured it out when he actively chose to channel his Ethera through the staff as opposed to simply using his body. Instantly, the area of effect associated with Nature's Bounty grew by almost ten feet. More than that, though, the associated atmosphere of Ethera felt heavier. Denser. More potent. Elijah couldn't be sure, but he interpreted that feeling as the spell being stronger, and not just in terms of its area of effect.

Which meant that the force he could bring to bear had just grown. Not only would his Grove and garden benefit from the increased power of Nature's Bounty, but he suspected that channeling Storm's Fury through the Staff of Natural Harmony would result in a more potent effect, as well.

"A grand achievement for one so young and inexperienced," came Nerthus's voice, though when Elijah looked up at the majestic tree at the center of the Grove, there was no physical representation of the spirit. Instead, the voice was disembodied, which somehow seemed even more magical. "I have chosen my guardian well, it seems."

Then, Nerthus's presence faded away before Elijah had a chance to ask any questions. He was about to head back to the cabin when a new notification flashed before his eyes, this one even more interesting than the one that had announced the completion of his staff.

23

SUPPLY RUN

Winter had come, blanketing the region around the settlement in a thick layer of snow. The temperatures had plummeted well below freezing, and as a result, food—as well as every other necessary resource—had grown scarce. Alyssa and a few of the other hunters with martial archetypes hunted as much as possible, and other members of the growing community frequently gathered supplies from the remnants of the town.

But the pickings were growing slimmer by the day. Already, the local market had been picked clean of nonperishable goods, and the gathering parties had been forced to range farther with every passing week. They'd found a few gas stations here and there, as well as a couple of fast-food restaurants, but for the most part, they had been forced to gather wild edibles like mushrooms and berries.

With winter having descended, even those sources of food had dried up.

Alyssa sat next to Carmen's forge, where her wife was busy shaping a hunk of metal into what would probably become a sword. She watched as the other woman's hammer repeatedly fell upon the hot steel. The spear that Alyssa favored—another of Carmen's creations—was never far away. They'd been attacked often enough that she didn't dare walk around unarmed.

Not anymore.

Finally, Carmen was satisfied with the shape, so she shoved it into the forge—which was really just a firepit—and let out a sigh. Then, she turned to Alyssa and asked, "What's wrong?"

"Nothing," Alyssa said. She sat in a camp chair she'd retrieved from the house when she and a few others had returned to gather any supplies they'd left behind. Most of the house had been ripped to pieces by some unknown monster, but the chair—along with a few other essentials—had survived.

"Yeah—not buying it," Carmen said. "C'mon. Lay it on me."

"Why does something have to be wrong? Can't I just want to watch my wife work?" she asked.

"Again—not buying it. You never stop moving unless something's gone wrong. So, what's going on?" Carmen asked.

Alyssa sighed. "Same as always. Not enough food," she said. "Not enough wood. Not enough of anything, really. We have almost three hundred people living here now, and unless something changes, there's no way we can survive the winter."

"Oh. That."

"Yeah. That," Alyssa agreed.

Carmen wiped the sweat from her brow, then grabbed a huge stump she often used as a chair. It had to weigh at least three hundred pounds, but with her enhanced Strength, she didn't even struggle with it. Carmen had always been a strong woman, but she'd begun to approach superhuman levels.

Of course, that had come at the cost of her other attributes, none of which had seen any significant investment. Despite Alyssa's words of caution, Carmen had no interest in increasing her Dexterity, Constitution, or the more ephemeral Ethera attributes.

"We're going to have to go on another supply run soon," Alyssa said. "I was talking to Roman about it, and he thinks we should go tomorrow."

"Miggy won't like that," Carmen said.

"And you?"

"I don't like it, either," she admitted. "But I'm an adult, and I know what's going on here. Either you do what needs to be done, or none of us survive."

"Someone else could go."

Carmen shook her head, then put her hand on Alyssa's thigh. "You're the highest level here," she said. "Face it—you're the most important person in this whole community."

"Roman—"

"Is an asshole who nobody likes," Carmen stated. "He tries. He works as hard as anybody. Harder, even. But think about it, Alyssa. Everyone sees you out there on the front lines, leading the charge. Meanwhile, Roman's in the back with all the noncombatants, firing away from relative safety. On top of that, he's the guy who's telling everyone they can only have so much food. That they have to work or get kicked out."

"This place would collapse without him."

"I know that. You know that. And deep down, most other people do, too. But just because they recognize that he's essential doesn't mean they like the guy. Hell, he's saved my life twice now, and I still barely tolerate him," Carmen said.

The fact that most people didn't particularly care for Roman wasn't news to Alyssa, though she certainly didn't think it was fair. Without his influence, the small community would have long since failed. People would have starved if he hadn't instituted rationing or insisted that everyone had to contribute in some way. Whether it was gathering or hunting, no one was exempt from food-procurement duties.

"He's a good man."

"Again, not arguing that he isn't," Carmen said, holding up her hands in surrender. "I'm just saying he's an asshole. And nobody likes assholes."

Alyssa shook her head, then leaned over, her head in her hands as she massaged her temples. She certainly hadn't signed up to lead a community, and she didn't think she was cut out for it. However, because she'd reached level nine—making her the highest-level person in the settlement—people looked to her for guidance. As she went, the community would follow.

"Doesn't matter," she said.

"I think it matters more than you want to admit, but okay," Carmen said. "So—how far do you think you'll have to go?"

Alyssa shrugged. "At least a few miles," she said. "Maybe farther. Last time he climbed the water tower, Rick said he thought he saw some buildings about ten miles to the north. So, at worst, we'll have to go there."

"Any signs it's inhabited?"

"Not by people," Alyssa answered.

Not for the first time, she tried to wrap her head around how much the world had been transformed. Before, Easton had been only a few miles from Seattle's city limits, but now, there was nothing but forest for dozens of miles all around, with only pockets of the abandoned remnants of civilization. Alyssa had confirmed it for herself when she'd climbed the water tower at the center of town.

It seemed that they'd managed to gather all the local survivors into one place, which was both horrifying and gratifying. Horrifying because it suggested that the mortality rate approached seventy or eighty percent. On the other hand, the fact that everyone was willing to gather in one spot and work together for the greater good was certainly a good thing. Alyssa had seen enough postapocalyptic movies where the world was ruled by warlords to be thankful that such a fate hadn't come to pass.

Perhaps it was different in more populated areas. Or maybe not. Either way, she couldn't concern herself with hypotheticals that couldn't be proved one way or another. Instead, she needed to focus on her own situation.

For a while, she and Carmen sat together, just enjoying one another's company. Miguel was in the main building with the other surviving children. Without the benefit of an archetype—the cutoff seemed to be fifteen years old—they weren't yet equipped to make it in the new world.

"Are you going to be back for Christmas?" Carmen asked.

"I hope so," Alyssa answered, fervently hoping that she could spend the holiday—if such a thing even mattered anymore—with her family. It was three days away—as far as they could tell, at least—and she wanted more than anything to be there for what would probably be a very subdued celebration. However, the needs of the many outweighed her desire for family time. She hoped Miguel understood why she just didn't have as much time for him as she would have liked.

Eventually, duty called, and Alyssa bade her wife goodbye. After that, she stopped by to see Miguel before reporting to the armory. She was the first of the hunters to do so, which gave her a few minutes to look her status over:

Name	Alyssa Hart		
Level	9		
Archetype	Warrior		
Class	N/A		
Specialization	N/A		
Alignment	N/A		
Strength	10		
Dexterity	10		
Constitution	10		
Ethera	7		
Regeneration	7		
Attunement	None		
Cultivation			
Body	Core	Mind	Soul
Unformed	Unformed	Unformed	Unformed

Unlike Carmen, Alyssa had chosen to spread the sixteen free attribute points out, allocating a few into each category. She'd brought all of her physical attributes to double digits, but Ethera and Regeneration had lagged a little behind.

The benefits were apparent, and she felt stronger, more coordinated, and far more durable than she ever had before. She'd never been in bad shape, but with the increased physical capability that came with her new attributes, Alyssa had no trouble throwing a grown man over her shoulder in a fireman's carry. She knew that because she'd been forced to do just that on more than one occasion, and even hindered by the extra weight, she could sprint at speeds appropriate for a professional athlete.

And during her frequent hunts, she'd also taken enough wounds to know precisely how much more durable she'd become. Attacks that would have once been debilitating were far less severe, and she healed from them far more quickly than ever before.

But even with her increased attributes, the most important change had come from her abilities:

Archetype: Warrior **A versatile melee archetype, proficient with most weaponry. Features bonuses to durability, Strength, and learning martial techniques.** **Required Aspect:** **[Martial]**	
Abilities	
Charge	**Dash forward at 200% your normal speed for three (3) seconds. Your next attack will do 30% more damage.**
Heavy Blow	**Increase the damage of your melee attacks by 5%. Toggled personal augmentation.**
Shockwave	**Stomp the ground, sending a wave of force to stun opponents. Incapacitates lesser enemies.**
Hardened Skin	**Increase your Constitution by one (1) point per level. Current: Nine (9). Toggled personal augmentation.**
Recover	**Focus your Ethera, tripling your Regeneration.**
Impale	**Strike an enemy, causing damage over time.**
Bulwark	**Summon a shield of Ethera to protect allies.**
Weapon Mastery	**Grants basic competence with any weapon.**
Champion's Shout	**Strike fear into your enemies' hearts, weakening their resolve.**
Enrage	**Channel Ethera into rage, increasing all physical attributes.**

All her abilities were powerful, though a few of them came with significant caveats. For instance, Recover allowed her to heal from grievous injuries in a fraction of the time that would normally be required, but it rapidly drained her Ethera, as well. The other abilities were also limited, either by Ethera, time, or an ephemeral cap on how many self-buffs she could maintain.

At present, she usually had Heavy Blows active, but she'd found a few occasions where Hardened Skin was more useful. The only one that didn't count toward her limit was Weapon Mastery, which seemed to always be active, regardless of the situation.

Alyssa was busy considering it when the others arrived. First, there was Tony—one of the town's Rangers. Thin and dark-skinned, he was level six, which made him the fourth-highest-level person in the community behind Alyssa, Carmen, and Roman.

"Hey," he said as he came into the room. Following him was Fiona, a mousy woman who'd chosen the Sorcerer archetype. Then, finally, Trish came into view. She was one of only three Healers in the settlement. Alyssa had argued against her inclusion, but Trish had insisted upon coming, citing the very probable need for a healer. Alyssa had reluctantly acknowledged that the blonde woman was right, but she'd have still preferred it if one of the other healers had been available.

They all exchanged greetings before Alyssa said, "I guess we need to get going. If we move quickly, we should be able to make it to the Robinson house before nightfall."

There wasn't much else to say, so they quickly set out, passing through the building's lobby, then crossing the parking lot and exiting through the gate. Often, Alyssa found herself marveling at how much had changed, and in only a handful of months.

Tony ranged ahead, using his abilities to stay hidden as he scouted their route. Periodically, he would return to the road to report his findings while the others moved at a much more sedate pace. Alyssa could have gone much faster, but neither Trish nor Fiona had invested heavily in their physical attributes. Even so, Alyssa knew that if they were attacked, both would prove their worth.

Gradually, they covered ground until, as the sun began to set, they reached a large log cabin. The mailbox labeled it as belonging to the Robinsons, though no one knew what had happened to the original owners. What they did know was that the house, with its sturdy walls, made for a great shelter, and it had often been used as such by foragers who needed to spend the night away from the settlement.

Though it was often referred to as a log cabin, the house was more of a mansion than anything else. The sort of place the incredibly wealthy built, and when they stayed there, they called it roughing it. So, to make it safe, Alyssa and the others had been forced to board the windows and block most of the doors.

That had been months back, and the house had proved its worth on more than one occasion. So, as the group settled in for the night, they had every reason to feel secure.

They weren't.

A little after midnight, something huge and scaly burst through the door, tearing it free of its hinges. Alyssa, who was the one who happened to be on watch at the time, sprang into action, using Champion's Shout. At the sound of Alyssa's raised voice, the creature stumbled a bit, but it was otherwise unaffected.

Shocked, Alyssa raised her spear and sprang forward, engaging the massive creature so the others would have a chance to respond.

24

THE MONSTER

Alyssa leaped toward the monster before she even took the time to properly analyze it. Using Impale, she thrust her spear forward, but to her horror, the creature's heavy scales turned the blade aside. Off-balance, she couldn't arrest her momentum quickly enough to keep herself from ramming into it shoulder first. It took the blow, skidding backward only a few scant inches.

She stomped on its talon-like foot, using Shock Wave at the same time. Disoriented, the monster lashed out with a backhanded blow that took Alyssa in the chest. She felt her ribs break before she flew backward, only slowing when she hit one of the room's couches. It flipped, and she tumbled to a stop a few feet later.

Owing to her enhanced Constitution, Alyssa barely maintained consciousness. However, pain lanced through her chest with every breath, and after only a couple of ragged gasps, she coughed up blood.

Knowing she didn't have much of a choice, she used Recover. In addition to rapidly draining her Ethera, the ability was only usable once every couple of days, so she usually kept it in reserve for emergencies. But with what felt like a punctured lung, she thought the current situation counted as just that. Instantly, she felt better, though it would still take some time for the increased Regeneration to heal the damage.

But it was enough to mend the punctured lung in short order, which was all that really mattered to get her back on her feet.

Using her spear as a lever, she pushed herself upright in time to see a Fireball hit the monster in the face. That brief bit of illumination showed her a creature that resembled nothing she'd ever seen before. With blue-green scales, plated ridges above its eyes, and a squashed visage, the thing was wholly unique. More, it was a little shorter than her, though from the muscles rippling beneath its scales, it wasn't difficult to see how it had managed to knock her across the room with a single blow.

The Fireball sent it stumbling backward, and Alyssa saw a blurry shadow materialize behind the monster. A second later, Tony appeared, stabbing his sword into the monster's back. Hissing loudly, it wheeled around much more quickly than any of them could have anticipated. Tony tried to retreat, but he was far too slow.

The monster's claw shot out, easily tearing through Tony's thin leather armor. It didn't stop there. In fact, it didn't even slow when it hit flesh, and an instant later, the claw burst through Tony's back. Blood splattered against the broken door, and the shocked Ranger desperately tried to wrench himself free.

But it was a futile effort.

The monster pulled him close. Another Fireball hit it in the back, but it paid no heed. Instead, it cocked its head to the side as it listened to Tony's increasingly desperate screams. Then, to Alyssa's horror, its tongue snaked out, running along Tony's face.

It tilted its head back and let out a hissing laugh.

Alyssa marshaled her courage and shouted, "Run! I'll hold it!"

Dashing forward on wobbly legs, she tried to bound over the couch, but she stumbled. She caught herself, but by that point, it was too late. The damage had been done. Alyssa's shout had gotten the creature's attention, and it responded by tossing Tony aside. He crumpled to the ground in a boneless heap.

Alyssa barely saw it.

Instead, she struggled to get her boar spear set. And to her eternal surprise, she managed to jam her foot down on the butt of the spear just in time. The stunned monster bounded forward, impaling itself with its own momentum. The blade bit deep before the shaft snapped.

And then it was on her.

In a panic, Alyssa used Hardened Skin, replacing Heavy Blows just before its claws reached her. She fell back, shielding her face with her forearms. The creature's claws shredded her leather armor like it wasn't even there. Then, it got to her flesh, which fared no better. Despite her enhanced Constitution, the monster's talons ripped through her with ease, sending great gouts of blood to coat the walls.

Alyssa went into shock, but she kept her wits about her enough to pull her machete from the sheath at her waist. With the monster's claws digging into her chest, she went to work. Screaming, she activated Enrage, flooding her body with her furious rage.

The ability to think rationally fled before the onslaught of emotion. The blade fell, dislodging one of the rigid scales above the monster's slitted eye. It howled in pain, trying to retract its claw, but Alyssa grabbed hold of its wrist and swung again.

And again. When she pulled the blade back, it was coated in blood. She swung again and was rewarded with a wet thunk.

At some point, her own screams joined the monster's cries. Vaguely, Alyssa recognized another Fireball splashing against the creature's back, but she couldn't be bothered to care. Her mind was swimming in a sea of fury, and the only thing keeping her conscious was the next swing.

And the next after that.

Over and over, Alyssa swung that machete. Each attack bit a little deeper until the monster's screams became whimpers.

Then, Enrage ran its course.

It only lasted a few short moments. Twenty seconds, at most. Normally, that was enough to win any battle. But this was no normal creature, and though she'd wounded the monster, she hadn't put it down.

Her shoulders sagged, and her next attack was like swinging through water. The results were predictable. Alyssa's machete hit the creature's wounded head, but robbed of any momentum, it did almost nothing. The scaled monster recognized the difference, and it reacted with alacrity, slinging Alyssa across the room, where she collided with one of the pillars holding the roof upright.

It splintered.

Someone screamed.

Another Fireball smashed into the monster, catching it off guard. It stumbled.

And Tony, who'd somehow clung to life and crawled into position, latched on to the monster's ankle and shouted, "Run!"

It came out in a croak that Alyssa, in her dazed, wounded, and drained state, barely understood. Another Fireball hit the monster, preventing it from rising. The flames splashed onto the floor, catching the rug on fire.

That was when Alyssa's struggling mind put things together. The glow she'd barely noticed wasn't from Fiona's Fireballs. Not directly. Rather, the entire cabin had caught fire, and it was on the verge of becoming a raging inferno.

Someone grabbed Alyssa by the armpits, and suddenly, she was being dragged across the floor.

Slowly.

So, so slowly.

She muttered, "Leave me . . . Save . . . Save yourself . . ."

But Trish wasn't going to do that. She couldn't move Alyssa, either. Not with enough speed. She needed a different strategy.

Fortunately, she was a Healer.

Often, Trish forgot that fact, largely because using her lone spell came with a significant cooldown. If she used Mend, she would be useless afterward. So, she had developed the habit of saving it for emergencies. However, unlike Alyssa, she was terrible at determining when there was no other choice, so she often waited too long or simply forgot to use it entirely. Some of that was mitigated by her husband's influence; so long as Roman—or someone else with a decent head for battle—was around, Trish was an extremely valuable asset.

Still, even Trish was capable of seeing that, if she was going to save Alyssa, she had little choice but to use her spell. So, that was what she did.

Vitality rushed into Alyssa, mending her broken bones, ruptured organs, and rent flesh. In less than a second, Alyssa was in perfect condition.

She shouted, "Fiona! Target the pillars!"

The Sorceress didn't hesitate to follow Alyssa's orders. Meanwhile, Alyssa found the remnants of her boar spear and threw it at the monster. The splintered shaft flew true, miraculously hitting the creature in its wounded skull. It howled, then tried to charge. However, with Tony still tangled in its legs, it quickly tipped over.

One look was all she needed to determine that the Ranger had died. He'd used the last of his energy to give them a chance, and Alyssa wasn't going to waste it. So, she grabbed Trish's arm and yelled, "Evacuate!"

Alyssa, Fiona, and Trish ran, making for the back door. Along the way, Fiona continued to use her spell to set the interior of the cabin on fire. And then, suddenly, they were free.

Stumbling in the snow, the trio went down in a heap, and a second later, the roof collapsed in a giant conflagration of burning wood.

Alyssa rolled over and pushed herself to her feet. If the monster could survive that, then they'd never had any chance to kill it. Still, she watched for a long few minutes as the building steadily succumbed to the fire.

"W-what the hell was that thing?" Fiona asked at last. Despite the battle, the small woman had escaped almost completely unscathed. But that wasn't a surprise. She had an ability that protected her from fire, and she'd never been in the thick of the fight.

Trish was a little worse off, but she'd escaped largely unharmed.

"I . . . I don't know," Alyssa said. "I've never seen anything like it."

"It felt wrong."

"Huh?" asked Alyssa, turning to Trish. The other woman had turned away, clearly struggling with what had happened. Alyssa reached out to comfort her, but Trish pulled away, retreating a couple of steps.

"You didn't feel it? Even just thinking about it makes me want to throw up," she said, gesturing toward the flames.

"I felt it," Fiona said.

Alyssa shook her head. "I don't know. I wasn't . . . I guess I just wasn't in any state to notice," she stated, watching the fire burn. As she did, she drew her backup weapon—the long dagger she kept strapped to her thigh. After all, even if the creature was dead . . .

Wait.

She hadn't felt an influx of experience. The monster hadn't died.

No sooner had that thought crossed her mind than a flaming figure burst free of the burning building. Its scales were half melted, and it screeched in obvious pain. But it wasn't dead.

Not yet.

It raced across the snow-covered ground. Alyssa reacted, trying to intercept it. Fiona shouted. And Trish froze.

The monster hit her with the force of a runaway car, ripping through her comparatively soft body with ease. If Alyssa had ever wondered about the effects of her inflated Constitution, she only needed to remember how Trish was practically torn apart. Alyssa had endured a similar attack, and though it was enough to have killed her without the Healer's intervention, she had more or less remained intact.

Trish couldn't make that claim.

In fact, she couldn't do anything as her body ragdolled across the terrain, leaving a wide smear of blood behind.

Alyssa shouted, then leaped upon the monster's back. Flames licked at her, but she didn't care. Her fury wasn't as all-encompassing as it had been under the effects of Enrage, but it wasn't far off, either. Her dagger rose, then fell. Over and over, as she dug through the monster's weakened scales.

It tried to dislodge her. It flailed, screeching and screaming.

But Alyssa wouldn't be denied.

And eventually, her blade bit into its brain. Still, it took three more blows before it finally went limp, falling to the melting snow.

Alyssa kept going until, at last, Fiona grabbed her by the arms and dragged her away. By that point, she had taken a few burns, but she wasn't concerned with that. Instead, she only cared about making the monster pay.

So, when at last it perished, all the fight went out of her.

Vaguely, she was aware of some notifications splashing across her inner eye, but she ignored them as she looked at Trish's limp body.

The woman was dead, practically ripped in two.

"Oh, God," she muttered. "Oh my God."

Fiona didn't respond because there was nothing else for either of them to say.

25

LADDER

Elijah wasn't sure what it meant. Certainly, on the most basic level, the list floating before his inner eye was easily understood. There was no mistaking that much. But the implications were far more difficult to figure out. Still, he studied it, starting with a simple message:

Five months have passed since the World Tree reached this world, giving inhabitants enough time to establish themselves. These are the future leaders of your planet:

Had it really been five months? It didn't seem like it. But then again, even before the onset of winter, the days had begun to blend together. So, the passage of so much time didn't come as too jarring of a surprise. Even so, it did give him hope that soon enough, winter would release the area from its cold grip.

When it did, he could hopefully progress past mere survival and to something more fulfilling. Perhaps he could even figure out a way to cross the strait.

In any case, Elijah moved on to the second notification, which was a list:

Planetary Power Rankings (Earth)

Oscar Ramirez—Level 26
Sadie Song—Level 25
Lisa Song—Level 24
Hu Shui—Level 24
Ram Khandu—Level 21
Anupriya Pandey—Level 19
Kimberly Jackson—Level 18
Michael King—Level 18
Gunnar Lindstrom—Level 17
Theresa Dupont—Level 16
. . .

...

...

Caleb Jameson—Level 11
Franklin Rich—Level 11

Elijah's eyes swept over the list, but unsurprisingly, he found that he didn't recognize any of the names. But if it represented the top one hundred people in the world—at least regarding levels—that wasn't unexpected. Still, Elijah was a little disappointed that his name wasn't on the list. Of course, that wasn't a surprise, either. Not really. It wasn't difficult to imagine the benefits of many people working together or using modern weapons, assuming those still worked. By contrast, Elijah was stranded on an island all alone, and he was preoccupied with mundane concerns like staying warm, finding water, or gathering enough food. It was only recently that he'd managed to branch out into woodworking, and even that was more to pass the time when the weather didn't cooperate.

So, discovering that he wasn't at the peak of humanity shouldn't have annoyed him. But it still did for some reason. And it only took him a few minutes to figure out why. First, he'd internalized the idea that he would be Nerthus's protector. Part of that was clearly rooted in the connection he felt to nature—and, subsequently, to the tree spirit—but it was also because Nerthus had helped him quite a bit, answering his questions and guiding his cultivation. So, if Elijah could repay the tree spirit by becoming its guardian, then he would.

In addition, Elijah suspected that, as the tree spirit matured—and his Grove right alongside it—he would be exposed to some benefits that might make him stronger. Or, at the very least, make the island much safer. If Elijah had encountered the Voxx, then surely the rest of humanity had, as well. And that wasn't even considering things like that giant flying creature that had downed the plane. No—it was a dangerous world out there, and having a safe home was incredibly important.

Finally, Elijah found the idea of quantifiable improvement to be somewhat habit-forming. That feeling he'd gotten as he improved his body cultivation, as he'd gained attribute points either via leveling or through rigorous exercise, or as he'd set the foundations for his soul's cultivation—it was all addictive in a way he couldn't really explain. And he wanted more. More levels. More spells. Better cultivation. And seeing that so many people had already exceeded his accomplishments was a little frustrating.

But it was also inevitable. Elijah was honest enough with himself to know that he had never been what anyone would categorize as the peak of humanity. He was smart and athletic, but he was never the smartest or most physically gifted. But could he change that?

Perhaps.

Either way, Elijah felt compelled to chase the people on that list, which somehow seemed like it might have been the point. He had no idea what the purpose of the System was, but it didn't take a genius to figure out that it wanted them to grow stronger.

Elijah studied the list for quite some time before, finally, dismissing the notification. When he did, he found that he could recall it with only a thought, much like he could with his status or his spell book.

As he gave the rankings some thought, he circled his Grove, flaring Nature's Bounty along the way. The saplings were on the cusp of reaching maturity, and Elijah found himself keenly looking forward to the completion of his Ancestral Circle. Once that was done, he would be free to explore the island a little more. As it was, he was limited to how far he could go because he had to leave enough time to get back to the cabin. But if he could teleport, that would change everything.

Once he completed two revolutions, Elijah headed back to the cabin. Once there, he made some crab-and-mushroom stew before settling down for the night. He had a blanket of rabbit furs that he'd stitched together with his natural cordage, so for the first time that day, he felt warm. As he lay there, he recalled the rankings a few times, but nothing had changed. So, he summoned his status to see his own progress:

Name	**Elijah Hart**
Level	**7**
Archetype	**Druid**
Class	**N/A**
Specialization	**N/A**
Alignment	**N/A**
Strength	**10**
Dexterity	**10**
Constitution	**11**
Ethera	**11**
Regeneration	**12**
Attunement	**Nature**
Cultivation	

Body	Core	Mind	Soul
Wood	Unformed	Unformed	Neophyte

He'd finally managed to reach his original goal of getting each of his attributes to double digits, but nothing else had changed. The fact that Constitution hadn't naturally gained any additional points seemed to support the idea that progressing past ten in any category required the investment of the free attribute points that came with leveling.

Or perhaps the consumption of natural treasures would help with that. Given that he spent a few hours of each day next to one of those natural treasures suggested that the benefits were more esoteric than a few attribute points, though. Maybe that was how people advanced their cultivation.

Or maybe those natural treasures could be turned into powerful items like his Staff of Natural Harmony.

The possibilities were endless, and without more information, Elijah had no way of knowing the truth of the matter. In fact, his ignorance had become one of his biggest weaknesses, though one without much in the way of solutions. He could only keep plugging along as he tried to survive at least until spring. Once the seasons turned, he could reevaluate his position.

So, he fell asleep, secure in the mandate to simply keep doing what he was doing. Hopefully, things could change as the temperatures rose.

The next morning, Elijah awoke to an intense blizzard that had already left the forest coated in ice and covered in a layer of deep snow. But he knew it wouldn't end soon, judging by the storm's fury. Thankfully, the cabin was well-placed, so his home was protected from the harsh winds and driving snow. Even so, it made everything more difficult. Even getting water became a chore, and not for the first time, Elijah found himself grateful for the combination of his Body cultivation and enhanced Constitution. Without it, he would no doubt have frozen, if for no other reason than because he didn't have proper clothing. The shirt he'd been wearing when he'd washed ashore had slowly been repurposed for various tasks, and his pants had been ripped and torn by the crabs. Where his shoes had gone, he had no idea, but he'd been barefoot from the very beginning.

That outfit—or lack thereof—would have been fine for a tropical island, but in the middle of a Pacific Northwest winter, it should have been a death sentence. Fortunately, his advancements had taken the bite out of the frigid temperatures, and any other issues that might've cropped up could be removed by Touch of Nature.

Still, being stranded in the middle of a blizzard wearing nothing but a pair of pants was anything but pleasant, even if it was no longer deadly.

The next couple of weeks were more of the same, with Elijah being more or less confined to the cabin. He still had to trudge through the snow to get water, and he kept up his efforts with the Grove. Otherwise, he remained secluded in the relative warmth of the cabin, covered in his makeshift rabbit-fur blanket as he maintained One With Nature and periodically pulsed Touch of Nature to stave off frostbite.

Over that time, Elijah lost any excess fat, giving his already compact frame a lean, stringy appearance. His sandy-blond curls continued to lengthen into a wild nest of hair, and his beard grew into something a lumberjack would be proud of. Meanwhile, to distract himself, Elijah explored his cultivation. First, he spent quite some time trying to familiarize himself with the new shape of his soul, which felt far more amorphous than the pathways had been. Because of that, the flow of Ethera was less constrained, which resulted in the gains he'd already seen. But beyond that, he was incapable of discovering a way to continue his advancement.

The same could be said for his Body, which was even less responsive than his Soul, leading him to the conclusion that he was missing something vitally important. But secluded as he was, without even Nerthus to guide him, Elijah had no idea how to progress. Thankfully, his Mind was a different story altogether, and after weeks of poking and prodding, he latched on to something that felt important.

In a lot of ways, it was an intuitive leap. But in others, it made so much sense that Elijah found himself wondering why it had taken him so long. Of course, the crux of the matter was that, like all the other facets of cultivation, it was incredibly uncomfortable, which meant that it wasn't something a person could just stumble upon. Instead, it required focused effort, which, once Elijah decided to pursue it, was one of the few things he had in abundant supply.

The technique—if it could even be called such a thing—was simple in that it only required him to flex his mind to such a point that the flow of ambient Ethera increased. In principle, easy. In practice, it was far from it, and on more than a few days, it resulted in a crippling headache.

But Elijah felt like he made progress all the same. He might not have been capable of reaching the levels of the people he saw on the rankings list, but he found himself driven by the hope that his cultivation might be even more valuable than a few extra levels. Besides, as uncomfortable—and often painful—as it was, it at least gave Elijah an opportunity for improvement, which, with the weather the way it was, was in short supply.

Then, one day, the weather began to change. At first, Elijah thought it was just a warm front coming through the area, but after a few more weeks of steadily warmer temperatures, he reasoned that winter had finally released the region from its grip. It still wasn't comfortable, but at least the frost melted, and the animals began to stir.

So it happened that a little over two months after the rankings had been released, spring managed to shoulder winter completely aside. And with that came the moment for which Elijah had been working for months—the completion of the Grove, heralded by a notification from the System:

Congratulations! Your Grove has reached maturity. Teleportation function of [Ancestral Circle] will be available after forging the bond with the Grove.

Elijah pumped his fist in celebration, grinning broadly as he threw the blanket aside. Thankfully, it was already morning, so he didn't have to wait before heading toward the Grove to check things out. So, he gathered his handwoven satchel and his staff before leaving the cabin behind.

The air still had a chill to it, and some of the snow remained unmelted. However, most of the ground was clear. As a result, he made good time as he traversed the forest, making his way to the Grove. To his surprise, the saplings—or trees now—looked to have grown ten feet overnight. That took him by surprise, but in a world of magic, his shock didn't last long.

The trees themselves were still dwarfed by Nerthus, though they were clearly from the same species. One day, perhaps they would attain sentience, as well. Or maybe not, considering that, regardless of how they looked, Nerthus felt different than the other trees. Either way, Elijah was more than a little excited to bond with his newly finished Grove.

Once he'd made his way to the center of the meadow, he settled down under Nerthus's broad limbs before dragging Ethera from his core and pushing it into Ancestral Grove.

Synergy found. Do you wish to bind yourself to the Grove of Nerthus?

Even though Elijah was a little wary of the Grove's name, Nerthus had been nothing but helpful. And besides, it wasn't like he had the desire or opportunity to grow another Grove. In his exploration of the island, he hadn't discovered enough free space to plant a circle of trees, and besides, he'd been working on the Grove for months, saturating it with his magic at every step of the way. Regardless of the name, it was as much his as it was Nerthus's glade.

So, Elijah consented to the binding.

A moment later, a presence erupted in his mind, sending him reeling until he collapsed to his knees.

Perhaps he should have been more careful, after all.

26

DOMAIN

It was like a bomb going off in Elijah's head. If he'd thought using One With Nature was a little overwhelming, then the deluge of sensory input that came when he'd completed the Grove nearly crushed his mind into pulp. He could feel everything, right down to the smallest insect, screaming inside his head. But more than that, he knew things he had no business knowing.

Like the existence of forty-two squirrels within a hundred yards of the Grove. Or exactly how many trees comprised the forest in that same area. Or how many leaves were on the ground. If he concentrated, he could even say precisely how many grains of dirt were within his range. And given that he could sense everything within a hundred yards of the outside edge of his Grove, that was a lot of dirt.

That sudden awareness washed over him, and for a long time, he was rendered insensate. Drool fell from the corner of his mouth as he lay there, staring up at the sky but seeing nothing.

Elijah very nearly lost himself to it.

Even as day wore into night, and the night into the next day, Elijah didn't move a muscle. Then, suddenly, he began to acclimate. The adaptation took another day, during which he gradually filtered the awareness down to a minimum. It was still there, hovering at the edge of his consciousness and threatening to overwhelm him. However, he kept it at bay via sheer concentration.

It wasn't pleasant, but he could do it.

Probably. So long as he didn't lose his grip. Which didn't seem all that likely. But he'd survived it once, and he could do it again, even if that definitely wasn't his goal.

But what if he increased his Mind's cultivation? Would that ease the burden? Or was that completely unrelated? He'd long since decided that the term didn't really refer to his mental capacity. Instead, it seemed wholly focused on his ability to draw Ethera into his Soul. But it couldn't hurt, could it?

So, sitting there, Elijah went back to his homemade Mind-cultivation technique. When he first pulled against the ambient Ethera, he nearly lost control and let the awareness blanket his consciousness once again. However, he barely managed to maintain the partition he'd created to hold it in place. Still, it made things that much more difficult because he had to split his attention into two directions.

Gradually, he funneled more and more Ethera through his mind and into his Soul. It had nowhere to go, so it slowly seeped from his pores and dissipated back into the air, but Elijah kept going. In some ways, it felt like lifting weights with his mind. Each pull was like a bench press repetition, though with the added difficulty that came with maintaining the partition, it was probably more like doing so with one hand while drawing a portrait with another.

Or something like that.

In any case, Elijah didn't have the mental capacity for metaphors. Instead, he focused his entire brain on the task at hand. And slowly, the depth of his pulls began to increase. Bit by bit, his capacity for input grew. However, as he worked, Elijah noticed an issue. The more Ethera he absorbed through his Mind, the flimsier the partition became. So, he had to spend almost as much concentration keeping it in place as he spent increasing his capacity.

It was as if, for every step forward, he took two steps back.

So, after a while, he started shifting some of the Ethera into the partition. It seemed counterintuitive, and Elijah had no real idea what he was doing. Instead, he was just going by instinct. Fortunately, it seemed like that was the last piece of the puzzle, and only an hour later, the Ethera took on a mind of its own. He barely even had to focus, and a river of Ethera flowed into his Mind.

Wider and wider, the aperture of his Mind grew until, at last, something shifted, and the flow stemmed down to a trickle, leaving placidity in its wake. It was only after a few minutes of that peace that he realized he had a new notification:

Congratulations! You have cultivated an Opal Mind!

"You did well," came the rough, yet curiously high-pitched, voice of the tree spirit, Nerthus. Elijah looked up from where he was sitting to see that the spirit had once again taken on its tiny humanoid form, but this time, it had descended from its customary tree branch to stand beside him. Only then did Elijah realize that it was resting a hand on his shoulder. Unknowable energy flowed from its touch; it felt like the natural Ethera he'd experienced when cultivating his Body of Wood, but it was far deeper and infinitely more powerful.

"What are you doing?" Elijah croaked, his throat raspy with thirst. "H-how long?"

"You have been cultivating for a week," Nerthus replied. "Before that, you were lying here in the Grove for three days."

"Ten days?" Elijah said. "I . . . How am I still alive?"

"I lent you some of my power," the spirit responded. "After all, you are the protector of my Grove. Or you will be. The bond goes both ways."

That was news to Elijah. He'd just wanted to empower his spell so he could teleport around. But now, it seemed that he'd made some kind of pact with a nature spirit of indeterminate power. That didn't seem like it was going to go so well, especially considering the disparity in Strength and Elijah's admitted ignorance.

"What does that entail?" he asked. "And I thought you said that completing the Ancestral Circle would bind us together."

"I may have stretched the truth. You must consent to the bond, lest I be expelled from your Ancestral Circle," Nerthus stated, looking down on him with its wooden eyes. Its face was capable of movement, but only just, so the effect was akin to talking to a puppet. "But it benefits you in a number of ways. I will manage the Grove, empowering it to levels far beyond what it could reach naturally. And you will guard me against all external threats."

"And this benefits me how?" Elijah asked.

Nerthus answered, "Cultivation beyond compare. You will advance faster and more easily than any of your contemporaries. In a year's time, this Grove will be home to the densest nature-attuned Ethera on this planet. And that is just the beginning. I will also prevent any intrusions from the Voxx. No towers. No portals. You will have a safe place to call home."

That certainly sounded good to Elijah, but he felt that his end of the bargain might prove more than a little difficult. After all, he wasn't very strong; indeed, he wasn't even on the power ladder, so he wasn't sure exactly how well he could protect himself, much less the Grove.

Likely seeing that Elijah wasn't convinced, Nerthus said, "I will also grow you a home. Yes—in a few months, you will have a home worthy of the dryads of Drathimar."

Elijah had no idea where Drathimar was, but in mythology, dryads were nature spirits. Perhaps they were just another race of creatures similar to the dwarves, gnomes, and goblins he'd seen across the strait.

Still, he wasn't convinced. So, he said, "I don't know. This doesn't—"

"Please," Nerthus pleaded, more emotion than it'd thus far shown evident in its voice. "If you do not agree, I will be cast back to my home world. It is terrible there. No chance of advancement at all. That is why I chose to . . ."

Its voice petered out, and Elijah expected that it was because the System didn't want Nerthus to say anything else.

"I'm not against it, okay?" he said. And it was true. The tree spirit had already helped him quite a bit, giving him as much information as it was allowed to give. And it had just kept him alive while he'd cultivated his Opal Mind. Couple that with how desperate it seemed, and Elijah really did want to help. He just wasn't sure he could protect himself, much less the tree spirit or its Grove. He said as much, adding, "What am I supposed to do if something attacks? If one of those Voxx things comes out of the ocean, I'm done for. The only reason I survived last time was because of the panther that lives here. And even that was probably only because I've been feeding it."

Nerthus cocked its head, saying, "Do not underestimate yourself. You have unlimited growth potential. You may be weak now, but in a month, you will be stronger. And a year, even more powerful. In a decade, you will have power incomprehensible to your current incarnation."

"If I survive."

"If you survive," it agreed. "However, I feel obliged to point out that you have survived this long, have you not? You have Strength of heart, conviction, and willpower; those will take you much further than anything else."

Elijah shook his head and looked around. It was a clear night, so the glade was well lit. However, he saw everything with far more acuity than he ever had before. Even in the light of day, his vision was never so sharp. Perhaps that was a result of his Mind cultivation.

"What about this . . . awareness?" Elijah asked, his thoughts barely brushing against the partitioned portion of his brain. Even that threatened to overwhelm him. "How do I deal with it?"

"Awareness?" the tree spirit asked. "Ah—it is called Locus. Or Presence, by some. It is your greatest asset, but it can be overbearing. I can guide you through learning to deal with it, though if you had asked me, I would have suggested that you partition your mind before the Grove's completion instead of after. People have died from less."

"I can believe it," Elijah muttered. Then, he asked, "Will you be able to give me more information if I agree to be your protector?"

Nerthus answered, "A little. Not much, though. The System is very strict with what information is to be made freely available to newly integrated worlds. As time goes by, those restrictions will lift, but it will be years before I could reveal everything I know without dire consequences."

Even a little more information would help because ignorance seemed to be the biggest threat to Elijah's survival. He'd managed to secure food, shelter, and water—the big three, as far as he was concerned—so basic necessities were covered. However, he would've died if it wasn't for the tree spirit's intervention, and all because he had no idea what he was doing when it came to the System and cultivation.

That alone was probably enough to make the choice for him, but it also came with other benefits. Like better cultivation and a home that would presumably improve upon his current situation.

And all it would take was for him to play security guard for a magic tree.

But wasn't that kind of in the job description for a druid, anyway?

He sighed, then said, "Okay. I'll do it."

The tree spirit managed to look relieved despite being unable to contort its face into an expression. It said, "Thank you. You will not regret this."

Then, a new notification appeared before Elijah's eyes. Instead of the unadorned boxes he normally saw, this one bore a golden border. It said:

Do you wish to become the Protector of the Grove, binding your fate to Nerthus, the ancestral tree spirit? This bond is irrevocable and unbreakable by normal means.

Elijah hesitated for only a moment before giving the notification his consent. And then . . . nothing happened.

"Uh . . ."

"Thank you!" exclaimed Nerthus. "You will not regret this! I can already see the home I will grow for you. You will be very pleased!"

Elijah couldn't help but smile at the excited tree spirit. Still, he asked, "Is that it? I expected more."

"The bond is more of a formality that lets me stay on this planet instead of being sent back home. The benefit to you is in the environment," Nerthus said, regaining some of its composure. "You should notice an increase in ambient Ethera within a day or two, and I will begin growing your home soon enough."

"I'm more interested in information at the moment," Elijah said. "This Locus sense or whatever—how do I deal with it? It's locked away for now, but you said it was important."

"Indeed, indeed. It is not meant for the mind of such a low-level druid," Nerthus said. Raising one wooden hand, it continued, "But that does not mean you cannot make it work. It merely requires practice."

"Well, considering I'm stranded on a deserted island, I've got nothing but time," Elijah said. "So, let's get to it."

27

LOCUS

Elijah let out a deep breath as he slowly opened the Ethera-bolstered partition in his mind. For the first few seconds, he only let a trickle of sensory input through while forcing the rest to remain sequestered away, but over the next couple of hours, he gradually released the rest. And to his surprise, it wasn't nearly as overwhelming as it had been before he'd cultivated his Opal Mind. At most, it was moderately distracting, though even that was manageable.

As far as Elijah could tell, the Locus gave him hyperawareness of everything within a hundred yards of his Grove. That didn't seem like much until he realized that it constituted over hundreds of thousands of square feet of dense vegetation and copious animal life. But it was more than just knowing things were there. He also felt a connection that hinted at something far deeper than mere awareness.

Nerthus had called it an undeveloped Domain, but that didn't really mean much to Elijah, save that he expected the connection to grow progressively stronger as he gained power. In addition, the tree spirit had claimed that the area would eventually grow to encompass the entire island. But not until he was far stronger and infinitely more capable of handling such a thing.

For now, though, Elijah needed to harness the awareness he did have. Eventually, over the next week, he learned to push all but the most basic information behind the partition. Certainly, if anything went wrong—or if there were intruders—he would feel it. But beyond a simple alarm, the connection was very much diluted—which allowed Elijah to function normally. Even so, that awareness in the back of his mind would definitely take some getting used to.

So it happened that he pushed himself to his feet and looked around. He'd been meditating for a few days, during which his basic needs were met by an influx of nature-attuned Ethera; that was one of the side benefits of the Grove. It didn't remove the need for sustenance—not entirely—but it did decrease his reliance on food and water. For instance, instead of being able to go without food for a week or two, he felt sure that he could abstain for at least a month, so long as he didn't leave the Grove during that time. With water, a week seemed to be his comfortable limit. After that, he suspected he would quickly become dehydrated.

Thankfully, Elijah didn't need to push those limits because, by acclimating himself to the Locus, he'd accomplished his most immediate task.

As he cast his gaze across the Grove, he couldn't help but marvel at the changes. Three new saplings grew nearby. They were only days old, but already, they had grown to a height of nearly ten feet. More than that, they didn't extend directly toward the sky; instead, they twisted in on one another, their thin branches intertwining until Elijah lost track of which one belonged to which tree. According to Nerthus, those three trees would grow into his new abode, and the spirit assured him that it would be a grand home indeed.

But it would take another month or two before it was finished. Until then, Elijah would continue to live in the decrepit old cabin.

With that in mind, Elijah trekked back to the stream, gathering mushrooms and berries along the way. Even though there was still a chill in the air, spring had begun to supplant winter, so there was a slightly larger selection than in weeks past. It was still sparse, but that would soon change along with the weather.

When he reached the stream, Elijah drank his fill and washed himself in the cold water before heading back to the cabin. The place reeked of rotten crab.

No surprise there—Elijah's forced cultivation hadn't been planned, and as a result, his stores of crabmeat had gone bad. Very, very bad, judging by the smell.

Even after he gathered the basket and dumped it into the ocean, the smell remained. And he suspected it would for some time. So, with that in mind, he made an executive decision to gather his things and prematurely move to the Grove. Fortunately, he didn't have much to gather—just the Staff of Natural Harmony, his various baskets, the rabbit-fur blanket, and a few tools. All in all, it only took one trip to transfer his belongings to the Grove.

When he arrived, Nerthus was waiting for him. The tree spirit still spent most of its time in its tree, but now that the ambient Ethera had thickened, it had a little more freedom of movement.

"Your home is not ready," it said.

"I know," Elijah replied. "But the cabin where I've been living isn't really . . . suitable for habitation anymore. So, with the weather turning, I think I'll be okay here until the house is done."

It probably wouldn't be pleasant if it started raining, but it was still better than smelling rotten crab for the next few weeks. On top of that, he was afraid that the smell would attract predators. So, it wasn't just a matter of comfort, but one of safety.

"I was wondering," Elijah said. "In my head, I've been using generic pronouns. Like *it*. But it occurs to me that I should ask if you're male, female, or agender."

Nerthus raised a hand of twisted branches, then said, "Your concept of male is the closest to reality. You may think of me in those terms."

"Good. Okay. So, I'm going to set my stuff up under your tree, okay? And just remember—this is temporary," he pointed out. "Oh, and is it okay if I build a fire? What with you being wood and all, I didn't want to offend you or anything."

"My people have been using fire for millions of years," said Nerthus. "No fire you could create on this world could burn the Ancestral Tree."

"Oh. Okay, then," Elijah said.

With that, Nerthus retreated back inside his tree, merging with it in only a second or two as Elijah set himself up beneath its expansive boughs. The tree's canopy wouldn't provide perfect protection from the elements, but it would be better than nothing. First, he deposited his meager belongings, then he set off back into the forest to gather rocks for a suitable firepit. As it turned out, the labor was quite a bit easier now that he had the benefit of a properly healthy body. He was sure that the Body of Wood contributed, as well, considering that he was far stronger than he'd ever been before. If he had to gauge it, he expected that his cultivation gave him at least a fifty percent boost to his physical capability, which put him firmly in the range of peak humanity. Probably even exceeding it, if ten really was the human limit without the interference of the System, as he suspected.

Once he finished the arduous labor involved in toting heavy rocks into the Grove, he arranged them in a circle around a pit he'd dug, then went back to his cabin where he gathered the firewood he'd already stockpiled. After that, it wasn't difficult to get the fire started—after all, he had plenty of experience by that point—and settled in for a meal of mushrooms and underripe berries.

As he ate, he also took some time to think about his future. With his fate intertwined with the island's—and Nerthus's—he knew he needed to get stronger. But the problem was that his neighbor, the panther, had already killed everything on the island higher level than the crabs. In most ways, he was grateful for his protector, but when it came to getting stronger, it was clear that the panther's presence had stunted his growth. Some familiar names on the ladder had dropped off, either dead or having hit some kind of wall in their leveling, but the ones that had remained continued to get stronger, with the leader, Oscar Ramirez, having reached level twenty-nine.

And there Elijah was, stuck at level seven.

He needed to get stronger, and the only way he was likely to reach any of his goals involved exploring the rest of the island. He still didn't even know how big it was, much less whether or not it was home to any viable threats. The panther couldn't be everywhere, after all. Surely, it had left something alive.

By the time he'd finished eating, night had already fallen. So, he resolved to begin his exploration of the island when the sun came up, which, the next morning, was exactly what happened. For the next week, Elijah charted the island, and he discovered a few things along the way.

First, it was a bit bigger than he'd first suspected. He couldn't be completely sure, but he judged it to be about six miles long, running from northwest to southeast and about half as wide. The biome remained consistent, and the area was as densely packed with vegetation as anything Elijah had ever encountered.

And thankfully, after about a mile, he started to encounter more wildlife, as well. The place was lousy with rabbits, marmots, and moles. He also saw a wide variety of birds, a few lizards that were quite a bit larger than they should have been, and a frog as big as a cocker spaniel. But none of them exuded an aura stronger than the crabs', so he left them alone.

That changed when, a few miles away from the Grove, Elijah heard a rustle in the bushes. He wheeled around, his staff in one hand and the stone-bladed hatchet he'd been using to cut a path through the vegetation in the other. It was just in time, too, because only a second later, a huge black bear burst through the underbrush. Elijah only had a brief moment to notice its unusual size and slavering jaws before he was forced to react.

The bear crashed into him, raking its claws across his shoulders. Elijah screamed in pain, swinging his hatchet instinctively. Despite his panic, his aim was true, and the hatchet found its way to the bear's snout. However, the small axe wasn't a real weapon, and under the influence of Elijah's enhanced Strength—after all, he was already operating at peak human level, and that was further augmented by One With Nature—the hatchet's stone blade shattered into pieces.

But it served the purpose of startling his attacker, and the creature reared back in pain and surprise. Elijah used that opportunity to kick out, his bare feet barely capable of pushing the bear off-balance.

By that point, he'd managed to regain some of his wits, and he used them to guide Ethera into Snaring Roots, binding the off-balance bear into place. Elijah scrambled back in a panicked crab walk made even more awkward than normal by the death grip he had on his staff.

Once he was a few feet away, he channeled more Ethera into Storm's Fury, pushing it through the Staff of Natural Harmony. When he released the spell, a thick blue bolt of lightning arced out, hitting the struggling black bear in the chest. The smell of charred flesh and burned hair filled the air as the bear let out a roar of furious agony. Elijah ignored it, dragging Ethera from his core and pushing it through his soul until the spell was charged once again. He let it loose, and another bolt of lightning hit the monstrous bear.

Then, he did it again.

And again.

Over and over until, by the tenth cast, the animal had been reduced to a twisting mass of dead flesh and charred fur.

Elijah sat there, panting in that curious exhaustion that seemed to come after every life-and-death experience. His muscles shook, and his heart was beating out of control—a feeling that he'd only experienced twice before. Once when he'd first learned that the cancer he'd been told was completely treatable was, in fact, terminal. And then once again after the death of the Voxx monster that had nearly killed him and the panther.

Slowly, Elijah got his thoughts back under control, and he studied his vanquished foe. The bear was far larger than a black bear should have been, but that didn't explain its aggressive behavior. Bear attacks weren't completely unheard-of, but this was different from a creature protecting its cubs or territory. For one, the thing was male, so the first excuse didn't seem applicable. And second, Elijah had found that, with One With Nature, most animals would simply ignore him unless he attacked them first. But this bear had instigated the encounter. That, coupled with its unrestrained aggression, suggested that something was wrong.

That suspicion was further supported when Elijah drew the stone-bladed knife that he'd secured to his waist via a makeshift belt woven from his homemade cordage and sliced into the bear's flesh. When he did, he saw that the expected red muscle was laced with black tendrils of what could only be called corruption.

It reminded Elijah of the Voxx, though he wasn't sure why he was so certain that it was related. It was just a feeling, but one he couldn't ignore.

After a little more inspection, he saw that the bear's eyes were clouded and milky white, and its saliva was flecked with fresh blood, almost as if it had been rabid. But even though his specialty had been marine life, Elijah had enough experience with land mammals to know that whatever had afflicted the bear hadn't been something as mundane as rabies. It was corruption, and given what he'd seen of the Voxx, it wasn't difficult to make the intuitive leap that they were the cause.

Still, he didn't even know if such a thing was possible. For all Elijah knew, it was just another strange mutation foisted upon the world by the touch of the World Tree. After all, if crabs could suddenly grow hundreds of times larger, then an aggressive black bear wasn't so far outside the realm of possibility that it could be completely discounted, regardless of Elijah's suspicions regarding corruption by the Voxx.

He needed confirmation, and the only way he was going to get it was to ask Nerthus. But first, he needed to heal the gashes in his chest. So, he channeled Ethera through his soul and into Touch of Nature. The wounds weren't too deep, so it only took two casts to mend his flesh. However, that ended up draining his core dry, so he had no choice but to wait a few minutes before he'd gathered enough Ethera to fuel the teleportation portion of Ancestral Circle.

When he finally cast the spell, it was as if one moment he was in the forest, and after a blink, he was back in the Grove. He'd used it before—without the ability to return to the Grove at will, his exploration would have been much slower—but Elijah didn't think he'd ever get used to the feeling.

Once he'd reoriented himself, he approached the Ancestral Tree, where he called out to Nerthus, who grew out of the trunk only a few moments later. Once he was fully present, Elijah explained the situation, then asked, "What do you think it is? I thought it felt like the Voxx, but I figured I'd ask before I jumped to any definitive conclusions."

Nerthus nodded. "Your instincts were correct," he said. "There must be a portal nearby. I knew there had to be at least one in the surrounding waters, but this is troubling."

Then, Nerthus explained how the existence of portals—dimensional rifts through which the Voxx could invade—had a corrupting influence on non-sentient life. Then, he said, "Fortunately, it seems to be a small one."

"How do you know?"

"If it was of significant size, the System would have contained it with a tower. If that were the case, we would know," Nerthus stated. "Because it is small, you should be able to take care of it."

"What? How? And why me?" Elijah asked.

"Because you are the Protector of the Grove," Nerthus answered. "It is a simple process. You must find the dimensional tear, enter it, and defeat the guardian. Once you have done so, you will gain a boon from the System."

"And . . . And you think I'm capable of that? I'm only level seven," Elijah stated.

"With your cultivation, you are much more powerful than your level," Nerthus said. "In any case, you wish to get stronger, correct? This is how you will do so."

Elijah sighed. That much was true, and the existence of these portals—or towers, if they were larger—suggested a reason for why the others on the ladder had grown so powerful. It was also gratifying to know that his cultivation meant that he was stronger than he might appear.

But in the end, Elijah knew he didn't have much choice. This was his island, and according to Nerthus's explanation, if the portal was left unchecked, its influence would grow until it enveloped the entire area. So, unless he wanted to run away—an impossibility because he didn't think crossing the strait was a good idea and because doing so would mean abandoning his Grove—he was stuck with dealing with it.

"Fine," he said. "Any advice?"

Nerthus cocked his head to the side, then said, "Try not to die. Your protection is needed if the Grove is meant to reach its potential."

Elijah shook his head, then said, "Thanks, I guess. I'll try to find it tomorrow then."

28

A PORTAL TO HELL

Elijah spent the rest of the day preparing his mind for what was coming. Nerthus couldn't tell him much about what he could expect to find on the other side of the dimensional portal, so he'd chosen the route of pessimism. Judging by his experiences with the Voxx and the corrupted bear, he thought expecting the worst was likely appropriate.

That night, he slept fitfully, and not just because he still wasn't used to sleeping under the open sky. Instead, his imagination had gone wild, conjuring one terrible setting after another until he felt like he was going to go mad. So, when morning dawned, he was more than ready to get things over with.

First, though, he had to find the portal. So, he returned to where he'd fought the bear, only to find that it had almost entirely rotted away during the night. All that was left were a few clumps of black fur and a couple of puddles of a semisolid slurry of flesh, blood, and corruption. The sight nearly made Elijah vomit, but he barely managed to keep his breakfast of berries and mushrooms from coming back up.

From there, he began his search. The island was only so big, but even with its limited size, the search proved frustrating, and it didn't bear fruit until four hours later when he felt something amiss. One With Nature was a versatile spell, giving him augmented physical ability as well as a watered-down connection with his surroundings. And it was via this sense that he found the first tendril of seeping corruption.

Pinpointing it was difficult, but the general direction was not. So, he picked his way through the forest, keeping that sickening corruption firmly in his senses. And when he stumbled across it, he once again felt the need to vomit. This time, though, he didn't manage to push through it, and he soon found himself heaving the contents of his stomach onto the forest floor.

The tendril wasn't all that noticeable—not to mundane senses. However, to the feelings that had come with his archetype, it was like bathing in raw sewage. To call it disgusting would have been underselling the repulsiveness to an extreme degree. When he looked around the meandering tendril of black rot snaking across the ground, Elijah felt like he had maggots burrowing into his skin.

But he pushed his disgust aside and followed the trail for a few dozen yards, and with each step, he felt the corruption more keenly until, at last, he found the source. It was a gaping rip in the very fabric of reality. With jagged edges of glowing purple light and a center of pitch black, it looked completely out of place amid the verdant forest.

Elijah took a deep breath that he regretted after being assailed by another wave of nausea. He wanted nothing more than to simply turn around and flee the alien thing. But he couldn't. He refused to back away. Not only because he really didn't have a choice, but also because he didn't want to be the kind of man who ran from his responsibilities.

He never had been, and he wasn't going to start now that the world had changed, either. So, after resolutely squaring his shoulders, Elijah stepped forward, his staff at the ready, and strode through the portal.

When he used the teleportation function of Ancestral Circle, it was no more uncomfortable than blinking. So, he'd expected that going through the portal would be somewhat similar. However, that expectation couldn't have been further from reality. For an instant, Elijah felt like he was being ripped into a million pieces and from every direction. Then, suddenly, the pain ceased, and he fell to the ground.

For a long moment, Elijah knelt on one knee, his breath coming in ragged gasps. Even the memory of that agony was enough to spike his heart rate. But over the next couple of seconds, even that faded away until he felt completely normal. That's when he took a moment to study his surroundings.

The ground was bare black stone, jagged and so shiny that it reminded him of obsidian. He looked up, and when he saw the alien landscape, Elijah couldn't stop himself from gasping. Huge peaks of gray rock stood against a black sky crisscrossed with rivers of deep-purple energy. By itself, that alien atmosphere was enough to tell Elijah that he was no longer on Earth. But the terrain was just as peculiar. The obsidian-like rock extended for thirty yards in every direction, but beyond that was lifeless gray stone. The only color came from what looked like purple anemones, their appendages waving in the motionless atmosphere.

But Elijah only had eyes for the hulking creature twenty feet away. In some ways, it resembled the scaled monster that had attacked him what felt like a lifetime before. However, where that creature's scales had shimmered with a green-blue luster, this new monster was black with purple markings running along its muscular shoulders.

It was also much smaller, only topping Elijah's compact frame by a few inches. But with its bulging muscles, it was much heavier than him.

It let out a hissing growl, staring at him with all four of its eyes. Had the other one possessed four eyes? Elijah couldn't remember. His fingers tightened around the Staff of Natural Harmony, and he held it before him. If everything went right, the monster wouldn't get anywhere near him. He just needed to keep his wits about him, and everything would be fine.

But as much as he wanted to believe that, it was difficult to keep it in mind when facing off against a monster out of his worst nightmares. It shifted forward, its muscles rippling beneath its scales as it dropped to all fours, like a gorilla.

Then, without any further delay, it sprang forward.

The thing exploded into motion so quickly that Elijah had no time to channel Ethera into Snaring Roots. Instead, all he could do was dive to the side, narrowly avoiding the monster's pounce. Even so, jagged rocks ripped at Elijah's bare shoulder as he rolled to safety. He managed to keep a grip on his staff, and by the time he reached his feet, he'd channeled enough Ethera into the spell.

Roots, thick and purple with three-inch thorns, erupted from the ground and snaked around the monster's legs. It yanked its limbs free, tearing the roots from the rocky land. However, the moment one root was destroyed, three more took its place. And after only a second, the monster's entire lower half was stuck in a quagmire of alien vegetation.

That was the difference his Soul cultivation and the Staff of Natural Harmony had made. Before, the roots were flimsy and easily broken, but now, he could pour enough Ethera into the spell that it was a much more formidable obstruction.

But Elijah knew it wouldn't last forever. So, he switched his focus to Storm's Fury, channeling as much Ethera as he could into the spell. In the second it took him to saturate the spell, the monster had begun to break loose. And if it managed that feat before he released the spell, Elijah knew he was doomed.

Just as it freed one leg, he loosed the spell, and purple lightning ripped forth, tearing a path from his staff to the black-scaled creature. With a crack of thunder, it punched the monster so hard that it was sent staggering backward. But even more importantly, that purple lightning raced through its body, leaving devastation in its wake.

Elijah wasn't finished, though.

Even as the monster convulsed, he charged another spell, releasing it just as the effects of the first faded. This time, the results were even more destructive, and by the time Elijah finished casting his third spell, the creature's flesh was smoking.

But Elijah refused to let up.

Seven more times, he cast Storm's Fury, never letting the monster recover or regain its feet. And when his Ethera ran dry, it was completely still.

It wasn't dead, though.

Elijah still hadn't gotten any sort of notification from the System, which meant that, for all the punishment he'd sent its way, it wasn't dead.

And that was a problem because Elijah's core was almost completely empty. He had just enough Ethera to fuel a heal but not enough to use Storm's Fury. And that meant he'd have to do things manually.

Elijah drew his stone-bladed knife before stalking forward. The jagged ground threatened to cut into his feet, but months of walking around barefoot had inured him to such discomfort. So, staff in one hand and knife in the other, he slowly approached the prone monster. The closer he drew, the worse it smelled, but he steeled himself against the disgust bubbling in his stomach.

Once he got close enough, he levered his staff under the creature's stomach and flipped it over. And for his trouble, he got a claw to the stomach.

It happened so quickly that Elijah had no chance to react. One second, the thing was completely inert, and the next, it was springing forward with flashing claws. Elijah stumbled, and the monster pounced on top of him. Luckily, Elijah had kept a grip on his weapons, and he managed to get his knife up just in time. Even more fortunately, the hardened scales on its stomach had been melted to such a degree that they offered little protection against even so pitiful a weapon as his knife. It sank deep even as Elijah blocked the creature's snapping jaws with his staff. The wood held firm, and the knife bit into the creature's vitals, ripping them apart without issue.

Elijah's arm pumped, repeatedly stabbing into the monster's stomach. It wasn't idle, though. No—it flailed and bit, ripped and clawed—but Elijah had steeled his will and cultivated his Body, which barely allowed him to survive long enough to destroy something vital. And then, suddenly, the Strength went out of the creature's powerful muscles, and it collapsed atop him.

With Strength enhanced by the System, his Body cultivation, and One With Nature, Elijah barely managed to push the creature aside. And as soon as he did, he pulsed Touch of Nature, partially healing the wounds he'd taken. He tried to cast the spell again, but his core was entirely dry.

So, as he lay there, waiting for his Ethera to recover, Elijah considered the fight. He couldn't think of anything he could have done differently, save for having better weapons or more Ethera. But even so, he'd only barely managed to survive. One less Storm's Fury, and he wouldn't have been able to punch through its scales. One misstep, and he'd have been ripped to pieces.

It was a grim reminder of just how little power he really had. Regardless of how much he'd advanced—and he felt that he'd done well with the situation he'd been given—he still had a long way to go.

But the notification he got after killing the monster was going to be a good start:

Congratulations! You have reached level eight, earning two (2) free attribute points. Would you like to allocate free attribute points?

Elijah did, adding two points to Ethera. It didn't seem like much, but if he'd had a couple of extra casts of Storm's Fury, he might not have had to kill the monster by hand. Or maybe it wouldn't have made any difference at all. He had no way of knowing. Not for the first time, he found himself wishing things were a little clearer. Perhaps if everyone had health points, like in a video game, things would've made a little more sense. As far as he could tell, though, even things like the relative value of his attributes didn't follow much logic. For instance, the points he'd spent in Ethera didn't result in a linear progression in terms of how many times he could cast his spells. The only quantifiable correlation was that more points meant more casts. Perhaps his cultivation threw things off. Or maybe it just wasn't linear. He had no way to know.

Such thoughts occupied his mind until he recovered enough Ethera to once again cast Touch of Nature, which, when channeled through his staff, was enough to push him to perfect health. After that, he rose to his feet and looked around for the exit. The portal through which he'd entered was nowhere to be seen, but in its place was a floating white crystal. When he looked upon it, he felt a draw unlike anything he'd ever felt. He needed to touch it. The need was so overwhelming that it completely abolished any sense of choice. He never even considered resisting it.

Elijah walked forward and laid his hand upon its smooth surface. Instantly, the alien landscape disappeared, replaced by a void, as if he floated between realities. It would have been maddening if it didn't feel so right.

Another notification bloomed in his mind's eye:

Congratulations! By closing a Minor Dimensional Rift, you have done a great service to your world. Thus, you have earned a reward. Lesser Attribute Potion awarded.

Elijah didn't have a chance to wonder what that meant before he was whisked away back to reality. An instant later, he was back in the forest, though when he looked around, the portal and tendrils of corruption were gone.

And in his hand was a small vial containing a glowing blue liquid. Without a doubt, it was the potion awarded by the System. Perhaps it would have been smart to wait. To investigate more. But the System had yet to lie, so he unhesitatingly popped the stopper off the vial, then upended the contents down his throat.

When he swallowed, he felt a budding warmth in the pit of his stomach, then received another notification:

You have consumed a Lesser Attribute Potion, receiving three (3) free attribute points. Would you like to allocate free attribute points?

Elijah pumped his fist. It was precisely what he'd hoped for, and he quickly allocated his points, pushing two into Ethera and bringing it up to fifteen. The final point he allocated into Regeneration, bringing it to thirteen total points.

Name	Elijah Hart		
Level	8		
Archetype	Druid		
Class	N/A		
Specialization	N/A		
Alignment	N/A		
Strength	10		
Dexterity	10		
Constitution	11		
Ethera	15		
Regeneration	13		
Attunement	Nature		
Cultivation			
Body	Core	Mind	Soul
Wood	Unformed	Opal	Neophyte

His reasoning was simple. He fully intended to spread his attribute points across each category on his status. However, for now, his spells were his most potent means of survival, so he intended to enhance the relevant attributes until he felt comfortable with where he was. Then, he'd push points into his physical attributes.

Once that was done, Elijah headed back to the Grove. He wished he could use Ancestral Circle to teleport back, but the spell had a significant cooldown that still hadn't lapsed. So, he was forced to go back on foot. Still, it wasn't an arduous journey, and soon enough, he was back in familiar territory.

29

ENVOY

I know it's not a new PlayStation, but . . . Happy birthday."

Miguel looked down at the weapon in his hands. It was a compound bow not unlike the one Roman still carried, but it had been made from scratch by Carmen. The same could be said for the wide variety of arrows in the paired quiver.

Alyssa and Carmen had gone back and forth trying to decide on an appropriate gift for Miguel's birthday. In the past, he'd usually gotten various electronics, games, or toys like Legos. But the world had changed, and not only were those things unavailable, but it was also irresponsible to devote any significant time to such frivolous pursuits.

Still, they wanted their son to have a childhood. Or whatever passed for one in the new world. So, in addition to the bow, they'd given him some homemade toys and scavenged board games. None were in perfect condition, but they were the best Alyssa could gather.

The young boy's face lit up, and he exclaimed, "I love it!"

Then, he threw himself at Carmen, wrapping his arms around her as he profusely thanked his mother. Then, he did the same for Alyssa, announcing that he was going to be a Marksman, just like Uncle Roman.

Carmen tousled his hair, then told him to go outside and practice. He'd already been taught the basics of the weapon—all the settlement's children had—and he was eager to test it out. So, he quickly scurried from the small cottage that Carmen had built, intent on following his mother's instructions.

That left the two women alone.

The moment he was gone, Alyssa's shoulders sagged. Carmen put her arm around the slenderer woman's shoulders and hugged her close as she said, "This was the right decision. Everything we've seen suggests that people get archetypes based on their past experiences. Being a Marksman will keep him off the front lines. It's a strong option."

Alyssa shook her head. "I just wish it wasn't necessary," she stated. It was a useless sentiment. As she well knew, the world had been irrevocably transformed, and there was nothing she could do about it. What she could do was prepare her son to thrive, at least as much as possible.

Leaning into Carmen, she thought about how far they'd come. It had been a difficult winter, and more than a few people hadn't made it. Some had starved. Others had passed away due to exposure. But most of the casualties had come at the hands of the wildlife. Many of the monsters they encountered were clearly mutated versions of Earth animals, but there were other, less natural creatures—like the bat monkeys they'd had to clear out of the station.

But deadliest of all were the scaled monsters like the one that had killed Trish and Tony. Fortunately, they hadn't encountered any others nearly that powerful; if they had, the settlement wouldn't have made it. But the ones they had fought were just as dangerous, especially considering that they often targeted people much less powerful than Alyssa.

And the results had been predictable. To date, they'd lost almost two dozen hunters and gatherers to the scaled monsters. But there was hope. The night that Trish had died, Alyssa had gained the ability to choose a class, and since then, ten others had done the same. It was slow going, but if everyone gained a class, there was a chance that they could stand up to the monsters.

So, even if there was hope for their continual survival, it was tempered by the reality of their losses. Still, with spring had come solutions to some of their problems. A few of the Scholars had planted some crops, and a couple of the Tradesmen had figured out how to get power from scavenged solar panels. The yield wasn't nearly what it should have been, but it was progress.

In short, after a hellish beginning to the end of the world, things had begun to look up. It was all different, but Alyssa thought they'd survived the worst of it.

Or at least she hoped so.

"How is Roman?" asked Carmen.

Alyssa sighed. "Outwardly? He's fine," she said. "He's doing everything right, and I think people recognize that."

"But?"

"He's still not over what happened to Trish."

"Who would be?" asked Carmen. It had been months, but the Healer's death still weighed heavily on the settlement's leader.

"I don't know. The problem isn't that he's still grieving. People expect that. It would humanize him. But he doesn't let it show. For all everyone knows, he just kept going like normal. Meanwhile, only those of us who really know him can see just how much he's hurting. I don't know what to do," she admitted. "I don't know how to help."

"It's not your responsibility," Carmen reminded her. "He's a grown man. If he doesn't want to address it, there's not really anything you can do."

Alyssa sighed, then pushed away from her wife's embrace. Standing, she said, "I know that. But I can't help but feel . . . I don't know . . ."

"He doesn't blame you, does he?" asked Carmen.

Alyssa shook her head. "No. I don't think so, at least. Maybe? I don't know. I blame myself, though."

"That's stupid. You couldn't have done anything differently," Carmen said without a hint of hesitation. "You did what you could. I know you don't want to hear this, but Trish was never cut out for this world. You saw that on the first day when she almost got killed. She was always going to end up—"

Just then, there was a knock at the door, cutting Carmen off. Their cottage only had three rooms—a common area and a pair of bedrooms—but each space was incredibly small. So, it only took Alyssa two steps to reach the door. When she opened it, she saw Fiona, who'd established herself in a position of some prominence after what had happened in the cabin. Since then, she'd become the highest-level mage type, and she'd distinguished herself on more than one occasion.

More importantly, she was Roman's right-hand woman.

"The chief needs you," she said. Looking past Alyssa at Carmen, she said, "Both of you."

"For what?"

Fiona shrugged. "No idea. He just said it's important" was her response, though Alyssa got the feeling that even if Fiona had known, she wouldn't have let loose with the information. She wasn't precisely hostile, but she wasn't friendly, either.

"Alright. Let's go then."

After letting Miguel know what was going on, the trio set off across the settlement. It had grown quite a bit, and the area surrounding the old police station now featured dozens of buildings and other homes. Most weren't more elaborate than four walls and a roof, but a few were a little more complex. It was further evidence that people had begun to adjust to the new world, especially considering that they'd started to move past the scarcity-induced policies of collective survival and into an economy based on barter. The various Tradesmen had begun to hawk their wares, and as a result, the availability of better weapons, armor, and other goods had taken a leap forward.

For her part, Alyssa favored the spear, largely because of the class she'd received at level ten. She'd had a host of options, but none seemed quite as powerful as the one she had chosen. As they walked, she looked at her class's description:

Class: Dragon Lancer
A powerful lancer meant to combat and kill the most dangerous foes.

Required Archetype:
Warrior

Required Achievements:
Slay a much more powerful creature with a spear or lance. Garner the loyalty of at least twenty people.

First Ability:
Descending Dragon

Attribute Allocation:
Physical

Compatibility: 97%

She'd gained a couple of levels since then, and her attributes had experienced a huge jump with each level. She had also gotten three new abilities: Descending Dragon, Heart of the Dragon, and Heroic Leap.

At first, she'd considered Descending Dragon a niche ability, but upon reaching level twelve and gaining Heroic Leap, she had been forced to reevaluate the synergy of her abilities. Heroic Leap was just what the name implied, and it allowed her to leap much higher and travel faster through the air than her attributes would normally allow. On its own, it was a useful way to close with her enemies, and it gave her far more mobility than she could have otherwise expected. However, where it really shone was when paired with Descending Dragon.

Descending Dragon	**Fall upon an enemy, dealing more damage based on distance fallen. Protected from falling damage while ability is active.**

Alyssa had no way to gauge precisely how much damage she could do with the ability, but she did know that she could obliterate normal beasts, so long as she used Descending Dragon at the apex of a Heroic Leap. If her timing was off, the resulting blow would be less powerful.

As for Heart of the Dragon, it temporarily enhanced her attributes. In a way, it was similar to Enrage, but the effect was far less potent. The other differences were more important, though. Not only did it last longer, but it didn't come with Enrage's fury, allowing her to keep her wits about her.

Before the trio reached their destination, she checked her status, as well:

Name	Alyssa Hart		
Level	12		
Archetype	Warrior		
Class	Dragon Lancer		
Specialization	N/A		
Alignment	N/A		
Strength	16		
Dexterity	12		
Constitution	12		
Ethera	7		
Regeneration	7		
Attunement	None		
Cultivation			
Body	Core	Mind	Soul
Unformed	Unformed	Unformed	Unformed

Unlike the first ten levels, after choosing her class, Alyssa's attribute allocation was automatic, and she'd gained two points in Strength as well as one each in Dexterity and Constitution per level. She worried a little about her low Regeneration and Ethera attributes, but at the moment, there wasn't much she could do about it. Perhaps she could figure it out sometime in the future, though. After all, she suspected that, at some point, she'd choose a Specialization, which would likely give her more options for improvement. There was also the question of the four aspects of Cultivation to worry about. No one had figured out what any of that meant, but she expected it would only be a matter of time before they did.

Soon, the group reached the central building that had once been the police station. It looked much the same as it always did, though construction had begun to add additional floors. With the abilities granted by the Tradesman archetype, the architects of that plan had promised that it would soon be completed. One of them had even confessed that he envisioned a future where it grew to the size of a skyscraper. Alyssa thought the man—named Toby—was a bit off in the head, but Carmen had insisted that it was theoretically possible, especially if one of the other Tradesmen reached level ten and took something like an Architect class.

For her part, Carmen had chosen the blacksmith class when she'd been offered the opportunity at level ten. She was the only member of the craftsman population to have reached such heights, but there were a few others who were snapping at the heels of her progress.

Once they entered the building, they had to pass through what had become a makeshift market slash headquarters, where people tried to organize the settlement's supplies, defense, and gathering missions. It was a mess, but the building was easily the most secure location within the settlement, and so it was the natural choice for such operations.

Soon, the trio found their way to the second level, where they passed a few old offices on their way to the one Roman had claimed. When they entered, Alyssa found her mind drifting back to what felt like ancient history. Roman looked much the same as he always did, which was to say he was lean, broad shouldered, and dark haired. But his face bore a few extra lines, no doubt due to worrying about all the people who'd entrusted him with their security.

The office, though, was almost identical to what it had been before the world had transformed. The same photos. The same old football memorabilia. The same hunting trophies. It was like stepping out of a time machine.

Beside the great wooden slab of a desk was a man Alyssa vaguely recognized, though she couldn't remember his name.

"What's up, chief?" she asked.

"Sit," he said, gesturing to the trio of chairs across from him. "We need to talk about something important."

Alyssa did as he bade, though she had to keep herself from wilting under the intensity of his gaze. She knew he didn't blame her for the death of his wife, but that didn't help much with her guilt. As a result, she found it difficult to look him in the eye.

Carmen had no such issues, and she plopped down in the chair, throwing her arm over the back in a display of comfort Alyssa wished she could emulate. Fiona took a seat, as well, looking like Carmen's exact opposite. Where Carmen's muscles had only grown larger and more defined, Fiona looked like she would blow away at the first hint of a breeze.

"Who's the stiff?" Carmen asked, gesturing to the man. "Derek or something, right?"

He adjusted his glasses and said, "Dirk, actually."

"Right. Sorry. I'm terrible with names. So, what's going on, boss?" asked Carmen.

"Right," Roman said. "Dirk here is a Scholar who just reached level ten."

"Okay? He's not the first," said Alyssa.

Indeed, there had been a couple of other Scholars who'd managed to climb to level ten. One had taken a Horticulturist class, while the other had become an Administrator. But both had other choices like Banker, Teacher, and Philosopher. It had become common practice to respect people's choices in regard to archetypes, but it was an undeniable fact that most of the townspeople looked down on Scholars because they offered little in terms of immediate survival. Some had found niches where they could be of use, but quite a few were nothing more than inferior laborers. There was even some sentiment that town should cease providing for them, and if they weren't already ingrained in the burgeoning society, the idea would have probably gotten a little more traction.

Roman had given voice to the idea on more than one occasion, though never where anyone but his inner circle—including Alyssa—could hear.

"He has a unique class choice," Roman said. Then, he told Dirk, "Go ahead. Tell them."

The bespectacled man once again adjusted his glasses, then cleared his throat before saying, "Right. So, it's called Envoy of the World Tree. The description is 'You have been chosen to represent the Cult of the World Tree. Doing so will legitimize your settlement and grant limited access to the Network.'"

"Uh . . . What the hell does that mean?" Alyssa asked.

"That's a damned good question," Roman answered. "Dirk?"

"I don't know. Not precisely. But you know how you kind of get an idea of what a class entails before you pick it?" he asked. They all had progressed past level ten, so they nodded. "Well, I get the impression that this one is . . . I don't know . . . necessary."

"How so?" asked Fiona, her first contribution.

"I have no idea. I just think it can help us survive somehow. The Network sounds like it might be some means of communication, right? So, maybe it will let us call for help."

Roman said, "That's what worries me."

Carmen asked, "Calling for help?"

Alyssa answered before Roman did, saying, "It could be dangerous. I know we haven't had much trouble with would-be warlords and the like, but we'd be stupid to assume they don't exist out there. Someone gets a little power, and then . . . Well, you know how it goes. It's been the same throughout human history. There are always people out there who will abuse power to enslave or oppress everyone else. And with everything else . . . I mean, does anyone here think there aren't bad actors out there? If we start calling for help, we might put a target on our backs."

"Exactly," Roman said. "Still, we can't ignore this. For all we know, we're completely wrong about how this works."

"I think we have to do it," said Carmen.

Fiona agreed. "We can't ignore a chance like this. We're already on the verge of ruin. Maybe this Network will give us a chance to do more than just survive."

Roman nodded. "I was thinking the same thing. So, Dirk, we're going to need you to take the class. But don't do anything else, okay? Not until we know what we're dealing with."

Dirk nodded. "Alright, here it goes."

30

THE NETWORK

Nothing happened—at least not outwardly, but Dirk's eyes briefly glazed over. It only lasted a second or two before he refocused. "It's done," he said.

"Well, that was anticlimactic," said Carmen, who, like everyone else, was on the edge of her seat after Dirk took the class. "That's it? What kind of ability did you get?"

"Not an ability," he said. "A spell."

"Yeah? What's it called?" she asked.

"Um . . . It's called Branch of the World Tree," Dirk answered. "It says that it imbues a crystal with a connection to the World Tree Network."

"A crystal? What kind of crystal?" asked Roman.

"You think I know?" Dirk responded. "I'm just as much in the dark as you are."

Alyssa said, "Okay. So, it seems we need to find a crystal. Any ideas where to find one?"

"How big?" asked Carmen.

Everyone looked at Dirk, who clearly did not like the attention. He said, "I have no idea. As large as we can find, I suppose."

"I think I've got something that will work," Carmen said.

"Really? What?" asked Alyssa.

"You remember that trophy we found last month?" she answered. "You know, the one with the giant golf ball?"

"You kept that?"

She shrugged. "It's sparkly."

Alyssa was about to respond, but then thought better of it. Instead, she just rolled her eyes. Carmen had always been something of a pack rat. Rarely did she encounter anything she wanted to toss out, and that clearly extended to the gaudy golf trophy they had found in one of the small town's more affluent houses.

"Plus, I thought I could reshape it," she said in a small voice. "Maybe into a dolphin."

"A . . . A dolphin?"

"You do have a birthday coming up," Carmen said, blushing. "And you like dolphins . . ."

Before Alyssa could respond to her wife's admission, Fiona cleared her throat and said, "As heartwarming as this is, can we get on with it? Where is this crystal? And if you can reshape it, why not do it in something that's . . . you know, not a golf ball?"

"I could just do a generic crystal," Carmen stated. She glanced at Dirk, as she continued. "Like a faceted gem." She held her hands about eight inches apart, adding, "About that big. Think that'd work?"

"I guess? Maybe. I don't know."

"You are tons of help," Carmen said. "Anyone ever tell you that? Helpful Dirk. That's what I'm going to start calling—"

"Enough, Carmen," said Roman. "He's doing everything he can."

Carmen started to respond—probably in a not-so-courteous way—so Alyssa grabbed her by the arm and tugged her away as she said, "Come on. Let's go get that crystal. Where do you want us to meet you?"

"In the lobby," Roman said.

"Ten-four, chief," Alyssa acknowledged, pulling Carmen out the door.

A few minutes later, the pair were in the small storehouse beside Carmen's forge, where she was muttering under her breath while searching through her materials. Eventually, she found the trophy—a gaudy thing that Alyssa couldn't believe anyone had ever commissioned—behind a bundle of iron rods.

Carmen easily pulled the dimpled sphere free of the base of the trophy, then tossed the faux marble aside. "Alright," she said. "You might want to look away."

Alyssa was well accustomed to Carmen's process. She had an ability she could use once a week that allowed her to reshape materials only using her hands. Aside from the significant cooldown, the other major downside was that it created a light bright enough to blind most normal people. To protect herself, Carmen pulled on a pair of old welding goggles, then used the ability.

Even with her back turned, Alyssa saw stars, and that was just from the indirect light. She couldn't imagine looking at it directly.

After a couple of minutes, Carmen announced, "Alright. I think that's the best I can do. Sucks I had to waste my cooldown on something like this, but whatever. For the greater good, right?"

"For the greater good," Alyssa echoed, grinning slightly as she turned to face her wife. In Carmen's hands was an oblong gem, faceted like a cut diamond. "Oh . . . Pretty."

"Would've been better as a dolphin."

"You know I don't even like dolphins, right?"

"Sure you do. You had all those figurines."

"Because they were my mom's . . ."

"Wait . . . Really?"

"Really."

"You mean I bought you that ridiculous dolphin blanket for nothing? And those matching slippers . . ."

"They were . . . uh . . . cute. I guess. And warm, which was the main purpose."

"God . . ."

"Don't worry about it. It's the thought that counts."

"That's what people say when they get shitty gifts," Carmen pointed out.

"Well . . . Yeah, but . . . I mean . . ."

"And moving right along . . ."

"Probably for the best," Alyssa acknowledged. "Come on. Roman's waiting on us."

"He can wait for all I care," groused Carmen. She'd never liked being at anyone's beck and call, which was why she had sought a field where she didn't really have to answer to anyone. Notably, she followed Alyssa, anyway. After all, like her wife, Carmen suspected that Dirk's spell would probably be important for the settlement's development.

It only took a couple of minutes for the pair to get back to the lobby, where they found the other three. Roman directed Carmen to set the crystal atop a stool someone had hunted down. When she did just that, they all stepped back, and Roman said to Dirk, "Alright. Do your thing."

Dirk stepped forward and held out his hand. As he did, he said, "I really hate that you're all staring at me . . ."

"Just do it," said Fiona.

He sighed, scrunched up his face, and laid his hand on the crystal. A second later, Alyssa felt something in the air move before the crystal lit up with blue light. Then, it started to morph, tendrils of the crystal growing downward to wrap around the stool. At the same time, the rest of the structure elongated before growing more tendrils.

"It looks like a tree . . ."

Alyssa glanced at Carmen, then back at the glowing crystal. The moment Carmen had said as much, Alyssa saw it, as well. And with every passing second, it grew clearer until, at last, the blue light faded. When it did, a crystalline tree was revealed. It was maybe six feet tall, with leafless branches stretching the same distance from the trunk.

"Uh . . . What now?" asked Carmen.

"I don't—"

Suddenly, someone new appeared before them. And everyone reacted with predictable aggression.

Carmen pulled a hammer from thin air, and Alyssa yanked a dagger from the sheath at her waist. Meanwhile, Roman, who'd taken the Assassin class, disappeared completely. When he reappeared a moment later, he had a pair of knives in hand.

Dirk was the only one who didn't move at all.

"Oh, isn't this embarrassing?" said the woman as a throwing knife passed right through her. "I suppose you didn't expect me to show up, huh?"

"What are you?" demanded Roman.

It was a valid question, considering that the woman was clearly inhuman, with light-green skin, pointed ears, and hair that looked more like vines than any tresses that Alyssa had ever seen. She wore a thin robe that left very little to the imagination.

"Oh. I guess you don't have wood elves here," she said. "No matter." She cleared her throat, then straightened her back. "I am Numa, and I am a representative of the Cult of the World Tree. You would know all about that, I'm sure."

"Uh . . . No," said Dirk.

"What? Really? Why did you take the class then?" Numa asked.

"They made me."

"We didn't make you!" Carmen barked. "We suggested."

"Ah. This . . . is a nice place you have here," said Numa, looking around. "Very chic."

"Oh, I'm sorry that it's not up to your standards," Carmen stated. "We've been a little too busy dealing with the fucking apocalypse to worry about making everything all nice and shiny."

"Apocalypse? Oh! This is a newly integrated world! That explains so much," she said. "In that case . . . Ahem. Welcome! Your world has been connected to the rest of the universe via the majesty of the World Tree. As an official settlement, you now have access to a host of features based on the level of your Envoy."

"He's level ten," said Alyssa. "What does that get us?"

"Ah, right. Not much, I'm afraid. You get access to the banking System, limited trade, and . . . Well, that's it. But if he reaches level fifty, you will unlock the teleportation System!" she said. "So, that's something to look forward to, right? We also have guides on a variety of subjects, classes, and of course, cultivation methods. For a price, obviously."

Alyssa addressed the obvious concern, saying, "I'm guessing you don't take dollars. What currency are we using here? Precious metals? Gems? We don't have much, but—"

"Etherium, of course."

"Uh . . . What the hell is etherium?"

"Solidified Ethera in the shape of coins," she said, holding up a small circular object the size of a half-dollar. "Copper is the lowest denomination, and it's denoted by a . . . well, copper color. Then silver. Gold after that. And finally, platinum. It takes a thousand copper to add up to a silver, a thousand silver to amount to the same value as one gold etherium, then a million gold coins to equal a single platinum. Most people only deal in copper and silver coins."

"And where do we get these coins? I don't suppose there's a class with a Mint ability, right?" said Fiona.

"Certainly not," said Numa with an indulgent smile. Alyssa didn't like how condescending the wood elf was, but then again, she probably had every right to be. As far as Numa was concerned, they were backward savages. It didn't matter that they'd had their world turned upside down; their lives were primitive by anyone's measure. "The answer to your question is the Branch of the World Tree. You merely need to touch it, and you will gain access to the banking System."

"We don't have anything to deposit," said Carmen.

"Oh, but you don't understand. Of course you don't," she said with a patient tone that reminded Alyssa of the way a kindergarten teacher would talk to a class full of five-year-olds. "That's okay. Each time you kill a hostile creature, it marks you. When you access the Branch of the World Tree, it reads those . . . ah . . . marks and rewards you appropriately. For instance, if you kill a reasonably weak creature, you might be credited with a single copper etherium. The more powerful the enemy, the higher the reward. And, of course, defeating one of the Voxx is even more valuable."

"Voxx?"

"Oh, dear. You don't know about the Voxx."

"Obviously," Carmen muttered.

"The Voxx are denizens of another reality," Numa said. "They infiltrate our universe via dimensional rifts. Some of those rifts are only active for long enough to admit a single Voxx. However, others remain in place until someone goes in and closes them. Then there are the towers, which can be divided into different grades of difficulty. Finally, there are primal realms, though I doubt you need to worry about those right now."

Alyssa nodded along as Numa explained it, and once the elf was finished, she asked, "So, we use those coins to buy the stuff you were talking about. What form does it take? And how does it arrive?"

"I don't understand," Numa said. Then, her already huge eyes widened, and she said, "Oh. I get it now. The information will be presented in the form of leaves, which will grow from this tree. Pluck them and you will be able to read their contents."

Alyssa realized then that she would get far more information by testing it out rather than relying on Numa's explanations. So, she stepped forward and asked, "I just put my hand on it?"

"Yes. Go ahead," the elven woman prompted with another condescending smile.

Alyssa suppressed the urge to roll her eyes, then put her hand on one of the crystalline branches. Immediately a new window flashed before her eyes:

Copper	Silver	Gold	Platinum
732	7	0	0

“Okay,” said Alyssa. “I guess I have a little over seven silver etherium. What can I get for that?”

“Seven? How . . .”

“You’re the expert,” she said. “So—what can I get?”

“For now? You’re limited to our basic guides. However, those should be quite sufficient for your current level of advancement,” Numa informed her.

“Okay? How do I access them?”

After that, Numa walked her through the process. It boiled down to simply thinking the word *market*, which pulled up the available guides. The wood elf also taught her how to access the other features of the Branch, but all of those were grayed out. Most she couldn’t even identify because they were hidden.

Still, she selected a dozen different guides, exhausting the limits of her currency. A few of them were for Carmen, and they detailed different crafting methods. However, the ones that really excited Alyssa were the ones meant to teach her about cultivation.

“I think this is going to change everything,” Alyssa said, pulling away.

The elf gave her an indulgent smile, saying, “Of course. That’s the point.”

31

INVADERS

Elijah heaved a rock above his head, pushing as high as he could. As soon as his elbows locked, he dropped it back to the ground. Once it settled into the soft, spongy forest floor, he bent down, his hands on his knees as he tried to catch his breath. If he'd had to guess, the rock weighed somewhere around a hundred and fifty pounds. Maybe two hundred, depending on the density.

Lifting that kind of weight might not have seemed all that impressive, but given his relatively small size, he was satisfied with the results of his training. Once he'd passed into double digits with his Strength and Constitution attributes, he'd been forced to expand upon his normal workout routine. Before, he'd relied on something he referred to as wilderness CrossFit, which included lots of calisthenics and endurance training, but now, if he wanted to push his limits, he needed to lift increasingly heavy things. And considering there were no weight sets or exercise machines lying around, he was forced to use the abundant rocks he found on the shore of his island.

Even so, over the past three weeks since he'd closed the minor dimensional rift, he'd made no verifiable progress in his attributes. And he was beginning to think that he never would—not without using his free points in the endeavor, at least.

Still, even though he didn't expect to see anything, he opened his status.

Name	Elijah Hart
Level	8
Archetype	Druid
Class	N/A
Specialization	N/A
Alignment	N/A
Strength	11
Dexterity	10

Constitution	11		
Ethera	15		
Regeneration	13		
Attunement	Nature		
Cultivation			
Body	Core	Mind	Soul
Wood	Unformed	Opal	Neophyte

The moment he saw that he'd gained a point in Strength, Elijah pumped his fist in the air and let out an inarticulate yell of satisfaction. It wasn't much, and he didn't think one point of Strength would even be noticeable. However, the fact that he could still train his attributes meant that he had another path he could follow. So, when he headed back to the Grove, he was in understandably high spirits that were buoyed even further when he saw that Nerthus was awake.

"Awake, huh?" Elijah said as he approached the Ancestral Tree.

"I do not sleep. I must go dormant while I process the ambient Ethera I absorb."

"Sounds like sleep to me," Elijah responded. "But call it what you want."

"Pardon, but you seem to be in high spirits. May I ask why?" asked the tree spirit, who was sitting on the tree's lowest branch, swinging his rootlike legs back and forth.

Elijah shrugged, then answered, "I just found out that I can continue to gain attribute points with training."

"Of course you can."

"You knew?"

"I did. Do not rely on it, though," Nerthus advised. "The higher you climb, the more effort it will take to gain even one attribute point."

Elijah sat on the mossy ground and leaned back on his hands. As he did so, he embraced the Ethera in his core, channeled it through his soul, and empowered Touch of Nature. The healing power of the spell washed through him, soothing the fatigue of his workout. So long as he only wanted to suffuse his body with formless healing, the spell was almost autonomous, and it didn't require much thought after activation. However, if he needed to heal a specific injury, he'd need to focus.

"How do they work, anyway? The attribute points. I mean, what is the relative value of one point?" he asked. He'd already surmised that ten points seemed to be the natural peak of human ability; however, gaining his eleventh point in Strength didn't seem to push him into superhuman levels.

Nerthus answered, "At ten, you are indeed at the peak of your race's normal potential. That is not to say that some members of your race haven't already exceeded that potential; they undoubtedly have. It is just exceedingly rare. In any case, your gains will continue at the same rate with each additional attribute point. However, you must understand that it is all relative."

That made some sense to Elijah. When he had first washed ashore, gaining a single point in Strength was an enormous boon. But even if each subsequent point meant the same gains, the increase wasn't as dramatic.

"I get it," he said. "When you can only lift forty pounds, suddenly being able to lift twenty more seems a lot bigger than if you started at two hundred. The gains are the same, but relatively speaking, one represents a fifty percent increase while the other is only like ten percent."

"Just so."

So, Elijah reasoned he wouldn't be throwing cars like a comic book superhero anytime soon. Disappointing, but it was also somewhat comforting. After all, he hadn't forgotten those people at the top of the leaderboard. If the gains were percentage based, he'd have no chance of standing up to any of them. But if each point defined a specific value, he wasn't quite as far behind as he'd thought.

Still, some of the people on the ladder were closing in on level thirty, which meant that they probably had more than forty more attribute points to work with. If someone went all in on one attribute, the results could be dramatic.

He said as much to Nerthus, ending with, "If I run into someone who spent all their points in Strength, I won't stand a chance."

"You will be less disadvantaged than you believe," Nerthus stated. "Without Constitution, they will quickly run out of energy. Without Dexterity, they will have no control. And without Ethera or Regeneration, their spells, techniques, and abilities will be limited in scope."

"You're saying a well-rounded approach is better than specialization."

"For you, yes. If you had allies, that would not be the case. Once you choose your class and specialization, your attribute allocation will become more specialized."

Elijah wanted to ask for further explanation, but he knew it would do no good. The tree spirit's restrictions had eased somewhat since Elijah had bonded with the Grove, but Nerthus was still limited as to what he could reveal.

Frustratingly, classes and specializations fell under the umbrella of taboo topics, and no matter how often Elijah asked, Nerthus steadfastly refused to reveal any details.

Soon enough, Nerthus retreated back into the Ancestral Tree, citing a need to rest, which was just as well because Elijah had plenty of tasks he still needed to accomplish. So, after Touch of Nature had renewed his body, he spent a couple of hours working on his garden. The berry bushes had already borne fruit, proving the value of Nature's Bounty. So, he'd doubled down, and over the past week, he'd expanded the garden. Hopefully, his efforts would be rewarded.

As he sat between the bushes, he glanced toward the three trees that would eventually become his home. Already, they'd twisted together so thoroughly that he had trouble telling where one ended and the others began. More, the branches had begun to grow outward in what Nerthus assured him would become the floor of his new home. He couldn't wait for it to be finished. Since spring had come, sleeping outside wasn't as torturous as it would've been in winter, but Elijah still found himself missing a roof over his head. Especially when it rained, which was a fairly frequent occurrence.

After he was satisfied that his garden was well saturated with his Ethera, Elijah gathered his fishing equipment and woven baskets and headed toward his fishing hole. With the onset of spring, the fish had come back to shallower waters, and he intended to supplement his diet accordingly.

But as he drew closer to the shore, his calm day was interrupted by the sound of agonized screaming.

Elijah reacted on instinct, sprinting through the forest until he came to the rocky shoreline where he saw a battle playing out. On one side were a trio of short figures—what looked like a gnome, a dwarf, and a green-skinned goblin. And on the other was the panther.

The gnome darted toward the panther, a pair of daggers in hand. She moved so quickly that Elijah could scarcely track her movements. To him, she looked like a blur as she crashed into the panther, where she repeatedly stabbed the big cat in the ribs. Before it could react, she dashed away.

A second later, the dwarf rammed his shield into the panther's face, sending it staggering backward. But the panther was only stunned for a brief moment before it pounced on the dwarf. The dwarf raised its shield and shouted something unintelligible, and a second later, a translucent half dome manifested before him. The panther crashed into it, and with the sound of breaking glass, the half dome shattered into a million pieces. Each piece homed in on the panther, cutting into its glossy black hide and sending gouts of blood splattering across the rocky shore.

But the cat paid its injuries no mind, and only an instant later, it raked its claws across the dwarf's face. Meanwhile, the gnome had returned to stab the distracted cat a dozen times in the space of a single second before springing backward in an acrobatic flip. The retreat was just in time to avoid the panther's reprisal, and when it tried to attack the gnome, its claws found nothing but air.

The moment it turned, the wounded dwarf slammed his shield into the panther's side, sending it skidding across the rocks. Meanwhile, the third member of the party raised a shining staff into the sky, and a beam of light descended upon the dwarf. Elijah gaped as he saw the dwarf's wounds heal in seconds.

The cat recovered from the dwarf's shield slam and, demonstrating an intelligence no animal should have, pounced on the healer. However, when the panther drew close to the goblin, it found that the dwarf had somehow interposed himself between the two. It was as if he'd simply teleported between them, and as a result, the cat once again took a shield to its face.

Like that, the battle continued, and Elijah watched as, slowly but surely, the trio wore the powerful panther down. After a few minutes, its glossy hide was wet with blood, and its agility had been almost completely negated by multiple injuries. Still, it fought on.

The problem was the dwarf. Every time the cat targeted one of the seemingly less durable members of the group, he was there to shield them from the panther's attacks. That was why, when Elijah chose to act, he aimed in his direction.

The panther once again pounced toward the healer, and Elijah watched as the dwarf readied himself to intervene. Just before he took that first step, Elijah cast Snaring Roots. A half dozen thick, spiny vines erupted from the ground, wrapping around his stubby legs. It only took him a moment to pull free, but Elijah's spell caused just enough delay that the cat finally reached the healer.

The results were explosively bloody.

The panther ripped through the goblin, sending a geyser of red blood splattering across the rocky shore. The goblin tried to cast a spell, but he was far too slow to complete the cast. He fell only a few moments later, well before the dwarf could extricate himself from Elijah's roots.

That's when Elijah felt something rip through his hip, the impact sending him spinning away and to the ground. As he skidded to a stop, he saw the gnome standing over him, a murderous gleam in her abnormally huge eyes. She stalked forward, absently twirling a wicked set of daggers as she spat, "You'll pay for that, human."

Elijah tried to clamor to his feet, but she dashed forward, peppering him with wounds as she stabbed him a half dozen times in the space of an instant. He cried out, blindly swinging his staff and, through blind luck, managed to connect. The gnome, who was barely the size of a preadolescent child, went staggering to the side. She quickly recovered, but by that point, Elijah had already empowered another cast of Snaring Roots.

Vines once again burst forth from the rocky ground, snaking around her legs and giving Elijah enough time to channel Ethera through his Staff of Natural Harmony as he cast Storm's Fury. Lightning burst forth from the end of the weapon and crashed into her. The momentum of the spell sent her flying through the air to collide with the warrior who was still engaged in his own fight against the panther.

The pair fell in a tangled heap, which gave the panther the opening it needed to swipe its claws across the gnome's throat. That attack opened the panther up to a counter from the dwarf, who bellowed something unintelligible before slamming his axe down on the panther's shoulder. It bit deep, and the panther let out an anguished whimper as it was driven to the ground.

Elijah aimed another cast of Storm's Fury at the dwarf, who took it far better than the gnome had. Instead of being thrown from his feet, he remained anchored to the ground. Then, still smoking from the bolt of lightning, he turned his attention toward Elijah.

Armed with a shield and axe, he strode forward.

Holding his staff before him, Elijah backed away. He still had enough Ethera to cast Storm's Fury a couple more times, but after that, he'd be done.

"Who are ye?" demanded the dwarf, his accent rendering his words barely intelligible.

"Uh . . ."

"Ne'er mind," the dwarf growled. "Don't matter none. Y' ain't gonna be 'round long 'nough fer it te matter."

Elijah summoned his Ethera and cast Storm's Fury, sending a bolt of lightning to crash into the dwarf. The dwarf took it on the shield, which was suddenly encased in a blue nimbus of energy. The dwarf was unhurt by the spell, so Elijah cast again. And again after that. Two more times, he cast Storm's Fury until the last of his Ethera petered out. But the additional casts were no more effective than the first, and the dwarf was almost entirely unharmed.

The warrior started to say something, but at that moment, the wounded panther pounced on his back, raking its claws across his shoulders and clamping its powerful jaws around the dwarf's head. He tried to fight back, but the panther was too strong. A few seconds later, the sound of cracking bone filled the air as the panther crushed the dwarf's skull.

Then, even as the dwarf fell free, the panther collapsed to the ground. Its breath came in ragged gasps as Elijah raced forward. When he reached the fallen cat, he tried to summon enough Ethera to power a cast of Touch of Nature, but his core was almost empty. So, without the ability to call upon magic, he clamped his hands around the panther's worst wounds as he tried to stem the flow of blood. But it was no use.

That's when the creature locked its eyes on his.

Suddenly, Elijah felt a push against his still active One With Nature. At first, it was like a feather brushing against his awareness, but over the next few seconds, the intensity of the contact increased until it felt like someone was swinging a hammer against his skull. Finally, it broke through, and he felt an alien presence invade his mind.

And suddenly, he knew what he had to do.

The panther knew it was dying, and it had used the last of its own Ethera to make its last wishes known.

"I . . . I can't," Elijah muttered, recoiling from the panther's last request. "I can't kill you . . ."

But that was what it wanted. It pushed harder, insisting. There were no words, just vague impressions. But still, the panther's wishes were clear. It wanted to die at Elijah's hands.

Elijah was no stranger to mercy killing. He'd spent much of his youth hunting with his father, and he had also seen plenty of animals euthanized during his time working at the zoo while in college. So, when he drew the flint-bladed knife from his belt, he did so with practiced surety.

The panther raised its chin, giving him free access to its throat. And Elijah stabbed out, raking the knife across its neck and severing its jugular vein. Blood gushed out, coating his hand.

The panther stared at him for a long moment before a wave of gratitude rushed through Elijah's thoughts. And then, it closed its eyes and went limp.

When it died, a series of notifications flew across Elijah's awareness. He ignored them.

Instead, he simply sat there on his knees, staring at the animal that had, for so long, protected him.

32

THE COST OF IMPROVEMENT

As Elijah knelt on the beach, he stared at the slain panther. But he didn't really see it. Instead, all he saw was what he'd just done. Strangely, he didn't feel the least bit guilty about the people he'd helped kill. They were invaders and defilers, and if he wanted to protect his island and the Grove, killing them was necessary. However, he couldn't help but keenly feel the loss of the panther who had, on more than one occasion, saved his life.

Was it silly to mourn the loss of a wild animal that, at any point, might have killed him? Maybe. But in those last moments, he had seen the creature's mind. He'd felt its soul. And in doing so, he'd forged a brief connection. Perhaps he was simply anthropomorphizing an animal, but as he looked at the panther, he felt a kinship that, in the end, had been reciprocated.

Until that moment, he hadn't realized just how much he'd leaned on the big cat's presence. Sure, it wasn't precisely a companion, but it had been with him since the very beginning. They had protected one another. And now, it was dead.

It took Elijah a long time to get past the poignant stabs of grief racing through his mind, but eventually, he forced himself to stand. As he did so, he felt a bolt of agony carve itself through his torso, and he realized that he'd been ignoring a serious wound in his side. Thankfully, his ill-advised moment of grief had given his Ethera the chance to regenerate, so he was free to use Touch of Nature to heal the injury—at least enough to ensure his survival. He did so, and the wound stopped bleeding. It would take a few more casts to completely heal himself, but he didn't have the Ethera to power such an effort.

Clutching his staff, he turned his attention to the three bodies. They had all been mauled beyond recognition, so Elijah didn't see much point in truly examining them. However, he wasn't above looting their corpses. For months, he'd been making do with homemade tools, so he was more than willing to plunder whatever valuables they had on them.

Of course, making that decision and actually following through with it were two very different things. While he might've been fine with killing the intruders, the process of rifling through the pockets of a bunch of corpses was a grim one, and by the time he'd finished, he'd emptied the contents of his stomach more than once. But the rewards, he thought, were worth that discomfort.

Glancing at the panther's corpse, he amended that thought. He'd have given everything if the panther could have survived just a little longer.

But that wasn't how things had turned out.

Not before whatever had transformed the world, and certainly not after. If he could soldier on through the deaths of his parents, he'd get through the loss of the panther.

To distract himself, he took stock of his looted treasures, which consisted of a couple of leather pouches, the dwarf's axe, two high-quality steel daggers, and the warrior's shield. None of the goblin healer's possessions had survived the panther's mauling intact, though Elijah took the time to remove his robes. He did the same with the other two invaders' clothing, which gave him plenty of material.

It was all too small to fit him, so he had no idea what he intended to do with it, but surviving in the wilderness was about resourcefulness. And he wasn't going to turn down a ready source of good cloth. The same could be said for the rest of their attire, and he picked up a couple of leather belts, as well.

In the end, it was a treasure trove, but one that had cost far more than it was worth.

Sighing, Elijah set about the task of getting rid of the bodies. The panther he took the time to bury, marking the grave with a small cairn made from the large rocks he found on the beach. It took a while, considering he had no tools, but he managed it all the same. Once he was finished, he just stared at the grave with a forlorn sense of sadness that he wasn't sure he'd get over anytime soon.

Disposing of the invaders' corpses was much easier, and after he'd toted the small corpses to what he'd begun to call Crab Beach, he simply threw them to the opportunistic scavengers. From experience, he knew the huge crabs would eat their way through the bodies in a matter of hours.

It was not a respectful end, but then again, Elijah didn't much respect them. Part of that was because of what he'd seen across the strait; the settlement had continued to grow, and the coalition of goblins, dwarves, and gnomes had likewise continued to despoil their environment. However, if he was honest with himself, most of Elijah's ire came from the fact that they had killed the panther.

Did it matter that the cat had probably attacked them first? No. Not really. After all, he'd coexisted with the panther for months, and it had never tried to kill him. Following from that was the perception that there must've been a reason for the battle that had ensued.

Whatever the case, the damage was done, and he needed to adjust accordingly. So, he spent the next hour searching for the means by which they'd reached his island. And soon enough, he found a small rowboat, which he pulled onto shore and stashed near the tree line where it wouldn't wash away with the tide.

After that, he returned to the Grove, where he settled down to go over the battle's other gains.

Congratulations! You have reached level nine, earning two (2) free attribute points. Would you like to allocate free attribute points?

That notification was quickly followed by another:

Congratulations! You have reached level ten, earning two (2) free attribute points [four (4) total]. Would you like to allocate free attribute points?

And unexpectedly, a third:

Congratulations! Upon reaching level ten, you are eligible to choose a class. Keep in mind that this decision will define your future. Choose wisely.

Then, there was a final notification:

Error. You may not accumulate kill energy until you have chosen a class. Please choose a class to progress further.

"Godamn it!" he growled, slapping his hand against the mossy turf around the Ancestral Tree. How much kill energy had he lost? Now more than ever, he needed to progress quickly and efficiently, and through no fault of his own, he'd wasted at least a level or two worth of energy.

Elijah's frustration finally spilled over, and he let out a wordless scream of pure anger. After spending months fighting tooth and nail just to survive the winter, he'd lost his protector. More than that, he'd set himself firmly at odds with the only people around. He was fine with that choice, but it was just one more issue to add to all the pressure on his shoulders. How was he supposed to survive if he didn't know any of the rules?

But it really wouldn't have mattered, would it? Even if he'd known that reaching level ten would require him to choose a class, he couldn't have changed anything. Still, it was frustrating, knowing what could have been. Then again, the kill energy he could've earned from the day's actions certainly wouldn't have let him catch up to the people on the ladder.

Those weren't his enemies, though. Aside from a salve for his competitive spirit, catching up to the people on the ladder wouldn't really affect him. But the trio he'd helped kill—they were a different story. Not only had they been well organized, but at an individual level, they'd all outpaced him in terms of power. He had no notion of what levels they were, but he knew beyond a shadow of a doubt that they were well beyond him.

So, he needed to get stronger, and fast. The first step on that journey was to choose a class. So, he moved on to the next notification:

Please choose a class from the listed options. Be aware that you may delay this choice until better options are available. However, you will not progress until you have chosen.

If his need to progress wasn't so urgent, Elijah might have taken the System up on that opportunity. The idea of getting better choices was certainly attractive enough to delay his own development. However, the looming threat of the settlement across the strait made it an impossibility. Further restricting his choices was the reality that, without the panther, his island had just gotten a lot more dangerous. After all, he'd seen the evidence of the cat's efforts every time he'd stumbled across one of the Voxx bodies. Now, without the panther patrolling the island, the responsibility for keeping it clear of the detestable creatures was left to him.

So, Elijah moved on to his choices, the first of which both excited and terrified him.

Class: Animist
The animist is a shape-shifter who can take on the characteristics of various beasts.

Required Archetype:
Druid

Required Achievements:
Create a bond with a guardian beast.

First Ability:
Shape of the Predator

Attribute Allocation:
Balanced

Compatibility: 99%

Elijah had been using magic since the very first day he'd arrived on the island. He'd healed himself from injury countless times. He had also cured himself of cancer. So, he thought he was used to the idea of magic being real. But upon reading a notification that told him that, if he chose that class, he could transform into an animal, he was taken aback. As such, it took him a few moments before he could look at the notification objectively.

The first thing he noticed was that his compatibility with the class was incredibly high. How the System came up with that number he had no idea, but a similar notification had given him his druid archetype. And that had worked out well. So, he had to believe that the System knew what it was doing.

Other than that, it didn't really give him much in the way of information. Without a description, the name of the first ability, Shape of the Predator, didn't really tell him much about what he could expect from the class. However, he did note that the attribute allocation was supposed to be balanced, whatever that meant.

He reread the description a few more times before moving on to the next class's notification:

Class: Fury
The fury is a spellcaster who harnesses the power of nature for offensive effect.

Required Archetype:
Druid

Required Achievements:
Kill ten (10) creatures of a higher level with offensive spells.

First Ability:
Cyclone

Attribute Allocation:
Ethera, Regeneration

Compatibility: 88%

The description for the fury was a little more informative than the one for the animist, and Elijah took it to mean that the class would give him more spells like Storm's Fury. The attribute allocation seemed to support that notion.

Surely, the idea of being a nature wizard had a certain appeal. However, his recent fight against the trio of invaders gave him some insight into what that might mean for his future. Seeing the panther rip through the healer so easily had definitely left a mark on his mind. If he chose to become a Fury, would that happen to him? The goblin healer had been very effective, so long as he'd had someone to protect him, but the moment he hadn't, the panther had ripped him apart without issue.

And Elijah didn't have some shield-bearing warrior to protect him. He was all alone, which meant that choosing the path of a dedicated spellcaster seemed like it might be the wrong way to go.

But then again, he kept going back to the listed ability, Cyclone. He'd seen the aftermath of plenty of tornados. What if that spell would let him summon something like that? The settlement across the strait would be gone in an instant.

Shaking his head, Elijah moved on to the final choice:

Class: Nurturer
The nurturer is a spellcaster who harnesses the power of renewal to promote growth and healing.

Required Archetype:
Druid

Required Achievements:
Completely heal a higher-level entity from near death.

First Ability:
Flower of Regrowth

Attribute Allocation:
Ethera, Regeneration

Compatibility: 72%

The moment Elijah read the name of the class, he knew what was in store, and the description did nothing to change his mind. It was a healer, not unlike the one he'd just watched die. Perhaps there was more to it than that—in fact, he was certain that would be the case—but it was similar enough that he didn't have to think about it too much before he rejected the class.

If he wasn't stuck on a deserted island with dangers all around him, Elijah would have probably picked the Nurturer as his class. The idea of healing people was a rewarding one. And given that he'd gained levels by healing the panther, it was a solid way to progress, as well. However, it came with the significant downside of being extremely vulnerable.

Elijah couldn't afford that, so he immediately struck the third option from his list of choices.

"Who am I kidding?" he muttered to himself. He'd made his choice the moment he'd read the description of the Animist. It wasn't because he relished the idea of turning into an animal. That was interesting and all, but the real reason he picked animist was because he'd seen the power the panther could bring to bear. On top of that, the attribute allocation was balanced, suggesting that it would be a jack-of-all-trades sort of situation.

Which was exactly what he needed, considering that he was all alone and had no one to depend on but himself.

So, without further deliberation, he chose his class.

You have chosen to become an Animist (Druid archetype).

A few more notifications popped up, but Elijah ignored them. Instead, he just stared at the one confirming his class, hoping all the while that he'd made the right choice. Because if he hadn't, his chances of survival were slim.

"Alright," he said to himself, clapping his hands together in anticipation. "Let's see what these new spells are."

33

SHAPE OF THE PREDATOR

Elijah opened his spell book and looked at the new additions:

Archetype: Druid The druid is the defender, ally, and cultivator of nature. Features bonuses to natural Regeneration, Ethera density, and One With Nature. Required Aspects: [Scholar], [Nature]	
Spells	
Touch of Nature	Harness the power of nature to heal yourself or an ally.
Snaring Roots	Call upon nature to summon a snarl of roots to bind your enemies' movements.
One With Nature	Draw power from nature.
Eyes of the Eagle	Briefly enhance your eyesight with the power of a fearsome raptor.
Ancestral Circle	Create a place of power.
Nature's Bounty	Encourage the growth of plants.
Storm's Fury	Call forth the power of a storm and harness its might.
Essence of the Boar	Harness the stamina of the boar, increasing Constitution attribute by five (5) points. Usable on allies.
Essence of the Monkey	Adopt the coordination of the monkey, increasing Dexterity attribute by five (5) points. Usable on allies.

Class: Animist The animist is a shape-shifter who can take on the characteristics of various beasts.	
Shape of the Predator	**Take on the shape of a mighty hunter, vastly increasing your Dexterity and Strength attributes and giving a minor increase to Constitution. Spellcasting is suspended while Shape of the Predator is active.**

Despite the lingering feelings of sadness, a sense of excitement washed over Elijah when he saw his new spells. Essence of the Boar and Essence of the Monkey were both impressive enough, but his eyes were immediately drawn to Shape of the Predator. Still, he forced himself to focus on what he considered the more mundane spells.

Essence of the Boar would increase his Constitution attribute by five points, while Essence of the Monkey would serve to do the same for his Dexterity attribute. The real question was whether he could keep them both active at the same time. Before, he'd been able to intuit that keeping One With Nature active was the limit of his current abilities, but now that he'd gained a class—or maybe it was because he'd gotten a couple of levels—he felt that those limits had been expanded. So, without further ado, he cast Essence of the Boar.

He immediately felt the effects as his fatigue washed away. Sure enough, when he opened his status, he saw that his attributes had increased according to the spell's description. That success prompted him to cast Essence of the Monkey, as well. However, that was when he got the first disappointment. He couldn't keep One With Nature, Essence of the Boar, and Essence of the Monkey active at the same time. Two seemed to be the limit.

Which presented something of a conundrum. Both Essence of the Boar and Essence of the Monkey gave quantifiable increases, while One With Nature was a bit more nebulous. Still, just because it wasn't reflected in his status didn't mean that it didn't come with benefits. One With Nature made him feel stronger, faster, and more durable, even if those gains weren't represented via the System.

So, the way he saw it, the choice was whether or not he wanted an all-around increase from One With Nature coupled with the specific increase that came with either Essence of the Boar or Essence of the Monkey. Or he could just remove all mystery from the equation and use his two newest spells to gain quantifiable increases in his attributes.

Elijah sat there for a long while as he considered the pros and cons of each combination. But in the end, he decided that he would always keep One With Nature active, largely because it didn't just come with benefits to his physical abilities. Rather, it also came with a more esoteric connection to the natural world that he'd begun to take for granted. Without it, he knew he'd feel a little lost.

As for his second available enhancement slot, he chose to use Essence of the Boar as a default, then switch to Essence of the Monkey as needed. That would protect him from any surprises by increasing his durability while giving him the flexibility to respond to threats according to the situation.

Satisfied with that strategy, Elijah shifted his focus to his status. Or more importantly, to the free attribute points he'd yet to allocate. However, to his surprise, he only had four unspent points. Frustrated, he cycled through his various notifications until he saw one he'd somehow ignored after choosing his class:

Class: Animist
Automatic attribute allocation:
+1 Strength, Dexterity, Constitution, Ethera, Regeneration

"What the . . ."

Elijah trailed off as he realized what it meant. His days of being able to guide his attribute allocation were over. Instead, because of his class, he'd get a single point in every attribute each time he gained a level. While that made sense, he found that he was a little disappointed. After all, he didn't like the idea of losing control over his own development.

Still, it only took him a few seconds to realize that that wasn't necessarily the case. When he'd closed the minor dimensional rift, he'd been awarded three free attribute points. So, if he wanted to keep a handle on his own progression, he would need to continue to do those sorts of things.

Which was probably going to happen sooner rather than later, considering that the panther was now dead. Because of that, the island didn't have any guardians left besides Elijah himself. He had no idea if the cat had been closing those rifts itself, but Elijah suspected that that was the case.

Suddenly, he started to realize that his progression had just become far more important than ever before. He needed levels as well as the attributes and additional spells that would come with them. Otherwise, he was going to be overrun by the Voxx, the invaders from across the strait, or both.

First, though, he needed to allocate his four free attribute points. To him, it felt like an easy decision. He had the means to augment his physical attributes, either directly via Essence of the Boar and Essence of the Monkey or indirectly by keeping One With Nature active. And it stood to reason that, as he leveled, he'd gain more enhancement slots as well as the spells to increase his other attributes.

But so far, his limiting factor had been Ethera. There was an argument to be made that Regeneration was just as valuable, but Elijah found himself discounting that line of thinking. If it came down to a fight, there just wasn't enough time for Regeneration to make much of a difference. However, being able to cast one more Storm's Fury could end up being the difference between life and death. So, he chose to allocate all four points into Ethera, thus increasing the number of spells he could use before his core ran dry.

Name	**Elijah Hart**		
Level	**10**		
Archetype	**Druid**		
Class	**Animist**		
Specialization	**N/A**		
Alignment	**N/A**		
Strength	**12**		
Dexterity	**11**		
Constitution	**12**		
Ethera	**20**		
Regeneration	**14**		
Attunement	**Nature**		
Cultivation			
Body	**Core**	**Mind**	**Soul**
Wood	**Unformed**	**Opal**	**Neophyte**

Looking at his status, Elijah felt a deep sense of pride. It felt like an eternity had passed since he'd washed ashore, and in that time, he'd been entirely remade. Certainly, he was still a long way from the superhuman levels that he'd imagined when he'd first accepted that magic was part of his new reality, but he was well on his way.

After letting loose a long sigh, he moved his focus to the most important item on his list. He opened the spell's description:

Shape of the Predator **Archetype: Druid** **Class: Animist** **Level: 10**

Take on the shape of a mighty hunter (Mist Panther), vastly increasing your Dexterity and Strength attributes and giving a minor increase to Constitution. Spellcasting is suspended while Shape of the Predator is active.	
Contagion	**Physical attacks made while in Predator form also inflict a minor infection.**

"Wow," Elijah breathed as he read the description. He would have been happy with the transformation alone, so he was ecstatic to find that another ability was included. He didn't know if it was just a characteristic of being a Mist Panther or if it was awarded as part of his Animist class progression, but he figured that time would answer that question. For now, he was eager to finally use the spell that he expected to define his class going forward. So, without further ado, he stood, then dragged Ethera from his core while focusing on Shape of the Predator.

By that point, he'd recovered all his Ethera, so his core was entirely full. However, the moment he cast the spell, that changed. His Ethera rushed out of him in a tidal wave, draining every last ounce of the energy and leaving it absolutely bare. However, Elijah barely noticed the headache that inevitably followed. Instead, he was entirely focused on the transformation that came soon after.

Unlike what he might've expected, it didn't hurt. Nor was it pleasant. It was just odd, feeling his bones rearrange themselves. He fell to all fours as his body continued to change. His organs shifted, his muscles reformed, and midnight fur sprouted all over his body. And after about thirty seconds, the transformation finished.

The moment it did, Elijah was overwhelmed by his own senses. He could smell everything. The small animals who made their home in the glade. The nearby bushes of his garden. The tree itself. He even smelled an acrid scent that he immediately interpreted as belonging to his human body.

But it wasn't just his sense of smell that had been enhanced. He also heard things he never knew were even there. The slight chitter of a squirrel that was at least a hundred yards away. The flap of a bird's wings. The scurrying insects underground. It was everything Elijah could do not to lose himself amid the cavalcade of sensory input.

His vision and sense of touch had been affected, as well, though not to the degree that his senses of smell and hearing had been enhanced. He collapsed to his stomach, burying his face between his paws as he struggled to adapt.

If he hadn't already experienced something similar when he'd cultivated his Neophyte soul, he never would have been able to endure it. However, because he'd done so, it only took him a few hours to come to terms with his new, much stronger senses. When he finally did, he couldn't help but marvel at just how much he'd never noticed before.

For a while, he just lay there, his tail wagging slightly as he took it all in.

Then, at last, he pushed himself to his feet and took his first steps as a Mist Panther. To his surprise, his body seemed to move of its own accord. Or, rather, like he'd been a panther all his life. A good thing, too, because he had not relished the idea of learning how to walk on four legs. But now, he could focus on everything else.

Without further delay, Elijah took off across the glade, moving far more quickly than he'd ever moved in all his life. When he reached the tree line, he bounded forward, kicked off one of the sturdy trees, then hit the ground running. That's when he noticed an enticing scent.

He followed it easily, and soon enough, it started getting stronger. With every step, the smell became more potent until, at last, he found the culprit. Without even thinking, Elijah pounced on the fat hare, clamping down on the back of its neck with his mighty jaws. Then, he shook it, breaking its neck.

Elijah didn't even realize what he was doing until he'd already consumed half of that rabbit. But when his mind caught up to his wild instincts, he recoiled. A moment later, he mentally canceled the spell.

His reversion to humanity took a lot longer than his transformation into a panther, and when it finally completed, the headache he'd felt coming when he'd first cast Shape of the Predator returned in force. When it did, he collapsed onto his rear and just sat there, burying his head in his hands until he'd regained enough Ethera to take the edge off.

Once he felt a little better, he looked around and realized that he'd traveled a lot farther than he'd intended. As a Mist Panther, he'd moved so quickly, and his mind had focused in on stalking the rabbit so thoroughly that he had completely lost track of anything else. That would be a danger he'd have to mitigate in the future.

The same could be said about the instincts that came with his transformation. It was perfectly natural for a panther to kill and eat raw animals. But for a human being? That was something entirely different, and the memory of that rabbit's raw flesh between his teeth twisted his stomach into knots.

Finally, the spell itself was incredibly Ethera hungry, draining every bit of the magical energy from his core. So, it was clear that he wouldn't be rapidly changing forms anytime soon. In fact, the next time he used Shape of the Predator, he intended to remain that way for a while, if just to get his proverbial money's worth out of the spell.

All in all, though, Elijah was impressed with the ability. It had performed far better than he could have expected, and the sense of power he'd felt as a mist panther was overwhelming. Perhaps if the spell had been available when he'd stumbled upon the battle between the trio of invaders and the island's guardian, then the panther might have survived.

Elijah sighed.

That wasn't fair. He had no reason to feel guilty. He had done everything he could, and even if he'd had access to Shape of the Predator, it wouldn't have made much difference. The invaders were simply too strong.

Or, rather, he was too weak.

But that was going to have to change. So, he pushed himself to his feet and returned to the Grove. There, he gathered his staff and set off toward the stream so he could wash the taste of raw rabbit out of his mouth. After that, he would come up with a plan that would hopefully shore up some of his weaknesses.

34

THE BLACK SHEEP

Eason Cabbot ran his hand along the thick bristles of his bloodred mohawk as he sat at the desk he'd been given. Ostensibly, he could have commandeered any building in the budding settlement of Ironshore—that was what his contract had said, at least—but he knew better than to make any power moves. For one, it wouldn't do much good. He was just the head of security, and as such, the miners and other settlers wouldn't follow him. For another, he had no aspirations of rule. Instead, he'd come to this out-of-the-way backwater of a newly integrated planet with one goal: to get strong enough to return home and claim his rightful place.

But it wasn't going well.

Certainly, there were opportunities for him and the mercenaries he'd brought with him. No restrictions on hunting. No guards to keep him from challenging any interdimensional rift he came across. And the local wildlife was just that—wild. Back home on Norat, everything was so restrictive. The rifts were well guarded, and the wildlife had long since been tamed. The only way to get ahead was to join a guild—or to convince his parents that he was worth their investment.

But that had never been possible for him. The sixteenth son of a minor noble house, gaining any degree of power was a tall hill to climb. More so because he'd taken a class that painted him as an uncontrollable barbarian. In his defense, though, Berserker was the most powerful class he'd been offered, and it wasn't even close. He would've had to have been a fool to take any of the others.

His parents didn't see it that way, though. Nor did his siblings. And as a result, Cabbot had been forced to take drastic measures—like joining a mercenary group called Black Sky and buying passage to the newly integrated world unimaginatively dubbed Earth. When he'd arrived only a few months before, he'd found that the settlement had only barely been developed. However, the miners had found signs that there was true iron beneath the local mountains, so there was every indication that Ironshore would turn out to be a profitable settlement.

Still, Cabbot didn't care about that. Certainly, he would gain a bonus based on the town's profits, but it was a pittance compared to what he'd need to get ahead. That was why he sought a shortcut.

And his eyes were set on the mist-wreathed island across the strait, which was why he'd sent a scouting team over. They'd been gone for three days, which meant that they were already two past due.

He rose, hopping down from the chair. It had been made for a much taller dwarf, and so, it was about two times too large for his diminutive stature. He'd commissioned some gnome-sized furniture, but the local carpenter was a busy goblin with a waiting list a mile long. It would take time to fill Cabbot's order, and in the meantime, he had to make do with what he had.

Which infuriated him.

Didn't these people know who he was?

But the answer to that question was a resounding no. To them, he was just the mercenary they'd hired to see to their security. Did it matter that he'd purposely stunted his own progression in hopes of securing just such an opportunity? If he'd let himself gain any more levels, he wouldn't have been able to make the trip at all. So, he was stuck at level twenty-five.

Hopefully, he wouldn't remain at that level for much longer. Already, he'd started to participate in local hunts, and it wouldn't be long before they started finding minor dimensional rifts. And with any luck, they'd discover a tower. Not only would the reward for a first clear be significant, but it would also be a perfect opportunity for him and his most trusted subordinates to quickly progress.

None of the local noncombatants knew that, though. And even if they did, it wouldn't matter. They had all the power. All the money. Sure, that would change if he ever pushed ahead and became an Ascendant, but that was a long way off. Most fighters never sniffed such a lofty status.

But Cabbot's parents had, even reaching the next tier of existence as Demigods. Two of his siblings were well on their way to that goal, as well. Not Cabbot, though. His parents wouldn't invest that kind of etherium or political capital into his progression, and so, he was forced to seek out other means of advancement.

He would prove them wrong, though.

All it would take was one lucky encounter, and he'd blow them all out of the water. Because while he hadn't gotten the same opportunities as his siblings—or even his contemporaries in the other noble houses—Cabbot had long known that he was special. Otherwise, he wouldn't have been offered such a powerful class. Sure, it came with weaknesses, but he could deal with those.

Mostly.

But it was fine. There were always going to be growing pains. And if it meant having killed a few of the wrong people while in a murderous rage that had begun as a bar fight, so be it. That was another reason he'd come to Ironshore. He wasn't afraid, per se. But getting out of Norat just seemed like a good idea.

Once again running his fingers over his mohawk, he checked his weapons. Using Arsenal, he pulled out a large two-handed axe. Then, making certain that it was in good condition, he checked the greatsword, as well. Then, the pair of shortswords. A few daggers. Finally, he inspected a large glaive.

Arsenal	**Store weapons in an extradimensional space. Limited to Unranked items.**

The ability was one of the most useful he'd been granted upon gaining his class, and though it precluded the use of higher-grade weapons, he had no complaints. Likely, that was because he couldn't afford anything better than Crude items for now, and those weren't enough better than peak Unranked items to matter.

Sure, they were usually much more durable, but with Arsenal, losing out on a little durability wasn't the detriment it otherwise would be. After all, if he destroyed one weapon, he could almost always just summon another.

After checking his weaponry, he crossed the small room—it really wasn't much bigger than a closet, which was something that would have to change, and soon—and left his office behind. When he did, he immediately stepped into a mud puddle.

Grimacing, he looked down at his boot. Like its partner, it was a Crude-grade item, but it had still been expensive. Besides, would it have killed Ramik to pave the roads? That seemed like a minimal level of development. The goblin who ran the town, though, clearly had other things on his mind because the settlement was still little more than a few hastily thrown-together buildings and an imported Branch.

Disgusted, Cabbot hopped over the mud puddle, then strode down the street. He had to avoid a few carts along the way, but miraculously, he managed to circumvent any more accidents as he trekked across Ironshore. Eventually, he reached the expansive barracks and went inside.

The front of the building was a tavern that a group of mercenaries ran during their off time. Cabbot didn't mind the split focus, mostly because they'd paid for the privilege. It wasn't much of an income stream—just a few copper etherium a week at present—but it didn't require any effort on his part. And over time, it would start to add up.

In any case, it was the only place in town to get a decent glass of gnomish whiskey. As tempting as that was, Cabbot resisted the urge as he passed through the tavern—called the Slow Dwarf—and entered the actual barracks. The room was long and lined with two rows of beds, each equipped with a sturdy footlocker and a cabinet for the mercenaries' other belongings. By no stretch of the imagination was it glamorous, but it was also temporary. As the town grew, the mercenaries would be given land and materials to have their own homes built.

If the planet's Ethera levels continued to rise, then those homes would be incredibly valuable going forward.

But that was a worry that wouldn't bear fruit for decades, if ever. So, Cabbot pushed that out of mind and continued on to the back of the building. Along the way, he greeted a few of the gnomes, but he all but ignored the goblins and dwarves. He wasn't quite as prejudiced as most of his race, but neither could he ignore the facts. By nature, goblins were tricky, crude, and often cruel, and dwarves weren't much better. That was just how it was, and no amount of goodwill or understanding was going to change reality. All Cabbot could do was recognize their obvious flaws and adjust his own expectations accordingly.

Soon enough, he reached his destination and knocked on the door. A moment later, it swung open to reveal a pink-haired gnomish woman. He grinned broadly and leaned against the doorframe. "Nirea! So good to see you! May I come in?" he asked.

"I was working."

"Right. That's what this is about," he said, pushing past her. She was just an Administrator, which meant that she didn't have the ability to stop him. Still, aside from being quite a beauty—which was what had caught his eye in the first place—she was an incredibly valuable member of the mercenary band. Without her, logistics would devolve into an unsolvable mess, which would, in turn, create an unmitigated disaster. Mercenaries were only as loyal as their last payday, and if the coins stopped flowing, they'd turn pretty quickly.

Nirea pointedly left the door open as she sighed and crossed the office to plant herself in her own gnome-sized chair. That she had one irritated Cabbot something fierce, but he nobly pushed his annoyance to the side.

"Have you heard from Dena and those two idiots she works with?" he asked without further preamble. Right to the point. Then, he'd get to personal matters.

"No. Dena, Braxon, and Vtigt are still missing. Do you want me to organize a search party?"

Cabbot shook his head, closing the door. What he had to say wasn't something he wanted the rest of the mercenaries to hear. "No. If they encountered what I think they found . . . no. We can't afford to lose anyone else."

"You think there's a guardian over there?"

Cabbot answered, "I do. It's the only thing that makes sense. Dena might've had bad taste in partners, but she was smart and capable."

"Highest level in the band."

"Was she?" he asked, a little surprised. That was certainly news to him.

"She found a minor dimensional rift last week. Then, she encountered a herd of lizard creatures. Ran on two legs, short arms, big teeth. She said they looked like six-foot birds, but with scales instead of feathers. They weren't that strong, but there were more than a dozen of them. She gained a level there and one in the rift."

"Oh."

"There are a few others who are on the verge of catching her, though. Well, now that she's . . . missing . . ."

Cabbot said, "Whatever's over there must be strong if it took out three of our higher-level fighters. If we go over there, we need to go in force. And we're not ready for that yet."

"When will we be?" she asked, drumming her fingers on the desk.

He sighed. That was certainly a good question, and one he couldn't really answer. The truth was that, though the presence of a guardian meant that there was probably some potent natural treasure on that island, they were ill-equipped to handle such a threat. Guardians weren't just powerful beasts. They were intelligent and cunning, and their sole purpose was to protect that natural treasure until it reached maturity. The World Tree permitted them to exceed the level restrictions imposed by the System, which meant that Cabbot and his mercenaries would almost assuredly be unprepared to face such a creature.

Dena and her two hangers-on had discovered that firsthand.

"Soon. We just need to get stronger," he said.

"Very well. What should I tell the others about Dena, Braxon, and Vtigt? They were popular, and their absence has already been noted."

"Tell them that they all received opportunities to go home," Cabbot stated.

"Lie?"

"Of course. To do otherwise would only invite a response. They'll go over to that island, and they'll die just like Dena and those other two idiots. If you think about it, we're saving lives," he said smoothly.

She thought about it for a moment, then said, "Very well."

"Now that business is done, perhaps you would like to accompany me—"

"My apologies, captain, but I have a good deal of work to do. We will have to do it another day."

Cabbot ground his teeth together, then once again ran his hand over his bristly mohawk. Then, he forced a smile he didn't feel before saying, "Alright then. I'll hold you to that."

Without anything else, he turned, opened the door, then strode away. However, he did hear something that sounded very much like *asshole* coming from the office he'd just left behind. Clearly, he'd misheard, though. Right. Obviously.

35

FIRST STEP

Carmen stood in front of her forge, staring at the flames. She had built the thing herself, and to exacting specifications. However, she knew just how much room there was for improvement. Still, as she walked around it and inspected the brickwork, she was more than happy with the results.

The forge itself was a little more than waist high, made of thick bricks she'd made herself using a local clay deposit she'd found near the lake. The process hadn't been as onerous as she'd expected, and it had been made even simpler via copious use of her archetype techniques. Idly, she inspected her technique list:

Archetype: Tradesman **A versatile crafter who can create a wide variety of goods.** **Required Aspect:** **[Scholar] [Magic]**	
Techniques	
Bond	**Using Ethera, bond two materials together.**
Fracture	**Harness Ethera to break a material.**
Summon Tool	**Summon one of the following temporary tools: mining pick, blacksmith's hammer, shears, knife, or woodsman's axe.**
Ethereal Infusion	**Imbue an item with Ethera.**
Minor Enchantment	**Imbue an item with the minor enchantment: durability.**
Decontaminate	**Remove contaminants from a raw material.**
Tradesman's Appraisal	**Gain basic information on your creation.**

Refine Material	Enhance the basic properties of a material. Only usable on pure substances.
Crafter's Stamina	Gain one (1) point of Constitution per level.
Resist Fire	Enhance resistance to fire and heat.
Shape	Reshape a material with raw Ethera.
Meld Metals	Create an alloy from two metals.
Minor Embellishment	Use a single embellishment to augment the grade of an unfinished item. Only usable on metallic weapons, armor, and tools.

Her techniques were mostly self-explanatory, though a few bucked that trend. Specifically, Ethereal Infusion, Minor Enchantment, and Minor Embellishment had required a little experimentation. Now, though, she felt confident that she understood them well enough to attempt something special.

And perhaps she would gain a level, as well, which would be quite a feat. As a Blacksmith, she didn't gain experience like the people with combat classes. Instead, her progression was predictably rooted in crafting. However, she couldn't simply make the same things over and over again. If she took that route, any progress would take forever. No—if she wanted to keep pace with powerful combatants like Alyssa, she had to continuously create new and unique items.

Which wasn't such an onerous task, considering that was the entire reason she'd taken the Tradesman archetype to begin with. For her whole life, Carmen had been fascinated with the idea of making things with her own two hands, which was why she'd chosen to pursue her postgraduate work specializing in primitive skills. And while she'd only had a very basic interest in smithing, when the Blacksmith class became available, it had felt like the best choice.

In any case, it gave her the opportunity to help without putting herself at personal risk. It wasn't that she was a coward. She would fight if she needed to. But with Miguel depending on her, throwing herself into battle just wasn't a viable option. One parent taking that path was bad enough—and worry for Alyssa often kept her awake at night—but two was infinitely worse. God forbid Alyssa was killed, but if it happened, Carmen had a responsibility to continue on without her, if only for Miguel's sake.

Besides, there was an argument to be made that, without the settlement's crafters, no one would have survived. Primitive though their situation was, at least they had shelter and equipment. Without those two things, few would have made it.

Now, though, Carmen wanted to do something more than build a log cabin or craft a mundane iron weapon. Instead, she wanted to make something special.

To that end, she gathered an old leaf spring she'd taken from one of the now-useless cars in town. Though it was rusty, it was still good steel, which was what she needed for the project she had in mind. She thrust it into the forge, then worked the attached bellows as she waited for the metal to heat to the proper temperature.

Slowly, the color changed. Starting at light yellow, it grew darker, progressing through a series of purples and blues on its way to a dark gray. That gray took on a red tint that gradually took over. When the metal became bright red, she knew it was ready to be manipulated. Using a pair of tongs, Carmen yanked it out of the forge, then placed the cherry red bar of steel on her anvil.

She used Summon Tool, and an unadorned blacksmithing hammer weighing about four pounds appeared in her hand. It was a little on the heavier side for what she needed, but with her inflated Strength, it felt almost too light. Still, when the heavy head fell on the bar of steel, the metal moved.

Over and over, she hammered against the steel until she saw the color fading back to gray. When it did, she thrust the bar back into the forge and repeated the process. Gradually, the bar of steel took on the shape of a tapered double-edged blade about a foot in length.

Once Carmen had hammered out the basic form, she dismissed the blacksmithing hammer, only to use Summon Tool again. This time, she came up with a much lighter hammer. It took a bit of concentration to make such a change, but she'd mastered it soon after receiving the technique. Thus armed, she started working on the profile of the blade, hammering it into a sloped surface that would eventually become a sharp edge.

Before the world's transformation, she would have done things slightly differently. But because of her techniques, Carmen could skip some steps—like building in a socket for the shaft she intended to attach. So, while the forging itself was slightly easier, the fact that she had to continuously use Ethereal Infusion, constantly bathing the piece in Ethera, made up for the decreased difficulty.

Gradually, the spearhead took shape. If she'd only wanted to hammer out something that would meet the basic standard of effectiveness, she could have been finished in less than an hour. However, because she wanted to create something at the height of her abilities, she was forced to take her time.

She fell into a rhythm. Hammering until the metal cooled, thrusting it back into the forge, working the bellows until it got hot enough to move, then repeating the process. Over and over until, at last, she was satisfied with the shape.

Then, Carmen got down to grinding.

She would have preferred a belt sander, but due to the lack of availability—and the fact that she hadn't had time to build one—Carmen was forced to do it the old-fashioned way. That meant repeatedly dragging the blade along the surface of a whetstone until the shape of the weapon was refined to her tastes.

That took even longer than the forging process, but with Ethereal Infusion coursing through her, she fell into something akin to a meditative state. Hours passed, and the sun eventually set, but she kept going by the light of the moon. Each pass along the whetstone took the tiniest portion of metal with it until, just before dawn, she had achieved perfection.

She looked up. The forge was still burning, but she didn't remember adding extra fuel. No one else was around, so she figured that she must've done it without thinking.

In any case, the blade was finished—except for the heat treat, but that would come later. For now, she needed to work on the haft.

For that, Carmen had chosen hickory she'd gathered from the local forest. But she wasn't just going to jam the two pieces together and call it a day. Instead, like she'd done with the steel, she'd used her Decontaminate and Refine Material techniques to purify and enhance the wood. As a result, it was a good deal more durable than it would've otherwise been. After that, she used a combination of Fracture and basic whittling skills to shape the raw limb.

In the end, she came up with a six-foot-long shaft that was about three-quarters of an inch wide. If the wood wasn't so durable, she would've gone slightly thicker, but because of her techniques, Carmen felt confident that it would survive just about any impact.

And she had plans to enhance it further.

Once the shaft was finished, Carmen set about heat treating the blade. Normally, she would have preferred to use oil for the quench, but it wasn't as if she could run down to the local big-box store and buy a drum of quenching oil, so she was forced to use water. Which was dangerous because it would cool the metal very quickly, and if there were any flaws in the blade, it stood the risk of shattering.

But Carmen had prepared as well as she could, so she could only hope it was enough.

With that in mind, she shoved the spearhead back into the forge, waited for it to reach critical temperature, then removed it. The moment it was out of the forge, she thrust it into a barrel of water she'd prepared.

Steam billowed, but because of her Resist Fire ability, Carmen was unaffected. Regardless, she was too focused on what she heard to pay any attention to the steam. She listened, but when she heard no cracking sounds, she let out a sigh of relief. Still, after the blade had cooled, she inspected it closely, looking for any flaws.

There were none.

So, she was free to move on to the next step, which involved shoving the two pieces together, then using Bond to meld them into one piece. If they were comprised of the same materials, it would have been simple. However, because the shaft was wood and the blade was high-carbon steel, it was a bit trickier.

Still, Carmen had spent quite some time preparing for just that problem by melding a wide variety of materials together. The trick was focus and patience. If she tried to do it all at once, just using the Bond technique without any direction, it would fail. But so long as she took her time, slowly guiding the two disparate materials into merging, it would create a seamless transition that was stronger than either of the individual materials.

With well-practiced resolve, she did just that, directing tiny tendrils of metal and wood into a series of microscopic braids. She couldn't see them, but so long as she maintained her focus, she could feel them. At the same time, she never let Ethereal Infusion drop, which added some degree of difficulty but would create much better results.

In the end, it took another four or five hours before she finished the process. Once it was done, she sagged in exhaustion, both mental and physical. But she was only getting started. Sure, the spear was fine as it was. It would do the job. Yet it required two more steps before she could call it complete.

First, though, Carmen needed some rest. She'd been at it for almost an entire day straight, and though her endurance was augmented by Crafter's Stamina, it could only do so much. So, she stashed the spear in a corner and headed home to eat and sleep. Fortunately, Alyssa had taken Miguel out into the wilderness, where she was teaching him the lessons her father had taught her. Hunting, fishing, tracking—all sorts of wilderness survival skills that were even more important now than they had been when she'd learned them.

Her meal wasn't terribly satisfying. Just a hunk of bread, a few berries Alyssa had gathered, and some dried meat. Normally, she would have taken the meal in one of the communal dining halls, but that would have come with a host of social obligations she had no time to meet. So, she suffered through her meal, then washed off as best she could before going to bed.

Sleep came fast and ended even more quickly, and soon enough she was back at the forge. Technically, she could have finished everything at the cabin, but she had no intention of taking her work home.

Sitting near the forge, she held the spear across her lap. After spending quite some time inspecting it for any flaws she might have missed, she decided that its quality was good enough to take the next step. It wasn't perfect, but it was the best she could do.

For now.

She felt positive that, one day, she could make something far more impressive. After all, the crafting guides Alyssa had bought from the Branch of the World Tree suggested the existence of rare, powerful materials. And she knew her journey as a crafter had only just begun.

No—there were many powerful items in her future. But every journey began with a single step, and her path as a blacksmith started with a single spear.

So, with that in mind, she took the next step.

Using a small knife, she started to carve. As she did, she kept two techniques active. The first, as always, was Ethereal Infusion, which bathed the entire weapon in Ethera. The second was Minor Embellishment, which had two requirements to activate. The first was to simply embrace the technique, using it the same way she used any other. The second requirement was to create some sort of flourish in her crafted product.

According to the crafting guides, it could be something as simple as embedding a jewel into a tiara, but it hinted that the more appropriate the embellishment was to the item, the more it would boost the eventual quality of the end result. However, the guide acknowledged that there was some debate on the subject, as well, and it said that some crafters had posited that the appropriateness of the embellishment was subject to the crafter's opinion. In short, if she thought it fit, then that was all that mattered.

Carmen wasn't sure about that, but it really wasn't all that important, either. She'd known from the very beginning what form the embellishment would take. So, she got to work, carving the shaft with fanciful designs that resembled Renaissance ornaments. But she didn't stop there, instead continuing onto the spearhead with an engraving tool.

Once she'd finished, Carmen set it on a nearby rack, then stepped back. From a distance, the designs weren't even visible. However, once someone drew close enough, they would see just how elaborate they were.

It was perfect.

But it wasn't done.

There were still three more steps. All were important, but one was far more critical than the other. So, Carmen chose to take care of that one—the Minor Enchantment—first. On the surface, it didn't seem all that difficult. All she had to do was carve the appropriate symbol into the surface of the weapon while channeling the technique. However, her tests had told her that it was far from simple, and she knew it would require every ounce of her concentration to get it right.

So, Carmen took another break, got some food, and even walked around the settlement for a bit. Once her head was clear, she returned to the forge, placed the spear across her lap, and got to work.

She'd left a small ring of virgin territory in the center of the spearhead, and she targeted that space with her engraving tool. As she did so, Carmen used Minor Enchantment. From experience, she knew it would only make the weapon more durable—a minor effect, just as the name implied—but it was worth it. The last thing she wanted was for the spear to snap at the wrong time, after all. So, Carmen put her all into it, doing her best to regulate the Ethera flowing through her so that she wouldn't overload the would-be enchantment.

It was no easy task, but she'd practiced enough that she managed it all the same. And then, after a few strokes of her engraving tool, she was finished.

Now, all she needed to do was sharpen the blade and seal the wooden haft with wax.

She took her time, partially because the tasks required it. But mostly, she was loath to finish the weapon. What if it didn't prove to be worth the trouble? What if it was just another spear? After everything she'd done, it was still made from mundane materials, after all. But part of her reticence was also because, despite the amount of effort it had taken, she had very much enjoyed the process.

There was something about the act of creating something from nothing that had always appealed to her, and the addition of magic—or Ethera, she supposed—just made it that much more impactful.

But still, she put the finishing touches on it, and just like that, the project was done. It was the product of three days of work and countless hours of practice. She'd arduously gathered the best materials she could, and she'd used every ability at her disposal. Looking back on the process, Carmen didn't think she could have done anything differently.

So, it was with some sense of satisfaction that she used Tradesman's Appraisal:

Congratulations! You have created a unique item, [Spear of the Dragon Lancer].

Overall Grade: Crude.

Enchantment Grade: F.

Carmen pumped her fist in celebration, letting out a whoop of excitement. Then, she did an awkward little dance. And as far as she was concerned, her celebration was well warranted. Until that moment, the best item she'd managed to craft had still never exceeded an unranked overall grade. That she'd stepped up to the next level was an enormous achievement.

Calling something crude wasn't really flattering, but it represented the first step of magical equipment. According to everything she'd read, it was an enormous leap forward in terms of effectiveness, and even though the Spear of the Dragon Lancer wouldn't have any fanciful magical powers, it would be nearly unbreakable and would feature a minor self-repair function.

In short, it was everything she'd hoped to achieve.

But having taken that first step, she couldn't help but look forward to the next. Sure, she'd made a crude magical item, and that was great. Better than great, really. But what would an item with a simple grade look like? Or a complex one?

Before, those goals had seemed almost unreachable. However, now that she'd taken the first step, those heights seemed much more attainable.

36

CLIMBING THE LADDER

Elijah stalked forward, his feet falling silently against the forest floor as he followed his prey through the forest. Even if it hadn't made so much noise, there was no mistaking the scent that it emitted. To Elijah's sense of smell, the odor was a combination of rotten eggs, something similar to cheap cigar smoke, and the sickly sweet scent of decomposing fruit. It was, to put it mildly, extremely off-putting, and he wanted nothing more than to get as far from the smell as he could manage.

But he couldn't do that.

No longer could he shirk his responsibilities as protector of his Grove. The panther was gone, and so, he needed to step up and fulfill his role. To that end, he followed the Voxxian creature through the forest.

It was small, barely as big as a midsize dog, and its sleek body was covered in blue-green scales that shimmered in the scant rays of light that managed to pierce the forest's canopy. In any other situation, the reptilian monster would have been beautiful, at least in its own odd way. However, with every step it took, the land was further despoiled.

It was a virus. A foreign entity that could only spread rot, disease, and destruction. With something like that, there was no coexistence. It was kill or be destroyed, with no compromise in between.

So, cloaked in Shape of the Predator, Elijah hunted.

It had been two days since he'd gained the spell, and in that time, he'd gained significant mastery over his new form. He knew he was no match for the panther that had died protecting the island from the invaders, but he was rapidly closing that gap. One day, he hoped he could rival its power.

But for now, he stalked the Voxxian monster.

When it leaped between two rocks, Elijah pounced. His claws flashed as he raked them across its scaly back, and to his surprise and satisfaction, they parted beneath his natural weapons. As Elijah's weight fell upon it, the monster screeched in pain and shock, but it quickly recovered and flexed its elongated neck as it tried to bite him. Elijah pressed down on it with every ounce of Strength he possessed, holding it there for a few long seconds before he brought his teeth to bear.

In only a moment, he'd clamped his jaws around its comparatively smaller skull. He squeezed, and his efforts were rewarded with the sound of cracking bone.

And the most repulsive taste imaginable.

It was like ash and oil mixed with rubber, and the moment it hit his tongue, he was forced to resist the urge to recoil. Instead, he redoubled his efforts, trying to end the fight before it could even begin. The monster struggled, wiggling beneath Elijah's comparatively larger form, but it was no use.

After a few more moments, the pressure finished its work, and the monster's skull collapsed entirely, squirting brains, blood, and whatever else the monster had inside its head into Elijah's mouth.

The second the monster was dead, Elijah bounded backward, spitting and hissing with every foot he could put between himself and the detestable creature. His efforts were useless, and the horrid taste remained. However, he still felt a deep sense of satisfaction as he watched the monster's death spasms.

Finally, once it was dead, he let his spell lapse, and over the next few moments, he reverted to his human form. It was still a strange transition, going from a four-legged mist panther to standing upright, and Elijah assumed that the process was helped along by magic. Otherwise, it would have assuredly been far more jarring.

Over the past couple of days, Elijah had learned a few things about his class's defining spell. First, as he'd discovered on that very first day, his clothing transformed with him. Where it went he had no idea, but he was grateful for the fact that he didn't have to walk around naked every time he transformed back into a human. By this point, his clothes didn't cover much—his shirt had been cannibalized for various projects, and his pants had been ripped to shreds below the knee—but he still appreciated the coverage all the same.

The second thing he had discovered was that his staff transformed with him, as well. Other weapons did not, though Elijah had no idea why that would be the case. The only answer that made sense was, as always, that it was all magic he didn't really understand. Hopefully, he would learn more as he made his way through the transformed world.

Finally, through trial and error, he'd learned that transforming into a mist panther vastly increased his Dexterity and Strength, which was reflected in his status. Numerically, the spell added ten points to both of those attributes while increasing his Constitution by a comparatively smaller three points. Considering that he couldn't cast any spells while transformed, the additional points in his physical attributes were a welcome—and wholly necessary—part of the ability.

Elijah leaned on his staff as he watched the monster's death throes. It was the fourth such creature he'd killed in the past two days, and the moment it had died, he received a new notification:

Congratulations! You have reached level eleven. Attribute points allocated according to your class.

Elijah was still of two minds about the fact that he had no say-so in his attribute allocation. However, he couldn't argue with the fact that, instead of two points, he received five with each level. They were spread across his entire status, but given the nature of his new class, the even distribution seemed appropriate. After all, he still had his druid spells, which required Ethera to cast, but he also needed the physical attributes if he was going to be effective in his mist-panther form.

He truly was a jack-of-all-trades, which was both comforting and disappointing. Comforting because he liked the idea of being capable of combating any situation that might come up, but disappointing because he knew he'd never be as powerful as a specialist.

Probably.

While that made sense, it functioned off of the assumption that the world—and classes—were balanced. There was no guarantee that that was the case, though. For all he knew, there were extraordinarily powerful classes that gave people godlike power. Or classes that gave people almost nothing. It was all a mystery to him, and aside from Nerthus, who seemed extremely restricted in what he could say, there was no one for Elijah to ask for advice. So, he had to discover most things for himself.

Unfortunately, one of those discoveries happened shortly after he reached level eleven. He'd fully expected to get another spell, much as he had with every other previous level. However, he quickly discovered that that wasn't the case.

He knew he should be happy with his additional attributes, but he'd been looking forward to getting a new spell. Sighing, he just shook his head and hoped that he would get one when he reached level twelve.

With that, Elijah set off back to the Grove, stopping by at the stream so he could rinse the foul taste of the Voxxian monster from his mouth. When he reached the Grove, he was unsurprised to find that the three trees that would eventually become his home had continued to grow, twining together to create a sizable floor. Suspended about ten feet off the ground, it spread out for around a hundred feet in every direction, meaning that, once it was finished, it would end up being quite a large house.

For now, though, he set himself up beneath what would eventually become the floor and leaned against one of the trunks. There, he focused his mind on the ambient Ethera and began to meditate. The process wasn't overtly effective, but the swirling Ethera did help him relax, which was sorely needed, given his situation.

After a while, Elijah slipped off into a fitful sleep, only waking when the sun rose the next morning. Starting that morning, his life took on a decided rhythm. Most of his time was spent hunting the Voxx. He had no idea where they were coming from, but he killed at least a couple each day. Most were small, but over the next few weeks, he managed to kill a couple that rivaled the one he'd fought in the minor dimensional rift in size.

When he wasn't hunting the Voxx, Elijah was either meditating, gathering food, or exploring his island. And slowly but surely, he made progress in each arena. So, by the time spring became summer, he'd managed to progress far more than he ever thought possible. Never was that more apparent than when he looked at the ladder:

Planetary Power Rankings (Earth)

Oscar Ramirez—Level 31
Sadie Song—Level 28
Lisa Song—Level 28
Hu Shui—Level 26
Ram Khandu—Level 25
Anupriya Pandey—Level 24
Kimberly Jackson—Level 24
Michael King—Level 23
Gunnar Lindstrom—Level 23
Niko Song—Level 23
. . .
. . .
. . .
Elijah Hart—Level 18

He thrust both of his hands into the air in celebration as he saw that he'd managed to break into the top one hundred. He was only five levels away from getting into the top twenty-five, too. However, getting to level twenty-three would technically put him on equal footing with a few of the top ten. How the System differentiated between people of the same level, he didn't know. Regardless, he didn't really care about rankings. He cared about power, and after his slow start, he'd truly begun to gain on the leaders.

Not that he was competing with the rest of humanity. Not really, at least. Instead, he just wanted enough Strength to do what was necessary. Hopefully, his latest gains would assist in that endeavor. He took a look at his status, feeling a deep sense of satisfaction at what he saw.

Name	**Elijah Hart**		
Level	**18**		
Archetype	**Druid**		
Class	**Animist**		
Specialization	**N/A**		
Alignment	**N/A**		
Strength	**19**		
Dexterity	**18**		
Constitution	**19**		
Ethera	**27**		
Regeneration	**21**		
Attunement	**Nature**		
Cultivation			
Body	**Core**	**Mind**	**Soul**
Wood	**Unformed**	**Opal**	**Neophyte**

His attributes were so much higher than they'd been even a few weeks before. However, he'd confirmed that each attribute point seemed to mean less and less as he grew in power. As far as he could tell, each point gave him the same benefit, but relative to his overall power, it just meant less. For instance, if each point of Strength let him lift an extra twenty pounds, that additional Strength would be a lot more noticeable when he could only lift forty total pounds than when his total capacity was in the hundreds of pounds.

In any case, Elijah was satisfied with his progress, especially considering that he'd had to do it all alone. Judging by the surnames of some of the other top one hundred, that wasn't the case with most people. For example, three people with the Song surname were in the top ten, suggesting that they were all leveling together. It didn't take a genius to reason that they all had complimentary classes and abilities, and even if they didn't, there was value in cooperation. Human beings were social animals, after all.

In addition to the extra attribute points that came with each level, Elijah had also gotten a few new spells. Instead of getting one every level, as he had for the first ten, he now got access to a new spell every other level. That meant that, since gaining his class, he'd gained four new spells.

He pulled up the individual spell descriptions:

Essence of the Wolf	**Channel the alacrity of the wolf, increasing movement speed by 20%. Combat cancels effect.**

The first spell, called Essence of the Wolf, was similar to the others in the essence line in that it enhanced his physical abilities. However, unlike Essence of the Monkey or Essence of the Boar, it didn't provide straight attribute bonuses. Instead, it simply made him run faster—a boon that he had used to great effect while exploring the island. Thankfully, it didn't take up one of his augmentation slots, so he didn't have to make a choice between using it or enhancing his other attributes. The only issue was that the benefits fell away when he entered combat.

Ward of the Seasons	**Harness the power of the seasons, increasing resistance to elemental damage (Water, Earth, Fire, and Air).**

The next new spell, which he'd gotten at level fourteen, was called Ward of the Seasons. It did take up one of his augmentation slots, so it was often forgotten. Certainly, he could see the benefits of the spell, which promised to decrease the damage he took from elemental spells. However, because he'd been fighting nothing but animals and Voxx, none of which had access to spells, he hadn't seen much use for it. Perhaps that would change in the future, though. For now, he mostly ignored it.

Guise of the Unseen	**Fade into your surroundings. Not usable in combat.** **Requires: Shape of the Predator.**

At level sixteen, he'd gotten an ability that was only usable when he took on the form of a mist panther. However, even with that limitation, it was incredibly useful. As a hunting cat, he was already incredibly stealthy, but using Guise of the Unseen made him all but completely undetectable. He'd tested it out against various animals, and unless he actively tried to be seen, he was almost entirely invisible. Of all his abilities, it was probably the one that had affected his everyday hunting the most.

Healing Rain	**Conjure a nourishing storm that heals allies.**

Once again, Elijah could see how his level-eighteen spell could be useful. He'd used it a few times, just to get a feel for it, and he'd discovered that it had a couple of points in its favor. First, it took almost no Ethera to cast, meaning that it was incredibly efficient. The downside to that was that it wasn't nearly as fast acting as Touch of Nature. A wound that Touch of Nature could heal in minutes took hours for Healing Rain to treat.

The second positive aspect of the spell was that the storm it conjured lasted for hours while covering an area that extended around twenty feet in each direction. So, if he ever encountered allies, he could heal multiple people at once with the spell. For now, though, Elijah used it to heal minor injuries and to stave off fatigue while Touch of Nature was more geared toward healing more urgent wounds.

Both had their places and were potent parts of his tool kit.

All in all, Elijah was satisfied with his progress. However, he couldn't help but feel that he wasn't going fast enough. The settlement across the strait had continued to grow, and despite his efforts, the infestation of the Voxx had only grown worse since the death of the panther. Unless something changed, and soon, he would be overwhelmed.

For now, though, he could only keep going the way he was and hope that it would be enough.

37

SURVIVAL ISN'T LIVING

Elijah bounded off the embankment, using his enhanced Strength to launch himself at the enormous crab. At some point within the past few weeks, the crabs had experienced another growth spurt, and they had reached absolutely gargantuan proportions. With claws as big as motorcycles and a body that would rival a Volkswagen Bus in size, it truly had earned the monster label.

With that increase in size came the mixed news that they'd begun preying on one another. Usually, when he came within a few hundred yards of the beach, his ears would be assaulted by the thunderous sounds of clacking claws and colliding car-sized crabs. On the surface, that didn't seem like such a bad thing, and usually, it made hunting the distracted or often-wounded creatures much easier. However, their increased size and decreased availability presented a new problem.

Food storage.

Ever since the very beginning, Elijah had depended on the crabs as his primary source of protein and fat. He'd supplemented it with various small game and fish, but crabmeat had always been the backbone of his diet. And though he often found himself looking at the lumpy bits of white meat with disgust, he knew he couldn't afford to ignore such a ready source of food.

However, because the crabs had grown so large and combative with one another, when he killed and harvested one, he was forced to make that meat last. Which wouldn't have been a problem if he had some means of refrigeration, but with spring already turning to summer, crabmeat was quick to spoil. So, he'd ended up wasting far more than he ate. Again, that wouldn't have been such a problem if they'd remained as numerous as before, but due to their habit of fighting and killing one another, that just wasn't the case anymore.

Still, that was a problem for another time, and Elijah focused on the fight at hand.

Or, rather, the slaughter.

For all their size, the mutated crabs were completely incapable of keeping up with Elijah's enhanced speed. Even if he'd been in human form, he could have run circles around the thing. The only dangerous bit came from how quickly it could bring its oversized claws to bear, but Elijah was an experienced enough crab hunter that he was never in any real danger.

First, he let his bounding leap take him to the top of the creature's muddy-brown shell. It spun in circles, trying to dislodge him, but he dug his claws into the surface and raced toward its head. Once there, he lashed out with his claws, severing the creature's eyestalks. It let out a whistling howl—a sound that enormous crabs apparently could make—as it tried to buck him off, but Elijah was already on the move, leaping from his perch and landing on the rocky shore.

Once there, he raced off into the nearby brush where he waited for the crab to lose interest. For all that the crabs had grown in size, their intelligence had not increased apace, and as a result, they were just as stupid as always. A good thing, too, because otherwise, Elijah would've had difficulty bringing them down.

Once the crab lost interest, it meandered around, confused and lacking the senses it needed to navigate the world. Even if Elijah left, it would soon succumb to some other predator—or to another crab. He didn't revel in the thing's suffering, but killing was a part of life in any ecosystem. If he wanted to survive, the crab needed to die by any means necessary. Suffering just didn't enter into his thought process. It couldn't.

Now that he was out of combat—a nebulous state that he couldn't really explain, save that he knew it when he felt it—Elijah embraced Guise of the Unseen, letting himself fade from view. It wasn't invisibility. Not exactly, at least. But it was the closest thing to it, and he knew that most creatures would have trouble detecting his presence unless he got really sloppy.

Which had happened more often than Elijah liked. While he had the instincts of a hunting cat to call upon, he was still new to it all. As such, he'd experienced almost as many failures as successes. So, he'd learned to handicap his prey any way possible. Thus, his attack on the crab's primary sensory organs.

He stalked forward, confident in his ability to remain undetected as he passed beneath the monster's shell. Because the crabs had a habit of standing extremely still when they couldn't see—it was a new development from the unmutated versions, but Elijah had observed it on enough occasions to trust it—he moved beneath the creature's body without hesitation. Once he reached the appropriate spot, he lashed out, plunging his claw deep into its relatively unprotected underbelly and destroying the nerve center closest to its head. With that done, he darted out from beneath it just before it collapsed.

It wasn't dead yet, but it was only a matter of time before it succumbed.

As he watched it slowly die, Elijah regretted that he couldn't have finished it off more quickly. Before, when he could simply flip the thing on its back, it was easy enough to destroy the second nerve cluster and kill it, but with how large it had grown, that was simply impossible. So, he had no choice but to watch it slowly perish.

However, only a few minutes into the process, an acrid scent wafted toward Elijah. The moment it hit his nostrils, he dashed away. It was just in time, too, because, only a second later, a Voxxian monster the size of a pony crashed into the spot he'd just vacated.

Like all the Voxx Elijah had seen, this newcomer was reptilian in appearance, with viridian scales, wicked talons, and sharp teeth. However, this one was also equipped with a thick, meaty tail that reminded Elijah of a crocodile.

Except for the spikes jutting from the end.

It recovered quickly, spinning around and using its tail as a weapon. Elijah leaped high into the air, avoiding a blow that would surely have skewered him, but the lizard-like Voxx was ready for that move, and it continued its spin by aiming a raking claw in his direction. Elijah tried to twist out of the way, but being suspended in midair, he had no leverage. So, although he managed to avoid the worst of it, he still took a blow to his side.

Blood gushed from the resultant wound, showering the Voxxian monster in red rain. It opened its mouth and screeched in obvious ecstasy as the momentum of the attack sent Elijah spinning through the air only to skid across the rocky beach before colliding with the dying crab.

He ignored his wound, leaping to his feet just in time to dodge the Voxxian monster's next blow, and he managed to clip it with a responding attack that easily parted the scales on its shoulder before landing lightly and taking off into the brush. The lizard-like Voxx crashed through the forest after him.

Elijah had come a long way since his first encounter with a Voxxian monster, and so he wasn't the helpless prey he'd once been. No—he'd spent weeks honing his skills as a hunter, and now that he'd recovered from the surprise attack, it didn't take him long to gather his wits and turn the tables on the creature.

And while he might've been comparatively vulnerable on the beach, he was completely at home in the forest that had been his home for the better part of a year. With the failure of its ambush, the monster never had a chance.

Over the next few minutes, Elijah engaged in hit-and-run tactics. He didn't try to kill the thing with a single blow. Instead, he utilized the death-by-a-thousand-cuts mentality. Soon enough, the wounds he'd opened with his first few attacks began to fester, and the monster stumbled. It quickly righted itself, but it was the beginning of the end.

Contagion, the passive ability that came with Shape of the Predator, usually didn't come into play. However, in a long and drawn-out confrontation, it showed its worth when the accelerated infection began to do its work. Elijah could have left it there and, like he'd done with the crab, simply waited on the monster to die. However, he chose to use the encounter to hone his skills. So, over the next hour, he continued to harass the creature until, at last, it fell over and died.

Elijah approached, ignoring the acrid scent assailing his nostrils as he beheld his handiwork. The Voxxian monster's scales had become a mass of shallow cuts, and the barely visible flesh beneath had turned a sickly green color with infection. It had been a useful fight, but even the day's two kills hadn't given him enough energy to gain a level.

Which was frustrating. It had been almost a week since he'd achieved level eighteen, and he'd yet to progress any further. That stall had already resulted in him falling off the ladder, which only exacerbated his annoyance.

After ensuring that the monster was dead, Elijah returned to the beach to find that his crab was already being consumed by another of the creatures. So, with a feline sigh, he set about repeating his actions, killing the oversized crab with little difficulty. Then, he let Shape of the Predator fall away, resuming his human form.

Of late, he'd spent most of his time as a mist panther, and as a result, returning to his natural body left him feeling momentarily awkward. Once he'd taken the time to harvest the huge crab's claws, he set off back to the Grove. Along the way, he stopped by to wash the blood from the wound on his side. Upon inspection, he saw that the monster's attack had actually exposed his ribs.

After cleaning up, he continued on his way, carrying an enormous crab claw on either shoulder. Once, he would've had trouble with such a feat of Strength. Certainly, when he'd first washed ashore, he'd have been entirely incapable of even dragging such heavy appendages. But now? With his increased Strength, the only barrier was how awkward the burden was to carry.

When he reached the Grove, he took a few moments to look around before heading to the underside of what would become his house. The roof still wasn't finished, so he'd yet to move in. However, it was growing closer to completion with every passing day. Still, he found it difficult to take pleasure in its construction.

Because he was frustrated with his slow progress.

Elijah had never been the most competitive person in the world. Sure, he wanted to win any competition he participated in, but losing hadn't put him in a foul mood. Not like it had with his sister. Indeed, she had always been the truly competitive one, and if Elijah was honest, he'd half expected to see her name at the top of the ladder. She was the high achiever, after all.

But now? Having tasted a bit of success, Elijah desperately wanted to continue climbing the ladder, and not just for the sake of doing so. He knew he needed to get stronger. The Voxx continued to assault his island, and even if they hadn't, there were the people across the strait to worry about. If he truly wanted to protect his Grove, he needed to grow more powerful, and fast.

And just when he'd started to roll, his progress had stalled.

His frustrations continued to mount as he stored his crab claws away in a woven basket he'd made for that very purpose. Then, he removed his clothing and cast Healing Rain. A small, localized storm cloud manifested, and a moment later, a steady drizzle fell from the sky. Elijah sat down and placed his hand over his wound before casting Touch of Nature. The combination of the two healing spells quickly mended his flesh, and soon enough, Elijah was entirely whole.

But he was still too frustrated to sink into meditation, so he took a few moments to inspect his garden. The berries he'd grown were almost ripe, which would be a boon for his food supply. To quicken the pace, he spent an hour steadily pulsing Nature's Bounty.

After that, Elijah made a circle around the Grove, using his spells to ensure that the trees continued their own growth. According to Nerthus, the Grove would continue to mature, and it would eventually encompass the entire island. Hopefully, at that point, the steady invasion of Voxx would cease.

Once he'd completed a few circuits around the Grove, Elijah retreated to his temporary home beneath what would become his permanent house and ate some stew he made from mushrooms, wild onions, and of course, crabmeat. It was not pleasant, but he ate it, anyway.

As he sat there spooning the vaguely edible concoction into his mouth, Elijah pondered the nature of life. Survival, he reasoned, wasn't enough. Not really. Eventually, endeavoring to simply live another day would lose its luster. He missed company. He missed good food prepared by people who actually knew what they were doing. He missed his family. He missed so many things about his old life.

Sure, he'd gotten a second chance when his terminal cancer had been cured. He even got magic powers out of the deal. But was he really living?

No. He certainly wasn't.

It was at that moment that Elijah resolved to change that. He still needed to ensure the Grove's survival, and eventually, he would have to do something about his aggressively industrious neighbors across the strait. But once he'd accomplished those goals, he decided to look for civilization, to find his sister, nephew, and sister-in-law, and to actually start living his life.

But as he looked up at the star-filled sky, he realized that those goals were probably a long way from becoming reality. For one, the world had been transformed. One of the very first notifications he'd read said that the Earth would experience selective randomization. And clearly, they had alien visitors. The fact that he'd helped kill a goblin, gnome, and dwarf proved that much. So, he reasoned that finding his way back to Seattle would probably be much more difficult than he could imagine.

Sighing, he lay back and closed his eyes. It would be difficult, sure. But that was fine. He had magic powers, after all. He could handle a little journey. With that in mind, he felt a little better about his situation.

38

TOWERS AND RIFTS

As summer laid its hand over the region, the island transformed. Flowers bloomed, fruit ripened, and wildlife became more active than ever before. Elijah was no exception, spending his days hunting and exploring. It wasn't long before he'd visited every corner of his island, and his efforts as a hunter were more successful than not. In short, he began to thrive.

However, despite his efforts in keeping the island clear of Voxx, he'd only barely progressed to level nineteen. Fortunately, that got him back on the ladder, if only into the ninety-ninth spot. Still, it was progress, and he appreciated the allocation of the additional attribute points that came with the level.

As he sat in his Grove, he looked at his status, a habit he'd developed over the months since he'd been stranded on the island. Barely a day went by when he didn't flick the window open and study his progress. Most of the time, there was nothing to see, but he still did it, nonetheless. That action came with varying degrees of pride and disappointment, depending on his mood.

Pride because he'd come a long way in a little more than a year. When he'd washed ashore, suffering from cancer treatments and terminal cancer, he'd been incredibly weak. In fact, he was so powerless that a few overgrown crabs had nearly killed him. Since that time, his Strength had grown by leaps and bounds, rendering survival trivial.

But he knew just how far he was behind the others at the peak. The ladder spoke for itself, after all. So, while his progress had been substantial, Elijah couldn't help but think that it wasn't enough.

The same could be said for the Grove, which had been transformed by his presence. What had been a simple field with a lone tree at the center had become a beautiful and thriving garden, ringed by a tower of trees and featuring lush vegetation that had been enhanced by his abilities. The only thing it was missing was a water feature until it could rival the elaborate and well-tended botanical gardens he'd visited before Earth was transformed.

But it wasn't enough—not to become the safe haven he and Nerthus had envisioned.

The coalition of dwarves, gnomes, and goblins across the strait had continued to settle the area, and their little town had become a thriving city with a population in the thousands. The surrounding landscape had been decimated, and though they hadn't covered everything with concrete like humanity was wont to do, it still smacked of the artificial. More, they'd begun to expand their efforts into the sea, sending sizable ships out that soon returned with massive whales in tow.

Elijah had never been a true conservationist, but there was enough of the marine biologist left in him that he saw whaling as an abominable practice. Once, humanity had driven the mighty creatures to near extinction, so he couldn't help but feel a sense of anger as he saw those carcasses being dragged into the strait.

But he couldn't do anything about it.

There were no regulations anymore. Not that he knew of, at least. And if the state of the crabs was any indication, those whales were probably more than capable of defending themselves. But that didn't really affect the way he felt about any of it.

The fact was that he was inadequate, and his efforts to change that had so far come up short.

So far.

He still had time, but the settlement continued to grow with every passing week. Soon, they would expand to his island. Why they hadn't done so, aside from sending the trio that had run into the panther, was a mystery he'd yet to solve.

Shaking his head, Elijah took one last look at his status:

Name	**Elijah Hart**
Level	**19**
Archetype	**Druid**
Class	**Animist**
Specialization	**N/A**
Alignment	**N/A**
Strength	**20**
Dexterity	**19**
Constitution	**20**
Ethera	**28**
Regeneration	**22**
Attunement	**Nature**

Cultivation			
Body	**Core**	**Mind**	**Soul**
Wood	**Unformed**	**Opal**	**Neophyte**

Sighing, he pushed himself to his feet and looked around. Behind him, his home was nearing completion. The branches had woven together, giving it a rounded shape that culminated in a leafy and impenetrable canopy that, when it was finished, would block out the elements. The interior construction—or growth, if he was being accurate—hadn't even begun, but according to Nerthus, that wouldn't take long to complete.

Almost as soon as he thought of the tree spirit, Elijah felt a stirring in the ambient Ethera that announced Nerthus's arrival. He looked up to see the vaguely humanoid knot of twisted roots and said, "You're popping up a little more often lately."

"The Ethera climbs a bit more each day," Nerthus said in his whispering-wind voice. "Soon, it will be capable of supporting my continuous presence."

Elijah nodded. "I have questions," he said.

"As is your habit," Nerthus replied from his perch.

"You've talked about those dimensional rifts," he started. "The one I closed was a minor version, right?"

"It was."

"But there are presumably major ones, as well, right? And you said something about towers before. Can you explain how that works?" Elijah asked.

Nerthus cocked his head to the side, then, after a moment, said, "Some."

Elijah gestured for him to go on, but when Nerthus clearly didn't take the hint, he said, "Okay? Go ahead."

"The minor dimensional rift is the second-weakest version of a Voxx incursion," he stated. "If left to its own devices, it will eventually spew forth a small horde of comparatively weak creatures."

"Second weakest? What's the weakest?" Elijah asked, already guessing the answer.

"The spontaneous manifestations. Singular Voxx who manage to tear through the dimensional membrane and invade the world. *Weak* is a bit of a misnomer, though. Typically, the creatures that come through spontaneous manifestations are much more powerful than those in minor rifts. These you have encountered, as well."

Elijah nodded along. That explained why he'd never been able to find the source of the monsters he routinely killed. If they were spontaneous manifestations, then there was no source. They simply appeared.

"What causes them?" he asked.

"A combination of factors I am prohibited from explaining to you."

Elijah sighed. It was so frustrating, having a source of information so close but being incapable of getting what he needed. It felt like reading a book that was missing pages.

"Okay, what comes after the minor dimensional rifts? Major ones?"

"No. After that comes average dimensional rifts. Then major. And finally, primal realms. There are more dangerous incursions but not on this planet. Not yet."

"What else can you tell me?"

"Average dimensional rifts are little different from the one you encountered. They act as a simple bridge between our two realities, and the creatures they manifest will be dependent on the region and ambient Ethera levels."

Elijah latched on to the last part, asking, "So, you're saying that as ambient Ethera levels rise, the Strength of the Voxx will rise, too?"

"Yes," Nerthus answered. "Until the planet stabilizes, you will face increasingly powerful Voxx."

Elijah sighed. "Fantastic," he muttered to himself. "Okay, so what about the major dimensional rifts? And the primal realms? Are there any of those around here?"

"No. You would know if you were anywhere near a primal realm."

"What—"

"I am prohibited from revealing anything else about primal realms."

Elijah shook his head, then asked, "What about major dimensional rifts, then?"

"Those are . . . different," said Nerthus.

"How so?"

For the first time, Nerthus looked flustered. "Towers," he said, obviously straining. "Look for towers."

"I don't—"

"I can say no more on the subject," Nerthus said. "Just . . . Just remember what I said."

Then, without any further warning, the little tree spirit retracted into his branch, disappearing entirely. Obviously, he'd overstepped, and as a result, he was incapable of sustaining his presence. Was that the secret, then? Was it a matter of energy keeping Nerthus from revealing too much? Elijah had no idea, and he suspected that it would be some time before he got any more answers.

However, the information Nerthus had revealed was incredibly useful. Because Elijah had seen something that might have been the top of a tower. During his exploration of the island, he'd seen a rocky spire a few hundred yards out to sea. At the time, he'd thought it just a curious rock formation, but now that he knew what to look for, he could easily imagine that it was the top of a tower.

Or perhaps he was just grasping at straws. After all, there was nothing else to suggest that there was a major dimensional rift near his island. But then again, perhaps its presence was the reason Nerthus had strained his limitations to give him the small but necessary bit of information that would steer him in the right direction.

But if there was a tower near the island, then it represented both a danger and an opportunity. Since the beginning, the ambient levels of Ethera had continued to rise, and according to Nerthus, the relative danger of the dimensional rifts rose right along with it. So, if there was a tower, it made far more sense to deal with it as soon as possible rather than let it continue to strengthen.

Or fester. That seemed a more accurate word, given the nature of the Voxx.

Was he ready to face such a challenge, though? His cautious nature screamed at him to avoid finding out. Hunting a few monsters that had manifested on his island was one thing, but to enter a major dimensional rift? That seemed like a recipe for disaster, especially considering that he'd nearly died in the minor version.

In fact, if he chose to combat the new threat—if it even it existed—he'd be skipping an entire level. Logically, he should look for an average dimensional rift, then work his way up from there. Instead, he was thinking about jumping from the lowest level threat to one of the highest, with nothing in between.

But was that accurate? He'd been hunting and killing Voxxian monsters for months, and he'd gained more than ten levels since defeating the minor dimensional rift. Maybe that would be enough to see him through.

Elijah sighed and sat down, leaning against the ancestral tree that was Nerthus's home. The reality of his situation was that he didn't have much in the way of options. He knew he wasn't ready to face the people across the strait. That was an indisputable fact that was supported by verifiable events. He had seen the panther in action, and he knew that, even now, he couldn't have stood up to it. And it had been killed by the people from across the strait.

Without Elijah's interference, they'd have done it without much difficulty, too.

That meant that they were still far above him in terms of power. And soon enough, they'd come to the island. He knew that as well as he knew anything else in the transformed world. Nerthus had said as much, but Elijah's surety came from observation. He'd seen them consume and destroy everything they saw, and it wasn't difficult to infer that, if they knew about the existence of the ancestral tree, they would aim their destructive tendencies in the island's direction.

The only thing standing in their way was Elijah himself. And he wasn't ready to fight them off. He'd long known that he needed to get stronger, and he'd diligently worked toward that goal ever since the panther's death.

But his progress had stalled.

He needed a jolt to get him back on track, and the unconfirmed presence of a tower represented just such an opportunity. It just made sense to challenge it. After all, defeating the minor dimensional rift had given him three free attribute points. What potential rewards might a more powerful rift offer?

Elijah shook his head. No matter how much he wanted to get stronger, there was no way he could convince himself to walk into unknown danger. He had no real context to guess what a major dimensional rift would entail, and if he went in blind, he would probably end up dead.

Certainly, he liked the idea of getting stronger at all costs. He wanted to gain levels, get attribute points, and learn new spells. But slow, steady, and alive was much better than quick and dead.

However, he did decide to check out the rocky pillar to see if it was, indeed, a tower. Scouting the area didn't mean throwing himself into danger. He would just investigate, then make further decisions from there.

With that in mind, he rose and cast Essence of the Wolf, then Essence of the Monkey, and finally, embraced One With Nature. Stretching, he reveled in the increased power of his enhancements, then cast Shape of the Predator. Over the past few weeks, he'd spent more time as a mist panther than as a human, and the transformation felt comfortable in a way his humanity couldn't match.

Perhaps it was the increased power, or maybe it was just easier to live as an animal. After all, with the transformation came the increased focus of a predator. And with so much stimuli tickling his senses, it was difficult to think about philosophical questions concerning loneliness, disappointment, and the future. Whatever the case, Elijah found it so much easier to focus on the task after the transformation completed.

He set off across the island, moving with incredible swiftness as he bounded over fallen trees, climbed hills, and leaped across wide depressions. Some of that speed came from the mist panther form, which increased his Dexterity and Strength attributes. Further adding to points to his status was Essence of the Monkey, which gave him an extra five points in Dexterity. The bonuses that came with One With Nature were a bit more nebulous in that it didn't award temporary bonuses to his attributes. Instead, it just made him stronger, more durable, and more coordinated than normal. Alone, none of the enhancements were too overwhelming, but when taken as a whole? The increased power was significant.

Finally, adding to his speed was Essence of the Wolf, which gave him an extra twenty percent movement speed. The end result was that he was more than twice as fast as he would've been without his various augmentations, and he covered the distance to the southern shore in a fraction of the time it would've taken him to travel the distance in his human form.

So, it was only about fifteen minutes before he reached his destination, which was a steep cliff that looked like someone had simply sliced into the side of a hill. As he stood at the top of the cliff, Elijah glanced down at the crashing waves more than a hundred feet below before letting his eyes wander out to sea.

In the distance—maybe two or three hundred yards away—he saw a rocky pillar jutting approximately fifty feet above the surface of the water. There were a few more fingers of stone surrounding it, but they barely crested the waves.

From a distance, the pillar looked natural. However, after Elijah let Shape of the Predator fall away and used Eyes of the Eagle to magnify his vision, he saw that beneath that rocky exterior was something that looked man-made. There were too many straight lines for it to be natural.

He couldn't be certain unless he dove into the sea, but Elijah's instincts—or maybe his sense for Ethera—told him that he'd found a tower.

39

THE ILLUSION OF PEACE

Elijah leaned against the ancestral tree, slowly chipping away at the hunk of wood that he hoped would one day become a recognizable figure. But even with the knives he'd taken from the invading trio that had killed the guardian panther, it was slow going. And the results of his attempts at carving were scattered at best.

Gradually, he whittled the hunk of wood down to a basic shape. When he finished, he hoped it would resemble the first Voxxian monster he'd encountered, but he knew enough to recognize that the best he could manage was a vague likeness. That was fine, though. It wasn't as if he intended to enter into some art competition. Instead, wood carving was just a way to pass the time.

After a couple of hours, he rose and crossed the Grove. As he did so, he snatched a handful of berries from the bushes he'd cultivated and popped them into his mouth. On the outside, they resembled blackberries, but they were far sweeter than any he'd ever tasted. More, only a few could sustain him for weeks—at least according to Nerthus, who, after a dormant week, had recently returned to dole out a few parcels of information. One such nugget was that the fruit grown within his Grove was abnormally nutritious. Eventually, it would pass from abnormal to overtly magical and would offer restorative powers.

But that was a long way off.

Still, Elijah appreciated the additional taste even if he didn't really need the enhanced nutrition. Because of his hunting prowess as a mist panther, food scarcity had ceased to be a threat to his survival. Of course, a lack of variety still haunted him to the point that, when he finally managed to make good on his internal promise to explore the transformed world, he fully intended to abstain from eating shellfish for the rest of his life.

But for now, crab remained the readiest source of fat and protein. He could hunt smaller game fairly easily, but doing so just wasn't worth the energy when he could quickly and easily kill crabs and harvest their meat.

After pausing to pulse Nature's Bounty next to the bushes, Elijah continued across the glade until he reached the trio of trees that had grown together into his home. It had only just reached the point where it was livable, and he was eager to give it a look. For a long few moments, he just stood and admired the creation, though.

The trees had grown together so seamlessly that, at first glance, they looked like the same organism. From those winding trunks grew a series of branches and roots that twisted around the base of the trees, creating what looked like a spiral staircase that led to the expansive floor suspended two dozen feet from the ground. From a distance, the structure of the house itself was hidden by leaves and branches, but up close, Elijah could see the solid walls that looked to him like a woven basket made of tree limbs.

With no more hesitation, Elijah mounted the steps, feeling the branches that comprised the staircase give slightly beneath his feet. He ran his hand along the tree trunk as he followed the spiral up and into the structure itself. When he did, he found his breath catching in his throat.

Flowers danced along the ceiling, slightly glowing with soft white light that illuminated the interior. Chairs, couches, and other furniture grew from the ground, their surfaces softened by moss and leaves. When Elijah reached down to touch the closest chair, he found that it felt little different from a modern version he might've had in his old apartment back in Hawaii.

"No," he said to himself as he sat down with a grateful sigh. "This is so much better."

Of course, that might've been due to the fact that he'd spent the past year with nothing but stumps and logs as furniture.

"I am glad you like it," said Nerthus as he suddenly grew out of the floor.

"I thought you couldn't leave the ancestral tree."

"That is true," said the tree spirit, but he didn't elaborate. That led Elijah to the conclusion that his home was somehow connected to the other tree, probably in a way Nerthus was prohibited from explaining. "Would you like a tour?"

Elijah nodded, and the little tree spirit led him deeper into the house, describing the home's features along the way. To Elijah's surprise, it wasn't devoid of amenities. In fact, Nerthus had somehow incorporated a kitchen into the design. Certainly, it didn't feature an electric stove or anything of that nature, but it did have a firepit where Elijah could cook his food and a few raised, flat surfaces where he could prepare his meals.

More importantly, it had what Nerthus described as a cold box. Set into the floor, it was only a couple of feet wide and half as deep, but when Elijah opened it, he felt a blast of cool air. It wasn't quite freezing, but it reminded Elijah of a small refrigerator.

"How is this possible?"

"Ethera," Nerthus said. "I noticed that you had a food-spoilage problem, so I took the liberty of addressing it. Are you pleased?"

Elijah nodded. "I definitely am," he said. Being able to preserve his food would free up quite a bit of time, much of which had been wasted due to the need to constantly acquire fresh meat. With the cold box to preserve the meat, a lot less would spoil.

Over the next few minutes, Nerthus showed Elijah through the tree house, and to his surprise, it featured a multitude of bedrooms in addition to the kitchen, living area, and even a bathroom.

"There is no running water as yet, but in a few months, I should have enough Ethera to manage it," Nerthus stated, almost apologetically.

"No, this is great," Elijah said. Indeed, he wasn't above hauling a little water if it meant having a comfortable place to do his business. After squatting in the woods for an entire year, even having an enclosed space seemed like a nearly unimaginable luxury.

All in all, the house seemed far more elaborate and comfortable than anything he could have expected. So, over the next hour or so, he engaged in the arduous process of moving in. First, he gathered a crab claw he'd harvested earlier that day and, after cracking the shell open, deposited a good portion of the meat in the refrigerated cold box. Then, after disposing of the remnants, he headed to the stream where he washed himself. It wasn't the same as using soap and water, but he did the best he could with his limited resources.

Once he'd removed the worst of the dirt and grime—as well as the scent of the raw crab—Elijah gathered the rest of his belongings. He didn't have much. Just a few baskets full of berries and mushrooms, his carving attempts, some honey he'd harvested from a hive a few days before, and the gear he'd looted from the invaders' corpses. He'd already made use of their clothing by picking out the stitches and adjusting it to fit his much larger frame, but there were a few strips of excess cloth he'd been using as rags.

After moving everything to the house, he looked around. On the one hand, he was grateful to finally have a real roof over his head and a comfortable, safe place to sleep. However, a wave of depression came with that satisfaction, largely because he had no one to share any of it with.

Elijah had never been what anyone would call a social person. He had friends and acquaintances, but he'd always been just as happy alone in the wilderness as he was accompanied by other people. Or that was what he'd thought before spending over a year with no one but an occasionally present tree spirit for company.

As he lay in his new bed, which was incredibly comfortable, and looked up at the softly glowing flowers, he found himself wishing someone else was there to appreciate it alongside him. His sister-in-law, Carmen, would have loved it. So would his nephew, Miggy. His sister, Alyssa, would act like she didn't find it all fascinating and beautiful, but Elijah knew her well enough to know just how false her act was.

Finally, his mind wandered to his ex-girlfriend, Lacey. They'd never been truly in love. Elijah could recognize that with the distance and time stretching between them. However, for years, she had been his closest friend. Breaking up with her had been one of the most difficult things he'd ever had to do, but at the time, he hadn't wanted to burden her with the reality of watching him slowly wither away and die.

Now, he regretted that they hadn't spent more time together.

He fell asleep thinking about the times they had shared, and his dreams followed along with that theme right up until something startled him awake. He bolted upright, already embracing the Ethera in his core and priming himself to cast Storm's Fury. Jerking his head around, he saw nothing but the unfamiliar confines of his new home, which was still softly lit by the white flowers growing out of the ceiling.

"What the . . ."

A wave of dense Ethera washed over him with enough force to send his mind reeling. Before, he would've said that it was impossible for there to be too much ambient Ethera. Clearly, that was false, and the excess left him feeling dizzy enough that, if he'd been standing, his knees would have already buckled. As it was, he had to grab the wall just to steady himself.

Over the next twenty seconds or so, the level of Ethera slowly fell until it reached something closer to normal. And then, just as Elijah was thinking about standing, another wave of dense energy swept through him, starting the process anew.

Again and again, the cycle repeated over the next few hours until, at last, normality reasserted itself. By that point, Elijah was a mess. He felt alternatingly drunk, hyperaware, and everything in between.

Still, once everything settled, he managed to push himself out of bed and stumble his way out of the house. Lurching down the steps proved to be particularly perilous, and he ended up falling down the last few steps. After hitting the ground, he simply lay there for a few moments before pushing himself to his hands and knees as he tried to master himself. The results were mixed, but after a while, he climbed back to his feet and staggered toward the ancestral tree.

When he reached the tree, Elijah called out for Nerthus, and only a few seconds later, the spirit grew out of the lowest branch. "How may I . . . Oh, dear . . ."

"What's going on?" Elijah slurred.

"It is a surge," Nerthus stated. "Please listen carefully because I do not have much time. The tower, you have found it, yes?"

"I . . . Yeah . . . I found it."

"Good. Over the next few hours, the island will be inundated by wave after wave of monsters," the tree spirit said. "After a period of calm, it will repeat unless you challenge and conquer the tower."

"Conquer it? I can't . . . I'm not . . ."

Elijah's mind spun. He'd decided not to investigate the tower further, and for good reason. He had no idea what dangers lay within, and as such, he felt like challenging it would be walking to his death.

"You must. Otherwise, this island will be overwhelmed and destroyed," Nerthus said. "Conquering it will—"

Nerthus collapsed, merging with the branch before he could get another word out. He was gone so suddenly that, for a long while, Elijah could only stare at that spot.

Until he felt something enter the Grove.

Elijah's head stopped spinning, and he whipped around, already embracing his various spells. First came Essence of the Monkey. Then Essence of the Wolf. One With Nature. And finally Shape of the Predator. Even as he felt himself transforming into a mist panther, he searched his surroundings for the intruder.

It didn't take long for him to find it.

The Voxxian monster, like all the others he'd encountered, was reptilian in nature. However, it stood on two legs and reached around four feet in height. So, given that size and power were correlated—at least as far as Elijah was concerned—he didn't think the creature would give him much trouble.

Then, a second presence appeared in his senses. And a third. A fourth. They kept coming until there were ten of the Voxx stalking forward. There were subtle variations between them, but for the most part, they were similar.

Fortunately, Elijah had embraced Guise of the Unseen the moment his transformation was complete, so he was hidden from view. However, their mere presence made his stomach roil, especially when he realized that they had taken a straight line that would soon bring them to the ancestral tree.

Perhaps it was just coincidence, but Elijah suspected that it was their goal.

And he couldn't let them reach it.

So, throwing his very valid fears into the back of his mind, Elijah crept forward, intending to massacre the creatures that dared to desecrate his Grove with their horrid presence.

40

PREAMBLE TO DISASTER

Elijah stalked forward, moving as quickly as he dared without rendering his Guise of the Unseen ineffectual. The ability was usually very effective, to the point where he could sneak up on most animals without fear of being detected, but it had its limits—chiefly, that if he moved too suddenly or into bright lights, he would be seen. It was still just before dawn, so bright lights were no threat, but he had to be careful to keep his movements under control as he hurried toward the invading Voxx.

The monsters approached with little care, crashing through the underbrush as they passed the ephemeral boundary of the Grove proper. They were already within his Domain, but they had yet to pass the circle of trees that constituted his Grove. Still, he could sense them very clearly.

More, Elijah knew—how, he wasn't sure—that they were weakened by the Grove. However, he also felt the Grove's power level dip, and he inferred that, if the Voxx were left to their own devices, they would slowly drain the Grove of all Ethera and consume whatever remained of the ancestral tree.

Elijah refused to let that happen.

Not because he wanted to fight them. He didn't, especially considering that he was outnumbered ten to one. But he also didn't have much of a choice. The Grove was more than just his home. It was a stronghold against the invaders and a fortress that protected Nerthus and the ancestral tree.

And he was meant to be their protector.

So, Elijah padded forward on silent paws until he reached the first monster. On all fours, Elijah was only a few feet tall at the shoulder, so the reptilian creature loomed over him. An air of corruption wafted from its viridian scales, accompanied by the sickly sweet smell of decay. If Elijah hadn't spent the last few months hunting similar creatures, he would have been overwhelmed by disgust. However, he'd grown accustomed to their stench, and so, he barely paid it any heed as he finally pounced.

The first attack was vicious, and Elijah's claws ripped through the monster's back legs. Its scales parted easily, and his efforts were rewarded with a screech of pain and a shower of black blood. It tried to whip around with a backhanded attack, but it didn't account for its injury. For all their magical toughness, the

Voxx were still physical creatures that were dependent on muscles, bones, and ligaments. So, the moment it tried to turn, its leg collapsed beneath it, sending it stumbling to the ground.

Of course, it quickly recovered—magical durability being what it was—but by that point, Elijah was already racing into the shadows. The monster howled in pain—or perhaps in an attempt to communicate with its fellows—but it was useless. Elijah darted from the darkness, targeting the second monster with a similar attack.

It was even more effective than the last, and Elijah felt his claws scraping against bone before he bounded away.

The third monster was clearly aware of his presence, but with Guise of the Unseen active, it couldn't pinpoint his location. So, it remained rooted in place, spinning around as it tried to look everywhere at once. It was a curiously human reaction, and if Elijah wasn't in the middle of a battle, he would have wondered at its origin. As it was, he baited the Voxxian monster by letting himself be seen, then melting back into the shadows. It responded with predictable fury, rushing toward the spot where Elijah had been seen, but by that point, he was already circling around.

His subsequent attacks ripped through both of the creature's hamstrings before Elijah dashed back into the underbrush, using the shadows and his ability for cover. The next few creatures were similarly easy to manipulate, giving Elijah confidence to push himself to do a little more damage with each ambush.

It was a mistake, as was made painfully obvious when he overplayed his hand and got a claw to his rib cage for his trouble. He went tumbling into the bushes, leaving a trail of blood as he barrel-rolled to a stop. Shaking his head, he pushed through the dizziness that came from blood loss, pain, and a budding concussion from where he'd hit his head multiple times while bouncing through the forest.

Knowing that he couldn't remain stationary for long, Elijah climbed to his feet and dashed away. It was just in time, too, because one of the remaining uninjured monsters—there were only two who were at full Strength—came into view only a moment later. It stopped, sniffing the air, then turned toward where Elijah was crouched.

A horrifying grin split its reptilian face before it let out a series of barking hisses. Elijah crept backward as those barks were answered by its fellows. The creatures were communicating. Were they pack hunters, like wolves? Or was their ability to communicate more advanced? Did they have intelligence on par with humans, perhaps?

It was a daunting prospect, but one Elijah had no time to contemplate.

Elijah ran, leaving a trail of blood behind him. Doubtless, the monsters could now track him—in fact, he was hoping that they would follow, forgetting the glade until the pesky mist panther was dealt with.

For a few seconds, the creatures kept up, but Elijah quickly outpaced them and, after a few more seconds, felt his speed increase as the System deemed him to have gotten out of combat. With that, the effect of Essence of the Wolf reasserted itself, and as a result, he tore through the forest with unprecedented speed that the Voxxian creatures couldn't hope to match.

He ran, but even as his injury sapped his life, he kept his wits about him, leading the monsters on a long and winding trail before finding his way to his old cabin. By the time he reached his former home, Elijah judged that he'd put enough distance between himself and the stalking Voxx to let Shape of the Predator fall away so he could heal himself.

The only problem was that he had no real notion of how much Ethera he had available. While in his predator form, he had no sense of his core. He knew his Ethera still regenerated while he was transformed, but with everything that had happened, he knew his sense of time was skewed.

Perhaps he had enough Ethera to heal himself, but would he have enough to resume his predator form?

Whatever the case, Elijah didn't have much choice. Shape of the Predator came with significant benefits, but in the months since he'd acquired the spell, he'd learned that its durability was grossly lacking. The form was meant for hit-and-run tactics, not standing toe-to-toe with powerful monsters. As a result, he was difficult to pin down, but when he actually took a hit, he had few defenses to mitigate the damage.

When he was only fighting one enemy, it wasn't such a problem. He could pounce, ravage the opponent, then retreat while Contagion did its work. But fighting multiple enemies at once had quickly shown him his limits. He could work around them, but doing so balanced him on a razor's edge of disaster.

Hence, the retreat.

Elijah felt himself resume his human form, and to his relief, he saw that his core had refilled almost entirely. So, he slapped his hand on his side and cast Touch of Nature, channeling the ability through his Staff of Natural Harmony. Enhanced by the staff, the spell quickly took effect. On the surface, the wound closed, but it would require at least one more cast before he was back to perfect health.

He couldn't afford that.

He had neither the time nor the spare Ethera to finish the job, so after making certain that he'd stopped the bleeding, he set off through the forest. In human form, he couldn't move nearly as quickly as he had as a mist panther, but he still put his high Dexterity and Strength, as well as the effects of Essence of the Wolf, to good use.

Still, it was a journey fraught with tension as he waited for his core to replenish. He tried to still his mind and funnel more Ethera through his mind and into his soul, but with his adrenaline pumping, it was an exercise in futility. Unable to still his thoughts, he was limited to his natural Regeneration.

Elijah could only hope that it would be enough.

Bounding over a fallen tree, he slid down a dew-slick hill before popping back to his feet and sprinting forward. Somewhere behind him, Elijah heard one of the monsters crashing through the brush. They didn't bother trying to conceal their presence, and instead of leaping over obstacles, they simply tore through them.

Elijah bent his mind toward pushing his limits, and at any moment, he expected to feel a wickedly sharp claw slice through his spine. While his body might be magically enhanced, Elijah didn't think he'd make it through that, regardless of how high his endurance or Regeneration was.

A few moments later, Elijah leaped over a familiar boulder and splashed down in the stream where he got most of his water. Fortunately, that was the moment where his Ethera regenerated enough to allow him to once again assume the Shape of the Predator. He embraced the spell, and his core emptied as his body transformed.

It took a subjective eternity as his form shifted from human to panther, but the transformation completed before his Voxxian stalker climbed over the boulder. With the metamorphosis finished, Elijah took off downstream, pushing himself to his top speed.

He left the frustrated monster behind, and when he'd managed to put quite a bit of space between his position and his pursuer, he dropped to his stomach and rolled, washing the blood away in the process before doubling back. As he did so, he cloaked himself in Guise of the Unseen and resumed his hit-and-run tactics.

When he reached the nearest monster, he saw that Contagion had already begun to work its gruesome magic. The creature was still moving forward, but the ability had sapped much of its Strength. If Elijah left it alone, there was every possibility that the infection would eventually kill it off.

But he wasn't going to take that chance. So, he climbed a tree, and when the monster passed beneath him, he pounced, raking his claws across its shoulders as he clamped his jaws down on the creature's head. It tried to throw him loose, but with Contagion coursing through its veins, it was incapable of displaying its former Strength. Elijah's jaws flexed, and a moment later, the monster's skull was crushed. It fell, dead before it hit the ground.

Elijah felt an influx of Ethera that pushed him closer to level twenty, but it wasn't quite enough to tip him over the edge.

But that was fine. He had nine more of the monsters to kill.

So, he set off through the woods, trying to ignore the foul taste in his mouth as he stalked the remaining Voxx. The first he found was one of the two uninjured, so he used similar tactics to what he'd employed at the start of the battle. Two quick claw strikes, and its hamstrings were severed. More importantly, it was infected with Contagion. Elijah moved on, disappearing into the shadows as he stalked the remaining monsters.

The next one he found was barely capable of standing on its own two feet. In his initial salvo, Elijah had severed the Voxx equivalent of one of the creature's Achilles tendons. That injury, along with the effects of Contagion, meant that its gait had been reduced to little better than an awkward stumble.

Elijah finished it off without any real difficulty.

The same could be said for the next, which fell almost as easily. The next few had huddled together as they searched for him, but their superior numbers did them little good as Elijah dashed in, slashed a few times, then used his superior speed to disappear into the forest. It took a few passes, but a few minutes later, they were all dead.

Over and over, Elijah killed the powerful monsters. With Contagion slowing them down and gradually sapping their Strength, they were no match for Elijah's combined advantages. There were a few close calls—especially when he found the lone uninjured monster—but he managed victory all the same.

He barely even took any additional wounds.

By the time it was all said and done, Elijah was absolutely exhausted, though. However, when he finally returned to his Grove, he couldn't help but feel a sense of accomplishment. Not only had he managed to defend his territory, but he'd also crossed over to level twenty. And with that came additional attributes.

Or more importantly, a new ability:

Predator Strike	**Ambush an enemy from stealth, causing increased damage. Only usable when under the effect of Shape of the Predator.**

When Elijah looked at the ability, he was elated. He'd been hoping for something he could use in his predator form, and reaching level twenty had given him precisely what he needed. He could only hope that it would be enough to get him through the ordeal laid out before him.

41

THE ENTRANCE

Elijah stalked the Voxxian monster as it, in turn, attempted to do the same to him. Of course, because he was cloaked in Guise of the Unseen, it had no clue where he was—which was precisely how Elijah liked it. As a mist panther, he was only marginally more durable than he was as a human, so caution was a necessity rather than a choice. Fortunately, his abilities made it easier.

Taking one careful step at a time, he silently closed with the monster. It was a bit bigger than the ten creatures he'd killed during the previous wave, but it was comparatively slower, as well. That meant that it was a perfect target for Elijah's brand of hunting, which involved rapid attacks and hit-and-run tactics that kept him out of harm's way.

However, this time, he had something different in mind.

Activating an ability was different than using a spell. Instead of dragging Ethera from his core, he harnessed the ubiquitous energy from his surroundings, funneling it through his mind and into his soul. From there, he let it seep into his body before darting forward and activating the ability. There were no mental commands. Instead, he simply acted according to the instincts that came with the ability.

Thus, he used Predator Strike for the first time.

His claws flashed toward the monster's spine—not an optimal target for his usual tactics, but Elijah trusted his instincts to guide him appropriately. He moved with unnatural speed, and just before his claws connected, he felt a surge of power burst forth. An instant later, he tore through the monster's back, slicing through its thick scales with ease. His claws crushed the creature's backbone, then severed its spinal cord before raking across its organs.

Elijah was so surprised by the sheer power of the attack that he almost forgot that the thing was still alive. Only at the last second did he remember to leap away. Fortunately, the lumbering creature, which was more than six feet tall and built like the world's most ill-proportioned bodybuilder, was slowed by the sudden obliteration of its spine, so even with Elijah's hesitation, its counterattack only found air.

But Elijah didn't melt back into the shadows like he normally would have. Instead, he slowly circled the Voxxian monster as it dropped to one knee. Then, unable to support itself, it fell forward.

Elijah watched as the thing struggled against its new infirmity, dragging its increasingly useless legs as it dug its claws into the loam-covered forest floor. It growled. It spat. It even barked something that might've been an attempt at communication. But Elijah simply continued to watch, waiting as Contagion, which was a passive ability that came with his transformation into a mist panther, took hold.

Gradually, the disease spread, further weakening the monster until it coughed up black blood. With a last surge of Strength, it tried to heave itself toward Elijah, but it came a half dozen feet short before, finally, it succumbed.

Elijah continued to circle, keeping his eyes and ears peeled just in case there were more monsters about. He felt nothing, but that wasn't an indicator that there were no more interdimensional invaders. In the past, he'd found a few spontaneous manifestations that specialized in stealth. If any of those had come with the second surge, he'd be far more pressed.

But Elijah found nothing.

The second surge had come a few hours after he'd killed the last of the previous wave of monstrous invaders, and according to Nerthus, that pattern would continue until he entered the tower. If he conquered it, then a period of peace would follow. If not, then the tower would disgorge a fresh wave the moment he failed.

And again every few hours after that, eventually taking over the entire area. They would eventually break down on their own—something about their natures being incompatible with Earth—but not before doing untold damage to the environment. If it happened enough throughout the world, then Earth would begin to change, eventually becoming inhospitable to the natives.

Of course, that would take hundreds of years, but according to Nerthus, it had happened often enough on other worlds that it was a very real danger for Earth's future. So, Elijah wasn't just tasked with fighting for his own island. Instead, he was fighting for the whole world.

Which was why he didn't let himself hesitate before transforming back into a human and gathering his woven satchel. It contained enough berries and mushrooms to last him about a week, which he hoped would be enough to conquer the tower. Nerthus had been silent on whether or not that was the case, which didn't fill Elijah with much confidence.

Once he'd slung the satchel across his back, he set off at a jog across the island. He was still under the effects of Essence of the Wolf, but he'd cast his other augmentations, as well. Including Essence of the Boar because, upon reaching level twenty, he'd gained another enhancement slot. Hopefully, he wouldn't need the extra Constitution that came with Essence of the Boar, but he suspected that was an impotent fantasy. Nerthus had spoken of the tower like it would be a challenge, and Elijah had learned to trust the little tree spirit's judgment. So, he was ready to be pushed to his limits.

Soon enough, Elijah reached the cliff that was his destination, and in the distance, he saw the pillar of stone protruding from the waves like a giant rocky finger. It was a foreboding sight, and not just because Elijah fully expected that entering the tower was extremely dangerous. That was part of it, but there was also a sense of unease that came with the mere sight of it.

Was that natural? Or was it part of its magic?

Elijah didn't know, and he suspected that he wouldn't soon find out. So, without further hesitation, he took a deep breath, then commenced with what would have once been an arduous climb. However, with the benefit of his increased attributes, the descent had become trivial, and soon enough, he found himself leaping into the water.

At first, Elijah tried to hold his satchel and staff above the waves, but it soon became clear that he was fighting a losing battle. So, even though he knew it would ruin most of the food inside, he stopped trying to keep the contents of the satchel dry. With the staff, at least, he was confident that it could endure the salt water fairly well. Even if it hadn't been a magical piece of equipment, it was well sealed.

Lowering his head, Elijah began to swim forward. His heart pounded as he imagined various sea creatures nibbling on his toes. Before Earth's transformation, he wouldn't have thought twice about swimming in the ocean. But now? With how much the wildlife had changed? It wasn't difficult to conjure a scenario where some overgrown fish decided that he looked like a viable meal.

Still, he didn't have much choice but to keep going forward. His Grove needed him, and if Nerthus was to be believed, so did the rest of the world. So, he pushed his fears to the back of his mind and continued with his swimming stroke.

After a while, he finally reached the pillar. Up close, he could clearly see the straight lines and the hints of intelligent design that marked it as an artificial creation. Of course, that wasn't entirely true, either. Not if one considered the towers to be natural. But Elijah didn't spend long pondering that distinction before he took a deep breath and dove into the water.

Fortunately, with his level of body cultivation, his senses had been greatly improved. Without Eyes of the Eagle, he couldn't really see farther, but obstructing forces like darkness and seawater were not the barriers to sight that they once might have been. So, when he dove beneath the waves, Elijah could see far more clearly than he'd expected.

Five smaller pillars surrounded the central column, though they didn't extend more than a foot or two above the surface. As he dove, Elijah saw that they were not, in fact, separate columns. Instead, the smaller pillars of stone connected to the larger, forming the head of a decorative staff.

Elijah categorized it that way because he quickly recognized that it was held by a giant stone hand that was, in turn, connected to an equally large arm that ended in a shoulder. Next came a torso that extended into the darkness hundreds of feet below.

He couldn't even see the seafloor.

But even so, Elijah kept going, using the shaft of the huge stone staff as a guide. Fortunately, with his enhanced attributes, he could swim far more quickly than he ever could have before becoming a druid, and as such, he quickly reached the bottom. There, he saw a landscape of flora that rivaled the island that had become his home. Seaweed danced upon the seafloor, mingling with multihued coral while giant crabs scuttled about. Fish—some of which he recognized but most species he'd never seen before—darted here and there, adding to the underwater ecosystem.

If Elijah had had a ready source of oxygen, he would have happily remained in place where he could simply observe the wondrous sight. However, the moment he'd dipped below the surface, the clock had begun to tick, and he only had a limited amount of time before even his enhanced body ran out of air. More, the tower still needed to be conquered, lest it spit more Voxxian monsters into the world.

So, without further hesitation, Elijah swam across the seafloor, carefully avoiding anything that looked particularly dangerous as he headed toward the base of what he now recognized was a giant headless statue.

When he reached his destination, Elijah was unsurprised to see what appeared to be a Greek-style temple, complete with a triangular pediment and carved columns. He was no expert on architecture, but Elijah recognized the style, nonetheless—which begged the question of how something so alien would adopt such a familiar form. Unfortunately, he didn't have the time to seek out an answer because his body had begun to protest the lack of oxygen.

So, he swam forward, intending to continue his investigation until he was forced to resurface. But soon enough, Elijah found what he was looking for in the entrance to the temple.

The portal, which extended from one column to the next, shimmered with unnatural light. Elijah kicked forward, but when he got close, he found himself hesitating. If he went in, there would be no going back. Either he conquered the tower—whatever that really meant—or he would die.

There was no in-between.

There would be no early exits.

Win or die. Those were the conditions Nerthus had described, and Elijah wasn't certain he wanted to commit to that. Not even to protect the Grove. Maybe not even to safeguard the world against an invasion of Voxx.

The smart thing to do was to head back to the island, use the boat he'd taken from the invaders to cross the strait to the mainland, then leave everything behind. He could survive the wilderness well enough, and he could start toward his goal of finding what remained of his family. Surely, they could use his help.

For a long moment, he considered abandoning his responsibilities. Did that make him a coward? Maybe. Or perhaps it simply made him smart. Because heading into unknown danger was not the intelligent thing to do, no matter how he spun it. Certainly, it might be necessary, but it definitely wasn't smart.

After a few more seconds, during which his oxygen levels continued to dwindle, Elijah made a decision. If he couldn't risk his life to protect the world—and all the people in it—he didn't deserve the second chance he'd been given. After all, he'd already made his peace with his own mortality. If he died now, he would do so trying to do the right thing.

So, he swam forward and passed through the portal.

A moment later, he fell into darkness. He tried to gasp, but he was still surrounded by water. However, unlike before, he could see nothing. Then, he remembered something his father had taught him a very long time ago.

Look for the bubbles.

The idea was simple. Bubbles would always rise to the surface. So, if he ever found himself underwater and unsure of which way to swim, he only needed to look for the bubbles. He pursed his lips and blew, resulting in a stream of bubbles that he then followed to the surface only ten feet above him.

When his head broke through, light pierced his eyes. For a second, he wondered why the light hadn't penetrated into the water, but that only lasted a moment before the need to breathe crashed into him. He took a series of deep, gulping breaths before finally taking stock of his surroundings.

He was in a cave. That much was immediately obvious. Stalactites descended from the ceiling, and a few dozen feet away, Elijah could see a rocky edifice that he hoped was the shore. So, he swam forward until he finally clapped his arm on the curiously porous rock. Like that, he remained stationary as he caught his breath.

After a few minutes, he climbed atop the boulder and pushed himself to his feet. When he did, he very nearly let out a gasp of surprise.

In the distance—maybe a quarter mile away across another expanse of water—he saw a village. That was odd enough, considering that he'd had to swim hundreds of feet below the surface to get to the portal. But what made it even stranger was that it was populated by what looked like humanoid walruses. The moment Elijah saw the creatures, a notification flashed before his eyes:

Welcome to The Keledge Tower, Level One. To advance to Level Two, complete the task before you.

Elijah shook his head, then looked at the next notification:

Task: Save the Ulthrak Village from annihilation.

Upon reading that message, he muttered, "This is a lot more involved than I expected."

42

A DRUID'S PURPOSE

Before Elijah swam to shore, he took a moment to take on the Shape of the Predator. However, the moment he did, he got a bit of a surprise when he suddenly realized that mist panthers were apparently very poor swimmers. He could stay afloat, and he could move a little, but his frantic flailing ruined any chance at maintaining Guise of the Unseen. So, he let the transformation drop and treaded water until he'd regained enough Ethera to comfortably approach the village.

By the time he did, he'd garnered enough attention from the village's occupants. Indeed, stealth had never been an option. A few of the larger creatures stood on the rocky shore, gesturing threateningly with long spears. So, when Elijah got close enough to stand, he did so, holding his hands up in a gesture of surrender.

He'd have preferred to find a different route on shore, but the lagoon was entirely enclosed. So, the stretch of beach before him—which was about three hundred yards long—was the only way out of the water.

"I come in peace," he said, hoping that there wasn't a language barrier. "I'm here to help."

That much was true. After all, the task he'd received from the tower had made it very clear that he needed to save a village. It didn't take a genius or a leap of logic to assume that the village in question lay before him. That meant that the humanoid walruses were the Ulthraks he needed to save.

Of course, that would almost assuredly require their cooperation, which was why he'd tried the peaceful approach. However, he had enough Ethera to fuel Shape of the Predator if they proved less than cooperative.

"Where'd you come from?" demanded the largest spear wielder. Like all the others, he had two arms, two legs, and opposable thumbs—which set him apart from Earth walruses—yet he still possessed the characteristic whiskers, tusks, and general girth of the creatures with which Elijah had associated him. The fact that he spoke English would have been surprising if not for two things. One, Elijah had heard the little dagger-wielding gnome speak English months before. And two, he'd grown used to the existence of Ethera-powered magic, so he didn't think anything could surprise him.

"Uh . . . The surface," Elijah said. "I don't—"

"It's a tower, Raji," said one of the other Ulthraks. "That's what old Migala's been tryin' to tell you. That's why we can't get out. That's why—"

"He's right," Elijah said, earning a glare from Raji. "My world . . . I don't know if you know anything about Earth, but this tower just popped up out of the ocean. If I don't conquer it, these things called the Voxx are going to overwhelm my home."

Honesty seemed like the best policy, especially when he got a distinct impression of danger from the overlarge Raji. Elijah had never been a great liar, anyway, and he had a feeling if he tried to make something up, he'd end up telling such an unbelievable tale that he'd end up with a spear in his gut.

Then, as Elijah was getting ready to defend himself, Raji's shoulders sagged, and he said, "I knew it. Didn't want to believe it, but . . . Well, what else could it be?"

"If you knew it, then why'd you argue with Migala all this time?" said the smaller Ulthrak. "I think you—"

Raji glared at the other humanoid walrus, which shut him up in a hurry. Elijah took that opportunity to ask, "What is going on here? I thought I was coming in here to fight corrupted reptiles from another dimension."

It sounded silly when Elijah said it, but it was the best way to describe what he'd expected out of the tower.

Raji answered, "You'd better come with us. Our survival likely depends on you."

If Elijah hadn't already been tasked with saving the village, he might've refused. However, he reasoned that completing his task would be a lot easier if he had cooperation from the people he was intended to save, so he just asked, "Are you Ulthraks, by the way? Is that your species, I mean?"

"We are."

"Oh. Okay, then. Lead on, I guess," Elijah stated, wading forward until he climbed onto shore. Once he did, Raji turned and led him into the village, which was a collection of huts that looked like they'd been built from whale bones and the hide of some sort of gray-skinned animal. And to Elijah's surprise, when he looked up, he saw stars winking back at him via a giant hole in the roof of the cavern.

He followed Raji through the village until they reached a hut that was much larger than any of the others. Along the way, they passed more of the Ulthrak villagers, many of whom were clearly female, while the smaller ones were obviously children. None of them looked particularly happy, and in fact, Elijah saw more than a few poorly dressed wounds among the villagers.

As he and Raji passed through the larger hut's door, he chanced a question, asking, "What happened here? Was there some sort of battle?"

"The water goblins," Raji said, crossing the single room and taking a seat on a large cushion. He gestured to another, saying, "Sit. I will explain everything."

"Not without me here, you won't, you big idiot," came a scathing voice from the entrance. Elijah's head whipped around, and he saw an old, incredibly thin Ulthrak standing nearby. His skin hung off of him in great bunches—like an obese man who'd recently lost most of his body weight—and he carried a crooked staff with an elaborate head of feathers. "You'll send our guest out to fight the goblins when he'd clearly be better suited for other tasks."

"He doesn't even know what's going on, Migala."

"More reason to use him to solve the real problems, hmm?"

"Just let me explain to him what's going on. Then, we'll let him pick his path. You know that's how this has to work. Curse the Gods for putting us in this situation."

"The Gods? No—curse our own weakness, Raji."

"That, too."

"Well, get on with it," said Migala, crossing the hut. He used the staff like a walking stick, but to Elijah's senses, it glowed with power. Migala must have noticed because he said, "Like my staff, hmm? Thinking about taking it? You wouldn't be the first to try."

Raji rolled his eyes—a strange sight, given he was a giant walrus man—and said, "Don't threaten him, Migala. We need his help to get out of this."

"You think there's any way out of this? No—we're doomed to a—"

Raji said, "Enough. Let me explain."

"He's too skinny. And he has so little power. A child could—"

"Enough!" Raji roared, and the smaller Ulthrak flinched back. "Enough."

"I just want to know what's going on," Elijah said. "Is this real?"

"Yes. And no," Raji stated. "The reality is that no one really knows. I remember my life. I remember fighting against the goblins. But I know that if I'm in a tower, I'm not the real me."

"Just spit it out, Raji," said Migala, who'd managed to regain some of his vigor.

"We are projections," Raji said. "Probably. If this tower is conquered, then our people will get some sort of benefit. It's all . . . fuzzy, like everything is obscured. I don't even think we're in our normal bodies."

Migala sighed. "Our people volunteered for this," he said. "We were given an opportunity to be recorded by the System, which we took in exchange for some sort of power. I don't know what. Like the big idiot there said, it's all a little fuzzy. Once the System had our souls in its grasp—"

"We're not souls, Migala."

"Sure. Our essences, then. Our reflections. Whatever the case, once it had us, we were put to work populating towers like this," he said. "For you, this is all real. But for us? When you die, we'll just loop back around and start all of this over again so the next group that comes in here will have a proper challenge. Until we satisfy the terms of our agreement. Then, this little piece will be reunited with the host, and . . . Well, the rest is all just conjecture based on blurry memories."

It was a lot to take in. If Elijah understood it right, then according to Migala, none of the people he'd seen were real. Instead, they were lifelike projections of people who actually existed—or at least had existed at some point.

"How does that even work? Do you just show up to some System kiosk and tell them you want to get recorded?" he asked.

Migala gave a derisive chuckle. "That's actually not that far off," he said. "There are people who—"

"We can't tell him any of that."

"Why not? I'm not—"

At that very moment, Migala simply ceased to exist. One second, the skinny Ulthrak was there, and the next, nothing of him remained.

"What the . . ."

"System sanction," Raji said. "Everyone has to follow the rules. I don't know anything about wherever you came from, but I'm guessing the System is fairly new to you."

"It is."

"The one thing you need to know is that the System likes its rules," Raji said. "Either you follow them, or bad things happen. Out there, you might just have a run of bad luck. Or you could end up being targeted by heaven's wrath. Probably the latter if you manage to get the System's attention. But for us, it's much, much worse. We're not physical beings, so we're easy to stamp out."

Elijah nodded. Nerthus had been prevented from answering his questions on more than one occasion, which supported Raji's explanation. Still, it seemed incredibly callous to end someone's existence over something so trivial. Sure, Migala hadn't been strictly real, but he'd clearly been capable of independent thought. Which made him real enough that Elijah felt sorry for him.

"What happens if you die?"

Raji shrugged. "I don't know," he said. "Nothing good, I'm sure. At best, I'll just cease to exist while my host continues living his life. Or hers, I suppose. But at worst? They'll be punished in some way. I feel like I used to know, but . . ."

"But it's all blurry. Yeah. You said that," Elijah said, nodding along.

"I see from your expression that you understand," Raji said. "We know we're not real, but we feel pain. We think. We have goals. We have lives. We love. We hate. And we want to live. Will you help us?"

Branching Task: Save the Ulthrak village or destroy them. Choose wisely because there are rewards at the ends of both paths.

There were probably plenty of people who would have chosen the second option. Certainly, it seemed easier. However, for Elijah, it was never really an option. There was no way he could just kill the Ulthraks he'd met. If they'd attacked him, it would have been a different story, but that wasn't how it had happened.

"Can you tell me how this all works?" Elijah asked. "Like I said, I came in here expecting to fight interdimensional reptiles."

Raji shook his head. "I can't tell you much," he said. "Not until you . . . Well, here's what I can tell you. These towers are just constructs meant to siphon Ethera from powerful interdimensional rifts. But left alone, a siphon isn't enough. It'll eventually overflow."

"The surges," Elijah said, remembering the waves of reptilian Voxx.

"That's just a side effect, but yeah. That's the gist of it. When someone like you comes in and challenges the tower, it has to spend that Ethera to run things," he explained. "And to provide rewards. So, most towers need to be constantly drained of Ethera, or . . . well, things overflow."

"But that means I'll have to keep challenging it if I want to keep this from happening again?" Elijah asked.

"In most cases, yes. There are ways around it, but . . . Well, I can't speak to that. So, will you help us?"

Elijah nodded. "I intend to, but I'm not sure what I can really do," he said. "I'm not a great fighter."

"Is the rest of your team going to join you? Did you get separated?"

"I don't have a team."

"You challenged a tower by yourself? Oh, that's not good."

"I'm beginning to realize that," Elijah said. "But I'm here now, and I don't think there's a way out unless I finish it. So, tell me what needs to be done, and I'll do what I can to help."

"What are your abilities?"

Elijah didn't want to reveal all his cards, so he chose to keep his ability to take on the form of a mist panther a secret. He said, "I can heal some, and I can—"

"You can heal? How often? And how efficiently?" the Ulthrak asked, his words tumbling out of his tusked mouth in a rapid stream.

"Um . . ."

"Never mind. We'll figure it out," Raji said, pushing his bulk upright. "Come with me."

With that, he strode from the building. Elijah sprang to his feet and hurried after him, catching up just in time to hear Raji tell the smaller Ulthrak from before to gather all the sick and wounded in the town square. The smaller walrus man rushed off, presumably to do as he was asked, and Elijah followed Raji into the center of the town, which was characterized by a tall tree with gleaming white leaves.

"So, what do you need? We don't have much coin, but—"

"I don't need anything," Elijah said. "Just . . . Uh . . . Just get everyone clumped around me, I guess."

Raji nodded, and over the next half hour, the square slowly filled with injured Ulthraks. Some were carried in on leather stretchers, while others hobbled close under their own power. Soon enough, they were clustered so close to Elijah that he began to feel a little claustrophobic. But he pushed that discomfort aside, knowing full well that Healing Rain had a very limited area of effect. So, he needed to get as many people under the clouds as possible, his comfort be damned.

Once everyone had been gathered, there were hundreds of Ulthraks in the square. "Is this everyone?" Elijah shouted over the din.

Raji nodded from afar.

Then, Elijah embraced the Ethera in his core, channeling it through his soul and into Healing Rain. When he cast the spell, a localized cloud materialized approximately twenty feet above him before dropping a steady drizzle on the area. It was only a couple dozen feet across, but it covered almost a third of the square.

Immediately, the injured and sick Ulthraks began to notice the effects of the Healing Rain. Someone gleefully shouted that their wounds had been healed, while others gasped in surprised relief.

Elijah just stood there, preparing to refresh the spell when necessary. He'd tested it many times, so he knew it would last quite a while before the spell faded.

In the meantime, he looked around, searching for someone who needed healing more urgently. And after only a moment, he sighted in on an Ulthrak woman who was covered in so many bandages that she looked like a slightly corpulent mummy. Elijah motioned for her to come closer, and she hobbled forward.

"What's your worst injury?"

"Gut wound," she muttered, grimacing with each word.

"Here," Elijah said, kneeling down and pressing his hand against her abdomen. He could practically feel the injury. While he knew it wasn't the most efficient use of his Ethera, Elijah used Touch of Nature, sending a powerful pulse of healing cycling through his staff, then through his hand and into her body. He tried to guide it to the wound in her stomach, but without actually inspecting the injury, it was safer to simply bathe the area in healing energy and hope for the best.

Still, the combination of the two spells—Healing Rain and Touch of Nature—did wonders, and in seconds, her eyes widened in shock. "It's . . . It's . . ."

"I know," Elijah said. And for the first time since gaining his archetype, he understood his place in the world.

He could fight.

He could kill.

But his true calling was preservation.

Sometimes, that would take the form of coaxing natural growth from the landscape, as he had in his Grove. Other times, he would be forced to defend the natural world, as he'd tried to do with the panther. But as he healed the Ulthrak woman's injuries, Elijah came to realize that he preferred the third option: mending the broken.

43

WHY WE FIGHT

They weren't real—not as he recognized reality, at least. Elijah knew that without a shadow of a doubt. However, that didn't seem to matter when he was surrounded by suffering people. Even if those people happened to be humanoid walrus. He had been at it for hours, and he was soaked with sweat that had mingled with precipitation from Healing Rain. He gasped, pulling his hand away from his latest patient.

He was tiny. Barely more than toddler-sized and with tiny nubs for tusks. He'd also been on the edge of death before Elijah had stepped in and cured some sort of infection by virtue of Touch of Nature. It had taken the last of his Ethera, but he'd finally done it. Everyone in the village who'd needed healing had gotten it.

And Elijah had been rewarded accordingly. He glanced at the notifications he'd so far ignored, and he couldn't help but give a tired smile as he slumped to the ground and leaned against the tree in the center of the square. It felt different from the vegetation on his island. Like the shadow of a tree.

Or a projection, which was probably more accurate.

He leaned his head back and stared at the arboreal canopy, watching the stark-white leaves dancing in the subtle breeze. Projection or not, it was definitely beautiful. He stared at it for a long few seconds before reading the notifications.

Congratulations! You have reached level twenty-one. Attribute points allocated according to your class.

Then, he moved on to the next one:

Congratulations! You have reached level twenty-two. Attribute points allocated according to your class.

Two levels in a single day. It was the fastest pace he'd managed since washing ashore, and he hadn't even gotten into a fight. That alone made him question his previous actions. If healing was so profitable, then what use did he have for killing?

Of course, he'd yet to kill anything simply to gain kill energy. The crabs and other animals he'd hunted he'd done so for food. The invaders he'd killed in order to protect the sanctity of his Grove as well as in a doomed attempt to assist the panther. And the Voxx—well, that was less about killing and more about simple extermination. He likened it to pest control. Unpleasant, necessary, and ultimately beneficial. Whatever the case, it wasn't as if he'd set out to murder hordes of creatures for the sake of quick leveling.

Elijah shook his head. He couldn't even fool himself. While he didn't think of himself as a bloodthirsty murderer, the reality was that he had enjoyed exterminating the Voxx. He had gotten satisfaction from hunting—and killing—the various animals that were his main sources of food. And the invaders? They were the enemy. He'd known it from the first moment he'd laid eyes on that settlement across the strait, and that impression had been further cemented when they'd tried to kill the panther.

No—he felt more guilty about killing crabs than he'd ever feel about taking out the invaders. That realization probably should have worried him, yet he was curiously ambivalent about it.

He let out a sigh and focused on his status:

Name	**Elijah Hart**		
Level	**22**		
Archetype	**Druid**		
Class	**Animist**		
Specialization	**N/A**		
Alignment	**N/A**		
Strength	**23**		
Dexterity	**22**		
Constitution	**23**		
Ethera	**31**		
Regeneration	**25**		
Attunement	**Nature**		
Cultivation			
Body	**Core**	**Mind**	**Soul**
Wood	**Unformed**	**Opal**	**Neophyte**

His attributes truly were beginning to round out, and though his physical abilities hadn't really kept pace with his expectations, he was satisfied. Originally, he'd thought that the threshold for peak humanity was the ten-point mark. However, he'd had to reassess that assumption when he'd nearly doubled that point total and he was still incapable of superhuman feats of physical prowess. Certainly, he felt confident that he'd reached at least Olympic-athlete levels of ability, but he wouldn't be lifting any cars anytime soon.

Before his latest burst of levels, he'd done a little testing, and as far as he could tell, it would take nearly triple his current totals to reach what he considered truly superhuman territory. For example, when he got to sixty Strength—assuming he didn't advance his body cultivation, which seemed likely considering that he still hadn't figured out how to do so—he estimated that he'd be capable of comfortably lifting around two thousand pounds.

Of course, that was assuming the gains would be linear. From one to ten, they hadn't been, but ever since, each point seemed to account for around twenty extra pounds of lifting capacity.

Then again, those were only estimates. It wasn't like he had a set of scales lying around, and "little rock" and "bigger rock" were not accurate units of measurement.

Perhaps when he reached civilization, he could remedy that lack of precision. The scientist in him wanted nothing more than to sit down and develop a way to accurately test his current capabilities while putting together a predictive model for what he might expect going forward.

But that would require his survival, which was anything but assured, given Raji's reaction to the fact that he'd entered the tower alone.

Knowing that he would need all the tools he could acquire, Elijah consulted his spell book and inspected his new spell:

Swarm	**Conjure a swarm of pests that infect your enemies with appropriate afflictions.**

"Nice," Elijah said, looking at the description. If it worked anything like Contagion, which was a passive trait that gave his claws the ability to infect his victims with a disease that sapped their Strength and slowly damaged them, the new ability would be a nice addition to his tool kit.

Looking around, he wished he had an opportunity to test it, though he quickly thought better of that desire. If he was forced into battle mode, it would probably mean that the Ulthraks he'd just spent hours healing would once again be injured.

"You've gotten stronger," came a soft voice from nearby. The child that had been his last patient had already scampered away, which meant that he'd thought he was alone. Clearly that wasn't the case, and he lowered his face and looked at the speaker.

"I . . . I recognize you, don't I?" he said, looking at the female Ulthrak. She was a bit smaller than males like Raji, but she was still quite bulky. Still, there was something undeniably feminine about her posture as well as her speaking voice.

"I was the first person you healed," she said. "I came to offer my gratitude."

With that, she held out a basket filled with some sort of fruit. Elijah took the container, saying, "Thank you."

"No—thank you," she said. "I . . . I don't think any of us would have survived without your efforts."

Elijah shrugged. "Anybody would have done the same."

Indeed, his experience was that most people tended to work together when faced with catastrophe. He'd seen as much after wildfires, volcanic eruptions, and hurricanes. When disaster struck, people tended to step up.

"I . . . disagree. I don't remember much about who I . . . was. Who I am, I suppose. But every instinct tells me that many people put in your situation would have simply killed us, taken our hides, and—"

Elijah gasped in horror. "Your hides?"

"Oh. I . . . Um . . . I shouldn't have said that . . ."

She backed away, suddenly afraid. Elijah held up his hands and said, "I'm not . . . I would never . . . I mean . . . W-why would anyone do that?"

"Ulthrak hides are extremely valuable," she said. "It is why the goblins hunt us. With Ulthrak-hide armor, they will be able to hunt, grow stronger, and expand their territory. Did you truly not know?"

Elijah shook his head. The mere notion of killing and skinning sentient beings was absolutely abhorrent. Even if the walrus beings' hides would make the best armor in the world, there was absolutely no way Elijah could ever use it. And he questioned the morality of anyone who could.

Of course, that wasn't really fair. If the choice was between that and death, many would choose the path that would lead them to survival.

But Elijah would rather die than take one step down that road.

He had no issues with killing for food. Or to protect himself or his territory. That was just natural. But hunting and murdering sentient beings just because they had some resource you wanted?

A shiver went up his spine.

"No. I definitely didn't know," Elijah said. He knew he couldn't say anything to put her at ease, so he simply shook his head and remained silent. He would have to let his actions speak for him. In that moment of silence, he latched on to something she'd said, so he asked, "How did you know I leveled? And what's your name?"

"Takha," she said. "My name is Takha. And I knew because I have an ability that lets me inspect things. The System provides a description."

"And what does it say about me?"

"That you are a level-twenty-two druid" was her answer. "I'm not powerful enough to gain any more information about you. But that staff . . ."

"What about it?"

"It glows with Ethera," Takha said. "Where did you get it?"

"I made it."

"Truly?" she said, her eyes widening. It was almost like watching a cartoon, her face was so expressive. "You are a great craftsman?"

Elijah shook his head and let out a slight chuckle. "I'm really not. I just needed a good walking stick. I guess I overshot that mark by a little."

Indeed, the fact that the staff could enhance his spells had been an incredible boon that had saved his life more than once.

Shaking his head, Elijah stood up. The skittish Takha flinched back, but he ignored the movement. She had every right to be afraid, given that she didn't really know him. He'd healed her, certainly, but who was to say that he wouldn't turn on her now that he knew the value of her hide? He never would, but caution was absolutely the right decision on her part.

"Now that everyone's healed, I think it's time to see what comes next."

"What do you mean?"

"The tower. I have to conquer it. I've chosen to save you all, but I still don't know what that really means. I hope Raji can point me in the right direction."

With that, he strode off, quickly passing through the small village to reach the largest hut in the village. The flap that served as the building's door hung open, so Elijah pushed through it. When he did, he saw that Raji was sitting in the center and eating something from a bowl.

He quickly pushed his bulk upright and said, "What can I do for you? Is everyone healed? I can't thank you enough for—"

"I need to know what the win condition for this place is."

"What?"

"The win condition. I need to save your village. That's my goal. So, how do I do that? I hoped the healing would satisfy the requirements, but that's obviously not it. So, spit it out. How do I ensure your survival?"

"The goblins," muttered Takha.

"No. It's too dangerous!" Raji interjected. "We need him to remain here where he can heal us. That will—"

"The goblins will keep coming. You know that, Raji. And we've already lost so many that we can't stand up to them. Every time they raid the village, we lose more people. Even if we can heal everyone who's injured, you know we can't save everyone," Takha said.

"I can't in good conscience—"

"Where are these goblins?" Elijah asked.

"You can't—"

"You know I'm not going to stay here indefinitely. I'm leaving, one way or another," Elijah stated. "I just need you to point me in the right direction, and I'll be out of your whiskers."

Raji shook his head. Elijah knew why the Ulthraks wanted him to stay. He'd already made it clear what he thought of Elijah trying to conquer the tower solo, but he'd also seen the good that could be done via Elijah's healing spells. Likely, he considered it the only way Elijah could lend any aid.

Of course, Elijah didn't think like that. Instead, he wanted to at least investigate the situation before he wrote it off as a lost cause. After all, he had abilities of which the Ulthraks were ignorant, and he felt confident that he could at least hold his own. Otherwise, Nerthus never would have sent him into the tower.

But he couldn't say that—not without revealing his secrets and losing any advantage he might have in the event of betrayal. He didn't want to think the Ulthraks would turn on him—he was an optimist, after all—but trust was earned, not freely given. And the humanoid walrus simply hadn't displayed anything but a willingness to take healing where it was offered.

"Fine," Raji said. "If you head to the other side of the village, you'll see a path that leads up to the surface. Once there, look to the west. That's where the goblins live."

Elijah nodded, then said, "Thanks."

Before he left, he looked down at his satchel. The mushrooms and berries he'd brought with him had been ruined by immersion in the salt water, so he asked, "Do you have any rations? I think I might be up there for a while."

Raji nodded, and Takha pushed the basket of fruit back into his hands. He hadn't even realized he'd left it behind. Nor did he remember seeing Takha retrieve it. Still, he took the fruit with a grateful nod as Raji left the hut. He returned a few moments later and handed a parcel to Elijah, saying, "Dried fish. It's not much, but it should last you a few days if you pace yourself."

"Thank you."

"Is there anything I can say to keep you from going?" Raji asked. "Our village isn't much, but you could stay here for a while longer. You would be safe, even if you couldn't leave."

Elijah answered, "No. This is something I have to do. But look on the bright side—if I'm successful, I'll conquer the tower."

Raji shrugged his massive shoulders, saying, "Doesn't matter. We'll just cycle. I'll forget this ever happened. At best, I'll finish whatever my commitment is and rejoin the real me. I don't know. Either way, win or lose, it's all the same. So long as we don't die."

"What happens then?"

"Nothing good," Raji said, and by the set of his tusks, Elijah knew he would get nothing else out of the big Ulthrak.

So, he once again thanked his hosts, then turned and left. As he did, he heard Raji remark, "No way he makes it."

Takha said, "I think he will."

"Then you're just as much an idiot as him," Raji responded. He said something else, but by that point, Elijah had gone out of hearing range.

He trekked through the village, then when he reached the edge, found the path leading into a tunnel that, in turn, rose at a gradual incline. Elijah followed it, and over the next twenty minutes, the path twisted and turned, steadily climbing until it finally led him to the surface. There, Elijah stopped to marvel at the sight before him.

To his left stretched a vast tundra of rolling white hills, and to his right was an expansive ocean. Huge blocks of ice floated nearby, completing the biome's appearance.

"This is all in a tower," he muttered to himself, glancing at the sky. Night still reigned, but on the distant horizon was the vague illumination that preceded a sunrise.

As the cold seeped into his bones, Elijah was suddenly aware of just how underdressed he was. In the fairly temperate summer of the Pacific Northwest, his ragged pants and barely there shirt offered plenty of protection. But in subzero temperatures? Even with his increased resistance to the elements that came with his enhanced Constitution, he knew he wouldn't last more than a few days before frostbite set in.

Sighing, he realized that he had no choice but to embrace Shape of the Predator, if only because, as a panther, he had thick fur that would protect him from the cold. So, he turned his attention to his rations, then dug into the fruit. He ate as much as he could stomach, then placed the dried fish in his satchel. He wrapped the bag as tightly as he could before finally embracing his spell and transforming into a mist panther.

Immediately, the cold felt less pervasive, placing his decision firmly in the good-idea column. Then, he dipped his head, grabbed the folded satchel containing his remaining rations between his jaws, and set off to the west. Hopefully, he would quickly find the so-called water goblins so he could at least scout things out.

After that, he'd make a plan for how he was going to defeat them.

44

GUERILLA WARFARE

The sun shone bright in the clear, blue sky as Elijah padded across the tundra. His steps were so light that he barely even left prints across the snow, but even as cautious as he was, he still moved quickly enough that, within a couple of hours of sunrise, he spotted the first sign of civilization when he saw a dark plume of smoke twisting in the air. Soon after, a series of buildings came into view.

Reminiscent of the architecture of the Ulthrak village, the buildings' walls were composed of thick gray hide stretched across a bone frame. However, the basic construction was where the resemblance ended. Instead of being low-slung dwellings, the ones arrayed around a shallow bay were octangular structures that stood on tall pylons. Between the buildings stretched a series of rope bridges, across which scurried a population of small blue figures.

Elijah stopped a few hundred yards away and, after letting Shape of the Predator lapse, returned to his human form. He crouched low, planting himself behind a snowdrift. Thus concealed, he waited on his Ethera to regenerate. As he did, he once again lamented his lack of appropriate clothing. With his Constitution, he could withstand the biting cold, but it wasn't pleasant. So, the few minutes he spent waiting left him shivering uncomfortably.

Still, he refused to accelerate his schedule, which hinged on him having a full core before he took even the most basic actions. So, he waited patiently, slowly pulling Ethera through the funnel of his mind. Without any outside stimuli to distract him, he could bolster his Regeneration via meditation. The effect wasn't so dramatic as to double the speed with which he could refill his core, but it was still significant enough to show a noticeable benefit.

Gradually, his core refilled, and when it reached saturation, he poked his head over the snowdrift and used Eyes of the Eagle to get a better look at the creatures he expected would be his opponents.

They were water goblins, he was certain. Blue skinned, with long arms and squat legs, they moved like primates. However, with Eyes of the Eagle, Elijah could see gills running just below their sharp jaws. In addition, they were equipped with bat-like ears, short, stubby noses, and sharp teeth. In short, aside from the gills, posture, and blue skin, they looked remarkably similar to the goblin intruder who'd helped kill the panther back on his island.

And yet, there was something different about them, too. They were more animalistic. Feral, almost. More than once, Elijah saw one member of the community growl and attack another. It was like they were primal versions of the comparatively more civilized goblin he'd previously encountered.

Or perhaps he was simply seeing what he expected to see. After all, he knew what these water goblins had done to the Ulthrak village. And he knew why.

The idea of anyone raiding a community of sentient creatures just to harvest their hides was absolutely abhorrent. Further disgusting Elijah was the giant whale carcass lying on the icy beach on the other side of the bay. Water goblins scurried all over it, hacking away with primitive tools they used to harvest meat, blubber, and skin. It didn't take him long to connect the gray hide that comprised the walls of the village's buildings with the similarly hued skin of the whale.

Of course, whaling wasn't terrible, in and of itself. People needed to eat, and in a primitive culture like the goblins', whaling may very well have been the only real source of food. However, judging by the gleeful shouts coming from the harvesting goblins, there was more to it than that. Besides, he was well aware of his own personal bias, which emanated from predatory whaling practices back on Earth.

Elijah watched and waited, spending quite some time studying the village. The goblins might have been primitive, but they were clearly sapient and organized, as evidenced by the community they had created. However, the longer Elijah watched them, the more he felt secure in his decision to side with the Ulthraks.

But for the life of him, he couldn't quite pinpoint why he felt that way. On the surface, they just looked like a normal—if primitive—people. Sure, he was probably biased against them due to what they'd done to the Ulthraks, but there was far more to it than that. He felt it in his bones that they were the enemy.

And then he realized what it was.

The blue-skinned goblins were all wearing leather armor.

Armor that was obviously made of Ulthrak hides.

The moment Elijah realized the origin of his disdain, the feeling intensified. No one had ever told him what it meant to be a druid, but his archetype wasn't simply a line on his status and a few useful spells. It meant more than that. Back in the Ulthrak village, he'd discovered that healing was part of it, but he was also a defender, wasn't he?

Looking at the goblins, he was reminded of how he felt about the settlement across the strait from his island. They weren't interested in living with the land. Nor were they concerned with conservation. Instead, they only took, harvesting whatever they needed and leaving nothing but devastation in their wake.

It wasn't environmentalism that he cared about. Not really—or not as he would have thought of it before the Earth's inclusion in the wider universe. Rather, it was about balance. And finding a way to live with the world in a mutually beneficial way rather than simply consuming whatever you needed to let you gain power.

As he sat there watching the village, Elijah considered his feelings. But by the time night fell, he'd gotten no closer to true understanding. However, what he had realized was that he needed to kill the goblins. Part of it was due to the task set by the System, but it was also because he needed to stay true to his druidic calling.

So, when night fell, he used Shape of the Predator and, leaving his pack of supplies behind the snowbank, set off toward the goblin village. As he did so, he cloaked himself with Guise of the Unseen.

Silent and all but invisible, he approached the village. Many of the goblins had already retired for the night, but there were a few still up and about. Guards, perhaps. Regardless, Elijah's vendetta was indiscriminate.

With surety of purpose, he stalked his first victim, passing under the houses as he crept from shadow to shadow. Soon enough, the blue goblin had separated itself, and he pounced, using Predator Strike.

It was over before the goblin ever knew what had happened. It fell, disemboweled by Elijah's first attack and with its throat slit by the second. Its aquamarine blood pooled on the snow as Elijah dragged it into the shadows beneath one of the buildings.

After that, Elijah continued his task, and the goblins fell, one after another. None of them even knew he was there, much less tried to defend themselves. Thus, the power of his class truly became evident.

As he swept through the village, silently slaughtering water goblins, he was too focused to consider the morality of his actions. However, after he'd killed the final creature, he stumbled across the building where they butchered and skinned the Ulthraks they'd taken prisoner.

After that, any sympathy he might've felt dissipated before the harsh reality of their actions. Only after he had seen that grisly charnel house did Elijah get a notification from the System:

Congratulations! You have completed Level One of the Keledge Tower. **Grade: A.** **To progress further, find the portal to Level Two.**

Then, a small box appeared before him. It was a simple metal cube about four inches wide, but it radiated enough Ethera to surprise Elijah. He leaned forward, sniffing it, but even with his panther's senses, he smelled nothing out of the ordinary. So, he let Shape of the Predator drop before reaching down and flipping the box's latch. It sprang open, revealing a simple pewter ring.

Elijah took it, resulting in a new notification:

Reward for completing Level One of the Keledge Tower:

Ring of Aquatic Travel

The ring itself was carved with fanciful whorls, but otherwise, it looked entirely ordinary. Elijah slipped it on but felt nothing. The last time Elijah had acquired a magical item, he'd gotten a description. But perhaps that was because he'd created the Staff of Natural Harmony himself. Either way, aside from making an inference based on the ring's name, Elijah had no idea what the ring really did.

He would do some testing once he made it out of the tower.

In the meantime, he needed to find the portal to the next level. To that end, he searched through the village once again. However, he found nothing, so he expanded his parameters to the small bay abutting the settlement.

The moment his feet touched the water, he felt a thrum of Ethera emanating from the center of the bay. It didn't take a leap of logic to recognize what it meant. The portal to the second level was down there.

Groaning, he said, "Swimming again? Ugh."

As much as he didn't want to do it, Elijah knew he didn't have much of a choice. So, after heading back to the snowbank where he'd spent most of the day observing the water-goblin village, he retrieved his supplies and ate his fill. Fortunately, the water of the bay was fresh, so he'd already sated his thirst.

Odd, sure. But he wasn't going to question something that worked in his favor. The last thing he wanted to do was melt snow just so he could get a drink.

With that done, Elijah checked to make sure that his Ethera had completely regenerated, then set off back to the bay. When he reached it, he waded in, and once the frigid water reached his midsection, he dove in.

It was not pleasant.

In fact, his entire body went numb after only a few seconds. With the knowledge that he didn't have much of a choice at the forefront of his mind, he forged ahead. Using the pulse of Ethera as his guide, he continued to swim until, a few dozen yards later, he was directly above it. Not wasting any time hesitating, Elijah dove.

It only took a few seconds to recognize the portal. This time, it presented itself as a stone doorway, its corners twisted in such a way that he struggled to make sense of it. But he didn't care about that. With the cold sapping his energy, Elijah didn't have the luxury of time on his side. So, he swam down and passed through the door.

Then, he was once again plunged into impenetrable darkness.

However, this time, it didn't fade.

Instead, a brief stab of light pierced Elijah's eyes, and suddenly, he felt an incredibly strong undertow pulling him down. He fought against it, using every point of his enhanced Strength attribute as he swam against the current, but it was useless. He couldn't escape. He couldn't even fight to a standstill.

Instead, the inexorable current continued to pull him into the watery abyss.

Panic suffused Elijah's mind as his oxygen ran out. But to his surprise, it didn't matter. That was when he remembered the name of his reward for completing the tower's first level. The Ring of Aquatic Travel clearly gave him the ability to survive underwater.

Still, as Elijah was slowly pulled ever downward, his panic did not subside. Even if he wasn't going to drown, he had no idea what to expect next.

Some indeterminate time later, Elijah hit something solid.

But it wasn't the silt he would have expected. Instead, it was stone. Gradually, his eyes began to adjust, and what he saw shocked him to his core.

45

UNDER THE SEA

Arrayed before Elijah was a maze of coral and seaweed. Even as he floated only a few feet above the seafloor, he forgot the conflict of the previous day. Instead, he focused entirely on the setting in front of him.

Elijah had been diving many times in the past. He had his scuba license, and he'd been an avid free diver before being stricken with cancer. More, he'd watched countless videos of the depths and studied even more photos and texts while earning his doctorate. However, he'd never seen anything like the landscape laid out before him.

Coral twisted hundreds of feet in the air, and the thick stalks of seaweed, barely waving in the current, looked like nothing so much as blades of grass. Huge schools of colorful fish flitted about, while Elijah caught sight of larger predators lurking within the forest of coral and seaweed. A shadow enveloped him, and he looked up.

A sea serpent the size of a bus slithered hundreds of feet above him, cutting through the water with speed that would have rivaled an airplane. Elijah stared as it darted into the seaweed forest and passed out of view.

That was when he noticed a notification waiting for him:

Welcome to The Keledge Tower, Level Two. To advance to Level Three, complete the task before you.

It was almost identical to the notification that had greeted him upon his entry into the tower, and it was followed by a description of the task in question:

Task: Reach the center of the Sea of Sorrows and defeat the Hegemonic Guardian.

Neither of those names sounded good. The words *sorrow* and *hegemony* did not fill him with the warm and fuzzies. But he knew he didn't have much in the way of choices. He couldn't very well turn back. Nor did he really want to. There was definitely something addictive about meeting the challenges laid out before him. In any case, there was every chance that the previous level had ceased to exist the moment he'd left it behind. Perhaps the scenario had already reset.

Looking back, his emotions felt a bit silly. If none of it was real—and it wasn't, at least according to the Ulthraks and his own deductive ability—then what did any of it matter? He shouldn't have cared if the walrus people lived or died. Nor should the goblins have infuriated him so thoroughly.

And yet, they had. He could only reason that there was more at play than he knew. But that wasn't exactly surprising, given that he knew almost nothing about what was going on. At times, Elijah felt like he was being led around by the nose, and he very much didn't like it.

For now, though, he needed to push those sorts of thoughts to the back of his mind and focus on accomplishing the task at hand and progressing to the third and final level of the tower. To that end, he sank to the seafloor and took cover behind a sizable rock so he could think about how he intended to accomplish the goals that had been thrust upon him.

And not for the first time, he realized just how out of his depth and unprepared he really was. Until that point, he'd leaned on his Shape of the Predator, which he'd found was incredibly powerful. It allowed him to remain undetected and, when the time was right, strike hard and fast before sinking back into the shadows.

But underwater, adopting that form just wasn't an option. When he'd tried to swim in his panther form, he'd barely been capable of remaining afloat. In theory, it ought to have been easy enough to adapt. After all, he knew how other animals swam, so it should have been a simple matter of practice before he mastered the necessary technique. But in this case, the instincts that came with the form had worked against him, inciting a simmering panic that had scuttled any attempt at rational thought. It had been all he could do to awkwardly paddle a few feet, much less swim through a territory the size of the Sea of Sorrows.

So, he was stuck in his human form.

Fortunately, he was extremely comfortable as a swimmer, and with the Ring of Aquatic Travel giving him the ability to breathe underwater, he felt confident that he could at least survive the environment.

However, he knew it wouldn't be so simple as to swim in the right direction. Never was that clearer than when he saw motion out of the corner of his eye. At first, he panicked, but that only lasted a split second before he realized that the creature he'd seen was hundreds of yards away.

It was an eel, but one with coloring he'd never seen. It was also the circumference of a horse, which made it the largest eel he'd ever even heard about. It swam from the forest of seaweed and coral, chased by a school of much smaller fish that resembled barracuda. The smaller fish nipped at the eel's tail, but it quickly started to outpace them.

Until a huge claw descended from above, snapping the eel in half.

Elijah tensed as the claw's owner splashed into the water from the surface, revealing its entire form.

It was a giant crab.

Because of course it was.

But if every crab he'd ever killed had all somehow combined into one, they wouldn't have reached half the size of this newcomer's claw, much less the rest of its body. If it was any smaller than an aircraft carrier, Elijah would have been shocked.

No—he was already shocked, regardless of his vehicle-based size estimations. The school of barracuda darted away, but the crab wasn't going to let even so small of a meal escape. It lashed out with its claw, and though it didn't make physical contact, the motion created an unnatural whirlpool that sucked the comparatively small fish into its gaping maw. The two halves of the still-writhing eel soon followed, and before long, nothing was left of the brief hunt.

Then, the crab floated up, eventually breaking through the surface. Where it went after that, Elijah couldn't see, and if he was honest, he had no interest in finding out.

Over the next hour, he settled in to watch the sea. And as he did, patterns became clear. For one, anything that ventured above the forest of kelp and coral was quickly killed and eaten by the crab, so trying to swim above the fray was impossible. Elijah had no idea if it was the same crab or if it was a series of the creatures, but it didn't really matter for his purposes.

Next, he saw that the ecosystem in the forest was, to put it mildly, one based on predation. If there were herbivorous creatures in there, Elijah never saw them. Instead, everything seemed out to kill everything else, which meant that the entire place was a natural battlefield of epic proportions.

And that posed quite a problem.

If he'd been capable of adopting his panther form, he could have simply snuck through. However, in his human form, he had no more ability in stealth than any other person. Certainly, he'd learned a few tricks over the past year of living in the wilderness, but most of his knowledge was useless in his current environment.

The third thing he was forced to realize was that he wasn't nearly as buoyant as he might have expected, which meant that swimming really was out of the question. In fact, after a little testing, he reasoned that it wasn't so different from the level of gravity on the moon.

And finally, he acknowledged that, once again, the water was free of salt, which seemed even more incongruous than the massive predators or clearly contrived scenario. But at least it meant that he wouldn't die of thirst if he remained on the level for too long.

Food would be an issue, though, largely because he'd lost his woven satchel sometime during the transition between levels. Hopefully, he would complete the task before he had to start considering eating the fish and other creatures he'd seen so far.

After a few hours, Elijah realized that he was stalling. He really didn't want to head into the forest of kelp and coral, largely because he felt incredibly vulnerable without his Shape of the Predator spell. He still had Storm's Fury, though he wasn't entirely certain it would work underwater. And he had his newest spell, Swarm. But other than that, he only had his staff to defend himself.

And he suspected that that wouldn't be enough.

Letting out a sigh that sent a series of bubbles drifting toward the surface, Elijah pushed the negative thoughts aside. He'd survived cancer. He had learned to thrive after being stranded on a deserted island. He'd killed a host of interdimensional lizards. He could stroll across the seabed and kill some boss monster. If that was what he had to do to survive, then that was what he was going to do.

The first order of business was to test Storm's Fury, though. So, he backed away from his rock and embraced the spell. To his shock, a veritable torrent of Ethera swept through his mind, and Storm's Fury activated in a fraction of the time it normally took. The moment the spell was saturated, he released his hold, and a thick bolt of white lightning tore across the water and hit the rock.

It shattered, sending bits and pieces slowly flying through the water.

Elijah grinned. It was definitely stronger, but he wasn't sure why. Was it the interaction with the water? Or was it the denser ambient Ethera? He had no way of knowing.

Testing it again, he fired off another spell. This time, though, he paid attention to the bolt of lightning itself. In its normal form, the lightning manifested from the sky, but when he channeled it through his Staff of Natural Harmony, it emanated from the head of the weapon. But it always took the form of a single, well-defined bolt of lightning.

Underwater, that changed. From that single bolt extended a series of smaller branches of electricity, suggesting that it could affect a wide area. The radius around the bolt wasn't large—maybe a few feet before those branches dissipated—but it was enough to excite Elijah about his chances of making it through the Sea of Sorrows.

He decided to test Swarm, as well.

To his surprise, though, when he tried, it wouldn't activate. It only took a moment for Elijah to realize that, like Shape of the Predator, the spell would take the bulk of his Ethera reserves to cast. So, he retreated a little and settled in to meditate on funneling Ethera through his mind and into his soul, after which it settled into his core.

He was well used to the process by that point, but he still reveled in the feeling of so much energy flowing through the ephemeral System.

Eventually, Elijah regenerated enough Ethera to fuel the spell. So, he rose and channeled it through his staff.

A moment later, a school of tiny fish—they looked a lot like piranhas—appeared and swept through the area. Without anything to attack, they dissipated only a few moments later.

Interesting. According to the spell's description, the creatures would infect his enemies with "appropriate afflictions," whatever that meant. Elijah didn't know, and he wouldn't find out until he used the spell on an enemy.

He hoped it wouldn't come to that, but given the nature of the tower, he suspected that his hopes would soon be dashed.

After testing the spell, Elijah settled in to once again regenerate his Ethera, and once his core was full, he finally set off, bounding across the seafloor with long, bouncy steps that helped him cover the ground very quickly. However, he chose to hesitate when he reached the edge of the kelp forest.

Was going in the right choice?

Maybe. Perhaps not. But he couldn't think of any other option. So, without further ado, he plunged ahead. This time, though, he kept his footsteps short, and he stayed as low as he could.

His attempts at stealth turned out to be useless.

Only ten steps into the kelp forest, he passed what he thought was an innocuous rock. But the moment his back was exposed, he felt the water stir. With instincts born of surviving for a year in the wilderness, he dove forward.

It wasn't enough.

Something clamped down on his side, ripping into the delicate flesh. His momentum tore him free, and whatever had attacked him pulled back. Blood as well as bits of skin and meat misted into the water as Elijah slapped his hand to his side and pulsed Touch of Nature.

He hit the seabed hard before bouncing into a tall stalk of kelp. Even as the spell stanched the bleeding, he got his first glimpse of his attacker.

It was a turtle, though a species Elijah did not recognize. The sharp beak and leathery skin were familiar, but its shell was made entirely from rock and coral. More, its legs were far longer than any snapping turtle Elijah had ever seen.

And finally, it was at least as big as he was, and it probably weighed at least three hundred pounds. Probably a lot more. In short, it looked like a primal version of a snapping turtle with a jagged boulder for a shell.

Elijah didn't hesitate to cast Storm's Fury the moment he recovered from his tumble. The monster—and that was the only way he could think of the creature—saw the spell coming, and displaying more intelligence than any reptile had a right to show, it twisted around to present its shell. The lightning hit it, splintering the shell and eliciting a burbling scream from the turtle.

It reacted instantly, leaping across the intervening space and latching on to Elijah's hastily raised arm. Bone crunched as its jaws closed, but Elijah kept his wits about him as he recast the spell.

The lightning hit the creature square between the eyes, but even though it was clearly hurt, the thing channeled its inner pit bull and refused to relinquish its grip. So, Elijah recast the spell. Once. Twice. Three more times. And as his Ethera dipped to dangerously low levels, the creature finally died.

But its jaws remained locked into place, and its weight tugged Elijah to the seafloor. Pain lanced through him. His arm was broken—probably in multiple places—and his side was still missing quite a bit of flesh.

He only had enough Ethera for two heals. Maybe three at most.

And he had a turtle latched on to his arm.

Prying it loose was the first order of business. Then, he intended to—

Just then, a school of small fish—maybe seven or eight inches long, with gold scales and red, beady eyes—swam into view. They made a beeline for the bloody water surrounding Elijah.

Recognizing them for the predatory scavengers they were, Elijah took aim with his staff and cast Storm's Fury.

Lightning arced out, taking the little creatures head-on. But the bolt of electricity was so powerful that it didn't stop after obliterating the first. No—it kept going, tearing through the school. That's when the little branches of lightning showed their worth, leaping out to fry most of the remaining fish.

The majority of the school died in an instant, but a few managed to survive. But suddenly alone, they weren't nearly as brave as they'd been only a moment before, and they quickly darted back under the cover of the kelp forest.

Elijah felt his shoulders sag.

He'd killed the little creatures, but that victory had come at a cost. His core was entirely empty now. So, he couldn't heal himself. Grimacing, he realized that he had no choice but to retreat. But first, he needed to pry the turtle's jaws apart. So, over the next couple of minutes, he awkwardly did just that. In the end, he had to lever his foot under one side while tugging the other in the opposite direction.

And just like that, he was free.

It only took one look at his arm to tell him that he'd severely underestimated the damage. He was a marine biologist, but he was familiar enough with mammalian physiology to know that, if he didn't have access to healing magic, he would lose the arm. It was already swollen to nearly three times its normal size, and bits of bone jutted through the purpling skin.

That served to further cement Elijah's decision to retreat.

Letting out a gurgling sigh, he returned to his previous spot and settled in to regenerate his Ethera. Without the adrenaline of the fight pumping through his veins, he felt every pulse of agony emanating from his arm. The only good thing he could say was that it at least served as a distraction from the injury on his right side.

Silver linings, he supposed.

As he sat there, he began to come to the realization that he might be on this current level of the tower for a little longer than expected.

46

SURVIVOR

Elijah knelt behind a fallen chunk of coral. In one hand, he clutched his staff, while the other kept him from drifting with the current as he watched the scene laid out before him. It had been nearly a week since he'd first entered the second level of the tower, and in that time, he'd been forced to learn to adapt to life in the sea.

At first, it had not gone well, and he'd spent most of the first few days recovering from the brief, intense battles that plagued every step into the kelp-and-coral forest. But with every fight, he drew a little closer to gaining enough power to traverse the sea with impunity. He still wasn't there yet, having only reached level twenty-three, but he felt like he was on the verge of gaining another level. And when he did, he would learn a new spell or ability. Hopefully, that would make his task easier to accomplish.

Which was why he was watching the giant eel lazily drifting back and forth in the current. It hadn't moved from the small clearing in some time, and Elijah knew that, if he was going to kill it, he needed to act soon, lest he lose his chance when the thing woke up and wandered off.

So, he screwed up his courage, then leaped up, grabbing a piece of branching coral, and dragged himself atop the edifice. Once there, he raised his staff and dragged Ethera from his core, channeled it through his soul, and cast Swarm. Instantly, a thousand piranha-like fish manifested and swept down into the clearing.

The eel never saw them coming. In seconds, the little fish, which were barely bigger than Elijah's fingers, had torn huge chunks from its flesh. More importantly, with each bite, they delivered an affliction that, so far as Elijah could tell, functioned like the necrotic damage associated with brown recluse spiders.

Only it was much accelerated and far more powerful. The degradation of the tissue surrounding such a bite would normally take as much as two weeks, but once magic became involved—as was the case with the fish conjured by Swarm—it only took moments. Instantly, the eel's brown-and-gray serpentine body was riddled with red blisters, which quickly turned white and soon after burst with pus and blood.

The eel didn't take the attack lying down, either. It twisted and struck, biting at the swarm of creatures. When its jaws clamped down on them, they burst into clear goo that dissipated only a second later. Over and over, the eel attacked the swarm of biting fish, but it only got a fraction of the creatures before the spell ended.

All the while, Elijah waited, hoping against hope that the damage would be enough to take the monster down. Because of the extreme Ethera cost, this was the first time he'd used the spell in battle, and though it hadn't disappointed, Elijah couldn't help but hold his metaphorical breath as the thing slowly succumbed to the necrotic venom.

Over the next few minutes, it thrashed and bucked, clearly in pain. Elijah hated watching the animal suffer, but he didn't dare intervene. He'd learned to fear the denizens of the Sea of Sorrows, and though his heart bled for his victims, it wasn't enough to throw himself into undue danger.

Gradually, the eel's thrashing ceased, and it sank to the silt-covered seabed.

But it was still alive. And worse, the sores that were the result of the creatures' bites had begun to close. If Elijah judged it correctly, it wouldn't be too much longer before the eel started to recover from its internal injuries, which were almost assuredly much more severe than the bites and burst blisters on its skin.

No—if he was going to kill the thing, he needed to act.

Fortunately, in the minutes since he'd cast Swarm, he'd recovered enough Ethera to fuel a few casts of Storm's Fury. Hopefully, that would be enough to end the monster's life and give him the kill energy he needed to progress.

If not, then he would have to find another vulnerable creature and start the process over again. It was not precisely the way Elijah wanted to live—after all, the eel was probably inedible, and even if it wasn't, there was no way he was going to use that much meat—but that was the reality that he'd been forced to confront.

Killing was necessary for survival.

It always had been, but that was even more true than it had been back on his island. There, he'd killed so he could eat. Or to protect the island and his Grove from the Voxx. But now, he was killing simply because he needed to grow more powerful. It wasn't exactly killing for the sake of killing, but it wasn't so far off that he didn't see the parallels, either.

Regardless, he had already come to terms with it. He'd resolved to survive by whatever means necessary, and so, that was precisely what he was going to do. However, he did recognize that there would come a point in time where he needed to have a better plan than that. In short, he needed a code by which he would live.

But for now, what he really needed most was for that eel to die, and no moral debate would change that. So, without further delay, he once again raised his staff, took aim at the eel, and used Storm's Fury.

Lightning, hot and furious, arced out from his Staff of Natural Harmony and hit the Eel directly in the forehead. The moment the spell hit, the creature seized, but Elijah knew it wouldn't be enough. So, he used the spell again, draining the last of his Ethera. More convulsions followed until, at last, it fell still and settled onto the seabed in a cloud of silt.

But the thing didn't die.

Elijah knew that because he hadn't received the expected influx of kill energy.

So, he had a choice. Either he could wait for his Ethera to regenerate and chance the monster healing the damage he'd just done. Or he could go down there and finish it off the hard way.

Both options had downsides, but considering that the downside of one of the choices was that he'd get eaten the moment he got within range of the creature, he chose the first option. So, once again, he settled down to wait. As he did, he focused on funneling as much Ethera as he could through his mind and into his core, but when the eel started to stir, he knew it wouldn't be enough.

Still, he refused to move.

Killing the eel was the goal, and he'd put everything he had into doing just that. But he refused to let that sway his judgment. Instead, he ignored the sunk cost and focused on the most important thing: staying alive.

So, he watched as, before he'd even regenerated enough Ethera to fuel two casts of Storm's Fury, the eel awoke. The moment it did, the creature swam away, taking Elijah's chance at gaining level twenty-four with it.

But at least he was still alive.

It was just further proof that, while his archetype was versatile and, in the right situation, deadly, it just didn't give him the kick he needed to easily kill most of the creatures in the Sea of Sorrows. If he'd had access to Shape of the Predator, things would be very different. He could have snuck up on the eel and ravaged it with Predator Strike, then finished it off with a combination of Contagion and the kind of hit-and-run tactics he'd used against the water goblins on the previous level.

But his mist-panther form was almost entirely incapable of swimming, which ruled that strategy out.

He sighed, sending a trail of tiny bubbles drifting toward the surface. It seemed that he wasn't going to progress via one big kill. Instead, he'd need to target the smaller creatures he'd been hunting since he'd entered the Sea of Sorrows.

Once the eel had been gone for a few minutes, Elijah climbed down from his perch and took a familiar route back to the shallow cave he'd been using as a temporary base of operations. When he got there, he looked at it with a sense of blended nostalgia and fatigue. The first because it reminded him of his earliest days on the island, when even killing a crab had been difficult. The second for the same reasons. It felt like it had been so long since he'd been able to just relax.

Survival, for all that it was periodically exciting, was incredibly exhausting, and at times, he longed for the days when he could just go home after a long day of work, kick off his shoes, and read a good book. Or watch some trash television. Or any of a number of other wastes of time that came from having most of his needs met.

It wasn't as if he intended to give up. He didn't. But he would've appreciated a short break, all the same.

That wasn't in the cards, though. He'd only made it a few miles into the kelp forest, and he knew he had at least that much left to go before he reached the center of the Sea of Sorrows. So, rest would have to wait.

Perhaps indefinitely, if his experiences since the world had been transformed were any indication.

But it wasn't that bad, really. With the water being fresh, he didn't run the risk of dehydration. And he'd killed enough fish, crustaceans, and other creatures that hunger wasn't an issue, either. Sure, he had to eat them raw—fire didn't burn underwater, after all—but ingesting unsafe food was nothing that a quick pulse of Touch of Nature couldn't take care of. So, he had no issues with meeting his basic needs.

As he settled into his cave to rest, Elijah let his mind drift until, at last, he fell asleep. He awoke some indeterminate time later—after all, without the steady rise and setting of the sun, he had no real concept of how much time had passed—he once again set off.

Soon enough, he was attacked by a small sea serpent, which he killed with a quick cast of Storm's Fury. Once it was dead, he ate a bit of its meat, then discarded the rest before moving on. He met a similar ambush by a sea spider with the same tactics, though he ended up having to bash the thing apart with his staff after it survived the onslaught of spells that drained his pool of Ethera.

He didn't eat any of the spider because, well, he drew the line at arachnids.

Like that, Elijah slowly progressed, and a day later, he finally achieved his goal.

Congratulations! You have reached level twenty-four. Attribute points allocated according to your class.

The notification came after he'd killed the second of a trio of giant, foot-long shrimp by clobbering them with his staff, and the shock of it very nearly got him killed when the lone survivor launched itself at him. Elijah barely managed to block its attack with his staff, knocking it aside before following up with a hastily cast Storm's Fury. It drained the last of his Ethera—he'd already cast it a handful of times, missing the little creatures more than he wanted to admit—but the resulting bolt of lightning took the stunned creature head-on, completely obliterating it.

Elijah's shoulders slumped. He'd been at it for hours, and after finally reaching his goal, his exhaustion finally caught up to him. However, he couldn't afford to rest. Not until he reached some modicum of safety. So, without even looking at his status or whatever new spell or ability he'd gained, he set off to find a safe haven.

It took longer than he hoped, but eventually, he found a dense clump of coral that seemed promising. So, he trudged into what turned out to be a tiny cave. The only problem was that it already had a resident in the form of a sizable catfish that did not appreciate being disturbed.

By that point, Elijah had enough Ethera to cast Storm's Fury a couple of times, but judging by the size of the thing—and the famous durability of catfish—he considered retreat a better option. So, after narrowly avoiding the creature's initial salvo, he leaped for the entrance and dragged himself out.

Thankfully, the catfish didn't follow.

After a few more failures, Elijah finally discovered another cave that would serve as a decent resting spot—at least for a few hours. So, he headed inside and spent the next few minutes arduously inspecting the interior for threats. He found none, so he dragged a few pieces of coral in front of the entrance and finally settled down to rest.

Though he struggled to keep his eyes open, Elijah forced himself to take a look at his status, just in case anything had changed:

Name	**Elijah Hart**
Level	**24**
Archetype	**Druid**
Class	**Animist**
Specialization	**N/A**
Alignment	**N/A**
Strength	**25**
Dexterity	**29 (24)**
Constitution	**30 (25)**
Ethera	**33**
Regeneration	**27**
Attunement	**Nature**
Cultivation	

Body	Core	Mind	Soul
Wood	Unformed	Opal	Neophyte

Unsurprisingly, aside from gaining two points in each attribute since he'd last checked, nothing had changed. And while he appreciated the additional attributes, Elijah was far more interested in his new ability. So, without further delay, he took a look at it:

Venom Strike	Imbues an attack with a fast-acting neurotoxin. Usable in all forms. Damage doubled when in Predator form.

Elijah didn't really know what to think of it. On the one hand, it certainly opened up a lot of possibilities—especially after he realized that the ability didn't actually take Ethera. Even though all he wanted was to rest, Elijah took a few minutes to try it out, and what he discovered was that even though it didn't use Ethera, it still had a cost. The first time he used the ability, he felt a sudden wave of fatigue. The second time, it was stronger. And the third nearly wiped him out.

It was an odd feeling—somewhere between the fatigue associated with a high fever and the result of a long workout. He could probably force himself to use it a few more times—especially if he was fresh—but eventually, he would simply collapse from exhaustion.

But that was fine. It just gave him one more tool to survive, and eventually, if he kept stacking advantages and abilities, he would make it out of the tower.

47

THE BITTER TASTE OF VICTORY

Elijah was exhausted.

It wasn't just the constant danger, though that was a big part of it. Nor was it the raw fish that had become his diet. He'd even grown accustomed to the taste of the water. No—what really got to him was the constant submersion. People just weren't meant to live underwater, as evidenced by the fact that his skin had started to break down only a few days into his time in the Sea of Sorrows. On top of that, if he didn't consistently use Touch of Nature to counteract some of the other effects—like the degradation of his muscles due to the decreased weight and the havoc submersion wreaked on his circulatory System—he would've already died.

But as valuable as Touch of Nature was, it did nothing to combat the psychological effects. Isolation was difficult on its own, but he'd been dealing with that for more than a year. However, when it was compounded by living for more than a month in such an alien environment, it became nearly unbearable.

There were only two reasons he'd managed to keep going. First—and most importantly—he didn't have any choice. He was a survivor, and after being given a second chance at life, Elijah simply refused to give in. With that driving him, he didn't really have any choice in the matter. The same factors that had driven him to enter the tower in the first place—chiefly, the fact that he would be overwhelmed by the Voxx if he didn't—kept him moving forward.

The second reason he'd managed to maintain his sanity was that, despite the hostility of the environment, he was consistently struck by the beauty all around him. He'd never been a particularly committed biologist. Certainly, he'd enjoyed his work well enough, but he wasn't nearly as driven as some of his colleagues. Work was work, and he was content with keeping it separated from the rest of his life.

However, spending so much time in the Sea of Sorrows had opened his eyes in a way that nothing else ever had. If he hadn't been trapped there, he might have even enjoyed himself. So long as he could get out of the water and enjoy dry land.

In any case, in the previous weeks, he had seen a host of things no one else ever had, and despite the fact that he desperately wanted to leave the Sea of

Sorrows, he couldn't help but appreciate it for the beauty it represented. Even the predators—especially them—filled him with awe.

But for now, he needed to focus on the task at hand. If he didn't, the sea wouldn't have to kill him because his foe would do the job instead.

Crouched behind a half-eaten carcass of what he thought had once been a whale, Elijah studied the creature he'd decided to kill. From Elijah's perspective, it looked like a giant isopod—with emphasis on the giant part. As seemed common within the Sea of Sorrows, and the transformed world at large, a creature that should have topped out at around twenty inches long had reached truly gargantuan proportions. If it was smaller than a minivan, Elijah would've been incredibly surprised.

More distressing than its size were the other addenda to its morphology. Chiefly, that its legs—all fourteen of them—were quite a bit longer than the species with which Elijah was familiar. That, in and of itself, wouldn't have been terribly distressing, but the limbs were also barbed, which told him all he needed to know about their purpose. Its shell also looked quite a bit thicker than it should've been, though, given Elijah's experiences with the crabs on his island, that was expected.

Otherwise, the creature looked much like its terrestrial relative, the humble wood louse—or the pill bug, as they were usually known. Though, instead of a black shell, the giant isopod was equipped with a much lighter-colored armor.

Regardless, Elijah had chosen the monster as his target for two reasons. First, after killing the whale and gorging itself, the isopod had grown quite lethargic. That would give him some leeway in his method of attack.

Most importantly, though, Elijah knew that if he didn't kill it, it would almost assuredly hunt him down. Because the overgrown crustacean was very territorial, and it killed anything that dared set foot—or fin—into its territory. The whale, as well as a dozen other, much smaller creatures, was proof enough of that.

No—if Elijah wanted to continue to progress toward the center of the Sea of Sorrows, he needed to get past the isopod. And if he couldn't? Then he had no business challenging the level's guardian in the first place.

But just because it was necessary didn't mean Elijah was looking forward to it. He wasn't. In fact, he was almost certain he was going to die in the effort. However, he was tired of the sea, and he knew that if he didn't make progress soon, his resolution to keep going would begin to wane. He wouldn't just give up, but every day he spent in that sea robbed him of some ineffable aspect of his motivation, and without that, he would lose focus and make mistakes that would eventually get him killed.

Still, he considered simply going back and continuing to hunt. There was no shortage of prey, and eventually, he would gain more levels. Though over the past few days, he'd gotten the feeling that kill energy was subject to diminishing returns. Killing things within the Sea of Sorrows would still let him progress, but the longer he stayed, the more it would take.

Elijah wasn't sure how he knew that—there was no numerical value or anything associated with how much kill energy he needed to level—but he knew it all the same.

Not for the first time, Elijah wished he had someone to explain everything to him. Or, failing that, a companion with which he could compare notes. Nerthus was great, and he'd been extremely helpful, but he was obviously very limited in what information he could pass on.

Shaking his head, Elijah realized that he was just stalling.

So, he stepped out from behind the whale and used Storm's Fury. Lightning lanced out from the tip of his staff, hitting the dormant monster directly in its eye. But Elijah didn't see it. Instead, he used the spell again, to similar results. The creature stirred, locking its eyes on Elijah. He tried to cast another instance of Storm's Fury, but he cut it off when the monster raced toward him. Propelled by its multitude of legs, the isopod could move incredibly quickly, and as such, Elijah knew he didn't have time to dawdle.

Instead, he turned and ran.

Moving quickly in the water required a curious mix of jumping, paddling, and running, but over the previous month, Elijah had been forced to master the awkward technique. As such, he managed to get away just before the isopod reached his previous position. Clicking its mandibles furiously, it dug its sharp legs into the silt and launched itself at Elijah.

But by that point, Elijah was already gone, darting between a pair of coral stalks and into a stand of kelp. The isopod thundered after him, crushing the coral and tearing through the waving kelp. Elijah never stopped moving, though he was careful not to outpace the monster.

Not that that was a real possibility. It was native to the environment, and despite its bulk, the thing was well equipped for rapid movement. So, Elijah struggled to stay ahead of it.

Leaping over a wide but relatively shallow chasm, Elijah landed with a roll before finding his feet and continuing his flight. A turtle not unlike the one who'd first greeted him snapped at him in passing, but by that point, Elijah was already gone. Just when he thought he was going to be caught, he got a boost of speed as the System finally judged that he'd left combat. The monster still chased him, but because he hadn't taken any hostile action or damage for a while, his Essence of the Wolf kicked in. Though it was expected—he'd tested it thoroughly—it still came as a welcome relief, and he quickly put some extra distance between himself and the giant sea louse.

After a few dozen more yards, he looked back to see that the creature had all but given up. So, mustering his Ethera, Elijah launched another Storm's Fury in its direction. From that distance, all he could manage was a glancing blow, but it was enough to renew the monster's ire.

Like that, Elijah ran the thing in circles until, at last, he came to the spot he'd prepared ahead of time.

It wasn't a very artful trap. Indeed, any creature with even basic intelligence would know to avoid it. But Elijah was banking on the creature being no more intelligent than the giant isopods with which he was familiar. So, he'd built the trap—which consisted of a few arduously sharpened bones arranged within a cave he had stumbled upon. The cave itself was characterized by a large overhang just above the entrance, and it was only just large enough for the monster to fit. Even though it was a tight fit, the monster still followed when Elijah dashed inside.

As he wove through the stakes and into the much narrower back of the cave, Elijah shot another Storm's Fury at the monster. It ran headlong into the cave, impaling itself on the angled stakes Elijah had carved from another whale carcass he'd stumbled upon a few days before.

But that wasn't enough to kill such a creature. Nor would it suffice to trap it. And with its long legs, it was only a matter of time before the thing escaped.

Elijah had a plan for that, too.

He had chosen his killing ground well, and though the cave hadn't initially had two openings, the wall at the narrow end was thin enough that it had only taken him a few hours to carve a hole big enough for him to fit through. So, he dragged himself through, then circled around to the entrance. Once there, he aimed his staff at the overhang above the entrance and let loose with another Storm's Fury.

He'd spent hours making certain that the overhang was weak enough that it would only take a single cast to send the rock and coral tumbling down. And that was precisely what happened, the ensuing avalanche sealing that side of the cave and trapping the giant isopod inside.

Elijah pumped his fist in celebration, but judging by the rumbling coming from within the cave, he knew he didn't have time to pat himself on the back. He still had a giant crustacean to kill.

So, he circled back around to what was now the lone exit. Then, he settled in to wait for his Ethera to regenerate. It only took a little while—after all, that was one of the reasons he'd led the creature on such a long chase—before he had enough Ethera to cast Swarm.

He pointed his staff into the hole and did just that.

He couldn't see the piranhas that the spell conjured, but he didn't need to because, only a second later, an unholy burbling screech came from within the cave. Elijah knew the conjuration wouldn't last long—just thirty seconds or so—but the screeching endured well after.

At the same time, the monster never stopped trying to escape. The other reason Elijah had circled the trap so many times was because he'd wanted to tire it out. He didn't know if it had worked, but with its massive size, even when it was exhausted and wounded, it was more than capable of breaking free.

But Elijah was committed now. Everything had gone precisely how he'd planned it. He just needed to finish things off.

Which was easier said than done, and over the next thirty minutes, he listened to the monster's screeches and attempts to escape its fate. At the same time, his Ethera continued to regenerate until, at last, he was able to cast Swarm once again.

The results were predictable.

More screeches. More localized earthquakes as the isopod tried to break free. But still it didn't die.

So, Elijah waited. And cast Swarm. Then waited some more.

By the time the monster finally keeled over, giving Elijah enough kill energy to progress to level twenty-five, it had nearly broken free of the trap. And it had taken seven casts of Swarm to do it in.

When it died, Elijah stood atop that half-destroyed mound, looking down at the massive monster he'd just killed, and basked in the satisfaction that, despite being handicapped by his inability to transform, he'd emerged victorious.

That was probably why he never saw his inevitable death bearing down on him.

48

DIVERGENT IDEAS

Alyssa swung her spear in a long arc, severing a series of saplings in one swing. As she did so, she let out a shout of anger and frustration.

"I'm going to go out on a limb here and say that Carmen didn't make that thing so you could use it to cut down trees," said Bryce, the party's Wizard. He specialized in long-casting, hard-hitting spells that could change the shape of any battle, but he exchanged that ability for any personal survivability. Most classes were equipped with some sort of ability that helped keep them alive, but Wizards were one of the few exceptions. As a result, he was definitely the kind of a glass cannon who was almost solely reliant on someone else to be effective.

"Like it matters," Kevin, the group's healer, said. He was a short, dumpy man with a crown of shaggy hair, and he'd taken the Rejuvenator class, which meant that he specialized in efficiency and healing over time. As with every other class, though, that specialization came at the expense of versatility. His healing spells took time to work their magic, and as a result, he wasn't great for emergency situations. But a healer was a healer, and they were rare enough that nobody could be particularly picky. "I've seen that thing go through a brick wall and not get a scratch. Wish I could convince her to make me something."

"If you're using a weapon, you're doing something wrong," Bryce stated. Tall, weedy, and awkward, he clearly hadn't allocated many of his attribute points into any of the physical categories. But from what Alyssa had seen, he had Ethera for days, and he regenerated it extremely quickly.

"Or you are," Kevin pointed out. "I mean, I'm dependent on jabronis like you to—"

"That word makes you sound like an idiot," said the final member of their party, Lisa. She occupied the scout role, but she was more of a damage dealer than anything else. Alyssa had no idea what the woman's class was—she wasn't keen on volunteering anything—but that wasn't a huge deal. She did her job, and that was all that really mattered.

"What word? Jabroni?" Kevin asked.

Bryce said, "I think it's cool. You should definitely keep using it at every opportunity."

"Do I sense some sarcasm?"

"From me? Noooo. I would never . . ."

"I hate you both," Kevin muttered.

"Samesies," Bryce said with a grin.

"That word makes you sound just as stupid as him," Lisa said. "In fact, I think being around you two is having a negative effect on my own intelligence. I'm going scouting." She looked at Alyssa, asking, "That alright, boss?"

Alyssa nodded, and the woman flitted off into the wilderness. If Alyssa really wanted to, she could have kept track of her. She certainly wasn't as adept at stealth as Roman. But that was fine. For a normal patrol, her skills were adequate for their purposes.

As the group continued on, Alyssa struggled to keep her mind on the task at hand. Not because of the banter between the remaining members of the patrol party but, rather, because her mind was nestled firmly back in Easton.

The settlement's name was no new addition—indeed, it had been in place since they'd made the connection to the World Tree—but Alyssa still had difficulty thinking of it as anything but the settlement. Easton had been the now-defunct town where they'd lived before the world's transformation, not the settlement they'd managed to cobble together from the ruins of a lost civilization.

In any case, Alyssa wasn't frustrated with names. In fact, she should have been happy. Things were looking up, and it appeared that they'd passed through the worst of the transition. The problem, though, was Roman.

He'd never been much for compassion, and after Trish's death, his heart had further hardened. He didn't care much for the sanctity of human life. Instead, he looked at everything with the eyes of a man who was only concerned with the prosperity of the settlement as a whole. That meant that, if someone couldn't pull their weight, Roman wanted to get rid of them.

The same could be said for any refugees who happened to stumble on them. Most recently, he'd turned a group of thirty away because they didn't possess what he considered useful classes. Or not enough of them, at least. If they couldn't contribute to Easton's immediate needs, then they had no place in the town. He'd turned them away without a second thought, and Alyssa hadn't found out about it until they were already gone.

When she chased them down, they'd been attacked by a herd of monsters, and the majority had been killed. She'd brought the survivors back to Easton, but saving those few wasn't enough to assuage her conscience.

And the worst of it was that she knew that, if another group came while she was gone, they'd be turned away, too.

She understood Roman's stance. There were only so many people they could support. Despite the fruition of the attempts to grow crops and their constant efforts to hunt more game, there was only so much food to go around. More, living conditions were still crowded, and while they were constantly building more houses, it was a slow process that had left quite a few people crammed into small domiciles.

They were surviving, but they were a long way from thriving. As a result, taking on more refugees was a bad idea. Alyssa knew that. But she didn't accept the ramifications. She would go without if it meant someone else had a chance to live, and she suspected that many of Easton's residents thought the same thing.

Or she hoped so, at least.

Before leaving on the current scouting expedition, she'd had another argument with Roman about it, but neither had been willing to budge. She trusted the man, and she knew he meant well, but they just couldn't come to a consensus about how to approach the subject. More than once, she'd thought about how much easier things would be if they simply broke apart and went their separate ways. If she hadn't had Carmen and Miguel to worry about, she might've already done it.

Shaking her head as she looked around, she realized how untrue that was. For better or worse, she cared about the people of Easton—too much to abandon them, especially over people she'd never even met. So, as much as she wanted to save everyone, Alyssa knew precisely where her priorities lay.

"You alright, boss?" asked Kevin.

"I'm fine, Kev," she said. "Just stressed is all."

"For what it's worth, we agree with you," Bryce said, adopting an uncharacteristically serious tone. As far as Alyssa knew, the man had approached the world like it was one of the video games he'd played before the world ended. It had served him well, giving him some insight into the inner workings of the System. However, it also meant that he sometimes failed to take things seriously, instead approaching it like he'd simply respawn if things went wrong. He wasn't the only one, either.

More than once, Alyssa had considered the possibility that the world's integration into the larger universe had been a large enough change that it had broken people's minds. Not completely. Not with the ones who'd survived, at least. But just enough that they weren't truly certain if what they saw was real.

Alyssa said, "You're a good man, Bryce. Don't let yourself forget that. Now, eyes up. You know how dangerous it is out here."

For the next hour, they continued on their patrol, passing through the old town along the way. The vegetation had experienced explosive growth over the spring and summer, and as a result, many of the buildings had been enveloped by creeping vines and blankets of moss. Thankfully, though, they didn't encounter any monsters.

They were out there, Alyssa was certain. They always were. In that respect, it wasn't unlike walking through the woods before the integration. Back then, animals were all around; they were just good at staying hidden. The mutated versions of the new world were the same, and most avoided humanity as much as possible.

The patrols were there to combat the other ones. The type that preyed on humans and killed indiscriminately. There were plenty of those, as well, which meant that the patrols were an absolute and dangerous necessity.

Almost an hour after she left them, Lisa returned. The slender girl—she couldn't have been older than nineteen—slipped from between a pair of overgrown buildings, saying, "Boss. You need to see this."

"What is it?"

"I genuinely don't know."

"That doesn't sound good," Alyssa muttered, but she directed the others to follow Lisa as the scout led them across the abandoned and mostly destroyed town. Along the way, Alyssa saw a few smaller animals, and she even caught sight of a couple of skeletons that had once been human beings. They hadn't had the chance to properly bury the people who'd died right after the integration, and so, they'd been left out to rot.

Or for the scavengers to gorge themselves.

Finally, Lisa pointed at the old hardware store and said, "In there."

"What?"

"I don't know. It's some kind of . . . I don't know. A hole in space or something. It's weird. Once I saw it, I didn't go any closer, but I wasn't so far away that I didn't feel it."

"Feel what?" asked Bryce. He carried a staff, though he didn't know how to use it. It was more of an affectation for the Wizard.

"The scaled monsters," she said. "Like that but different. Wrong, you know?"

They all nodded. Each of them had felt it, so they knew precisely what she was talking about.

"Okay," Alyssa said. "Bryce and Kev, to the rear. Lisa, flanking. If something comes, I'll pin it down. Everyone else, do what you do."

They'd drilled the strategy dozens of times, and it worked great against the comparatively weak wildlife. Against the scaled monsters—the Voxx, Alyssa had read in one of the guides she'd bought off the Branch—it was only moderately effective. It was fine when they only faced the weaker versions, but against something like the creature that had killed Trish, it would be woefully inadequate. If they fought something like that, Alyssa intended to tell her team to run while she tied it up.

They probably wouldn't obey that order, though.

In any case, they couldn't leave something like that free, let alone something that sounded suspiciously like the dimensional rifts Alyssa had read about. She'd made those guides available for anyone who wanted to read them, but few people had the time or the inclination to learn more than was absolutely necessary. Survival was enough to occupy the whole of their minds.

"Follow."

Then, Alyssa advanced, passing through the shattered frame that had once held a pane of glass. When she stepped inside, she was assailed by a musty smell and a subtle undercurrent of what she could only interpret as corruption. Overgrown with moss and fungi, the interior of the old hardware store looked like it had been abandoned for decades rather than a little less than a year.

An effect of the ambient Ethera, she reasoned.

What remained of the shelves were empty, having been picked clean by scavenger teams, so there was nothing useful—aside from a few mushrooms that looked like an edible variety. She marked them in her mind, intending to direct the gatherers to the small cache of potential food.

Slowly, they advanced. The store was a local mom-and-pop operation—or at least it had been before the world ended—so it didn't take long to reach the rear. When the group did, Alyssa saw the anomaly that had garnered Lisa's attention.

Suspended a few inches above the floor, it was a gaping hole with jagged, purple-glowing edges that looked like some interdimensional being had ripped a hole in the fabric of reality. The interior of the portal—and that was clearly what it was—was pitch-black, offering no visibility.

"We have to go in," she said.

"W-what?" asked Kevin.

"That sounds like the kind of thing someone says before they're violently murdered," Bryce pointed out.

"I hate to agree with him, but Bryce is right," Lisa agreed.

"Wait, why do you hate to agree with me? I'm smart," he argued.

"You're stupid smart. Like, you know plenty of things, but . . . Well, you're stupid, too."

"That makes no sense."

"Doesn't have to."

"Shut up," Alyssa said. "That's a dimensional rift. A minor one, by the looks of it. If we don't close it, it's going to burst, and we'll get a flood of those scaled monsters. If we go in, though, we can close it. And we'll be rewarded for it, too."

"No offense, boss, but we'd have to be alive to get a reward," Bryce said.

"That's the idea, yeah."

"But if it's got one of those big monsters inside . . ."

"It won't. It'll be one we can handle."

"You know that?" he asked.

"No," Alyssa said. "Not for sure. But everything I've read suggests we should be able to do this. More importantly, we're here. If we take the time to go back, it might burst. If that happens, people will die."

"And if we go in there, we might be the ones to die," said Kevin.

"Maybe," Alyssa acknowledged. "But maybe not."

"Fine. I'm in," said Bryce. Kevin looked at him like he'd said something crazy. "Look—we've got the boss here. If we're ever going to earn our pay—"

"We don't get paid," Kevin pointed out.

"Whatever. You know what I mean. If we're ever going to do something like this, now's the time when we've got the best chance of surviving. Plus, I'm close to leveling."

"This isn't a game, Bryce," said Kevin.

"I'm aware," he replied, a bit of steel in his voice. Like everyone else, he'd lost people, and every now and again, he let the carefree mask slip.

"I'm going in," Alyssa said, cutting the conversation off. "You can come in with me if you want. Or not. If you don't—"

"We're obviously coming with you, boss."

"Yeah."

Lisa added, "I'm in."

"Alright. Let's do this," Alyssa said, forcing a smile. She appreciated their loyalty and faith, but she also knew what was probably on the other side of that gate.

So, she took a deep breath, then stepped forward into hell.

After a blink-and-you'll-miss-it period of black nothingness, Alyssa stumbled into a rocky landscape. Upon crossing that threshold, the first thing she saw was a sky of roiling purple fire, but soon after, she took in the gray terrain with rivers of purple liquid cutting through it. More importantly, she saw the creature.

Even as the others staggered out of the gate, the viridian monster—four arms, two legs, and a face like a salamander—rumbled forward. It was big. A little over six feet tall and bulging with rippling muscles.

Alyssa didn't hesitate to act.

Using Heroic Leap, she launched herself into the sky. The monster stopped its charge, seemingly surprised by what it saw. At the apex of her leap, she used Descending Dragon, which sent her plummeting toward the ground like a falling meteor. She led the way with the Spear of the Dragon Lancer, which sliced through the monster's scales, pierced through its thick muscles, and erupted from between its four shoulder blades. Then, her weight hit it, knocking it onto its back.

The blade of her spear bit deep into the ground, pinning the creature in place.

However, Alyssa didn't escape unharmed. The moment she landed on its chest, the Voxxian monster went insane and, with all four of its clawed hands, tried to rip her to pieces. She sprang away in a backflip that sent a cascade of blood raining onto the landscape, then landed on unsteady legs.

Then, she felt the familiar sensation of Kevin's healing spells layering onto her. One after another, and the wounds the monster had ripped open began to mend. Still, it would take more than a few minutes for her to completely heal, and the monster wouldn't remain pinned in place for long.

That's where the other two members of the party came in.

Bryce had begun casting the second he'd stepped through the portal, and he would be occupied for a few more seconds still. Meanwhile, Lisa had circled around to the back, unnoticed by the monster. And even as Alyssa gathered herself for another pass at the creature, Lisa struck.

Once. Twice. Her swords arched out, biting deep under the influence of her abilities.

The Voxxian monster screamed in pain, terror, and rage, ripping itself free of Alyssa's spear. Before Lisa could react, it wheeled around, catching her with a backhand that sent her sprawling. Alyssa bounded forward, dragging her trusty machete from the sheath at her hip. As she did, she used Heart of the Dragon and Enrage in conjunction, sending her attributes skyrocketing.

Her first attack hit the creature's shoulder, and the blade didn't stop until it was embedded in its collarbone. She tried to yank the weapon free, but it was stuck fast. So, she let it go and kicked out, taking the monster in the stomach.

It staggered back but recovered quickly. Still, with Alyssa's attributes so enhanced, it was no match for her. She raced forward—not at the monster, but at the spear she'd left embedded in the rocky ground. When she reached the weapon, she wrapped her fingers around the familiar haft and yanked it free.

That was when Heart of the Dragon ran its course. Her attributes plummeted, eliciting a gasp and a stumble at exactly the wrong time. She twisted around, trying to get her spear up, but the Voxxian monster was already upon her.

It tackled her to the ground, then raised its talons high into the air. They fell. Alyssa screamed as she was torn to pieces. Kevin screamed as he tried to layer his healing spells on her, and for a moment, they did the trick. She healed almost as quickly as the monster could tear through her body.

But it was short-lived, obviously the result of some ability that accelerated the healing-over-time effects upon which he relied so heavily.

Then, Lisa was back, her swords moving in a blur as she sliced into the creature's back. It wasn't much damage—not really. But it was enough to get its attention. The moment it turned to her, Alyssa kicked away. It paid her no mind, intent as it was on getting to Lisa. For her part, the young scout bounded away, barely faster than the scaled monster.

That was the opening Bryce needed.

He let loose with his spell, and a huge ball of molten rock descended from the sky. When it hit the Voxxian monster, it sent out a shock wave powerful enough to nearly knock the recovering Alyssa from her feet. Lisa stumbled to her knees before pitching forward onto her chest.

And the monster was buried under a pile of lava.

The spell only lasted a moment before it dissipated, and when it did, a sizable crater—at least ten feet wide and a few feet deep—was revealed. The monster wasn't dead, though. It pushed itself to unsteady feet, then looked around.

Its scales were smoking, and it was clearly wounded. But it was still standing.

Alyssa, who was still healing, intended to put an end to that.

So, she bounded forward in a loping run. She couldn't use Descending Dragon so soon, but Heroic Leap had no cooldown. She intended to use that to her advantage. Before she did, though, she used Heavy Blows, then Charge. Finally, she kicked off the ground, using Heroic Leap, sending her rocketing through the air. Before she reached the monster, she threw Bulwark out behind it, then used Champion's Shout.

The creature froze for a split second, which allowed Alyssa to once again stab it in the chest. As she did, she used Impale, which, in the event that it didn't immediately die, would cause damage over time.

Her momentum knocked the monster back, but it could only go a few inches before it hit her Bulwark, which acted as an anvil.

And she was the hammer.

Bones cracked on both sides, but Alyssa had the benefit of Kevin's healing. She reared back, yanking her spear free before stabbing it again. Then again after that. Three times, she managed to wound it before the monster knocked her free.

The moment Alyssa was clear, another spell—this time, sharpened spikes of ice ascending from the ground—exploded into the creature. Seeing that it was distracted, both Alyssa and Lisa hit it again. This time, its responses were sluggish, and they managed to do quite a bit more damage than the first few forays.

But still, the monster was dangerous and immensely powerful, and they were both forced to retreat a moment later. That's when Bryce shouted, "After this, I'm out!"

Then, a giant earthen worm burst forth from the ground, wrapped itself around the monster, and squeezed. It screamed, but its bestial cries fell on deaf ears. Bryce's summon only lasted a few seconds before it fell apart, but by then, the monster was barely standing.

Alyssa approached with steady resolve, and when she got in range, she thrust her spear forward with deadly accuracy. The creature tried to respond, but it was far too sluggish. The blade took it in the throat, and Alyssa ripped it free a moment later, leaving a jagged wound behind.

That was the last straw, and it tipped forward, falling flat on its face. A few seconds later, it bled out, sending a deluge of experience to blanket the group. The moment the monster died, a pure-white crystal appeared before Alyssa. She reached out, touching it, prompting a notification:

Congratulations! By closing a Minor Dimensional Rift, you have done a great service to your world. Thus, you have earned a reward. Minor attribute potion awarded.

Alyssa also gained a level, pushing her to level fourteen and granting a new ability. She didn't take the time to inspect it, instead focusing on the vial of white liquid in her hand. She looked around, seeing that all the others were holding similar rewards.

"Well, I guess we win," said Bryce, raising his arms in a sarcastic cheer. "Yay, us."

49

GUARDIAN

Elijah was in mid-celebration when he felt something about the current change. No stranger to ambushes, he wheeled around, ready to defend himself. But when he did, he saw nothing but a gaping maw filled with jagged teeth. Panicked, he tried to dash away, but he only took a single step before the maw closed around him.

He let out a gurgling scream as the jaws clamped down on him, but he kept enough of his wits about him to grab hold of whatever he could and drag himself forward. The creature's teeth ripped a ragged wound down his side and very nearly tore his leg off, and yet, he still managed to pull himself to safety. With terror and agony tearing through his mind, Elijah barely managed to slap a hand on his side and cast Touch of Nature before the creature's bulbous purple tongue shifted and forced him down its slimy throat.

Crushing pressure encapsulated him, breaking bones and making him feel like an overfilled balloon on the verge of bursting. Somewhere in the back of his mind where the terror, pain, and panic couldn't reach him, Elijah recognized what was happening as the muscles in the creature's throat slowly pushed him down its esophagus.

But he could barely think, much less acknowledge that seemingly useless information. Somehow, he managed to recast Touch of Nature. The healing spell wasn't enough to keep up with the crushing damage, but it was barely capable of keeping him alive and conscious.

Pain, he would later acknowledge, was not something to which one could really grow accustomed. Elijah learned the truth of that as he was slowly but surely crushed as the creature swallowed him. Without his consistent use of Touch of Nature or the ability to breathe underwater that had been granted by the Ring of Aquatic Travel, he would have perished. The same could be said about his Constitution, which had been further enhanced by Essence of the Boar.

Still, Elijah couldn't think straight enough to be grateful. In fact, if death would have closed in on him, he might have been thankful.

Yet, held at bay by his healing spell, death did not come, and eventually, Elijah broke free of the esophagus and fell into a pit of acid. Screaming while he recast Touch of Nature, Elijah dragged himself forward, crawling across the fleshy innards of the monster until, at last, the sting of the acid began to dissipate.

But just because the acid wasn't eating through him at a visible rate, that didn't mean it wasn't still killing him. Away from the center of what must have been the monster's stomach, the acid had been diluted by the water, but it was still there, slowly dissolving his flesh.

Through the pain, Elijah forced himself to focus just enough to take stock of his Ethera. It was dangerously low. And he knew he couldn't keep using Touch of Nature. He'd run out of Ethera, and then, he'd die a slow and agonizing death. But with Healing Rain, there was a possibility that he could keep pace with the damage being wreaked on his body.

So, he cast it.

Apparently, being underwater wasn't enough to stop the spell from activating, and as the rain—Elijah didn't question how that was possible—fell, he felt the healing magic begin to take hold.

But just because he was constantly regenerating didn't mean that the pain had stopped. Indeed, it only meant that, so long as he could keep Healing Rain active, the damage was negated by the Regeneration.

Still, the cycle of damage and Regeneration hurt. A lot. And as a result, Elijah started to go into shock. And that shock eventually ushered him into unconsciousness. When he awoke some indeterminate time later, his Healing Rain had run its course, and the acid had gained some ground. So, he recast the spell and tried to force himself to remain conscious long enough to utilize the Ethera that had regenerated while he'd been unconscious.

To that end, he cast Touch of Nature, marginally healing the wound in his side. It didn't do much. In fact, the spell didn't even completely close the wound. But it was progress, and in his situation, that was all he could really hope for.

From that point on, Elijah's world devolved into a cycle of hellish agony and healing. It was not pleasant. In fact, it was the worst experience of his life. And given that he'd gone through multiple rounds of radiation and chemotherapy, that was saying something. For a long time, he was incapable of rational thought. Instead, he focused the entirety of his consciousness on maintaining the cycle.

Heal. Regenerate. Heal some more. Cast Healing Rain. Keep healing. Regenerate. Hours must have passed. Perhaps days. Elijah had no means of keeping track. But gradually, he gained ground until, at last, the wound on his side had healed as much as it could when encased in a pool of diluted acid.

Then, he started on his leg.

The monster's teeth had ripped a long, jagged wound that ran from mid-ankle all the way to his knee, exposing muscle, bone, and everything else skin was supposed to hide. Resting his hand on the injury, he began the cycle anew.

By the time he finished, weeks had to have passed, but it might as well have been an eternity. With the ubiquitous pain keeping him from resting, his mind had descended well past the dividing line between sanity and madness. The only thing that had kept him from plunging headlong into insanity was the focus he'd had to maintain. Otherwise, he would have long since succumbed.

But it still took its toll, and as he finally saw the wound in his leg heal, the only thought on his mind was vengeance against the monster who was responsible for shoving him into a pit of hell.

And without the need to use all his Ethera on healing, he had options available. The first thing he tried was Swarm, but his conjured piranhas only lasted a quarter of their usual time before the acid did them in.

That was fine, though. He had other spells.

After renewing Healing Rain, Elijah cast Shape of the Predator. He still couldn't swim, but what he had in mind only required him to stand still and attack. He could do that.

And so he did, ripping into the monster's innards with his claws. But it wasn't enough. The creature was tough, and even though he spent the entirety of Healing Rain's duration furiously digging into the thing's flesh, the only effect was a shallow divot.

Transforming back into his human form, Elijah renewed Healing Rain and forced himself to think. With the pain of his skin being constantly dissolved by the acid and rebuilt by Healing Rain, his thoughts were sluggish. Still, he could think just clearly enough to recognize that he was missing something incredibly important. Though, try as he might, he couldn't put his finger on it.

Then, like a lightning bolt, it hit him.

Venom Strike. The ability he'd yet to use because he had no interest in getting close to monsters when he was in his human form. But now? He was already close. Too close, really. To focus his mind, he pulled up the ability's description:

Venom Strike	**Imbues an attack with a fast-acting neurotoxin. Usable in all forms. Damage doubled when in Predator form.**

Double damage when in Predator form. That was all Elijah needed to set his path. Still, he couldn't immediately take the first step down that road. Instead, he had to wait until he'd regenerated enough Ethera to fuel the transformation into his Predator form. Then, he needed to cast the spell directly after renewing Healing Rain. Otherwise, he would lose ground to the acid still steadily eating away at his skin.

So, he waited.

In agony.

Compared to the time he'd already spent in the creature's stomach, it was nothing. But with the plan for his eventual escape taunting him, Elijah could barely stand it. It felt like an eternity. Still, in the back of his mind, buried beneath a mountain of pain, he knew that if he jumped the gun, he would only make things worse.

With that firmly entrenched in his mind, he continued to wait. And suffer.

Eventually, though, Elijah recovered enough Ethera to power his transformation into a mist panther. Still, he waited until he could renew Healing Rain before he initiated the spell. As usual, the transformation didn't take long, and as soon as it was complete, he used Venom Strike.

Then, he attacked.

The effect was immediate, and the monster's response nearly threw Elijah from his feet. He clung to the fleshy stomach lining with his claws and attacked once again. And again after that. He kept digging into the monster's innards, with each swipe of his claws bearing with it a refreshed Venom Strike.

Each attack drained a bit of his stamina, and within thirty seconds, he could barely hold himself upright. So, he switched back to his human form to wait for the neurotoxin to take hold.

The moment he did, though, he realized his mistake. In the ubiquitous pain clouding his mind, Elijah hadn't considered the fact that, as a human, he didn't have any claws, and so, the moment he switched back, the monster's convulsions sent him flying back into the dense acid in the center of the stomach.

If he'd been in agony before, there was no word capable of describing what he felt as he plunged into the more concentrated acid. He flailed, watching his skin melting away with every passing moment. Then, the most powerful shudder yet rocked the stomach, and suddenly, Elijah was flying forward. He hit the esophagus, and it opened. A second later, a powerful current pushed him into the fleshy hose until, at last, he passed the teeth that had ripped him to pieces.

And just like that, he was free.

Tumbling down through the water, he hit a stand of coral that scraped much of his melted skin from his shoulder, then settled into the silt where he lay, completely incapable of moving. Even as unconsciousness started to close in, Elijah managed to cast Healing Rain.

Then, darkness enveloped him.

It only lasted a few moments, and when he awoke, the blessed lack of acid was enough to jolt him back to reality. He still hurt, but it was the pain of more mundane injuries rather than the constant agony of being dissolved.

Opening his eyes, Elijah tried to sit up but immediately wished he hadn't. More agony lanced through his body as he collapsed onto the ground. Checking his Ethera, he saw that he had enough to fuel a few casts of Touch of Nature—maybe he'd been out longer than he thought. So, he flopped his arm over his stomach and cast the spell. A wave of healing magic swept through him, making him feel slightly better, but it was directionless and only resulted in a slightly better overall condition.

Still, it was better than nothing, especially when combined with the ongoing Regeneration from the still-active Healing Rain. And after his time being slowly digested within the monster's stomach, the small relief the spell brought with it was more than welcome. He cast the spell three more times before his Ethera ran dry. Then, he lay back and waited for his core to regenerate. As he did so, he focused on the funnel of his mind, trying to force more and more ambient Ethera into his soul.

It was mildly successful, though the improvement over his normal meditative Regeneration was barely noticeable. It might've even been his imagination at work. Whatever the case, he resolved to keep it up on the off chance that he wasn't imagining things.

Gradually, his core refilled until, at last, he could continue his efforts to heal his ravaged body. One cast of Touch of Nature after another, and after using two cores' worth of Ethera, he felt well enough to sit up. His body protested as he levered himself upright and looked down at his arm.

It was a withered mass of flesh that looked like nothing so much as a melted candle.

Groaning, Elijah grabbed it and resumed his healing. With each cast of Touch of Nature, his arm looked a little better. More, he slowly regained feeling as the nerves and muscles rebuilt themselves. However, when he finally finished the healing process, his arm still bore significant scarring.

Fortunately, the rest of his body had escaped that fate, though his clothing and hair had long since dissolved.

His staff had survived, though, and once he picked himself up, he found it only a few feet away. So, naked as the day he was born—and even more hairless—Elijah started toward the creature that had fallen only a few dozen yards away.

The neurotoxin of Venom Strike had nearly killed the monster that had tried to eat him, but the job still wasn't finished. With vengeance in his heart, Elijah aimed to change that.

50

VENGEANCE AND MERCY

Elijah rolled his shoulders as he strode forward, but in the back of his mind, he realized that the effect was probably ruined by the curious, bouncing gait required to walk across the seafloor. He didn't care, though. Instead, he only had eyes for the monster that had tried to eat him.

It was an orca.

Or that was the closest analogue Elijah could conjure. The thing was at least a hundred feet long, with the same sturdy yet sleek black-and-white body as the familiar marine mammals. But like all the other animals he'd seen in the sea—and on the island, come to that—everything about it seemed more exaggerated. From its huge jagged teeth to its slightly more angular body, it was like a cartoon version of the creatures with which he was familiar.

And it was obviously dying.

The thing was still breathing, but it couldn't move more than a few feet in any direction. So, as Elijah approached, it only succeeded in flopping around a bit. Still, it was a monster that probably weighed dozens of tons, so there was a very real danger of being crushed. With that in mind, Elijah took great care as he drew closer.

But it didn't even acknowledge his presence. Instead, it seemed wholly focused on its own agony as Elijah's repeated usage of Venom Strike slowly ate away at it. Given the orca's massive size, Elijah knew its death would not be quick. Instead, it was in for a slow and agonizing process.

There was a part of him that thought it served the creature right. After spending what felt like an eternity being digested by the sea mammal, Elijah thought it had gotten its just deserts. However, the marine biologist inside of him rejected that idea. As much as he wanted to take pleasure in its suffering, Elijah couldn't shed the lessons he'd learned at his father's knee.

Killing wasn't wrong. Instead, death and predation were necessary parts of nature. Elijah had never shied away from hunting or fishing. But his father had taught him that any responsible hunter tried to minimize his prey's suffering. So, as much as Elijah wanted to anthropomorphize the enormous killer whale and assign blame, the reality was that the thing had merely been acting according to its nature. There was no sapience there. It was just an animal, and so, it couldn't be blamed for its actions.

Taking vengeance on the creature was an exercise in futility. It would never understand its mistake. There was no lesson to be taught. No reform to be found. And, even though Elijah knew he'd feel a certain satisfaction when the thing was dead, he also knew himself well enough to recognize the fact that, with the benefit of time and distance, he would regret it if he let the thing suffer more than necessary.

So, it was with mercy on his mind that Elijah raised his staff and conjured his Swarm of piranhas, which wasted no time before tearing into the monster. It wasn't enough to finish it off. Nor was the second cast. Or the third. Soon, it became clear that, if he wanted to hasten the monster's death, he would have to do so up close.

That was why he found himself leaping from a hastily climbed stalk of coral onto the orca's back. It didn't react. Instead, the creature only continued its weak convulsions as Elijah climbed toward its head and then, when he reached his destination, transformed into a mist panther.

Immediately, he felt awkward, and his instincts screamed at him to somehow get out of the water. He pushed through that and embraced Guise of the Unseen. Before the fact that he was out in the open and standing atop a giant killer whale could degrade his stealth, Elijah reached back with his claw and used Predator Strike to gouge a massive hole in the orca's head.

That woke it up, and its bucking sent Elijah spinning through the water before he landed in a cloud of silt. With the panic of his feline instincts threatening to overwhelm him, Elijah transformed back into his human form. Then, after he healed the minor damage he'd sustained—just a few bruises—he waited for his Ethera to regenerate enough that he could repeat the process. When his core was saturated with Ethera, he climbed the coral stalk, leaped onto the orca's back, and repeated his previous strike. This one went a good deal deeper, but the result was much the same, and he ended up back on the sea floor.

It took three more uses of Predator Strike before Elijah broke through the monster's thick skull. After that, it only took one more attack to destroy its brain. And just like that, a wave of kill energy swept through him, giving him two levels and a new ability.

More importantly, he also received an update to his task, congratulating him on killing the guardian. Now, he just needed to reach the center of the Sea of Sorrows in order to complete the second level of the Keledge Tower.

Elijah's shoulders sagged, and he took a moment to dig a bit of the monster's brain out. One look at the black tendrils that had infested the creature's flesh, and he knew he couldn't eat any of it. Which was a shame, considering that he had no idea how long it had been since he'd eaten anything.

Perhaps his body was more magical than he'd originally thought. Or maybe his constant usage of his healing spells had helped keep him on his feet even as he starved. It was even possible that his perception of time had been skewed by the persistent agony he'd endured. He had no idea, but regardless of how he'd managed to live through his ordeal, he was now starving.

So, without hesitation, Elijah slid off the monster's back and immediately set off through the Sea of Sorrows. Eventually, he stumbled across a school of midsize fish that he killed with a trio of Storm's Fury casts. Then, like the starving man he was, he tore into them with reckless abandon.

Elijah had never been a huge fan of raw fish, but in that moment, he considered it the best meal he'd ever had. He gorged himself, then gathered a few of the fish he hadn't already eaten before moving on.

Like that, he kept going for the next few hours until he finally found a shallow cave in which he could rest. Once he'd blocked the entrance, Elijah settled in to inspect the ability he'd received upon reaching level twenty-six.

It was a spell:

Aura of Renewal	**Tap into the power of nature to increase your Regeneration by ten (10) points. Usable on allies.**

Elijah let out a chuckle that came out in a gurgle and sent a stream of bubbles drifting toward the ceiling of the small cave. That certainly would have come in handy while he was being digested. He just stared at the spell and shook his head before mentally canceling one of his other augmentations—Essence of the Monkey—and replacing it with his new spell.

Essence of the Monkey was great for when he was on land, but in the Sea of Sorrows, both Aura of Renewal and Essence of the Boar seemed much more important. Those two took up his only available enhancement slots, leaving Essence of the Monkey as the odd one out. Hopefully, though, he would get another slot sometime soon. At least Essence of the Wolf seemed to be a different category—perhaps because its effect was restricted to out of combat—so he didn't have to make the choice between more Constitution or faster movement speed.

In any case, Aura of Renewal was a nice addition. Still, he couldn't help but wonder what the future might hold. Perhaps he would get an augmentation that would enhance his Ethera next so he could complete the set. As he thought about his attributes, he couldn't help but toggle open his status:

Name	Elijah Hart		
Level	27		
Archetype	Druid		
Class	Animist		
Specialization	N/A		
Alignment	N/A		
Strength	28		
Dexterity	27		
Constitution	33 (28)		
Ethera	36		
Regeneration	40 (30)		
Attunement	Nature		
Cultivation			
Body	Core	Mind	Soul
Wood	Unformed	Opal	Neophyte

As always, his attributes had gone up by a single point for each of his two levels. It wasn't enough that he could notice the difference from before he'd killed the orca, but looking back to when he'd first entered the Keledge Tower, Elijah certainly felt stronger, more durable, and more coordinated. And he could cast his spells more often, which spoke to the size of his core. Finally, he felt certain that, without those few points he'd gained in Regeneration, he never would have survived the killer whale's stomach acid. So, while he hadn't made huge strides, they were enough to make the difference between life and death.

Which was all Elijah could really ask for, all told. Aside from maybe asking not to spend weeks being digested by a giant orca. That would've been nice, too, but maybe that would've been expecting a little too much, given the world in which he now lived.

Such thoughts occupied Elijah's mind as he settled in to rest and recover as much as he could. He slept, albeit fitfully, and soon enough, the urge to continue to the next and final level of the tower grew overwhelming. So, after once again gorging himself on the leftover fish, he used Touch of Nature to remove any chance of food poisoning, then set off.

The next day stretched his capabilities. Not by pitting him against powerful monsters. By that point, he'd spent long enough in the Sea of Sorrows that he felt almost as comfortable in that submerged environment as he did on his own island. Rather, the problem was his own body, which, despite his increased attributes, had been ravaged by malnourishment as well as the acid that had slowly eaten away at him. In fact, when he looked down at his thin limbs and exposed ribs, he suspected that he weighed less than he had at any time since the plane crash that had stranded him on the island.

And that was more than a little distressing because, at that time, he'd been fresh off his third round of chemotherapy.

Curiously, the problem didn't present itself in a way he might have expected. He was just as strong as ever before, but he could only show that Strength in extremely short bursts before he grew exhausted. The same could be said for his ability to traverse the Sea of Sorrows. He could only go for an hour or two before he needed to rest, which was a far cry from what he'd experienced before his bout of whale digestion.

But gradually, as he continued to eat his weight in slain monsters—from fish to turtles and everything in between—his endurance returned. By the end of that first week after his encounter with the killer whale, he'd reached what he thought of as the halfway point in his quest to recover his stamina. A week after that, he finally felt fully recovered—a feeling that was supported by his increased weight.

It was just in time, too, because that was when he finally reached the center of the Sea of Sorrows, which presented itself as a huge hole in the seabed that stretched hundreds of yards across. It didn't take a genius to guess that, in order to reach the third level, he would have to take the plunge and dive into the hole.

Still, he couldn't help but hesitate, especially when he found himself at the edge of the hole and looking down into the shadowy abyss.

Could he have been wrong about it being his goal? Of course. But given the saturation of Ethera in the area, he didn't think so. He'd also circled the pit, searching for anything else that might qualify as his destination. But he'd found nothing but more coral and kelp.

No—it was the right place, but knowing that did nothing to assuage the fear coursing through Elijah's veins. The first level had been fairly easy. The second had stretched him to his limits. And it stood to reason that the difficulty would only increase going ahead.

But as he kept reminding himself, there was no choice in the matter. He couldn't go back. Even the teleport associated with Ancestral Circle was disabled within the tower, which he'd confirmed at some point during the cycle of healing and dissolution he'd experienced in the whale's stomach.

The only way out was through.

So, he squared his shoulders, then dove into the abyss.

51

THE PRIMORDIAL JUNGLE

Elijah dove, slicing through the water with ease. Then, when he'd gone a few hundred feet, gravity shifted, and he was suddenly falling in the other direction. Inexplicably panicked, he desperately treaded water as he searched for some landmark in the abyssal darkness. Looking down, he saw nothing but blackness. The same was true when he spun left, then right. But when he tilted his head up, he saw a glimmer of light. So, with no other guide, he swam toward it. Gradually, he drew closer to the surface until, finally, he broke free in the middle of a storm.

That was a far cry from the Sea of Sorrows, which had been a strangely navigable underwater seascape.

Even with only a glance as evidence, Elijah knew that the new environment of the third level was markedly different. For one, it was clear that he would no longer have to live beneath the waves. Above him was a gray sky filled with storm clouds, and in the distance, he saw a strip of dense jungle that stretched from one end of the horizon to the other.

Struggling to stay afloat, Elijah knew the dangers of a storm on the open sea, so he started paddling to shore. It was difficult, and not just because of the violent current tugging against him. In addition to that riptide, he also had to deal with the inevitable effects of spending weeks in what amounted to a low-gravity environment. His muscles hadn't exactly atrophied, but he'd certainly grown used to using them less. And so, the way ashore was awkward and filled with frustration.

Still, he persisted, and after what felt like hours, he finally dragged himself onto a muddy beach.

Then, he collapsed, taking huge, gulping breaths as he tried to acclimate to what should have been his natural environment. It took some time, but eventually, he forced himself to his hands and knees. Then, a few minutes after that, he pushed himself upright and looked around.

The first thing he noticed was that a small metallic box had, at some point, appeared before him. It didn't take a genius to figure out that it was his reward for defeating the Keledge Tower's second level. So, he reached out with shaking hands and popped it open. Inside was another ring, which he promptly collected. Even as the box dissolved, Elijah read the notification that had accompanied the acquisition of the ring:

Reward for completing Level Two of the Keledge Tower: **Ring of Anonymity**

"What the hell does a Ring of Anonymity do?" he asked aloud, slipping the dark-green circlet around his pinkie finger. It shrank, sizing itself to fit, then disappeared from his sight. He could still feel it, so he knew it remained around his finger, but he couldn't see it at all. A moment later, he received another notification:

Ring of Anonymity Equipped. Choose Mode: **Anonymous** **False Identity (Unchosen)** **Deactivated (Currently Active)**

Elijah had no idea what any of that meant. So, he selected False Identity, which prompted yet another notification:

Specify False Identity: **?**

Intuitively, Elijah knew that he could create a pseudonym. But more than that, he could choose a new archetype, which he most certainly did not want to do. He suspected that it was only for display purposes, but he resolved not to use it until he knew for sure. The last thing he wanted was to screw things up. Besides, it wasn't as if anonymity would do much for him while he was still in the tower.

So, he left the ring Deactivated and moved on to the next two notifications he'd received. Both were expected.

Welcome to The Keledge Tower, Level Three. To conquer the tower, complete the Task before you.

It was almost identical to the notifications he'd gotten upon reaching the previous levels, so he shifted his attention to the next:

Task: Before you lies the Primordial Maze. There are many paths to completion, but some are more dangerous than others. Choose wisely, reach the center, and conquer the Tower.

Elijah read the message a few times, but it seemed straightforward enough. Before he could embark on that Task, though, he needed to get his feet under him. His time in the Sea of Sorrows had definitely taken its toll, and though he'd managed to recover somewhat, he was still naked, rail thin, and unaccustomed to existing on land.

With that in mind, Elijah slowly acclimated to his new environment. First, he worked up to standing, then walking, and finally, to doing the calisthenics routines he'd created when he'd first been stranded on the island. It took almost two days, during which his ability to go without food was tested, but eventually, he managed to recover some semblance of his former conditioning.

Thankfully, he didn't have to go without water, though. Not only was the rain constant, but the water in which he'd entered the level was fresh. So, that was one thing he didn't have to worry about.

His nudity, though, was unavoidable.

Which was how, two days later, he found himself standing on the muddy beach and staring ahead at a dense jungle. Somewhere ahead of him was the entrance to the Primordial Maze, which he would have to traverse before he could conquer the tower and get back to his island.

And given his experiences in the previous levels, he expected that the maze would be huge. Even if it was no larger than the Sea of Sorrows, it would take weeks—or maybe even months—to reach the center, and that was assuming he could find his way at all. More, he felt certain that there would be plenty of monsters within.

But at least he had all his abilities available. In the Sea of Sorrows, he'd learned a lot about using his caster form, but the jungle—and presumably the maze, as well—was tailor-made for his Predator form.

So, without further hesitation, Elijah cast Essence of the Wolf to increase his movement speed, then used Aura of Renewal to help him stave off fatigue, and finally Essence of the Monkey to augment his Dexterity. Only once he finished casting his enhancements did he use Shape of the Predator to transform into a mist panther. The moment the transformation completed, he felt infinitely more comfortable. Some of that was due to his glossy black fur, but there was also some ephemeral quality about the jungle that made him feel more at home.

He took a deep breath—oh, he'd certainly missed that when he was underwater—then activated Guise of the Unseen before setting off into the jungle. If he'd been in human form, he might've found the dense foliage difficult to traverse. Certainly, with the impenetrable canopy above him, Elijah would've felt at least a little claustrophobic. But as a panther? It wasn't even a factor.

He went a little more than a quarter of a mile before he smelled another animal. It was musty and unfamiliar, which triggered Elijah's curiosity. So, he stalked toward it, keeping low as he passed broken branches and fallen trees. Along the way, the smell grew stronger until, finally, he reached a massive pile of dung.

That certainly didn't bode well, but after giving it a quick sniff, he determined that he'd been tracking a carnivore. A few hundred yards later, he stumbled upon a giant track. It was at least four feet across, with three distinct claws that marked it as either a giant reptile or some sort of bird. In fact, to Elijah, it reminded him of a turkey's tracks, only hundreds of times larger.

Cautiously, he continued to follow the trail until he heard something crashing through the jungle ahead of him. Elijah didn't let himself react. Instead, he simply continued to follow until, at last, he saw his quarry.

And it was terrifying.

With its huge jaws, pebbled skin, powerful hind legs, and comparatively small forelegs, the massive reptile could only be described as a *Tyrannosaurus rex*. And it was happily feeding on some smaller, unidentifiable reptile.

Clearly, the primordial label extended to the jungle surrounding the maze.

Elijah shivered, then backed away. He had killed creatures just as large as the dinosaur—the killer whale had been much bigger, and even the giant isopod had rivaled the tyrannosaur in size. But there was just something about seeing the terrifying subject of countless movies and books that sent a jolt of fear up his spine.

He backed away, careful not to make a sound that might interfere with Guise of the Unseen. Then, once he'd made it a few dozen yards away, he turned and sped across the jungle. His haste was probably why, five minutes later, he fell afoul of a different sort of threat.

The sound of cracking bone echoed across the jungle as something reached up and grabbed him around the foot. Elijah let out a scream as he instinctively tried to tug his limb free, but all he did was make it worse. Something thudded into his side, piercing his hide, and he looked down to see that the thing that had clamped around his foot was what looked like a crude bear trap made of bone.

Something else hit him, this time in the shoulder, eliciting another cry of pain as it dug deep into the muscle. If Elijah hadn't had the benefit—if it could be called that—of spending days being steadily digested within the orca's stomach, the pain might've kept him from thinking straight.

It still hurt, but the agony didn't send him careening down the path of panic.

So, even as another something hit him in the back leg, he shifted form and cast Touch of Nature. He followed it up with Healing Rain before reaching down and prying his foot loose. He cast Touch of Nature again, mending the fractured bone enough that he could put weight on it. In the meantime, he heard something shout as another projectile went wide.

It was only then that he recognized that someone was shooting arrows at him.

He shouted, "I come in peace!"

He only got a roar in response as something that looked like a mix of ape and Sasquatch crashed through the forest, making a beeline toward him. Elijah didn't need more than a glance to confirm that he had no chance in a physical confrontation. The thing was at least eight feet tall, and beneath its shaggy red fur, it was thick with muscle. More, it was armed with a giant flint-headed spear.

So, Elijah took aim with his staff and cast Snaring Roots, which he'd largely ignored during his time in the Sea of Sorrows. Vines, thick and thorny, erupted from the ground and snaked around the creature's legs. It tripped, tumbling face-first into the ground, where even more vines enveloped it.

Elijah didn't dare stick around for a fight. He'd already used a lot of Ethera, and judging by the Sasquatch ape's size, it would take more than a few casts of Storm's Fury to take it out. However, he wasn't going to let it off completely unharmed. So, he hobbled forward, reared back with his staff, and after activating Venom Strike, smacked it across the back of the head. The already prone monster was driven down by the force of the blow.

But Elijah knew he hadn't done any real damage. Not yet. Eventually, Venom Strike would take effect, but because he'd activated it in his human form as opposed to as a mist panther, it wouldn't be nearly as dramatic as when he'd used it against the killer whale. So, after taking his swing, Elijah took off through the forest, bounding over the fallen trees and jumping across various depressions.

In a way, he felt like he was back on his island.

But clearly, the level of danger in the Primordial Maze was at least as high as it had been in the Sea of Sorrows he'd left behind. Monsters were one thing, but what really frightened him was a creature who could use tools like traps and the arrows still sticking out of him.

52

WILD

Once Elijah had gone a few hundred yards, he stopped and yanked the arrows out. There were three of them, but only one had penetrated more than an inch. Whether he could blame the ape creature's poor equipment or his own enhanced Constitution he had no idea, but whatever the reason for the projectiles' poor performance, he wasn't going to complain.

Normally, he wouldn't have removed the arrows, a caution borne out by the veritable fountain of blood that came with the most serious wound when he yanked the arrow free. But with Touch of Nature, he was capable of stemming the flow of blood in only an instant. It was especially effective with such a small wound, and after two casts, he'd completely healed the two most serious injuries. However, doing so drained most of his Ethera, so he had no choice but to continue his flight until he regenerated enough to finish the job.

So, that was what he did.

He knew he was leaving a trail a mile wide for the Sasquatch monster to follow him, but he didn't have much of a choice in the matter. He could only hope that his use of Venom Strike would slow it down enough so that he could get away.

Minutes passed, and to his surprise, Elijah wasn't forced to endure any further attacks. Soon, he regenerated enough Ethera to finish healing, though he kept running for almost an hour more until, at last, he used Shape of the Predator to return to his panther form and slink into the shadows.

Only once he'd climbed a tree did he let himself relax.

A little.

Even though he'd managed to escape with his life, Elijah knew precisely how close to the edge he'd gotten. One little mistake, and he would have died. And it'd been like that since he'd first stepped foot in the tower. Even back on the first level, the goblins were more than capable of killing him. Certainly, he'd easily massacred that village, but if he'd stepped one foot out of line, they would have fallen on him without mercy. And it was a fool's hope to expect quarter from such monsters.

No—he was walking a fine line, and even if he hadn't recently spent an untold number of days being digested in the stomach of a killer whale, he'd have been close to his breaking point. A person wasn't meant to endure so much constant stress.

But what choice did he have?

He couldn't afford to just break down. He didn't get the luxury of taking a break. He couldn't just call for a time-out. Even if he could find somewhere relatively safe, there was always the danger that some powerful predator would find him. And it wasn't as if he could just turn around and go home, either. Even if he could exit the Keledge Tower without conquering it, his reasons for challenging it in the first place hadn't changed. Either he won, or his island—and, eventually, the world—would be overrun with horrible monsters from another dimension.

He transformed back into his human form and muttered, "How is this my life now?"

Indeed, as he used Touch of Nature to complete the healing he'd begun during his flight, Elijah wondered how the rest of the world was faring. Were they fighting monsters, too? What about his sister? What about Carmen, his sister-in-law? Or his nephew? His ex-girlfriend back in Hawaii? The list went on and on, but it was a pointless exercise because he had no way of getting any answers.

Eventually, Elijah came to the conclusion that feeling sorry for himself was just as pointless as wondering how the rest of the world had dealt with the transition. So, he forced his mind to other topics—like the task before him. He'd already gotten turned around, so he didn't know which way was which. The sun still hadn't made an appearance, and despite being on the new level for a few days, night still hadn't fallen. It seemed reasonable to conclude that it never would. Instead, the whole level seemed eternally mired in a rainy afternoon.

After a while, Elijah transformed back into a panther, then climbed down from his perch. Over the next day, he scouted the area, but he still hadn't found the maze. So, he kept going, switching his focus to survival rather than exploration. He'd established that he could go without food for quite some time, but there were repercussions for doing so. With that in mind, he began his first hunt.

It didn't take long before he found another dinosaur. This one was clearly herbivorous, but Elijah couldn't identify it. Regardless, it was quadrupedal and the size of a large cow, which meant that it had plenty of edible meat. Most importantly, it didn't seem terribly dangerous, which meant that he could avoid tainting the meat with Venom Strike.

Instead, he crept forward, dipping below a series of low-hanging vines as he prepared to pounce. The creature, which resembled a triceratops, but without the natural armor or horns, remained completely unaware as Elijah stalked closer. When he got within a few feet, he embraced Predator Strike and leaped forward, slicing his claws across the monster's back leg.

The joint exploded, but Elijah had let the animal's ponderous size fool him into thinking that it was slow. It wheeled around, using its head as a club, and it would have connected if the thing's leg hadn't completely given out. As it was, the blow still came close enough that Elijah had to spring backward out of range.

The animal bellowed, either in agony or rage, as it tried to run away in a three-legged gait. It moved relatively quickly for its impairment, but Elijah was much faster. He darted in, slicing his claws across the other back leg. He didn't cut nearly as deeply, but he still severed the monster's hamstring. Not enough to completely immobilize it, but it was further slowed, which allowed Elijah to dart in once again and nip at the front leg.

This attack wasn't nearly as effective, but with the dinosaur so thoroughly wounded, Elijah had the luxury of time. So, over the next few minutes, he continuously harassed the injured animal until, at last, he disabled the third limb. Soon after, the creature collapsed. But as Elijah found out when he tried to finish it off, his prey wasn't completely defenseless. He darted in, and it once again swung its head around, taking him in the side and sending him rolling across the jungle until he hit a tree.

Growling, he found his feet.

He'd sustained a few broken ribs, and though they were painful, he couldn't afford to switch back to his human form and heal. Soon, the jungle's scavengers and other predators would smell the blood in the air, and when they did, they would descend upon the scene. If Elijah was there when that happened, he'd be forced to flee. So, without the option to heal himself, he once again started circling the immobilized monster.

It tried to track him, but with its injuries, it could only do so much. So, when Elijah found a blind spot, he pounced. This time, he leaped atop the creature's back and clamped his jaws down on the base of the thing's skull. At first, Elijah couldn't get through the dinosaur's tough, pebbly skin, but he leveraged his enhanced Strength to great effect, and soon enough, he crushed the thing's spine.

It went limp, but it was still alive.

Elijah ended its life a few moments later when he raked his claws across its throat and watched it bleed out.

Then, without bothering to shift back to his human form, Elijah tore into the creature's haunches, eating as much as he could handle before dashing away.

Over the next few days, he followed the same pattern. Hunting, eating, and surviving—it was so easy to lose himself in the animalistic instincts that came with his predator form. Soon enough, he found that he only canceled Shape of the Predator when he was injured and needed healing. Otherwise, he remained in his predator form at all times.

And gradually, he lost track of time. At some point, he gained another level, but he didn't really notice it. He was too busy living the life of an apex predator.

Later, he would recognize his descent into animalism as a coping mechanism, but it wasn't until, weeks later, he stumbled upon the maze that he was shocked out of it. Suddenly, as he stood in front of that gate, his humanity came rushing back, and when it did, it brought with it the memory that he wasn't just there to survive. He had a goal.

He had a Task.

To remind himself, he summoned the notification he'd read just after entering the jungle:

Task: Before you lies the Primordial Maze. There are many paths to completion, but some are more dangerous than others. Choose wisely, reach the center, and conquer the Tower.

How long had it been since he'd assumed his human form? It had felt like . . . he didn't know how long. Days, at least. Weeks, probably. It might have even been months. In his panther form, and with the sameness of the gray days, time was difficult to judge. But he knew it had been far too long.

So, with some regret, Elijah forced himself back into the shape of a human being. Even as he changed, he felt a sudden sense of loss. The world seemed so much less alive. There were no interesting smells. He couldn't see nearly as well. And standing on two legs, he felt so weak. So awkward.

So human.

His heartbeat quickened. His breath came in sudden, sharp, and shallow pants as a formless panic began to overwhelm him. Nothing seemed to make sense, and if he'd had the Ethera for it, he would have immediately shifted back to the Shape of the Predator.

Leaning on his staff, he struggled to get his breathing under control. As he wrangled his emotions, Elijah saw his feelings for the danger they represented. It was so easy to be an animal. It was a much simpler life to surrender to the mechanics of survival and let everything else fall away.

But he was not an animal.

"Human," he muttered, his voice ragged from lack of use. The word felt thick on his tongue, and it certainly didn't come easily. It was like his mind was fighting him. Still, he persisted: "I am . . . human."

He repeated the words a few more times, and with each iteration, he felt a little more in control. The panic receded, and he felt more comfortable in his own body.

Elijah looked down. He had gained weight, and his body was corded with lean muscle. His memory of his self-image was a little fuzzy, but he suspected that he was even healthier than he'd been before he'd entered the tower. For as much as it was psychologically dangerous, living as a panther had done wonders for his physique.

He forced a chuckle. "The Tarzan workout, I guess," he rasped.

Then, he studied the arched entrance to the maze. It was constructed of thick, rugged stone, and it looked as if it had existed for thousands of years. The same could be said for the connected wall, which was covered in vines and moss. Both parts of the structure were at least fifty feet tall.

Looking at the maze, Elijah's first idea was to simply climb the walls. It still wouldn't be easy to traverse, but it would still be much easier if he could get a top-down view. So, he approached the wall and tried just that. However, ten feet up, he started feeling heavier. At first, it was just a minor increase, but with every foot he ascended, his weight increased until he could barely hold on. He'd only made it twenty feet before he could climb no higher.

"Should've expected that," he said to himself. It felt good to speak, especially after his stint as a panther. It reminded him that he was still human. In any case, it seemed like he had no choice but to traverse the maze the old-fashioned way.

With the completion of his Task in mind, Elijah stepped through the gate and entered the Primordial Maze. He could only hope that it would prove less dangerous than the jungle, but even as that thought crossed his mind, he recognized how ridiculous it was. There was no way things would get easier now that he was on the home stretch. If anything, he was in for a steep increase in difficulty.

53

THE TOWER

Alyssa said, "We don't have a choice."

"It's almost fifty miles away," Roman pointed out. "It's not our problem."

Alyssa looked around at the others. Carmen was there representing the noncombatants, but the rest of the council were Roman's allies. He had handpicked most of them because they agreed with his philosophy of blatant self-interest. Not on a personal level, but rather when it came to the way they ran Easton. That meant that, of the eight members of the council, Alyssa only had one ally.

She resisted the urge to scream. The formation of the council was supposed to have been a compromise, a way to solve the rift between Roman and her. But in her frequent absence, the former police chief had managed to stack the deck against her. A few of her people had been intimidated into stepping down, and one had been outright bribed. The replacements were loyal only to Roman.

No—that wasn't quite right. They didn't care about him. They cared about themselves, and it didn't matter if that came to the detriment of everyone else. To Alyssa's sensibilities, they were selfish and cowardly.

But she couldn't really argue with their reasoning—not on a purely logical level. It didn't make much sense to put their lives on the line in order to help people who couldn't do anything for them. And if they responded to this new threat, they would certainly be putting themselves, as well as all of Easton, at risk.

Choosing not to act carried with it its own risks, though.

"You heard the Envoy," she said, gesturing to Dirk. He claimed to be completely neutral, and as an Envoy of the Cult of the World Tree, that was precisely what he was supposed to be. However, he was clearly Roman's stooge. He'd proved that a hundred times over. "This tower is a threat to our survival. If nothing is done, it's going to overflow. We'll be inundated by more Voxx. You have to see that it's better to take care of it before circumstances force our hand."

"And I'm sure the proximity of the refugee camp has nothing to do with your stance," one of Roman's flunkies said. "Pardon me if I don't share your bleeding heart and—"

"Enough," Roman interrupted. The woman snapped her mouth shut. The former police chief took a deep breath, then continued, "Compassion is commendable. You know I don't want anyone to die unnecessarily, Alyssa. But the fact remains that if we attack this tower, we'll have to send some of our best. That will leave us vulnerable, and not just to the wildlife. You know what's coming our way."

Alyssa looked away. They'd recently received word that there was a roving band of warriors making their way across the landscape. They'd already sacked a half dozen towns, and there was a good chance that they'd soon target Easton. The group—no, it was an army, by all accounts—might never find the settlement, but they had to be ready to fight in the event that they were attacked.

It had been so much easier when all she had to worry about was patrolling the surrounding area. But as Dirk had leveled, he'd unlocked more features of the Branch of the World Tree, including the ability to communicate with other nearby settlements. And to Alyssa's surprise, there were dozens of them, though none as large or successful as Easton.

But with that communication had come trade, dependence, and news.

And it had unlocked Roman's ambition. It was an open secret that he wasn't content with ruling Easton. He wanted his own kingdom. Sure, he couched that ambition in a desire to save as many people as possible. After all, Easton was far safer than anywhere else with whom they had been in contact. It only made sense that he take them all under his wing.

Of course, if he had his way, that would mean the virtual enslavement of anyone who didn't offer immediate benefit to society. Alyssa had fought against it, and she'd been mostly successful, but the more power Roman got, the less capable she was to fight against the worst of his nature.

"Then we should send our best," Alyssa said. "Get through it quickly, gain the benefits, and be better prepared to meet the army coming our way. Or do you want to fight a war on two fronts? Think about it. What's going to happen when that tower bursts? Even if we fight off the waves of Voxx, we'll be weakened when that army gets here. They'll roll over us."

"Unlikely," one of the others scoffed.

Alyssa shook her head. Of the people present, only she and Roman fought with any regularity. The others were just sycophantic bureaucrats. They all had combat classes, but they used any excuse to avoid anything that might put them in danger. They were cowards, and as such, Alyssa had no respect for them.

Certainly, they served a purpose. Someone had to tend to the minutiae required to run the city whose population had grown into the thousands. However, recognizing that they weren't completely useless didn't equate to respect.

Either way, that lack of combat experience meant that they wavered between looking down on those who protected them and putting far too much trust in those same people's abilities.

"You know I'm right, chief," she said.

Roman locked his eyes on hers, but he didn't change his expression. She couldn't read him. Not anymore. Not since Trish's death. His thoughts and emotions had become a mystery to her.

After a moment, he asked, "How do you propose we do this?"

"You and me, at minimum," she said. They were the two highest-level people in the city. "A healer. Maybe two. And at least a couple of damage dealers. The tower won't allow more than six people inside at a time."

He nodded, but before he could speak, one of his sycophants spat, "You can't be serious? We would be defenseless!"

"There are more than a thousand warriors in this city," Roman stated. "Surely they can defend you while we're gone. Perhaps you can even defend yourself, Mr. Adams."

"You've got a combat class, don't you?" asked Alyssa. "A warrior variant, right? We could use you in the tower. Unless you think you're needed here, of course."

"I . . . I don't . . ."

"We should take Verin Watson," Roman stated. "She got some sort of Priest class, and she's probably the most versatile healer we have in the city."

The woman in question was one of the newer arrivals, though Alyssa didn't know much else about her.

"I want Bryce Caraway."

"The Wizard?"

"Yeah. He's one of our hardest hitters," she stated.

"That's four. You know another healer?"

"Could take Kevin Tate," she suggested. "I've worked with him."

"No. I think I have someone else that would work," he said. "In fact, I think I can fill our other two slots. So, I suggest you spend the night saying your goodbyes and preparing. We leave in the morning."

And just like that, Alyssa had won the argument, though she wasn't certain if she would grow to regret it. The minor dimensional rift had been difficult enough to overcome, but a tower was supposed to be far more dangerous. The guides she'd purchased from the Branch had been limited in what information they contained, but one thing seemed certain—if they were going to challenge a tower, it was going to be deadly.

After Roman had agreed to the plan, the meeting concluded, and Alyssa and Carmen quickly left the former police station behind. Having grown to five stories tall, it was unrecognizable, as was the rest of the city. The collection of log cabins had been replaced by more permanent brick buildings, and though none of them had much artistry to be seen, there were a couple that had been designed by Architects. Those were clearly higher-quality, and there was a hope that soon enough, the rest of the city would follow suit.

After traversing the city, Carmen and Alyssa retreated to their home. It still wasn't huge, but they'd had a host of modern amenities installed. Running water, central heating, and a working kitchen, complete with ethera-powered appliances, meant that it was almost as comfortable of a home as the one they'd abandoned shortly after the world had transformed. In that respect, the Branch of the World Tree had proved invaluable, if only for the guides it made available. Without them, Easton would've still been stuck in the Stone Age.

Once they got home, Carmen said, "I don't like this. You saw that, right?"

"What?" Alyssa asked, plopping down on one of the couches. She'd gone to the meeting straight from a patrol, so even with her inflated Constitution, she was absolutely exhausted.

"Roman. He didn't want you to bring your people even though it made sense," she pointed out. "Why would he do that?"

Alyssa shrugged. "Probably because he thinks his people would be better," she answered.

"Or he's going to betray you," Carmen stated.

"Oh, come on. This is Roman. He's the chief. He's a good man."

"Who wants to let people die just because he doesn't consider them useful."

Alyssa sighed. "It's not like that. We have limited resources, and—"

"I know more about our resources than you do. I go to almost all those sham council meetings, you know. And we could have taken those refugees in. It would've meant people had to cut back a little, but we could have done it."

"Yeah? And what about the next group? We'd cut back a little for them, too. And the next after that. Until, suddenly, we have people starving or sleeping in the streets. It's a slippery slope, Carmen."

"I'm aware."

Alyssa rubbed her eyes. "I don't want to argue about this again," she said. "I trust Roman. Besides, he needs me."

"For now," Carmen pointed out. "But fine. Just promise you'll stay on your guard in there."

"I will."

"Did you see it?" asked Carmen in a different tone.

"What?"

"The ladder."

"Oh. He's . . . He's still on there," Alyssa said, referring to her brother's placement on the worldwide power rankings. How he'd managed to even survive, much less climb to such heights, was a mystery to her. When she'd first noticed his name on the list, she had wanted to pick up right then and there and try to find him. But it didn't take long for reason to take over when she realized that she didn't even know where to start. The world had been entirely transformed, and there was no telling where Elijah had ended up. However, she took more than a little comfort from the confirmation that he wasn't just alive, but he was also thriving.

She could only wish that everyone could say the same.

After that, they moved on to more pleasant topics, like the fact that Miguel had won an archery competition among the town's children. There were only a couple hundred, and half of those weren't old enough to compete. But still, it was quite an accomplishment.

As the afternoon turned to night, Miguel got home from the school the town had set up. He eagerly told his mothers about his exploits at the competition, and Alyssa made it clear that she wished she'd been able to attend. Carmen had been there, but that was because, as a crafter, she didn't have to leave the city. Eventually, Alyssa had to break the news that she was once again leaving. Miguel took it well—he was proud that his mother worked so hard to protect everyone—but he was still disappointed.

In the end, the family spent a nice night together, though. Which made it that much more difficult when, the next morning, Alyssa found herself waiting near the southern gate. Slowly, the members of the group trickled in. Bryce was the first to arrive, followed by the healer, Verin. She was a matronly woman, but she looked solid enough. And judging by the spring in her step, she wouldn't slow them down.

Next came a man who introduced himself as Trace. He also claimed to be their scout, with the Outlaw class. The next to last to arrive was a woman with the Disciple class, which apparently was a healer variant that also specialized in unarmed combat. Alyssa had no idea how that worked, but the woman—named Chen—seemed pleasant enough.

Finally, Roman arrived, flanked by a pair of his sycophants. Alyssa had never even learned their names.

Alyssa looked around at her party. Of them all, she was the most heavily armored, but that was no surprise. Carmen had made her a full suit of actual plate armor, and just like her spear, it could take a significant beating. Chen and Trace both wore leather armor, while Roman had equipped a chain mail hauberk, heavy leather gloves, and a pair of armored pants. Bryce wore heavy robes, as much because he didn't have the Strength to accommodate heavier armor as because he thought it appropriate for his Wizard class. Finally, Verin's armor was almost as heavy as Alyssa's, and the older woman had a wicked-looking morning star at her waist.

All in all, they looked like a well-equipped party.

"Everyone have rations?" she asked, looking from one to the other. Each had a sizable pack on their back, and they all confirmed that they'd packed plenty of dried meat, hardtack, and extra bottles of water. "Alright, let's get this thing going."

She and Roman had agreed that, while he was the highest-ranking official in the city, she would command the party during combat, largely because she had far more experience than the rest of the group combined.

"This is going to be so awesome," Bryce muttered.

The others looked at him like he was crazy, but no one argued. Instead, everyone but Trace followed. The Outlaw ran ahead, scouting their path.

And like that, they slowly made their way across the wilderness toward the south. The tower had appeared almost fifty miles away, so it took them two days of hard travel to reach it. When they did, the group took the opportunity to rest for a day before finally approaching it.

To Alyssa, it looked like a ruin, though it was almost entirely intact. The impression of age was due to the thick moss coating the weathered stones. Vines cascaded from the crown, blending it in with the surrounding forest.

"And if we go in that thing, we're going to what? Teleport somewhere else? How does this thing even work?" asked Trace.

Alyssa told him what she knew, which was precious little. The towers were constructs meant to contain the surging Ethera that came with powerful dimensional rifts. If they conquered them, it would drain the rift for a time, removing the possibility that it would spill over.

"So, those Voxx creatures we've killed, they're just . . . What? Constructs?" asked Bryce.

"I don't know. I don't think so, though. In truth, I only know as much as I've read in the guides I've bought from the Branch," Alyssa admitted. "But I think it's more like these creatures are alien enough that they need all that Ethera to cross over. Again, I might be wrong, though. The guides weren't very specific."

"It doesn't matter," Roman said. "We have a job to do, so let's do it. We'll leave the conjecture to the Scholars."

"Agreed," she said. Then, to Trace, she added, "You found the entrance, right? Lead on."

"Aye, cap'n," he said with a mock salute. "Right this way, m'lady."

"Is it captain? Or lady?" asked Bryce.

"Don't humor him," Chen said.

"Give me a shot, and you'll find I'm quite humorous," Trace said with an exaggerated wink.

"That makes no sense."

"I stand by it," he said. Then, he thrust a finger to the sky and shouted, "Onward!"

Alyssa glanced at Roman and asked, "He's the best you could find?"

"He's . . . an acquired taste. But he's a fantastic fighter. Stealthiest man I've ever seen, too."

"If you say so," Alyssa said, watching the ridiculous Outlaw march off.

They followed Trace around the tower until they found him standing by a large crack in the masonry. Inside was completely dark, and Alyssa could tell by the ambient Ethera that they'd found the entrance to the tower. In truth, she'd expected something more grandiose, but she had no idea why she might've thought that.

In any case, she once again asked if everyone was ready, and when they confirmed that they were, she said, "Okay. You all know the order. Wait two seconds, then follow. When you get inside, step to the left so the next person in line doesn't trample you. Everyone got it?"

They all said they did, which was unsurprising. They'd been over it more than once, after all.

So, with that confirmed, Alyssa took a deep breath, then ducked into the tower.

54

ZOMBIE APOCALYPSE

Unlike when she'd entered the minor dimensional rift, Alyssa didn't stumble.

Not physically, at least. But her mind certainly hit a speed bump as she beheld the landscape before her. At its most basic level, it looked like a city, not dissimilar from any of the dozen or so major population centers she had visited before the world had changed. Skyscrapers stretched high into the air, surrounded by comparatively squat structures. Streets cut between them, populated by a multitude of densely packed cars. The whole thing was surrounded by a river, making the city accessible only via a trio of bridges.

"Do you recognize it?" asked Roman from beside her. She turned, noting that the other four were also staring at the city.

She shook her head. "No. But I haven't been everywhere."

"Did you read the notification?" was his next question.

"Not yet."

"You should."

Alyssa conceded with a nod, then focused on the notification that had popped up upon entry into the tower:

Welcome to The Zombie Apocalypse, Level One. To advance to Level Two, complete the task before you.

Alyssa stared at that notification for a long moment before moving on to the second:

Task: Enter the City.

It seemed simple enough, but just because it was easily understood didn't mean that it wouldn't be a difficult task. Alyssa glanced around at her immediate surroundings. Clearly, they'd arrived in the outskirts of the city, but more immediately, she and the others stood in the center of a wide street that would have been at home in any low-income neighborhood. What looked like a service station occupied one corner, while an obvious pawnshop sat across from it.

The other two corner lots were vacant, though they featured a few overturned and rotting couches and a multitude of burning barrels. It was clearly the sort of area where homeless people tended to congregate.

But there were no people around.

In fact, aside from a gentle wind that sent the pawnshop's sign to flapping, there was no sound at all. To call it eerie would have been a vast understatement.

And Bryce, at least, agreed, saying, "This looks like the opening scene from *28 Days Later*. You know, that horror movie where Cillian Murphy wakes up in the hospital and walks around an abandoned London."

"You're just saying that because of the tower's name," Trace said.

"They weren't zombies in that movie," Bryce pointed out. "They were infected by the Rage virus."

"Oh, come on—they were zombies, and you know it. Just because they call them a different name doesn't mean—"

"Enough."

Bryce cut off at Roman's single word. "Sorry," he muttered.

"I didn't think I would need to remind you people that this is probably the most dangerous place you've ever been," he went on. "So, perhaps you should take it seriously."

Alyssa wanted to say something, but she held her tongue. She knew Bryce well enough to recognize his coping mechanisms, which included babbling about whatever useless facts had taken hold of his mind. But Roman was right. They needed to focus, and that included refraining from talking about twenty-year-old movies, even if the comparison did seem fairly apt.

Instead of commenting on it, she chose to address the topic at hand. "So, we have three options," she said, pointing at the city in the distance. "Three bridges into the city."

"Shouldn't we just go for the closest one?" asked Chen, her arms crossed.

"You think it'll be that simple?" asked Trace. "Because I don't."

"I don't think anyone believes this will be simple," Roman stated. "But that doesn't mean it won't be straightforward."

Alyssa said, "That's not necessarily true, chief. The guides I bought said that these tower tasks can be incredibly complex. I read about one where the tower climbers had to fight a war that lasted weeks."

It was true, but that tower had been on the verge of being a Primal Realm, so it was larger and more complicated than normal. According to her research, towers could be divided into five levels of power, which coincided with the grades associated with items. The lesser dimensional rifts were better categorized as unranked and crude, but any tower that manifested was at least considered simple grade. But that was just the minimal level of power, and there were also stronger towers that were classified as complex, then sophisticated, miraculous, deific, and transcendent.

And that wasn't even considering the Primal Realms, which were akin to entirely separate worlds, complete with indigenous populations. Like intelligent creatures found in towers, the denizens of Primal Realms were still manifestations of Ethera whose sentience was based on copying existing people's souls, but the explanations she'd found in the guides were a little fuzzy on how all of that worked.

"What grade do you think this is?" asked Bryce. They'd all read the same guides, so theoretically, they should've all had the same information.

"No way to know," she said. It would take someone with a powerful analysis skill to determine that. Abilities like that came from classes subordinate to the scholar archetype. Roman's policy on the uselessness of those people meant that no one in Easton had received any skills that could manage the sort of analysis they needed.

It was shortsighted and more than a little moronic, but Alyssa's efforts could only affect so much change, especially considering that she had so many other responsibilities. When weighed against keeping the town safe via her frequent patrols, making sure that scholars were properly appreciated seemed particularly low priority. She always intended to use her influence to change things, but she had so far been too busy to implement any of her plans.

That would probably come back to bite them sometime in the future, but for now, she needed to focus on the tower.

Over the next few minutes, the group came to a consensus. Without any other information, one choice was much the same as any other. So, they opted to aim for the closest bridge in the hope that it would help them conquer the tower more quickly.

As he had outside, Trace ranged ahead, plotting a course and scouting for dangers, while the rest of the party followed. Alyssa took the lead, with the others coming soon after. Roman brought up the rear, often remaining completely undetected.

Which was incredibly unnerving. Alyssa knew she was higher level than the other man, but if Roman wanted to remain hidden, she would never see him. Even though she trusted him—they were friends and colleagues, after all—she still couldn't escape the wave of anxiety his undetectable presence brought with it.

About thirty minutes into their trek through the outskirts of the city, they rounded a corner to find Trace waiting. He held one finger over his lips, indicating that they should remain silent, then motioned for them to follow. They all did, taking great care not to make any noise. They'd all spent time on patrol, so they knew how to stay quiet.

Because the people who hadn't learned that lesson hadn't survived long.

Alyssa and the others followed Trace for a few minutes as he led them down an alley that ran parallel to the river surrounding the city proper. It terminated in a dead end, where Alyssa saw a dumpster. Trace pointed to her, then Roman, before pointing to the dumpster. Then, he climbed atop it, giving him just enough clearance to see over the wall at the end of the alley.

Roman, then Alyssa echoed his path, climbing onto the top of the dumpster next to him. It was a close fit, but they squeezed in, maintaining their silence the whole way.

When Alyssa looked over the top of the wall, she almost let out a gasp. Fortunately, she kept her wits about her, stifling any audible reaction. Still, she could feel her heart beating out of her chest as she beheld a sea of rotting corpses.

Most lay on the asphalt surface of a wide street, and the blanket of cadavers stretched as far as Alyssa could see in either direction. Death had become an undeniable part of her life. Indeed, even before the end of the world, she'd spent a good portion of her childhood hunting with her father and brother. So, she'd never considered herself squeamish around dead bodies. Then, in her time as a police officer—especially when she'd worked in Seattle—she'd seen her fair share of death. Most of the time, the victims died of natural causes, but she'd seen the results of quite a few violent deaths, as well.

But nothing could have prepared her for what she saw stretched out before her, and she wasn't ashamed to admit that, upon seeing it, she very nearly lost control of her stomach. Still, Alyssa was nothing if not in control of herself, so she managed to push her nausea aside and focus on the multitude of corpses.

None were in good condition, exhibiting the kind of rot one would expect from a few weeks' worth of decomposition. In a way, that helped her separate them from their obvious humanity. It was easier to look at rotting corpses and see things rather than the people they'd once been.

A tug at her arm got her attention, and she turned to Trace. The man's face had gone pale, clearly indicating that he was just as uncomfortable as she was. He extended his arm, pointing toward the corpses. Alyssa followed his gesture, a little unsure of what he intended to point out. However, it only took a couple of seconds before she realized what he wanted her to see.

One of the corpses was moving.

Zombies. It was so easy to forget what the tower was called, which in turn had prompted her to take the pile of corpses at face value. But now? It all made horrible sense. Those weren't just a bunch of dead bodies. No. They were enemies, and after only a few more moments, she realized that they were blocking the way to the bridge, which stood only a couple hundred yards away.

Alyssa continued to watch, and over the next few minutes, she caught sight of more movement. None of the zombies moved much—just a twitch here or there—but after seeing the first, the rest were easily noticeable.

Finally, she turned away and silently climbed down. There, she settled in to think. It only lasted a few minutes before Roman and Trace got her attention and motioned for her to follow. She did, and they returned with the others to relative safety. They didn't stop there, though. Instead, they retreated another few hundred yards until Roman finally said, "I think this is far enough away."

"What did you see?" asked Verin, her hand resting on her morning star's grip.

Roman told them, explaining what they faced. He ended by asking, "Any ideas? Let's get them all out there so we can figure out how we're supposed to do this."

There were a few suggestions, each of them viable enough to work. Most hinged on setting some sort of trap for the zombies, and Verin actually suggested that she get their attention, then lead them away so the rest of the team could progress.

"Nobody's sacrificing themselves," Alyssa said with a roll of her eyes.

"I'm prepared for it," the Priest said. "I knew I probably wasn't going to live through—"

"No."

She looked disappointed, which prompted Alyssa to wonder what, precisely, the woman had been through if she was so quick to suggest martyring herself. However, she didn't pursue the matter, largely because she needed to focus on other things.

"Okay, so here's what I think we should do . . ."

As Alyssa explained her plan, the others nodded along. It took elements of the others' plans, but notably, it wouldn't require anyone to sacrifice themselves. When she'd finished, Roman said, "I wish explosives still worked. They wouldn't last long if I could've brought a few drums of homemade napalm in here."

Alyssa couldn't disagree, but one of the first things they'd discovered after the world had transformed was that explosives didn't work anymore. Not to any degree of success. They could still set fires the normal way, but any explosion that exceeded a certain threshold had been significantly diminished. In some cases, like with firearms, that meant that they'd been weakened enough that they quickly became largely useless. In others, as with internal combustion engines, they didn't work at all. But bombs were definitely off the table.

"Yeah," Alyssa agreed. "But we have to work with what we've got."

"I want to go on record as saying that I really like this plan," said Trace. "Normally, I'd be the bait, so this is a nice change of pace."

"The boss doesn't work like that, man," Bryce pointed out. "She's—"

"Not the time, Bryce," said Alyssa.

"But—"

"Not the time."

He sighed, but he didn't argue. Instead, he and the others headed toward a nearby building. It was a two-story brick structure that, if they weren't in the middle of a magical tower, Alyssa would've pinned as being built in the fifties. It was the sort of relic she recognized as belonging to a bygone, more prosperous era. The entirety of the outskirts was like that. Sure, there were more modern prefabricated buildings, but there were also long stretches that suggested that the area had once seen some degree of prosperity. Time had taken its toll, though, and over time, the middle class had shifted farther from the city, and they were replaced by a slightly less fortunate population. Over and over, the process had repeated until, at last, it descended into poverty.

Or that was what the landscape suggested. Alyssa knew it wasn't real. It was just a detailed projection, not so different from an elaborate movie set, with plenty of detail but none of the real history.

In any case, the others climbed to the roof of the three-story building while Alyssa set off toward the mass of zombies. Once she'd reached her destination, she settled down to wait for a little more than half an hour, just to ensure that the rest of the party would be ready. As she waited, she made certain that Hardened Skin was still active. If everything went as she hoped, she wouldn't need either of her self-buffs, but if things went wrong, she would appreciate the defensive ability far more than the offensive Heavy Blows.

Steeling her nerves, she embraced Heart of the Dragon, as well. The increase to her capabilities wasn't massive—only a few points to each physical attribute—but it was enough that she noticed the difference. Fortunately, the ability only produced a minor drain on her energy levels. Even in battle, she could keep the ability active for hours before she began to experience noticeable fatigue.

Hopefully, the upcoming fight wouldn't take that long.

With her abilities active, Alyssa stepped out from around the corner and started yelling. The living corpses responded immediately, pushing themselves to their feet. She retreated a few feet around the corner of a building, then waited. The moment she saw the first zombie step into view, she started jogging back toward the building where she had left the rest of her party. The distance went by in a flash, and before she knew it, she was in front of the building.

But there was a problem.

The zombies weren't the shambling mass portrayed in most movies, but they weren't exactly fast, either. The result was that she'd left them behind. So, she headed back, finding that they'd only reached the halfway point. Some had lost interest altogether and were heading back to their original location. That changed when Alyssa let out another shout, and when she saw that she once again had a trail of zombies, she took off at a light jog. Every few yards, she looked back and let out another yell, and like that, she led the horde back toward the building.

When she finally reached it, she once again assured herself that the zombies were on their way. Then, she used Heroic Leap, launching herself into the air. With her inflated Strength, as well as the enhancement of the ability, she reached the roof. As she climbed to her feet, she noted that Bryce was already in the middle of casting one of his spells.

Meanwhile, Roman had drawn his bow and was steadily picking off the zombies at the fringe of the mass. After ensuring that the others knew their roles, Alyssa headed to the roof access and hefted her spear. Behind her, Bryce finished casting his spell, and there was the sound of a massive explosion. But Alyssa tried to ignore it. Bryce and Roman had their task, and she had hers.

Beside her stood Trace, while the pair of healers had positioned themselves behind her. However, Alyssa noticed that both looked eager for a fight. Verin had her morning star in hand, while Chen had adopted a fighting stance.

Another explosion sounded before Roman shouted, "They're in the building!"

The plan was simple. Under no circumstances could Bryce kill all the zombies. His spells were powerful, but he'd run out of Ethera well before they were all dead. The same was true of Roman with his arrows. So, they were always going to have to fight hand to hand. Knowing that, Alyssa planned to mitigate the weight of the zombies' numbers by forcing them into the stairwell, which would not only funnel them into a single file line, but it would also slow them down.

With that in mind, Alyssa had placed herself at the door where she intended to use her abilities as well as inflated attributes to hold the line long enough to finish the horde off.

It was some time before the first zombies broke through the door, but Alyssa was ready. She thrust her spear forward, sweeping the blade across its neck and decapitating it. She'd seen enough movies to know that was the surest method to deal with the creatures. Even as the monster fell, another took its place. Alyssa's spear whipped out, spearing the zombie through the head. It dropped, just like the first.

Two more appeared, trying to squeeze through the doorway at the same time. Alyssa decapitated one, while Trace stepped forward and sliced the top of the other's head off. They both fell.

So it began, but judging by the numbers she'd seen, the battle was far from over.

As it turned out, her prediction was correct. On and on it went, and the bodies piled up, blocking the door. Every now and then, zombies would manage to crawl through, but it was enough to give them plenty of rest.

After a few hours, Roman announced that the flow of zombies had slowed to a trickle and that the building was probably full of the creatures. That meant that it was time for phase two.

Alyssa turned to Bryce, who'd stopped casting for the past hour so he could regain his Ethera. She asked, "You ready?"

"Definitely not."

"It'll be fine."

"You have no way of knowing if that's true," he stated.

"Bryce, I—"

He rolled his eyes. "I know," he said. "This is how it's got to be. Just don't let them eat my brains."

To Roman, Alyssa asked, "Is the ladder clear?"

He nodded, saying that it was.

"Alright, then. Let's get this thing going," she said.

With that, Roman, the two healers, and Trace headed to the back of the building, where they descended a ladder. They wouldn't stop there, either. Over the next few minutes, Alyssa watched the piled corpses, just in case other zombies broke through. They didn't, and soon enough, enough time had passed for Alyssa to say, "Alright. Use it."

"On it, boss," Bryce said, extending his hand toward the bodies.

He muttered something under his breath, though as far as Alyssa knew, there was no verbal component to his spells. Instead, he just had to wait for them to gather enough Ethera. Once the spell was saturated, he would unleash it. Still, he was fully committed to the image he'd created, so he maintained that the incantation was a necessary part of decent spellcasting.

And considering that Bryce was the highest level pure spellcaster in Easton, Alyssa couldn't really gainsay him. In any case, he was effective, so she didn't push it.

After about thirty seconds, he finished his spell, and a huge stream of fire burst forth from his extended hand. It was hot enough that, even from five feet away, Alyssa felt her skin on the verge of blistering. She stepped back, watching as the fire melted the bricks around the doorway and burned the corpses to ash. The stream continued for almost fifteen seconds until, at last, the flames petered out. Bryce's shoulders sagged as he said, "That was . . . a lot of Ethera."

Then, he looked at the results of the spell, saying, "Effective, though."

And he wasn't wrong. Dozens of zombies had been so thoroughly burned that nothing but charred bones remained. More importantly, a few of the flames persisted as more mundane fire. That was due to the others' preparation. While Alyssa had been acting as bait, the rest of the party had scoured the building for anything flammable, which they placed in such a way as to catch the entire building on fire.

One cast wouldn't be enough, but they didn't intend for it to be, either.

"You still have enough Ethera, right?"

"One more cast. Not Stream of Flame, though. I can only cast Meteor Strike."

"That'll have to do," she said. "Do it."

"Already gathering Ethera."

Alyssa watched the half-melted doorway, but Stream of Flame had done its work well. Much of the brickwork had collapsed, blocking the way. The zombies soon piled up on the other side, and eventually, she knew they would manage to break through. But for now, Alyssa and Bryce were safe.

Then, the Wizard dropped a meteor on them.

It was only a yard or two across, and it certainly didn't hit with the force of a real meteor. However, it didn't need to, either. When it hit, the stairwell collapsed, as did a good portion of the roof. Alyssa had expected it, so she grabbed the much taller Bryce around the waist, throwing him over her shoulder in a fireman's carry, then sprinted across the roof.

Using Enrage, she increased her attributes to unreal levels, and when she reached the edge of the roof, she used Heroic Leap, sending her sailing through the air for over thirty feet before she landed on the neighboring roof.

As she skidded to a stop, she was greeted by the sound of a collapsing building, and when she turned around, she saw the fruits of their labor. The fires from Stream of Flame had spread throughout the building, weakening it enough that Meteor Strike was sufficient to tear it down.

With all those zombies inside.

"I just got a lot of experience," Bryce said.

"Good. I think we're going to need it going forward," she said. Then, looking around, she added, "Let's go find the others."

55

THE PRIMORDIAL MAZE

Elijah was afraid he would once again lose himself if he shifted back into his predator form, so as he headed through the maze's entrance, he did so as a human. Holding his staff in front of him like a spear, and naked as the day he was born, he crept forward one tentative step at a time.

But nothing attacked.

He knew it was coming, though. So, he maintained vigilance as he continued toward the first intersection. He kept close to the moss-covered wall, dragging his hand along the ancient brickwork until he reached his destination. Taking a deep breath to steady his nerves, Elijah peeked around the corner and saw nothing but more of the maze. No monsters. No giant predators. Just a long, empty corridor that looked no different from the way he'd come. Looking back in the opposite direction, he saw much of the same.

Glancing up at the overcast sky, he let out a sigh of mingled relief and disappointment. Relief because he truly didn't want to fight any more monsters. Certainly, gaining a few extra levels would be beneficial, but as had happened in the Sea of Sorrows, his progress while in the Primordial Jungle had slowed to a crawl as the diminishing returns began to take effect. Killing the same creatures over and over was no way to advance.

More than that, though, he was just tired of the constant killing. That was one of the reasons his panther instincts had taken over. In his predator form, Elijah didn't have to worry about stress or morality or anything else. He could just hunt, eat, and live. Everything else had faded into the background. And while that had made his journey through the Primordial Jungle much easier to endure, it certainly wasn't a state to which he wanted to soon return. He was a human, not a panther, and though it was sometimes beneficial to let his identity slip toward the latter, it was also dangerous.

Elijah knew just how close he'd come to letting his human identity disappear, which was a horrifying testament to his adaptability.

So, he was relieved that no foes were in evidence.

However, he couldn't help but feel a little disappointment, too—mostly because it meant that he probably had starvation ahead of him. After all, the jungle, for all its seeming normalcy, was an artificial space. There was no fruit.

No edible fungi. If he wanted to eat, he had to kill. And without any other creatures around, Elijah had no source of food.

He wouldn't die, but the prospect of slowly wasting away was distressing enough that he turned around, intending to exit the maze and gather some food to carry with him. The meat would likely spoil quickly, but a quick pulse of Touch of Nature would take care of any problems that might present. So long as he got some calories in him, he would be okay.

But as soon as he turned around, he saw a very big problem.

The exit had disappeared. The corridor he'd just traversed was a dead end.

"Damn it," he muttered, his voice sounding odd in his own ears. Or maybe it was the silence of the maze that rendered it strange.

Elijah had been in a few jungles in his time. Not only had he lived in Hawaii, but he'd also visited the Amazon during college. And one of the many things that set a natural, Earthly rainforest apart from his current location was the ubiquitous presence of insects. Even so, Elijah had yet to feel the sting of a single mosquito. No biting flies. No spiders in their webs. Nothing but dead air and rain.

If he let himself notice it, Elijah found the whole thing incredibly disturbing. Forests should be alive, but the Primordial Jungle and the attached maze were anything but living ecosystems. Never had anything felt less real than the moment he realized that.

But that was what it was, wasn't it? The whole tower was just a manifestation of Ethera. That was Elijah's understanding, at least. Perhaps there were more steps involved, but he felt confident in that basic assertion.

Then again, aside from satisfying his intellectual curiosity, knowing that didn't change anything. The dangers were still present, and they would certainly kill him if he didn't treat them as reality. So, with that in mind, he turned back toward the center of the maze and sank to his haunches to think about how he wanted to attack the challenge before him.

Elijah was no expert on mazes, but he was familiar enough with them to know a few basic strategies for the traversal of a labyrinth. First among them was what was known as the right-hand rule, which was a technique that, fittingly, given the name, would require Elijah to keep in contact with the right-hand wall at all times.

The right-hand rule wasn't foolproof, though, and stood a chance of getting him even more lost than if he just wandered around aimlessly. So, he wracked his brain for another method, and over the next few minutes, he came up with what he felt was a viable solution.

Basically, it came down to mapping the maze by keeping track of which paths he'd taken and how many times he had taken them. So, each time he reached a path, he would make one of three marks. The initial mark would come during the first encounter. The second would, predictably, come if he crossed that path again. And the third would be for dead ends. So long as he prioritized unmarked paths, he felt that he could eventually find his way to the center.

There were two major problems, though. First, he suspected that using this method would be extremely time-consuming and require quite a lot of back-tracking. Yet, he didn't see any option that wouldn't have that issue, so he could discount that as unavoidable. The second problem was that he didn't have any way to mark the paths.

That was easily solvable, though. The walls were helpfully covered in moss into which it was easy to scrape a pattern. So, he settled on one line for the first crossing of a path, two lines for the second, and a giant *D* for dead ends.

"Keeping it simple," he muttered to himself.

Then, he stopped hesitating and got to moving, marking his first path. Over the next few hours, he continued that pattern, carving a single line each time he reached an intersection and chose a direction. Eventually, he crossed paths he'd taken before and marked them appropriately, as well. The same was true of dead ends.

Like that, he kept going for some time until, at last, his fatigue finally caught up to him. So, knowing that he wasn't likely to traverse the labyrinth in a single day, he settled down to rest. When he awoke, Elijah continued on as he had before.

And so, his days took on a pattern where he kept to his strategy. Each time he passed one of his markings, he made sure to refresh them by using his staff to recarve the appropriate lines in the moss. Otherwise, after only a few days—or even weeks—they would have grown over.

It was in the second week when the hunger got overwhelming, and he resorted to eating the moss. It wasn't tasty, and Elijah felt certain that it wasn't really edible. However, he had Touch of Nature on his side to deal with any lethal side effects, and it was the only real solution to his hunger problem. He had no idea if he really got any nutrients from it, but it did fill his stomach. So, it had that going for it. And with the ubiquitous rain, at least water wasn't an issue.

Boredom was the real killer, and Elijah occupied his mind in a few ways. Most of the time, he dwelled on thoughts of the world at large. Largely, he worried about his sister and her family, but he did give some thought to the rest of the population.

One thing he'd discovered since being stranded on the island was that his mind often drifted to his past, and when that happened, his memories seemed far more vivid than they ever had before. That was the nature of extended solitude, he supposed, and he appreciated the ability to remember the good times he'd had with his family and friends. However, it also highlighted just how lonely of an existence he led.

One day, he'd leave his island. And when he finally found his family, he would no longer take them for granted.

Before that, he had to complete the tower, though. Not only was it the only way of protecting his island from an invasion of Voxx, but now that he was committed, there was no way out but through. And to do that, Elijah suspected he would have to be much stronger.

With that in mind, he focused on his neglected cultivation. Upon reaching the Opal stage with his mind, his ability to regenerate Ethera had received quite a boost due to the widening of the aperture through which the ambient energy was funneled into his soul. By comparison, his soul cultivation had decreased the casting time of his spells. Finally, his body reaching the Wood stage had made him stronger and more durable, almost as if it had made each point of his attributes count for more.

He had no idea how to improve his core cultivation. Although, he suspected that when he did finally figure it out, it would be even more impactful than the rest of his improvements. Part of that certainty came from a suspicion that it was all meant to work together. So, when he reached the first stage of improvement with all of them, the whole would add up to more than the sum of its parts. However, the majority of his surety was rooted in the feeling he got from his unimproved core. It was the battery upon which everything about him was built. He was all but useless without it. So, it stood to reason that any improvement to his core would be incredibly impactful.

It was a shame, then, that Nerthus had refused to give him any information on how to improve it. Perhaps he could figure it out on his own at some point.

All of that and more flitted through Elijah's mind as he slowly traversed the labyrinth, making his marks along the way. Days passed into weeks, and as he'd expected, his time in the maze eventually eclipsed the one-month mark—at least as far as he could count the days. In the absence of a sun, he'd taken to marking the days via how often he slept. It wasn't exact, but at least it gave him some degree of context.

As he went, the monotony of the labyrinth dulled the edge of his mind until, suddenly, everything changed when he stumbled across a dead body.

The corpse was unidentifiable, but given its general size and the color of what little fur was left, he suspected that it might have been one of the giant primates that called the jungle their home. His time in the jungle was a bit of a blur, but he remembered enough of it that he could confidently label the primates as deadly foes.

And something had killed one.

Had it simply wandered into the labyrinth and died of hunger, thirst, or some combination of the two? Maybe. But given the state of the corpse, it was clear that something else was within the maze. Something that had probably killed and then feasted upon the fearsome Sasquatch ape.

Elijah knelt beside the body, then, with a shake of his head, started rummaging for anything useful. It was disgusting, and it took far longer to sift through the pile of meat, fur, and bones, but eventually, Elijah came away with a simple stone knife and a collection of broken sticks and string that might've once been a bow. There were no arrows. Nor did he find a quiver.

Not that he would've used such a crude weapon. Perhaps if he'd taken the Ranger class in the very beginning, but he currently had much more potent means of attack. If it came down to a battle, he would rely on his spells or his predator form.

After looting the corpse, Elijah backed away. He had a choice to make. He had to keep moving forward, but the question was what form he would take while doing so. There were benefits to both options, and as Elijah settled down into a squat, he considered the choices before him.

His human form gave him the opportunity to carry the items he'd looted. Neither the knife nor the broken bow were immediately useful, but he didn't have to get creative to think of ways that could change. The knife, especially, was invaluable—especially after he'd lost all the equipment he'd brought with him. Only his staff had survived so far.

But as a panther, he didn't really need tools or weapons. More, he could traverse the maze almost undetected, which seemed much increasingly important now that he knew he wasn't alone within the labyrinth.

Clearly, his panther form was better suited for the task. However, Elijah found himself hesitating. Did he dare risk letting those animalistic instincts overwhelm him again? If they took hold, there was every chance they'd never let him go.

For a long time, Elijah thought it over, but in the end, he decided that he couldn't simply ignore such the defining feature of his class. Shape of the Predator was part of him, and he couldn't run from it. Instead, he needed to use it to his advantage. He had to control the wild nature of his panther form rather than let it control him.

With that in mind, Elijah renewed his enhancements, casting Essence of the Monkey, Aura of Renewal, and Essence of the Wolf. Then, for the first time in more than a month, he embraced Shape of the Predator and took on his mist-panther form.

56

CROSSING OVER

Alyssa sagged to one knee, propping herself up with the Spear of the Dragon Lancer. Looking around, she saw that the rest of her party looked just as exhausted as she felt. No one seemed nearly as drained as Bryce, though. But that wasn't surprising, considering that, as they cleared their way to the first bridge, he'd become their most powerful weapon. Despite his clear weaknesses—long cast times and horrible physical attributes—the Wizard's spells had torn through the zombies in a way none of the others could replicate.

Again—not terribly surprising, considering that they'd taken great pains to put him into optimal situations, setting numerous traps and guarding his back along the way. But it was still impressive, nonetheless. Now, though, they'd finally reached their goal.

"How many do you think we killed?" asked Chen, her leather armor ripped and her hands bloody. During the short campaign, the woman had put her martial arts prowess on display, and while she wasn't as powerful of a healer as some Alyssa had seen, she made up for it in versatility. She wasn't the strongest combatant, but she was far from weak, either.

"Thousands, at least."

"I figured we would have gotten more experience," Bryce said. "But after that first bump, it's been . . . I don't know. Underwhelming."

"Speak for yourself, beanpole," said Trace as he wiped viscera from one of his blades. "I got a whole level."

"I got two, but—"

"And you're complaining?" Trace asked, shaking his head in derision. "You kids today. No sense of—"

"We're like the same age," Bryce interrupted.

"I'm an old soul."

"You're an idiot."

Trace shrugged. "A badge I wear with honor," he said. "Nobody's looking out for the fool, right? Being underestimated is a weapon just like any other. You should write that down."

Bryce shook his head. "That would mean a lot more if I thought it was intentional," he said. "Acting like an idiot is one thing. Actually being dumb is something else."

Before Trace could respond, Roman cleared his throat. He'd taken a back seat during the fighting, but he was still the leader of Easton. So, he had no trouble getting everyone's attention.

"We still have a bridge to cross," he said. "We need to find somewhere to rest that isn't covered in corpses. Then, we need to move on. I don't want to be in here any longer than necessary."

Alyssa voiced her agreement, and the others fell into line soon after. A few minutes later, they'd found their way to an old gas station, where they settled in for some rest. Roman sat next to her on the counter and offered her a piece of dried meat. She took it, pulling a bottle of water from her own pack.

"That was unpleasant," Roman said, his eyes trained on the others, who'd all congregated in a different corner. Once again, Trace and Bryce were having an animated discussion, though Alyssa couldn't make out the subject.

"It's probably going to get worse when we cross the bridge," she said. "I don't know how it'll be presented, but the guides were all pretty clear about the increasing difficulty. The farther you progress, the worse it'll get."

Roman sighed, then ran his hand through his hair. He looked extremely tired, but that wasn't so different than everyone else. They'd been fighting for what felt like an entire day, and while they'd done everything they could to mitigate the danger, there'd still been a few close calls. And Alyssa knew better than anyone how thoroughly life-and-death situations could drain a person's energy.

"It's hard to believe, you know."

"What?"

"This," Roman said, gesturing to their surroundings. "Magic towers and spells and zombies. It really wasn't that long ago that the worst I had to worry about was a domestic-abuse call. I mean, I moved out of Seattle to get away from the stress of living in a big city. Now, I'm responsible for thousands of people. If I make the wrong choice, people die. Even if I make the right decisions, people die. All I can do is mitigate it. I can't stop it. Not completely."

That had been true even before the world had changed. Sometimes, bad things happened, and there was nothing anyone could do to stop it. It was a lesson she'd been forced to learn when her parents had died, but it had really been driven home during her time as a police officer.

"You're doing the best you can," she said, reaching out to grip his shoulder reassuringly. He flinched at her touch, but she pretended not to notice as she went on: "You care, Roman. That's what matters. You just want what's best for everyone."

"I do," he agreed. "But sometimes . . . Sometimes, I'm afraid of what it's doing to me. To us. Before all of this, I would have tried to save everyone. Rationally,

I know that it would've eventually killed us all. We don't have the resources to support everybody. But still . . ."

Alyssa shook her head. "The fact that you're worried about it means you're a good man, chief. You're just trying to make the best of a bad situation. We all are. So long as you keep working toward the greater good, I don't think anyone has a right to criticize you. Not unless they've been in your shoes. Not unless they've had to make the same choices you've had to make."

Not unless they'd experienced the same losses, Alyssa left unsaid. Trish's death had come close to breaking Roman. He'd put on a strong front, and he had kept going despite his grief. But Alyssa knew him well enough to recognize how close he'd come to falling off the edge. That he'd somehow climbed his way out of that pit was just further evidence that he was worthy of her respect.

Despite their frequent disagreements.

For the next few hours, everyone rested. Fortunately, they'd killed most of the zombies, so they were undisturbed. It was a necessary break, and when Roman finally called for everyone to gather up, they did so with renewed vigor.

"We're crossing the bridge. I want you all to be ready for anything," he said.

Alyssa added, "Same formation as before. Roman in the back. Me in the front. Trace, you stick close for now, though. We don't want you crossing before we do."

She recognized that crossing the bridge likely constituted progressing to the tower's next level, and she didn't want the group separated.

After everyone had received their instructions, the party set out across the corpse-strewed outskirts, and they reached the bridge only half an hour later. It was no different than a thousand other bridges across the world, which meant that it was four lanes wide, about a quarter mile long, and supported by thick concrete pylons.

The city beyond was wreathed in fog, though, so despite the sun hanging high in the sky, none of them could see what awaited. That mist had grown steadily thicker the closer they drew to the city proper.

Alyssa took the lead, and the others followed her across the bridge. For most of its length, it was no different from the outskirts. However, when they passed the three-quarter mark, she got a notification:

Congratulations! You have completed Level One of The Zombie Apocalypse. Grade: C.

To progress further, continue across the bridge.

An instant later, a small box appeared in front of Alyssa. It was silver with red trim, but it looked no different than any other metallic box she had seen.

She stopped, then knelt beside it. From her guides, she knew that it was the reward for completing the tower's first level, so she didn't hesitate to flip the latch and open the lid.

Reward for completing Level One of The Zombie Apocalypse:

Pendant of Ethereal Regeneration

"What is it?" asked Roman as Alyssa retrieved the silver necklace. She held it up so the others could see it, but there really wasn't much to see. Just a blue gem set in silver and attached to a thin chain.

Alyssa told them what it was called, then said, "I don't know what it does. What should we do with it?"

"Give it to one of the healers. Probably Verin," Trace said.

They all looked at him in surprise, and he said, "What? If it comes down to that thing making the difference, I'd rather her have it so she can heal my ass."

"It makes sense," said Alyssa. If it did what they expected it would do—help to boost Ethera Regeneration—she certainly had no use for it. Only a couple of her abilities even used Ethera, with the rest taking stamina.

The others all agreed, and the pendant went to Verin. The older woman protested, saying that it should go to someone else, but they all insisted.

Once Verin had accepted it and verified that it enhanced her Regeneration attribute by three points, the group continued across the bridge. The moment they reached the other side, another pair of notifications crossed Alyssa's vision. The first welcomed her to the second level of the tower, while the second gave her the task of reaching the capital.

They'd barely made it a few dozen yards into the city when the heavy slap of skin against asphalt alerted them that they weren't alone. Alyssa whipped around, her spear at the ready, and she was just in time to see a bulky figure emerge from the mist. It didn't even attempt to dodge, instead ramming into her spear with the speed of an Olympic sprinter.

The blade cut deep, but the attacker kept coming, sliding past the blade and up the shaft. Before it could reach her, Alyssa spun. Using all her Strength, she flung the monster off her spear. It hit the ground and rolled to a stop.

But it wasn't dead.

It pushed itself to its feet just in time to catch an arrow in the eye. Trace flashed in from the side, dragging his sword across its hamstrings. And then, Verin was on it, swinging her morning star with all her might. The spiked head took the creature in the face, once again knocking it to the ground, where another arrow hit it. At the same time, Chen aimed an axe kick at its already damaged skull. Her heel hit with enough force to crack bone.

Still, it didn't die.

In fact, it seemed mostly unaffected by the deluge of attacks.

The creature lunged to its feet, pouncing on Chen before she had a chance to react. Another arrow hit it, and Alyssa rushed forward, using Charge to enhance her speed. She knew she wouldn't get there in time, though.

The thing reared back and then, with the speed of a striking snake, descended upon Chen's exposed jugular vein. It only took an instant before Alyssa rammed her spear into it, but by that point, it had already ripped the woman's throat out. She fell away, limp and dying. Verin tried to cast a heal, but the impaled monster took her with a backhand before Alyssa could drive it away.

The older woman went tumbling across the asphalt, but Alyssa couldn't do anything to help. Instead, she rammed her spear farther into the monster's chest until the blade got lodged in its ribs.

She shouted, "Burn it!"

Bryce had finally finished his spell. With the influx of experience during the first level, he'd earned a new one, which he let loose at Alyssa's prompting. A fireball the size of a softball arced through the air, taking the monster in the shoulder. It quickly caught fire, and though it went wild, screeching in pain, Alyssa's spear kept it under control.

A few moments later, it died, falling to the ground. The flames remained, continuing to burn through the monster's body. It was a bulky thing, with the sort of muscles that would've qualified it to compete as a professional wrestler, and though it looked vaguely human, it clearly wasn't.

With maggoty-white skin, huge eyes, and pointed ears, it was something else entirely.

Alyssa only took it in at a glance before she turned her attention to her fallen comrades. When she did, she saw Verin kneeling beside Chen's still form. The older woman's hands glowed with blue light, but no matter how much she tried, it wouldn't make the jump into Chen's body.

Because the younger woman had already died.

Tears fell down Verin's cheeks as the woman continued to attempt her casting. But it was too late. She knew it. Everyone did. Still, she tried. Over and over again until Roman rested his hand on her shoulder, saying, "She's gone."

Verin didn't respond. Instead, she rose, then collapsed against the man's chest. He wrapped his arm around her, comforting the Priest as best he could. After a moment, he looked at Trace and said, "Find us somewhere to rest. We need to get our bearings."

As Alyssa watched the man disappear into the mist, she realized what had happened. On the surface, they were powerful enough to fight the monster. However, because of the nature of the previous level, where the zombies were all relatively weak, they'd gotten sloppy. And this new enemy had taken advantage of it.

That was her fault.

She was the battle leader, and now, because of her failure, one of their number was dead. She had always known it was possible. Likely, even. But knowing it was coming and watching someone die were two very different things. It was especially impactful because, at the end of the day, Chen had been her responsibility.

Then and there, she vowed to keep everyone else alive as they climbed the tower. But in the back of her mind, she couldn't help but doubt herself. Did she have the ability to follow through with that promise?

Maybe.

Maybe not.

Only time would tell.

With that in mind, she collected Chen's body, and when Trace returned, the subdued but alert group followed him into the lobby of one of the skyscrapers. Once inside, they found their way to a side room, where they blockaded the door with disused furniture.

Thus secured, they turned their attention to saying goodbye to the woman. Verin was the most affected, but none of them could look at their party member's corpse without at least some guilt. As it turned out, Roman had known the woman best, and he handled the impromptu eulogy.

"She was a good person. I didn't know her for long. She only arrived at Easton a little less than a month ago," he said. "But she led a group of forty people across the wilderness, personally keeping most of them alive. She was a protector and a healer, and she will be missed."

He delivered the short speech in a dry, emotionless voice, but Alyssa knew Roman well enough to recognize his guilt. Probably because she felt it, too.

For a long while, they just sat there, stunned. It hadn't been that long ago that they'd been joking among one another. Now, though? None of them even considered making flippant remarks. Eventually, they started planning for the immediate future. They had a destination, though they didn't know where it was, so finding the capital was the first order of business. Next, once it was found, they needed a safe way to make the journey. None of them thought that the monster that had attacked them was the only enemy, after all. Likely, there were a lot more of them out there.

In the end, it came down to taking the journey in steps. They intended to go from one building to another, using Trace and Roman as scouts. It wasn't elaborate, and it certainly wasn't a perfect plan, but it was the best any of them could come up with.

So with that established, the group set out, leaving the corpse of one of their own behind. Alyssa could only hope that it would be the last time they would be forced to do so.

57

PACK HUNTERS

As Elijah padded down the corridor, a chill ran up his spine, raising his hackles. Cloaked in Guise of the Unseen, he was safe from observation, but he still felt like something was watching him. Over the past few days, an eerie ambiance had blanketed the labyrinth, setting him on edge even if nothing had outwardly changed. When he looked around, the same moss-covered walls and endlessly twisting turns greeted him.

And yet, he felt like he'd been enveloped by a formless and persistent fear.

Since finding that first body—or hunk of flesh, fur, and bone, really—he had come across a half dozen more, all in various states of decay. The lack of scavenging insects pushed him even closer to the edge, and he knew it wouldn't take much to shove him over.

Still, the only way out was through, he kept telling himself. But increasingly, he'd done so with fatalistic despair rather than the stoic determination that had once accompanied the mantra.

He reached out with one paw, scratching a second line next to the one he'd left in his first passing. Then, he chose the other direction, keeping to his pattern. With how much time had passed, he suspected that he was getting closer to his destination. He only had to keep going—even if it felt increasingly futile.

Perhaps the labyrinth was endless.

Maybe he had missed some key detail that would have seen him completing the level without issue.

Elijah's greatest fear was that it was all just an elaborate death trap.

But still, he continued on, and the days continued to pass. Eventually, he grew accustomed to the fear, and he barely even hesitated when he saw new bodies. The only thing that kept him going was a single-minded refusal to quit.

And it almost got him killed when he turned a corner and very nearly walked into the center of a recently concluded hunt. The most intact simian body he'd yet seen within the maze lay in the middle of the corridor, surrounded by the creatures who'd obviously killed it.

At first, Elijah thought they were terrestrial birds, though that impression was based more on the way they moved than how they looked. It was only when he looked a little closer that he realized that they were four-foot-tall reptiles that stood on two legs.

In real life, raptors had not been the devastating predators portrayed in popular media. Instead, they were much smaller than how they were usually depicted, and they were primarily scavengers. However, these creatures very much resembled the fearsome dinosaurs he'd seen in movies and on television, though they differed in a one major way—they looked like they'd been made of twisted roots, with thorns for teeth and tufts of moss in place of feathers. Still, there were six of the creatures huddled around and tearing chunks of flesh from the carcass.

Elijah backed away, praying that his Guise of the Unseen was enough to keep him hidden. And to his surprise, he made it back around the corner without gaining their attention. When he did, he let out a feline sigh, then sank to his haunches.

He had a choice to make. Either he could backtrack and try to find another way through the maze; there were still plenty of untapped routes. Conversely, he could follow the root raptors. Guise of the Unseen seemed to be up to the task of keeping him hidden, but it would only take a single misstep to ruin the effect.

And then he'd have to deal with an entire pack of the creatures.

The first option was safer, but no matter how he looked at it, Elijah felt it was the wrong move. He'd been trekking through the maze for so long, and he'd barely seen anything break up the monotony. And given that the environment was a manufactured level of the tower, it suggested that there would be no coincidences. If something changed, it was meaningful.

So, it stood to reason that the root raptors were important. Following them was the right choice, even if it was more dangerous than the alternative.

With that in mind, Elijah ensured that his enhancements and Guise of the Unseen were active, then stepped around the corner where he settled down to wait.

The raptors never noticed him, due in no small part to their grisly feast. They tore the simian corpse apart, seemingly reveling in the dismantling as much as they enjoyed the meal. Or perhaps Elijah was anthropomorphizing them. Either way, he forced himself to watch the ghastly scene, and soon enough, one of the creatures let out a piercing cry. The others stopped, whipping around to the leader, and when it took off at a run, they followed.

And just like that, Elijah was alone.

He was tempted to run after them, but that was a good way to get detected. So, he approached the corpse, took a few nips from the leftover meat, then sniffed around. Beneath the overwhelming smell of blood was a wet, musty scent that he instinctively knew belonged to the raptors. After finding that scent, it was easy enough to follow their trail.

As he did, Elijah continued to mark each turn, but he had a sneaking suspicion that if he continued to track the root raptors, he would find his way to his destination.

So it went for the next few hours until he found the scene of another massacre. This time, there were two of the simians, but to Elijah's surprise, there were also a pair of raptor bodies.

And one of them was still alive.

So, once Elijah ensured that there were no other root raptors around, he approached the survivor. It had been pierced through by four arrows, and its labored breathing was shallow. Sap-like blood stained the ground, telling Elijah that the creature was on the verge of death. He had no issues with speeding it along on its way to whatever afterlife awaited the tower's denizens.

He stepped forward, reared back one forepaw, then activated Predator Strike. He swept his claws forward, ripping through it with a combination of his considerable Strength and the augmentation provided by his ability.

It never even knew what killed it.

Elijah's attack destroyed its elongated head, shattering it into a thousand splintered and sap-covered pieces.

He received some kill energy, but it wasn't enough to send him to the next level. So, after ensuring that there was nothing useful around the corpses, he continued to follow the trail.

Over the next few hours, he came across three more scenes of slaughter, each with two or more simian corpses. However, there weren't any other dead or dying raptors. Seeing that, he didn't spend much time investigating them.

As he went, though, the eerie ambiance of the labyrinth continued to grow more and more palpable until every third or fourth step was punctuated by a glance to his rear. He didn't see anything, but he couldn't shake the feeling that something was following, that some monster was stalking him.

He strained his senses, but he came up empty.

Until, at last, he caught a whiff of something familiar.

It was just a stray scent, but the moment it wafted beneath his nose, he recognized it. Without hesitation, Elijah leaped to the side, and he was just in time to avoid a descending thornlike claw. He skidded to a stop, then used the wall to reverse directions. His claws flashed with Venom Strike before he collided with his attacker. He barreled into it, his claws digging deep and delivering their poisonous payload before he bounded away.

He slid to a stop, then reversed course. Crouching low, he saw the creature pick itself up. The thing was clearly a raptor, but instead of only being four feet tall, it was at least half again that height, with wicked claws and gnashing teeth.

More distressingly, as the thing rose, the remaining pack of root raptors appeared from around the corner. They didn't stop when they reached the larger monster, instead tearing across the ground with clearly murderous intent.

Elijah knew he couldn't stand up to so many, so he wasted no time before turning tail and running away. At first, the creatures kept pace, but the moment the System deemed that he'd left combat, his Essence of the Wolf took effect, and he left them behind.

But that wasn't enough.

Elijah knew it.

These monsters would have to die if he was going to complete the Primordial Maze. It was no different than when he'd had to kill the guardian in the Sea of Sorrows. The only question was how he was going to do it.

Had they always known he was there? Were they simply leading him along so that their alpha could kill him off? Had he walked into a trap? Or was there some other explanation? He didn't know.

But what Elijah did know was that he had an opportunity. If he could kill a few of the smaller raptors off, he might have a chance to kill the larger one.

To that end, Elijah poured on the speed, hoping to separate the pack. He was certain that the neurotoxin from Venom Strike wouldn't kill the alpha. His claws had barely even nicked it, suggesting that its Constitution—if monsters even had such attributes—was extremely high. However, the poison would slow it down, he was sure. He hoped that would prevent it from keeping pace, giving him the opportunity he needed to thin the pack.

Once he'd been running for a few minutes, he rounded a corner, then leaped onto the wall. His claws dug into the vines, and he pulled himself up. Immediately, his weight increased, but he didn't have to go far. Just a few extra feet, and then Elijah once again embraced Guise of the Unseen.

The muscles in his paws strained under his increased weight, but he pushed through it long enough for the raptors to come tearing past him. They kept going, with a couple lagging a little behind.

When the last one passed beneath him, he pounced, falling upon it with Predator Strike. His descending claw ripped through its spine, flattening it against the ground. Then, he snapped out, his jaws closing around the nape of its neck. Then, he squeezed, and the base of its skull shattered.

But Elijah wasn't finished.

He leaped, bounding off the wall and attacking the next closest creature. This time, it didn't go quite as well, but he wasn't aiming to take it out all at once. Instead, he used Venom Strike, and even though he only managed a glancing blow on the quick monster, he accomplished his goal of infecting it with the ability's neurotoxin.

He got one more attack in on a third creature, but by that point, he'd started to push his luck. So, having done what he'd intended to do, he turned and took off back in the direction he'd come. However, he turned down one of the two-stripe routes, taking a different path and putting more distance between himself and the pursuing pack of root raptors.

A few minutes later—well after the effect of Essence of the Wolf returned to speed him along his way—Elijah received a pulse of kill energy as one of the monsters died. A couple of minutes after that, yet another went down.

That left only a few more.

However, when he tried to repeat his tactic, he was distressed to find that the raptors were ready for him. He barely escaped alive, but even so, he sustained a couple of wounds from their vicious claws. Clearly, his Constitution was too low to stand up to them in a stand-up fight. Taking them head-on was a good way to get ripped to pieces.

Fortunately, Elijah was slightly faster, an advantage that was further enhanced when Essence of the Wolf took effect. Still, the fact that they could learn was a disappointing discovery. That meant he couldn't just keep doing the same thing over and over.

But Elijah's class, if nothing else, was versatile.

If he couldn't kill them in his panther form, then his caster form would pick up the slack.

So, once Elijah judged he was far enough ahead, he shifted back to human form, then adjusted his enhancements, exchanging the extra Dexterity of Essence of the Monkey for more Constitution via Essence of the Boar. Then, he cast Healing Rain and settled in to wait at the end of a long corridor.

The remaining raptors appeared only a minute or so later, and he wasted no time before channeling Storm's Fury through his Staff of Natural Harmony. Lightning tore across the intervening distance between them, hitting the first monster and knocking it back into the other members of its pack. They went down in a heap, and Elijah cast Snaring Roots, further entangling them. Finally, he brought another Storm's Fury to bear, intending to keep casting until he finished them off.

The first monster died after the third cast. It took two more to kill the fifth, but by that point, the third and final root raptor had regained its feet and closed the distance. Elijah didn't have enough Ethera to cast his spell again, so he reared back and swung his staff with every ounce of Strength he could muster. The monster wasn't expecting the vicious attack, so it took the blow directly in its open mouth.

The impact cracked its lower jaw, and the momentum of the attack sent it skidding across the ground. Elijah's every instinct told him to leap upon it and finish it off, but his rational mind screamed at him that doing so would be a terrible idea. The alpha couldn't be that far behind, and even if it didn't catch up anytime soon, the little raptor was more than capable of ripping him to fleshy ribbons.

So, once again, Elijah turned tail and ran.

It didn't matter how long it took to kill the thing. Hit and run. That was his game. Standing and fighting was too dangerous.

His feet slapped against the ground as he sprinted to safety. The raptor recovered its feet before Elijah turned a corner, and to his distress, Essence of the Wolf didn't kick in. Without that extra movement speed, he couldn't outrun it. Not in human form, at least.

But he could still ambush the thing.

So, as he turned the corner, he reached out, grabbing one of the vines attached to the wall, and forced himself to a stop. Then, he hefted his staff and waited.

The raptor came screaming around the corner only to once again find itself on the wrong end of Elijah's staff. This time, though, the attack carried with it a Venom Strike, infecting the monster with a neurotoxin that would eventually kill it. Having delivered that blow, Elijah once again sprinted away.

A minute later, Essence of the Wolf took effect, telling him that his strategy of slowing the monster down had been successful. A couple of minutes after that, he received another dose of kill energy.

Just like that, he'd finished the pack off.

Now, Elijah only needed to take out the alpha. Something told him that doing so would be much more difficult than killing the pack of smaller creatures.

58

A RARE OPPORTUNITY

"Are you certain?" asked Cabbot, using the same imperious tone he'd heard from his father on so many occasions. The effect, in his opinion, was ruined by a lack of a throne room. Or perhaps by the presence of his disgustingly common office, with its mismatched oversize furniture, bare walls, and the stubborn draft that kept the space annoyingly cool. Still, he sat in his dwarf-sized chair, back straight and chin held high—just like he'd been taught.

Nirea shook her head. "I'm sorry, but there's no certainty to be had in a situation like this," she said. "We caught only a trace, and it is unclear how old it is."

He leaned forward. "But you're sure of the trail's origin, right?" he said, a little eagerness peeking through.

"The trackers are," she answered.

Cabbot's heartbeat sped up at the confirmation. A dragon? A real one, and not some lowly drake? On a freshly integrated backwater like Earth? It didn't seem possible. In fact, it was so improbable that, despite Nirea's insistence, his skepticism persisted. Still, even the possibility of something like that was enough to excite him in ways he didn't want to acknowledge.

If it was a real dragon's trail, then it presented a unique opportunity. Dragons were an Elder race, and as such, even the weakest among them were nearly unassailable for someone like Cabbot. He'd heard of whole continents being decimated after a dragon's descent. But Earth, being newly integrated, couldn't support power like that. If a true dragon fell upon the baby planet with its full might intact, the entire world would know about it.

Right before their death.

They probably wouldn't even recognize the surge of Ethera for the danger it would represent. Newly integrated planets were slowly introduced to Ethera for a reason. It was why each world was transformed the moment it was touched by the World Tree, but that was just setting the table for a slow and steady rise of Ethera levels.

If a fully developed member of one of the elder races descended upon Earth so soon after its initial transformation, the planet would be destroyed by the flood of potent Ethera that came with the creature's aura. That was why the planet represented such a unique opportunity for someone like Cabbot.

On his own planet of Norat, he was still a weakling. But on Earth? He was already near the peak. The natives would quickly catch up, though. The environment was carefully cultivated to drive them to progress. So, Cabbot could feel his lead dwindling by the day—which was why he needed to seize every opportunity that presented itself.

There was the island across the narrow strait, but he was still wary of whatever Guardian called it home. He'd contemplated sending more explorers to check it out, but a combination of caution, fear, and the necessity of fulfilling his duties to Ironshore had kept him from committing even one team to such an endeavor. After all, Guardians were normally tethered to their natural treasures, but it wasn't completely unheard-of for one to go on the offensive if it felt threatened.

Cabbot had no intention of prompting such a reaction. He still intended to take the island—and whatever treasure it housed—but he would only do so once he'd had the chance to progress a little more.

And the potential dragon represented just such an opportunity.

Because if one was here, that meant it was young and inexperienced. Vulnerable—at least as much as any dragon ever was.

"What do you want to do?" asked Nirea.

Cabbot shifted in his overly large chair as he thought about her question. His people had a long history of hunting powerful beasts. It was one of the reasons they'd risen to such prominence. He knew what he needed to do, but he also knew it would take almost every coin of etherium he'd earned since coming to Earth. It wasn't a huge sum, but a combination of his pay, the profits from the Slow Dwarf tavern, and the proceeds from selling a few minor treasures had left him far richer than when he'd arrived. He had intended to use that money to commission some new equipment—like some Simple-Grade armor or a piece of jewelry that might grant him an attribute point or two.

But if he could capture a dragon and drain its essence, the gains would far outstrip anything he could get from mere equipment. After that, all it would take was commissioning a decent Alchemist to create an appropriate potion, and his cultivation would see marked progression. He might even develop a proper core—something that would, even in optimal conditions, take months. Realistically, he didn't expect to reach the first stage of core development for years.

If he could accelerate that process with a potion created from a real dragon's essence, he would put himself on a path that would eventually take him to the peak of the new world.

So, there really was no choice to make. Only one option was viable.

"Do nothing. Not yet," he said. "I need to go to the Branch. When I return, we will act."

With that, he pushed himself from the chair, dropping a few extra inches to the office floor. Normally, that would have annoyed him something fierce, but he was too excited to let his ill-fitting office get to him. He didn't even bother flirting with Nirea or asking her out. He knew she was hesitant to acquiesce to his advances—probably because she didn't want to seem like she was getting special treatment—but he knew she would give in eventually.

Right now, though, he couldn't be bothered to care about issues of the heart. He had a lot to do and not much time to accomplish his goals. After all, there was no guarantee that the dragon wouldn't move on, and quickly.

So, he pushed past Nirea, then left the office behind. Nimbly, he leaped over the mud puddle in front of his office, then trekked across town to the budding town's central building. The broad, low-slung building was a combination of warehouse and administrative hub, but more importantly than that, it housed the imported Branch of the World Tree, which made it the settlement's most important location.

Cabbot strode through the front doors, taking a well-trod path through the building until he was forced to a stop at the end of the line leading to the Branch. Sighing, he considered using his position as the leader of the security forces to bully his way to the front of the line, but like everyone else, he knew that would be counterproductive. Before the World Tree, everyone was equal. To the being that connected their universe, a king was no different than a beggar.

That attitude had affected its Attendants and Envoys, and even the elder races would think twice before offending a World Tree Ambassador. So, Cabbot impatiently waited in line as a parade of brutish dwarves, cunning goblins, and gnomes moved into the room housing the Branch. And after forty-five minutes, he reached the front of the line, where he met one of the Envoys.

The lowest-ranked members of the Cult of the World Tree were still afforded a significant degree of authority. At the dwarven woman's word, he could be barred from access. So, Cabbot put on his most winning smile, pushed his innate—and well-earned—prejudice against dwarves aside, and said, "Good afternoon! I trust your day's going well, honored Envoy."

The dwarven woman barely even looked at him before saying, "I'm fine. You understand the rules?"

Cabbot did. He'd been introduced to his family's Branch of the World Tree as a child, and he'd visited it—or others like it—on numerous occasions. So, he knew the rules as well as anyone.

After confirming that he knew how to conduct himself, Cabbot retrieved a handful of copper etherium from his purse and handed them over. The woman took the offering with equanimity, then waved him forward. He suppressed his annoyance, then stepped into the room.

Even though he'd seen many Branches over the course of his life, he still found the sight breathtaking. A crystalline tree sprouted from the center of the room. It wasn't large—barely the size of a sapling—but it was still awe-inspiring, largely because of the Ethera swirling through its branches.

He strode forward confidently, ignoring the pair of Envoys standing guard. So close to the Branch, they wielded enviable power, but even if they hadn't, it would not have mattered. With a flick of thought, they could bar him from accessing the Branch, which would be absolutely disastrous. Not only would it cut him off from ever leaving Earth, but it would also prevent him from ever earning etherium through hunting. He could still get by—after all, people could pay him via their own coins—but it would still be incredibly inconvenient. Besides, losing access to the World Tree carried with it a certain stigma, and most people shied away from anyone so tarnished.

So, Cabbot remained on his best behavior as he approached the Branch and laid his hand on the trunk. Instantly, he saw his etherium totals:

Copper	Silver	Gold	Platinum
212	44	3	0

Upon seeing his amassed wealth, Cabbot felt a mingled sense of satisfaction and disappointment. The first was due to the fact that, aside from a single gold etherium, he'd earned it all himself. However, the latter emotion came from the reality that, no matter how he looked at it, he was poor. His parents—even his siblings—had multiple platinum etherium available to them. And here he was, after months of effort, with only a few measly gold coins to his name.

Of course, that still put him head and shoulders over most combatants his level, but to him, it wasn't enough to simply be better than the unwashed masses. He was meant for much greater things, and he knew it. The world just needed to catch up and recognize that he was better than everyone else.

The System knew. That was why it had given him such a powerful class. Now, he just needed to prove that he was worth it.

To do that, he needed to contact a few old acquaintances back on Norat. So, he navigated past the Knowledge Base, through the Market—where everything was overpriced, anyway—and to the Communications Apparatus. From there, he cycled through his contacts and settled on the person he thought could help him. He initiated the messaging function, detailing what he needed.

Fortunately, Erlych didn't take long to respond, and when he saw the payment on offer, he was quick to acquiesce to Cabbot's requirements. Soon enough, the transfer went through, and Cabbot headed to the Transfer Portal to await his goods.

A few minutes later, the boxes arrived, accompanied by a foursome of robed figures. They were all Ritualists, though due to the planetary restrictions, they were even lower level than Cabbot. He hoped they would be powerful enough to accomplish his goals.

"Where may we set up?" asked one of the male gnomes. He was obviously the leader.

Cabbot answered, "I will show you to the barracks where you can wait until we track the creature down."

"How will you capture the beast?"

Cabbot hadn't told them what sort of creature it was, but they had to have guessed. Otherwise, their presence wouldn't be necessary. He said, "I'm an Eason."

"Oh. Very well, then."

It was telling that the simple mention of his house was enough to allay any worries. Telling but unsurprising. The Eason reputation was well-earned, and even a black sheep like Cabbot had all the expertise he needed to capture any beast—even one as powerful as a dragon.

Still, after showing the Ritualists to the barracks and getting them set up in one of the attached apartments meant for officers, he took the time to lay out his plans. The idea wasn't terribly complicated. He simply needed to lure the dragon into a trap. To do so, he'd need a reasonably powerful natural treasure—young dragons were notoriously curious, and they would be attracted to any fluctuation in Ethera, which meant manipulating it into position was the easy part.

More difficult was the method meant to capture it. The Entrapment Ritual was a family secret, and one Cabbot had learned as a child. He'd since put it into use on multiple occasions, which meant that, with the materials he'd gotten from Erlych, it would be easy enough for him to empower the ritual.

Cabbot hoped that would be the case, at least, because he'd just used every etherium coin at his disposal. Even the coppers. So, if it didn't work, he would be back to square one.

With that in mind, he gathered the scouts who'd found the dragon's trail and set off into the surrounding wilderness, hopeful that he'd taken the first steps toward realizing his vast potential.

59

A MIGHTY HUNTER

The alpha never showed up, much to Elijah's chagrin. He was keyed up and ready to fight, and the moment he regained enough Ethera, he resumed his predator form before retracing his steps. It wasn't easy, finding his way back to the site of the original ambush, but the marks he'd previously left at every intersection proved their worth. Eventually, he arrived, and to his mingled disappointment and relief, the alpha was nowhere to be seen.

But its scent was everywhere.

Elijah crept through the area, sniffing everything, but with how ubiquitous the odor was, he couldn't get a read on where it had gone. Still, that didn't mean he knew nothing. It probably wasn't back the way he'd come, so it had to have gone forward. He left the site behind and continued in much the same way he'd spent the past month progressing through the labyrinth.

And like that, he kept going, moving slowly and methodically. Never did he drop his guard, though. The giant root raptor had surprised him once, and he wasn't going to let it happen again.

It wasn't long before Elijah felt that same formless fear that had preceded his previous encounter with the alpha raptor. But no matter how closely he looked, there was nothing following him. Did the thing have some sort of concealment skill, just like Elijah's Guise of the Unseen? Or was that aura of terror simply that pervasive?

Elijah had no idea.

But he couldn't keep his hackles from rising as he continued through the maze. Nor was he surprised when, finally, the creature attacked. It leaped at him from behind, leading the way with its mighty daggerlike talons. Even though Elijah was on guard for an attack, he was caught by surprise, and so, he barely managed to avoid being gored by those wicked claws. Still, the creature's natural weapons scraped against his ribs, and the impact sent him tumbling across the ground. Elijah regained his feet just in time to dart beneath the raptor's next attack.

He lashed out with his own claws, raking them across his foe's ankles in an effort to render it immobile. But his attempts only scattered a few wood chips across the ground. He didn't stop moving, though, dashing past the much larger figure. He leaped, bounded off the wall, and sent himself flying toward the still-turned raptor. He activated Venom Strike, then latched on to the monster's back. Holding on with his front claws, he kicked with his back legs, digging into the raptor's lower back. In addition, he latched on to it with his jaws, activating Venom Strike again.

And again.

The raptor wheeled around, trying to dislodge Elijah, but it was useless. Not until Elijah's repeated usage of his ability drained his energy and fatigue began to set in. His muscles went slack, and a second later, the raptor's wild bucking sent him flying through the air to crunch against the moss-covered wall.

Elijah narrowly retained his consciousness. As the giant root raptor spun about and charged, he could barely lift his head, much less dodge the creature's attack. He'd overreached, and now, he was a sitting duck.

With exhaustion setting in, Elijah knew his panther form was useless. So, without any further hesitation, he resumed his human form. It took a second for the transformation to complete, and by that point, the raptor was upon him. Elijah didn't have time to use his staff. He simply raised his hand and cast Storm's Fury as the raptor clamped down on his shoulder, its teeth digging in down to his navel.

Lightning descended from the sky, tearing into the monster's back, but rather than dislodge the creature, the resulting convulsions tightened its jaws. Razor-sharp teeth ripped into Elijah's vulnerable flesh, but he cast the spell again.

At the same time, he slapped his hand against his side, casting Touch of Nature. It did almost nothing as the raptor ripped his flesh to shreds. So, he cast it again. He summoned Healing Rain, too. But he knew he wasn't going to last much longer. Already, he could feel the weakness of blood loss setting in, and that was saying nothing for whatever damage its teeth were inflicting upon him.

But Elijah couldn't give up. Not after he'd come so far. He refused.

Even as he rapidly descended into shock, Elijah's mind whirled, searching for some solution. And the only thing he could come up with was a gamble. If he did it, he wouldn't have anything left. Not for a while.

He didn't have a choice, though.

So, as he bled out, he cast Swarm.

A thousand biting flies manifested in a cloud, then descended upon the raptor. They tore into its most vulnerable places. Some targeted its fleshy eyes, while others flew into its half-open mouth and down its throat, biting all the way. The shock of it sent the monster reeling backward, and suddenly, Elijah was free.

The raptor bucked, throwing its head back and snapping at the biting flies. But its efforts were useless. The little creatures were too small and far too numerous. They could only last so long, though, and after a little more than thirty seconds, they dissipated.

For a moment, the raptor was confused by their sudden disappearance, but soon enough, it locked its eyes back on Elijah, who still hadn't moved. His still-active Healing Rain helped with some of his injuries, but he was too drained to make a break for it. So, devoid of Ethera and with exhaustion weighing him down, Elijah just glared at the raptor in defiance.

Then, he screamed.

It was a wordless roar, but it still took the raptor by surprise. It took a step back, and then, miraculously, it stumbled.

That's when Elijah saw the black tendrils creeping up its neck. It tried to right itself, but it stumbled again. Then, it fell on its side. The monster's fore-claws scraped against the ground as it attempted to drag itself forward, to finish the job it had started. And yet, it couldn't. With every passing second, the neurotoxin from Elijah's Venom Strike coursed through its veins. That, combined with the afflictions from Swarm, slowly killed it.

When it died only half a minute later, Elijah received a huge burst of kill energy that pushed him into level twenty-nine. He barely noticed, though. He was far too focused on his own plight.

He was naked, bleeding like a stuck pig, and completely drained of energy and Ethera. If he hadn't had the presence of mind to cast Healing Rain in the middle of battle, he would have already died. The same could be said for his choice to use Essence of the Boar and Aura of Renewal. Without either, he'd have died.

He still might.

But no matter what else, he'd won. He had beaten the raptor, and in his increasingly delirious state, that was all that really mattered.

Gradually, with the aid of Healing Rain, the bleeding slowed, then stopped. At the same time Elijah's Ethera regenerated enough that he could use Touch of Nature. He didn't dare look down at the gaping wound stretched across his chest. Instead, he just put his hand into position and cast the spell. It didn't do much, but it did help him feel slightly better.

Over the next day—or it might have been longer—Elijah healed himself every time he regenerated enough Ethera to fuel Touch of Nature. At the same time, he kept Healing Rain going. And between the two—as well as the increased Regeneration provided by Aura of Renewal—he was slowly healed.

For the first few hours, it was touch and go, and he very nearly slipped into unconsciousness on more than one occasion. However, he forced himself to stay awake, and at some point, he passed from critical condition to something a little less serious. When he was finally healthy, he took a moment to inspect the site of the injury, and he found the puckered flesh of a long, wide scar that extended from his collarbone, across his pectoral muscle, and almost to his navel.

It went well with the acid scars on his right arm.

"How is this my life now?" he muttered to himself, running his fingers along that scar. It was difficult to wrap his mind around how many times he'd nearly died since entering the tower. But unless he was completely off base, that was the last challenge he'd have to complete.

Maybe.

Certainly, the pack of raptors and their alpha felt like a threat on par with the guardian of the last level. However, he had to acknowledge that there was every possibility that, with the increased difficulty of the third level, he might have to fight something even more fearsome. If that turned out to be the case, Elijah was not confident in his ability to survive.

But as had been his mantra since entering the tower—and even before, really—he didn't have much choice but to keep moving forward. Sometimes, a man had to do difficult things if he wanted to survive, and there was no point whining about it, even in his own head. So, once he was healed, Elijah pushed himself to his feet and stretched his stiff muscles.

After checking to see if the raptor had anything useful on its body—and finding nothing—Elijah shifted back into his mist-panther form and continued his exploration of the labyrinth. On the surface, it was no different than before he'd killed the raptor, but somehow, it felt safer. He felt stronger.

That was when he remembered that he'd gained another level. Elijah opened his status to make sure:

Name	**Elijah Hart**
Level	**29**
Archetype	**Druid**
Class	**Animist**
Specialization	**N/A**
Alignment	**N/A**
Strength	**30**
Dexterity	**29**
Constitution	**35 (30)**
Ethera	**38**
Regeneration	**42 (32)**
Attunement	**Nature**

Cultivation			
Body	**Core**	**Mind**	**Soul**
Wood	**Unformed**	**Opal**	**Neophyte**

Sure enough, he'd passed the threshold into level twenty-eight, gaining another point in all his attributes. With Aura of Renewal, his Regeneration had passed the forty-point mark, too. Which was incredible, considering where he'd started. However, Elijah was more interested in the new ability he knew was waiting on him:

Calamity	**Bury your enemies beneath the power of nature. Conjure a natural disaster appropriate to your environment. Only usable in caster form.**

That sounded good. Really good, in fact. He wanted to use it immediately, but Elijah suspected that it would be quite attention getting. The last thing he wanted was to bring more enemies down on his head—after all, he knew that at least the primitive ape creatures had some sort of presence within the maze. So, he refrained from shifting back into his human form and trying it out.

Instead, Elijah continued through the labyrinth. As he went, he realized something was wrong. He couldn't put his finger on it. There was no odor to indicate any other creatures were around. No formless fear to herald the arrival of another raptor. Nothing.

And then it hit him.

It had stopped raining.

In fact, when he looked up, Elijah saw sunlight peeking through the clouds. He had no idea what it meant, but he couldn't help but bask in the sudden cessation of precipitation. Like that, he stood, tilting his feline face toward the sky and bathing in the warmth of a weak ray of sunlight.

However, eventually, he remembered his task and set off again. With every step, it felt like the light grew stronger until, when he looked up a few hours later, he saw nothing but blue skies.

That had to be a good thing, he thought, continuing on. It still took him a further day of exploration, but it felt like no time at all until he finally reached the center of the maze.

Elijah's shoulders sagged in relief as he looked across a wide, grassy clearing and saw a simple stone arch. He didn't need a notification to tell him that he had reached his destination.

Once he'd established that there were no threats within the clearing, he shifted back to his human form and stepped forward. A notification flashed before his eyes, verifying what he'd suspected:

Congratulations! You have completed Level Three of the Keledge Tower.
Grade: S.

To exit the tower, step through the portal.

Then, consistent with what had happened when he'd completed the other two levels, a small metallic box appeared before him. He bent down and opened it, revealing a small crystalline splinter. When he picked it up, another notification flashed before him:

Reward for completing Level Three of the Keledge Tower:

Shard of the World Tree

As before, it didn't come with any explanation or description. But something called the Shard of the World Tree couldn't be trivial. In any case, he hadn't challenged the tower to get rewards. He'd done it to prevent his island from being overrun. So long as he'd accomplished that goal, that was all he really cared about. Anything else was just icing on the cake.

After collecting his reward, Elijah took a deep breath, then stepped through the portal.

60

THE PRICE OF VICTORY

Elijah burst through the surface and took a deep breath of freedom. Bobbing up and down with the waves, he lay back and stared at the winter sun for a few seconds before the frigid water began to affect him. Once numbness started to set in, he swam toward his island. When he got within a few dozen yards, he circled around to avoid the cliff, then finally climbed onto the rocky shore.

Nearby, a giant crab was busy picking meat from a huge skeleton that, to Elijah's trained eye, looked like it had belonged to some sort of enlarged sea snake. But he didn't pay any attention to the pervasive stench of the decaying corpse. Instead, he simply sank to his knees and wept.

He had won.

He had survived.

But months of life-or-death battles had taken their toll, both on his body and his psyche. Most of all his psyche. Until that moment, he'd refused to acknowledge the stress weighing him down, but now that he was reasonably safe, he could allow himself to acknowledge it.

And it was overwhelming enough to drive him to tears of mingled relief and horror.

Elijah wasn't sure how long he knelt, weeping, on the rocky shore. But by the time his tears dried, he was shivering with the winter cold. It had been late summer when he had entered the tower, but clearly, the world had continued its steady march through time, and the seasons had turned.

Thankfully, with his increased endurance, it wasn't nearly as deadly as it probably should have been. Still, it wasn't comfortable, and so, hefting his staff in one hand and the Shard of the World Tree in the other, he pushed himself to his feet and crossed the island.

Before he'd challenged the tower, Elijah's territory had only extended a couple hundred yards around his Grove. However, the moment he'd climbed ashore, he'd known that his Domain had grown to encompass the entire island. Because of that, he could feel everything around him. Normally, it was just background noise not dissimilar from the ambient sound of any forest, but with a bit of mental effort, he could know the island down to its most minuscule detail.

He chose to keep the partition of his mind firmly in place, mostly because it would have overwhelmed his mind with the sheer amount of knowledge. Instead, he let himself feel the area around him in a fifteen-foot radius, which seemed to be the limit without getting everything jumbled up.

In any case, Elijah trekked across the island. With his increased attributes and Essence of the Wolf pushing his speed to new heights, he covered the few miles with some alacrity, and soon enough, he arrived at his Grove. The sight of the familiar trees and his home nearly brought him to tears.

Again.

He'd never been much of a crier, but spending months being abused both physically and psychologically could change that kind of thing in a hurry. And so, as he walked toward the ancestral tree at the center of the Grove, he let himself bask in the emotions.

"Nerthus?" he called, laying his hand on its trunk. He could feel it, and not just the Ethera coursing through it. No—he could feel the life. The tree's glacial thoughts. Its emotions, such as they were. It was content and, to Elijah's surprise, joyous.

"You made it!" came the gnarled but high-pitched voice of the tree spirit. Elijah looked up to see that Nerthus's form had reached almost three feet in height, and he was currently sitting on the same branch where he usually appeared.

"I did," Elijah said. "I . . . I didn't . . ."

And then, once again, he collapsed to his knees. This time, there were no tears. Just a mental acknowledgment of everything he'd experienced. It was one thing to fight a few Voxxian invaders or giant crabs. But it was something else entirely to endure what he had in the tower.

He looked up and said, "That was the worst experience of my life."

But if Elijah was honest, that wasn't necessarily true. Certainly, it had been extremely stressful. And he could have done without all the pain. But there had also been triumphs, as he'd felt after healing the Ulthrak village and defeating the giant isopod. Aside from the constant threat of death, he'd even enjoyed the Sea of Sorrows, after a fashion.

As he thought about it, Elijah realized that he much preferred his experiences in the tower over the time he'd spent slowly dying of cancer. Back then, he'd had no agency. No control. He was just waiting to die. But in the tower, he had the ability to fight. His survival was in his own hands. And that made all the difference.

The real question was whether or not he would do it again. After all, as far as he knew, the same dangers would soon return. The Ethera would build, and the tower would need to be reconquered.

And Elijah only had to think about it for a moment to realize that, when the time came, he wouldn't hesitate to go back in there. Partially because it was his responsibility, but also due to the sheer amount of progress he'd made. Growing stronger was addictive and rewarding in its own right, after all.

"Pardon," said Nerthus, interrupting his reverie. "But . . . But what is that in your hand?"

"Oh," said Elijah. He'd intended to ask the tree spirit about his rewards, but in the wake of his relief at finally conquering the tower, he'd forgotten. Still, he clutched the Shard of the World Tree in his fist. He held it up, saying, "I got this for beating the final level."

Nerthus gasped, then collapsed into convulsions. No—wait. He wasn't convulsing. He was trembling while he knelt, his head on the branch.

"Uh . . . What's going on, Nerthus?"

"The . . . The . . . Is that . . . That is a piece of the World Tree."

"Yeah? That's what the notification said. What's it do?" he asked.

"I . . . It is . . ."

The tree spirit clearly couldn't find the words. So, Elijah said, "Calm down. Just breathe. Wait—do you breathe?"

"No."

"Then do . . . whatever you do to calm down. Meditate or whatever."

It took a few more minutes to get Nerthus to relax, and even that was only partially successful. In the end, he was still trembling—with fear or excitement, Elijah wasn't sure—but he was at least able to talk.

"It is a Shard of the World Tree," the tree spirit explained. "A holy artifact for . . . for any . . ."

He sighed, then admitted, "I lack the vocabulary to explain what that means to me and my people. And anyone who venerates nature."

"What is the World Tree?" Elijah asked. The name had popped up more than once, but he'd never gotten a decent explanation as to what it was.

"It is the beginning and the end," Nerthus said. "It is the source of all life."

"Oh . . . That clears it up . . ."

Nerthus glared. "The World Tree is a universe unto itself," he said. "It runs parallel to our own, connecting everything and everyone. Without it, there would be no System. No communication or travel between worlds. It is the most important being in existence. That shard represents the tiniest sliver of its power. Normally, only the elder races would ever get the chance to see one, and even then, it is rare."

Elijah looked down at the small crystalline object. It was white, with green veins pulsing through it, but to his senses, it was just an ordinary crystal. He didn't even feel any Ethera in it.

"What does it do, though?"

"It . . . I don't know," Nerthus admitted. "Not for sure. But there are legends . . ."

"Legends? What kind of legends?" Elijah asked.

"I think that it could change everything," Nerthus stated. "Oh, yes. I feel it now. If my tree absorbs the shard, it will enhance the Grove's power."

"What does that mean?"

"I don't know," Nerthus admitted. "Denser Ethera. Stronger vitality. And perhaps . . . perhaps more."

"But it won't hurt, right?" Elijah asked. As it was, he had no real use for the shard. If it had emitted even a little Ethera, he might've been more hesitant to let the tree absorb it. But at the end of the day, the Grove was his home, and anything that benefited it did the same for him.

"No. Not us."

Elijah shrugged. "Suppose that's all I need to know," he said. Perhaps he was making a mistake. There was a chance that the Shard of the World Tree could help him more directly sometime in the future. But as he offered the crystalline shard to Nerthus, he felt good about the choice.

Nerthus backed away. "No. Do not offer it to me," he said, trembling. "I could . . . but . . . no. No, I mustn't. Press it against the trunk of the tree. Yes. Do it soon."

Elijah shrugged, then did just that, and when he held the splinter against the ancestral tree, it trembled. Then, in the space of a second, the Shard was gone. A moment later, a burst of Ethera swept out of the tree, and a notification appeared in Elijah's mind's eye.

The Shard of the World Tree has been absorbed by an Ancestral Tree.

"I really hope that was a good thing," Elijah said.

"Oh, it is!" Nerthus responded. "I can already feel it. And . . . Oh, that is surprising . . ."

"What is?" Elijah asked, a little alarmed. The last thing he needed was more surprises.

"The ancestral tree is changing."

Elijah looked up, saying, "Looks the same to me."

"For now, the transformation is . . . Well, it's more like an evolution. Think of it in terms of your cultivation, though all branches at once."

"And again, this is good, right?" he asked.

"Better than good. It is life-changing."

"How so?"

"My progression is tied to the tree. The stronger it gets, the more powerful I become."

"Tell me I didn't just create a monster," Elijah muttered.

"Oh, no. I am a natural spirit. As such, there is a limit to how much influence I can exert in the physical world. Tending to the tree—and by extension, the Grove—is my purpose. If I ever reached the Transcendent stage, that would change, but only minutely."

Elijah knew he wouldn't get much more information on the subject out of Nerthus, so he nodded. "So, what can you tell me about the two other items I got in the tower," Elijah said, holding up the hand where he wore both rings. The Ring of Aquatic Travel was visible, but the Ring of Anonymity was not, though he could still feel it on his pinkie finger. "The first one lets me breathe underwater, but the other is kind of a mystery."

"I see only one."

"Oh. Sorry," Elijah said, pulling the ring off his finger. The moment he did, it became visible. "Called the Ring of Anonymity."

"Not uncommon in the wider universe," Nerthus said. "But it surprises me to see one here, given how new this world is."

"What does it do?"

"Precisely what its name implies. You can use it to conceal your identity. Does it have one or two options?"

"Three. Anonymous, False Identity, and Deactivated," Elijah said.

"Good, good. That means it is at least Simple grade. Perhaps even the lower reaches of Complex," Nerthus stated. "The ring will allow you to either conceal or falsify your identity at will."

"Like a disguise?"

"No. It only affects the response when others use an identification ability," Nerthus stated. Then, seeing that Elijah had no idea what he was talking about, he went on to explain that some classes and archetypes had abilities that allowed them to identify people and objects.

"So, it's useless for me right now," Elijah said, shaking his head. He put the ring back on. "Not really anyone around here to hide from, right?"

"Just so. However, you may want to familiarize yourself with its use. If I may be so bold as to make a suggestion, you may wish to create a benign false identity that you can use when you eventually encounter civilization," Nerthus said. "Druids are not common, and there are those who might target you for the archetype."

Elijah nodded, then with a little focus on the Ring of Anonymity, brought up the item's governing notification. After a little fiddling, he found that he could not only change his apparent level, but he could also choose from a long list of identifiers ranging from Fighter to Merchant and everything in between. For a long while, Elijah perused the list, as much to get a sense for what was out there as to find a viable alternative identity. The sheer breadth of options was overwhelming, and according to Nerthus, it represented only a fraction of what was really possible.

In the end, Elijah chose to reduce his apparent level and adopt the identity of a generic and nonthreatening healer with an imminently common name.

Ring of Anonymity Equipped. Choose Mode:

Anonymous
Mike Smith—Level 18 Healer (Currently Active)
Deactivated

With that done, he left the tree spirit to his own devices and, for the first time in months, returned to his home. Once there, he wasted no time before heading to the bathroom. One good thing about his monthslong stay in the tower was that it had given Nerthus plenty of time to complete the tree house. And that meant that it was now equipped with an actual running water.

When Elijah stepped under the stream of water—which was more like a natural waterfall than anything else—he felt much of his tension wash away alongside all the dirt and grime he'd accumulated. Unfortunately, there was no soap—Elijah had some ideas about how to remedy the lack, but he'd had no time to put his plans into place—but it was still the most wonderful shower he'd ever experienced.

After that, he ambled toward his bed and, for the first time in months, felt secure enough to fall into a deep and dreamless sleep.

61

SAFE AND SOUND

Elijah chipped the last bit of wood away, then ran his thumb over the pawn's head before holding it out to inspect. It wasn't perfect, but his whittling skills had improved since he'd first washed ashore. And using the knife he'd taken from the gnomish invader was much better than using the flint-bladed knife upon which he'd once relied. So, at least the chess piece was recognizable.

He set it down on the homemade board, where it joined all the others he'd carved. Finally, after four nights of work, he'd finished the set.

Leaning back in the chair, he looked down at the small pile of wood shavings and sighed. It had been almost a week since he'd returned from the tower, and he'd spent much of that time in total relaxation. Sure, he still had to pick the incredibly nourishing berries from his garden, and he'd spent a little time fishing, as well, but after spending the past few months in a struggle for survival, none of that seemed so onerous.

But as he sat there, Elijah had to admit something to himself.

He was devastatingly bored. At first, whittling his chess board had been enough to stave off his boredom, and because of that, he'd stretched the process out quite a bit. However, now that he was finished, he couldn't help but wonder what he was supposed to do with all his free time.

If he'd been back home in Hawaii, he might've gone out hiking. Or hung out with his friends and coworkers. Perhaps gone on a date with Lacey. Maybe he would have planted himself in front of his laptop and watched some trashy television or the latest, greatest prestige drama. He could've gone to a football game. He could've played basketball. Or headed down to the gym to work out. The modern world was replete with near infinite ways to waste time and relax, but stranded on his island, opportunities for recreation were slim.

Which was why he'd long since taken to carving various bits of wood.

Still, that could only occupy him for so long before he started to go a little crazy.

The fact was that, with his basic needs met and with the safety his home represented, boredom had truly begun to set in.

Sighing, Elijah decided to do something he'd been putting off for some time. So, he rose from his seat—which had been grown from the floor—and prepared for a little excursion. Or, more accurately, a project that had been sitting in the back of his mind for months before he'd entered the tower.

To put it simply, he wanted to make some soap.

At the most basic level, he understood the process well enough. He needed to make some lye, then melt some fat and add the two together. He'd even seen it done a few times when he was young. But vague memories were not enough to make him confident that he could do it. Still, he was willing to try.

So, the first thing he did—after slipping on some shorts he'd cobbled together from the last remnants of the cloth he'd taken from the invaders—was grab his equipment. Staff in one hand and the axe he'd taken from the dwarf in the other, he descended from his tree house and into the early morning air. It was cold, but judging from the lack of bite in the wind, winter was close to giving way to spring.

His first task in his quest for soap was simple: find lots of wood.

So, axe in hand, he set off into the forest and set about the arduous process of gathering fallen branches, which he dragged back to his old cabin. It was just as decrepit as always, but at least the smell of rotten crab had dissipated in the months since he'd last visited. Once there, he cleared an area, then after it was free of debris, he started piling his branches. It took most of the day to get enough, but by the time he'd finished, he had plenty for a sizable bonfire.

He lit it, then sat back to watch as the flames enveloped the meticulously stacked branches. Once that was done, he found a large tree whose trunk was nearly two feet across, then set about cutting it down.

With his enhanced Strength, Elijah was only held back by his tools. Luckily, the dwarven axe was well-made, and the tree fell after only a couple of hours. By that point, night had begun to take hold, so he retreated back to his tree house, where he spent the night whittling before going to sleep.

The next morning, he returned to cut the fallen tree into two sections before rolling them next to the remains of the bonfire. Elijah added some additional branches, then started the process of turning the rounds of lumber into a pair of barrels, which, over the next few days, he accomplished by slowly chipping away at the interiors of both. It really wasn't so different from how he'd created his bowls, just on a much larger scale.

In the end, it was an entire week before he was satisfied, and by that point, he'd managed to accumulate a huge pile of wood ash. So, after lining the bottom of the largest barrel with sticks, then layering some pine straw over that, he started shoveling ash inside. Once the barrel was full, he took the smaller barrel, which he estimated would probably hold about twenty gallons of water, to the stream, where he filled it.

Then, Elijah started pouring water into the larger barrel, stopping only when he'd created a soupy mess that he covered with a layer of sticks and moss.

With that done, he dropped off his tools at his tree house, then shifted into a panther and went on the hunt.

Given his awareness of everything on the island, locating his prey was laughably easy, and he quickly hunted down and killed a large boar. The only tricky part was avoiding its lethal tusks, but Elijah was experienced enough with hunting dangerous prey that he had no issues with that.

Once the animal was dead, he shifted back into human form and dragged the three-hundred-pound carcass back to the cabin, where he processed it. The meat and edible organs went back to the tree house's cold storage, but he had other plans for the layer of fat he took from the animal's back.

After cutting it into chunks, he gathered the old pot he'd long ago found in the cabin, then started melting the fat down over a smaller fire he'd built. Once it had turned to liquid, he poured it through a piece of cloth—again, taken from the clothing he'd looted from the invaders—and into one of his bowls.

He repeated that process a couple of times until he had nothing but pure fat, which he left to cool and harden.

With that done, his next task was to gather something to make the eventual product smell a bit better. For that, he harvested some pine oil before retiring for the night. The next day, he poked a hole in the bottom of his large barrel and drained the ash water into the smaller receptacle.

The dark-brown color looked right, but he needed to check if it was appropriately alkaline. To do that, he tasted it. Normally, he'd never have done that—that was a good way to get your tongue melted—but he had access to Touch of Nature, so he wasn't afraid of playing loose and fast with his own health.

Fortunately for his tongue, it was only slightly alkaline. Unfortunately for his project, that meant he needed to repeat the process. So, he filled the barrel—better categorized as a lye hopper, considering its use—with more ash, then poured the water back in. It took three more rounds over the next week to get it where he wanted, but by the time he'd finished, he was satisfied with the results.

So, after straining it a couple of times, he boiled the resulting liquid into a more concentrated solution.

Finally, he was ready to make his soap.

The remaining process involved melting the fat, then adding the lye water before spending the next three hours stirring it. During that time, he added a bit of pine oil and a few pinches of salt he'd gotten by boiling seawater. Eventually, the mixture took on a pudding-like consistency, telling him that it was ready. Upon reaching that point, Elijah poured the white substance into a mold he'd whittled for that purpose and took it back to his tree house.

After that, it was just a matter of waiting a few weeks until everything hardened.

All in all, it had taken Elijah a week to finish the project. But now? He was back to having nothing to occupy his time. So, without anything else to focus on, he returned to his Grove and, while flaring Nature's Bounty, circled through the garden. He was on his third revolution when he noticed that the ancestral tree had subtly changed.

Before, it had taken the appearance of a massive and ancient oak tree. It wasn't one, but that was how it had looked. But now? Its brown-gray bark had begun to skew closer to white, and its leaves—the presence of which was more than a little incongruous, given the season—were distinctly lighter. In addition, the Ethera in the area felt noticeably thicker than before.

He shook his head, knowing that the Shard of the World Tree was responsible.

Was that the extent of the changes he could expect? Or was there more in store?

There was no way to know, but Elijah couldn't help but wonder if he'd made a big mistake. In any case, after finishing his rounds, he set off to explore more of the island. He was aware of everything in his territory—which stretched across the whole island—but there was a distinct difference between that awareness and actually laying eyes on it. To Elijah, it felt like the difference between seeing photos of something and experiencing it.

So, with that in mind, he began a thorough exploration of the territory he'd claimed. That occupied him for the next few days, though when he reached the cliff overlooking the tower, he got an incredible surprise.

He could feel the seafloor.

His Domain only extended a few feet past the cliff, but it had definitively grown. Which, according to Nerthus, should not have been possible. So, Elijah used Ancestral Circle to teleport back to his Grove, then marched toward the ancestral tree to demand some answers.

Nerthus responded to his calls with some alacrity, and when Elijah told him what was happening, the tree spirit said, "It must be the shard. The boundaries of your Domain are no longer as fixed as they once were."

"Does this mean it'll keep growing forever?"

"No. This planet is too large, and the Ethera is too diffuse," Nerthus answered. "But with luck, your territory will soon encompass the tower. If that happens, you will not need to conquer it again."

"I don't understand," Elijah admitted.

"The excess Ethera the tower is meant to contain will go to fueling your Grove," Nerthus said. "It's not dissimilar from how the Grove prevents the manifestation of other dimensional rifts."

That was when Elijah realized that, since returning from the tower, he'd yet to see or feel any other Voxx incursions. When he asked Nerthus about it, the tree spirit explained that his Grove drained any dimensional disturbances of Ethera, keeping them from forming.

"It won't completely disable the tower, but it will keep it from overflowing," Nerthus finished. "Assuming that your Domain grows that large, of course."

That was a weight off Elijah's shoulders. Even if he was a little bored, he'd been dreading going back into the tower. If it was necessary, he'd already decided he would do it, but now, it didn't seem like he'd have to.

Not unless he wanted to.

It was just a seed of a feeling, but Elijah had begun to move past some of the more horrible aspects of his time in the tower. He could acknowledge that they were terrible, but time had begun to heal those wounds and blur the memories. Instead, he'd started to focus on how much he had grown as well as the triumph he'd felt upon conquering it.

"That is not uncommon," Nerthus said when Elijah had explained what he was feeling. "This universe is built on Strength, and the most efficient way to progress is to challenge dimensional rifts and conquer towers."

"I see," Elijah said. "What is to prevent me from conquering it again, then?"

Indeed, if that was the best way to grow stronger, then it made sense to simply repeat the process over and over.

"Diminishing returns," Nerthus said. "Doing so will not gain as much kill energy. Of course, you can still earn money, but—"

"Money? I didn't get any money."

"Of course not."

"Explain."

Nerthus sighed. "The System rewards killing Voxx more than anything else, and the same goes for killing creatures in the towers," he said. "Some of that reward comes via kill energy—which is just another form of Ethera, by the way—but the bulk of the reward is monetary. If you wish to collect your reward, you only need to go to a Branch of the World Tree, which will read your status and give you your reward in the form of currency."

"I . . . And where do I find a Branch of the World Tree?"

"Major population centers," said Nerthus.

"Like the settlement across the strait?"

"Perhaps, if they imported one. For natives, someone will have to first join the Cult of the World Tree as an Envoy, which will grant a spell to grow a Branch," Nerthus explained. "It really is exciting. Most people in the wider universe never get to see such a thing."

"So, you're saying that when I reach one of these Branches, it'll be able to tell what I've killed, and they'll just give me a bunch of money," Elijah summarized.

"Yes."

"Well, that's good to know," he said. He had no idea how the System's monetary System had been implemented in the world at large, but he suspected that, as was always the case in any society, money would be incredibly important going forward.

Not that it did him much good. He was still stuck on his island, and though he felt confident about crossing the strait, he certainly couldn't do so until his domain rendered the tower safe.

So, he really wasn't any better off than before. But on the bright side, at least he'd have some soap in a couple of weeks.

62

CURIOSITY

Saraalinisa looked around with wide eyes, her every footfall accompanied by fresh awe. The trees were so green, the local fauna so varied—it was so distinctly wild that she could not help but wonder if the curated forests of her homeland even qualified for the label. The Empire of Scale was one of the oldest in existence, and though there were plenty of untamed lands within its borders, the inhabited territory was so thoroughly controlled that it could scarcely even be called wild.

Or that was true of any place Saraalinisa had been allowed to roam unsupervised. That was why she had begged her mother to allow her to visit the newly integrated world called Earth. If she was ever to realize her potential as a true dragon, she needed to experience a world without the protection and guidance of her ever-present chaperones.

It had taken some time to convince her mother—a powerful elder dragon in her own right—but in the end, her logic was unassailable. No one truly progressed beneath the shelter of a powerful wing. Instead, a hatchling had to experience the world for herself, lest she be unprepared for the challenges inherent in evolution.

Earth represented a perfect opportunity. Even though Saraalinisa was barely more than a hatchling, she was still a member of an elder race. That meant that she was at the pinnacle of what could exist on a newly integrated world. Of the inhabitants of Earth, only truly mighty Guardians could rival her power, and those posed no threat to her. Indeed, they would be more likely to assist than attack.

No—she was in no real danger. Otherwise, her mother never would have allowed her to visit the planet.

So, the juvenile dragon was more than a little surprised when she caught an ephemeral whiff of something extremely interesting. Since coming to Earth, she had sensed plenty of spikes of Ethera. The world was still in flux, and as such, the ambient Ethera was unsettled. However, there was a distinct difference between wild Ethera and what she felt in the distance. It wasn't just powerful. It was enticing in a way she couldn't quite understand. As a result, Saraalinisa was moving before she had a chance to examine her curiosity.

Her form was large—at least for the tiny world in which she found herself—but she moved through the forest with sinuous speed. A few local animals fled before her, and rightly so. While she was barely more than a hatchling, on Earth, she was mighty, and the wildlife could sense that they were in the presence of an apex hunter.

It reminded her of her youth, when she was little more than a clever lizard. That was decades ago, but she still remembered it with some degree of fondness. Back then, she had fought, tooth and claw, for every advantage. And through some twist of fate, she'd managed to survive. She had thrived, steadily growing in power and intelligence until, at last, sapience had bloomed.

That was when her mother had found her. From then on, she had been coddled as she was ushered into juvenility. She had grown into a mighty—if young—dragon. Still, Saraalinisa had a long way to go before she could truly claim her birthright, and when she did, she would need to be much, much stronger.

Those thoughts and more slithered through her mind as she stalked through the forest. Every now and then, she came across particularly slow animals, which she used to satisfy her budding hunger. The furry little creatures went down in a single gulp, reminding her of what she had left behind. They were not unpleasant; in fact, despite the gamy tinge to the meat, she enjoyed the little morsels. However, they were nothing compared to the feasts her mother's servants prepared on a daily basis.

Gradually, she drew closer to the curious ethereal aroma, and with every step, it grew more potent until she could think of little else. In the back of her mind, Saraalinisa knew she should have maintained caution, but a combination of the overwhelmingly enticing smell, her natural curiosity, and the certitude in her own might pushed it aside.

Still, she maintained her wits enough that, when she reached the source, she recognized it for the danger it represented. But by that point, she could not stop, and she ran headlong into the trap. Even as the ethereal bonds snapped around her, she fought against them, ripping them to pieces with her claws and teeth. If she was a little older, she might have won free. However, the trap had been well designed, and soon enough, she found herself pressed against the loamy forest floor. Incapable of moving, she tried to use her natural gifts, but only a tiny gout of golden flame came from her snout. And even that petered out after only a few seconds.

That was when she realized what was happening.

The trap was draining her Ethera. Panic enveloped her heart as she recognized the dangerous situation for what it was. She writhed and snapped, but her efforts were useless. Steadily, the trap siphoned her Strength away until exhaustion gripped her in its claws. She still tried to fight it, but soon enough, she could not even force herself to move. And then, darkness began to close in until, at last, she succumbed to unconsciousness.

The last thing she saw before she passed out was a grinning gnome with a bloodred mohawk.

Cabbot let out a sigh of relief as he looked at the gold dragon he'd trapped. It was still alive—no trap he could set would be sufficient to drain such a creature's vitality—but it would remain unconscious until he released it. Which he wouldn't. Instead, he had plans.

"That what I think it is?" asked Brogan, the gnomish tracker who'd first found the dragon's trail.

"You knew we were hunting a dragon," Cabbot said, glancing at the shaggy-haired gnome.

"Aye. But I thought it was a dragonkin. Like a wyrm or a drake or somethin'," the scout said. "Didn't think we were huntin' a real dragon. And a gold one at that. You sure you want to deal with that kind of weight?"

Cabbot rolled his eyes. Dragons were powerful enough, but they had to work within the confines dictated by the World Tree, just like everyone else. Sure, if he was stupid enough to ever go to the Empire of Scale—or one of their subordinate territories—he might be in trouble. But he didn't think so. Earth was an unclaimed planet, and as such, he could do whatever he wanted.

Even if half the universe would look down on him for it.

The other half, on the other hand, would be jealous of the opportunity. But that was the nature of things, and just by virtue of his birth, he knew which side he fell on.

"I think we'll be just fine," Cabbot said. Then, to the others, he said, "Now, bind it, pack it away, and get it to the ritual chamber."

Brogan spat, then asked, "You ain't gonna help?"

"I have better things to do" was Cabbot's answer. The other gnome didn't seem to like that very much, but Cabbot was banking on Brogan knowing who held the purse strings. "Just get it done."

"Aight," he said. Then to his helpers, he said, "C'mon boys. You heard 'im. Let's do it."

Cabbot stayed around long enough to ensure that they weren't going to mess it up, then retreated through the forest, eventually arriving back in Ironshore. Once he did, he quickly made his way to the barracks, where he collected the Ritualists he'd hired. They'd been cooling their heels for weeks while Cabbot and the others hunted the dragon down, and so, they were eager to finish the job.

To that end, Cabbot led them into the mines and to the specially prepared chamber where they would drain the dragon's essence. There, they set up their rituals as Cabbot waited for the scouts to bring the creature along. Once they were finished, the leader asked, "What do you intend to do with the essence? I can offer you—"

"I have big plans," Cabbot stated. "Very big plans."

"Do you need the services of an alchemist?"

Cabbot shook his head. "No. I intend to use an old friend," he said. "He is an Ascendent alchemist working for the Ferdan Family."

"Oh," said the robed gnome. "Impressive. Making Ascendent as a craftsman is no small feat. He must be talented."

"Indeed."

"What of the other materials?" the ritualist leader asked. Cabbot still hadn't learned his name. Nor did he want to. Ritualists who specialized in essence draining were not looked upon favorably in most circles. They were necessary, but most people were uncomfortable with the process. Some people even called it a violation of a creature's soul.

A ridiculous superstition, as far as Cabbot was concerned.

"I hadn't thought about that," he said. It would be a shame if such a potent resource went to waste. "Do you have something in mind?"

"I do. Our . . . organization will be happy to take them off your hands," he said, greedily rubbing his hands together. "You will be compensated, of course. Not only will we pay . . . ah . . . handsomely for those resources, but we will also be in your debt. I don't think I need to remind you of how useful that could be, considering the nature of our relationship."

Indeed, the only reason Cabbot had known to call on Erlych in the first place was because he'd used them before. Not on anything so taboo as a dragon—or any other sentient race—but that relationship was the poorly concealed secret to his family's power. After all, being able to trap powerful monsters was useless without the means to eke out every ounce of benefit, which was where the ritualists came in.

Or rather, the Cult of the Devourer. The Ritualists came from a comparatively weak sect within the cult, but they were clearly adherents of the religion. Cabbot didn't know much about them, save that they worshipped an ancient Transcendent being whose power was built on consuming the power of others. He'd never researched more than that because, well, he found the notion far too enticing to trust.

The Cult of the Devourer wasn't exactly illegal, but the organization was certainly frowned upon in most societies. However, that didn't stop people from seeking out their services; they just didn't talk about it at parties.

In any case, Cabbot knew just how valuable a good relationship with the cult could be, so he said, "That's fine with me. Just let me know what you're willing to pay for the carcass, and we'll address this once you've had a chance to examine it."

"The creature is not an it," the ritualist leader stated.

"What?"

"They have an identity. A gender. They are a living, thinking, and self-aware being with a soul," he responded. "To refer to them as an it robs them of dignity."

"You're about to drain it of its essence," Cabbot stated. "It won't have any dignity left when you're done."

"Yes. Our tenets require that we acknowledge what we're taking," he responded. "Make no mistake. A sapient being will die, their soul stripped away so that we may progress. That is as the Devourer dictates."

Cabbot resisted the urge to roll his eyes. He'd seen the creature. It was nothing more than a giant unthinking lizard. Perhaps it would one day be more—or it would've been before he captured it—but for now, it was just another monster.

He wasn't going to say that, though. Not to a gnome who could, with a single order, ruin all Cabbot's plans. So, he just nodded his head in acquiescence, saying, "If you say so."

After that, the conversation petered out until a couple of hours later when the hunters arrived. Between them they carried a sizable litter, the contents of which was covered in a heavy tarp. It was curious, but at a glance, there was no way anyone could have identified the bulky burden as a living dragon.

At the ritualists' direction, the trackers turned porters deposited the creature in the center of the room, where the ritualists had drawn their glyphs and sigils. After that, they hurried away, clearly wanting nothing to do with what was going to happen next.

"How long?" asked Cabbot before they could get started.

"Days, at least. Maybe weeks. It depends on how much power she has."

Cabbot nodded, then said, "Then let's hope for weeks. I'll leave you to it, then."

The lead ritualist nodded, but before Cabbot could leave, he said, "Think on what I said. No power comes without sacrifice."

Cabbot didn't respond, instead pretending that he hadn't heard. As he left the ritual chamber behind, passing into the mines, the whole of his mind was occupied as he considered everything he stood to gain.

63

A PLEA FOR HELP

Though it took almost three weeks to fully harden, the soap turned out exactly as Elijah had hoped, which was to say that, while it was a little harsh, it did the job. So it was that, after spending almost two years on his island, he was finally able to reach a reasonable level of cleanliness. After that, he collapsed onto the bed, which was made of pleasant-smelling moss and leaves. He looked up at the softly glowing flowers above him and let out a satisfied sigh.

It had taken a long time, but he'd finally achieved a level of comfort that should have been impossible. So, of course it couldn't last.

"Elijah," came Nerthus's soft voice.

Elijah looked up to see the tree spirit standing in his doorway. "What?" he asked. Then, seeing the troubled expression on Nerthus's face, he sighed and said, "Please don't tell me the tower is about to burst again."

"It's called a Surge," Nerthus said. "But no. The local tower should be subdued for some time yet. Perhaps for as long as the Grove persists, if your Domain continues to grow."

The boundaries of Elijah's territory had continued to expand, but the growth was slow, and even if it kept going at the same rate, it would take months for the tower to be subsumed into his Domain. Hopefully, it would happen quickly enough that Elijah wouldn't be forced to challenge it again. He could acknowledge that his previous experience within the tower had been valuable for his personal growth, but that didn't mean he was eager for a repeat.

"Here's hoping, then," Elijah said, making a show of crossing his fingers. Nerthus clearly didn't understand the gesture.

"Yes. Of course. The reason I've disturbed your rest is more troubling than the tower, though," Nerthus said, nervously looking down as he shuffled from one foot to the next.

"That doesn't sound good," Elijah said, sitting up. "What's going on?"

"I have been . . . contacted by a powerful being," Nerthus explained. "And she made a request that I don't think we should turn down."

Elijah didn't like the way that sounded. He sat up. "Powerful being? That's a bit vague, man. Can't you be a little more specific?" he asked.

In a clear effort to compose himself, Nerthus took a deep breath. "A dragon."

"What? A dragon? Like a huge reptile with wings and—"

"Dragons are technically not reptilian, though they do share some characteristics," he said. "But if you ever meet one—which seems likely, if you are to fulfill the request—you should not liken them to lizards."

"Why?"

"Because they are touchy about that sort of thing, and you do not wish to anger a dragon."

"I think I probably already know the answer to this," Elijah said. "But why not?"

"Because a suitably upset dragon is fully capable of destroying this entire planet."

"Gotcha. Don't piss dragons off," Elijah said. "So—if they're so powerful, then why would one need to make a request of me?"

Nerthus answered, "Because this planet is young. Its Ethera is weak enough that a fully grown dragon couldn't survive here. However, that is not to say that they couldn't destroy this whole planet from afar. Or if they set foot on the surface."

Elijah sighed. He certainly didn't like the sound of that. Nor was he thrilled with the implications behind the statement. It felt like Nerthus was telling him that if he didn't do what this dragon asked, then he would run the risk of having his entire planet destroyed.

"What does this dragon want?"

"Something was stolen from her," Nerthus said. "In fact, it is, at this moment, only a few miles away. She wishes for you to retrieve it."

That sounded very vague to Elijah, and he said as much before asking what, precisely, had been stolen.

"Her daughter," Nerthus said. "She is barely past the hatchling stage, though even that should have been plenty to survive a new planet such as this. However, she was abducted soon after her arrival and brought to the settlement across the strait."

"Why?" Elijah asked. "I mean, if dragons are so powerful, why would anyone do something so stupid?"

Nerthus sighed. "I have mentioned this a few times, but this universe can be roughly divided into two philosophies," he said. "On one side, there are those who see the world as theirs by right. They consume, using any means they can to progress. On the other are those like you who, instead, seek to harmonize with the natural world.

"The first way is faster, but it comes at a cost. Once a resource is used, it is gone. These devourers must continuously seek new sources of power," Nerthus went on. "They are, in a very real way, a spreading virus that will consume the universe. The worst of them adhere to the Cult of the Devourer, a Transcendent being older than your world and much more powerful than anything you can imagine."

"But these . . . devourers, their way works, right?"

"Certainly."

"And the other side?" Elijah asked, already guessing the answer. Still, he wanted it confirmed.

"Preservationists seek to cultivate relationships with sources of power," he said. "For instance, if a devourer were to encounter this Grove, he would harvest the ancestral tree and use the wood to fuel his own advancement."

"How?"

"Potions. Rituals to temporarily provide an ideal cultivation environment. Sacrifices. They might even consume the wood via mastication," Nerthus explained. "The methods are many and varied. But the results are the same. They get a little stronger, and this Grove would cease to exist. Once they'd wrung every ounce of power from it, they would move on to the next. And the next after that. Over and over until they reached the pinnacle or there was nothing left."

"So, I'm already a preservationist, huh?" Elijah asked. "Or does harvesting the berries in this Grove mark me as a devourer? What if I was to—"

"You wouldn't have been offered the druid archetype if you were the sort who might become a devourer."

"Oh."

"But most people are somewhere in between," Nerthus admitted. "And though I may not like it, I can't blame people for grasping at power. However, there are those who take things too far. That is what we're dealing with here."

"How so?"

"Dragons are some of the most powerful creatures in the known universe," Nerthus answered. "The people who kidnapped the young one intend to drain her."

"Drain her? That's . . . Wait . . . They're going to use a sentient creature as fuel?" Elijah asked. "That's . . . I mean . . . Is that even allowed?"

"Of course not!" Nerthus exclaimed. "But there are those who will do anything for power."

Elijah shook his head. The idea was abhorrent, but he could understand the motivation. On Earth, people had done horrible things for money and power, so the idea that some would be willing to sacrifice a sapient creature just to enhance their own cultivation wasn't all that surprising. Greed, it seemed, was a constant, even in the wider universe.

"What am I supposed to do?" asked Elijah.

"The task is simple. Retrieve the young one."

He waved his hand, and a notification bloomed before Elijah's eyes.

A powerful entity has offered you a Task:

Obejective:
Rescue the child.

Reward:
Blessing of the Dragon Kirlissa

Do you accept?

"This looks like the tasks I did in the tower," Elijah said. Then, he looked up at Nerthus and asked, "How?"

"Sufficient power gives you the option of offering official tasks through the System," he said. "I am merely the vessel by which the dragon acted."

"What is the Blessing of the Dragon?"

Nerthus shook his head. "That I do not know," he said. "It could be a useful item. It could be etherium. Or anything else. There is no limit, save for the level of power of the offered reward."

"Which is?"

"Enough to make a difference. Not enough to change the fate of this world," Nerthus said. "So, will you take the task?"

"I have one more question," Elijah said. "Why me?"

Nerthus cocked his head to the side as if confused. Then, he said, "Because you are a druid."

"Yeah, no—I know I am. But what difference does that make? I'm sure there are lots of druids."

"No. There aren't. Perhaps a few thousand satisfied the requirements of that archetype. Of those, only a couple hundred managed to survive. It is a prestigious and rare archetype. Even more so because you have managed to gain power so quickly. Usually, druids are much slower and far less combative. The more action oriented of the archetype tend to die early deaths."

"Oh. That's . . . I don't know if I should feel good about myself for surviving or terrible for all the people who died."

"Both," said Nerthus.

"Still—that doesn't answer the question. What makes me being a druid so important?" Elijah asked.

"Dragons trust druids."

"Why?"

"Mutual benefit and aligned philosophies," Nerthus stated. "That is not to say they are one entity. Dragons tend to be . . . proud, and though dragons and druids have often allied with one another, there is still some level of animosity. However, with something of this nature, there is no better ally than a druid."

Elijah still didn't quite understand. It was just an archetype, which, in turn, was just a means to get some useful spells. But he wasn't going to argue with the tree spirit's assertion.

"Okay—I thought of another question. How did the dragon contact you?"

"Very painfully," Nerthus answered. "I barely survived the touch of her mind."

"Oh."

"So, will you accept the task?" the tree spirit asked.

Elijah was torn. He had seen how powerful the people across the strait were when they'd killed the guardian. So, what chance did he have of going up against an entire settlement? But then again, could he sit on the sidelines and let an innocent person die? Sure, that person was a dragon, but that didn't really matter.

She was just a child. What kind of monster would he have to be to ignore her plight?

And then there was the reward. The Blessing of the Dragon was a bit ambiguous, but Nerthus seemed convinced that it would be worth it. Besides, if dragons were so powerful, then a blessing bearing their name was clearly something worth pursuing.

Just like that, Elijah knew what he would do. So, he accepted the task, then told Nerthus his decision. The tree spirit seemed relieved, but he was also clearly worried.

"I need to get ready," Elijah said.

And so he did. He didn't have much in the way of supplies to gather, but he did grab his staff. One thing he'd discovered was that, so long as he was wearing an item—even if it was something like a knife stuck to his belt or a pack secured to his back—it would transform right alongside him.

That would have been good to know before he'd challenged the tower, but back then, he'd assumed it was just his staff that transformed with him. So, he'd never even tried it. Now he knew, though, and so, he could prepare accordingly.

After stuffing one of his woven satchels full of berries and mushrooms, Elijah stuck his pilfered knife into a homemade sheath at his waist. Then, after checking everything a second time, he bade goodbye to Nerthus, who wished him luck. Then, he set off across his island.

Soon enough, he reached his destination.

The boat hadn't been in the water since he'd helped kill the trio of invaders who'd infiltrated his island, and the months that had passed since then had left it a little worse for wear. Still, it wasn't rotted, so he figured it would hold together at least long enough for him to reach the other shore.

However, Elijah wasn't going to set off until after dark. So, he settled down to wait. In that time, he focused on what he planned to do. He didn't know the layout of the settlement—which, by that point, had become a proper city, with thousands of residents—but he hoped he could figure things out when he got there.

It wasn't much of a plan, but he didn't know how else to accomplish the task at hand.

Eventually, night began to fall, accompanied by a light drizzle. Elijah looked to the west and saw dark clouds on the horizon. There was a storm coming, and he could only hope that he had the means to survive it.

64

IRONSHORE

Rain fell in heavy drops that reminded Elijah that spring would soon overtake winter. But it had yet to arrive, as evidenced by the biting cold that refused to relinquish its grip. Elijah ignored it as he pushed the small boat out into the sea. He had endured worse, and he knew his suffering had just begun.

He could only hope that it would be worth it.

Once the water reached his waist, he climbed into the boat, grabbed the oars, and started to row. With his enhanced Constitution, it was trivial to send the vessel cutting through the waves, and soon enough, he was skipping along the surface with some speed. Still, the strait was wide, and even as the darkness of full night enveloped him, he continued to row toward his destination.

Even with his augmented Strength, it took Elijah over two hours to cross the strait, partially due to the distance, but also because the boat itself had never been built for speed. Still, he made it without much difficulty.

Upon reaching the shore, which was just as rocky as that of his island, he climbed out of the boat and dragged it out of the sea. For his point of ingress, Elijah had chosen a spot about a mile up the shore from the edge of the settlement. He'd done so in an effort to avoid detection; after all, the town was well lit, and it would have been tempting fate to assume he could arrive at the dock unseen.

Thankfully, the tree line was only a few feet from the shore, which allowed Elijah to quickly drag the boat under cover. Once that was taken care of, Elijah recast his enhancements—Essence of the Wolf, Essence of the Monkey, and Aura of Renewal—before casting Shape of the Predator. As always, One with Nature was still active, as well.

Once he'd assumed the form of a mist panther, he set off through the forest. As he slowly padded through the woods, nimbly leaping over fallen trees and across the dips in the terrain, he sorely missed the awareness of his Domain. He hadn't felt it back in the tower, but in the weeks since returning to the island, he'd grown used to knowing everything about his surroundings. Fortunately, One With Nature acted as a watered-down version of the skill. The breadth of knowledge it granted was far more limited, and it only extended a dozen yards around him, but it was much better than nothing.

Gradually, he covered the ground between his landing spot to the clearing surrounding the city. As he did, he tried to plan for what he would find. A hundred possibilities flitted through his mind, but they were all useless until he knew what obstacles might bar his way.

He reached the edge of the forest, then bounded up a tree until he was twenty or thirty feet from the ground. From that elevated position, he gazed out across the clearing at the settlement. The first thing he noticed was that it was far more developed than he'd expected. The buildings weren't so different from what he might've seen from industrious humans, though the few residents he saw put the lie to that image.

Gnomes, dwarves, and goblins made up the majority of the population, but he also saw a couple of creatures he could only categorize as dark elves. Because of their onyx skin, refined features, tapered ears, and stark-white hair, Elijah couldn't think of them as anything else.

After watching for a while, Elijah resigned himself to the inevitable. He could only glean so much information from afar; he would have to enter the settlement if he wanted to find the dragon's daughter and complete the task he'd been given. So, after only a little more hesitation, he descended from his perch and embraced Guise of the Unseen before setting off across the clearing.

However, after only a few feet, he felt something in the ambient Ethera shift, a feeling that was quickly followed by a sense of vague unease. When he felt that, he stopped in his tracks and retreated a few feet until he felt things return to normal. It took a few more passes before he found the line of demarcation. After a few more minutes of study—during which he followed the line across the clearing—he determined that it surrounded the settlement.

With that in mind, and without any other indications as to the purpose, Elijah set out to test it further. As he did, he determined that it clearly wasn't dangerous, but there was something about it that tickled at the back of his mind. So, after finding a hollow that was out of the line of sight of the settlement, he shifted back to his human form. Then, he crossed the line, and just as he'd expected, he felt nothing.

That cemented it.

The line wasn't so different from the boundaries of his Domain. However, instead of granting awareness, it was meant to keep the wildlife away. Perhaps it even prevented dimensional rifts from forming. He didn't know enough to draw any further conclusions, so he retreated out of sight and waited for his Ethera to regenerate. Once it did, he once again assumed the form of a mist panther and stalked forward.

After crossing the line, the sense of unease returned, but it wasn't enough to dissuade him from continuing. Perhaps that was because he wasn't truly an animal. Or maybe his attributes protected him. It might've even been One With Nature keeping the boundary from fully affecting him.

Whatever the case, it was easily endured, so he continued to stalk toward the settlement.

As he drew closer, more of the town's details became apparent. It was lit by what looked like gas lamps, though the light was different enough that Elijah thought they must have been powered by Ethera. The buildings themselves were made from a mixture of quarried stone and wood from the surrounding forests and, from an architectural perspective, were entirely unimpressive in their mundanity.

Elijah padded forward, keeping low and trusting the shadows and Guise of the Unseen to keep him hidden. Even so, he took great pains to avoid the residents. By that point, it was well past midnight, so there weren't many out and about, but there were enough that Elijah had to choose his route into the city with care. Fortunately, there were no active defenses or guards; otherwise, he might've been found.

Over the next few hours, Elijah explored the city, and as he did, he was struck by just how normal everything seemed. The residents were all mythological creatures—at least from his perspective—but they acted much as he'd have expected from humans. He saw them eating, drinking, laughing with their friends, and enjoying all sorts of leisure activities. He passed a few taverns, and he even crept into a couple of domiciles to see them sleeping. It was all just so normal.

And even when he was focused on the task before him, Elijah couldn't help but be reminded of just how lonely he was. It had been more than a year since he'd spoken to another human being, much less done something so mundane as hung out at a bar. Once, Elijah had taken that sort of thing for granted, but now, he knew just how valuable companionship really was.

More, the city—and the normalcy of its atmosphere—suggested that the world hadn't fared as poorly as he had expected. Certainly, people had died, but if the collection of gnomes, goblins, and dwarves could live normal lives, then so could the human population that had been lucky enough to have survived the world's transition.

Seeing the city also awakened within him a resolve to find other survivors. To search out his family. Before, it had seemed impossible. Now, though, he felt confident that he could traverse the world with some degree of safety. After all, he'd survived the Sea of Sorrows and the Primordial Jungle. Surely, that was more dangerous than whatever he'd find in Earth's wilderness.

In any case, Elijah couldn't focus on that. Instead, he continued to search the settlement for any hints as to where he might find the dragon's daughter. Despite his efforts, as dawn approached, he still hadn't discovered any leads. So, with the population beginning to stir, he had no choice but to retreat, quickly returning to the forest and settling in to observe the town by the light of day.

Soon enough, the sun rose, and the town came to life as hundreds of people set about their daily tasks. Elijah focused on two groups in particular, though. One headed into the surrounding forests, while another went to the mine behind the town.

After finding a secluded cave a few miles away from the city, Elijah settled in for a few hours' worth of sleep. When he awoke, he took off through the forest to search out the townspeople who'd gone into the woods. The first group he found were loggers, while the second were clearly hunting the local wildlife.

From a perch on the thick branch of an oak tree, Elijah watched as the hunters took down a bear the size of a compact car. The beast put up a decent fight, but the group of five hunters were well prepared and clearly practiced at their craft. So, the animal fell without inflicting much damage on its killers. After that, they set about processing the creature, and when they finished and headed back to the town, they left nothing behind.

After seeing that, Elijah continued to search the forest, and he came across more hunts in progress. None of them even vaguely suspected he was around, which, though unsurprising, was gratifying. Emboldened by that success, he followed each of the hunting parties until he could confirm that they weren't keeping the dragon's daughter hidden away. It took most of the day, but by the time the sun set, he'd ruled the hunters out as the kidnappers.

So, with night falling, he retreated to his cave and got a few more hours of rest.

When he awoke, it was nearly midnight. While he'd slept, the rain had returned in full force, which provided that much more cover as he crept toward the mine. It was situated at the base of one of the surrounding mountains, and the entrance was guarded by a few scattered buildings.

Elijah searched them, though he found nothing but administrative facilities that looked strangely reminiscent of what he'd expect from a similar human-run operation, a couple of storehouses filled with various mining supplies, and a guard post manned by a couple of dozing goblins. He also made a couple of discoveries along the way. First, the System's translation feature apparently extended to the written word, so he had no issues reading the files in the administrative room. Second, that ability gave him a little context for the mining operation—chiefly that the settlement was called Ironshore, was run by a group known as the Green Mountain Mining Guild, and that they were almost exclusively interested in something called true iron.

None of that was pertinent to his task, so he only spent a few minutes reading the files. Still, it was nice to get some information about his neighbors.

He crept past the goblin guards, entering the mine. At first, he took things slowly, but after a few minutes, it became clear that the mine was entirely deserted. So, he sped up, abandoning Guise of the Unseen in favor of alacrity. He passed carts and piles of ore along the way, but for the first hour or so, he found nothing out of the ordinary. As far as he could tell, it was just a regular mine.

Then, Elijah noticed that the density of the ambient Ethera began to rise. As he continued on, he came to a fork in the tunnel. Down the left path, the Ethera remained mostly stable, but to the right, it continued to thicken. Reasoning that that had to mean something, he chose the right path.

Over the next hour, he was confronted with a few more such choices, and each time, he decided to follow the Ethera, deciding that it was probably the best strategy. Along the way, he paid special attention to the senses granted by One With Nature—a good strategy because, otherwise, he never would have found his quarry.

He was slowly padding down the mine shaft when he felt something that shouldn't have been there. To his left, he could sense the normal life—insects and the like—that indicated there should be a tunnel there, but when he looked, he saw nothing but a solid wall of rock. Curious, Elijah reached out with a paw, and to his shock, he saw it pass through the wall.

He snatched his paw back, then inspected it. It seemed the same as always, and he hadn't felt any pain to indicate that it was dangerous. So, it only took a few seconds for him to conclude that the wall was some sort of illusion.

Still, even though such an explanation made perfect sense, Elijah felt a tremble of fear as he pushed through. Nothing bad happened, and he sighed in relief as he stepped into a new tunnel.

However, this one was different. Rougher. It didn't bear the same wooden beams that supported the integrity of the rest of the tunnels. Likely, that was because it was so small. The rest of the mine's passages were at least twenty feet across and just as high, but this new tunnel was maybe a quarter of that. Wide enough to permit passage of a couple of the small gnomes or goblins, but wider-shouldered dwarves would have to traverse it single file.

Elijah padded down the tunnel as it sloped dramatically downward, twisting and turning every few steps. Then, finally, he reached a point where it opened into a wide chamber.

It only took him a few seconds to confirm that he'd found his destination because in the center of the room lay a large, curled form that could only be a young dragon.

65

THE RITUAL

Golden scales glinted in the flickering light of a dozen torches, giving the illusion that the figure was moving. But aside from the gentle rise and fall of her chest, the dragon was entirely motionless. The creature had been described as little more than an infant, and yet, she was at least seven feet long, from delicate snout to tapered tail. With wings folded against her back, she had the sinuous shape of a serpent, and yet, four legs were tucked under her form.

In short, she was a stunning creature, and for a moment, Elijah could only stare in awe. And then, as he continued to study the scene before him, anger started to overwhelm the sense of astonishment.

Because she was clearly injured, with one of her legs bearing an obvious break. Blood coated one of her folded wings, and a long gash stretched from the base of her tail to her ribs. Even more disturbingly, a half dozen hooded figures that, from their size, had to be goblins or gnomes, were busy drawing complex symbols on the stone ground.

Or a few of them were, at least. The others followed behind, sprinkling glittering dust on the still-wet paint.

No.

Wait.

Elijah caught another whiff, and he instantly recognized the smell. Blood, mixed with something else and pulsing with Ethera.

A low growl escaped from between his lips, though he was thankfully far enough away that the gnomes didn't hear.

It didn't take much intuition to see what was happening. The gnomes—or goblins, perhaps—were setting up a ritual of some sort. That tracked with what Nerthus had described. They wanted to harvest the dragon, taking whatever made her special in order to enhance their own cultivation. Or perhaps to sell it. He didn't know which, but it really didn't matter, either. Even if he hadn't had the task spurring him forward, there was no way he could see what was happening and not act.

As he crouched low to the ground, his tail swished back and forth. Then, he pounced, using Predator Strike. His claw ripped through the gnome's robes, cutting deep before shattering his ribs. Without stopping, he snapped out, clamping his jaws on the screaming figure's head, then bit down.

The creature's skull shattered.

But Elijah wasn't finished. Instead, he bounded toward the next closest figure, and when they turned, he saw nothing but wide-eyed surprise. He pounced on her, then swiped his claws across her exposed throat. He felt a slight resistance at the last second, but it wasn't enough to stop him.

With two down, Elijah was gone before the rest even knew what had happened. He melted into the shadows, letting Guise of the Unseen settle onto his shoulders. Nestled in darkness, he knew he was completely undetectable.

One of the remaining four figures whipped around, saying, "What . . ."

Another locked eyes on Elijah's second victim, and upon seeing the bright-red blood pooling around her fallen body, she screamed, "Rayna!"

"Don't move," said the third, his voice full of authority. He raised his hand, and Elijah felt Ethera gathering at his fingertips. That was enough to mark him as his next victim.

Elijah darted from the shadows, then used Predator Strike and Venom Strike at the same time. However, he was surprised when his claw met stiff resistance; it wasn't enough to stop his attack entirely, but it was plenty to prevent a mortal strike.

Still, his claw traced a line across the gnome's shoulder, sending a spray of blood arcing through the air. Elijah never stopped moving, instead melting into the shadows with Guise of the Unseen.

Against animals, such a strategy wouldn't have been possible. But the gnomes' senses just weren't sharp enough to track him—especially after he started attacking the torches. One after another, they fell. They weren't extinguished, but it was enough to deepen the shadows.

Meanwhile, the neurotoxin of Venom Strike had begun to do its job. The leader fell, seizing as he hit the ground. Pink foam escaped his mouth as he rasped, "Poison . . ."

Elijah didn't pay attention.

Instead, he stalked his remaining prey. There were only three left, and they planted themselves with their backs against the wall. All three were gnomes. One male. Two female. As if that mattered. With what they'd done to the dragon, they deserved whatever he could dish out, regardless of gender.

Elijah circled to the right, careful to avoid the guttering torches. He could taste the gnomes' fear. He could feel it in his bones. And there was a part of him that reveled in it, that felt justified in striking terror into the hearts of people who thought nothing of killing and harvesting a sapient creature.

He padded closer, staying close to the ground.

Then, he pounced, once again using Predator Strike. And just like before, he was met with significant resistance that slowed his claws. It didn't matter. One strike followed the next, and he could feel the invisible shield weakening. Finally, he broke free and gutted one of the females, raking his claws across the gnome's midsection. Her innards spilled out, filling the chamber with the foul stench of ruptured intestines.

But the kill had taken too long, giving the remaining two a chance to respond.

And respond they did. Elijah felt something slam into his ribs, flipping him over and sending him sprawling across the ground. He recovered quickly, but judging by the burning pain on his side, he'd picked up a serious wound. Even more distressingly, another unseen force slammed into him a second later. Then another.

Elijah rolled with the momentum, then launched himself at the wall and used it to spring into another attack. His claws raked across an invisible shield, doing nothing. He'd learned his lesson, though, so he kept moving, diving back into the shadows.

"It's bleeding! Just follow the trail!" screeched the remaining female.

Elijah kept going, moving as quickly as he could. But he didn't need to inspect his wounds to know that he might have bitten off more than he could chew. So long as he could strike from the shadows, his mist-panther form was deadly. However, in a straight-up fight, it left a lot to be desired, at least in regard to durability.

"Where did it go?!"

"Over there!"

Something thudded into the wall across the room.

"Did you get it?"

"I don't know!"

They were jumping at shadows, which Elijah understood. The combination of his black coat and the dying light of the flickering torches had created a nearly perfect environment for him. But even if he could easily remain undetected and escape if he so desired, the gnomes were still alert enough to see him coming.

But Elijah refused to abandon his task.

So, he continued to circle, trusting that his Aura of Renewal–enhanced Regeneration could keep him alive, even with his wounds.

"Is it gone?" asked one, her voice trembling.

The other hissed, "I have no idea!"

"What was it? It looked like a big cat," the female whispered. "But how? With the barrier—"

That's when Elijah pounced, his claws raking across her shield. He could feel it weakening with every subsequent attack. He could use Venom Strike and Predator Strike in tandem, and perhaps he could get through, but that would leave him dangerously close to exhaustion. No—it was better to hit and run, over and over, until she was vulnerable.

So, that's what Elijah did. Each swipe he took came with the risk of taking another hit himself. But so long as he kept moving, he felt confident in his chances. The gnomes weren't fighters. He could tell that much. That made them prone to panic, and more, the constant flow of adrenaline would eventually take its toll.

After twenty minutes, they tried to escape.

That was the opening Elijah needed to finish the female off. He pounced on her, driving her to the ground. Her partner continued running toward the tunnel as Elijah's claws flashed. Once. Twice. Three times. She screamed. Elijah paid it no mind as he finally broke through her shield and eviscerated her small body.

She died soon after he clamped down on the back of her neck, crushing her vertebrae and severing her spinal cord.

The final gnome only made it a few feet into the tunnel before Elijah caught up. However, when he leaped upon the lone survivor's back, he got a surprise when the creature disappeared, reappearing a few feet away. As Elijah recovered, the gnome raised his hands. Ethera gathered in a flash, and then, suddenly, Elijah felt something at his feet. He looked down to see ethereal chains encircling his legs. He tried to pull free, but it did no good.

"Stupid animal," the gnome panted, his shoulders sagging. "Suppose it's not all bad, though. You're what? Level twenty-nine? Decent materials. Bones for weapons. Pelt for a—"

Elijah wasn't going to listen to that. Instead, seeing that he couldn't escape the gnome's spell, he knew he had no choice but to play his ace. So, he shifted back to human form, pointed his staff at his enemy, and cast Storm's Fury.

Lightning lashed out, and the shocked gnome went flying backward, hitting the wall of the narrow tunnel and collapsing to the ground. But it didn't kill him.

"What? That's not—"

Elijah cast again, but even though the gnome was once again knocked back into the wall, he didn't look all that injured. So, after focusing on his core, Elijah decided to use something with a little more oomph.

He cast Swarm.

At first, it didn't seem like anything had happened, but then, a buzzing sound filled the air. The gnome said something derisive, but Elijah paid no attention. He knew what was coming.

"Ow!" said the short figure, slapping a hand against his neck. It was prelude to disaster—at least from the gnome's perspective—and a second later, a swarm of stinging flies descended upon him. Elijah had no idea why the shield did nothing to stop them, but he wasn't going to argue with it. Instead, he watched with stoic fury as the swarm's afflictions took hold.

The gnome screamed.

Elijah watched.

Even after the spell holding him in place faded, he didn't move until, at last, the swarm dissipated, leaving only a diseased corpse behind. Once he was certain that the gnome was dead, as evidenced by the influx of kill energy that pushed him closer to level thirty, he slapped a hand over his side and cast Touch of Nature. The bleeding stopped, but he didn't dare use more than one cast, lest he not have enough Ethera to heal the dragon.

With that, he dragged the gnome's body back to the ritual chamber, then cast Healing Rain. Clouds swirled, covering the center of the room and enveloping the dragon in rejuvenating precipitation. Perhaps more importantly, it washed away the glittering paint the ritualists had been using to draw symbols on the ground. With that done, Elijah set his sights on the corpses; he looted them, coming up with a couple of purses containing a few strange coins, the robes, and a pair of new knives. He slipped his ill-gotten gains into his woven pack, then headed toward the prone dragon.

He laid a hand on the golden scales, feeling her breathing. She was warmer than he'd expected, hammering home the fact that she was not a cold-blooded reptile. More, he felt the mass of Ethera swirling in her body. It was no wonder the gnomes had been trying to harvest her. It didn't excuse their actions, but he understood.

Taking a deep breath, Elijah channeled Ethera into Touch of Nature, sending a jolt of healing through the creature. When that did nothing, he cast it again. Then again after that. Two more times he cast, but the dragon was unaffected.

He wanted to do more, but his core was dry.

So, Elijah waited, and just like he'd done with the panther what felt like an eternity ago, he healed the creature each time his Ethera recovered enough to facilitate a cast of Touch of Nature.

It took two more hours before the dragon awoke.

And she did so with explosive violence, raking her claws across his chest and tearing open a gaping wound. Elijah sprang backward, but he knew he could do nothing to stop the vicious monster he'd made the mistake of saving.

Her eyes were wild as she stepped on his chest, and smoke curled up from her flared nostrils.

"Human," she growled, her voice deep but feminine. "Why? What?"

Elijah channeled Touch of Nature through his body as he choked out, "I . . . was sent . . . to rescue you."

That's when her eyes lost their wildness, and she glanced around. When she saw the bodies of the gnomes, her expression softened, and she stepped back.

"Oh," she said. Then, she collapsed, once again losing consciousness.

Elijah shook his head, then used the last of his pool of Ethera to cast Touch of Nature on himself. After that, he just lay there, his breath shallow as he tried to deal with the pain of the wound she had caused. Once he'd regained enough Ethera, he cast the spell again. It took two more casts before the wound closed.

But by that point, he heard voices coming from the entrance tunnel.

Glancing at the dragon, he saw that she was still unconscious. And after his battle against the gnomes and the misunderstanding with the dragon, he was in no shape to fight. He'd healed enough to get around, but anything beyond that would take some time and more than a few more casts of Touch of Nature.

Which left him with only one option, though he had no idea if it would work. But given the situation, he didn't think he had much choice.

So, Elijah painfully pushed himself to his feet before staggering to where the dragon had collapsed. Then, he knelt beside her form, placed his hand on her side, and used the teleport function of Ancestral Circle.

He felt the spell tugging at him—and him alone. But he wouldn't allow that. Instead, he forced more Ethera into the spell so it would accept the dragon, as well. It wasn't so different than when he used the same method to bolster the effect of Nature's Bounty. Though it was significantly more difficult, and at first, the spell refused to cooperate. But then, suddenly, it snapped into place.

Elijah screamed as pain tore through him, and just as the spell enveloped the pair of them, he saw a group of gnomes and goblins appear at the mouth of the tunnel.

Then, he was gone, and for a split second, he felt like he was being ripped into a thousand pieces.

He thudded to the ground as he and the dragon appeared in his Grove.

Blood spurted from a hundred wounds. Vaguely, he heard someone shouting his name, but by that point, the blood loss had begun to take hold. Still, before he passed out, he managed to use the very last bit of his Ethera to cast Healing Rain.

Then, everything went black.

66

TASK COMPLETE

Elijah awoke and, for a long time, just lay there unmoving. His body was still a mess—he didn't need to inspect his wounds to recognize that much—but he didn't feel like he had the energy to do anything about it. Nor did he have any idea how much time had passed. But one thing he did know was that he'd survived, and judging by the steady sound of heavy breathing nearby, the dragon had, as well.

For a while, that was enough.

Soon enough, though, Elijah's eyes fluttered open, and he saw a clear blue sky looking down on him. After taking a deep breath, he cast Healing Rain and watched the clouds coalesce above him before they dumped their regenerative payload on him.

Then, he began the arduous process of healing himself via Touch of Nature. He felt terrible, and his limbs refused to respond to his instructions. So, he channeled the spell without direction, letting the formless healing energy flood his body. It was inefficient, but given the sheer volume of his injuries, there wasn't that much wasted Ethera.

He wasn't sure precisely how long he lay there, but it was at least one day. Maybe more, considering that, while waiting for his Ethera to regenerate, he often dozed off. It wasn't outside the realm of possibility that, on a few of those occasions, he slept through an entire night. But eventually, Elijah healed enough to sit up.

Predictably, when he did, he saw the familiar confines of his Grove staring back at him. He glanced down at his previously unblemished arm, where he saw a series of pale, thin scars marring his skin.

Elijah sighed. At the rate he was picking up scars, he'd soon become a malformed mess.

Glancing to his side, he saw a mass of golden scales. But given that the dragon was still alive—he could see that she was still breathing—he reasoned that he should take care of himself first, then heal her once he was healthy. So, Elijah continued on his long road of Regeneration, renewing Healing Rain every time it fell away and using Touch of Nature in the interim.

And over the next day, he gradually returned to health.

Then, he started in on the dragon. With the benefit of time on his side, Elijah could better gauge what was happening, and it didn't take him long to recognize that the dragon's pool of vitality—or life energy—was far larger than his own. When he healed her, it was like trying to fill a swimming pool with a bucket. He was making progress, but it was going to take a long time.

So, he bent himself to the task.

Fortunately, he was in his Grove, so food was no issue. And it only took a quick trip up to his tree house to get water—Nerthus had told him that it would be difficult to exhaust its water stores, so his basic needs were easily met.

However, beyond satisfying those necessities, he had a hard time focusing on anything but the task in front of him. That got a little better as the days passed, which hinted that the issue was related to forcing Ancestral Circle to teleport both him and the dragon, but beyond that, he was unsure what else to expect.

And so, time went as he slowly healed the dragon, one Touch of Nature at a time. In a way, it reminded him of how he'd healed the guardian panther so long ago. But as difficult as it had been to heal the panther, it couldn't even begin to compare—at least in terms of how much Ethera it took—to doing the same for the young dragon.

But Elijah persisted.

Curiously, Nerthus remained absent. At first, Elijah didn't even spare the tree spirit's absence a second thought. After all, he'd only had a handful of conversations with him since making first contact. However, as days passed without Nerthus making an appearance, Elijah started to worry.

Not that it did any good. The tree spirit showed up when he wanted to, and there was nothing Elijah could do to change that.

So, he pushed that from his mind and focused on healing the dragon. And finally, a week later, Elijah succeeded.

Thankfully, the dragon didn't respond as she had in the ritual chamber. Instead, after her eyes fluttered open, she craned her long neck and looked around before focusing on Elijah. She stared at him for a long moment before saying, "I apologize for my actions, druid."

Then, she collapsed into unconsciousness once again. Over the following few days, she awoke a few more times, but she didn't speak again until, as far as Elijah could tell, she'd finally reached perfect health.

At that point, she said, "Where am I? What happened to the devourers?"

"You're in my Grove," Elijah answered. Aside from shifting to a more comfortable position, she still hadn't moved. "You're safe."

"How did we escape? The leader would not have allowed me to leave without a fight."

"I used a spell to teleport us here," Elijah said.

She narrowed her eyes, then leaned closer, and for a moment, Elijah felt like he was being sized up by a much larger predator. Then, she said, "You are not strong enough to do that."

He sighed, then sat down. "You're not wrong about that," he admitted. "It nearly ripped me to pieces." He raised his arm, showing off the pattern of thin scars. "And I have the scars to show for it."

"I see."

"So, how did you get caught? No offense, but those guys didn't seem all that strong," Elijah said. "And you . . . Well, you're a dragon."

Before, he hadn't really understood why Nerthus had spoken of dragons with such reverence. However, after seeing the one before him, he thought he'd begun to understand just how much more powerful the species was. She was only a child, and yet, Elijah was certain that if she so wished it, she could tear him to pieces with only minimal effort.

"They trapped me," she said. "I was . . . foolish and hubristic. Despite my mother's words of caution, I thought this world beneath me. I was wrong."

Elijah didn't probe the topic any further. Instead, he changed the subject, asking, "So, what do I call you?"

"I am Saraalinisa."

"Uh . . . Mind if I just call you Sara?" he asked. "Because that's a mouthful."

She cocked her massive head to the side as if thinking it over, then said, "I suppose that will do."

"So, what happens now? Because I just checked, and my task isn't complete."

"Task? Wait . . . Did my mother send you?"

"Are you going to eat me if I say she did?" Elijah asked.

"What? No!" Sara shouted. "Why would I eat you?"

"You attacked me for healing you back in the ritual chamber," Elijah reminded her. "Just covering my bases here."

"Bases?"

"Don't worry about it. My point is that I really don't want to get attacked again. So . . . Uh . . . Please don't. Because I don't think I can stop you if you want to eat me."

"I'm not going to eat you!"

"That sounds like what someone who intended to eat me would say."

It was a strange thing, watching a dragon roll her eyes. Curiously human, but also undeniably alien. Either way, Elijah found it disconcerting. "I have no intention of eating you," she said. "So, please—just leave it at that."

"Fair enough. My original question still stands. I'm not saying the only reason I rescued you was to complete that task, but I'm not saying it didn't play a huge part in my decision," he said.

"What was the objective?"

"It just said to rescue the child."

"Child? Ugh. She would phrase it like that," Sara said. "I'm almost a century old, and she still treats me like an infant." She let out a snort. "So infuriating!"

"Again—please don't eat me."

"I am not going to eat you!"

"Good. Because I'm sure I don't taste very good. Too little fat."

"What is wrong with you?" she asked.

"Nothing. I just don't want to get eaten. Plus, I've been living on this island alone for close to two years at this point. I mean, I did talk to some nice walrus people, but they weren't real, so I contend that doesn't count. There's Nerthus, too, but he's a tree. Or a tree spirit, I guess. I'm not sure where he ends and the tree begins, if I'm honest. He'd probably tell me if I asked, but that just felt a little rude, you know?"

"What is a walrus? And why would they not be real?" she asked.

"Uh . . . Never mind. My point is that I really, really don't want to get eaten. I can't stress that enough."

"I swear not to eat you."

"Even if you're annoyed with me? Because—"

"No matter what, I won't eat you. There. Satisfied?"

"Well, not really. Who knows if you're a liar? I mean, you seem trustworthy as far as giant golden dragons are concerned, but I'll admit that I'm not the best judge of character. I mean, I had this girlfriend back in high school who was sleeping with half the football team, and I never—"

"Can you please stop babbling?" Sara interrupted.

"Oh, right. Just haven't had a lot of conversational opportunities lately. So, about my quest? Or task, I guess. Not sure if there's a difference, but we mustn't get the terminology wrong."

Sara sighed, a bit of a spark escaping from between her lips.

"Don't roast me, either."

The dragon didn't respond, which Elijah thought was moderately concerning. Instead, she asked, "How did my mother contact you?"

"She didn't. She talked to Nerthus."

"This is the tree spirit you mentioned?" she asked.

Elijah nodded, then hiked his thumb in the direction of the ancestral tree. "Lives over there. But sometimes, he visits me in the tree house."

Sara nodded, then pushed herself to her feet. When she did, Elijah could only stare in awe. Her form was even more magnificent than he'd first thought.

"Stop staring. It's weird."

"Don't stare. Gotcha," he said, though he didn't look away.

Sara let out a huff, then headed toward the ancestral tree. When she reached it, she called out, "Tree spirit! Speak to me!"

Nerthus appeared only a moment later, and Elijah groaned, "Oh, come on. I tried to get you to come out like ten times over the past week, and nothing. But she calls for you one time, and you just pop right up?"

"She's a dragon," he said unapologetically, as if that was explanation enough. Looking at Sara, Elijah couldn't really argue with that assessment.

"Please contact my mother and tell her I am safe," Sara said.

Nerthus disappeared, merging with his branch. He was gone for only about thirty seconds before he reappeared, saying, "Your mother wishes for your return. Consent and Elijah will complete his task."

"But she said I could stay on this—"

"She was very specific about the conditions. She said—and I quote, 'You have visited the new world. Return and continue your training.' The Great—"

"Ugh. Fine. I'll go. Just do it."

"Wait, what's going on?" Elijah asked.

"The tree spirit is going to use his connection to the World Tree to send me home," Sara said. "Once I'm back in Kabalis, you'll get your reward."

"Ah. Makes sense, I guess," he said, tapping his lip. "Except for, you know, the whole thing! You're just going to connect to the World Tree? And what the hell, Nerthus? Could you have just sent me away?" He sighed, then before either Sara or Nerthus could respond, Elijah said, "You know what? Never mind. The answer's probably just magic, anyway. Right? It's magic."

"It's not not magic," said Nerthus.

"Fine. Carry on, I guess. Stupid trees and magic and dragons . . ."

He looked up at Sara, then held up his hands, "Not you. Obviously. As the only dragon I've ever met who—let's remember—promised not to eat me, I'm very much on your side. And your mom's. And any other dragon out there, I guess. Let's just say I'm pro-dragon all the way."

To drive his point home, he held up two thumbs.

Sara, for her part, just shook her head, then placed her foreleg on the tree's trunk. Looking down at Elijah, she said, "You're weird. But thank you."

Without waiting for a response, she disappeared. Nerthus wilted, merging with his tree without another word. That left Elijah alone.

Again.

"What's new?" he muttered to himself. However, at least he'd completed his task, which was important enough. He couldn't help but think that he'd have traded the reward for a little company, though.

Congratulations! You have completed a Task. Stand by for reward . . .

Elijah held his breath until the next notification flashed before his eyes:

Blessing of the Dragon Kirlissa received. Please choose which form it takes:

Core Advancement
Item (Wings of the Dragon)
Spell (Firestorm)

Elijah sank to his knees as he read the notification. He'd anticipated that the reward to be good, but the Blessing of the Dragon exceeded his expectations. The first option was something he'd sought—without any luck—for quite some time.

The second option was a little less exciting, but the name was evocative enough that he was practically drooling at the possibilities. However, the third choice was probably the most straightforward—a new spell, and the name Firestorm suggested that it was a powerful one.

Still, Elijah only looked at the options for a moment before making his decision.

You have chosen:

Core Advancement

Elijah grinned. And then, something exploded inside of him, driving him back into unconsciousness.

67

DRAGON CORE

Elijah awoke suddenly, springing upright the moment awareness returned. However, despite his alarm, he was in no danger. In fact, he felt better than he had in . . . well, ever. Sitting beside the ancestral tree, he glanced down at his hands but saw no difference. One still bore the acid scars he'd gotten in the Sea of Sorrows, while the other, like most of the rest of his body, was riddled with thinner, much lighter scarring from overstepping in his use of Ancestral Circle.

It took only a second more for him to realize that he was, once again, completely nude.

Sighing, Elijah muttered, "Of course I'm naked. Again."

The loss of what amounted to rags wasn't a big deal, and due to looting the ritualists, his collection of cloth was much deeper than it once had been. However, he really hated sewing—especially since he didn't have proper tools, instead relying on bone hooks and homemade twine in place of thread—so he wasn't looking forward to putting a new outfit together.

If only the robes hadn't been sized to fit gnomes, he could've just used them as they were. But that wasn't the case, so it looked like he had a good deal of sewing in his future.

For now, though, the day was warm enough that his nudity wasn't terribly uncomfortable. Certainly, he'd have once been a bit self-conscious about it. But there was no one else around—aside from Nerthus's inconsistent presence—and after spending so much time in the tower without any clothes, he'd gotten over any shyness he might've once fostered.

In any case, he had other things on his mind. Chiefly, the pair of notifications clamoring for his attention. The first was:

Congratulations! You have cultivated a Dragon Core! Current stage: Hatchling.

"What does that even mean?" he said to himself. However, aside from the obvious—that he'd managed to reach the first stage of cultivating his core—he had no idea what it meant. "Okay, so . . . tabling that for later. Moving on . . ."

He pushed past that notification and opened the next:

You have reached the first threshold. Current stage: Cultivator.

Elijah knew that he'd accomplished something important, but he wasn't certain how to categorize it. So, lacking any further information, he opened his status:

Name	**Elijah Hart**		
Level	**29**		
Archetype	**Druid**		
Class	**Animist**		
Specialization	**N/A**		
Alignment	**N/A**		
Strength	**30**		
Dexterity	**29**		
Constitution	**30**		
Ethera	**38**		
Regeneration	**32**		
Attunement	**Nature**		
Cultivation Stage: Cultivator			
Body	**Core**	**Mind**	**Soul**
Wood	**Hatchling**	**Opal**	**Neophyte**

As expected, he'd gained a single point in every attribute when he'd gained level twenty-nine. But that certainly didn't account for how much stronger he felt. If he had to compare it to something, he would've likened it to how he'd felt after cultivating his body of wood. Though there was more to it than that, Elijah sensed.

So, he took a moment to look at his spell book. And at first, it looked no different—at least until he reached Shape of the Predator:

Shape of the Predator	Take on the shape of a peerless hunter, vastly increasing your Dexterity and Strength attributes and giving an average increase to Constitution. Spellcasting is suspended while Shape of the Predator is active.

There were a couple of changes. First, it had once featured the world *mighty* to describe the transformation, but now it used the term *peerless*. Second, it described the increase to his Constitution as average instead of minor, suggesting that it would be more impactful.

If he'd had any doubts about the general power of his spells, though, they were allayed when he reached his various Essence spells, the benefits of which had all doubled. So, instead of Essence of the Monkey increasing his Dexterity by five points, it now would enhance the attribute by ten points. Perhaps his other spells would see a similar increase in their potency.

But he wanted to check things out, just in case. So, after stopping by the tree house and wrapping one of the robes around his waist, Elijah headed to the beach where he usually hunted the giant crabs. Fortunately, there was one there, and even more luckily, the unnatural growth that had transformed the species seemed to have run out of steam. As a result, the one in front of him was no larger than a truck.

A good thing, too. When the crabs had continued to grow, he'd spent more than a couple of sleepless nights worrying about world-devouring crabs. Thankfully, it seemed that such a future would remain in his nightmares, where such things belonged.

In any case, Elijah used his Essence spells to increase his Regeneration and Dexterity, then applied One With Nature before pointing his staff at the crab. First, he used Snaring Roots, and at his command, thick vines erupted from the rocky shore to grab the crab's legs. It tried to tug free, but most of the vines remained intact. And those that broke were quickly replaced by more of the same.

That was a marked improvement over the previous incarnation of the spell, which had been weak enough that he'd often forgotten to use it. Now, though, that seemed to have changed, and it was potent enough to at least slow down powerful enemies. Idly, he wondered how it would fare against something like the Voxxian monster that had nearly killed the panther.

Shaking his head, he knew that such a matchup wouldn't end well. He had no idea how strong either creature had been, but he was well aware of just how poorly he'd stand up to either the Voxxian monster or the guardian panther. He'd gotten stronger, but that kind of power seemed to be out of his reach.

For now.

Elijah watched as the crab continued to struggle, but it seemed incapable of escape. From experience, though, Elijah knew that it wouldn't last forever. Instead, the spell had a duration of around a minute before it would start to lose steam. So, he quickly raised his staff and channeled Storm's Fury though it.

The bolt of lightning that tore out of the Staff of Natural Harmony was thicker and brighter than any he'd summoned before, and when it hit the crab, it sent bits and pieces of the creature's shell flying away from the point of impact. At the same time, the creature collapsed into a seizure as the powerful electrical current coursed through its body. The aroma of cooking crab filled the air, telling Elijah just how much stronger his spell was.

Still, he needed more tests. So, he aimed another couple of casts at the crab, killing it.

"Solid improvement," he muttered to himself. Indeed, the spell had never been the most potent, and before, it had taken at least eight casts to kill one of the crabs, depending on how strong the individual monsters were. Having that number cut in half was a remarkable increase in power.

Still, he had more spells to test. So, over the next few hours, he did just that, finding another crab on the other side of the island so he could determine how much stronger Swarm had become. Curiously, the afflictions it inflicted weren't that much stronger, but the size of the swarm itself had grown by nearly half.

However, the biggest change came when he finally decided to test Shape of the Predator. The transformation occurred much as it always did, but instead of sprouting fur, he grew glistening black scales. Looking down at his claws, he saw that they were far longer, as well, and upon seeing that, he quickly sought out a small pool of water so he could look at his reflection.

When he did, he let out a reptilian hiss.

He certainly didn't look like a panther anymore. Indeed, if he had to describe the new expression of Shape of the Predator, he would have said it was a curious mixture of alligator, wolf, and panther. More than anything, the new form looked like some undiscovered dinosaur, swift, sleek, and more than anything else, deadly.

The next big shock came when he used Guise of the Unseen. Instead of simply melting into the shadows as he normally did, he watched his blurry reflection fade away entirely. No—that wasn't necessarily true. He didn't become invisible. Instead, the ability acted more like a chameleon's color-changing defense mechanism, though it was obviously aided by Ethera, because, if he stood still, his scales were almost completely indistinguishable from their surroundings.

So, not only would he gain far more attributes, but the viability of Guise of the Unseen had seen a significant boost, as well.

Elijah tracked down another crab, but this time, he only intended to use abilities native to Shape of the Predator. Chiefly, Venom Strike, Predator Strike, and Guise of the Unseen. However, when he pounced, using Predator Strike, his claws went through the animal's shell like it wasn't even there. He destroyed the monster's frontal nerve center with that single attack, and it collapsed in a heap, still alive but incapable of moving anything but its back legs.

Silently apologizing for the creature's suffering, he proceeded with checking Venom Strike's viability, as well, and he got the results he had expected. The crab died only thirty seconds after Elijah had used Venom Strike, which injected it with a much more potent neurotoxin.

He still had one spell to test, but because Calamity had a significant dormant period after being cast, he chose not to experiment. After all, it would be quite an issue if he needed the powerful spell and didn't have it available. So, as he had since acquiring the spell, he kept it in his back pocket, just in case he needed it going forward.

Once he'd finished testing his Strength, Elijah returned to the Grove. There, he found Nerthus waiting for him in the tree spirit's customary spot on one of the ancestral tree's branches.

"Thanks for bailing on me, man," Elijah said. "Do you have any idea how many questions I have? I mean, could you always use the World Tree like that? And—"

"What happened to you?" Nerthus interrupted. "I . . . You . . . You are different."

"Right. Yeah," Elijah said. "Well, the Blessing of the Dragon—you know, the reward for my task? It gave me three options. I could have taken an item called Wings of the Dragon, and—"

"You refused?! Wings of the Dragon are some of the most sought-after items in the universe!" Nerthus exclaimed. "They allow for true flight. Do you know how rare that is at your stage?"

"Right. Maybe I should've taken that, but I don't think so. The other option was a spell called Firestorm. I've gotta tell you—that one tempted me," he said.

"As well it should!" Nerthus shouted, clearly excited.

"Well, I thought the other option was better," Elijah said. "I upgraded my core."

"W-what? How? That should not be possible on this world . . . The Ethera is too thin."

Elijah shrugged. "Don't know what to tell you. That was the reward," he said. "It's at the hatchling stage, if that means anything to you."

"Hatchling? That doesn't . . . I've never heard of that . . . What kind of core did you get? A nature core? Tree? Perhaps the predator core?"

"Dragon."

"W-what?"

"That's what it said on the box," Elijah stated. Then he read the notification aloud, "Congratulations! You have cultivated a Dragon Core! Current Stage: Hatchling."

Nerthus fell off his tree. Elijah rushed over to make sure the tree spirit was unhurt, but he found the small creature muttering to himself.

"That isn't possible. You can't be . . . No. They wouldn't . . . But she would have the power to . . . Oh, dear . . ."

"Calm down, man. What's going on? Is a Dragon Core really that rare?" Elijah asked.

Nerthus fixed him with a look of disbelief, then said, "It is beyond rare. As far as I know, it may well be unique."

"Oh. Well. That's good, then."

"Good? Good?! It is unprecedented!"

"That's what I said. It's good. Maybe I'll be able to get off this island now," Elijah said. His brief trip across the strait had reawakened his need for human companionship. Seeing all those people living normal lives—he wanted something like that. Certainly, he had no intention of abandoning his Grove, but he could always return with Ancestral Circle. "Anyway—what's so good about it?"

"Oh . . . Yes. Right. Where to begin?"

"How about you start with why you just about have a seizure every time someone says the word *dragon*, and then we can move on from there."

68

LONG OVERDUE

"First, you must understand the fundamental races that comprise the universe," Nerthus stated. "Humans are one. Obviously. But there are also elves, dwarves, gnomes, goblins, kysar, and elementals, with each race having various branches. For instance, elves have three main variants—wood elves, dark elves, and high elves. Each of the other races have at least as many varieties who have followed different evolutionary paths."

"Okay," Elijah said. "When you say races, I'm guessing you're not talking about ethnicity."

"I am not. Though most races can reproduce with one another, creating even more diversity, each is fundamentally different from the other."

"Gotcha. Lots of interbreeding. A bunch of half elves and demignomes running around. Not really my thing, but someone has to be into that kind of thing, right?" Elijah asked. Nerthus just looked at him like he'd gone a little crazy. "Sorry. This is the second-longest conversation we've had, and like I said before, it's kind of gotten to me."

"Right."

Elijah apologized again, then said, "Carry on."

Nerthus continued to explain the shape of the universe and its inhabitants, once again pointing out the difference between devourers and preservers, though Elijah got the feeling that neither group was exactly codified. They were just labels that probably meant different things to different people.

He also talked about how there were thousands of worlds, adding, "The older they are, the more connected to the World Tree they are. That makes the overall Ethera in those worlds thicker and the denizens more powerful on average."

"And I'm guessing the World Tree is where the System comes from?"

"No. Though it is dependent on the World Tree to spread, the System is not of the World Tree. Instead, it is the result of multiple Transcendents working together," Nerthus answered. "They worked for eons until, at last, they created the System."

"Oh. Why?"

"To help people resist the Voxx, of course," Nerthus said. "But I digress. You wish to know of dragons. They are what's known as an elder race. There aren't many, and even the youngest among them is capable of feats few of the fundamental races can match. To those of us following a nature path, they are as gods."

That certainly explained Nerthus's reaction.

Elijah asked, "So, what does it mean that I have a Dragon Core? And why do I feel so much better now? It's like I got twenty or thirty percent stronger in the blink of an eye."

Indeed, during his testing, he'd experimented with his attributes by lifting progressively heavier rocks, which was where he'd gotten his estimate. It wasn't exactly scientific, but he felt confident in the assessment.

"You passed the first threshold," said Nerthus.

Elijah rolled his eyes. "You say that like it's supposed to mean something to me. Come on, man. I have no idea what any of this stuff means," he groaned.

"It is the System's way of measuring your overall cultivation," he said. "There are nine stages, starting with Cultivator and ending with Supremacy. It is the first half of Godhood."

"Wait—are you saying I can become a god?"

"Indeed. How do you think the originators gathered enough power to create the System? Of course, they went far beyond our current measurements, but—"

"I can become a god, though? Like, you're not screwing with me, are you?"

"Yes. Though, I caution you that such a journey will take you millennia. However, with a Dragon Core, if you progress that far, you will be one of the more powerful deities," Nerthus said.

"In plain terms, what does core cultivation do?"

"It increases the density and quality of your stored Ethera, making your spells, abilities, and techniques more powerful. Different types of cores represent differing degrees of improvement. For instance, if you were to have cultivated a nature core and reached the seed stage, you would have experienced a five or six percent increase in the power of your spells. Higher stages result in larger increases, though I can't speak to anything after the sapling stage."

"Uh . . . Are you sure about those numbers?"

"Quite. Why do you ask?"

"It's just that . . . Well, I can't say that this is the case for everything, but my Essence spells—they increase my attributes by set amounts—all experienced a bigger increase than what you're describing."

"Oh? That should be expected, with a Dragon Core. They are some of the most powerful beings in the universe, after all. How large of an increase did those abilities experience? Ten percent? Fifteen?"

"Um . . . higher. A lot higher."

"Thirty?"

Elijah gestured for the tree spirit to keep going. Nerthus went pale—quite a feat, considering that he was made of tree bark—and Elijah took pity on him. He said, "Double."

"D-double?"

"Yeah. For those spells, at least. I can't tell for sure with the others, though."

"That's not . . . That isn't possible."

"You've said that a couple of times already. I don't think you really know what that word means." Nerthus looked like he was on the verge of having a seizure, so Elijah changed the subject: "So, you said dragons are only one of the elder races, right? What are the other ones?"

Nerthus shook his head, muttering to himself, but after a few seconds, he looked up and answered, "Demons are one. Angels are another. And mechaniques, though they are exceedingly rare."

"Demons?" Elijah said. Then, he held his hands up to his head with his index fingers pointing skyward. "Like, horns, forked tails, and cloven hooves?"

"Indeed," Nerthus answered. "They are the sworn enemies of angels, though they rarely come into actual conflict. Long ago, they reached an agreement to remain on their respective sides of the universe. If they hadn't, there's every chance that nothing would have survived the ensuing war. Mechaniques, by comparison, are a race of awakened golems. No one knows how they reached that stage, and any attempts to replicate the feat have met with failure. There are a handful of other elder races that have died out, as well."

"That's . . . a lot to take in." The idea that angels and demons were real had been more of a surprise than seeing gnomes and dwarves. "So, is there a reason why some of our religious stories and myths mention these elder races? Or the foundational races, come to that."

"Before the planet's integration, it would have been incredibly difficult for them to reach your planet. However, difficult does not mean impossible. Likely, this planet has been visited sometime in the past, which is the source of your myths, legends, and religions."

Elijah shook his head. If the rest of the world knew that, then there were probably some religions that would experience quite a bit of upheaval. The only thing that made it any more palatable was that the way Nerthus described deities was more like Greek gods, rather than any of the omnipotent monotheistic versions. The first was frightening, but the second was far more so. The idea that a flawed being could reach that level of power was one of the most horrifying things Elijah could imagine.

"What does this mean for me, though?" he asked.

"Druids are already rare," Nerthus said. "But a druid with a dragon core? If there is another one in the entire universe, I would be shocked. You must keep this to yourself. Otherwise, the Grove will be in danger."

"Why?"

"Some will see it as an obstacle to overcome," Nerthus said. "Strength invites challenge. However, dragons have their own enemies. We have spoken of this, but you must understand that the most extreme devourers can and will attempt to harvest anything they can find that will increase their power. That was why the young dragon was trapped. That is why you must be careful. Even if only your core is of the dragon, it is still valuable in the extreme."

Elijah sighed. "Understood," he said, thinking that it sounded like more trouble than it was worth. However, he only needed to remember the challenges he'd faced so far to recognize the necessity to gather as much Strength as he could. That included his Dragon Core, regardless of the problems that came with it.

"Alright, I only have a couple more questions," Elijah said. Indeed, he'd been compiling them since the very beginning, and now that Nerthus was willing to explain some things, he intended to take full advantage. "You've mentioned that the World Tree let you connect with Sara's mother. How?"

"The World Tree connects everything. You merely need to know how to tap into it. Your spell, Ancestral Circle, does this."

"I really don't understand."

"You don't need to," Nerthus said. "And I haven't the time to explain it in the sort of depth understanding would require."

"Alright. No need to get snippy," Elijah said. "And I see you're getting a bit antsy to get back in your tree, so I've only got one more question."

Nerthus sighed, "Very well."

"Why aren't we being inundated by powerful beings?" Elijah asked. "Those gnomes had some Strength, but the fact that, after less than two years, I could kill them like that suggests that they weren't very powerful. But that doesn't make sense. How come there aren't stronger people here taking over the world?"

"Two reasons. First, there's no motivation to," Nerthus stated. "This world may one day be valuable, but for now, getting here and taking over is far more trouble than it's worth. That may change in the future, but for now, only the people who want to escape their old lives would come here. Second, the low density of ambient Ethera is uncomfortable for anyone above a certain level or cultivation threshold."

"What about Sara? How was she trapped?"

"She is a child, and according to her mother, she was reckless. For someone with the right skills, that is all that's necessary. Let that be a lesson to you, Protector of the Grove. No matter how strong you become, a moment of inattention is all it will take to bring you low."

"That's a cheery thought."

"You must excuse me," Nerthus said. "I have stayed far longer than I should. If the Ethera levels continue to rise, I should soon be capable of leaving the tree permanently. However, I should point out that I will never be able to leave the Grove."

"Oh. That sucks."

Nerthus cocked his head to the side, then said, "No. Not really. This is a great thing, tending a druid's Grove. At heart, I am still a tree, and trees were never meant to roam. Goodbye, for now."

"Yeah. See you later, Nerthus."

With that, the tree spirit retreated to the ancestral tree, laid his hand on the trunk, and then merged with it. The process was a bit of a mind bender, but Elijah had seen it often enough that it didn't really seem that odd to him anymore.

"What a weird world . . ."

After that, Elijah stood, grabbed the pack that had been discarded when he'd returned to the Grove, and headed back to his tree house, where he intended to get started on sewing his new clothing. Halfway up the stairs, he stopped midstep as he felt something he had hoped he would never feel.

Someone had landed on his island.

No. Not just one person. A veritable army of gnomes, goblins, and dwarves had invaded his Domain. He could feel them all so thoroughly that it almost felt like he was standing right there beside them.

Ten.

Twenty.

Thirty.

The numbers didn't stop climbing until he reached fifty, all having been carried ashore by a small fleet of rowboats.

Elijah was vaguely aware that one of them was shouting orders, but his Domain didn't extend to interpretation of sound. It didn't matter, though. Even as they spread out, he hopped down the steps and checked his enhancements. They were all still active.

With that confirmed, he was ready to defend his Domain, and he quickly shifted into Shape of the Predator. Once he'd taken on his new form, he set off across the island he knew so well.

69

DEFENSE

Elijah darted through the dark forest like a ghost, letting Guise of the Unseen hide him. The ability didn't just change the color of his scales or use the shadows to obscure him. Instead, it also harnessed his Ethera to muffle every other aspect of his presence. He was quieter. His odor less pronounced. Even the air moved a little less while he was cloaked in the ability.

Still, it wasn't perfect, and at the speed he dashed beneath the trees, he knew he was vaguely visible. Fortunately, the awareness that came with his Domain helped him avoid anything—whether it was wild animals or his prey—so he remained as unseen as the name of his ability would suggest.

Fifty invaders was a daunting number. In the ritual chamber, he'd fought against six, and he'd only narrowly managed to survive. And who knew if these newcomers would be more suited to a fight? After all, he hadn't forgotten the battle that had killed the panther. That trio of combatants had been far stronger than the ritualists. So, Elijah knew he needed to be prepared for the worst.

Both Shape of the Predator and Essence of the Monkey provided double their previous attribute enhancements, and One With Nature probably did so, as well, even if it wasn't displayed in his status. So, his effective Dexterity—and Strength—had more than doubled with the formation of his Dragon Core. And that wasn't even considering the even more ephemeral increase he'd gotten from passing the first threshold.

No—he was more powerful than ever before. The only problem was that he expected that he would need it if he was going to repel the invasion. One against fifty weren't good odds, no matter how much stronger he felt. Even with his advantages, if he made one small mistake, he would become easy prey.

So, knowing how close to the edge he needed to walk, he let himself slip into the instincts that had come with Shape of the Predator. They'd let him survive the Primordial Jungle, so Elijah reasoned that they would stand him in good stead against the invaders. Hopefully, he would retain enough of his rational mind to pull out of it once everything was done.

With that out of the way, his gait became even more graceful, his movements more silent as the animalistic part of his mind took full advantage of his improved attributes. He never slowed, springing over natural gullies, bounding past boulders, and climbing and leaping from tree to tree when there was no other option.

He covered almost three miles in a little more than a quarter of an hour—a mighty feat, considering the terrain—and during that time, few of the island's residents even knew of his passing. It was a heady feeling, knowing just how efficient a predator he had become. But soon, he pushed those emotions to the side as he finally reached his destination.

The beach was one of the more accessible on the island, with a long, open stretch of shore marred only by the occasional rock or piece of driftwood. There were a dozen boats, each a copy of the one Elijah had used to cross the strait. With a clear night sky lit by a carpet of stars as well as the silvery light of a gibbous moon, there was plenty of illumination for him to study his prey.

Most of them were diminutive gnomes, but there were a few green-skinned goblins and broad-shouldered dwarves mixed in, as well. More importantly, they were kitted out for battle, with most of them wearing one sort of armor or another. Elijah saw more than a few wearing sturdy plate, while most wore chain mail mixed with hardened leather. Even the ones Elijah marked as casters wore armored robes and carried staves. The rest were armed with a wide variety of weapons ranging from axes to swords and shields, with quite a few wielding bows mixed in.

They didn't look so much like the small army he'd expected as they seemed to be a collection of individuals. Elijah could only hope he would be able to use that to his advantage. So, he watched from the tree line, keeping low to the ground with Guise of the Unseen masking his presence.

And as they started setting up tents a few dozen yards from shore—far enough to keep dry during high tide, but not nearly enough for Elijah's preference—an idea began to take shape. And the more he thought about it, the more sense it made. So, once Elijah was satisfied with his plan, he set off back the way he'd come. As he did, he kept a proverbial eye on the invaders via the senses granted by his Domain, but they continued setting up their camp.

When they'd first arrived, Elijah had thought they had somehow followed the metaphysical trail he'd left behind after rescuing Sara. However, the fact that they seemed keen on sticking around for at least a little while suggested a different motivation, though Elijah wasn't clear on what, precisely, that was. Sure, he felt confident that it had something to do with the ancestral tree, but beyond that, he was completely ignorant.

In any case, he didn't expect he would ever find out. With any luck, he'd be rid of them in only a few hours. With that in mind, he continued to dash through the woods until, at last, he reached a familiar beach on the other side of the island. Fortunately, he only had to follow the beach for a few minutes in order to find his quarry.

One of the huge crabs stood before him, busy tearing into some carcass that had washed ashore. Elijah wasted no time before bounding toward the creature, then tapping it on its leg. Then, as the monster skittered around, he sprang backward out of range of its claws. He took off down the beach, the crab in tow. Every now and then, when the crustacean started to lose interest in the chase, he'd circle around and reengage. Even before reaching the first threshold and having his spells and abilities enhanced by the Dragon Core, he'd been capable of running circles around the crabs. He could even manage it in his human form, so doing it as the scaled predator barely required any focus.

Elijah led the creature along the beach until he saw another crab. When he did, he repeated the process, nipping at its armored legs before dashing along. It followed, just like the other, though it was about thirty feet in front of the first.

He kept going, leading the creatures along as he gradually circled the island. It took hours, but the only really tricky part had come when he reached the western cliffs. There, he'd had to switch to his human form and swim while keeping the crabs engaged via Storm's Fury. He lost one along the way, but by that point, he'd grabbed three others, and he reached the next beach without any further issue.

As soon as his Ethera allowed, he switched back to the predator form and continued along until he felt the invaders' camp looming ahead of him.

Throughout the process, Elijah had let his mind wander slightly. However, with the invaders so close, he reengaged his focus and stalked forward. He knew he had to time things correctly. Otherwise, the crabs would lose interest.

By that point, the invaders had finished setting up their camp, and they'd set out a few sentries, one of which was only a couple dozen feet in front of him. The scout wore stiff leather armor and was armed with a bow, but more importantly, he was clearly alert.

It didn't help.

Elijah circled, staying low and hidden by the terrain, until he saw the gnome's back. Then, using Predator Strike, he pounced. The first attack met little resistance, but it wasn't immediately fatal. He let out a high-pitched scream but was quickly silenced by a claw to the throat.

Without skipping a beat—and knowing just how tight his window was—Elijah clamped his jaws around the scout's thin arm, bit through the bone, then repeated the action on the other limbs. In short order, he had five pieces of gnome piled before him.

More troublingly, the crabs were almost upon him, and the gnome's scream had roused the camp. That was fine, though. Elijah shifted back to his human form, grabbed one of the limbs, and tossed it in the direction of the skittering crabs.

Then, he repeated the action, scattering the bloody chunks of gnome in a rough line that led directly to the camp. After that was done, he ran off, bounding across the rocky shore and into the tree line. No one had ever seen him.

His breath coming shallow and fast, Elijah circled the camp. Even in his human form, he was no slouch when it came to remaining hidden, and soon enough, he found himself on the other side of the camp.

It was at that moment that the crabs came into view, having followed Elijah's trail of gnome parts. When the invaders saw the massive monsters, they let loose with a wide variety of attacks. Mages cast fireballs, archers shot arrows, and the heavily armored warriors rushed to what they thought were the front lines.

That left the other scouts on a proverbial island where, even if they shouted an alarm, they would get little support.

And Elijah was more than willing to take advantage of that.

In his caster form, he wasn't nearly as deadly as he would be as the scaled predator, but he was still much stronger than an average human. And he had a big, sturdy stick. So, when he rushed the gnome, swinging his staff like a baseball bat, the little scout fell without a word. He hadn't died—he'd only been knocked unconscious—but that was fine. Elijah had no qualms about finishing the job with the knife at his belt.

After slitting the invader's throat, he took a look back at the camp. They were handling the crabs well enough, and though the crustaceans had little hope of actually hurting the invaders, they were extremely durable. And there were half a dozen of them, which meant that the camp's damage was spread out enough that it gave Elijah plenty of time to kill the lone remaining scout.

This one went much the same as the last, though it took two staff strikes to put the goblin down. Still, Elijah managed, then slit the green-skinned creature's throat before turning back to the camp.

Three of the crabs had been killed, and the rest were on their last legs. Not surprising, considering the overwhelming Strength of the force. However, Elijah had never meant for the crabs to be anything but a distraction. His real attack was forthcoming.

He only wished he'd had the chance to test it, but between the rescue, his subsequent recovery, and gaining his Dragon Core, it wasn't possible. In his defense, his island had been relatively safe since the very beginning, so he hadn't expected a small army of invaders to land on his shores. Still, as he gathered his Ethera, he vowed to never let it happen again. From now on, he'd test his abilities and spells as soon as he could.

Once he'd shifted enough Ethera into the appropriate spell, he cast Calamity, hoping it would be just as devastating as the description implied.

70

THE BOSS

Mist swirled around Alyssa as the monster launched itself at her. Moving far more quickly than any normal human could have managed, she raised her Spear of the Dragon Lancer just in time to intercept its snapping jaws. Still, its momentum hit her like a truck, sending her tumbling onto her back. The monster followed, raking its claws across her breastplate. The metal held, but only barely, and Alyssa used the creature's inertia against it as she rolled, kicking up as she sent it flying past her. It hit a nearby wall, shattering glass and distorting the steel frame of a floor-to-ceiling window.

Even as it skidded across the building's lobby, an arrow followed. Just before it hit, the projectile split into three, each of which slammed into its chest. A stream of pale blood arced into the air as the monster screamed. A blur materialized behind it, and suddenly, its head was rolling to a stop at Trace's feet.

The Outlaw disappeared a second later, but Alyssa didn't see it. Instead, she was too busy pushing herself to her feet so she could face the next threat. There were three enemies, each advancing with cautious implacability. They looked much the same as all the other monsters they'd faced in the city—pale-white skin, with almost human features and abnormally muscular bodies—but Alyssa wasn't concerned with their appearance. She had already seen enough of them, after all.

Stomping down, she used Shock Wave, the ability sending out a wave of force that briefly stunned them. Then, she thrust her spear forward in a move that might've looked odd from a full fifteen feet away. As she lunged, she used Unstoppable Thrust, sending a thick wave of ethereal force piercing through them.

Unstoppable Thrust	**Thrust with a spear or lance, hitting all enemies in a straight line.**

It wasn't enough to kill the monsters, but it certainly did plenty of damage. More importantly, it kept them off-balance as she used Heroic Leap, pushing herself high into the air. Then, she fell upon them with Descending Dragon, skewering the centermost monster with her spear. Even as the blade exploded through its skull, she let loose with Champion's Shout, striking fear into the remaining creatures.

It wouldn't last long. She knew that. But then again, she didn't need much time to wrench her spear free and sweep it out in a wide arc that hacked into the second monster's neck. She used that momentum to sweep the legs out from under the third monster, which she dispatched with a two-handed thrust to its inhuman face.

But that's where her luck ran out.

Something rammed into her back, sending her sprawling across the concrete sidewalk. The metal of her armor screeched in protest as she tried to twist around, but her assailant had timed its attack well. Without looking back, she used Bulwark, hoping to superimpose the invisible shield between herself and her attacker.

But without being able to see, her aim was off, and she placed the shield behind the pale-skinned monster. So, she improvised, gathering her limbs beneath her and pushing up with all her might. As she did, she once again activated Heroic Leap. Bones crunched—hers as well as the monster's—but she gritted her teeth through the pain and sent an elbow back to hit the monster again.

It let loose with what sounded like a combination of a dog's yelp and a human's scream, but it didn't loosen its grip. If anything, it clung to her back with even more fervor, its claws digging deep into her flesh.

Then, heat washed over her, and the monster's screams ceased.

"Stay still!" yelled Bryce. Then, Alyssa screamed as something ripped the claws free. Bryce called out, "Need a heal!"

"I'm almost out of Ethera!" responded Verin.

But despite the healer's lack of fuel, a spell of Regeneration washed over Alyssa. The wounds in her back closed, though she knew that a single spell wouldn't entirely heal the damage. In fact, if she moved too violently, the lacerations would reopen. Still, it was better than nothing.

She used Recover, sending her Regeneration through the roof.

With that done, she levered herself to her feet. Wobbling, Alyssa thrust the butt of her staff into the ground and looked around. The monsters were dead, and everyone had survived.

For now.

She'd lost track of how long they'd been there. Time was difficult to track in the mist, and even without it, there was no night or day to mark the time. Still, she suspected it had been days, at least. Maybe as much as a week, based on how often they'd been forced to rest, and barely an hour of it had passed without significant combat.

But according to Trace, they'd finally reached their destination. More importantly, they'd done so without losing anyone else. Sure, they'd all been injured, but they'd made it.

Letting out a deep sigh to steady her nerves and help herself deal with the pain of her persistent wounds, Alyssa looked around. Everyone was there, and aside from Roman, they were all looking to her for direction.

She said, "Into the building. Find us a defensible position."

"But the capital is right there . . ."

She glared at Trace. The man's armor had definitely seen better days, but due to Verin's ministrations, he was whole. The same could be said for all the others. For her part, Alyssa's armor was mostly intact, though she'd lost one of her vambraces during a previous fight. Still, for her next suit of armor, Alyssa intended to ask Carmen to make her a more robust backplate. The current level of protection back there was woefully insufficient, as she'd discovered when the latest monster had sunk its claws into her back.

Aside from the terrible state of their armor, everyone looked exhausted. And given what had happened the last time they'd gone from one level of the tower to another—which was what she assumed would happen when they reached the capital—Alyssa wanted everyone in the best shape possible. That meant rest and repast.

No one spoke much over the next couple of hours. By that point, they didn't have much to say. For her part, Alyssa watched for any sign of attack, planting herself in the doorway as the rest of her team prepared for what was to come. She was so focused on the lobby of the building—which looked like every upscale office building she'd ever seen—that she didn't even notice Roman until he put a hand on her shoulder.

She flinched, moving with incredible speed as she extricated herself from his grip. She had her spear up and at his neck in only an instant. The moment she realized what she'd done, she retracted the blade and apologized.

Roman shook his head, saying, "No need to apologize. We're all on edge. I shouldn't have snuck up on you."

Alyssa sighed, then resumed her vigil. Roman joined her.

"What do you think we'll find on the next level?" she asked at last.

"More monsters," he stated. "Beyond that . . . I don't know. But I don't think we're done with this one."

"Really?" she asked.

"You read the guides. There's probably some kind of guardian."

"Boss monster!" supplied Bryce from across the room.

She turned her head and glared at him. "Don't eavesdrop."

"Sorry, boss."

"Right," Roman said, running his hand through his hair. "There's probably something we'll have to beat before we advance. Maybe it's another horde of monsters. Or it might be a bigger, badder monster. But I don't think we're done with this level. Not by a long shot."

Alyssa didn't know how to respond to that. She was already prepared for something worse, so it didn't really matter if they met it at the end of the second level or the beginning of the third. She just said, "We'll beat whatever we find. We don't have a choice."

Roman didn't say anything after that, instead giving Alyssa's shoulder another squeeze before heading back to rest with the others. At one point, he might have tried to relieve her, but he'd learned firsthand that doing so wouldn't do any good. She had a responsibility, and with her heavy armor, Recover ability, and high level, she was the best person for the job. So, if someone wanted to replace her as the group's guardian, they'd have to physically drag her out of the way.

No one was willing to try that.

After a couple more hours, Alyssa's wounds had healed, and everyone had recovered enough that they felt confident in moving forward. So, they set off from the skyscraper's lobby and down the wide street. The evidence of the previous battle remained, but they all ignored it. Instead, they kept moving along the route defined by Trace's scouting, and soon enough, the capital came into view.

"Familiar," she muttered.

And it was. The building before them lay at the center of a wide plaza whose details were lost to the mist. However, the building itself was almost a perfect replica of the US Capitol building, though even larger than the real thing. Still, Alyssa was less concerned with that than the creature planted at the base of the steps.

"Eyes up," she said a little louder, hefting her spear. "Boss monster ahead."

The monster in question looked a lot like the others they'd fought, though where they were roughly human sized, this new creature was the size of a giant. If it was less than fifteen feet tall, Alyssa would have been surprised, and its frame bulged with dense muscle. More, the pale skin was riddled with raised green veins.

And what's even worse, it had clearly noticed them because it pushed itself to its feet—an act that made Alyssa reassess her previous estimate of the thing's height; it was at least twenty feet tall, and maybe even larger. A shiver of fear slid up Alyssa's spine, but she suppressed it.

"You all know what to do."

Indeed, the group had been working together for long enough that they were all extremely familiar with the most effective strategy.

Alyssa stepped forward. The monster echoed the motion, cocking its head to the side as if surprised that she wasn't running in fear. She hefted her spear in both hands. Then, she used Heart of the Dragon, flooding her body with Ethera and inflating her physical attributes.

Meanwhile, Roman stepped to the side, raising his bow. He drew an arrow from the quiver at his waist, but he didn't draw it back. Not yet. At the same time, Bryce started casting a spell while Trace slipped away unnoticed, fading into the mist.

Finally, Verin slipped her morning star from her waist and cast her own spell. Alyssa felt the woman's heal-over-time spell hit her, followed by a second effect. Thus prepared, she trotted forward.

The monster was only forty yards away, so it wasn't long before Alyssa used Heroic Leap, following it up with Descending Dragon. Predictably, the monster was taken by surprise—even if it had expected her descent, it certainly didn't envision the sheer ferocity of her first strike. Still, it managed to dodge to the side at the last second, so Alyssa's spear—which had been aimed at its head—hit its meaty shoulder instead.

The blade tore through pale flesh, spraying Alyssa with a fountain of blood. She bounded backward, leaving the spear embedded in the monster; she might have been capable of dislodging it, but she wasn't sure of it. So, she'd chosen not to try.

Flipping, she used her newest ability. Leathery wings manifested, spreading out from her shoulder blades and allowing her to glide away. It was perfectly timed, too, because, only a second later, the monster charged forward, trampling the spot where she would have landed. Instead, it caught nothing but air, and Alyssa canceled the ability. She landed on its shoulders, grabbed the spear, and used Enrage. With her increased Strength, she yanked it free, then used Heroic Leap to send herself flying away.

Predictably, the monster attempted to follow, but she'd used Bulwark the moment her feet left its bulbous flesh. So, it hit the low wall, tipped over, and landed on its face. That's when Bryce finished his spell.

The ground beneath the monster erupted, and suddenly the earthworm wrapped itself around its torso. The creature screamed in pain as the worm squeezed, its rocky flesh contracting until bones started to break.

But it didn't last long before, with a mighty shove, the monster broke free. Rocks and earth exploded in every direction as a roar of fury filled the air.

Before it could rise, Roman shot it.

Once. Twice. Thrice the thwap of his bowstring sounded, and suddenly, three arrows sprouted from the monster. It seemed stunned, looking down at them in confusion. They had barely even pierced its skin, much less done any damage.

Then, they exploded into whirlwinds of shadow that enveloped the thing.

Another arrow hit its leg, and arcane black chains shackled it to the ground. Another arrow took it in the head, piercing one of its eyes. It stumbled, clearly blinded by Roman's newest ability. He hadn't revealed its name, but Alyssa thought of it as Blinding Shot. He'd kept most of the rest of his ability names a secret, as well, but they were certainly effective at hindering the creature.

Still, Roman didn't have the ability to finish it off.

And Bryce had only just begun casting his latest spell.

Fortunately, that was when Trace made himself known. He launched himself from the mist as if he'd only just manifested from nothing. His swords flashed as he fell on the creature, stabbing down into its chest. Then, he raced away, disappearing back into the mist. The blinded monster never even knew he was there.

But it wasn't dead. Like Roman, Trace kept his ability names close to his chest. However, Alyssa had seen the Outlaw's blades rip through lesser creatures with ease, so she knew just how much damage he could do.

The monster had to be on its last legs.

Alyssa just needed to finish it off.

So, she strode forward, and when she reached the hobbled creature, she used Unstoppable Thrust. A wave of piercing force ripped through it, sending more blood to spray across the plaza. Then, she used Heroic Leap, sailing high into the air. When she started to fall, she summoned an invisible Bulwark before kicking off the plane of Ethera with yet another Heroic Leap.

Twice more she repeated the action until she was more than a hundred feet in the air. Then, at last, she used Descending Dragon.

Descending Dragon	**Fall upon an enemy, dealing more damage based on distance fallen. Protected from falling damage while ability is active.**

She fell, leading the way with her spear. Just before she reached the monster, its eyes cleared, and for the briefest of moments, it saw its doom.

The Spear of the Dragon Lancer bit into the monster's skull with enough force to shatter it entirely. But Alyssa's attack didn't end there. Instead, her knee took it in the chest, obliterating flesh and bone alike before cracking the plaza's stone tiles and digging a shallow crater in the ground below.

When the dust settled, she rose, covered in the creature's blood and having defeated the guardian of the tower's second level.

Without any of them, it wouldn't have been possible. Roman had hobbled it. Both Bryce and Trace had weakened it so that Alyssa could finish it off. It was a team effort, but to anyone who saw her rising from that crater, it was clear who'd shouldered the bulk of the load.

Alyssa looked around, then down at her gore-covered body before letting out a resigned sigh. "I really need a shower."

71

CURSED

Standing in the center of camp, Cabbot shouted, "They're just crabs, you idiots! Just kill them!"

Even as he said it, the whole of Ironshore's defense force waged war against the remaining three pests. They weren't terribly dangerous—not unless his idiotic soldiers made a bunch of mistakes, which, given their performance so far, wasn't outside the realm of possibility—but they were difficult to kill. Still, despite taking the camp by surprise, the attack hadn't claimed any casualties.

He turned to Nirea, demanding, "Have you heard from those idiot scouts? Why didn't they warn us?"

She looked up, tucked a vivid pink lock of hair behind her ear, then said, "No contact. They are presumed incapacitated, though we won't know for certain until we investigate further."

The gnomish woman was an Administrator, which was supposed to be an extremely valuable addition to any force. However, from what Cabbot could tell, she was mostly a waste of resources. All she ever did was tell him things he could have figured out on his own. She was lucky she was beautiful. Otherwise, Cabbot would've already gotten rid of her.

"Well, investigate, then!" he growled. "Figure it out!"

"Yes, sir," she said, and then, without any further conversation, she strode away.

"Not now!" he spat, though by that point, she was too far away. He looked around, seeing that he was safe. At least the idiots had managed to repel a few scavengers; if they hadn't . . .

He looked around at the battle-hardened combatants. They were all of a level with him, though he knew most had fairly common classes. Not like him.

The Berserker class had never been his goal, but after seeing his other options, he'd made the only choice that made any sense. And since then, he'd come around to its benefits. However, that didn't mean he was completely comfortable with some of its downsides. That would take years of pain and effort—neither of which really appealed to him.

Still, it was a powerful class with great attribute bonuses that put him above any other elite in Ironshore. And even if he'd lost the opportunity the captured dragon represented, he was still on a fresh world with plenty of chances to improve.

So long as he could find whatever natural treasure made the island so special. And it was special. He knew that from the moment he set foot on shore. The Ethera was thick, feeling almost solid to his senses, and the crabs' advanced mutation was even further evidence that there was something worth harvesting in the area.

He just had to find it.

But to do that, he needed to establish a foothold. Cabbot might've been impatient, but he was anything but foolish. The first step was to create a defensible position. Then, he would send the scouts to map the interior of the island. Meanwhile, his underlings would begin the process of subduing the local fauna.

And when the time came, he would reap the benefits.

Really, it was probably for the best if a few of his soldiers died. That meant that he'd have to worry less about appeasing them. After all, natural treasures were finite, and Cabbot had no desire to split the benefits with anyone else, least of all the sorts of idiots he'd been able to recruit for an expedition into a newly integrated backwater.

Finally, one of the dwarven warriors—Rockbeard, unless Cabbot was mistaken—finished off the final crab with a vicious overhead swing of his axe. And then, everything went quiet. A few of the soldiers who knew how to harvest monsters rushed forward, intending to tear the crabs to pieces in hope of finding something useful.

The shells were durable enough that some of the craftsmen back in Ironshore might be able to use them for armor. The meat would probably be edible, as well, and given the thickness of the ambient Ethera, a decent chef might be able to make something worthwhile with it.

But Cabbot wasn't concerned with any of that. The real prize was whatever treasure had given the island its increased Ethera density. Unless it turned out that the crabs were more valuable than he expected. If that happened, he would take his cut.

"Mr. Cabbot," came Nirea's voice.

Cabbot whipped around and demanded, "What?"

"We found one of the scouts," she said. "Or what was left of him. Initial findings suggest that he was killed before the—"

At that moment, the Ethera in the air stirred. Cabbot only had a moment to activate his ability, Death Wish, before the world came alive with wind, lightning, and trembling earth. He activated Blood Shield, as well, enveloping himself in a bubble of red-tinged force. It was just in time, too, because a second later, an enormous bolt of lightning descended upon Nirea, tearing through her before ripping a hole in the rocky shore. The force of the lightning bolt sent her flying through the air, where the wind cut through her, leaving a trail of blood behind. She landed before taking another bolt of lightning, but by that point, Cabbot knew she was already dead.

All around him, chaos reigned as the earth was ripped asunder and a violent thunderstorm tore across the sky. Blades of wind whipped through the air, drowning out the screams of agony coming from anyone who hadn't raised some sort of defenses in time. The warriors fared the best, with the healers following soon after. But the mages took the worst of it. At the end of the day, ethereal shields—which were a staple among the mage variants—could only take so much before they broke.

And break they did. Cabbot fell to the ground, curling up in the fetal position as the entire camp was torn apart by the fury of nature. It only lasted a handful of seconds before it dissipated, but by that point, the damage had been done.

When Cabbot pushed himself upright, he saw nothing but carnage. Most of his soldiers had survived, but there were enough casualties that he had to wonder if he'd made a mistake by coming to what had been described as a cursed island.

"Report!" he screamed, his voice shaking as he let his abilities lapse.

But that's when he remembered Nirea's fate. She'd taken care of all the administrative functions, so when she'd stupidly allowed herself to be killed, her failure had robbed him of necessary utility.

Looking around, Cabbot felt something sting him. He slapped his hand against his neck. "Sound off!" he shouted. Then, something else stung him.

A moment later, a wave of dizziness swept over him. He looked up to see a swarm of biting flies descending upon the camp. And as his stomach twisted with nausea, he couldn't help but wonder if the island was, indeed, cursed, as so many back in Ironshore suspected.

Elijah didn't stay to watch his Swarm fall upon the camp. Calamity had been incredibly effective, and it had killed a few of the invaders by itself. However, like the crabs, it was only ever intended to be part of the first wave of attacks. A distraction meant to break through their defenses and allow Swarm to do its work.

The only downside was that Calamity had a significant recharge period before it would once again be available—a trade-off that was probably responsible for its incredibly low Ethera cost. By comparison, Swarm had a high cost but could be cast back-to-back if he had the available Ethera.

Which he didn't.

In fact, Elijah's core had been almost entirely drained by the sequence of attacks, so he had no choice but to retreat. As he ran through the forest, he wondered how effective Swarm would be. He knew the force had plenty of healers among their number, but he also had no clue whether they could cure the Swarm's afflictions. Even if they managed it, there would be a cost.

And that was fine with Elijah. Despite hoping otherwise, he'd known from the moment the invaders landed on the shores of his island that he wouldn't win the battle in a single day. Indeed, he expected it to take quite a bit longer than that. But the first strike was important because he hoped it would set the tone for the rest of the conflict. He needed to keep them off-balance so he could continue to wage guerilla warfare.

The worst that could happen was if they chose to break camp and head back to Ironshore. That would let them regroup, resupply, and replenish their numbers. If they returned after that, then they would be prepared for Elijah's tactics.

Of course, they didn't even know who he was. Even if they suspected his presence—as opposed to some guardian—they would only think he was a caster. They didn't know about his predator form, which gave him the continued advantage of surprise.

All in all, Elijah was happy with how things had gone. He just hoped his advantage would continue. To that end, he retreated from the shore, racing through the forest with experienced ease. All the while, he kept his mind trained on the devastation he'd wreaked on the camp.

There were thirty-one survivors, and if his senses were anything to go by, they hadn't escaped unscathed. Only a couple seemed completely healthy, and the healers were in the process of healing the afflictions. It was no easy task, either, and it took multiple casts for each of the affected.

Once Elijah was about a mile away, he settled down to rest. Glancing up at the forest's canopy, he saw sunlight beginning to peek through the leaves. It had been an exhausting night, but he'd only just begun with the defense of his island.

There were still more than thirty left, and Elijah knew he and his Grove wouldn't be safe until they were all dead. So, he rested. He regenerated his Ethera. And, more importantly, he considered the tactics he would need to employ if he was going to survive the incursion.

Cabbot looked around at the devastated camp. Almost twenty dead, all because his moronic and lazy scouts hadn't been paying attention. If they hadn't already paid for their inattention with their lives, he would have killed them.

"Sir," said Iros, one of the goblin mages. He'd just been healed, but his skin still bore the marks of that damnable infection. Even Cabbot hadn't been capable of resisting it, and though it hadn't killed him, he still felt weak. And judging by the way Iros swayed on his feet, the goblin was just as affected. "We should go back. We need to regroup."

"Regroup? No."

"But, sir . . ."

"Look around, Iros," Cabbot said, sweeping his arm to indicate the ruined camp. Most of the tents had been trampled by the crabs, and the dead bodies still hadn't been recovered. Multiple people lay on the ground, groaning in pain, too ill to rise. Healers knelt beside some, but Cabbot suspected that, before they got to everyone, a few more would perish. But that was expected. And, in his mind, it was acceptable.

After all, the fewer people who lived, the fewer times he had to split the reward for their efforts. More, Cabbot thought of it as trimming the fat. Without the weak to hold the rest of them back, the group would be capable of so much more.

"What am I looking at?" asked the goblin.

"If the natural treasure's guardian is powerful enough to do this, then think about what it must be guarding," Cabbot said. It was well-known that a guardian's Strength was directly linked to its treasure.

Iros's face split into a jagged-toothed grin as he processed Cabbot's statement. "I see," he said. Then, his grin faded before he continued, "But, sir . . . what if it's too powerful for us to kill? Remember what happened to Dena and her group."

"We don't know what happened to those three. For all we know, they ended up getting killed by some sea monster," Cabbot said. "But it doesn't matter. Those idiots were always too confident for their own good. And, anyway, we're prepared now. We know the guardian's tricks. We can defend against it. Get the shield arrays set up. Use the coins if you need to."

Iros said, "Aye, sir."

Cabbot nodded, then said, "This time tomorrow, we'll all be taking whatever this island has to offer." He looked around at the rest of the group. "Well, those of us who survive."

Once they defeated the guardian, Cabbot intended to make certain that there weren't many left to split the spoils.

72

A TEST OF MIGHT

Alyssa stepped through the doors and felt the familiar moment of nothingness before the interior of the Capitol building came into focus. Once, she'd visited Washington, DC, and while there, she'd taken a tour of the US Capitol building. So, the sight that greeted her was easily recognizable.

The expansive lobby was festooned with white marble, with a foursome of comparatively small statues standing before square columns. Behind and between those was the much larger replica of the *Statue of Freedom*, which depicted a robed woman wearing an elaborate headdress. Behind that sculpture was a pair of identical staircases that met on an elevated platform.

"It looks like the Capitol Visitor Center," she said once the others had joined her.

"Like, the US Capitol? But that wasn't Washington, DC, out there," remarked Bryce. "I mean, I've never been, but . . . Well, I've seen movies."

"It wasn't," agreed Roman, clutching his bow while looking around. "I'm willing to bet that the rest of this building doesn't exactly match up with the real thing, either."

Alyssa didn't say anything else, but she suspected Roman was right. The levels for the towers could take just about anything for inspiration, so it wasn't surprising that it had used one of Earth's most iconic buildings. However, she did wonder if it would have presented itself similarly if the tower climbers hailed from another country. If they'd been French, perhaps it would have resembled the Louvre. Or Buckingham Palace for a group of Englishmen.

She shook her head. There were too many possibilities to consider, and regardless of how interesting it was, it seemed a fruitless endeavor to do so. Understanding the nature of towers wouldn't help them survive what was coming. What could help them, though, was the silver box that suddenly appeared before her.

Alyssa knelt, flipped the latch, and opened the box to reveal a long, thin dagger. She looked at the notification that had appeared directly after she'd stepped into the building:

Congratulations! You have completed Level Two of The Zombie Apocalypse. Grade: B.

To progress further, defeat the Final Guardian.

It was an expected message, though Alyssa had to admit that she felt a sense of accomplishment when she saw that the group had been given a higher grade than after the last level. She wasn't certain what it really meant, but she suspected that the reward's power was dependent on their grade.

In any case, she moved to the next notification:

Reward for completing Level Two of The Zombie Apocalypse:

Stiletto of Sundering

"It's called a Stiletto of Sundering," she said, reaching out to pick the weapon up. When her fingers closed around the hilt, she felt a brief jolt of Ethera, suggesting that it was an incredibly powerful weapon. Even her spear, which, according to Carmen, was the strongest weapon created by any of Easton's crafters, didn't come with that sort of feeling.

She glanced back at her companions, wondering who should get the item. Verin and Bryce were out, largely because Byrce had no martial ability and Verin favored her morning star. Alyssa also ruled herself out as the recipient. She could use a dagger well enough due to her Novice level of Weapon Mastery, but she preferred to use the spear. A dagger would only be a backup weapon for her.

But both Roman and Trace could make use of it.

In Roman's case, he typically used his bow. However, he had a couple of abilities meant for use in melee combat. As for Trace, the Outlaw favored longer blades, but Alyssa suspected that he could use daggers just as effectively as he used his swords.

"I'm thinking it should go to you or Trace," she said to Roman. "Up to you."

Without hesitation, Roman said, "Trace. He can make better use of it."

The Outlaw narrowed his eyes. "You sure, chief?"

Roman nodded. "Consider it a loan. When we get back to Easton, we'll redistribute these rewards for the greater good."

Trace shrugged. "Sounds fine to me."

Then, he accepted the offered Stiletto of Sundering, letting out a slight gasp when he took hold of the hilt. He didn't say anything else, though, so everyone quickly moved past it. Alyssa told everyone what the level's task was, but no one was terribly surprised. According to the guides they'd all read, most towers required a show of Strength before the climbers could claim the final reward.

After taking a few minutes to collect themselves, they began their progress through the building, using a similar strategy to what they'd established in the city. Trace and Roman acted as scouts, while the others took the only route available to them—up the stairs and down the wide hall. Alyssa noticed that each side of the corridor was lined with paintings, though they'd been slashed to pieces, obscuring the subjects.

After a few hundred feet—which would make it an incredibly long hall—Alyssa started to notice the blood. At first, there were only a few drops here and there, but soon enough, the group came across huge standing puddles of red liquid. More, the walls were stained with patterns of splattered blood.

"Okay, this is starting to freak me out," Bryce muttered, almost under his breath.

Alyssa was tempted to tell him to stay quiet, but she refrained from doing so because, if she was honest, she felt just as uneasy as he did. Still, they kept going, with Roman and Trace periodically returning to report that the way forward was more of the same. As they went, they passed a multitude of side rooms, but none were occupied.

Not anymore, at least. But judging by the amount of blood in each of what appeared to be well-appointed offices, they once had been. Clearly, the building had been the subject of a massacre of epic proportions.

Gradually, Alyssa led the others down the hall, eventually reaching an intersection. Roman and Trace had already explored all three directions and passed on which way would lead them to their destination, so Alyssa didn't hesitate before continuing forward. Over the next few hours, they experienced more of the same. Eventually, blood covered everything, and they found themselves walking through what felt like a half-congealed bog.

Finally, Roman appeared before them and whispered, "This is going to be an issue."

"What is it?"

"You've got to see it. I can't really . . . I can't really describe it."

After being assured that there were no enemies around, Alyssa left the other two behind and followed Roman. The journey took another few minutes, during which they were accompanied by the squelching sounds of their footsteps, but soon enough, they found Trace standing before a pair of massive wooden doors.

And the Outlaw looked like he'd seen a ghost.

Roman held a finger up to his lips, indicating that she should remain silent. Then, he pushed one of the doors open—just a crack—and gestured for her to take a look. Alyssa leaned forward, pressing her eye to the opening.

Her eyes widened in horror.

At first, she wasn't certain what she was looking at. At a glance, it looked like a pile of meat, misshapen and with a series of odd bulges. However, after she saw it quiver, Alyssa recognized that some of those bulges were human limbs attached to a bulbous mass of naked fat and muscle.

And it was huge. At least forty feet across and just as wide. The sight was so grotesque that she almost didn't recognize the setting. Then, her thoughts caught up, and everything clicked into place.

She pulled away, and Roman gently pulled the door back into place. Then, the trio retreated to where they'd left the other two. When they arrived, Alyssa finally asked, "Was that the Senate Chamber?"

Roman nodded. "Yeah. I think the scale is off a little, but I recognize it from the State of the Union."

"And that monster?" Alyssa asked.

It was Trace's turn to answer, and he said, "It's people."

"What?"

"It's a big ball of people. I don't know if they're zombies like we saw outside or whatever. But those are people. I think . . . I think it's all the people who were in these offices," he said. "I . . . I got close. Closer than I wanted. And I saw them. The faces. The arms and legs. The . . . T-the everything. They looked like they were in pain."

"It's not real," Alyssa said, reaching out to pat him on the shoulder.

He yanked away. "It was real enough for me."

She didn't persist, instead turning to Roman. "How do we kill it, then?"

"Overwhelming force?" he said. "With all the blood, I don't think we can get this place to catch fire. So, I think we're just going to have to hack it to pieces. Drop a Meteor on it. That sort of thing."

"And we think that'll work?"

"I know just as much as you do," he replied. "But I don't think this is the kind of thing we can outthink. If we want to win, we're going to have to do it in a straight-up fight."

"Against that thing?" she asked, a shiver of fear traveling up her spine. "We'll lose."

"I think you're underestimating what we can do," Roman stated. "You destroyed that last monster. Besides, we don't have a choice. Not unless you can think of a way to make this work."

Alyssa shook her head, but she didn't immediately respond. Her first inclination was to set a trap for the thing, but there were two issues that made that impossible. For one, it was so huge that any trap would have to be absolutely enormous. They didn't have the means to create something like that. For another, there were no materials to construct anything of note. They couldn't even dig a basic pit because, under all the blood and the floor, they found only concrete.

No—it was like Roman had suggested. If they were going to conquer the tower, they'd have to do so in a straight fight against the abomination. So, Alyssa turned her mind to creating a battle plan where they might stand a chance of survival. She didn't get far, though, because the reality was that none of them had seen the thing in action, so they had no context for its capabilities. Without that, any plan was largely useless.

Still, they could follow some basic parameters, which she explained to the others. In the end, the fight would likely require a lot more improvisation than Alyssa would like, but that was unavoidable.

She hated going into it half-cocked, but there really wasn't any choice in the matter. That monster was between them and conquering the tower, which meant that, one way or another, it needed to go down.

So, without further ado, the group set off for the tower's version of the Senate Chamber. When they reached the double doors, Alyssa once again asked if everyone was ready. They all confirmed that they were as prepared as they could be, so after taking a few steadying breaths, she slowly pushed the doors open.

"Can you hit it from here?" whispered Alyssa, glancing from Roman to Bryce.

The latter shook his head in the negative, but Roman confirmed that he could shoot the monster from that distance. It was only a hundred yards—at most—so that wasn't that surprising. Ever since he'd gained his class, Roman's ability with the bow had grown by leaps and bounds, and Alyssa had seen him hit targets from hundreds of yards away.

"Okay," Alyssa said. "Start casting."

Bryce did as he was told, closing his eyes as he mumbled his spell. At the same time, Roman raised his bow, nocked an arrow, and drew it back to his cheek. Ethera gathered as he used some ability. He exhaled, then loosed the arrow.

It flew with unerring accuracy, and when it hit the bulbous monster, it did so with an explosion of force that tore a massive divot out of the bulging mass of flesh at its side. It let loose with a thousand screams, each one loud enough to set Alyssa's ears to ringing.

Then, it rolled around, and she saw its faces.

Hundreds of them, all connected by flaps of moist skin. Men. Women. Fat and thin. Beautiful and ugly. It didn't matter. They'd all merged into one. Every eye locked onto the party standing at the open door. Then, it heaved its bulk into motion, rolling across the ground and crushing chairs and desks along the way.

It moved with alacrity that belied its size. When it drew near enough, Alyssa used Bulwark, hoping to trip it up as she had with the previous monster. But it rolled over the shield like it wasn't even there, the monster's shapeless bulk conforming to the immovable plane of Ethera with ease.

Alyssa cursed. Bryce was a long way from finishing his spell. He needed more time, and she was the only one who could give it to him.

"Keep me alive," she muttered to Verin.

Before they could object to the alteration of the plan—which had hinged on them staying safe in the hall while Bryce and Roman peppered it with attacks—Alyssa dashed forward. The plan hadn't been a bad one, per se. However, the moment it moved past her Bulwark, she knew it wouldn't work. The thing was like a boneless slug, and it could easily conform to the confines of the hall.

So, it was better that she fight the battle in the open. Hopefully, that would allow her to use her mobility and keep it occupied while Bryce and Roman did their job.

With Heroic Leap, she soared into the sky, hoping that she had what it took to survive.

73

HIT AND RUN

Sunlight streamed through the forest canopy, casting the undergrowth in deep shadow. Elijah stepped lightly, his feet making no sound as he slowly approached the trio of invaders. The closest was a slight gnome with bushy turquoise hair, while her two escorts were both dwarves with magnificent black beards. The pair of dwarves both held wicked axes, and the gnome wore a robe and carried an elegant staff that was taller than she was.

"I don't like this," growled one of the dwarves, peering intently into the shadows. "I feel like I'm bein' watched."

"This place is cursed," said the other.

"You always say that," the gnome responded, rolling her large eyes.

Elijah took another slow step, carefully placing his paw on the loamy ground.

"I do not."

"She's right, Biko," the other dwarf said. "It's just like that cave we found last month. You said that was cursed, too, and how'd that turn out?"

"That was different. How was I s'posed to know there was ghouls around?"

"Ghouls are common on newly integrated worlds," the gnome stated. "Did you even read the pamphlet I made before we came here?"

Another step.

"Biko can't read."

"Can so!"

Then another.

"Sure, buddy. We all believe that," said the second dwarf, patting the other on the shoulder.

Finally, Elijah was in range. He used Predator Strike, then pounced. His claws met some resistance from the mage's shield, but it wasn't enough to keep him from ripping out her throat. Even as she fell, Elijah kept moving, disappearing into the shadows. The moment he was out of sight, he bounded up the trunk of a tree, then out onto a limb.

Meanwhile, the dwarves reacted, charging noisily into the brush but finding nothing.

"Oh, gods . . ."

"What was that?!"

"Looked like a giant lizard."

"Weren't no lizard. That was a—"

Elijah leaped from the branch, using Venom Strike as he dropped onto the smarter dwarf's shoulders. In less than an instant, his teeth sank into his neck, and then he was gone, bounding back under cover.

"It bit me! It bit me!"

"Ain't nothin' but a scratch . . ."

"I don't feel so good . . ."

Elijah raced from the scene, getting far enough away to use Guise of the Unseen. Once he did, he wheeled around and crept back to where the dwarf had fallen to his knees. He fumbled at his belt pouch, grabbing a small vial and tipping it back. Even as he did, Elijah darted forward, using Predator Strike before slashing his claws across Biko's hamstrings. Even as the short figure fell forward, Elijah dashed behind a tree.

"Gimme that potion! It got me! It got me, Tor!"

Whatever the other dwarf had drunk had clearly counteracted the neurotoxin inflicted by Venom Strike, but he was still a little unsteady. He turned left, then right, holding his axe before him. He used some sort of ability, but Elijah couldn't tell what it did. Probably something defensive, given their obvious role.

Elijah didn't care.

All he needed was to break the skin, and he doubted anything but a powerful mage's shield could stop that. So, he once again used Venom Strike, then dashed from under cover and leaped at Tor's face. His claws barely managed to pierce the dwarf's skin, but it was enough to deliver the toxic payload before he bounded off.

Tor coughed, then pitched forward onto his face. The potion obviously hadn't completely cleared the neurotoxin, and the extra dose had pushed him over the edge. Even as he fell into a seizure, Elijah circled the remaining dwarf, who, due to his torn hamstrings, was having trouble remaining upright.

Coming at him from behind, Elijah once again used Venom Strike before raking his claws across the dwarf's back. Before Biko could turn around, Elijah had already bounded up the nearest tree, where he waited for the neurotoxin to finish the dwarf off.

It took less than a minute before the final bit of kill energy swept through him. Elijah's shoulders sagged as he sank to his stomach in exhaustion. Using so many abilities so close together had really taken it out of him. But still, he'd managed to win the fight, which meant that there were only twenty-eight more.

After a few minutes of rest, Elijah leaped from the branch and headed toward the next group. The bulk of the invaders were still in camp, but after they'd recovered from Elijah's first attack—mostly, at least—they had begun to send groups out to scout their surroundings. At present, there were two other groups out and about, which meant that Elijah had his targets.

Gradually, he stalked his prey—another group of three, consisting of a pair of goblins and a gnome—and, when the time was right, he pounced. The fight went much as the last had, and over the next couple of minutes, he took them down. The only dangerous bit came when the mage's shield managed to block his first attack, but Elijah was quick enough to adjust. The next attack took the mage out, and the remainder of the battle followed the script he'd used during the first encounter.

The next group fell, as well, and soon enough, Elijah was alone within the forest.

With the invaders confined to their camp, he decided to head back to the Grove, where he ate a meal of berries and mushrooms. He'd have loved to eat something warm, but he didn't want to give away his position with a fire. If the invaders were even moderately observant, they could follow a plume of smoke right to the Grove.

"Wait . . ."

There was an opportunity there, wasn't there? If he could count on the invaders coming to a certain spot, then couldn't he take advantage of their predictability?

It was worth a shot.

Elijah thought he could kill them using his current tactics, but only if they didn't adjust. So long as they kept to groups of three or less, he would be fine. But if they increased their numbers? Things would get much more difficult. Wouldn't it be better if he could take some of them out of the fight without his direct intervention? At worst, it would force them to focus more on the environment.

With that, Elijah cemented his plan and set off across the island. He didn't intend to go far—just a mile from the camp—but once he reached the clearing, he got to work. First, he started digging. With his enhanced Strength and sharp claws, he was almost as efficient as a small backhoe, and within an hour, he'd completed his first pit. Then, he dug a handful more, arranging them in a semicircle.

It took half a day, but the invaders remained idle, giving him the opportunity to complete his undertaking. Once the pits had been dug—each one reaching a depth of almost ten feet—he set off into the forest to gather sticks. Doing this required that he shift back into his human form, but he didn't mind. He had plenty of Ethera available, so he could shift back into his predator form at a moment's notice.

Fortunately, Elijah's enemies remained sequestered in their camp. Likely, they knew that something was hunting them and, as a result, were reluctant to leave—especially with night coming. That played right into Elijah's plans, giving him hours to finish building his traps.

He'd based the design on a medieval fortification called a trou-de-loup—or a wolf hole—which consisted of a dense pattern of conical pits, at the bottoms of which would be punji sticks. In some cases, rotting meat or feces would be smeared on the wooden stakes, but Elijah had neither the time nor the inclination to go to those lengths. In any case, he suspected that any long-running infection that came from such tactics would be easily cured by the healers among the invaders.

No—all he cared about was creating more chaos. With any luck, he could repeat his actions from before, using Calamity and Swarm to further whittle their numbers down. And if he was truly fortunate, he'd kill them all in one go.

After sharpening the stakes with his knife, Elijah jammed them into the bottoms of the pits, then went about gathering some firewood, which he arranged in another shallow pit at the center of the arrayed traps. By that point, it was already night, which gave him only a few short hours to finish the project.

The last piece that would bring everything together required him to weave a series of flimsy mats from grass he gathered from nearby. Once he'd done that, morning was only about an hour off, so he quickly covered them with a thin layer of dirt and loose grass that he hoped would disguise his traps.

Finally, with his traps built, Elijah lit the fire before stacking a series of green limbs onto the pile. As the fire filled the air with a thick plume of dark smoke, the invaders set out from their camp en masse.

They were going in the wrong direction at first, but as Elijah continued to stoke the fire, adding more green limbs, they clearly noticed the plume of smoke and changed directions. And just like that, Elijah's plan was on.

He retreated into one of the trees, climbing until he had a good view of the clearing. Then, he waited.

It only took them an hour to reach the clearing. All of them, advancing in a line. They did so cautiously, but none of them even looked at the ground. Elijah's previous efforts to kill their scouts bore fruit when the first few—a couple of gnomes and a goblin—fell into one of the traps.

They screamed, and the group panicked. One of the gnomes—a fellow with a vivid-red mohawk—started shouting something Elijah couldn't hear, gesturing violently.

That was when Elijah leaped down from the tree, shifted into his human form, and for the second time in the past three days, used Calamity.

The sky tore apart as thick storm clouds rolled in. The earth rumbled, and the wind whipped into a frenzy. That was enough to send the remaining invaders into a panic. They scattered.

Unfortunately, the clearing was absolutely lousy with traps, and it only took a couple of seconds before the panicked invaders ran afoul of the previous night's efforts. A full half of the group fell into traps as Calamity tore the area asunder, peppering it with lightning, blades of hurricane-force winds, and a minor earthquake. As before, it only lasted for a few seconds before it dissipated, but by that point, the damage was done.

Elijah cast Swarm.

Thousands of biting flies manifested, then swept down on the trapped invaders. Some tossed out fireballs and other spells meant to mitigate the mass of insects, but their efforts were all for naught. A handful of gnomes and goblins had managed to avoid the traps, but all except one had fallen to Calamity.

Elijah crouched at the tree line, watching as Swarm did its work. Slowly, the kill energy flooded in, pushing him past level thirty.

And just like that, the invaders were finished. Only one remained. A few others were still alive, but he was the only one upright and mostly healthy. The same gnome that seemed to be in charge, pulsing with red energy, stood amid the carnage. He looked around, panicked and furious, screaming something unintelligible. Elijah ignored him, instead letting himself regenerate his Ethera as he inspected his new spell:

Shape of the Guardian	**Take on the form of a stalwart guardian, vastly increasing your Strength and Constitution attributes. Spellcasting is suspended while Shape of the Guardian is active.**

Another shape-shift, but unlike Shape of the Predator, it didn't cost nearly as much Ethera. As Elijah inspected the new spell, he briefly forgot that there was still one invader left. And because of that brief lack of attention, the red-glowing gnome finally saw the man who'd torn his small army apart.

He shouted in rage, then raced toward Elijah's position.

74

A LONG TIME COMING

Using Descending Dragon, Alyssa rocketed toward the bulbous mass of sweaty flesh. It reacted far more quickly than she could have anticipated, and even as she fell, a series of appendages thrust upward, each one tipped with a yellow pustule. They burst, spraying her with a sticky goo that immediately set her armor to smoking. Through some miracle, she avoided getting it into her eyes, but the rest of her body was fair game.

She screamed in mingled agony and anger, but her spear remained steady, tearing into the bulky monster and carving a huge gash into its moist form. The moment she landed, she tried to kick off, intending to use Dragon Wings to glide away to safety. However, the monster was too fast, and its multitude of disparate arms whipped out, grabbing at her legs. Caught off-balance, she tumbled forward, slamming face-first into the naked flesh.

The thing let out a multitude of screeching laughs, then wrapped its arms around her, hugging her close. The skin split, then the flesh beneath opened, as well, trying to swallow her whole. Panicked, Alyssa summoned another Bulwark directly below her, and miraculously, the invisible shield locked into place, preventing the flesh from closing around her.

Activating Enrage, she let loose with Champion's Shout, flooding her body with Strength even as the latter ability stunned the monster's grasping limbs. With that small opening, she shoved herself upright and leaped away, sprouting wings a second later.

But her victory was short-lived, as a tendril of pure muscle lashed out, smashing against her lower half and sending her off course. Before she could right the proverbial ship, Alyssa crashed into the ground, destroying one of the desks before rolling to a stop against another.

With her vision blurred and her thoughts slowed by a probable concussion, Alyssa struggled to rise. She heard someone shout something, but her sluggish mind couldn't wrap itself around the meaning. Then, a wave of vitality swept through her. Her thoughts cleared, and her agony faded under Verin's ministrations.

Shaking her head, she looked up to see that the monster was on fire, with a full quarter of its flesh resembling something with the consistency of melting rubber. The smell of cooking flesh—which was disturbingly like grilled pork—filled the air, but despite the obvious damage wreaked by Bryce's fiery spell, the monster was far from dead.

And it was just as clearly pissed off.

Each of its faces screamed in fury while its various appendages waved in formless anger. It rolled forward, intent on crushing the author of its pain. Bryce tried to run, but he tripped over something Alyssa couldn't see. Roman shouted something, but he'd dashed away in the opposite direction.

Bryce never stood a chance.

He yelled, casting another spell, but it was the quick-casting variety, and the fireball connected with barely a sizzle before the bulbous monster rolled over him. It quivered in obvious ecstasy as a squelching sound filled the air.

A second later, Alyssa saw the melted flesh begin to reform. Most of it was featureless, but she couldn't mistake the growing presence of Bryce's agonized face.

Fury, disgust, and fear coursed through Alyssa's mind as her Enrage reached new heights. She threw herself to her feet, then raced across the Senate Chamber. The monster turned in her direction, quivering eagerly as it likely contemplated adding yet another body to its mass. When she got close enough, Alyssa activated three abilities, all in quick succession.

First, Champion's Shout to briefly stun the monster. Then, Impale to add a damage-over-time component to her next ability. Finally, she aimed a lancing strike in the direction of the monster's injured side, shouting a wordless war cry as she unleashed Unstoppable Thrust, sending a concentrated spear of Ethera to tear through its mass.

Blood misted into the air as a layer of flesh was carved from its body. It screamed.

But Alyssa wasn't finished. Once again, she used Heroic Leap. This time, though, she didn't go upward. Instead, she used it to send herself into a horizontal Charge. Her spear took the creature in the injured side, slicing deeper than ever before. She landed amid the bloody muscle with a wet squelch, pulled her spear back, and stabbed again.

And again after that.

Vaguely, she recognized Roman's arrows joining her barrage of spear strikes. With every passing second, she was battered by the creature's nearest limbs. But none could dislodge her. Over and over, she brought her weapon to bear.

She didn't escape unscathed, but Verin healed her from a distance. In the meantime, she also activated Recover almost by instinct. Slowly, she carved her way into the monster until, at last, she found something that seemed important.

It was a concentrated ball of dense flesh that looked like a mass of wriggling worms. Was it the brain? Or was it the creature's original form? Alyssa didn't care.

She attacked it, using Impale to increase the damage.

Those wriggling worms shot out, but most of them hit her armor. The ones that found skin tried to burrow into her, but with Hardened Skin enhancing her Constitution, they couldn't find any purchase. She ignored the pain, stabbing and slicing with her spear until, at last, the thing fell still.

A second later, the flesh lost cohesion and fell apart. Alyssa tumbled to the ground as she was buried beneath hundreds of bodies. She panicked, slicing the cadavers apart with every ounce of fury she could muster. But they were dead, and as such, they were no match for her blade.

They were heavy, though, and it took her a few minutes to carve her way free. When she finally did, she found Roman and Verin waiting for her.

And they looked almost disappointed.

Or was that sadness? They had lost Bryce, after all. Maybe they felt guilty. She started to say something, but then, something rammed into her back.

Alyssa twisted, but her body failed her.

She flopped to her side, confused as to what had happened. Was there another monster?

No . . .

She had felt the experience from killing the monster. They'd conquered the tower. More, she could see the reward box sitting only a few feet away, gleaming in the ambient light.

She tried to roll over, but her body wouldn't respond. Recover had faded. So had her passive augmentations.

"W-what . . ."

Roman crossed his arms, saying, "Again."

"You got it, chief."

Another stab, this time in her kidney. Alyssa coughed up blood, but she couldn't move.

"Damn nice knife here," came Trace's voice as he circled into Alyssa's field of vision. He looked like he hadn't even fought in the previous battle. He tossed the Stiletto of Sundering into the air, letting it flip before its hilt fell back into his hand. "Interesting effect. Did you know I have an analysis ability? Part of being a proper Outlaw is recognizing which goods are worth stealing, after all. And this one is a real gem. Doesn't do much damage. Not really. But it debuffs the shit out of you. Forcibly deactivates self-buffs and decreases attributes. Not by a lot. Really hits the ol' Constitution hard, though. Just enough that my ability could put you down."

Roman growled, "Enough with the monologue."

"Sorry, chief."

It took all her Strength, but Alyssa managed to croak, "W-why . . ."

Roman sighed. "Do you think I don't see what you've done?" he asked. "Always putting yourself out there, taking extra patrols, saving people . . . And all the while, I'm doing what's necessary. I'm making the hard decisions, the unpopular choices. And people hate me for it as much as they love you. I can't have it. I won't stand for division."

Alyssa tried to move, to do something, but whatever Trace's ability was, it robbed her of any control over her own body. She didn't think it was permanent. It would wear off. So, she just needed to keep Roman talking. She spat, "Is . . . it . . . about . . . Trish . . ."

Roman's placid expression changed in an instant, taking on a pained and furious visage. "It's not about that," he growled.

"It is . . ."

She saw his knuckles whiten around the grip of his bow. He took a couple of deep breaths, then looked from Trace, who seemed as calm as if he was on a walk in the park, to Verin, who was clearly uncomfortable. But she seemed stoic. Committed. Alyssa didn't think she was going to step in to help.

Roman closed his eyes and took yet another deep breath. And when he once again opened his eyes, it was as if his anger had simply washed away. "Believe what you want," he said. "This isn't personal."

If Alyssa could have moved, she would have laughed in his face. She could see it in his expression. He blamed her, whether or not he wanted to admit it aloud.

He sighed. "But it doesn't matter. You're going to die here, Alyssa. I wish it hadn't worked out this way. You're a good person. One of the best. I know you want to help," he said. "And believe me, you dying here today—that'll help Easton more than anything else you could do."

"I . . . I don't . . ."

"You know it's true. Your death will make sure we're all united to face the difficulties to come," he said, stepping forward. He knelt beside the box, then unlatched it. A notification flashed across Alyssa's eyes. Everyone froze, clearly reading the same notification Alyssa had just received.

Congratulations! You have completed Level Three of The Zombie Apocalypse. Grade: A.

To exit the tower, step through the portal.

It was an expected message, though Alyssa had to admit that she felt a sense of accomplishment when she saw that the group had been given a higher grade than after the last level. She wasn't certain what it really meant, but she suspected that the reward's power was dependent on their grade.

In any case, she moved to the next notification:

Reward for completing level three of The Zombie Apocalypse:
Seal of Authority

"Oh, that's a good one, chief. Lets you establish the town as an official city with the System. Don't know what that means, but it's probably good," said Trace.

"If you're going to do it, just do it," said Verin. "I didn't agree to this so I could watch her suffer. It's inhumane."

"F-fuck you," Alyssa spat, with some of the feeling coming back to her legs. Just a few more moments, and she'd be able to move. And when she regained mobility, she would end all three of them. The Priest would have to go first. Then the Outlaw. She'd save Roman for last, and she intended to take her time with the traitor. "Fuck you all."

"Best get on with it, Chief," Trace said. "The effect won't last much longer. She's already getting feeling back."

Roman shook his head, pocketing the Seal of Authority. It was a simple item the size and shape of a coin, though she couldn't see it well enough to recognize more than that. Once he'd put it away, he stepped forward. He held a hand out toward Trace, and the Outlaw responded by handing him one of his swords, hilt first.

"For what it's worth, I wish I didn't have to do this. Even with . . . everything that's happened, I still consider you a friend."

Then, Ethera swirled around him as he raised the sword in a two-handed grip. Even as it fell, Alyssa tried to squirm out of the way. She desperately attempted to activate an ability. Hardened Skin. Heroic Leap. Shock Wave. Anything. But none of them responded any more than her paralyzed body.

The sword fell, biting deep into her exposed neck. She didn't even feel it.

Nor did she immediately die. Blood pooled beneath her, and she tried to speak. Nothing came out but a wordless gurgle. Roman raised the sword again, and just like it had the first time, it fell upon her neck.

Still, she lived.

Barely. Darkness had begun to creep around her eyes, which flicked from one person to another. Trace looked unconcerned. Roman was stoic yet regretful. But Verin—she had tears in her eyes. She didn't look away, though.

The sword came down again, and at last, her head fell free. It rolled a foot or so away, and for a few seconds, Alyssa's awareness persisted. But then, finally, her life winked out.

Her last thoughts were of impotent anger and revenge.

75

PROTECTOR OF THE GROVE

The charging gnome was shorter than any of the others Elijah had seen, a fact he'd tried to disguise with a very ridiculous mohawk that extended almost a foot higher than was reasonable. Still, the diminutive man moved with enough alacrity that Elijah almost didn't have time to respond. At the last second, he pointed his staff in the gnome's direction, casting Entangling Roots.

The spell took hold, transforming the targeted area into a quagmire of thorny roots. They reached up, wrapping around the racing gnome's legs and digging into his flesh. But he never stopped moving, ripping free and leaving quite a bit of blood behind. He was unaffected, though, moving just as quickly as before.

Next came Storm's Fury, sending a bolt of lightning in the gnome's direction. It hit, and the attack was effective. The gnome—Cabbot, Elijah thought he'd heard someone say back in the camp—tumbled backward from the force of the lightning's impact, flipping end over end until he came to a rest after ten feet.

Elijah watched as Cabbot staggered to his feet, his clothing smoking and the flesh on one side of his face charred. Only a moment later, the red energy cloaking his form pulsed, and the blistered and black flesh flaked away, leaving unmarred skin behind.

He was healing, and at a rate Elijah thought impossible. Even with Touch of Nature combined with Healing Rain, if he'd tried to heal that much damage, it would've taken hours. Perhaps days. But Cabbot had accomplished the feat in only seconds.

Seeing that, Elijah turned to run.

He couldn't keep up to that kind of power. Not in a straight-up fight. Instead, he intended to use the same strategy he'd used before, harassing the gnome with hit-and-run tactics until he went down.

However, before he could get more than a few steps, something hit him in the back. He went flying through the air, then hit the ground where he tumbled, end over end, until he hit the tree line. Thankfully, he didn't collide with a tree. Instead, he was slowed by the underbrush, and about ten feet into the forest, he came to a stop on his back.

He felt something wet.

Confused—there was no water around—he reached down, dipping his fingers into the puddle below. Pulling his hand away, he held it up in front of his face. And all he saw was red.

Blood.

He was bleeding.

That didn't seem right. There was something he needed to do. Some way he should have responded. But in his foggy state, Elijah couldn't solve that seemingly insurmountable puzzle.

Then, by instinct more than conscious thought, he cast Touch of Nature. The healing power coursed through him, reversing the effects of his concussion and clearing his thoughts. But it did little for the gaping wound in his side.

"You ruined everything!" came a shout, accompanied by something—Cabbot, his slowed mind reasoned—crashing through the underbrush.

Elijah used Touch of Nature again, but it was like trying to fill a bucket one thimbleful at a time. The bleeding slowed, but it didn't even come close to stopping.

He tried to rise, but his legs didn't seem to work. So, all he managed was to awkwardly lever himself into a sitting position. When he did, he saw the gnome, still pulsing with angry red energy, charging through the forest, an enormous bloody axe raised above his head.

Cabbot's murderous intentions were clear.

Elijah's options were nearly nonexistent. In fact, he only had one, and it was untested. But he had no choice. So, without any other options, Elijah embraced his newest spell. Ethera raced through his body, transforming it with every passing millisecond. Scales sprouted, muscles inflated, and his skeleton twisted into the appropriate shape. After only a second, he had assumed Shape of the Guardian.

<table>
<tr><td colspan="2">Shape of the Guardian
Archetype: Druid
Class: Animist
Level: 30

Take on the form of a stalwart guardian, vastly increasing your Strength and Constitution attributes. Spellcasting is suspended while Form of the Guardian is active.</td></tr>
<tr><td>Guardian's Renewal</td><td>Instantly and completely regenerate. Cooldown affected by Regeneration attribute. Current cooldown: Once Per Week.</td></tr>
</table>

Elijah gasped as the notification flashed before his eyes. Whether it was a sign from the System or his subconscious mind reminding him that his shapeshifting forms came with innate abilities, he had no idea. But regardless of whence it had come, Elijah wasted no time before using Guardian's Renewal.

As the description promised, his wounds instantly healed. The exhaustion he'd felt from his days of fighting a guerilla war disappeared. And just like that, he was ready to meet the gnome on equal footing.

However, the transformation had clearly surprised Cabbot, who'd stumbled to a stop.

"W-what . . ."

Elijah didn't wait for him to regain his composure. Instead, he pushed himself to his feet and raced forward. Or he tried to, at least. His new form was enormous and powerful, and the sudden disparity between his Strength and Dexterity made him clumsy. As a result, he found himself stumbling.

Cabbot took that as an opportunity to regain his momentum. Fury evident in his expression, he leaped forward, hefting his axe in a herculean swing that took Elijah by surprise.

He tried to dodge, but he still hadn't managed to master his new form. So, he once again stumbled, and Cabbot's axe took him in the hip. A loud clang filled the forest as Cabbot's momentum took him tumbling past Elijah's surprised form. The blow hadn't even drawn blood. Instead, the axe had gotten lodged in Elijah's scales.

With a sweep of his powerful foreleg, he knocked the weapon aside, then turned to face Cabbot.

"What are you?" the gnome demanded, pulling another weapon out of nowhere. This one was a plain-looking greatsword with a blade almost twice Cabbot's size. He held it easily, though, evidence of his inflated Strength attribute.

"A druid," Elijah growled, speaking before he thought better of it. He'd never even tried in his predator form, so the ability to do so surprised him. "And you're trespassing in my Grove."

Cabbot took a step back, and the red light enveloping his form flickered, then dimmed slightly. "A d-druid? Here? How?"

Elijah tried to shrug his massive shoulders. It was difficult, given his new anatomy. As far as he could tell, the Guardian form was a mixture of dinosaur, ape, and bear. But that was inadequate to describe what he felt. He could move on two legs, but he was much more comfortable using his long arms to move in an apelike gait. Perhaps he would know more about the form when he had a chance to study it further.

For now, though, he had a gnome to kill.

Cabbot easily interpreted the situation, and as a result, his light flared as he charged forward. This time, his attacks were more measured, but his blade was incapable of doing more than chipping Elijah's scales. At least at first.

With each ineffectual attack, Cabbot's fury rose. With it, he grew stronger. Faster. And less controlled. In seconds, he'd become a whirling dervish of slashing blades. Elijah tried to respond in kind, but a combination of his mismatched attributes, inexperience with his new form, and the gnome's rapid movements rendered his own counterattacks ineffective.

Each miss brought with it more frustration, and soon enough, Elijah was roaring like the beast he appeared to be. If he'd been in his Predator Form, he could have easily kept up. But it came with its own weaknesses—chiefly, that if he was hit, he probably wouldn't survive. By comparison, the Guardian Form lived up to its name, and it traded coordination for explosive Strength and durability.

In any case, he was stuck in the form because he didn't have the Ethera to fuel another transformation, and he couldn't endure the gnome's attacks as a human. No—he had to remain in the Guardian form for now.

Which meant that the two combatants reached something of a stalemate.

The fight wore on. Minutes passed, becoming more than an hour. The whole time, Elijah stoically withstood the gnome's ferocious attacks. Eventually, though, the everlasting battle took its toll. Not on Elijah, who was well suited to such a fight—not only due to his Guardian form, but also because of his experiences in the tower. There he'd learned to endure, and against Cabbot, he put those hard-won lessons to good use.

As he did, he slowly grew more used to his new body. He knew it would take quite some time before he was nearly as comfortable in the Guardian form as he was as a human or in the Predator shape, but he did improve, even clipping Cabbot a few times.

Still, the biggest deciding factor was that the gnome's abilities clearly weren't made for a long, drawn-out battle. As it wore on, it became obvious that he was fighting against impotent frustration as much as he fought Elijah. And in the end, his abilities began to peter out. The red light dimmed, and his movements slowed.

Still, Elijah didn't dare make his move.

He knew that the moment he did, it would reignite the gnome's fury. So, he had to make that first major blow count. Cabbot flailed against inevitability. Eventually, his sword broke, and he produced another axe from thin air. That broke, too. However, with every passing minute, the gnome's attacks grew weaker until they were incapable of even chipping Elijah's scales.

Still, he waited.

And waited.

The gnome continued, but Elijah knew how to be patient.

Then, finally, the light winked out, and Elijah struck.

With his Strength attribute so thoroughly inflated, he was well into superhuman territory. And even if he didn't have the Dexterity to control his power, he didn't really need to, either. Not with Cabbot having slowed to more normal speeds.

Elijah lashed out with his foreclaw. It was a simple jab, but it took Cabbot directly in the face. The gnome flipped backward, then hit one of the nearby trees. It shuddered with the impact, and Cabbot crumpled.

The red light flickered back into being, but Elijah had no intention of letting the gnome get going. Using his explosive Strength, he rushed forward. Then, clasping his hands together, he brought both fists down on the injured figure. Red light flared again, and bones snapped back into place. Elijah hit him again.

And again.

Over and over, his attacks barely outpaced the Berserker's Regeneration.

Slowly, Elijah gained ground. He shattered bones, over and over, and then, suddenly, the red light disappeared.

Kill energy rushed into Elijah—less than he would have expected—as the gnome finally died. Elijah sighed, the sound coming out in a growling hiss, then let his shoulders sag. He still wasn't finished.

There remained a few survivors who'd managed to live through the barrage of Calamity, Swarm, and his traps. So, after letting himself resume his human form, he looked down at his body. There were hundreds of tiny cuts where his scales had been chipped. Shaking his head, Elijah used Touch of Nature, healing the minor damage, then marshaled his resolve.

Most of the fighting force was dead, but as he'd suspected, a few had managed to survive—all of which were still impaled on the stakes he'd planted at the bottom of the pits. After taking a deep breath, he used Storm's Fury to finish them off. It wasn't pretty, and it usually took more than one cast, but he did what he had to do.

He would have preferred something more humane. The gnomes and goblins certainly suffered more than Elijah would have liked. But in the end, he needed to protect his Grove. That meant finishing the job he'd started.

When he reached the last one, though, he hesitated. She was a goblin, with huge green ears and sharp teeth. But unlike the others, she hadn't fallen into one of the traps.

He pointed his staff at her and demanded, "What's your name?"

"Calix," she coughed, spitting blood. She was either a mage or a healer, judging by her robes and the staff lying nearby. But she was just as clearly out of Ethera—using it was probably the only reason she'd survived so long.

"Do you want to live, Calix?" he asked.

"I . . . I do . . ."

Elijah stepped forward, then put his hand on her shoulder. The battle against Cabbot had gone on long enough that he'd managed to regenerate most of his Ethera, so he had no issues with casting Touch of Nature. It took four pulses—and half of his remaining Ethera—but in only a few seconds, Calix was healthy.

"W-why?" she asked, looking up at him with mingled fear and awe.

"You need to go home," he said. "When you get there, I want you to let everyone in that town know what happens to anyone who comes to my island. You come here, you die. Period. This is the last bit of mercy I'll give. Do you understand?"

"I . . . I . . ."

"And if I hear about you trying to harvest sentient creatures as fuel for your advancement, I will come for you. If that happens, Ironshore will not survive. Do I make myself clear?"

She nodded eagerly.

"Go," he growled.

Calix didn't need any further prodding. After all, Elijah had killed almost fifty people in less than two days, so it wasn't surprising that she was far too frightened to do anything but flee. However, before she got more than a few steps, she did manage to stop, turn, and ask, "W-what are you?"

Elijah thought about it for a second before he said, "I am the Protector of the Grove. Challenge me at your own risk."

ABOUT THE AUTHOR

Nicholas Searcy is the author of Death: Genesis, Mistrunner, and Path of Dragons, originally released on Royal Road. He enjoys writing, reading, spending time with family, sports, and, of course, a good cup of coffee.